NOT ONE OF US

NOT ONE OF US

STORIES OF ALIENS ON EARTH

EDITED BY
NEIL CLARKE

NIGHT SHADE BOOKS
NEW YORK

Night Shade books may be purchased in bulk at special discounts for sales promotion, corporate gifts, fund-raising, or educational purposes. Special editions can also be created to specifications. For details, contact the Special Sales Department, Night Shade Books, 307 West 36th Street, 11th Floor, New York, NY 10018 or info@skyhorsepublishing.com.

Night Shade Books® is a registered trademark of Skyhorse Publishing, Inc. ®, a Delaware corporation.

Visit our website at www.nightshadebooks.com.

10 9 8 7 6 5 4 3 2 1

Library of Congress Cataloging-in-Publication Data is available on file.

ISBN: 978-1-59780-957-3

Cover illustration by Jacques Leyreloup
Cover design by Claudia Noble

Please see page 593 for an extension of this copyright page.

Printed in the United States of America

If you find a bit of yourself in these stories,
this book is for you.

CONTENTS

Introduction

Throughout the science fiction landscape, aliens have been used to illustrate our own best and worst traits, but from a distance that makes it more palatable than a closer look in the mirror. They are portrayed as invaders, refugees, saviors, observers, outsiders, opportunists, and sometimes as beings that barely notice our existence. Yet, outside of the stories, the idea that aliens are visiting Earth is pretty much consigned to conspiracy theories and myths. While many governments and private organizations have investigated claims and made contingencies for the possibility, we have no credible evidence to suggest that we have been visited by beings from other worlds.

But how would we react if they did? What would they do? And why are they here?

Our history is littered with examples of how we have treated our own kind in similar situations, and it isn't always pretty. Will we behave any differently if and when aliens do make contact? Science fiction challenges us to think about those possibilities, often drawing on history in a way that causes us to see things from another perspective. Traversing those paths can evoke multiple emotions, with some tales experienced as entertaining, thoughtful, and sometimes downright terrifying.

For example, one of the most popular tales of alien invasion is *War of the Worlds* by H. G. Wells. Wells followed in the vein of classic invasion literature of the time, but through the Martians, he created a power that mirrored the attitudes of the British Empire. This allowed him to turn the spotlight on the problems caused by imperialism and social Darwinism, calling into question issues of race, ethnicity, and class in his time. Written sometime between 1895 and 1897, it has never been out of print and has been adapted for several films and other performances, including a famous panic-inducing radio program in 1938. While Wells was not the only one writing about these things, his allegorical approach has actually proven more enduring.

And while invasion stories might be one of the first to come to mind, the science fiction field, both in print and film, have covered a wide spectrum of scenarios that led to aliens being on Earth. For example, "Who Goes There?" by John W. Campbell—the story that inspired the movie *The Thing*—was about a twenty-million-year-old survivor of a crashed ship that essentially feeds on people. Is it a monster or something just trying to survive? But when Peter Watts chose to tell the tale from "the monster's" perspective, we see a creature that is trying to help save us from our own isolated minds and become part of something greater. It simply cannot understand why we resist its own sacred communion, and believes it has a responsibility to help us evolve . . .

The movie *E.T.* provides yet another look at the alien trapped on Earth, but this time centered on an alien who just wants to go home after being mistakenly left behind by an interrupted research expedition. Our government plays the part of the monster in this particular scenario as they try to capture him throughout the film. The heart of the tale is one of a forbidden friendship between children and the alien—who can be seen as childlike itself—and their efforts to help him return to his kind. Another film, *District 9*, portrays yet another refugee scenario, which plays upon the themes of social segregation and xenophobia and is heavily influenced by the era of South African apartheid. These might be more challenging stories to tell—and sell—had the aliens been replaced with humans, which makes the art that much more poignant in its allegorical connection. It aims for subtle and overt and ultimately succeeds.

Arthur C. Clarke's novel *Childhood's End*—also made into a TV miniseries of the same name—gives us a tale of the alien as potential savior. Here, they come to Earth to help bring about an almost utopian age under their supervision, but in the process, humanity begins to lose its identity and culture. While the aliens' motivations may be well-meaning and driven by a higher-power, the consequences are significant and frightening. You can't help but question the trade-off by the end of the book.

Or sometimes the underlying issues are far more simplistic. For example, another take on the "alien as savior" trope is Superman, a refugee alien whose powers grant him the ability to combat the forces of evil; or Doctor Who, a time-traveling alien that acts as a guardian of Earth. Here, the alien hero is a reassuring presence, a role often symbolizing a protective parent-child relationship, and in these specific stories we see that common bond. The alien is something larger than life, able to take on the over-whelming dangers and provide hope and escape where needed.

For others, however, these portrayals have been significantly problem-atic. Despite being alien, they often appear human, typically representing some of us much more than others. You can see this in the recent decision to have Doctor Who's latest incarnation be female, which created some controversy, but was also met with high praise or ambivalence from oth-ers. Given the alien's frequent role in demonstrating our own problems, it is not surprising that it should start addressing this one, particularly now. Science fiction has always embraced the unknown, the uncomfortable, and the controversial. There hasn't been a time when social and political issues haven't influenced the genre, period. Science fiction is, by nature, a literature that constantly challenges us. The best of those stories become timeless.

In exploring the often popular first contact theme, this avenue allows the author to illustrate the difficulties two groups can have because of culture, language, and tradition. One of my favorite stories involving this subject closes out this anthology, but for me, the more interesting aspect is what happens *after* we've found each other. I find things really get moving after the diplomats, scientists, and linguists have started the ball rolling and the two societies have to learn to coexist in spite of all our issues.

Ultimately, their journey is our own, whether it be stories of hope, where we find a way to live, work, and love together; or stories of persecution simply for being different. Aliens are the ultimate outsiders, a sentiment to which many of us can can relate.

Maybe someday, one of them will read this book.

Neil Clarke
May 2018

Note: The title of this book is shared by a Peter Gabriel song and a small press science fiction magazine, both of which are significant in their own ways. I admire both, but neither are connected to this anthology.

Carolyn Ives Gilman is a writer of science fiction. Her most recent novel, *Dark Orbit*, is a space exploration adventure that raises questions about consciousness and perception. Her short fiction has received nominations for both the Nebula and Hugo awards. In her professional life she is a historian who writes nonfiction about North American frontier and Native history, most recently for the National Museum of the American Indian (Smithsonian Institution). She lives in Washington, DC.

Touring with the Alien

CAROLYN IVES GILMAN

The alien spaceships were beautiful, no one could deny that: towering domes of overlapping, chitinous plates in pearly dawn colors, like reflections on a tranquil sea. They appeared overnight, a dozen incongruous soap-bubble structures scattered across the North American continent. One of them blocked a major interstate in Ohio; another monopolized a stadium parking lot in Tulsa. But most stood in cornfields and forests and deserts where they caused little inconvenience.

Everyone called them spaceships, but from the beginning the experts questioned that name. NORAD had recorded no incoming landing craft, and no mother ship orbited above. That left two main possibilities: they were visitations from an alien race that traveled by some incomprehensibly advanced method; or they were a mutant eruption of Earth's own tortured ecosystem.

The domes were impervious. Probing radiation bounced off them, as did potshots from locals in the days before the military moved in to cordon off the areas. Attempts to communicate produced no reaction. All the domes did was sit there reflecting the sky in luminous, dreaming colors.

Six months later, the panic had subsided and even CNN had grown weary of reporting breaking news that was just the same old news. Then, entry panels began to open and out walked the translators, one per dome. They were perfectly ordinary-looking human beings who said that they had been abducted as children and had now come back to interpret between their biological race and the people who had adopted them.

Humanity learned surprisingly little from the translators. The aliens had come in peace. They had no demands and no questions. They merely wanted to sit here minding their own business for a while. They wanted to be left alone.

No one believed it.

A very was visiting her brother when her boss called.

"Say, you've still got those security credentials, right?" Frank said.

"Yes . . ." She had gotten the security clearance in order to haul a hush-hush load of nuclear fuel to Nevada, a feat she wasn't keen on repeating.

"And you're in D.C.?"

She was actually in northern Virginia, but close enough. "Yeah."

"I've got a job for you."

"Don't tell me it's another gig for Those We Dare Not Name."

He didn't laugh, which told her it was bad. "Uh . . . no. More like those we *can't* name."

She didn't get it. "What?"

"Some . . . neighbors. Who live in funny-shaped houses. I can't say more over the phone."

She got it then. "Frank! You took a contract from the frigging *aliens?*"

"Sssh," he said, as if every phone in America weren't bugged. "It's strictly confidential."

"Jesus," she breathed out. She had done some crazy things for Frank, but this was over the top. "When, where, what?"

"Leaving tonight. D.C. to St. Louis. A converted tour bus."

"*Tour* bus? How many of them are going?"

"Two passengers. One human, one . . . whatever. Will you do it?"

She looked into the immaculate condo living room, where her brother, Blake, and his husband, Jeff, were playing a noisy, fast-paced video game, oblivious to her conversation. She had promised to be at Blake's concert tomorrow. It meant a lot to him. "Just a second," she said to Frank.

"I can't wait," he said.

"Two seconds." She muted the phone and walked into the living room. Blake saw her expression and paused the game.

She said, "Would you hate me if I couldn't be there tomorrow?"

Disappointment, resignation, and wry acceptance crossed his face, as if he hadn't ever really expected her to keep her promise. "What is it?" he asked.

"A job," she said. "A really important job. Never mind, I'll turn it down."

"No, Ave, don't worry. There will be other concerts."

Still, she hesitated. "You sure?" she said. She and Blake had always hung together, like castaways on a hostile sea. They had given each other courage to sail into the wind. To disappoint him felt disloyal.

"Go ahead," he said. "Now I'll be sorry if you stay."

She thumbed the phone on. "Okay, Frank, I'll do it. This better not get me in trouble."

"Cross my heart and hope to die," he said. "I'll email you instructions. Bye."

From the couch, Jeff said, "Now I know why you want to do it. Because it's likely to get you in trouble."

"No, he gave me his word," Avery said.

"Cowboy Frank? The one who had you drive guns to Nicaragua?"

"That was perfectly legal," Avery said.

Jeff had a point, as usual. Specialty Shipping did the jobs no reputable company would handle. Ergo, so did Avery.

"What is it this time?" Blake asked.

"I can't say." The email had come through; Frank had attached the instructions as if a PDF were more secure than email. She opened and scanned them.

The job had been cleared by the government, but the client was the alien passenger, and she was to take orders only from him, within the law. She scanned the rest of the instructions till she saw the pickup time. "Damn, I've got to get going," she said.

Her brother followed her into the guest room to watch her pack up. He had never understood her nomadic lifestyle, which made his silent support for it all the more generous. She was compelled to wander; he was rooted in this home, this relationship, this warm, supportive community. She was a discarder, using things up and throwing them away; he had created a home that was a visual expression of himself—from the spare, Japanese-style furniture to the Zen colors on the walls. Visiting him was like living inside a beautiful soul. She had no idea how they could have grown up so different. It was as if they were foundlings.

She pulled on her boots and shouldered her backpack. Blake hugged her. "Have a good trip," he said. "Call me."

"Will do," she said, and hit the road again.

The media had called the dome in Rock Creek Park the Mother Ship—but only because of its proximity to the White House, not because it was in any way distinctive. Like the others, it had appeared overnight, sited on a broad, grassy clearing that had been a secluded picnic ground in the urban park. It filled the entire creek valley, cutting off the trails and greatly inconveniencing the joggers and bikers.

Avery was unprepared for its scale. Like most people, she had seen the domes only on TV, and the small screen did not do justice to the neck-craning reality. She leaned forward over the wheel and peered out the windshield as she brought the bus to a halt at the last checkpoint. The National Park Police pickup that had escorted her through all the other checkpoints pulled aside.

The appearance of an alien habitat had set off a battle of jurisdictions in Washington. The dome stood on U.S. Park Service property, but D.C. Police controlled all the access streets, and the U.S. Army was tasked with maintaining a perimeter around it. No agency wanted to surrender a particle of authority to the others. And then there was the polite, well-groomed young man who had introduced himself as "Henry," now sitting in the passenger seat next to her. His neatly pressed suit sported no bulges of weaponry, but she assumed he was CIA.

She now saw method in Frank's madness at calling her so spur-of-the-moment. Her last-minute arrival had prevented anyone from pulling her aside into a cinderblock room for a "briefing." Instead, Henry had accompanied her in the bus, chatting informally.

"Say, while you're on the road . . ."

"No," she said.

"No?"

"The alien's my client. I don't spy on clients."

He paused a moment, but seemed unruffled. "Not even for your country?"

"If I think my country's in danger, I'll get in touch."

"Fair enough," he said pleasantly. She hadn't expected him to give up so easily.

He handed her a business card. "So you can get in touch," he said.

She glanced at it. It said "Henry," with a phone number. No logo, no agency, no last name. She put it in a pocket.

"I have to get out here," he said when the bus rolled to a halt a hundred yards from the dome. "It's been nice meeting you, Avery."

"Take your bug with you," she said.

"I beg your pardon?"

"The bug you left somewhere in this cab."

"There's no bug," he said seriously.

Since the bus was probably wired like a studio, she shrugged and resolved not to scratch anywhere embarrassing till she had a chance to search. As she closed the door behind Henry, the soldiers removed the roadblock and she eased the bus forward.

It was almost evening, but floodlights came on as she approached the dome. She pulled the bus parallel to the wall and lowered the wheelchair lift. One of the hexagonal panels slid aside, revealing a stocky, dark-haired young man in black glasses, surrounded by packing crates of the same pearly substance as the dome. Avery started forward to help with loading, but he said tensely, "Stay where you are." She obeyed. He pushed the first crate forward and it moved as if on wheels, though Avery could see none. It was slightly too wide for the lift, so the man put his hands on either side and pushed in. The crate reconfigured itself, growing taller and narrower till it fit onto the platform. Avery activated the power lift.

He wouldn't let Avery touch any of the crates, but insisted on stowing them himself at the back of the bus, where a private bedroom suite had once accommodated a touring celebrity singer. When the last crate was on, he came forward and said, "We can go now."

"What about the other passenger?" Avery said.

"He's here."

She realized that the alien must have been in one of the crates—or, for all she knew, *was* one of the crates. "Okay," she said. "Where to?"

"Anywhere," he said, and turned to go back into the bedroom.

Since she had no instructions to the contrary, Avery decided to head south. As she pulled out of the park, there was no police escort, no helicopter overhead, no obvious trailing car. The terms of this journey had been carefully negotiated at the highest levels, she knew. Their security was to be secrecy; no one was to know where they were. Avery's instructions from Frank had stressed that, aside from getting the alien safely where he wanted to go, insuring his privacy was her top priority. She was not to pry into his business or allow anyone else to do so.

Rush hour traffic delayed them a long time. At first, Avery concentrated on putting as much distance as she could between the bus and Washington. It was past ten by the time she turned off the main roads. She activated the GPS to try and find a route, but all the screen showed was snow. She tried her phone, and the result was the same. Not even the radio worked. One of those crates must have contained a jamming device; the bus was a rolling electronic dead zone. She smiled. So much for Henry's bugs.

It was quiet and peaceful driving through the night. A nearly full moon rode in the clear autumn sky, and woods closed in around them. Once, when she had first taken up driving in order to escape her memories, she had played a game of heading randomly down roads she had never seen, getting deliberately lost. Now she played it again, not caring where she ended up. She had never been good at keeping to the main roads.

By 3:00 she was tired, and when she saw the entrance to a state park, she turned and pulled into the empty parking lot. In the quiet after the engine shut off, she walked back through the kitchen and sitting area to see if there were any objections from her passengers. She listened at the closed door, but heard nothing and concluded they were asleep. As she was turning away, the door jerked open and the translator said, "What do you want?"

He was still fully dressed, exactly as she had seen him before, except without the glasses, his eyes were a little bloodshot, as if he hadn't closed them. "I've pulled over to get some sleep," she said. "It's not safe to keep driving without rest."

"Oh. All right," he said, and closed the door.

Shrugging, she went forward. There was a fold-down bunk that had once served the previous owner's entourage, and she now prepared to use it. She brushed her teeth in the tiny bathroom, pulled a sleeping bag from her backpack, and settled in.

M orning sun woke her. When she opened her eyes, it was flooding in the windows. At the kitchen table a yard away from her, the translator was sitting, staring out the window. By daylight, she saw that he had a square face the color of teak and closely trimmed black beard. She guessed that he might be Latino, and in his twenties.

"Morning," she said. He turned to stare at her, but said nothing. Not practiced in social graces, she thought. "I'm Avery," she said.

Still he didn't reply. "It's customary to tell me your name now," she said.

"Oh. Lionel," he answered.

"Pleased to meet you."

He said nothing, so she got up and went into the bathroom. When she came out, he was still staring fixedly out the window. She started making coffee. "Want some?" she asked.

"What is it?"

"Coffee."

"I ought to try it," he said reluctantly.

"Well, don't let me force you," she said.

"Why would you do that?" He was studying her, apprehensive.

"I wouldn't. I was being sarcastic. Like a joke. Never mind."

"Oh."

He got up restlessly and started opening the cupboards. Frank had stocked them with all the necessities, even a few luxuries. But Lionel didn't seem to find what he was looking for.

"Are you hungry?" Avery guessed.

"What do you mean?"

Avery searched for another way to word the question. "Would you like me to fix you some breakfast?"

He looked utterly stumped.

"Never mind. Just sit down and I'll make you something."

He sat down, gripping the edge of the table tensely. "That's a tree," he said, looking out the window.

"Right. It's a whole lot of trees."

"I ought to go out."

She didn't make the mistake of joking again. It was like talking to a person raised by wolves. Or aliens.

When she set a plate of eggs and bacon down in front of him, he sniffed it suspiciously. "That's food?"

"Yes, it's good. Try it."

He watched her eat for a few moments, then gingerly tried a bite of scrambled eggs. His expression showed distaste, but he resolutely forced himself to swallow. But when he tried the bacon, he couldn't bear it. "It bit my mouth," he said.

"You're probably not used to the salt. What do you normally eat?"

He reached in a pocket and took out some brown pellets that looked like dog kibble. Avery made a face of disgust. "What is that, people chow?"

"It's perfectly adapted to our nutritional needs," Lionel said. "Try it."

She was about to say "no thanks," but he was clearly making an effort to try new things, so she took a pellet and popped it in her mouth. It wasn't terrible—chewy rather than crunchy—but tasteless. "I think I'll stick to our food," she said.

He looked gloomy. "I need to learn to eat yours."

"Why? Research?"

He nodded. "I have to find out how the feral humans live."

So, Avery reflected, she was dealing with someone raised as a pet, who was now being released into the wild. For whatever reason.

"So where do you want to go today?" Avery said, sipping coffee.

He gave an indifferent gesture.

"You're heading for St. Louis?"

"Oh, I just picked that name off a map. It seemed to be in the center."

"That it is." She had lived there once; it was so incorrigibly in the center there was no edge to it. "Do you want to go by any particular route?"

He shrugged.

"How much time do you have?"

"As long as it takes."

"Okay. The scenic route, then."

She got up to clean the dishes, telling Lionel that this was a good time for him to go out, if he wanted to. It took him a while to summon his resolve. She watched out the kitchen window as he approached a tree as if to have a conversation with it. He felt its bark, smelled its leaves, and returned unhappy and distracted.

Avery followed the same random-choice method of navigation as the previous night, but always trending west. Soon they came to the first ridge of mountains. People from western states talked as if the Appalachians weren't real mountains, but they were—rugged and impenetrable ridges like walls erected to bar people from the land of milk and honey. In the mountains, all the roads ran northeast and southwest through the valleys between the crumpled land, with only the brave roads daring to climb up and pierce the ranges. The autumn leaves were at their height, russet and gold against the brilliant sky. All day long Lionel sat staring out the window.

That night she found a half-deserted campground outside a small town. She refilled the water tanks, hooked up the electricity, then came back in. "You're all set," she told Lionel. "If it's all right with you, I'm heading into town."

"Okay," he said.

It felt good to stretch her legs walking along the highway shoulder. The air was chill but bracing. The town was a tired, half-abandoned place, but she found a bar and settled down with a beer and a burger. She couldn't help watching the patrons around her—worn-down, elderly people just managing to hang on. What would an alien think of America if she brought him here?

Remembering that she was away from the interference field, she thumbed on her phone—and immediately realized that the ping would give away her location to the spooks. But since she'd already done it, she dialed her brother's number and left a voicemail congratulating him on the concert she was missing. "Everything's fine with me," she said, then added mischievously, "I met a nice young man named Henry. I think he's sweet on me. Bye."

Heading back through the night, she became aware that someone was following her. The highway was too dark to see who it was, but when she stopped, the footsteps behind her stopped, too. At last a car passed, and she wheeled around to see what the headlights showed.

"Lionel!" she shouted. He didn't answer, just stood there, so she walked back toward him. "Did you follow me?"

He was standing with hands in pockets, hunched against the cold. Defensively, he said, "I wanted to see what you would do when I wasn't around."

"It's none of your business what I do off duty. Listen, respecting privacy goes both ways. If you want me to respect yours, you've got to respect mine, okay?"

He looked cold and miserable, so she said, "Come on, let's get back before you freeze solid."

They walked side by side in silence, gravel crunching underfoot. At last he said stiffly, "I'd like to re-negotiate our contract."

"Oh, yeah? What part of the contract?"

"The part about privacy. I . . ." He searched for words. "We should have asked for more than a driver. We need a translator."

At least he'd realized it. He might speak perfect English, but he was not fluent in Human.

"My contract is with your . . . employer. Is this what he wants?"

"Who?"

"The other passenger. I don't know what to call him. 'The alien' isn't polite. What's his name?"

"They don't have names. They don't have a language."

Astonished, Avery said, "Then how do you communicate?"

He glowered at her. She held up her hands. "Sorry. No offense intended. I'm just trying to find out what he wants."

"They don't want things," he muttered, gazing fixedly at the moonlit road. "At least, not like you do. They're not . . . awake. Aware. Not like people are."

This made so little sense to Avery, she wondered if he were having trouble with the language. "I don't understand," she said. "You mean they're not . . . sentient?"

"They're not conscious," he said. "There's a difference."

"But they have technology. They built those domes, or brought them here, or whatever the hell they did. They have an advanced civilization."

"I didn't say they aren't smart. They're smarter than people are. They're just not conscious."

Avery shook her head. "I'm sorry, I just can't imagine it."

"Yes, you can," Lionel said impatiently. "People function unconsciously all the time. You're not aware that you're keeping your balance right now—you just do it automatically. You don't have to be aware to walk, or breathe. In fact, the more skillful you are at something, the less aware you are. Being aware would just degrade their skill."

They had come to the campground entrance. Behind the dark pine trees, Avery could see the bus, holding its unknowable passenger. For a moment the bus seemed to stare back with blank eyes. She made herself focus on the practical. "So how can I know what he wants?"

"I'm telling you."

She refrained from asking, "And how do *you* know?" because he'd already refused to answer that. The new privacy rules were to be selective, then. But she already knew more about the aliens than anyone else on Earth, except the translators. Not that she understood.

'm sorry, I can't keep calling him 'him,' or 'the alien,'" Avery said the next morning over breakfast. "I have to give him a name. I'm going to call him 'Mr. Burbage.' If he doesn't know, he won't mind."

Lionel didn't look any more disturbed than usual. She took that as consent.

"So where are we going today?" she asked.

He pressed his lips together in concentration. "I need to go to a place where I can acquire knowledge."

Since this could encompass anything from a brothel to a university, Avery said, "You've got to be more specific. What kind of knowledge?"

"Knowledge about you."

"Me?"

"No, you humans. How you work."

Humans. For that, she would have to find a bigger town.

As she cruised down a county road, Avery thought about Blake. Once, he had told her that to play an instrument truly well, you had to lose all awareness of what you were doing, and rely entirely on the muscle memory in your fingers. "You are so in the present, there is no room for self," Blake said. "No ego, no doubt, no introspection."

She envied him the ability to achieve such a state. She had tried to play the saxophone, but had never gotten good enough to experience what Blake described. Only playing video games could she concentrate intensely enough to lose self-awareness. It was strange, how addictive it was to escape the prison of her skull and forget she had a self. Mystics and meditators strove to achieve such a state.

A motion in the corner of her eye made her slam on the brakes and swerve. A startled deer pirouetted, flipped its tail, and leaped away. She continued on more slowly, searching for a sign to see where she was. She could not remember having driven the last miles, or whether she had passed any turns. Smiling grimly, she realized that driving was *her* skill, something she knew so well that she could do it unconsciously. She had even reacted to a threat before knowing what it was. Her reflexes were faster than her conscious mind.

Were the aliens like that all the time? In a perpetual state of flow, like virtuoso musicians or Zen monks in *samadhi?* What would be the point of achieving such supreme skill, if the price was never knowing it was *you* doing it?

Around noon, they came to a town nestled in a steep valley on a rushing river. Driving down the main street, she spied a quaint, cupolaed building with a "Municipal Library" sign out front. Farther on, at the edge of town, an abandoned car lot offered a grass-pocked parking lot, so she turned in. "Come on, Lionel," she called out. "I've found a place for you to acquire knowledge."

They walked back into town together. The library was quiet and empty except for an old man reading a magazine. The selection of books was sparse, but there was a row of computers. "You know how to use these?" Avery said in a low voice.

"Not this kind," Lionel said. "They're very . . . primitive."

They sat down together, and Avery explained how to work the mouse and get on the internet, how to search and scroll. "I've got it," he said. "You can go now."

Shrugging, she left him to his research. She strolled down the main street, stopped in a drugstore, then found a café that offered fried egg sandwiches on Wonder Bread, a luxury from her childhood. With lunch and a cup of coffee, she settled down to wait, sorting email on her phone.

Some time later, she became aware of the television behind the counter. It was tuned to one of those daytime exposé shows hosted by a shrill woman who spoke in a tone of breathless indignation. "Coming up," she said, "Slaves or traitors? Who *are* these alien translators?"

Avery realized that some part of her brain must have been listening and alerted her conscious mind to pay attention, just as it had reacted to the deer. She had a threat detection system she was not even aware of.

In the story that followed, a correspondent revealed that she had been unable to match any of the translators with missing children recorded in the past twenty years. The host treated this as suspicious information that someone ought to be looking into. Then came a panel of experts to discuss what they knew of the translators, which was nothing.

"Turncoats," commented one of the men at the counter watching the show. "Why would anyone betray his own race?"

"They're not even human," said another, "just made to look that way. They're clones or robots or something."

"The government won't do anything. They're just letting those aliens sit there."

Avery got up to pay her bill. The woman at the cash register said, "You connected with that big tour bus parked out at Fenniman's?"

She had forgotten that in a town like this, everyone knew instantly what was out of the ordinary.

"Yeah," Avery said. "Me and my . . . boyfriend are delivering it to a new owner."

She glanced up at the television just as a collage of faces appeared. Lionel's was in the top row. "Look closely," the show's host said. "If you recognize any of these faces, call us at 1-800- . . ." Avery didn't wait to hear the number. The door shut behind her.

It was hard not to walk quickly enough to attract attention. Why had she left him alone, as if it were safe? Briefly, she thought of bringing the bus in to pick him up at the library, but it would only attract more attention. The sensible thing was to slip inconspicuously out of town.

Lionel was engrossed in a website about the brain when she came in. She sat down next to him and said quietly, "We've got to leave."

"I'm not . . ."

"Lionel. We have to leave. Right now."

He frowned, but got the message. As he rose to put on his coat, she quickly erased his browser history and cache. Then she led the way out and around the building to a back street where there were fewer eyes. "Hold my hand," she said.

"Why?"

"I told them you were my boyfriend. We've got to act friendly."

He didn't object or ask what was going on. The aliens had trained him well, she thought.

The street they were on came to an end, and they were forced back onto the main thoroughfare, right past the café. In Avery's mind every window was a pair of eyes staring at the strangers. As they left the business section of town and the buildings thinned out, she became aware of someone walking a block behind them. Glancing back, she saw a man in hunter's camouflage and billed cap, carrying a gun case on a strap over one shoulder.

She sped up, but the man trailing them sped up as well. When they were in sight of the bus, Avery pressed the keys into Lionel's hand and said, "Go on ahead. I'll stall this guy. Get inside and don't open the door to anyone but me." Then she turned back to confront their pursuer.

Familiarity tickled as he drew closer. When she was sure, she called out, "Afternoon, Henry! What a coincidence to see you here."

"Hello, Avery," he said. He didn't look quite right in the hunter costume: he was too urban and fit. "That was pretty careless of you. I followed to make sure you got back safe."

"I didn't know his picture was all over the TV," she said. "I've been out of touch."

"I know, we lost track of you for a while there. Please don't do that again."

As threats went, Henry now seemed like the lesser evil. She hesitated, then said, "I didn't see any need to get in touch." That meant the country was not in peril.

"Thanks," he said. "Listen, if you turn left on Highway 19 ahead, you'll come to a national park with a campground. It'll be safe."

As she walked back to the bus, she was composing a lie about who she had been talking to. But Lionel never asked. As soon as she was on board he started eagerly telling her about what he had learned in the library. She had never seen him so animated, so she gestured him to sit in the passenger seat beside her while she got the bus moving again.

"The reason you're conscious is because of the cerebral cortex," he said. "It's an add-on, the last part of the brain to evolve. Its only purpose is to monitor what the rest of the brain is doing. All the sensory input goes to the inner brain first, and gets processed, so the cortex never gets the raw data. It only sees the effect on the rest of the brain, not what's really out there. That's why you're aware of yourself. In fact, it's *all* you're aware of."

"Why are you saying 'you'?" Avery asked. "You've got a cerebral cortex, too." Defensively, he said, "I'm not like you."

Avery shrugged. "Okay." But she wanted to keep the conversation going. "So Mr. Burbage doesn't have a cortex? Is that what you're saying?"

"That's right," Lionel said. "For him, life is a skill of the autonomic nervous system, not something he had to consciously learn. That's why he can think and react faster than we can, and requires less energy. The messages don't have to travel on a useless detour through the cortex."

"Useless?" Avery objected. "I kind of like being conscious."

Lionel fell silent, suddenly grave and troubled.

She glanced over at him. "What's the matter?"

In a low tone he said, "He likes being conscious, too. It's what they want from us."

Avery gripped the wheel and tried not to react. Up to now, the translators had denied that the aliens wanted anything at all from humans. But then it occurred to her that Lionel might not mean humans when he said "us."

"You mean, you translators?" she ventured.

He nodded, looking grim.

"Is that a bad thing?" she asked, reacting to his expression.

"Not for us," he said. "It's bad for them. It's killing him."

He was struggling with some strong emotion. Guilt, she thought. Maybe grief.

"I'm sorry," she said.

Angrily, he stood up to head back into the bus. "Why do you make me think of this?" he said. "Why can't you just mind your own business?"

Avery drove on, listening as he slammed the bedroom door behind him. She didn't feel any resentment. She knew all about guilt and grief, and how useless they made you feel. Lionel's behavior made more sense to her now. He was having trouble distinguishing between what was happening to him externally and what was coming from inside. Even people skilled at being human had trouble with that.

The national park Henry had recommended turned out to be at Cumberland Gap, the mountain pass early pioneers had used to migrate west to Kentucky. They spent the night in the campground undisturbed. At dawn, Avery strolled out in the damp morning air to look around. She quickly returned to say, "Lionel, come out here. You need to see this."

She led him across the road to an overlook facing west. From the edge of the Appalachians they looked out on range after range of wooded foothills swaddled in fog. The morning sun at their backs lit everything in shades of mauve and azure. Avery felt like Daniel Boone looking out on the Promised Land, stretching before her into the misty distance, unpolluted by the past.

"I find this pleasant," Lionel said gravely.

Avery smiled. It was a breakthrough statement for someone so unaccustomed to introspection that he hadn't been able to tell her he was hungry two days ago. But all she said was, "Me, too."

After several moments of silence, she ventured, "Don't you think Mr. Burbage would enjoy seeing this? There's no one else around. Doesn't he want to get out of the bus some time?"

"He *is* seeing it," Lionel said.

"What do you mean?"

"He is here." Lionel tapped his head with a finger.

Avery couldn't help staring. "You mean you have some sort of telepathic connection with him?"

"There's no such thing as telepathy," Lionel said dismissively. "They communicate with neurotransmitters." She was still waiting, so he said, "He doesn't have to be all in one place. Part of him is with me, part of him is in the bus."

"In your *head?*" she asked, trying not to betray how creepy she found this news.

He nodded. "He needs me to observe the world for him, and understand it. They have had lots of other helper species to do things for them—species that build things, or transport them. But we're the first one with advanced consciousness."

"And that's why they're interested in us."

Lionel looked away to avoid her eyes, but nodded. "They like it," he said, his voice low and reluctant. "At first it was just novel and new for them, but now it's become an addiction, like a dangerous drug. We pay a high metabolic price for consciousness; it's why our lifespan is so short. They live for centuries. But when they get hooked on us, they burn out even faster than we do."

He picked up a rock and flung it over the cliff, watching as it arced up, then plummeted.

"And if he dies, what happens to you?" Avery asked.

"I don't want him to die," Lionel said. He put his hands in his pockets and studied his feet. "It feels . . . good to have him around. I like his company. He's very old, very wise."

For a moment, she could see it through his eyes. She could imagine feeling intimately connected to an ancient being who was dying from an inability to part with his adopted human son. What a terrible burden for Lionel to carry, to be slowly killing someone he loved.

And yet, she still felt uneasy.

"How do you know?" she asked.

He looked confused. "What do you mean?"

"You said he's old and wise. How do you know that?"

"The way you know anything unconscious. It's a feeling, an instinct."

"Are you sure he not controlling you? Pushing around your neurotransmitters?"

"That's absurd," he said, mildly irritated. "I told you, he's not conscious, at least not naturally. Control is a conscious thing."

"But what if you did something he didn't want?"

"I don't feel like doing things he doesn't want. Like talking to you now. He must have decided he can trust you, because I wouldn't feel like telling you anything if he hadn't."

Avery wasn't sure whether being trusted by an alien was something she aspired to. But she did want Lionel to trust her, and so she let the subject drop.

"Where do you want to go today?" she asked.

"You keep asking me that." He stared out on the landscape, as if waiting for a revelation. At last he said, "I want to see humans living as they normally do. We've barely seen any of them. I didn't think the planet was so sparsely populated."

"Okay," she said. "I'm going to have to make a phone call for that."

When he had returned to the bus, she strolled away, took out Henry's card, and thumbed the number. Despite the early hour, he answered on the first ring.

"He wants to see humans," she said. "Normal humans behaving normally. Can you help me out?"

"Let me make some calls," he said. "I'll text you instructions."

"No men in black," she said. "You know what I mean?"

"I get it."

When Avery stopped for diesel around noon, the gas station television was blaring with news that the Justice Department would investigate the aliens for abducting human children. She escaped into the restroom to check her phone. The internet was ablaze with speculation: who the translators were, whether they could be freed, whether they were human at all. The part of the government that had approved Lionel's road trip was clearly working at cross purposes with the part that had dreamed up this new strategy for extracting information from the aliens. The only good news was that no hint had leaked out that an alien was roaming the back roads of America in a converted bus.

Henry had texted her a cryptic suggestion to head toward Paris. She had to Google it to find that there actually was a Paris, Kentucky. When she came out to pay for the fuel, she was relieved to see that the television had moved on to World Series coverage. On impulse, she bought a Cardinals cap for Lionel.

Paris turned out to be a quaint old Kentucky town that had once had delusions of cityhood. Today, a county fair was the main event in town. The RV park was almost full, but Avery's E.T. Express managed to maneuver in. When everything was settled, she sat on the bus steps sipping a Bud and waiting for night so they could venture out with a little more anonymity. The only thing watching her was a skittish, half-wild cat crouched behind a trashcan. Somehow, it reminded her of Lionel, so she tossed it a Cheeto to see if she could lure it out. It refused the bait.

That night, disguised by the dark and a Cardinals cap, Lionel looked tolerably inconspicuous. As they were leaving to take in the fair, she said, "Will Mr. Burbage be okay while we're gone? What if someone tries to break into the bus?"

"Don't worry, he'll be all right," Lionel said. His tone implied more than his words. She resolved to call Henry at the earliest opportunity and pass along a warning not to try anything.

The people in the midway all looked authentic. If there were snipers on the bigtop and agents on the merry-go-round, she couldn't tell. When people failed to recognize Lionel at the ticket stand and popcorn wagon, she began to relax. Everyone was here to enjoy themselves, not to look for aliens.

She introduced Lionel to the joys of corn dogs and cotton candy, to the Ferris wheel and tilt-a-whirl. He took in the jangling sounds, the smells of deep-fried food, and the blinking lights with a grave and studious air. When they had had their fill of all the machines meant to disorient and confuse, they took a break at a picnic table, sipping Cokes.

Avery said, "Is Mr. Burbage enjoying this?"

Lionel shrugged. "Are you?" He wasn't deflecting her question; he actually wanted to know.

She considered. "I think people enjoy these events mainly because they bring back childhood memories," she said.

"Yes. It does seem familiar," Lionel said.

"Really? What about it?"

He paused, searching his mind. "The smells," he said at last.

Avery nodded. It was smells for her, as well: deep fat fryers, popcorn. "Do you remember anything from the time before you were abducted?"

"Adopted," he corrected her.

"Right, adopted. What about your family?"

He shook his head.

"Do you ever wonder what kind of people they were?"

"The kind of people who wouldn't look for me," he said coldly.

"Wait a minute. You don't know that. For all you know, your mother might have cried her eyes out when you disappeared."

He stared at her. She realized she had spoken with more emotion than she had intended. The subject had touched a nerve. "Sorry," she muttered, and got up. "I'm tired. Can we head back?"

"Sure," he said, and followed her without question.

That night she couldn't sleep. She lay watching the pattern from the lights outside on the ceiling, but her mind was on the back of the bus. Up to now she had slept without thinking of the strangeness just beyond the door, but tonight it bothered her.

About 3:00 AM she roused from a doze at the sound of Lionel's quiet footstep going past her. She lay silent as he eased the bus door open. When he had gone outside she rose and looked to see what he was doing. He walked away from the bus toward a maintenance shed and some dumpsters. She debated whether to follow him; it was just what she had scolded him for doing to her. But concern for his safety won out, and she took a flashlight from the driver's console, put it in the pocket of a windbreaker, and followed.

At first she thought she had lost him. The parking lot was motionless and quiet. A slight breeze stirred the pines on the edge of the road. Then she heard a scuffling sound ahead, a thump, and a soft crack. At first she stood listening, but when there was no more sound, she crept forward. Rounding the dumpster, she saw in its shadow a figure crouched on the ground. Unable to make out what was going on, she switched on the flashlight.

Lionel turned, his eyes wild and hostile. Dangling from his hand was the limp body of a cat, its head ripped off. His face was smeared with its blood. Watching her, he deliberately ripped a bite of cat meat from the body with his teeth and swallowed.

"Lionel!" she cried out in horror. "Put that down!"

He turned away, trying to hide his prey like an animal. Without thinking, she grabbed his arm, and he spun fiercely around, as if to fight her. His eyes looked utterly alien. She stepped back. "It's me, Avery," she said.

He looked down at the mangled carcass in his hand, then dropped it, rose, and backed away. Once again taking his arm, Avery guided him away from the dumpsters, back to the bus. Inside, she led him to the kitchen sink. "Wash," she ordered, then went to firmly close the bus door.

Her heart was pounding, and she kept the heavy flashlight in her hand for security. But when she came back, she saw he was trembling so hard he had dropped the soap and was leaning against the sink for support. Seeing that his face was still smeared with blood, she took a paper towel and wiped him off, then dried his hands. He sank onto the bench by the kitchen table. She stood watching him, arms crossed, waiting for him to speak. He didn't.

"So what was that about?" she said sternly.

He shook his head.

"Cats aren't food," she said. "They're living beings."

Still he didn't speak.

"Have you been sneaking out at night all along?" she demanded.

He shook his head. "I don't know . . . I just thought . . . I wanted to see what it would feel like."

"You mean *Mr. Burbage* wanted to see what it would feel like," she said.

"Maybe," he admitted.

"Well, people don't do things like that."

He was looking ill. She grabbed his arm and hustled him into the bathroom, aiming him at the toilet. She left him there vomiting, and started shoving belongings into her backpack. As she swung it onto her shoulder, he staggered to the bathroom door.

"I'm leaving," she said. "I can't sleep here, knowing you do things like that."

He looked dumbstruck. She pushed past him and out the door. She was striding away across the gravel parking lot when he called after her, "Avery! You can't leave."

She wheeled around. "Can't I? Just watch me."

He left the bus and followed her. "What are we going to do?"

"I don't care," she said.

"I won't do it again."

"Who's talking, you or him?"

A light went on in the RV next to them. She realized they were making a late-night scene like trailer-park trash, attracting attention. This wasn't an argument they could have in public. And now that she was out here, she realized she had no place to go. So she shooed Lionel back toward the bus.

Once inside, she said, "This is the thing, Lionel. This whole situation is creeping me out. You can't make any promises as long as he's in charge. Maybe next time he'll want to see what it feels like to kill *me* in my sleep, and you won't be able to stop him."

Lionel looked disturbed. "He won't do that."

"How do you know?"

"I just . . . do."

"That's not good enough. I need to see him."

Avery wasn't sure why she had blurted it out, except that living with an invisible, ever-present passenger had become intolerable. As long as she didn't know what the door in the back of the bus concealed, she couldn't be at ease.

He shook his head. "That won't help."

She crossed her arms and said, "I can't stay unless I know what he is."

Lionel's face took on an introspective look, as if he were consulting his conscience. At last he said, "You'd have to promise not to tell anyone."

Avery hadn't really expected him to consent, and now felt a nervous tremor. She dropped her pack on the bed and gripped her hands into fists. "All right."

He led the way to the back of the bus and eased the door open as if fearing to disturb the occupant within. She followed him in. The small room was dimly lit and there was an earthy smell. All the crates he had brought in must have been folded up and put away, because none were visible. There was an unmade bed, and beside it a clear box like an aquarium tank, holding something she could not quite make out. When Lionel turned on a light, she saw what the tank contained.

It looked most like a coral or sponge—a yellowish, rounded growth the size of half a beach ball, resting on a bed of wood chips and dead leaves. Lionel picked up a spray bottle and misted it tenderly. It responded by expanding as if breathing.

"*That's* Mr. Burbage?" Avery whispered.

Lionel nodded. "Part of him. The most important part."

The alien seemed insignificant, something she could destroy with a bottle of bleach. "Can he move?" she asked.

"Oh, yes," Lionel said. "Not the way we do."

She waited for him to explain. At first he seemed reluctant, but he finally said, "They are colonies of cells with a complicated life cycle. This is the final stage of their development, when they become most complex and organized. After this, they dissolve into the earth. The cells don't die; they go on to form other coalitions. But the individual is lost. Just like us, I suppose."

What she was feeling, she realized, was disappointment. In spite of all Lionel had told her, she had hoped there would be some way of communicating. Before, she had not truly believed that the alien could be insentient. Now she did. In fact, she found it hard to believe that it could think at all.

"How do you know he's intelligent?" she asked. "He could be just a heap of chemicals, like a loaf of bread rising."

"How do you know *I'm* intelligent?" he said, staring at the tank. "Or anyone?"

"You react to me. You communicate. He can't."

"Yes, he can."

"How? If I touched him—"

"No!" Lionel said quickly. "Don't touch him. You'd see, he would react. It wouldn't be malice, just a reflex."

"Then how do you . . . ?"

Reluctantly, Lionel said, "He has to touch you. It's the only way to exchange neurotransmitters." He paused, as if debating something internally. She watched the conflict play across his face. At last, reluctantly, he said, "I think he would be willing to communicate with you."

It was what she had wanted, some reassurance of the alien's intentions. But now it was offered, her instincts were unwilling. "No thanks," she said.

Lionel looked relieved. She realized he hadn't wanted to give up his unique relationship with Mr. Burbage.

"Thanks anyway," she said, for the generosity of the offer he hadn't wanted to make.

And yet, it left her unsure. She had only Lionel's word that the alien was friendly. After tonight, that wasn't enough.

Neither of them could sleep, so as soon as day came they set out again. Heading west, Avery knew they were going deeper and deeper into isolationist territory, where even human strangers were unwelcome, never mind aliens. This was the land where she had grown up, and she knew it well. From here, the world outside looked like a violent, threatening place full of impoverished hordes who envied and hated the good life in America. Here, even the churches preached self-satisfaction, and discontent was the fault of those who hated freedom—like college professors, homosexuals, and immigrants.

Growing up, she had expected to spend her life in this country. She had done everything right—married just out of high school, worked as a waitress, gotten pregnant at 19. Her life had been mapped out in front of her.

She couldn't even imagine it now.

This morning, Lionel seemed to want to talk. He sat beside her in the co-pilot seat, watching the road and answering her questions.

"What does it feel like, when he communicates with you?"

He reflected. "It feels like a mood, or a hunch. Or I act on impulse."

"How do you know it's him, and not your own subconscious?"

"I don't. It doesn't matter."

Avery shook her head. "I wouldn't want to go through life acting on hunches."

"Why not?"

"Your unconscious . . . it's unreliable. You can't control it. It can lead you wrong."

"That's absurd," he said. "It's not some outside entity; it's *you*. It's your *conscious* mind that's the slave master, always worrying about control. Your unconscious only wants to preserve you."

"Not if there's an alien messing around with it."

"He's not like that. This drive to dominate—that's a conscious thing. He doesn't have that slave master part of the brain."

"Do you know that for a fact, or are you just guessing?"

"Guessing is what your unconscious tells you. Knowing is a conscious thing. They're only in conflict if your mind is fighting itself."

"Sounds like the human condition to me," Avery said. This had to be the weirdest conversation in her life.

"Is he here now?" she asked.

"Of course he is."

"Don't you ever want to get away from him?"

Puzzled, he said, "Why should I?"

"Privacy. To be by yourself."

"I don't want to be by myself."

Something in his voice told her he was thinking ahead, to the death of his lifelong companion. Abruptly, he rose and walked back into the bus.

Actually, she had lied to him. She *had* gone through life acting on hunches. *Go with your gut* had been her motto, because she had trusted her gut. But of course it had nothing to do with gut, or heart—it was her unconscious mind she had been following. Her unconscious was why she took this road rather than that, or preferred Raisin Bran to Corn Flakes. It was why she found certain tunes achingly beautiful, and why she was fond of this strange young man, against all rational evidence.

As the road led them nearer to southern Illinois, Avery found memories surfacing. They came with a tug of regret, like a choking rope pulling her back toward the person she hadn't become. She thought of the cascade of non-decisions that had led her to become the rootless, disconnected person she was, as much a stranger to the human race as Lionel was, in her way.

What good has consciousness ever done me? she thought. It only made her aware that she could never truly connect with another human being, deep down. And on that day when her cells would dissolve into the soil, there would be no trace her consciousness had ever existed.

That night they camped at a freeway rest stop a day's drive from St. Louis. Lionel was moody and anxious. Avery's attempt to interest him in a trashy novel was fruitless. At last she asked what was wrong. Fighting to find the words, he said, "He's very ill. This trip was a bad idea. All the stimulation has made him worse."

Tentatively, she said, "Should we head for one of the domes?"

Lionel shook his head. "They can't cure this . . . this addiction to consciousness. If they could, I don't think he'd take it."

"Do the others—his own people—know what's wrong with him?"

Lionel nodded wordlessly.

She didn't know what comfort to offer. "Well," she said at last, "it was his choice to come."

"A selfish choice," Lionel said angrily.

She couldn't help noticing that he was speaking for himself, Lionel, as distinct from Mr. Burbage. Thoughtfully, she said, "Maybe they can't love us as much as we can love them."

He looked at her as if the word "love" had never entered his vocabulary. "Don't say *us*," he said. "I'm not one of you."

She didn't believe it for a second, but she just said, "Suit yourself," and turned back to her novel. After a few moments, he went into the back of the bus and closed the door.

She lay there trying to read for a while, but the story couldn't hold her attention. She kept listening for some sound from beyond the door, some indication of how they were doing. At last she got up quietly and went to listen. Hearing nothing, she tried the door and found it unlocked. Softly, she cracked it open to look inside.

Lionel was not asleep. He was lying on the bed, his head next to the alien's tank. But the alien was no longer in the tank; it was on the pillow. It had extruded a mass of long, cordlike tentacles that gripped Lionel's head in a medusa embrace, snaking into every opening. One had entered an ear, another a nostril. A third had nudged aside an eyeball in order to enter the eye socket. Fluid coursed along the translucent vessels connecting man and creature.

Avery wavered on the edge of horror. Her first instinct was to intervene, to defend Lionel from what looked like an attack. But the expression on his face was not of terror, but peace. All his vague references to exchanging neurotransmitters came back to her now: this was what he had meant. The alien communicated by drinking cerebrospinal fluid, its drug of choice, and injecting its own.

Shaken, she eased the door shut again. Unable to get the image out of her mind, she went outside to walk around the bus to calm her nerves. After three circuits she leaned back against the cold metal, wishing she had a cigarette for the first time in years. Above her, the stars were cold and bright. What was this relationship she had landed in the middle of—predator and prey? father and son? pusher and addict? master and slave? Or some strange combination of all? Had she just witnessed an alien learning about love?

She had been saving a bottle of bourbon for special occasions, so she went in to pour herself a shot.

To her surprise, Lionel emerged before she was quite drunk. She thought of offering him a glass, but wasn't sure how it would mix with whatever was already in his brain.

He sat down across from her, but just stared silently at the floor for a long time. At last he stirred and said, "I think we ought to take him to a private place."

"What sort of private place?" Avery asked.

"Somewhere dignified. Natural. Secluded."

To die, she realized. The alien wanted to die in private. Or Lionel wanted him to. There was no telling where one left off and the other began.

"I know a place," she said. "Will he make it another day?"

Lionel nodded silently.

Through the bourbon haze, Avery wondered what she ought to say to Henry. Was the country in danger? She didn't think so. This seemed like a personal matter. To be sure, she said, "You're certain his relatives won't blame us if he dies?"

"Blame?" he said.

That was conscious-talk, she realized. "React when he doesn't come back?"

"If they were going to react, they would have done it when he left. They aren't expecting anything, not even his return. They don't live in an imaginary future like you people do."

"Wise of them," she said.

"Yes."

They rolled into St. Louis in late afternoon, across the Poplar Street Bridge next to the Arch and off onto I-70 toward the north part of town. Avery knew exactly where she was going. From the first moment Frank had told her the destination was St. Louis, she had known she would end up driving this way, toward the place where she had left the first part of her life.

Bellefontaine Cemetery lay on what had been the outskirts of the city in Victorian times, several hundred acres of greenery behind a stone wall and a wrought-iron gate. It was a relic from a time when cemeteries were landscaped, parklike sanctuaries from the city. Huge old oak and sweetgum trees lined the winding roadways, their branches now black against the sky. Avery drove slowly past the marble mausoleums and toward the hill at the back of the cemetery, which looked out over the valley toward the Missouri River. It was everything Lionel had wanted—peaceful, natural, secluded.

Some light rain misted down out of the overcast sky. Avery parked the bus and went out to check whether they were alone. She had seen no one but a single dog-walker near the entrance, and no vehicle had followed them in. The gates would close in half an hour, and the bus would have to be out. Henry and his friends were probably waiting outside the gate for them to appear again. She returned to the bus and knocked on Lionel's door. He opened it right away. Inside, the large picnic cooler they had bought was standing open, ready.

"Help me lift him in," Lionel said.

Avery maneuvered past the cooler to the tank. "Is it okay for me to touch him?"

"Hold your hand close to him for a few seconds."

Avery did as instructed. A translucent tentacle extruded from the cauliflower folds of the alien's body. It touched her palm, recoiled, then extended again. Gently, hesitantly, it explored her hand, tickling slightly as it probed her palm and curled around her pinkie. She held perfectly still.

"What is he thinking?" she whispered.

"He's learning your chemical identity," Lionel said.

"How can he learn without being aware? Can he even remember?"

"Of course he can remember. Your immune system learns and remembers just about every pathogen it ever met, and it's not aware. Can *you* remember them all?"

She shook her head, stymied.

At last, apparently satisfied, the tendril retracted into the alien's body.

"All right," Lionel said, "now you can touch him."

The alien was surprisingly heavy. Together, they lifted him onto the bed of dirt and wood chips Lionel had spread in the bottom of the cooler. Lionel fitted the lid on loosely, and each of them took a handle to carry their load out into the open air. Avery led the way around a mausoleum shaped like a Greek temple to an unmowed spot hidden from the path. Sycamore leaves and bark littered the ground, damp from the rain.

"Is this okay?" she asked.

For answer, Lionel set down his end of the cooler and straightened, breathing in the forest smell. "This is okay."

"I have to move the bus. Stay behind this building in case anyone comes by. I'll be back."

The gatekeeper waved as she pulled the bus out onto the street. By the time she had parked it on a nearby residential street and returned, the gate was closed. She walked around the cemetery perimeter to an unfrequented side, then scrambled up the wall and over the spiked fence.

Inside, the traffic noise of the city fell away. The trees arched overhead in churchlike silence. Not a squirrel stirred. Avery sat down on a tombstone to wait. Beyond the hill, Lionel was holding vigil at the side of his dying companion, and she wanted to give him privacy. The stillness felt good, but unfamiliar. Her life was made of motion. She had been driving for twenty years—driving away, driving beyond, always a new destination. Never back.

The daylight would soon be gone. She needed to do the other thing she had come here for. Raising the hood of her raincoat, she headed downhill, the grass caressing her sneakers wetly. It was years since she had visited the grave of her daughter Gabrielle, whose short life and death were like a chasm dividing her life into before and after. They had called it crib death then—an unexplained, random, purposeless death. "Nothing you could have done," the doctor had said, thinking that was more comforting than knowing that the universe just didn't give a damn.

Gabrielle's grave lay in a grove of cedar trees—the plot a gift from a sympathetic patron at the café where Avery had worked. At first she had thought of turning it down because the little grave would be overshadowed by more ostentatious death; but the suburban cemeteries had looked so industrial, monuments stamped out by machine. She had come to love the age and seclusion of this spot. At first, she had visited over and over.

As she approached in the fading light, she saw that something was lying on the headstone. When she came close she saw that some stranger had placed on the grave a little terra-cotta angel with one wing broken. Avery stood staring at the bedraggled figurine, now soaked with rain, a gift to her daughter from someone she didn't even know. Then, a sudden, unexpected wave of grief doubled her over. It had been twenty years since she had touched her daughter, but the memory was still vivid and tactile. She remembered the smell, the softness of her skin, the utter trust in her eyes. She felt again the aching hole of her absence.

Avery sank to her knees in the wet grass, sobbing for the child she hadn't been able to protect, for the sympathy of the nameless stranger, even for the helpless, mutilated angel who would never fly.

There was a sound behind her, and she looked up. Lionel stood there watching her, rain running down his face—no, it was tears. He wiped his eyes, then looked at his hands. "I don't know why I feel like this," he said.

Poor, muddled man. She got up and hugged him for knowing exactly how she felt. They stood there for a moment, two people trapped in their own brains, and the only crack in the wall was empathy.

"Is he gone?" she asked softly.

He shook his head. "Not yet. I left him alone in case it was me . . . interfering. Then I saw you and followed."

"This is my daughter's grave," Avery said. "I didn't know I still miss her so much."

She took his hand and started back up the hill. They said nothing, but didn't let go of each other till they got to the marble mausoleum where they had left Mr. Burbage.

The alien was still there, resting on the ground next to the cooler. Lionel knelt beside him and held out a hand. A bouquet of tentacles reached out and grasped it, then withdrew. Lionel came over to where Avery stood watching. "I'm going to stay with him. You don't have to."

"I'd like to," she said, "if it's okay with you."

He ducked his head furtively.

So they settled down to keep a strange death watch. Avery shared some chemical hand-warmers she had brought from the bus. When those ran out and night deepened, she managed to find some dry wood at the bottom of a groundskeeper's brush pile to start a campfire. She sat poking the fire with a stick, feeling drained of tears, worn down as an old tire.

"Does he know he's dying?" she asked.

Lionel nodded. "*I* know, and so he knows." A little bitterly, he added, "That's what consciousness does for you."

"So normally he wouldn't know?"

He shook his head. "Or care. It's just part of their life cycle. There's no death if there's no self to be aware of it."

"No life either," Avery said.

Lionel just sat breaking twigs and tossing them on the fire. "I keep wondering if it was worth it. If consciousness is good enough to die for."

She tried to imagine being free of her self—of the regrets of the past and fear of the future. If this were a *Star Trek* episode, she thought, this would be when Captain Kirk would deliver a speech in defense of being human, despite all the drawbacks. She didn't feel that way.

"You're right," she said. "Consciousness kind of sucks."

The sky was beginning to glow with dawn when at last they saw a change in the alien. The brainlike mass started to shrink and a liquid pool spread out from under it, as if it were dissolving. There was no sound. At the end, its body deflated like a falling soufflé, leaving nothing but a slight crust on the leaves and a damp patch on the ground.

They sat for a long time in silence. It was light when Lionel got up and brushed off his pants, his face set and grim. "Well, that's that," he said.

Avery felt reluctant to leave. "His cells are in the soil?" she said.

"Yes, they'll live underground for a while, spreading and multiplying. They'll go through some blooming and sporing cycles. If any dogs or children come along at that stage, the spores will establish a colony in their brains. It's how they invade."

His voice was perfectly indifferent. Avery stared at him. "You might have mentioned that."

He shrugged.

An inspiration struck her. She seized up a stick and started digging in the damp patch of ground, scooping up soil in her hands and putting it into the cooler.

"What are you doing?" Lionel said. "You can't stop him, it's too late."

"I'm not trying to," Avery said. "I want some cells to transplant. I'm going to grow an alien of my own."

"That's the stupidest—"

A moment later he was on his knees beside her, digging and scooping up dirt. They got enough to half-fill the cooler, then covered it with leaves to keep it damp.

"Wait here," she told him. "I'll bring the bus to pick you up. The gates open in an hour. Don't let anyone see you."

When she got back to the street where she had left the bus, Henry was waiting in a parked car. He got out and opened the passenger door for her, but she didn't get inside. "I've got to get back," she said, inclining her head toward the bus. "They're waiting for me."

"Do you mind telling me what's going on?"

"I just needed a break. I had to get away."

"In a cemetery? All night?"

"It's personal."

"Is there something I should know?"

"We're heading back home today."

He waited, but she said no more. There was no use telling him; he couldn't do anything about it. The invasion was already underway.

He let her return to the bus, and she drove it to a gas station to fuel up while waiting for the cemetery to open. At the stroke of 8:30 she pulled the bus through the gate, waving at the puzzled gatekeeper.

Between them, she and Lionel carried the cooler into the bus, leaving behind only the remains of a campfire and a slightly disturbed spot of soil. Then she headed straight for the freeway.

They stopped for a fast-food breakfast in southern Illinois. Avery kept driving as she ate her egg muffin and coffee. Soon Lionel came to sit shotgun beside her, carrying a plastic container full of soil.

"Is that mine?" she asked.

"No, this one's mine. You can have the rest."

"Thanks."

"It won't be him," Lionel said, looking at the soil cradled on his lap.

"No. But it'll be yours. Yours to raise and teach."

As hers would be.

"I thought you would have some kind of tribal loyalty to prevent them invading," Lionel said.

Avery thought about it a moment, then said, "We're not defenseless, you know. We've got something they want. The gift of self, of mortality. God, I feel like the snake in the garden. But my alien will love me for it." She could see the cooler in the rear view mirror, sitting on the floor in the kitchen. Already she felt fond of the person it would become. Gestating inside. "It gives a new meaning to *alien abduction*, doesn't it?" she said.

He didn't get the joke. "You aren't afraid to become . . . something like me?"

She looked over at him. "No one can be like you, Lionel."

Even after all this time together, he still didn't know how to react when she said things like that.

Nancy Kress is the author of thirty-three books, including twenty-six novels, four collections of short stories, and three books on writing. Her work has won six Nebulas, two Hugos, a Sturgeon, and the John W. Campbell Memorial Award. Her most recent work is *Terran Tomorrow*, the conclusion of her Yesterday's Kin series. Like much of her work, this series concerns genetic engineering. Kress's fiction has been translated into Swedish, Danish, French, Italian, German, Spanish, Polish, Croatian, Chinese, Lithuanian, Romanian, Japanese, Korean, Hebrew, Russian, and Klingon, none of which she can read. In addition to writing, Kress often teaches at various venues around the country and abroad, including a visiting lectureship at the University of Leipzig, a 2017 writing class in Beijing, and the annual intensive workshop Tao Toolbox, which she taught every summer with Walter Jon Williams.

Laws of Survival

NANCY KRESS

My name is Jill. I am somewhere you can't imagine, going somewhere even more unimaginable. If you think I like what I did to get here, you're crazy.

Actually, I'm the one who's crazy. You—any "you"—will never read this. But I have paper now, and a sort of pencil, and time. Lots and lots of time. So I will write what happened, all of it, as carefully as I can.

After all—why the hell not?

I went out very early one morning to look for food. Before dawn was safest for a woman alone. The boy-gangs had gone to bed, tired of attacking each other. The trucks from the city hadn't arrived yet. That meant the garbage was pretty picked over, but it also meant most of the refugee camp wasn't out scavenging. Most days I could find enough: a carrot stolen from somebody's garden patch, my arm bloody from reaching through the barbed wire. Overlooked potato peelings under a pile of rags and glass. A can of stew thrown away by one of the soldiers on the base, but still half full. Soldiers on duty by the Dome were often careless. They got bored, with nothing to do.

That morning was cool but fair, with a pearly haze that the sun would burn off later. I wore all my clothing, for warmth, and my boots. Yesterday's garbage load, I'd heard somebody say, was huge, so I had hopes. I hiked to my favorite spot, where garbage spills almost to the Dome wall. Maybe I'd find bread, or even fruit that wasn't too rotten.

Instead I found the puppy.

Its eyes weren't open yet and it squirmed along the bare ground, a scrawny brown-and-white mass with a tiny fluffy tail. Nearby was a fluid-soaked towel. Some sentimental fool had left the puppy there, hoping what? It didn't matter. Scrawny or not, there was some meat on the thing. I scooped it up.

The sun pushed above the horizon, flooding the haze with golden light.

I hate it when grief seizes me. I hate it and it's dangerous, a violation of one of Jill's Laws of Survival. I can go for weeks, months without thinking of my life before the War. Without remembering or feeling. Then something will strike me—a flower growing in the dump, a burst of birdsong, the stars on a clear night—and grief will hit me like the maglevs that no longer exist, a grief all the sharper because it contains the memory of joy. I can't afford joy, which always comes with an astronomical price tag. I can't even afford the grief that comes from the memory of living things, which is why it is only the flower, the birdsong, the morning sunlight that starts it. My grief was not for that puppy. I still intended to eat it.

But I heard a noise behind me and turned. The Dome wall was opening.

Who knew why the aliens put their Domes by garbage dumps, by waste pits, by radioactive cities? Who knew why aliens did anything?

There was a widespread belief in the camp that the aliens started the War. I'm old enough to know better. That was us, just like the global warming and the bio-crobes were us. The aliens didn't even show up until the War was over and Raleigh was the northernmost city left on the East Coast and refugees poured south like mudslides. Including me. That's when the ships landed and then turned into the huge gray Domes like upended bowls. I heard there were many Domes, some in other countries. The Army, what was left of it, threw tanks and bombs at ours. When they gave up, the refugees threw bullets and Molotov cocktails and prayers and graffiti and candlelight vigils and rain dances. Everything slid off and the Domes just sat there. And sat. And sat. Three years later, they were still sitting, silent and closed, although of course there were rumors to the contrary. There are always rumors. Personally, I'd never gotten over a slight disbelief that the Dome was there at all. Who would want to visit us?

The opening was small, no larger than a porthole, and about six feet above the ground. All I could see inside was a fog the same color as the Dome. Something came out, gliding quickly toward me. It took me a moment to realize it was a robot, a blue metal sphere above a hanging basket. It stopped a foot from my face and said, "This food for this dog."

I could have run, or screamed, or at the least—the very least—looked around for a witness. I didn't. The basket held a pile of fresh produce, green lettuce and deep purple eggplant and apples so shiny red they looked lacquered. And peaches . . . My mouth filled with sweet water. I couldn't move.

The puppy whimpered.

My mother used to make fresh peach pie.

I scooped the food into my scavenger bag, laid the puppy in the basket, and backed away. The robot floated back into the Dome, which closed immediately. I sped back to my corrugated-tin and windowless hut and ate until I couldn't hold any more. I slept, woke, and ate the rest, crouching in the dark so nobody else would see. All that fruit and vegetables gave me the runs, but it was worth it.

Peaches.

Two weeks later, I brought another puppy to the Dome, the only survivor of a litter deep in the dump. I never knew what happened to the mother. I had to wait a long time outside the Dome before the blue sphere took the puppy in exchange for produce. Apparently the Dome would only open when there was no one else around to see. What were they afraid of? It's not like PETA was going to show up.

The next day I traded three of the peaches to an old man in exchange for a small, mangy poodle. We didn't look each other in the eye, but I nonetheless knew that his held tears. He limped hurriedly away. I kept the dog, which clearly wanted nothing to do with me, in my shack until very early morning and then took it to the Dome. It tried to escape but I'd tied a bit of rope onto its frayed collar. We sat outside the Dome in mutual dislike, waiting, as the sky paled slightly in the east. Gunshots sounded in the distance.

I have never owned a dog.

When the Dome finally opened, I gripped the dog's rope and spoke to the robot. "Not fruit. Not vegetables. I want eggs and bread."

The robot floated back inside.

Instantly I cursed myself. Eggs? Bread? I was crazy not to take what I could get. That was Law of Survival #1. Now there would be nothing.

Eggs, bread . . . crazy. I glared at the dog and kicked it. It yelped, looked indignant, and tried to bite my boot.

The Dome opened again and the robot glided toward me. In the gloom I couldn't see what was in the basket. In fact, I couldn't see the basket. It wasn't there. Mechanical tentacles shot out from the sphere and seized both me and the poodle. I cried out and the tentacles squeezed harder. Then I was flying through the air, the stupid dog suddenly howling beneath me, and we were carried through the Dome wall and inside.

Then nothing.

A nightmare room made of nightmare sound: barking, yelping, whimpering, snapping. I jerked awake, sat up, and discovered myself on a floating platform above a mass of dogs. Big dogs, small dogs, old dogs, puppies, sick dogs, dogs that looked all too healthy, flashing their forty-two teeth at me—why did I remember that number? From where? The largest and strongest dogs couldn't quite reach me with their snaps, but they were trying.

"You are operative," the blue metal sphere said, floating beside me. "Now we must begin. Here."

Its basket held eggs and bread.

"Get them away!"

Obediently it floated off.

"Not the food! The dogs!"

"What to do with these dogs?"

"Put them in cages!" A large black animal—German shepherd or boxer or something—had nearly closed its jaws on my ankle. The next bite might do it.

"Cages," the metal sphere said in its uninflected mechanical voice. "Yes."

"Son of a bitch!" The shepherd, leaping high, had grazed my thigh; its spittle slimed my pants. "Raise the goddamn platform!"

"Yes."

The platform floated so high, so that I had to duck my head to avoid hitting the ceiling. I peered over the edge and . . . no, that wasn't possible. But it was happening. The floor was growing upright sticks, and the sticks were growing crossbars, and the crossbars were extending themselves into mesh tops . . . Within minutes, each dog was encased in a cage just large enough to hold its protesting body.

"What to do now?" the metal sphere asked.

I stared at it. I was, as far as I knew, the first human being to ever enter an alien Dome, I was trapped in a small room with feral caged dogs and a robot . . . what to do now?

"Why . . . why am I here?" I hated myself for the brief stammer and vowed it would not happen again. Law of Survival #2: Show no fear.

Would a metal sphere even recognize fear?

It said, "These dogs do not behave correctly."

"Not behave correctly?"

"No."

I looked down again at the slavering and snarling mass of dogs; how strong was that mesh on the cage tops? "What do you want them to do?"

"You want to see the presentation?"

"Not yet." Law #3: Never volunteer for anything.

"What to do now?"

How the hell should I know? But the smell of the bread reached me and my stomach flopped. "Now to eat," I said. "Give me the things in your basket."

It did, and I tore into the bread like a wolf into deer. The real wolves below me increased their howling. When I'd eaten an entire loaf, I looked back at the metal sphere. "Have those dogs eaten?"

"Yes."

"What did you give them?"

"Garbage."

"Garbage? Why?"

"In hell they eat garbage."

So even the robot thought this was Hell. Panic surged through me; I pushed it back. Surviving this would depend on staying steady. "Show me what you fed the dogs."

"Yes." A section of wall melted and garbage cascaded into the room, flowing greasily between the cages. I recognized it: It was exactly like the garbage I picked through every day, trucked out from a city I could no longer imagine and from the Army base I could not approach without being shot. Bloody rags, tin cans from before the War, shit, plastic bags, dead flowers, dead animals, dead electronics, cardboard, eggshells, paper, hair, bone, scraps of decaying food, glass shards, potato peelings, foam rubber, roaches, sneakers with holes, sagging furniture, corn cobs. The smell hit my stomach, newly distended with bread.

"You fed the dogs that?"

"Yes. They eat it in hell."

Outside. Hell was outside, and of course that's what the feral dogs ate, that's all there was. But the metal sphere had produced fruit and lettuce and bread for me.

"You must give them better food. They eat that in . . . in hell because they can't get anything else."

"What to do now?"

It finally dawned on me—slow, I was too slow for this, only the quick survive—that the metal sphere had limited initiative along with its limited vocabulary. But it had made cages, made bread, made fruit—hadn't it? Or was this stuff grown in some imaginable secret garden inside the Dome?

"You must give the dogs meat."

"Flesh?"

"Yes."

"No."

No change in that mechanical voice, but the "no" was definite and quick. Law of Survival #4: Notice everything. So—no flesh-eating allowed here. Also no time to ask why not; I had to keep issuing orders so that the robot didn't start issuing them. "Give them bread mixed with . . . with soy protein."

"Yes."

"And take away the garbage."

"Yes."

The garbage began to dissolve. I saw nothing poured on it, nothing rise from the floor. But all that stinking mass fell into powder and vanished. Nothing replaced it.

I said, "Are you getting bread mixed with soy powder?" Getting seemed the safest verb I could think of.

"Yes."

The stuff came then, tumbling through the same melted hole in the wall, loaves of bread with, presumably, soy powder in them. The dogs, barking insanely, reached paws and snouts and tongues through the bars of their cages. They couldn't get at the food.

"Metal sphere—do you have a name?"

No answer.

"Okay. Blue, how strong are those cages? Can the dogs break them? Any of the dogs?"

"No."

"Lower the platform to the floor."

My safe perch floated down. The aisles between the cages were irregular, some wide and some so narrow the dogs could reach through to touch each other, since each cage had "grown" wherever the dog was at the time. Gingerly I picked my way to a clearing and sat down. Tearing a loaf of bread into chunks, I pushed the pieces through the bars of the least dangerous-looking dogs, which made the bruisers howl even more. For them, I put chunks at a distance they could just reach with a paw through the front bars of their prisons.

The puppy I had first brought to the Dome lay in a tiny cage. Dead.

The second one was alive but just barely.

The old man's mangy poodle looked more mangy than ever, but otherwise alert. It tried to bite me when I fed it.

"What to do now?"

"They need water."

"Yes."

Water flowed through the wall. When it had reached an inch or so, it stopped. The dogs lapped whatever came into their cages. I stood with wet feet—a hole in my boot after all, I hadn't known—and a stomach roiling from the stench of the dogs, which only worsened as they got wet. The dead puppy smelled especially horrible. I climbed back onto my platform.

"What to do now?"

"You tell me," I said.

"These dogs do not behave correctly."

"Not behave correctly?"

"No."

"What do you want them to do?"

"Do you want to see the presentation?"

We had been here before. On second thought, a "presentation" sounded more like acquiring information ("Notice everything") than like undertaking action ("Never volunteer"). So I sat cross-legged on the platform, which was easier on my uncushioned bones, breathed through my mouth instead of my nose, and said, "Why the hell not?"

Blue repeated, "Do you want to see the presentation?"

"Yes." A one-syllable answer.

I didn't know what to expect. Aliens, spaceships, war, strange places barely comprehensible to humans. What I got was scenes from the dump.

A beam of light shot out from Blue and resolved into a three-dimensional holo, not too different from one I'd seen in a science museum on a school field trip once (no, push memory away), only this was far sharper and detailed. A ragged and unsmiling toddler, one of thousands, staggered toward a cesspool. A big dog with a patchy coat dashed up, seized the kid's dress, and pulled her back just before she fell into the waste.

A medium-sized brown dog in a guide-dog harness led around someone tapping a white-headed cane.

An Army dog, this one sleek and well-fed, sniffed at a pile of garbage, found something, pointed stiffly at attention.

A group of teenagers tortured a puppy. It writhed in pain, but in a long lingering close-up, tried to lick the torturer's hand.

A thin, small dog dodged rocks, dashed inside a corrugated tin hut, and laid a piece of carrion beside an old lady lying on the ground.

The holo went on and on like that, but the strange thing was that the people were barely seen. The toddler's bare and filthy feet and chubby knees, the old lady's withered cheek, a flash of a camouflage uniform above a brown boot, the hands of the torturers. Never a whole person, never a focus on people. Just on the dogs.

The "presentation" ended.

"These dogs do not behave correctly," Blue said.

"These dogs? In the presentation?"

"These dogs here do not behave correctly."

"These dogs here." I pointed to the wet, stinking dogs in their cages. Some, fed now, had quieted. Others still snarled and barked, trying their hellish best to get out and kill me.

"These dogs here. Yes. What to do now?"

"You want these dogs to behave like the dogs in the presentation."

"These dogs here must behave correctly. Yes."

"You want them to . . . do what? Rescue people? Sniff out ammunition dumps? Guide the blind and feed the hungry and love their torturers?"

Blue said nothing. Again I had the impression I had exceeded its thought processes, or its vocabulary, or its something. A strange feeling gathered in my gut.

"Blue, you yourself didn't build this Dome, or the starship that it was before, did you? You're just a . . . a computer."

Nothing.

"Blue, who tells you what to do?"

"What to do now? These dogs do not behave correctly."

"Who wants these dogs to behave correctly?" I said, and found I was holding my breath.

"The masters."

The masters. I knew all about them. Masters were the people who started wars, ran the corporations that ruined the Earth, manufactured the bioweapons that killed billions, and now holed up in the cities to send their garbage out to us in the refugee camps. Masters were something else I didn't think about, but not because grief would take me. Rage would.

Law of Survival #5: Feel nothing that doesn't aid survival.

"Are the masters here? In this . . . inside here?"

"No."

"Who is here inside?"

"These dogs here are inside."

Clearly. "The masters want these dogs here to behave like the dogs in the presentation."

"Yes."

"The masters want these dogs here to provide them with loyalty and protection and service."

No response.

"The masters aren't interested in human beings, are they? That's why they haven't communicated at all with any government."

Nothing. But I didn't need a response; the masters' thinking was already clear to me. Humans were unimportant—maybe because we had, after all, destroyed each other and our own world. We weren't worth contact. But dogs: companion animals capable of selfless service and great unconditional love, even in the face of abuse. For all I knew, dogs were unique in the universe. For all I know.

Blue said, "What to do now?"

I stared at the mangy, reeking, howling mass of animals. Some feral, some tamed once, some sick, at least one dead. I chose my words to be as simple as possible, relying on phrases Blue knew. "The masters want these dogs here to behave correctly."

"Yes."

"The masters want me to make these dogs behave correctly."

"Yes."

"The masters will make me food, and keep me inside, for to make these dogs behave correctly."

Long pause; my sentence had a lot of grammatical elements. But finally Blue said, "Yes."

"If these dogs do not behave correctly, the masters—what to do then?"

Another long pause. "Find another human."

"And this human here?"

"Kill it."

I gripped the edges of my floating platform hard. My hands still trembled. "Put me outside now."

"No."

"I must stay inside."

"These dogs do not behave correctly."

"I must make these dogs behave correctly."

"Yes."

"And the masters want these dogs to display . . ." I had stopped talking to Blue. I was talking to myself, to steady myself, but even that I couldn't manage. The words caromed around in my mind—loyalty, service, protection—but none came out of my mouth. I couldn't do this. I was going to die. The aliens had come from God-knew-where to treat the dying Earth like a giant pet store, intrigued only by a canine domestication that had happened ten thousand years ago and by nothing else on the planet, nothing else humanity had or might accomplish. Only dogs. The masters want these dogs to display—

Blue surprised me with a new word. "Love," it said.

aw #4: Notice everything. I needed to learn all I could, starting with Blue. He'd made garbage appear, and food and water and cages. What else could he do?

"Blue, make the water go away." And it did, just sank into the floor, which dried instantly. I was fucking Moses, commanding the Red Sea. I climbed off the platform, inched among the dog cages, and studied them individually.

"You called the refugee camp and the dump 'hell.' Where did you get that word?"

Nothing.

"Who said 'hell'?"

"Humans."

Blue had cameras outside the Dome. Of course he did; he'd seen me find that first puppy in the garbage. Maybe Blue had been waiting for someone like me, alone and nonthreatening, to come close with a dog. But it had watched before that, and it had learned the word "hell," and maybe it had recorded the incidents in the "presentation." I filed this information for future use.

"This dog is dead." The first puppy, decaying into stinking pulp. "It is killed. Non-operative."

"What to do now?"

"Make the dead dog go away."

A long pause: thinking it over? Accessing data banks? Communicating with aliens? And what kind of moron couldn't figure out by itself that a dead dog was never going to behave correctly? So much for artificial intelligence.

"Yes," Blue finally said, and the little corpse dissolved as if it had never been.

I found one more dead dog and one close to death. Blue disappeared the first, said no to the second. Apparently we had to just let it suffer until it died. I wondered how much the idea of "death" even meant to a robot. There were twenty-three live dogs, of which I had delivered only three to the Dome.

"Blue—did another human, before you brought me here, try to train the dogs?"

"These dogs do not behave correctly."

"Yes. But did a human not me be inside? To make these dogs behave correctly?"

"Yes."

"What happened to him or her?"

No response.

"What to do now with the other human?"

"Kill it."

I put a hand against the wall and leaned on it. The wall felt smooth and slick, with a faint and unpleasant tingle. I removed my hand.

All computers could count. "How many humans did you kill?"

"Two."

Three's the charm. But there were no charms. No spells, no magic wards, no cavalry coming over the hill to ride to the rescue; I'd known that ever since the War. There was just survival. And, now, dogs.

I chose the mangy little poodle. It hadn't bit me when the old man had surrendered it, or when I'd kept it overnight. That was at least a start. "Blue, make this dog's cage go away. But only this one cage!"

The cage dissolved. The poodle stared at me distrustfully. Was I supposed to stare back, or would that get us into some kind of canine pissing contest? The thing was small but it had teeth.

I had a sudden idea. "Blue, show me how this dog does not behave correctly." If I could see what it wasn't doing, that would at least be a start.

Blue floated to within a foot of the dog's face. The dog growled and backed away. Blue floated away and the dog quieted but it still stood in what would be a menacing stance if it weighed more than nine or ten pounds: ears raised, legs braced, neck hair bristling. Blue said, "Come." The dog did nothing. Blue repeated the entire sequence and so did Mangy.

I said, "You want the dog to follow you. Like the dogs in the presentation."

"Yes."

"You want the dog to come when you say 'Come.'"

"Love," Blue said.

"What is 'love,' Blue?"

No response.

The robot didn't know. Its masters must have had some concept of "love," but fuck-all knew what it was. And I wasn't sure I knew anymore, either. That left Mangy, who would never "love" Blue or follow him or lick his hand because dogs operated on smell—even I knew that about them—and Blue, a machine, didn't smell like either a person or another dog. Couldn't the aliens who sent him here figure that out? Were they watching this whole farce, or had they just dropped a half-sentient computer under an upturned bowl on Earth and told it, "Bring us some loving dogs"? Who knew how aliens thought?

I didn't even know how dogs thought. There were much better people for this job—professional trainers, or that guy on TV who made tigers jump through burning hoops. But they weren't here, and I was. I squatted on my haunches a respectful distance from Mangy and said, "Come."

It growled at me.

"Blue, raise the platform this high." I held my hand at shoulder height. The platform rose.

"Now make some cookies on the platform."

Nothing.

"Make some . . . cheese on the platform."

Nothing. You don't see much cheese in a dump.

"Make some bread on the platform."

Nothing. Maybe the platform wasn't user-friendly.

"Make some bread."

After a moment, loaves tumbled out of the wall. "Enough! Stop!"

Mangy had rushed over to the bread, tearing at it, and the other dogs were going wild. I picked up one loaf, put it on the platform, and said, "Make the rest of the bread go away."

It all dissolved. No wonder the dogs were wary; I felt a little dizzy myself. A sentence from a so-long-ago child's book rose in my mind: Things come and go so quickly here!

I had no idea how much Blue could, or would, do on my orders. "Blue, make another room for me and this one dog. Away from the other dogs."

"No."

"Make this room bigger."

The room expanded evenly on all sides. "Stop." It did. "Make only this end of the room bigger."

Nothing.

"Okay, make the whole room bigger."

When the room stopped expanding, I had a space about forty feet square, with the dog cages huddled in the middle. After half an hour of experimenting, I got the platform moved to one corner, not far enough to escape the dog stench but better than nothing. (Law #1: Take what you can get.) I got a depression in the floor filled with warm water. I got food, drinking water, soap, and some clean cloth, and a lot of rope. By distracting Mangy with bits of bread, I got rope onto her frayed collar. After I got into the warm water and scrubbed myself, I pulled the poodle in. She bit me. But somehow I got her washed, too. Afterwards she shook herself, glared at me, and went to sleep on the hard floor. I asked Blue for a soft rug.

He said, "The other humans did this."

And Blue killed them anyway.

"Shut up," I said.

The big windowless room had no day, no night, no sanity. I slept and ate when I needed to, and otherwise I worked. Blue never left. He was an oversized, all-seeing eye in the corner. Big Brother, or God.

Within a few weeks—maybe—I had Mangy trained to come when called, to sit, and to follow me on command. I did this by dispensing bits of bread and other goodies. Mangy got fatter. I didn't care if she ended up the Fat Fiona of dogs. Her mange didn't improve, since I couldn't get Blue to wrap his digital mind around the concept of medicines, and even if he had I wouldn't have known what to ask for. The sick puppy died in its cage.

I kept the others fed and watered and flooded the shit out of their cages every day, but that was all. Mangy took all my time. She still regarded me warily, never curled up next to me, and occasionally growled. Love was not happening here.

Nonetheless, Blue left his corner and spoke for the first time in a week, scaring the hell out of me. "This dog behaves correctly."

"Well, thanks. I tried to . . . no, Blue . . ."

Blue floated to within a foot of Mangy's face, said, "Follow," and floated away. Mangy sat down and began to lick one paw. Blue rose and floated toward me.

"This dog does not behave correctly."

I was going to die.

"No, listen to me—listen! The dog can't smell you! It behaves for humans because of humans' smell! Do you understand?"

"No. This dog does not behave correctly."

"Listen! How the hell can you learn anything if you don't listen? You have to have a smell! Then the dog will follow you!"

Blue stopped. We stood frozen, a bizarre tableau, while the robot considered. Even Mangy stopped licking her paw and watched, still. They say dogs can smell fear.

Finally Blue said, "What is smell?"

It isn't possible to explain smell. Can't be done. Instead I pulled down my pants, tore the cloth I was using as underwear from between my legs, and rubbed it all over Blue, who did not react. I hoped he wasn't made of the same stuff as the Dome, which even spray paint had just slid off of. But, of course, he was. So I tied the strip of cloth around him with a piece of rope, my fingers trembling. "Now try the dog, Blue."

"Follow," Blue said, and floated away from Mangy.

She looked at him, then at me, then back at the floating metal sphere. I held my breath from some insane idea that I would thereby diminish my own smell. Mangy didn't move.

"This dog does not be—"

"She will if I'm gone!" I said desperately. "She smells me and you . . . and we smell the same so it's confusing her! But she'll follow you fine if I'm gone, do you understand?"

"No."

"Blue . . . I'm going to get on the platform. See, I'm doing it. Raise the platform very high, Blue. Very high."

A moment later my head and ass both pushed against the ceiling, squishing me. I couldn't see what was happening below. I heard Blue say, "Follow," and I squeezed my eyes shut, waiting. My life depended on a scrofulous poodle with a gloomy disposition.

Blue said, "This dog behaves correctly."

He lowered my platform to a few yards above the floor, and I swear that—eyeless as he is and with part of his sphere obscured by my underwear—he looked right at me.

"This dog does behave correctly. This dog is ready."

"Ready? For . . . for what?"

Blue didn't answer. The next minute the floor opened and Mangy, yelping, tumbled into it. The floor closed. At the same time, one of the cages across the room dissolved and a German shepherd hurtled toward me. I shrieked and yelled, "Raise the platform!" It rose just before the monster grabbed me.

Blue said, "What to do now? This dog does not behave correctly."

"For God's sakes, Blue—"

"This dog must love."

The shepherd leapt and snarled, teeth bared.

I couldn't talk Blue out of the shepherd, which was as feral and vicious and unrelenting as anything in a horror movie. Or as Blue himself, in his own mechanical way. So I followed the First Law: Take what you can get.

"Blue, make garbage again. A lot of garbage, right here." I pointed to the wall beside my platform.

"No."

Garbage, like everything else, apparently was made—or released, or whatever—from the opposite wall. I resigned myself to this. "Make a lot of garbage, Blue."

Mountains of stinking debris cascaded from the wall, spilling over until it reached the dog cages.

"Now stop. Move my platform above the garbage."

The platform moved. The caged dogs howled. Uncaged, the shepherd poked eagerly in the refuse, too distracted to pay much attention to me. I had Blue lower the platform and I poked among it, too, keeping one eye on Vicious. If Blue was creating the garbage and not just trucking it in, he was doing a damn fine job of duplication. Xerox should have made such good copies.

I got smeared with shit and rot, but I found what I was looking for. The box was nearly a quarter full. I stuffed bread into it, coated the bread thoroughly, and discarded the box back onto the pile.

"Blue, make the garbage go away."

It did. Vicious glared at me and snarled. "Nice doggie," I said, "have some bread." I threw pieces and Vicious gobbled them.

Listening to the results was terrible. Not, however, as terrible as having Vicious tear me apart or Blue vaporize me. The rat poison took all "night" to kill the dog, which thrashed and howled. Throughout, Blue stayed silent. He had picked up some words from me, but he apparently didn't have enough brain power to connect what I'd done with Vicious's death. Or maybe he just didn't have enough experience with humans. What does a machine know about survival?

"This dog is dead," Blue said in the "morning."

"Yes. Make it go away." And then, before Blue could get there first, I jumped off my platform and pointed to a cage. "This dog will behave correctly next."

"No."

"Why not this dog?"

"Not big."

"Big. You want big." Frantically I scanned the cages, before Blue could choose another one like Vicious. "This one, then."

"Why the hell not?" Blue said.

I t was young. Not a puppy but still frisky, a mongrel of some sort with short hair of dirty white speckled with dirty brown. The dog looked liked something I could handle: big but not too big, not too aggressive, not too old, not too male. "Hey, Not-Too," I said, without enthusiasm, as Blue dissolved her cage. The mutt dashed over to me and tried to lick my boot.

A natural-born slave.

I had found a piece of rotten, moldy cheese in the garbage, so Blue could now make cheese, which Not-Too went crazy for. Not-Too and I stuck with the same routine I used with Mangy, and it worked pretty well. Or the cheese did. Within a few "days" the dog could sit, stay, and follow on command.

Then Blue threw me a curve. "What to do now? The presentation."

"We had the presentation," I said. "I don't need to see it again."

"What to do now? The presentation."

"Fine," I said, because it was clear I had no choice. "Let's have the presentation. Roll 'em."

I was sitting on my elevated platform, combing my hair. A lot of it had fallen out during the malnourished years in the camp, but now it was growing again. Not-Too had given up trying to jump up there with me and gone to sleep on her pillow below. Blue shot the beam out of his sphere and the holo played in front of me.

Only not the whole thing. This time he played only the brief scene where the big, patchy dog pulled the toddler back from falling into the cesspool. Blue played it once, twice, three times. Cold slid along my spine.

"You want Not-Too . . . you want this dog here to be trained to save children."

"This dog here does not behave correctly."

"Blue . . . How can I train a dog to save a child?"

"This dog here does not behave correctly."

"Maybe you haven't noticed, but we haven't got any fucking children for the dog to practice on!"

Long pause. "Do you want a child?"

"No!" Christ, he would kidnap one or buy one from the camp and I would be responsible for a kid along with nineteen semi-feral dogs. No.

"This dog here does not behave correctly. What to do now? The presentation."

"No, not the presentation. I saw it, I saw it. Blue . . . the other two humans who did not make the dogs behave correctly . . ."

"Killed."

"Yes. So you said. But they did get one dog to behave correctly, didn't they? Or maybe more than one. And then you just kept raising the bar higher. Water rescues, guiding the blind, finding lost people. Higher and higher."

But to all this, of course, Blue made no answer.

I wracked my brains to remember what I had ever heard, read, or seen about dog training. Not much. However, there's a problem with opening the door to memory: you can't control what strolls through. For the first time in years, my sleep was shattered by dreams.

I walked through a tiny garden, picking zinnias. From an open window came music, full and strong, an orchestra on CD. A cat paced beside me, purring. And there was someone else in the window, someone who called my name and I turned and—

I screamed. Clawed my way upright. The dogs started barking and howl-ing. Blue floated from his corner, saying something. And Not-Too made a mighty leap, landed on my platform, and began licking my face.

"Stop it! Don't do that! I won't remember!" I shoved her so hard she fell off the platform onto the floor and began yelping. I put my head in my hands.

Blue said, "Are you not operative?"

"Leave me the fuck alone!"

Not-Too still yelped, shrill cries of pain. When I stopped shaking, I crawled off the platform and picked her up. Nothing seemed to be bro-ken—although how would I know? Gradually she quieted. I gave her some cheese and put her back on her pillow. She wanted to stay with me but I wouldn't let her.

I would not remember. I would not. Law #5: Feel nothing.

We made a cesspool, or at least a pool. Blue depressed part of the floor to a depth of three feet and filled it with water. Not-Too considered this a swimming pool and loved to be in it, which was not what Blue wanted ("This water does not behave correctly"). I tried having the robot dump various substances into it until I found one that she disliked and I could tolerate: light-grade motor oil. A few small cans of oil like those in the dump created a polluted pool, not unlike Charleston Harbor. After every practice session I needed a bath.

But not Not-Too, because she wouldn't go into the "cesspool." I curled myself as small as possible, crouched at the side of the pool, and thrashed. After a few days, the dog would pull me back by my shirt. I moved into the pool. As long as she could reach me without getting any liquid on her, Not-Too happily played that game. As soon as I moved far enough out that I might actually need saving, she sat on her skinny haunches and looked away.

"This dog does not behave correctly."

I increased the cheese. I withheld the cheese. I pleaded and ordered and shunned and petted and yelled. Nothing worked. Meanwhile, the dream continued. The same dream, each time not greater in length but increasing in intensity. I walked through a tiny garden, picking zinnias. From an open window came music, full and strong, an orchestra on CD. A cat paced beside me, purring. And there was someone else in the window, someone who called my name and I turned and—

And woke screaming.

A cat. I had had a cat, before the War. Before everything. I had always had cats, my whole life. Independent cats, aloof and self-sufficient, admirably disdainful. Cats—

The dog below me whimpered, trying to get onto my platform to offer comfort I did not want.

I would not remember.

"This dog does not behave correctly," day after day.

I had Blue remove the oil from the pool. But by now Not-Too had been conditioned. She wouldn't go into even the clear water that she'd reveled in before.

"This dog does not behave correctly."

Then one day Blue stopped his annoying mantra, which scared me even more. Would I have any warning that I'd failed, or would I just die?

The only thing I could think of was to kill Blue first.

B lue was a computer. You disabled computers by turning them off, or cutting the power supply, or melting them in a fire, or dumping acid on them, or crushing them. But a careful search of the whole room revealed no switches or wires or anything that looked like a wireless control. A fire in this closed room, assuming I could start one, would kill me, too. Every kind of liquid or solid slid off Blue. And what would I crush him with, if that was even possible? A piece of cheese?

Blue was also—sort of—an intelligence. You could kill those by trapping them somewhere. My prison-or-sanctuary (depending on my mood) had no real "somewheres." And Blue would just dissolve any structure he found himself in.

What to do now?

I lay awake, thinking, all night, which at least kept me from dreaming. I came up with two ideas, both bad. Plan A depended on discussion, never Blue's strong suit.

"Blue, this dog does not behave correctly."

"No."

"This dog is not operative. I must make another dog behave correctly. Not this dog."

Blue floated close to Not-Too. She tried to bat at him. He circled her slowly, then returned to his position three feet above the ground. "This dog is operative."

"No. This dog looks operative. But this dog is not operative inside its head. I cannot make this dog behave correctly. I need a different dog."

A very long pause. "This dog is not operative inside its head."

"Yes."

"You can make another dog behave correctly. Like the presentation."

"Yes." It would at least buy me time. Blue must have seen "not operative" dogs and humans in the dump; God knows there were enough of them out there. Madmen, rabid animals, druggies raving just before they died or were shot. And next time I would add something besides oil to the pool; there must be something that Blue would consider noxious enough to sim-ulate a cesspool but that a dog would enter. If I had to, I'd use my own shit.

"This dog is not operative inside its head," Blue repeated, getting used to the idea. "You will make a different dog behave correctly."

"Yes!"

"Why the hell not?" And then, "I kill this dog."

"No!" The word was torn from me before I knew I was going to say anything. My hand, of its own volition, clutched at Not-Too. She jumped but didn't bite. Instead, maybe sensing my fear, she cowered behind me, and I started to yell.

"You can't just kill everything that doesn't behave like you want! People, dogs . . . you can't just kill everything! You can't just . . . I had a cat . . . I never wanted a dog, but this dog . . . she's behaving correctly for her! For a fucking traumatized dog and you can't just—I had a dog I mean a cat I had . . . I had . . ."

—from an open window came music, full and strong, an orchestra on CD. A cat paced beside me, purring. And there was someone else in the window, someone who called my name and I turned and—

"I had a child!"

Oh, God no no no . . . It all came out then, the memories and the grief and the pain I had pushed away for three solid years in order to survive . . . Feel nothing . . . Zack Zack Zack shot down by soldiers like a dog Look, Mommy, here I am Mommy look . . .

I curled in a ball on the floor and screamed and wanted to die. Grief had been postponed so long that it was a tsunami. I sobbed and screamed; I don't know for how long. I think I wasn't quite sane. No human should ever have to experience that much pain. But of course they do.

However, it can't last too long, that height of pain, and when the flood passed and my head was bruised from banging it on the hard floor, I was still alive, still inside the Dome, still surrounded by barking dogs. Zack was still dead. Blue floated nearby, unchanged, a casually murderous robot who would not supply flesh to dogs as food but who would kill anything he was programmed to destroy. And he had no reason not to murder me.

Not-Too sat on her haunches, regarding me from sad brown eyes, and I did the one thing I told myself I never would do again. I reached for her warmth. I put my arms around her and hung on. She let me.

Maybe that was the decision point. I don't know.

When I could manage it, I staggered to my feet. Taking hold of the rope that was Not-Too's leash, I wrapped it firmly around my hand. "Blue," I said, forcing the words past the grief clogging my throat, "make garbage."

He did. That was the basis of Plan B: that Blue made most things I asked of him. Not release, or mercy, but at least rooms and platforms and pools and garbage. I walked toward the garbage spilling from the usual place in the wall.

"More garbage! Bigger garbage! I need garbage to make this dog behave correctly!"

The reeking flow increased. Tires, appliances, diapers, rags, cans, furniture. The dogs' howling rose to an insane, deafening pitch. Not-Too pressed close to me.

"Bigger garbage!"

The chassis of a motorcycle, twisted beyond repair in some unimaginable accident, crashed into the room. The place on the wall from which the garbage spewed was misty gray, the same fog that the Dome had become when I had been taken inside it. Half a sofa clattered through. I grabbed Not-Too, dodged behind the sofa, and hurled both of us through the onrushing garbage and into the wall.

A broken keyboard struck me in the head, and the gray went black.

Chill. Cold with a spot of heat, which turned out to be Not-Too lying on top of me. I pushed her off and tried to sit up. Pain lanced through my head and when I put a hand to my forehead, it came away covered with blood. The same blood streamed into my eyes, making it hard to see. I wiped the blood away with the front of my shirt, pressed my hand hard on my forehead, and looked around.

Not that there was much to see. The dog and I sat at the end of what appeared to be a corridor. Above me loomed a large machine of some type with a chute pointed at the now-solid wall. The machine was silent. Not-Too quivered and pressed her furry side into mine, but she, too, stayed silent. I couldn't hear the nineteen dogs on the other side of the wall, couldn't see Blue, couldn't smell anything except Not-Too, who had made a small yellow puddle on the floor.

There was no room to stand upright under the machine, so I moved away from it. Strips ripped from the bottom of my shirt made a bandage that at least kept blood out of my eyes. Slowly Not-Too and I walked along the corridor.

No doors. No openings or alcoves or machinery. Nothing until we reached the end, which was the same uniform material as everything else. Gray, glossy, hard. Dead. Blue did not appear. Nothing appeared, or disappeared, or lived. We walked back and studied the overhead bulk of the machine. It had no dials or keys or features of any kind.

I sat on the floor, largely because I couldn't think what else to do, and Not-Too climbed into my lap. She was too big for this and I pushed her away. She pressed against me, trembling.

"Hey," I said, but not to her. Zack in the window Look, Mommy, here I am Mommy look . . . But if I started down that mental road, I would be lost. Anger was better than memory. Anything was better than memory. "Hey!" I screamed. "Hey, you bastard Blue, what to do now? What to do now, you Dome shits, whoever you are?"

Nothing except, very faint, an echo of my own useless words.

I lurched to my feet, reaching for the anger, cloaking myself in it. Not-Too sprang to her feet and backed away from me.

"What to do now? What bloody fucking hell to do now?"

Still nothing, but Not-Too started back down the empty corridor. I was glad to transfer my anger to something visible, real, living. "There's nothing there, Not-Too. Nothing, you stupid dog!"

She stopped halfway down the corridor and began to scratch at the wall.

I stumbled along behind her, one hand clamped to my head. What the hell was she doing? This piece of wall was identical to every other piece of wall. Kneeling slowly—it hurt my head to move fast—I studied Not-Too. Her scratching increased in frenzy and her nose twitched, as if she smelled something. The wall, of course, didn't respond; nothing in this place responded to anything. Except—

Blue had learned words from me, had followed my commands. Or had he just transferred my command to the Dome's unimaginable machinery, instructing it to do anything I said that fell within permissible limits? Feeling like an idiot, I said to the wall, "Make garbage." Maybe if it complied and the garbage contained food . . .

The wall made no garbage. Instead it dissolved into the familiar gray fog, and Not-Too immediately jumped through, barking frantically.

Every time I had gone through a Dome wall, my situation had gotten worse. But what other choices were there? Wait for Blue to find and kill me, starve to death, curl up and die in the heart of a mechanical alien mini-world I didn't understand. Not-Too's barking increased in pitch and volume. She was terrified or excited or thrilled . . . How would I know? I pushed through the gray fog.

Another gray metal room, smaller than Blue had made my prison but with the same kind of cages against the far wall. Not-Too saw me and raced from the cages to me. Blue floated toward me . . . No, not Blue. This metal sphere was dull green, the color of shady moss. It said, "No human comes into this area."

"Guess again," I said and grabbed the trailing end of Not-Too's rope. She'd jumped up on me once and then had turned to dash back to the cages.

"No human comes into this area," Green repeated. I waited to see what the robot would do about it. Nothing.

Not-Too tugged on her rope, yowling. From across the room came answering barks, weirdly off. Too uneven in pitch, with a strange undertone. Blood, having saturated my makeshift bandage, once again streamed into my eyes. I swiped at it with one hand, turned to keep my gaze on Green, and let Not-Too pull me across the floor. Only when she stopped did I turn to look at the mesh-topped cages. Vertigo swooped over me.

Mangy was the source of the weird barks, a Mangy altered not beyond recognition but certainly beyond anything I could have imagined. Her mange was gone, along with all her fur. The skin beneath was now gray, the same gunmetal gray as everything else in the Dome. Her ears, the floppy poodle ears, were so long they trailed on the floor of her cage, and so was her tail. Holding on to the tail was a gray grub.

Not a grub. Not anything Earthly. Smooth and pulpy, it was about the size of a human head and vaguely oval. I saw no openings on the thing but Mangy's elongated tail disappeared into the doughy mass, and so there must have been at least one orifice. As Mangy jumped at the bars, trying to get at Not-Too, the grub was whipped back and forth across the cage floor. It left a slimy trail. The dog seemed oblivious.

"This dog is ready," Blue had said.

Behind me Green said, "No human comes into this area."

"Up yours."

"The human does not behave correctly."

That got my attention. I whirled around to face Green, expecting to be vaporized like the dead puppy, the dead Vicious. I thought I was already dead—and then I welcomed the thought. Look, Mommy, here I am Mommy look . . . The laws of survival that had protected me for so long couldn't protect me against memory, not anymore. I was ready to die.

Instead, Mangy's cage dissolved, she bounded out, and she launched herself at me.

Poodles are not natural killers, and this one was small. However, Mangy was doing her level best to destroy me. Her teeth closed on my arm. I screamed and shook her off, but the next moment she was biting my leg above my boot, darting hysterically toward and away from me, biting my legs at each lunge. The grub, or whatever it was, lashed around at the end of her new tail. As I flailed at the dog with both hands, my bandage fell off. Fresh blood from my head wound blinded me. I stumbled and fell and she was at my face.

Then she was pulled off, yelping and snapping and howling.

Not-Too had Mangy in her jaws. Twice as big as the poodle, she shook Mangy violently and then dropped her. Mangy whimpered and rolled over on her belly. Not-Too sprinted over to me and stood in front of me, skinny legs braced and scrawny hackles raised, growling protectively.

Dazed, I got to my feet. Blood, mine and the dogs', slimed everything. The floor wasn't trying to reabsorb it. Mangy, who'd never really liked me, stayed down with her belly exposed in submission, but she didn't seem to be badly hurt. The grub still latched onto the end of her tail like a gray tumor. After a moment she rolled onto her feet and began to nuzzle the grub, one baleful eye on Not-Too: Don't you come near this thing! Not-Too stayed in position, guarding me.

Green said—and I swear its mechanical voice held satisfaction, no one will ever be able to tell me any different—"These dogs behave correctly."

The other cages held grubs, one per cage. I reached through the front bars and gingerly touched one. Moist, firm, repulsive. It didn't respond to my touch, but Green did. He was beside me in a flash. "No!"

"Sorry." His tone was dog-disciplining. "Are these the masters?"

No answer.

"What to do now? One dog for one . . ." I waved at the cages.

"Yes. When these dogs are ready."

This dog is ready, Blue had said of Mangy just before she was tumbled into the floor. Ready to be a pet, a guardian, a companion, a service animal to alien . . . what? The most logical answer was "children." Lassie, Rin Tin Tin, Benji, Little Guy. A boy and his dog. The aliens found humans dangerous or repulsive or uncaring or whatever, but dogs . . . You could count on dogs for your kids. Almost, and for the first time, I could see the point of the Domes.

"Are the big masters here? The adults?"

No answer.

"The masters are not here," I said. "They just set up the Domes as . . . as nurseries-slash-obedience schools." And to that statement I didn't even expect an answer. If the adults had been present, surely one or more would have come running when an alien blew into its nursery wing via a garbage delivery. There would have been alarms or something. Instead there was only Blue and Green and whatever 'bots inhabited whatever place held the operating room. Mangy's skin and ears and tail had been altered to fit the needs of these grubs. And maybe her voice box, too, since her barks now had that weird undertone, like the scrape of metal across rock. Somewhere there was an OR.

I didn't want to be in that somewhere.

Green seemed to have no orders to kill me, which made sense because he wasn't programmed to have me here. I wasn't on his radar, which raised other problems.

"Green, make bread."

Nothing.

"Make water."

Nothing.

But two indentations in a corner of the floor, close to a section of wall, held water and dog-food pellets. I tasted both, to the interest of Not-Too and the growling of Mangy. Not too bad. I scooped all the rest of the dog food out of the trough. As soon as the last piece was out, the wall filled it up again. If I died, it wasn't going to be of starvation.

A few minutes ago, I had wanted to die. Zack . . .

No. Push the memory away. Life was shit, but I didn't want death, either. The realization was visceral, gripping my stomach as if that organ had been laid in a vise, or . . . There is no way to describe it. The feeling just was, its own justification. I wanted to live.

Not-Too lay a short distance away, watching me. Mangy was back in her cage with the grub on her tail. I sat up and looked around. "Green, this dog is not ready."

"No. What to do now?"

Well, that answered one question. Green was programmed to deal with dogs, and you didn't ask dogs "what to do now." So Green must be in some sort of communication with Blue, but the communication didn't seem to include orders about me. For a star-faring advanced race, the aliens certainly weren't very good at LANs. Or maybe they just didn't care—how would I know how an alien thinks?

I said, "I make this dog behave correctly." The all-purpose answer.

"Yes."

Did Green know details—that Not-Too refused to pull me from oily pools and thus was an obedience-school failure? It didn't seem like it. I could pretend to train Not-Too—I could actually train her, only not for water rescue—and stay here, away from the killer Blue, until . . . until what? As a survival plan, this one was shit. Still, it followed Laws #1 and #3: Take what you can get and never volunteer. And I couldn't think of anything else.

"Not-Too," I said wearily, still shaky from my crying jag, "sit."

D ays" went by, then weeks. Not-Too learned to beg, roll over, bring me a piece of dog food, retrieve my thrown boot, lie down, and balance a pellet of dog food on her nose. I had no idea if any of these activities would be useful to an alien, but as long as Not-Too and I were "working," Green left us alone. No threats, no presentations, no objections. We were behaving correctly. I still hadn't thought of any additional plan. At night I dreamed of Zack and woke in tears, but not with the raging insanity of my first day of memory. Maybe you can only go through that once.

Mangy's grub continued to grow, still fastened onto her tail. The other grubs looked exactly the same as before. Mangy growled if I came too close to her, so I didn't. Her grub seemed to be drying out as it got bigger. Mangy licked it and slept curled around it and generally acted like some mythical dragon guarding a treasure box. Had the aliens bonded those two with some kind of pheromones I couldn't detect? I had no way of knowing.

Mangy and her grub emerged from their cage only to eat, drink, or shit, which she did in a far corner. Not-Too and I used the same corner, and all of our shit and piss dissolved odorlessly into the floor. Eat your heart out, Thomas Crapper.

As days turned into weeks, flesh returned to my bones. Not-Too also lost her starved look. I talked to her more and more, her watchful silence preferable to Green's silence or, worse, his inane and limited repertoires of answers. "Green, I had a child named Zack. He was shot in the war. He was five." "This dog is not ready."

Well, none of us ever are.

Not-Too started to sleep curled against my left side. This was a problem because I thrashed in my sleep, which woke her, so she growled, which woke me. Both of us became sleep-deprived and irritable. In the camp, I had slept twelve hours a day. Not much else to do, and sleep both con-served energy and kept me out of sight. But the camp was becoming dis-tant in my mind. Zack was shatteringly vivid, with my life before the war, and the Dome was vivid, with Mangy and Not-Too and a bunch of alien grubs. Everything in between was fading.

Then one "day"—after how much time? I had no idea—Green said, "This dog is ready."

My heart stopped. Green was going to take Not-Too to the hidden OR, was going to—"No!"

Green ignored me. But he also ignored Not-Too. The robot floated over to Mangy's cage and dissolved it. I stood and craned my neck for a better look.

The grub was hatching.

Its "skin" had become very dry, a papery gray shell. Now it cracked along the top, parallel to Mangy's tail. She turned and regarded it quizzically, this thing wriggling at the end of her very long tail, but didn't attack or even growl. Those must have been some pheromones.

Was I really going to be the first and only human to see a Dome alien?

I was not. The papery covering cracked more and dropped free of the dog's tail. The thing inside wiggled forward, crawling out like a snake shedding its skin. It wasn't a grub but it clearly wasn't a sentient being, either. A larva? I'm no zoologist. This creature was as gray as everything else in the Dome but it had legs, six, and heads, two. At least, they might have been heads. Both had various indentations. One "head" crept forward, opened an orifice, and fastened itself back onto Mangy's tail. She continued to gaze at it. Beside me, Not-Too growled.

I whirled to grab frantically for her rope. Not-Too had no alterations to make her accept this . . . thing as anything other than a small animal to attack. If she did—

I turned just in time to see the floor open and swallow Not-Too. Green said again, "This dog is ready," and the floor closed.

"No! Bring her back!" I tried to pound on Green with my fists. He bobbed in the air under my blows. "Bring her back! Don't hurt her! Don't . . ." do what?

Don't turn her into a nursemaid for a grub, oblivious to me.

Green moved off. I followed, yelling and pounding. Neither one, of course, did the slightest good. Finally I got it together enough to say, "When will Not-Too come back?"

"This human does not behave correctly."

I looked despairingly at Mangy. She lay curled on her side, like a mother dog nursing puppies. The larva wasn't nursing, however. A shallow trough had appeared in the floor and filled with some viscous glop, which the larva was scarfing up with its other head. It looked repulsive.

Law #4: Notice everything.

"Green . . . okay. Just . . . okay. When will Not-Too come back here?"

No answer; what does time mean to a machine?

"Does the other dog return here?"

"Yes."

"Does the other dog get a . . ." A what? I pointed at Mangy's larva.

No response. I would have to wait.

But not, apparently, alone. Across the room another dog tumbled, snarling, from the same section of wall I had once come through. I recognized it as one of the nineteen left in the other room, a big black beast with powerful-looking jaws. It righted itself and charged at me. There was no platform, no place to hide.

"No! Green, no, it will hurt me! This dog does not behave—"

Green didn't seem to do anything. But even as the black dog leapt toward me, it faltered in mid-air. The next moment, it lay dead on the floor.

The moment after that, the body disappeared, vaporized.

My legs collapsed under me. That was what would happen to me if I failed in my training task, was what had presumably happened to the previous two human failures. And yet it wasn't fear that made me sit so abruptly on the gray floor. It was relief, and a weird kind of gratitude. Green had protected me, which was more than Blue had ever done. Maybe Green was brighter, or I had proved my worth more, or in this room as opposed to the other room, all dog-training equipment was protected. I was dog-training equipment. It was stupid to feel grateful.

I felt grateful.

Green said, "This dog does not—"

"I know, I know. Listen, Green, what to do now? Bring another dog here?"

"Yes."

"I choose the dog. I am the . . . the dog leader. Some dogs behave correctly, some dogs do not behave correctly. I choose. Me."

I held my breath. Green considered, or conferred with Blue, or consulted its alien and inadequate programming. Who the hell knows? The robot had been created by a race that preferred Earth dogs to whatever species usually nurtured their young, if any did. Maybe Mangy and Not-Too would replace parental care on the home planet, thus introducing the idea of babysitters. All I wanted was to not be eaten by some canine nanny-trainee.

"Yes," Green said finally, and I let out my breath.

A few minutes later, eighteen dog cages tumbled through the wall like so much garbage, the dogs within bouncing off their bars and mesh tops, furious and noisy. Mangy jumped, curled more protectively around her oblivious larva, and added her weird, rock-scraping bark to the din. A cage grew up around her. When the cages had stopped bouncing, I walked among them like some kind of tattered lord, choosing.

"This dog, Green." It wasn't the smallest dog but it had stopped barking the soonest. I hoped that meant it wasn't a grudge holder. When I put one hand into its cage, it didn't bite me, also a good sign. The dog was phenomenally ugly, the jowls on its face drooping from small, rheumy eyes into a sort of folded ruff around its short neck. Its body seemed to be all front, with stunted and short back legs. When it stood, I saw it was male.

"This dog? What to do now?"

"Send all the other dogs back."

The cages sank into the floor. I walked over to the feeding trough, scooped up handfuls of dog food, and put the pellets into my only pocket that didn't have holes. "Make all the rest of the dog food go away."

It vaporized.

"Make this dog's cage go away."

I braced myself as the cage dissolved. The dog stood uncertainly on the floor, gazing toward Mangy, who snarled at him. I said, as commandingly as possible, "Ruff!"

He looked at me.

"Ruff, come."

To my surprise, he did. Someone had trained this animal before. I gave him a pellet of dog food.

Green said, "This dog behaves correctly."

"Well, I'm really good," I told him, stupidly, while my chest tightened as I thought of Not-Too. The aliens, or their machines, did understand about anesthetic, didn't they? They wouldn't let her suffer too much? I would never know.

But now I did know something momentous. I had choices. I had chosen which room to train dogs in. I had chosen which dog to train. I had some control.

"Sit," I said to Ruff, who didn't, and I set to work.

Not-Too was returned to me three or four "days" later. She was gray and hairless, with an altered bark. A grub hung onto her elongated tail, undoubtedly the same one that had vanished from its cage while I was asleep. But unlike Mangy, who'd never liked either of us, Not-Too was ecstatic to see me. She wouldn't stay in her grub-cage against the wall but insisted on sleeping curled up next to me, grub and all. Green permitted this. I had become the alpha dog.

Not-Too liked Ruff, too. I caught him mounting her, her very long tail conveniently keeping her grub out of the way. Did Green understand the significance of this behavior? No way to tell.

We settled into a routine of training, sleeping, playing, eating. Ruff turned out to be sweet and playful but not very intelligent, and training took a long time. Mangy's grub grew very slowly, considering the large amount of glop it consumed. I grew, too; the waistband of my ragged pants got too tight and I discarded them, settling for a loin cloth, shirt, and my decaying boots. I talked to the dogs, who were much better conversationalists than Green since two of them at least pricked up their ears, made noises back at me, and wriggled joyfully at attention. Green would have been a dud at a cocktail party.

I don't know how long this all went on. Time began to lose meaning. I still dreamed of Zack and still woke in tears, but the dreams grew gentler and farther apart. When I cried, Not-Too crawled onto my lap, dragging her grub, and licked my chin. Her brown eyes shared my sorrow. I wondered how I had ever preferred the disdain of cats.

Not-Too got pregnant. I could feel the puppies growing inside her distended belly.

"Puppies will be easy to make behave correctly," I told Green, who said nothing. Probably he didn't understand. Some people need concrete visuals in order to learn.

Eventually, it seemed to me that Ruff was almost ready for his own grub. I mulled over how to mention this to Green but before I did, everything came to an end.

Clang! Clang! Clang!

I jerked awake and bolted upright. The alarm—a very human-sounding alarm—sounded all around me. Dogs barked and howled. Then I realized that it was a human alarm, coming from the Army camp outside the Dome, on the opposite side to the garbage dump. I could see the camp—in outline and faintly, as if through heavy gray fog. The Dome was dissolving.

"Green—what—no!"

Above me, transforming the whole top half of what had been the Dome, was the bottom of a solid saucer. Mangy, in her cage, floated upwards and disappeared into a gap in the saucer's underside. The other grub cages had already disappeared. I glimpsed a flash of metallic color through the gap: Blue. Green was halfway to the opening, drifting lazily upward. Beside me, both Not-Too and Ruff began to rise.

"No! No!"

I hung onto Not-Too, who howled and barked. But then my body froze. I couldn't move anything. My hands opened and Not-Too rose, yowling piteously.

"No! No!" And then, before I knew I was going to say it, "Take me, too!" Green paused in mid-air. I began babbling.

"Take me! Take me! I can make the dogs behave correctly—I can—you need me! Why are you going? Take me!"

"Take this human?"

Not Green but Blue, emerging from the gap. Around me the Dome walls thinned more. Soldiers rushed toward us. Guns fired.

"Yes! What to do? Take this human! The dogs want this human!"

Time stood still. Not-Too howled and tried to reach me. Maybe that's what did it. I rose into the air just as Blue said, "Why the hell not?"

Inside—inside what?—I was too stunned to do more than grab Not-Too, hang on, and gasp. The gap closed. The saucer rose.

After a few minutes, I sat up and looked around. Gray room, filled with dogs in their cages, with grubs in theirs, with noise and confusion and the two robots. The sensation of motion ceased. I gasped, "Where . . . where are we going?"

Blue answered. "Home."

"Why?"

"The humans do not behave correctly." And then, "What to do now?"

We were leaving Earth in a flying saucer, and it was asking me?

Over time—I have no idea how much time—I actually got some answers from Blue. The humans "not behaving correctly" had apparently succeeding in breaching one of the Domes somewhere. They must have used a nuclear bomb, but that I couldn't verify. Grubs and dogs had both died, and so the aliens had packed up and left Earth. Without, as far as I could tell, retaliating. Maybe.

If I had stayed, I told myself, the soldiers would have shot me. Or I would have returned to life in the camp, where I would have died of dysentery or violence or cholera or starvation. Or I would have been locked away by whatever government still existed in the cities, a freak who had lived with aliens none of my story believed. I barely believed it myself.

I am a freak who lives with aliens. Furthermore, I live knowing that at any moment Blue or Green or their "masters" might decide to vaporize me. But that's really not much different from the uncertainty of life in the camp, and here I actually have some status. Blue produces whatever I ask for, once I get him to understand what that is. I have new clothes, good food, a bed, paper, a sort of pencil.

And I have the dogs. Mangy still doesn't like me. Her larva hasn't as yet done whatever it will do next. Not-Too's grub grows slowly, and now Ruff has one, too. Their three puppies are adorable and very trainable. I'm not so sure about the other seventeen dogs, some of whom look wilder than ever after their long confinement in small cages. Aliens are not, by definition, humane.

I don't know what it will take to survive when, and if, we reach "home" and I meet the alien adults. All I can do is rely on Jill's Five Laws of Survival:

#1: Take what you can get.

#2: Show no fear.

#3: Never volunteer.

#4: Notice everything.

But the Fifth Law has changed. As I lie beside Not-Too and Ruff, their sweet warmth and doggie-odor, I know that my first formulation was wrong. "Feel nothing"—that can take you some ways toward survival, but not very far. Not really.

Law #5: Take the risk. Love something.

The dogs whuff contentedly and we speed toward the stars.

Steve Rasnic Tem is a past winner of the World Fantasy, Bram Stoker, and British Fantasy awards. He has published over four hundred and thirty short stories. Some of his best stories are collected in *Figures Unseen: Selected Stories*, published in April 2018 by Valancourt Books. *The Mask Shop of Doctor Blaack*, a middle grade novel about Halloween, will appear Fall 2018 from Hex Publishers. A handbook on writing, *Yours To Tell: Dialogues on the Art & Practice of Writing*, written with his late wife Melanie, appeared from Apex Books last year. Also appearing last year was his science fiction horror novel *Ubo* (Solaris Books), a finalist for the Bram Stoker and Locus Awards.

At Play in the Fields

STEVE RASNIC TEM

After years of repetition, waking up in some altered state had become the expected outcome of long, uninterrupted slumber. Since childhood, Tom had come to think of sleep as practically a means of transportation. If ill or depressed he'd take to his bed for that healing power of sleep, reviving at some point forward in time, in a better place, a healthier frame of mind.

So when he regained consciousness this time in a brilliant haze of light he was not extremely concerned, even when he saw an enormous plant maybe eight feet tall—some sort of succulent bromeliad, he believed—moving about in the room, its long fleshy leaves touching tables and racks, picking up bottles and tools, its flexible stamen waving. Near the top of the plant the leaves had widened into shoulders, where some sort of brightly lit chandelier was mounted.

Clearly he should have screamed, or been overwhelmed by anxiety, and in some compartment of his mind he was. But the trauma was muted, the terror inaccessible.

The plant waved a cluster of long filaments in Tom's direction, emitting a high-pitched, scraping sound. Now feeling the beginnings of concern, he attempted to escape. But he appeared to be paralyzed, his limbs oblivious to urgent commands. He wasn't strong enough to even cover his ears.

The scraping ceased. "I apologize," said a voice inside his head. "I had not activated your implant."

Tom managed to twist his neck slightly in order to find the source of the voice, whether a presence or some visible speaker grille. He found nothing, but noticed that the handles on the tools, the vessels on the tables, were distorted, as if melted. He was hallucinating, then. Maybe he'd eaten something toxic.

The plant moved with unbelievable rapidity, as an octopus had moved across the ocean floor in a nature documentary he'd seen recently, and now leaned over him. "I will help you into a sitting position," it—the voice inside his head—said.

The leaves were cool and firm against his skin. One curled its tip around his shoulder and pulled, while another supported his back, and yet another pressed against his forehead as if to prevent his skull from flopping forward, which seemed unnecessary until he was actually upright and felt the heaviness. He noticed among the fleshy leaves numerous strands of wire or cable of varying thickness, some lit with flickering arrays, some ribbed, some featureless. Whatever they were, these additional appendages were not organic.

Now Tom *was* unsettled. But something was obviously working in his system to suppress the panic.

"Please maintain a state of calm. I will ask you questions. There are no right or wrong answers. I will help you make a safe transition into your next phase. You are feeling some anxiety. For your safety we treated your systems to decrease your level of anxiety. These treatments did not affect your cognitive abilities in any way."

Tom was now very clear about one thing—the voice was coming from inside this gigantic plant. "I will begin. What is the last thing you remember before you . . ." There was a pause, and a little bit of that scraping noise bled through. "Before you entered your sleep phase."

Tom used to exercise to help him sleep. Sometimes he tried heated milk, medications. But not the last time. The last time he'd been lying on a bed before surgery. "I was hooked up to an IV. They were going to do something with my inner ear. The right, no, the left side. I had been losing my balance for a very long time. That last month it had gotten much, much worse—just sitting up made me ill. The surgery was supposed to be . . . um." He swallowed. His mouth was like a cloth pocket containing a dried-out, forgotten tongue. The plant inserted a long straw into his mouth. He searched apprehensively for the other end of the straw, but could not find it. His mouth filled with cool liquid. "The surgery was supposed to be a simple procedure. Later, I woke up, but I didn't really wake up. Everything was so hazy, and the room seemed to be full of people—at least I could hear their . . . distorted echoes—but I couldn't see anyone." He could feel that distant fear approaching. It would arrive very soon now.

"We have repaired . . . your condition," it said. "I will answer those questions I have answers for. But please answer these first."

Tom took a deep breath and looked around. The room appeared sterile, and there were recognizable tubes, containers, liquids, instruments—with handles and other attachments distorted and unlike anything he'd ever seen before. But they made a kind of sense, given the nature of the creature before him, who gave an impression of floating on a mop of fine roots. He understood now that this plant-thing was in constant, subtle movement—its leaves, stems—gently flowing, changing shape in a way that emphasized this impression of floating. He also saw that a thin layer of greenish liquid coated the floor, streaked and shiny like some sort of lubricant.

There were objects on tables around the room. Tom thought he recognized the shell of an old toaster, some random auto parts, maybe a radio, what might have been a fragment of toilet bowl—all so stained and rusty, so worn that they might have been dredged out of the ocean mud.

"You were *suspended.*"

"What? What do you mean?"

"You were placed in a state . . . cannot translate . . . cannot translate. You were placed in a condition of suspended animation. The technology was primitive then, but there have been . . . cannot translate. There have been survivors. Cannot translate. Did they make promises to you concerning the eventual outcome?"

"What? No . . . I told you. It was just supposed to be a simple procedure. No one said anything about suspended animation or anything like that. I didn't agree to anything but my ear operation!"

There was a very long pause. Tom felt increasingly uncomfortable, but periodic waves of cold moving through his body calmed him. Finally the plant spoke again. "Many of the records from this facility . . . cannot translate. Incomplete. Your record is incomplete. But they indicate that a mishap occurred. An anomalous event. An error was made during surgery. You could not be revived. Subsequently an agreement was reached."

"An agreement with whom? I told you I didn't agree to anything."

Another long, uncomfortable silence. "The agreement was signed by a Richard Johnston."

"My dad. He was my next of kin."

"He was told, according to the fragment remaining, that your life might not end. Your body would be suspended, until your condition could be rectified."

"He always believed in that sort of thing. They probably offered him all kinds of money, but he asked for this instead. He couldn't fix me, so he had them send me into the future. That's the way he thought about things."

"Are you stating that you would not have chosen this for yourself?"

"No, never. I am, was, a fatalist. There were so many diseases then. If it hadn't been a botched surgery, it would have probably been some terrible plague. Dying in your sleep would be so much better. Those last forty years, epidemics killed so many. And maybe that was actually a blessing."

"A blessing?"

"I know that sounds harsh, but sometimes you have to step back, view history with a bit of perspective. That's what I used to do—I taught high school history. There were too many people, and with the droughts, the infestations, many crops were lost. People came up from Latin America looking for food—Mexico was just a rest stop. Refugees were pouring out of Asia into Europe, away from flooded coastal cities everywhere. No way could all those people be fed. The fields were empty, and then the fields were filled with bodies. They deserved better. My father would have agreed with that much. People deserve better."

"Your father thought you deserved better. So he sent you forward—"

"To where?" Anxiety was beginning to fill him. "To when? *When* is this?"

"Cannot translate. Cannot translate," the plant's heavy leaves rose and fell, rhythmic and graceful as some deep jungle ballerina. "To here. To now."

It was easier just to imagine yourself a new person than to attempt to adjust, carrying around the old self's vague memories, as if you'd read them in a book. "Therapy has been performed," according to the implanted translator, but details were untranslatable, answered instead by a series of random sounds. It bothered him, certainly, to have been tampered with, and to wake up owing someone for his revival. But it was all the life he had.

Loss and displacement aside, the most difficult thing that first year was coping with the apparent limits of the translator. Although the quality improved, there were always gaps where a lengthy period of attempted communication resulted in a disappointingly blunt "cannot translate," or worse, absolute silence.

Despite his plant-like appearance, it soon became apparent that the alien was not botanical in nature, nor bird, reptile, fish, or mammal or anything else he could compare it to on Earth. Obviously there was a cybernetic component, whether attached or integrated Tom couldn't say.

Of more practical concern was that Tom had nothing to call him—and he didn't want to use some disrespectful coinage or 'pet' name. Nor could he determine where the alien was from, or even the name of the van-like contraption they used to travel around together on the surface of a transformed Earth.

Tom understood that he was still in St. Louis, Missouri, but nothing was recognizable. Quakes and floods had distorted the town's profile, and the fact that the suspension facility where he'd been found had been relatively intact was, in the translator's terms, "an unlikely reality." The alien said the area was "architecture in recombination with landscape," a complexly ridged, sculptural field of debris and trash split by a narrow stream that was a vastly diminished and relocated Mississippi River.

The Gateway Arch was gone as well, and the companion had acquired a video so that Tom could watch in awe as the keystone failed and dropped out, the disconnected legs twisting away and falling in opposite directions, the translator narrating the analysis in an annoyingly detached, analytical monotone.

But at least Tom was finally allowed to drive the van. He stood before the segmented dashboard, his hands on the sections as the companion had demonstrated, maneuvering over the broken landscape. Despite having fewer appendages than the controls had been designed for, he was still able to make turns and stops, in most directions, just more slowly. Each day they returned to a predetermined location the companion picked via some untranslatable criteria.

As they came over the final rise from the lab, the clean, geometric lines of the excavation fields were clearly distinguishable from the muddle of destruction. It looked like a typical archaeological dig, he supposed, not having ever been on one during his own lifetime. (He'd have to stop thinking that way—it wasn't as if he'd died.)

Eight or nine aliens traveled their particular areas of the field, trailed by assistants like himself intent on the debris at their feet—picking things up, examining them, recording the scene, stealing glances at the others, but keeping on task. He supposed a lucky alien might unfreeze an actual archaeologist to assist him. Otherwise he had to settle for, say, a high school history teacher.

The natives—the people indigenous to this time, smaller than Tom and the other assistants who'd been suspended—looked like children playing in the fields of debris. They climbed up and down the rubble, scrambling frantically over each other in their search for objects for survival or trade. At first he thought they were scavenging for food, but after having sifted through tons of debris himself he discovered there was almost nothing organic left in the ruins of the city.

A swollen version of the alien vans sped rapidly into the center of the dig. The natives surrounded it in an eye blink. A panel slid aside, disgorging dozens of green and brown packages. A swarm of natives hauled the parcels away like hungry insects. The aliens were feeding them.

From the patch directly in front of him, he picked up a small metallic jar and was looking at it when broad hands attached to skinny arms snatched it away. He had an impulse to chase after the native, who was now scrambling up a ridge, but thought better of it.

Angrily, he looked over at his companion for some help. A group of natives circled the alien as if he were some giant corn plant (extinct since Tom's own era) and they worshippers anticipating his moves, interpreting what he considered worthy of his attentions.

No alien ever made a move to stop the natives, or even alter their path. Other than supplying food, the aliens ignored them. And Tom had to concede the natives deserved every liberty they could take. Manners had become a luxury.

He went back to work, picked up a piece of hammer, a bowl, a cupboard door, a jar rattling with something mummified inside. He catalogued, reported, added some objects to the stack they would take back to the lab. He still didn't really know what they were looking for—the companion's criteria had been untranslatable, so everything seemed of potential interest. Back at the lab he would study the recordings, flagging anything different from what they had seen before.

He found a telescoping handle with a bowl-like end closed with some sort of shutter. A visual record sent to the van came back as audio from his implant: "a device used for the capture and inspection of rat corpses. Decontaminated and safe to collect." It was dated from after his time. The function of most unfamiliar objects he found was easier to guess—these were things made by human beings for human use, after all. People used tools, ate, bathed, and relieved themselves with generally recognizable equipment.

When he found an old plastic pull-toy, he began to speak of toys his father had made for him. Every day he made more of these sometimes stressful but highly addictive recorded narratives.

A rhythmic crunching noise surprised him. One of his fellow assistants was jogging across the debris field toward him. "The name's Franklin!" the man shouted. "So, how long were you under?"

Tom's companion swiveled toward the noise, but made no attempt to discourage this meeting. Franklin looked like an old man—like Tom did, he knew, suspension being less the fountain of youth than had probably been promised. Franklin was all skin and bone, but he moved with easy, un-self-conscious energy.

"Do you know *when* this is?" Tom asked eagerly.

Franklin laughed. "Sorry. No, I don't think any of us do. 'Cannot translate,' which is what they say if there's something they don't want you to know."

"I don't think my companion would lie—I don't think he even *can*."

"But he can leave out the details, or say nothing at all. Surely he's like all the other flowers in this petunia patch, and you get these long, silent, brooding spells?"

"Well, yes. But there's no way for us to know what that silence actually means, or how it functions for them. They're not plants, by the way."

Franklin made a dismissive gesture with his hands. Or Tom thought it was dismissive—it had been a very long time since he'd actually witnessed a non-verbal human gesture. "Oh, I know. But you have to call them *something*, and they certainly look like plants. They look, well, they're identical, aren't they?"

Tom looked around and saw that his companion was now standing with Franklin's. They were as motionless as . . . as houseplants. Perhaps they were watching, but Tom sensed it was more complicated than that. "Mine is bluer around the base above the filaments, and slightly less symmetrical. He feels—I don't know—older than some of the others. They're not identical at all—you just have to study them to recognize the differences."

"I gather you call yours 'the companion.'"

"That's the way I *think* about him—it's better than 'the alien.' But I don't call him anything, at least when I speak to him. I just pretend I'm speaking to myself out loud."

"I call mine *Audrey*. It makes the conversation go more easily, to have an actual name."

"Audrey?"

"*The Little Shop of Horrors?* 'Feed me!'? That giant man-eating plant? Did you ever see it? There was a revival, very popular when I died, if you'll excuse the expression."

"That must have been after my time. When I—died—the refugees were just crossing into Arizona, Texas."

"They'd made it to St. Louis by the time I passed. By that time it made no difference—if they were from California, Arizona, Mexico or Latin American—they were all refugees. Starving, desperate, disease-ridden human beings. What were the rest of us supposed to do?"

Tom had no answer, and did not want to know what Franklin might have participated in. They both stood quietly looking around at the natives, as if anything but silence would be somehow disrespectful, and it occurred to Tom that this might offer another explanation for the aliens' long non-responsive silences. An alien drifted slowly by, several natives trailing excitedly. Franklin gazed after them, looking troubled.

"Have you tried to talk with one of them?" Tom asked. "A native?"

"Only at first. How much do you know about them?"

"Very little—they hardly ever speak, and when they do I can't understand them. But they're what's left of us."

"No, *we're* what's left of us—the ones from another time, the ones that were suspended. That's who we are, the survivors from that time. These people, they're from *this* time, and this, my friend, is a whole other world. You know they hate us, don't you? At least the ones who understand enough."

"No, I don't," Tom said firmly. "Why would they hate us?"

"Because we got to miss the worst of it. They don't look like much, but they're not dumb—it takes some smarts to survive this long in this environment. And we got to skip what they went through, and what their fathers and mothers went through, and who knows how many generations back, and now we're helping their invaders."

"They're hardly invaders, Franklin."

Franklin looked at Tom for a moment as if he felt sorry for him. "Then tell me, Tom. Who's in charge here?"

During the next few months Tom became obsessed with the complexities of reconstituting a vanished world from its pieces—his world, and that world which had evolved into being while he slept. A thick but feather weight oval so transparent it might be invisible proved to be a lamp. Nearby he found a piece of rainbow—he held the iridescent fragment against the sun and it began to vibrate with colors that filled the air. Alarmed, he dropped it, and heard a nearby laugh. When his eyes readjusted he saw Franklin a few yards away, scraping busily at the ground but sparing a glimpse Tom's way.

"Happened to me, too. It's a piece of something they were developing for energy storage. A lot of innovation was going on during my time, desperate attempts to save us all. I doubt that thing, or that lamp you found earlier, were ever finished. Least I never saw them. We were so *clever*, you know? Hard to understand how we failed so catastrophically."

Perhaps it was this, or Tom's growing fatigue over the futility of attempting to reclaim a lost world while not really living in *this* one, that made the day feel endless. Tom looked at his companion with growing suspicion. The creature's silences, his awful impenetrability. His invasion of Tom's life. The alien *was* in charge of him—he set the pace and the daily priorities.

And yet Tom would have no purpose at all if they had not brought him back from the darkness. They might be occupiers, but they kept him occupied.

At the end of that long day Franklin came to Tom and dropped a battered coin into his hand. It was inscribed *The Day of the Triffids.* "Just scan it with the lab recorder," he said. "It'll start playing on the monitor. It's a classic—and you may find it amusing."

As Tom watched the movie back at the lab he decided it was clumsy, but when an actor told an actress, "Keep behind me. There's no sense in getting killed by a plant," he laughed out loud.

"This amuses you," the companion said, behind him. Tom jumped up, alarmed.

"Some of the lines, yes, they made me laugh." Then, "but it's just a silly movie," he said unnecessarily.

"Cannot translate." Then a bit later, "You are uncomfortable."

"Yes. Just a bit. I didn't know you were there."

"You may always ask questions if you are uncomfortable."

"Yes, I know." Tom hesitated. "I wanted to ask you if you had considered that—that we might not welcome your help here?"

Again the awkward silence. And a few "Cannot translate" statements followed by a series of untranslatable sounds before the companion began to speak. "I—apologize. You have been—influenced—so you will not harm us. There has been—debate."

"You mean whatever you've done to us wouldn't let us try."

"Cannot translate. It would not. Cannot translate."

It made Tom uncomfortable that he'd never known where to look when he spoke to the companion. He didn't know where the eyes—or whatever the alien used for visual input—were located. He'd looked in numerous places for them. Today he simply looked away. "It is our world."

"You look out at the world, the sky, and you think that you see your-selves," the companion replied. "You do not. Cannot translate. You witness our silences, our—soft—pauses between the efforts to communicate with you, and you think that they are about you. Cannot translate. They are not."

There was something different about the companion. He moved more slowly across the ragged ridge, pausing now and then with his fila-ments trembling. Sometimes he stood for half an hour or more, fully exposed to the hot afternoon sun. The group of natives who normally followed the companion avoided him.

Tom discovered the door lying flat on the hillside under a thin layer of broken concrete. The companion paused but passed quickly. It was just a door, and they had examined many doors. Tom pried it up and verified that it was attached to nothing, like opening a door in the ground to more ground.

He lingered over it, brushing at it, touching it with his palms. The paint was worn, but still apparent. Blue. It was a sky-blue door. After a lengthy brushing, the scratches on its surface became legible:

The Collier family lived here 200 years. It sheltered & nourished us. God bless our home.

Tom loaded the door into their van to take back to the lab. He'd started back to the fields when Franklin ran up to him.

"Audrey died!"

"I—" He didn't know what to say. "I imagined they had a very long life-span. Was there an accident?"

"No. I'd noticed some color changes, some fading, and the tips of the appendages? I'd been seeing some transparency there the past few months. Then one evening last week Audrey was silent and still for a very long time, and the next morning I found him in that same position, as if he'd just been switched off."

Tom saw some aliens off in the distance, their filaments floating gently back and forth, pushed by the breeze, natives running between them like children playing among trees. "I'm sorry, Franklin. What did you do?"

"I couldn't even get out of the lab—all the security was keyed to Audrey. But the next morning a group of them arrived with Audrey's replace-ment. You know, I've been noticing the differences since I first met you. Audrey's coloring was a little different, a little more orange. This new one acts differently, moves differently, I don't know, I'm thinking I may not like this one as much."

"Maybe they're more complex than you thought."

Franklin nodded, a bit wide-eyed, but Tom wasn't convinced he was actually listening. "Hey, have you seen the hands?"

"The hands?"

"Well, obviously you haven't. The natives built them, fairly recently, I think."

Tom followed Franklin down the slope and through labyrinthine mounds of debris until they reached a small clearing on the edge of the dig. A few natives working on something scattered as the two men approached.

He couldn't quite tell what he was looking at until he shifted angles. In the middle of the clearing it appeared the natives had built several tall, narrow mounds of refuse. But as he moved sideways the constructions became clear: eight or nine giant hands rising out of these fields of destruction.

Tom and Franklin approached as closely as they dared. It was obvious that whatever held these sculptures together was nothing more than a complex interlocking and placement of parts. They were meant to be temporary, and might dissolve at any moment into the rubble field they'd come from.

"Look at the way the palms are curved," Tom said. "There's no tension in them—no matter how tightly they were put together, those palms are relaxed, ready to accept whatever might fall into them. These aren't the desperate hands of someone needing rescue, or begging. They're just hands that have been raised, hands that are showing themselves."

"Do they make you feel guilty?" Franklin asked nervously. "These hands make me feel guilty. Not so much for surviving—these people survived. But for missing the worst of it. I don't know what to do about that."

Tom nodded. "I think you just do your work, continue to piece things back together. Sometimes the best thing is just doing the only thing that's left."

Franklin was silent for quite some time, then said, "They told me Audrey had lived a very long time. They said that most of the ones who come here to explore what's been left of us were at the very end of those long lives. They won't be seeing their homes again, Tom. They're spending their final days with us."

The companion had not taken him out to the St. Louis fields in several weeks. Tom was glad to be able to catch up on his research, his endless cataloging, but he was worried.

The companion had been standing beside him for days, as if unable to leave his side. Had he moved at all? When he could detect even the slightest of movements he would return to his labor, satisfied. There was increased transparency in the leaves, the filaments, even the mechanical threads, even in that chandelier-looking device whose function Tom had never determined. The companion had remained silent. Even a "cannot translate" would have been welcomed.

The transparent tips of the leaves were frayed, and their ragged failure seemed like movement, but Tom doubted it really was. They looked like jewelry in the hazy bright light of the lab.

Tom propped the blue door up against the lab wall to get a good view of it. The companion would be able to see it also, if the companion was seeing anything now. Then Tom began to speak, adding to the hundreds of hours of testimony he'd already made.

"My father believed every human being deserved two things—meaningful work and a home to live in or come back to when the world felt unsafe. My mother tended to agree but her practical nature told her that not everyone got what they deserved, and when survival was at stake self-fulfillment was a luxury.

"The fact that they never managed to own their own home caused my father great shame. He was a smart man but not formally educated. He read in libraries and watched educational shows and devoured the newspaper.

"He worked a lot of jobs and some were more interesting than others but he never found one that brought him joy. Mother always said his standards were too high and there wasn't a job invented that would make him happy.

"But he was determined that one day we would have a house of our own and toward that end he found what he thought was the perfect front door. On a demolition job he discovered this thick door with carved panels and an elaborate brass doorknob. He took it home to our little rented duplex, leaned it against the wall, and announced to the family that we were going to have a great house someday and that this would be the front door.

"The next morning he replaced the door to the duplex with this new one. It didn't quite fit and he had to trim it and make some adjustments to the frame. He had an extra key made and gave it to the owner because, of course, it was actually *his* house. The owner wasn't very happy but my dad could be pretty charming.

"From then on, wherever we moved my father carried that door. Sometimes he had to cut it to fit a smaller opening and sometimes he had to add lumber to one end to widen it or make it taller. After a few years with all those alterations it didn't look so elegant, but it was still strong, and it was *our* door. I'm sure we were evicted more than once because of it, but he was stubborn. I think the uglier it became, the more he liked it.

"Dad used to tell me stories about early civilizations, about the night watch, and how people would lock themselves in at night behind a good door to protect themselves from wild animals and thieves. I think those stories are one reason I became a history teacher. He said the world wasn't like that anymore, that you didn't have to be so afraid. But by the time I was an adult it was obvious those times of the nightly lock-in had come again.

"My father desperately wanted to make his mark but didn't know how. He said we should leave behind more than a few scattered bones in a field, that we all deserved better. He thought you should feel that your limited time here mattered. That you had opened doors.

"For me the worst thing about those last few years of my old life was that mattering didn't seem possible anymore. It appeared to be too late to make a difference. Has that changed? Can you tell me that?"

For a long time Tom waited there by that beautiful, unknowable alien thing. The answer finally came, faintly, as if across some vast distance.

Cannot translate.

Robert Reed is a prolific author with a fondness for the novella. Among
Reed's recent projects is polishing his past catalog, then publishing those
stories on Kindle, using his daughter's sketches for the covers. His novella,
"A Billion Eves," won the Hugo for Best Novella in 2007. His latest novel
is *The Dragons of Marrow*.

The Ants of Flanders

ROBERT REED

INTRUDERS

The mass of a comet was pressed into a long dense needle. Dressed with
carbon weaves and metametals, the needle showed nothing extraneous
to the universe. The frigid black hull looked like space itself, and it carried nothing that could leak or glimmer or produce the tiniest electronic
fart—a trillion tons of totipotent matter stripped of engines but charging
ahead at nine percent light speed. No sun or known world would claim
ownership. No analysis of its workings or past trajectory would mark any
culpable builder. Great wealth and ferocious genius had been invested in a
device that was nearly invisible, inert as a bullet, and flying by time, aimed
at a forbidden, heavily protected region.

The yellow-white sun brightened while space grew increasingly dirty.
Stray ions and every twist of dust was a hazard. The damage of the inevitable impacts could be ignored, but there would always be a flash of radiant light. A million hidden eyes lay before it, each linked to paranoid minds
doing nothing but marking every unexpected event. Security networks
were hunting for patterns, for random noise and vast conspiracies. This
was why secrecy had to be maintained as long as possible. This was why
the needle fell to thirty AU before the long stasis ended. A temporary mind
was grown on the hull. Absorbed starlight powered thought and allowed a
platoon of eyes to sprout. Thousands of worlds offered themselves. Most
were barren, but the largest few bore atmospheres and rich climates. This
was wilderness, and the wilderness was gorgeous. Several planets tempted
the newborn pilot, but the primary target still had its charms—a radio-
bright knob of water and oxygen, silicates and slow green life.

Final course corrections demanded to be made, and the terrific momentum had to be surrendered. To achieve both, the needle's tail was quickly reconfigured, micron wires reaching out for thousands of miles before weaving an obedient smoke that took its first long bite of a solar wind.

That wind tasted very much like sugar.

The penguins were coming. With their looks and comical ways, Humboldt penguins meant lots of money for the Children's Zoo, and that's why a fancy exhibit had been built for them. People loved to stand in flocks, watching the comical nervous birds that looked like little people. But of course penguins were nothing like people, and while Simon Bloch figured he would like the birds well enough, he certainly wasn't part of anybody's flock.

Bloch was a stubborn, self-contained sixteen-year-old. Six foot five, thick-limbed and stronger than most grown men, he was a big slab of a boy with a slow unconcerned walk and a perpetually half-asleep face that despite appearances noticed quite a lot. Maybe he wasn't genius-smart, but he was bright and studious enough to gain admission to the honors science program at the Zoo School. Teachers found him capable. His stubborn indifference made him seem mature. But there was a distinct, even unique quality: because of a quirk deep in the boy's nature, he had never known fear.

Even as a baby, Bloch proved immune to loud noises and bad dreams. His older and decidedly normal brother later hammered him with stories about nocturnal demons and giant snakes that ate nothing but kindergarteners, yet those torments only fed a burning curiosity. As a seven-year-old, Bloch slipped out of the house at night, wandering alleys and wooded lots, hoping to come across the world's last T. rex. At nine, he got on a bus and rode halfway to Seattle, wanting to chase down Bigfoot. He wasn't testing his bravery. Bravery was what other people summoned when their mouths went dry and hearts pounded. What he wanted was to stare into the eyes of a monster, admiring its malicious, intoxicating power, and if possible, steal a little of that magic for himself.

Bloch wasn't thinking about monsters. The first penguins would arrive tomorrow morning, and he was thinking how they were going to be greeted with a press conference and party for the zoo's sugar daddies. Mr. Rightly had asked Bloch to stay late and help move furniture, and that's why the boy was walking home later than usual. It was a warm November afternoon, bright despite the sun hanging low. Three hundred pounds of casual, unhurried muscle was headed east. Bloch was imagining penguins swimming in their new pool, and then a car horn intruded, screaming in the distance. And in the next second a father down the street began yelling at his kid, telling him to get the hell inside now. Neither noise seemed remarkable, but they shook Bloch out of his daydream.

Then a pair of cars shot past on Pender. Pender Boulevard was a block north, and the cars started fast and accelerated all the way down the long hill. They had to be doing seventy if not a flat-out eighty, and under the roar of wasted gas he heard the distinct double-tone announcing a text from Matt.

It was perfectly normal for Bloch's soldier-brother to drop a few words on "the kid" before going to bed.

"So what the hell is it," Bloch read.

"whats what," he wrote back. But before he could send, a second cryptic message arrived from the world's night side.

"that big and moving that fast shit glad it's probably missing us aren't you"

Bloch snorted and sent his two words.

The racing cars had disappeared down the road. The distant horn had stopped blaring and nobody was shouting at his kids. Yet nothing seemed normal now. Bloch felt it. Pender was hidden behind the houses, but as if on a signal, the traffic suddenly turned heavy. Drivers were doing fifty or sixty where forty was the limit, and the street sounded jammed. Bloch tried phoning a couple friends, except there was no getting through. So he tried his mother at work, but just when it seemed as if he had a connection, the line went dead.

Then the Matt-tones returned.

"a big-ass spaceship dropping toward us catching sun like a sail are you the hell watching?????"

Bloch tried pulling up the BBC science page. Nothing came fast and his phone's battery was pretty much drained. He stood on a sidewalk only four blocks from home, but he still had to cross Pender. And it sounded like NASCAR out there. Cars were braking, tires squealing. Suddenly a Mini came charging around the corner. Bloch saw spiked orange hair and a cigarette in one hand. The woman drove past him and turned into the next driveway, hitting the pavement hard enough to make sparks. Then she was parked and running up her porch steps, fighting with her keys to find the one that fit her lock.

"What's happening?" Bloch called out.

She turned toward the voice and dropped the key ring, and stuffing the cigarette into her mouth, she kneeled and got lucky. Finding the key that she needed, she stood up and puffed, saying, "Aliens are coming. Big as the earth, their ship is, and it's going to fucking hit us."

"Hit us?"

"Hit the earth, yeah. In five minutes."

On that note, the woman dove into her house, vanishing.

Perched on a nearby locust tree, a squirrel held its head cocked, one brown eye watching the very big boy.

"A starship," Bloch said, laughing. "That's news."

Chirping in agreement, the squirrel climbed to its home of leaves.

An image had loaded on the phone's little screen—black space surrounding a meaningless blur painted an arbitrary pink by the software. The tiny scroll at the bottom was running an update of events that only started half an hour ago. The starship was huge but quick, and astronomers only just noticed it. The ship seemed to weigh nothing. Sunlight and the solar wind had slowed it down to a thousand miles every second, which was a thousand times faster than a rifle slug, and a clock in the right corner was counting down to the impact. A little more than four minutes remained. Bloch held the phone steady. Nothing about the boy was genuinely scared. Racing toward the sun, the starship was shifting its trajectory. Odds were that it would hit the earth's night side. But it was only a solar sail, thin and weak, and there was no way to measure the hazard. Mostly what the boy felt was a rare joyous thrill. If he got lucky with the stop lights, he could run across the intersection at the bottom of the hill, reaching home just in time to watch the impact on television.

But he didn't take a step. Thunder or a low-flying jet suddenly struck from behind. The world shook, and then the roar ended with a wrenching explosion that bled into a screeching tangle of lesser noises. Brakes screamed and tires slid across asphalt, and Bloch felt something big hammering furiously at the ground. A giant truck must have lost control, tumbling down the middle of Pender. What else could it be? Fast-moving traffic struggled to brake and steer sideways. Bloch heard cars colliding, and the runaway truck or city bus kept rolling downhill. Turning toward the racket, toward the west, he couldn't see Pender or the traffic behind the little houses, but the mayhem, the catastrophe, rolled past him, and then a final crash made one tall oak shake, the massive trunk wobbling and the weakest brown leaves falling, followed by a few more collisions of little vehicles ending with an abrupt wealth of silence.

The side street bent into Pender. Bloch sprinted to the corner. Westbound traffic was barely rolling up the long gentle hill, and nobody was moving east. The sidewalk and one lane were blocked by a house-sized ball of what looked like black metal. Some piece of Bloch's brain expected a truck and he was thinking this was a damn peculiar truck. He had to laugh. An old man stood on the adjacent lawn, eyes big and busy. Bloch approached, and the man heard the laughter and saw the big boy. The man was trembling. He needed a good breath before he could say, "I saw it." Then he lifted a shaking arm, adding, "I saw it fall," as he slapped the air with a flattened hand, mimicking the intruder's bounce as it rolled down the long hill, smacking into the oak tree with the last of its momentum.

Bloch said, "Wow."

"This is my yard," the old man whispered, as if nothing were more important. Then the arm dropped and his hands grabbed one another. "What is it, you think? A spaceship?"

"An ugly spaceship," Bloch said. He walked quickly around the object, looking for wires or portholes. But nothing showed in the lumpy black hull. Back uphill were strings of cars crushed by the impacts and from colliding with each other. A Buick pointed east, its roof missing. Now the old man was staring at the wreckage, shaking even worse than before. When he saw Bloch returning, he said, "I wouldn't look. Get away."

Bloch didn't stop. An old woman had been driving the Buick when the spaceship came bouncing up behind her. One elegant hand was resting neatly in her lap, a big diamond shining on the ring finger, and her head was missing, and Bloch studied the ripped-apart neck, surprised by the blood and sorry for her but always curious, watchful and impressed.

People were emerging from houses and the wrecked cars and from cars pulling over to help. There was a lot of yelling and quick talking. One woman screamed, "Oh God, someone's alive here." Between a flipped pickup and the Buick was an old Odyssey, squashed and shredded. The van's driver was clothes mixed with meat. Every seat had its kid strapped in, but only one of them was conscious. The little girl in back looked out at Bloch, smiled and said something, and he smiled back. The late-day air stank of gasoline. Bloch swung his left arm, shattering the rear window with the elbow, and then he reached in and undid the girl's belt and brought her out. What looked like a brother was taking what looked like a big nap beside her. The side of his face was bloody. Bloch undid that belt and pulled him out too and carried both to the curb while other adults stood around the van, talking about the three older kids still trapped.

Then the screaming woman noticed gasoline running in the street, flowing toward the hot spaceship. Louder than ever, she told the world, "Oh God, it's going to blow up."

People started to run away, holding their heads down, and still other people came forward, fighting with the wreckage, fighting with jammed doors and their own panic, trying to reach the unconscious and dead children.

One man looked at Bloch, eyes shining when he said, "Come on and help us."

But there was a lot of gasoline. The pickup must have had a reserve tank, and it had gotten past the van and the Buick. Bloch was thinking about the spaceship, how it was probably full of electricity and alien fires. That was the immediate danger, he realized. Trotting up ahead, he peeled off his coat and both shirts, and after wadding them up into one tight knot, he threw them into the stinking little river, temporarily stopping the flow.

The screaming woman stood in the old man's yard. She was kind of pretty and kind of old. Staring at his bare chest, she asked, "What are you doing?"

"Helping," he said.

She had never heard anything so odd. That's what she said with her wrinkled, doubtful face.

Once more, Bloch's phone made the Matt noise. His brother's final message had arrived. "Everythings quiet here everybodys outside and I bet you wish you could see this big bastard filling the sky, B, its weird no stars but the this glow, and pretty you know???you would love this"

And then some final words:

"Good luck and love Matt."

Tar and nanofibers had been worn as camouflage, and an impoverished stream of comet detritus served as cover. A machine grown for one great purpose had spent forty million years doing nothing. But the inevitable will find ways to happen, and the vagaries of orbital dynamics gave this machine extraordinary importance. Every gram of fuel was expended, nothing left to make course corrections. The goal was a small lake that would make quite a lot possible, but the trajectory was sloppy, and it missed the target by miles, rolling to a halt on a tilted strip of solid hydrocarbons littered with mindless machinery and liquid hydrocarbons and cellulose and sacks of living water.

Eyes were spawned, gazing in every direction.

Several strategies were fashioned and one was selected, and only then did the machine begin growing a body and the perfect face.

B randishing a garden hose, the old man warned Bloch to get away from the damn gas. But an even older man mentioned that the spaceship was probably hot and maybe it wasn't a good idea throwing cold water near it. The hose was grudgingly put away. But the gasoline pond was spilling past the cotton and polyester dam. Bloch considered asking people for their shirts. He imagined sitting in the street, using his butt to slow things down. Then a third fellow arrived, armed with a big yellow bucket of cat litter, and that hero used litter to build a second defensive barrier.

All the while, the intruder was changing. Its rounded shape held steady but the hull was a shinier, prettier black. Putting his face close, Bloch felt the heat left over from slamming into the atmosphere; nevertheless, he could hold his face close and peer inside the glassy crust, watching tiny dark shapes scurry here to there and back again.

"Neat," he said.

Bystanders started to shout at the shirtless boy, telling him to be careful and not burn himself. They said that he should find clothes before he caught a cold. But Bloch was comfortable, except where his elbow was sore from busting out the van window. He held the arm up to the radiant heat and watched the ship's hull reworking itself. Car radios were blaring, competing voices reporting the same news: a giant interstellar craft was striking the earth's night side. Reports of power outages and minor impacts were coming in. Europe and Russia might be getting the worst of it, though there wasn't any news from the Middle East. Then suddenly most of the stations shifted to the same feed, and one man was talking. He sounded like a scientist lecturing to a class. The "extraordinary probe" had been spread across millions of square miles, and except for little knots and knobs, it was more delicate than any spiderweb, and just as harmless. "The big world should be fine," he said.

On Pender Boulevard, cars were jammed up for blocks and sirens were descending. Fire trucks and paramedics found too much to do. The dead and living children had been pulled out of the van, and the screaming woman stood in the middle of the carnage, steering the first helpers to them. Meanwhile the cat litter man and hose man were staring at the spaceship.

"It came a long ways," said the litter man.

"Probably," said the hose man.

Bloch joined them.

"Aren't you cold?" the hose man asked.

The boy shrugged and said nothing.

And that topic was dropped. "Yeah, this ship came a long ways," the litter man reported. "I sure hope they didn't mean to do this."

"Do what?" asked his friend.

"Hurt people."

Something here was wrong. Bloch looked back at the Buick and the sun, waiting to figure out what was bothering him. But it didn't happen. Then he looked at the spaceship again. The shininess had vanished, the crust dull and opaque except where little lines caught the last of the day's light.

Once again, Bloch started forward.

The two men told him to be careful, but then both of them walked beside the sixteen-year-old.

"Something's happening," the hose man said.

"It is," his buddy agreed.

As if to prove them right, a chunk of the crust fell away, hitting the ground with a light ringing sound.

Bloch was suddenly alone.

Radio newscasters were talking about blackouts on the East Coast and citizens not panicking, and some crackly voice said that it was a beautiful night in Moscow, no lights working but ten centimeters of new snow shining under a cold crescent moon. Then a government voice interrupted the poetry. U.S. military units were on heightened alert, he said. Bloch thought of his brother as he knelt, gingerly touching the warm, glassy and almost weightless shard of blackened crust. Another two pieces fell free, one jagged fissure running between the holes. Probe or cannon ball or whatever, the object was beginning to shatter.

People retreated to where they felt safe, calling to the big boy who insisted on standing beside the visitor.

Bloch pushed his face inside the nearest gap.

A bright green eye looked out at him.

Swinging the sore elbow, Bloch shattered a very big piece of the featherweight egg case.

B eautiful," bystanders said. "Lovely."
   The screaming woman found a quieter voice. "Isn't she sweet?" she asked. "What a darling."

"She?" the hose man said doubtfully.

"Look at her," the woman said. "Isn't that a she?"

"Looks girlish to me," the litter man agreed.

The alien body was dark gray and long and streamlined, slick to the eye like a finely grained stone polished to where it shone in the reflected light. It seemed to be lying on its back. Complex appendages looked like meaty fins, but with fingers that managed to move, four hands clasping at the air and then at one another. The fluked tail could have been found on a dolphin, and the face would have been happy on a seal—a whiskerless round-faced seal with a huge mouth pulled into a magnificent grin. But half of the face and most of the animal's character was focused on those two enormous eyes, round with iridescent green irises and perfect black pupils bright enough to reflect Bloch's curious face.

The egg's interior was lined with cables and odd machines and masses of golden fibers, and the alien was near the bottom, lying inside a ceramic bowl filled with a desiccated blood-colored gelatin. The body was too big for the bowl, and it moved slowly and stiffly, pressing against the bone-white sides.

"Stay back," bystanders implored.

But as soon as people backed away, others pushed close, wrestling for the best view.

The screaming woman touched Bloch. "Did she say something?"

"I didn't hear anything."

"She wants to talk," the woman insisted.

That seemed like a silly idea, and the boy nearly laughed. But that's when the seal's mouth opened and one plaintive word carried over the astonished crowd.

"Help," the alien begged.

People fell silent.

Then from far away, a man's voice shouted, "Hey, Bloch."

A short portly figure was working his way through the crowd. Bloch hurried back to meet Mr. Rightly. His teacher was younger than he looked, bald and bearded with white in the whiskers. His big glasses needed a bigger nose to rest on, and he pushed the glasses against his face while staring at the egg and the backs of strangers. "I heard about the crash," he said, smiling in a guarded way. "I didn't know you'd be here. Did you see it come down?"

"No, but I heard it."

"What's inside?"

"The pilot, I think."

"An alien?"

"Yes, sir."

Mr. Rightly was the perfect teacher for bright but easily disenchanted teenagers. A master's in biology gave him credibility, and he was smarter than his degree. The man had an infectious humor and a pleasant voice, and Bloch would do almost anything for him, whether moving furniture after school or ushering him ahead to meet the ET.

"Come on, sir."

Nobody in front of them felt shoved. Nobody was offended or tried to resist. But one after another, bodies felt themselves being set a couple feet to the side, and the big mannish child was past them, offering little apologies while a fellow in dark slacks and a wrinkled dress shirt walked close behind.

To the last row, Bloch said, "Please get back. We've got a scientist here."

That was enough reason to surrender their places, if only barely.

The alien's face had changed in the last moments. The smile remained, but the eyes were less bright. And the voice was weaker than before, quietly moaning one clear word.

"Dying."

Mr. Rightly blinked in shock. "What did you just say?"

The creature watched them, saying nothing.

"Where did you come from?" the litter man asked.

The mouth opened, revealing yellow teeth rooted in wide pink gums. A broad tongue emerged, and the lower jaw worked against some pain that made the entire body spasm. Then again, with deep feeling, the alien said to everybody, "Help."

"Can you breathe?" Mr. Rightly asked. Then he looked at Bloch, nervously yanking at the beard. What if they were watching the creature suffocate?

But then it made a simple request. "Water," it said. "My life needs water, please, please."

"Of course, of course," said the screaming woman, her voice back to its comfortable volume. Everyone for half a block heard her declare, "She's a beached whale. We need to get her in water."

Murmurs of concern pushed through the crowd.

"Freshwater or salt," Mr. Rightly asked.

Everybody fell silent. Everybody heard a creaking noise as one of the front paddle-arms extended, allowing the longest of the stubby, distinctly child-like fingers to point downhill, and then a feeble, pitiful voice said, "Hurry," it said. "Help me, please. Please."

Dozens of strangers fell into this unexpected task, this critical mercy. The hose man returned, eager to spray the alien as if watering roses. But the crashed ship was still warm on the outside, and what would water do to the machinery? Pender Slough was waiting at the bottom of the hill—a series of head-deep pools linked by slow, clay-infused runoff. With that goal in hand, the group fell into enthusiastic discussions about methods and priorities. Camps formed, each with its loudest expert as well as a person or two who tried making bridges with others. Mr. Rightly didn't join any conversation. He stared at the alien, one hand coming up at regular intervals, pushing at the glasses that never quit trying to slide off the distracted face. Then he turned to the others, one hand held high. "Not the Slough," he said. "It's filthy."

This was the voice that could startle a room full of adolescents into silence. The adults quit talking, every face centered on him. And then the cat litter man offered the obvious question:

"Where then?"

"The penguin pool," said Mr. Rightly. "That water's clean, and the penguins aren't here yet."

The man's good sense unsettled the crowd.

"We need a truck," Mr. Rightly continued. "Maybe we can flag something down."

Several men immediately walked into the westbound lanes, arms waving at every potential recruit.

Mr. Rightly looked at Bloch. "How much do you think it weighs?"

Bloch didn't need urging. The hull was cooling and the interior air was hot but bearable. He threw a leg into the shattered spaceship and crawled inside. Delicate objects that looked like jacks lay sprinkled across the flat gray floor. They made musical notes while shattering underfoot. A clean metallic smell wasn't unpleasant. Bloch touched the alien below its head, down where the chest would be. Its skin was rigid and dry and very warm, as if it was a bronze statue left in the sun. He waited for a breath, and the chest seemed to expand. He expected the body to be heavy, but the first shove proved otherwise. He thought of desiccated moths collecting inside hot summer attics. Maybe this is how you traveled between stars, like freeze-dried stroganoff. Bloch looked out the hole, ready to report back to Mr. Rightly, but people were moving away while an engine roared, a long F-350 backing into view.

Two smiling men and Mr. Rightly climbed inside the ship, the egg, whatever it was. One of the men giggled. Everybody took hold of a limb. There was no extra room, and the transfer was clumsy and slow and required more laughs and some significant cursing. Mr. Rightly asked the alien if it was all right and it said nothing, and then he asked again, and the creature offered one quiet, "Hurry."

Other men formed matching lines outside, and with the care used on babies and bombs, they lifted the valiant, beautiful, helpless creature into the open truck bed, eyes pointed skyward, its tail dangling almost to the pavement.

Mr. Rightly climbed out again. "We'll use the zoo's service entrance," he announced. "I have the key."

The hose man finally had his target in his sights, hitting the alien with a cool spray. Every drop that struck the skin was absorbed, and the green eyes seemed to smile even as the voice begged, "No. Not yet, no."

The hose was turned away.

And the screaming woman ran up, daring herself to touch the creature. Her hands reached and stopped when her courage failed, and she hugged herself instead. Nearly in tears, she said, "God bless you, darling. God bless."

Bloch was the last man out of the spaceship.

Mr. Rightly climbed up into the truck bed and then stood, blinking as he looked at the destruction up the road and at the shadows cast by the setting sun. Then Bloch called to him, and he turned and smiled. "Are you warm enough?" he asked.

"I'm fine, sir."

"Sit in the cab and stay warm," he said. "Show our driver the way."

Their driver was three weeks older than Bloch and barely half his size, and nothing could be more astonishing than the extraordinary luck that put him in this wondrous place. "I can't fucking believe this," said the driver, lifting up on the brake and letting them roll forwards. "I'm having the adventure of a lifetime. That's what this craziness is."

There was no end to the volunteers. Everybody was waving at traffic and at the truck's driver—enthusiastic, chaotic signals ready to cause another dozen crashes. But nobody got hit. The big pickup lurched into the clear and down the last of the hill, heading east. People watched its cargo. Some prayed, others used phones to take pictures, catching Bloch looking back at the children and the paramedics and the bloody blankets thrown over the dead.

"Can you fucking believe this?" the driver kept asking.

The radio was set on the CNN feed. The solar sail had reached as far as Atlanta. Power was out there, and Europe was nothing but dark and China was the same. There was a quick report that most of the world's satellites had gone silent when the probe fell on top of them. There were also rumors that an alien or aliens had contacted the US government, but the same voice added, "We haven't confirmed anything at this point."

They crossed Pender Slough and Bloch tapped the driver on the arm, guiding them onto Southwest. The driver made what was probably the slowest, most cautious turn in his life. A chain of cars and trucks followed close, headlights and flashers on. Everything they did felt big and important, and this was incredible fun. Bloch was grinning, looking back through the window at his teacher, but Mr. Rightly shot him a worried expression, and then he stared at his hands rather than the alien stretched out beside him.

"Hurry," Bloch coaxed.

The zoo appeared on their left. An access bridge led back across the slough and up to the back gate. Mr. Rightly was ready with the key. Bloch climbed out to help roll the gate open, and a couple trailing cars managed to slip inside before a guard arrived, hurriedly closing the gate before examining what they were bringing inside.

"Oh, this gal's hurt," he called out.

Bloch and his teacher walked at the front of the little parade, leading the vehicles along the wide sidewalk toward the penguin exhibit.

Mr. Rightly watched his feet, saying nothing.

"Is it dead?" Bloch asked.

"What?"

"The alien," he said.

"No, it's holding on."

"Then what's wrong?"

Mr. Rightly looked back and then forward, drifting closer to Bloch. With a quiet careful voice, he said, "She was rolling east on Pender. That means that she fell from the west."

"I guess," Bloch agreed.

"From the direction of the sun," he said. "But the big probe, that solar sail . . . it was falling toward the sun. And that's the other direction."

Here was the problem. Bloch felt this odd worry before, but he hadn't been able to find words to make it clear in his own head.

The two of them walked slower, each looking over a shoulder before talking.

"Another thing," said Mr. Rightly. "Why would an alien, a creature powerful enough and smart enough to cross between stars, need water? Our astronauts didn't fly to the moon naked and hope for air."

"Maybe she missed her target," Bloch suggested.

"And there's something else," Mr. Rightly said. "How can anything survive the gee forces from this kind of impact? You heard the sonic booms. She, or it . . . whatever it is . . . the entity came down fast and hit, and nothing alive should be alive after that kind of crash."

Bloch wanted to offer an opinion, but they arrived at the penguin exhibit before he could find one. Men and the screaming woman climbed out of the trailing cars, and like an old pro, the pickup's driver spun around and backed up to the edge of the pond. Half a dozen people waved him in. In one voice, everybody shouted, "Stop." Night was falling. The penguin pool was deep and smooth and very clear. Mr. Rightly started to say something about being cautious, about waiting, and someone asked, "Why?" and he responded with noise about water quality and its temperature. But other people had already climbed into the truck bed, grabbing at the four limbs and head and the base of that sad, drooping tail. With barely any noise, the alien went into the water. It weighed very little, and everyone expected it to float, but it sank like an arrow aimed at the Earth. Bloch stood at the edge of the pool, watching while a dark gray shape lay limp at the bottom of the azure bowl.

The screaming woman came up beside him. "Oh god, our girl's drowning," she said. "We need to jump in and help get her up to the air again."

A couple men considered being helpful, but then they touched the cold November water and suffered second thoughts.

Another man asked Mr. Rightly, "Did we screw up? Is she drowning?"

The teacher pushed his glasses against his face.

"I think we did screw up," Mr. Rightly said.

The body had stopped being gray. And a moment later that cute seal face and those eyes were smoothed away. Then the alien was larger, growing like a happy sponge, and out from its center came a blue glow, dim at first, but quickly filling the concrete basin and the air above—a blue light shining into the scared faces, and Bloch's face too.

Leaning farther out, Bloch felt the heat rising up from water that was already most of the way to boiling.

The woman ran away and then shouted, "Run."

The driver jumped into his truck and drove off.

Only two people were left at the water's edge. Mr. Rightly tugged on Bloch's arm. "Son," he said. "We need to get somewhere safe."

"Where's that?" Bloch asked.

His teacher offered a grim little laugh, saying, "Maybe Mars. How about that?"

THE LEOPARD

Any long stasis means damage. Time introduces creeps and tiny flaws into systems shriveled down near the margins of what nature permits. But the partial fueling allowed repairs to begin. Systems woke and took stock of the situation. Possibilities were free to emerge, each offering itself to the greatest good, yet the situation was dire. The universe permitted quite a lot of magic, but even magic had strict limits and the enemy was vast and endowed with enough luck to have already won a thousand advantages before the battle had begun.

Horrific circumstances demanded aggressive measures; this was the fundamental lesson of the moment.

The sanctity of an entire world at stake, and from this moment on, nothing would be pretty.

"Did you feel that?"

Bloch was stretched out on the big couch. He remembered closing his eyes, listening to the AM static on his old boom box. But the radio was silent and his mother spoke, and opening his eyes, he believed that only a minute or two had passed. "What? Feel what?"

"The ground," she said. Mom was standing in the dark, fighting for the best words. "It was like an earthquake . . . but not really . . . never mind . . ."

A second shiver passed beneath their house. There was no hard shock, no threat to bring buildings down. It was a buoyant motion, as if the world was an enormous water bed and someone very large was squirming under distant covers.

She said, "Simon."

Nobody else called him Simon. Even Dad used the nickname invented by a teasing brother. At least that's what Bloch had been told; he didn't remember his father at all.

"How do you feel, Simon?"

Bloch sat up. It was cold in the house and silent in that way that comes only when the power was out.

She touched his forehead.

"I'm fine, Mom."

"Are you nauseous?"

"No."

"Radiation sickness," she said. "It won't happen right away."

"I'm fine, Mom. What time is it?"

"Not quite six," she said. Then she checked her watch to make sure. "And we are going to the doctor this morning, if not the hospital."

"Yeah, except nothing happened," he said, just like he did twenty times last night. "We backed away when the glow started. Then the police came, and some guy from Homeland, and Mr. Rightly found me that old sweatshirt—"

"I was so scared," she interrupted, talking to the wall. "I got home and you weren't here. You should have been home already. And the phones weren't working, and then everything went dark."

"I had to walk home from the zoo," he said again. "Mr. Rightly couldn't give me a ride if he wanted, because he was parked over by the crash site."

"The crash site," she repeated.

He knew not to talk.

"You shouldn't have been there at all," she said. "Something drops from the sky, and you run straight for it."

The luckiest moment in his life, he knew.

"Simon," she said. "Why do you take such chances?"

The woman was a widow and her other son was a soldier stationed in a distant, hostile country, and even the most normal day gave her reasons to be nervous. But now aliens were raining down on their heads, and there was no word happening in the larger world. Touching the cool forehead once again, she said, "I'm not like you, Simon."

"I know that, Mom."

"I don't like adventure," she said. "I'm just waiting for the lights to come on."

But neither of them really expected that to happen. So he changed the subject, telling her, "I'm hungry."

"Of course you are." Thankful for a normal task, she hurried into the kitchen. "How about cereal before our milk goes bad?"

Bloch stood and pulled on yesterday's pants and the hooded Cornell sweatshirt borrowed from the zoo's lost-and-found. "Yeah, cereal sounds good," he said.

"What kind?" she asked from inside the darkened refrigerator.

"Surprise me," he said. Then, after slipping on his shoes, he crept out the back door.

M r. Rightly looked as if he hadn't moved in twelve hours. He was standing in the classroom where Bloch left him, and he hadn't slept. Glasses that needed a good scrubbing obscured red worried eyes. A voice worked over by sandpaper said, "That was fast."

"What was fast?" Bloch asked.

"They just sent a car for you. I told them you were probably at home."

"Except I walked here on my own," the boy said.

"Oh." Mr. Rightly broke into a long weak laugh. "Anyway, they're gathering up witnesses, seeing what everybody remembers."

It was still night outside. The classroom was lit by battery-powered lamps. "They" were the Homeland people in suits and professors in khaki, with a handful of soldiers occupying a back corner. The classroom was the operation's headquarters. Noticing Bloch's arrival, several people came forward, offering hands and names. The boy pretended to listen. Then a short Indian fellow pulled him aside, asking, "Did you yourself speak to the entity?"

"I heard it talk."

"And did it touch you?"

Bloch nearly said, "Yes." But then he thought again, asking, "Who are you?"

"I told you. I am head of the physics department at the university, here at the request of Homeland Security."

"Was it fusion?"

"Pardon?"

"The creature, the machine," Bloch said. "It turned bright blue and the pond was boiling. So we assumed some kind of reactor was supplying the power."

The head professor dismissed him with a wave. "Fusion is not as easy as that, young man. Reactors do not work that way."

"But it asked for water, which is mostly hydrogen," Bloch said. "Hydrogen is what makes the sun burn."

"Ah," the little man said. "You and your high school teacher are experts in thermonuclear technologies, are you?"

"Who is? You?"

The man flung up both hands, wiping the air between them. "I was invited here to help. I am attempting to learn what happened last night and what it is occurring now. What do you imagine? That some cadre of specialists sits in a warehouse waiting for aliens to come here and be studied? You think my colleagues and I have spent two minutes in our lives preparing for this kind of event?"

"I don't really—"

"Listen to me," the head professor insisted.

But then the ground rose. It was the same sensation that struck half a dozen times during Bloch's walk back to the zoo, only this event felt larger and there wasn't any matching sense of dropping afterwards. The room remained elevated, and everyone was silent. Then an old professor turned to a young woman, asking, "Did Kevin ever get that accelerograph?"

"I don't know."

"Well, see if you can find either one. We need to get that machine working and calibrated."

The girl was pretty and very serious, very tense. Probably a graduate student, Bloch decided. She hurried past, glancing at the big boy and the college sweatshirt that was too small. Then she was gone and he was alone in the room with a couple dozen tired adults who kept talking quietly and urgently among themselves.

The head physicist was lecturing the bald man from Homeland. The bald man was flanked by two younger men who kept flipping through pages on matching clipboards, reading in the dim light. An Army officer was delivering orders to a couple soldiers. Bloch couldn't be sure of ranks or units. He had a bunch of questions to ask Matt. For a thousand reasons, he wished he could call his brother. But there were no phones; even the Army was working with old-fashioned tools. The officer wrote on a piece of paper and tore it off the pad, handing it to one scared grunt, sending him and those important words off to "The Site."

Mr. Rightly had moved out of the way. He looked useless and exhausted and sorry, but at least he had a stool to perch on.

"What do we know?" Bloch asked him.

Something was funny in those words.

Laughing along with his teacher, Bloch asked, "Do you still think our spaceship is different from the big probe?"

As if sharing a secret, Mr. Rightly leaned close. "It came from a different part of the sky, and it was alone. And its effects, big as they are, don't compare with what's happening on the other side of the world."

The professors were huddled up, talking and pointing at the ground.

"What is happening on the other side?"

Mr. Rightly asked him to lean over, and then he whispered. "The colonel was talking to the Homeland person. I heard him say that the hardened military channels didn't quit working right away. Twenty minutes after the big impact, from Europe, from Asia, came reports of bright lights and large motions, from the ground and the water. And then the wind started to blow hard, and all those voices fell silent."

Bloch felt sad for his brother, but he couldn't help but say, "Wow."

"There is a working assumption," Mr. Rightly said. "The Earth's night side has been lost, but the invasion hasn't begun here. Homeland and the military are trying not to lose this side too."

Thinking about the alien and the dead kids, Bloch said, "You were right, sir. We shouldn't have trusted it."

Mr. Rightly shrugged and said nothing.

Some kind of meeting had been called in the back of the room. There was a lot of passion and no direction. Then the Homeland man whispered to an assistant who wrote hard on the clipboard, and the colonel found new orders and sent his last soldier off on another errand.

"What's the alien doing now?" Bloch asked.

"Who knows," Mr. Rightly said.

"Is the radiation keeping us away?"

"No, it's not . . ." The glasses needed another shove. "Our friend vanished. After you and I left, it apparently punched through the bottom of the pond. I haven't been to the Site myself. But the concrete is shattered and there's a slick new hole reaching down who-knows-how-far. That's the problem. And that's why they're so worried about these little quakes, or whatever they are. What is our green-eyed mystery doing below us?"

Bloch looked at the other faces and then at the important floor. Then a neat, odd thought struck him: the monster was never just the creature itself. It was also the way that the creature lurked about, refusing to be seen. It was the unknown wrapped heavy and thick around it, and there was the vivid electric fear that made the air glow. Real life was normal and silly. Nothing happening today was normal or silly.

He started to laugh, enjoying the moment, the possibilities.

Half of the room stared at him, everybody wondering what was wrong with that towering child.

"They're bringing in equipment, trying to dangle a cable down into the hole," Mr. Rightly said.

"What, with a camera at the end?"

"Cameras don't seem to be working. Electronics come and go. So no, they'll send down a volunteer."

"I'd go," Bloch said.

"And I know you mean that," Mr. Rightly said.

"Tell them I would."

"First of all: I won't. And second, my word here is useless. With this crew, I have zero credibility."

The physicist and colonel were having an important conversation, fingers poking imaginary objects in the air.

"I'm hungry," Bloch said.

"There's MREs somewhere," said Mr. Rightly.

"I guess I'll go look for them," the boy lied. Then he walked out into a hallway that proved wonderfully empty.

Every zoo exists somewhere between the perfect and the cheap. Every cage wants to be impregnable and eternal, but invisibility counts for something too. The prisoner's little piece of the sky had always been steel mesh reaching down to a concrete wall sculpted to resemble stone, and people would walk past all day, every day, and people would stand behind armored glass, reading about Amur leopards when they weren't looking at him.

Sometimes he paced the concrete ground, but not this morning. Everything felt different and wrong this morning. He was lying beside a dead decorative tree, marshaling his energies. Then the monster came along. It was huge and loud and very clumsy, and he kept perfectly still as the monster made a sloppy turn on the path, its long trailing arm tearing through the steel portion of the sky. Then the monster stopped and a man climbed off and looked at the damage, and then he ran to the glass, staring into the gloomy cage. But he never saw any leopards. He breathed with relief and climbed back on the monster and rode it away, and the leopard rose and looked at the hole ripped in the sky. Then with a lovely unconscious motion, he was somewhere he had never been, and the world was transformed.

Cranes and generators were rumbling beside the penguin pond. Temporary lights had been nailed to trees, and inside those brilliant cones were moving bodies and purposeful chaos, grown men shouting for this to be done and not that, and goddamn this and that, and who the hell was in charge? Bloch was going to walk past the pond's backside. His plan, such as it was, was to act as if he belonged here. If somebody stopped him, he would claim that he was heading for the vending machines at the maintenance shed—a good story since it happened to be true. Or maybe he would invent some errand given to him by the little physicist. There were a lot of lies waiting inside the confusion, and he was looking forward to telling stories to soldiers holding guns. "Don't you believe me?" he would ask them, smiling all the while. "Well maybe you should shoot me. Go on, I dare you."

The daydream ended when he saw the graduate student. He recognized her tight jeans and the blond hair worn in a ponytail. She was standing on the path ahead of him, hands at her side, eyes fixed on the little hill behind the koi pond. Bloch decided to chat with her. He was going to ask her about the machine that she was looking for, what was it called? He wanted to tell her about carrying the alien, since that might impress her. There was enough daylight now that he could see her big eyes and the rivets in her jeans, and then he noticed how some of the denim was darker than it should be, soaked through by urine.

The girl heard Bloch and flinched, but she didn't blink, staring at the same unmoving piece of landscape just above the little waterfall.

Bloch stopped behind her, seeing nothing until the leopard emerged from the last clots of darkness.

Quietly, honestly, he whispered, "Neat."

She flinched again, sucking down a long breath and holding it. She wanted to look at him and couldn't. She forced herself not to run, but her arms started to lift, as if ready to sprout wings.

The leopard was at least as interested in the girl as Bloch was. Among the rarest of cats, most of the world's Amur leopards lived in zoos. Breeding programs and Russian promises meant that they might be reintroduced into the Far East, but this particular male wasn't part of any grand effort. He was inbred and had some testicular problem, and his keepers considered him ill-tempered and possibly stupid. Bloch knew all this but his heart barely sped up. Standing behind the young woman, he whispered, "How long have you been here?"

"Do you see it?" she muttered.

"Yeah, sure."

"Quiet," she insisted.

He said nothing.

But she couldn't follow her own advice. A tiny step backward put her closer to him. "Two minutes, maybe," she said. "But it seems like hours."

Bloch watched the greenish-gold cat eyes. The animal was anxious. Not scared, no, but definitely on edge and ready to be scared, and that struck him as funny.

The woman heard him chuckling. "What?"

"Nothing."

She took a deep breath. "What do we do?"

"Nothing," was a useful word. Bloch said it again, with authority. He considered placing his hands on her shoulders, knowing she would let him. She might even like being touched. But first he explained, "If we do nothing, he'll go away."

"Or jump us," she said.

That didn't seem likely. She wasn't attacked when she was alone, and there were two of them now. Bloch felt lucky. Being excited wasn't the same as being scared, and he enjoyed standing with this woman, listening to the running water and her quick breaths. Colored fish were rising

slowly in the cool morning, begging out of habit to be fed, and the leopard
stared down from his high place, nothing moving but the tip of his long
luxurious tail.

Voices interrupted the perfection. People were approaching, and the
woman gave a start, and the leopard lifted his head as she backed against
a boy nearly ten years younger than her. Halfway turning her head, she
asked the electric air, "Who is it?"

Soldiers, professors, and the Homeland people—everybody was walking
up behind them. If they were heading for the penguin pond, they were
a little lost. Or maybe they had some other errand. Either way, a dozen
important people came around the bend to find the graduate student and
boy standing motionless. Then a soldier spotted the cat, and with a loud
voice asked, "How do you think they keep that tiger there? I don't see bars."

Some people stopped, others kept coming.

The head physicist was in the lead. "Dear God, it's loose," he called out.

Suddenly everybody understood the situation. Every person had a unique
reaction, terror and flight and shock and startled amusement percolating
out of them in various configurations. The colonel and his soldiers mostly
tried to hold their ground, and the government people were great sprint-
ers, while the man who had ordered the woman out on the errand laughed
loudest and came closer, if not close.

Then the physicist turned and tried to run, his feet catching each other.
He fell hard, and something in that clumsiness intrigued the leopard, causing it to slide forwards, making ready to leap.

Bloch had no plan. He would have been happy to stand there all morning
with this terrified woman. But then a couple other people stumbled and
dropped to their knees, and somebody wanted people to goddamn move
so he could shoot. The mayhem triggered instincts in an animal that had
killed nothing during its long comfortable life. Aiming for the far bank of
the pond, the leopard leapt, and Bloch watched the trajectory while his own
reflexes engaged. He jumped to his right, blocking the cat's path. Smooth
and graceful, it landed on the concrete bank, pulling into a tuck, and with
both hands Bloch grabbed its neck. The leopard spun and slashed. Claws
sliced into one of the big triceps, shredding the sweatshirt. Then Bloch
angrily lifted the animal, surprised by how small it felt, but despite little
exercise and its advanced years, the animal nearly pulled free.

Bloch shouted, "No!"

The claws slashed again.

Bloch dove into the pond—three hundred pounds of primate pressing the cat into the carp and cold water. The leopard got pushed to the bottom with the boy on top, a steady loud angry-happy voice telling it, "Stop stopstopstopstop."

The water exploded. Wet fur and panicked muscle leaped over the little fake hill, vanishing. Then Bloch climbed out the water, relieved and thrilled, and he peeled off his sweatshirt, studying the long cuts raking his left arm.

Eyes closed in terror, the young woman hadn't seen the leopard escape. Now she stared at the panicked fish, imagining the monster dead on the bottom. And she looked at Bloch, ready to say something, wanting very much to thank the boy who had swept into her nightmare to save her life. But then she felt the wet jeans, and touching herself, she said, "I can't believe this." She looked at the piss on her hand, and she sniffed it once, and then she was crying, saying, "Don't look at me. Oh, Jesus, don't look."

H e slept.

The medicine made him groggy, or maybe Bloch was so short of sleep that he could drift off at the first opportunity. Whatever the reason, he was warm and comfortable in the army bed, having a fine long dream where he wrestled leopards and a dragon and then a huge man with tusks for teeth and filthy, shit-stained hands that shook him again and again. Then a small throat was cleared and he was awake again.

A familiar brown face was watching him. "Hello."

"Hi."

The physicist looked at the floor and said, "Thank you," and then he looked at the boy's eyes. "Who knows what would have happened. If you hadn't been there, I mean."

Bloch was the only patient in a field hospital inflated on the zoo's parking lot. One arm was dressed with fancy military coagulants, and a bottle was dripping antibiotics into Bloch's good arm. His voice was a little slow and rough. "What happened to it?"

Bloch was asking about the leopard, but the physicist didn't seem to hear him. He stared at the floor, something disgusting about the soft vinyl. "Your mother and teacher are waiting in the next room," he said.

The floor started to roll and pitch. The giant from Bloch's dream rattled the world, and then it grew bored and the motion quit.

Then the physicist answered a question Bloch hadn't asked. "I think that a machine has fallen across half the world. This could be an invasion, an investigation, an experiment. I don't know. The entire planet is blacked out. Most of our satellites are disabled, and we can barely communicate with people down the road, much less on the other side of the world. The alien or aliens are here to torture us, unless they are incapable of noticing us. I keep listening for that god-voice. But there isn't any voice. No threats or demands, or even any trace of an apology."

Rage had bled away, leaving incredulity. The little man looked like a boy when he said, "People are coming to us, people from this side of the demarcation line. Witnesses. Just an hour ago, I interviewed a refugee from Ohio. He claims that he was standing on a hilltop, watching the solar sail's descent. What he saw looked like smoke, a thin quick slippery smoke that fell out of the evening sky, settling on the opposite hillside. Then the world before him changed. The ground shook like pudding and trees were moving—not waving, mind you, but picking up and running—and there were voices, huge horrible voices coming out of the darkness. Then a warm wind hit him in the face and the trees and ground began flowing across the valley before him and he got into his car and fled west until he ran out of gas. He stole a second car that he drove until it stopped working. Then he got a third and pushed until he fell asleep and went off the road, and a state trooper found him and brought him here."

The physicist paused, breathing hard.

He said, "The device." He said, "That object that you witnessed. It might be part of the same invasion, unless it is something else. Nobody knows. But a number of small objects have fallen on what was the day side of the Earth. The military watched their arrival before the radars failed. So I feel certain about that detail. These little ships came from every portion of the sky. Most crashed into the Pacific. But the Pender event is very important, you see, because it happened on the land, in an urban setting. This makes us important. We have a real opportunity here. Only we don't have time to pick apart this conundrum. The quakes are more intense now, more frequent. Ground temperatures are rising, particularly deep below us. One hypothesis—this is my best guess—is that the entity you helped carry to the water has merged with the water table. Fusion or some other power source is allowing it to grow. But I have no idea if it has a different agenda from what the giant alien is doing. I know nothing. And even if I had every answer, I don't think I could do anything. To me, it feels as if huge forces are playing out however they wish, and we have no say in the matter."

The man stopped talking so that he could breathe, but no amount of oxygen made him relax. Bloch sat quietly, thinking about what he just heard and how interesting it was. Then a nurse entered, a woman about his mother's age, and she said, "Sir. She really wants to see her son now."

"Not quite yet."

The nurse retreated.

"Anyway," the physicist said. "I came here to thank you. You saved our lives. And I wanted to apologize too. I saw what you did with that animal, how you grabbed and shook it. You seemed so careless, so brave. And that's one of the reasons why I ordered the doctors to examine you."

"What did you do?" Bloch asked.

"This little hospital is surprisingly well-stocked," the physicist said. "And I was guessing that you were under of some kind of alien influence."

Bloch grinned. "You thought I was infected."

The little man nodded and grimaced. "The doctors have kept you under all day, measuring and probing. And your teacher brought your mother, and someone finally thought to interview the woman. She explained you. She says that you were born this way, and you don't experience the world like the rest of us."

Bloch nodded and said nothing.

"For what it is worth, your amygdala seems abnormal."

"I like being me," Bloch said happily.

The physicist gave the floor another long study. Then the ground began to shake once again, and he stood as still as he could, trying to gather himself for the rest of this long awful day.

"But what happened to the leopard?" Bloch asked.

The man blinked. "The soldiers shot it, of course."

"Why?"

"Because it was running loose," the physicist said. "People were at risk, and it had to be killed."

"That's sad," the boy said.

"Do you think so?"

"It's the last of its kind," Bloch said.

The physicist's back stiffened as he stared at this very odd child, and with a haughty voice, he explained, "But of course the entire world seems to be coming to an end. And I shouldn't have to point out to you, but this makes each of us the very last of his kind."

THE PENDER MONSTER

Bloch was supposed to be sleeping. Two women sat in the adjoining room, using voices that tried to be private but failed. Fast friends, his mother and his nurse talked about careers and worrisome children and lost men. The nurse's husband had abandoned her for a bottle and she wanted him to get well but not in her presence, thank you. Bloch's father died twelve years ago, killed by melanoma, and the widow still missed him but not nearly as much as during those awful first days when she had two young sons and headaches and heartaches, and God, didn't she sound like every country song?

It was the middle of a very dark night, and the warm ground was shaking more than it stood still. The women used weak, sorry laughs, and the nurse said, "That's funny," and then both fell into worried silence.

Bloch didn't feel like moving. Comfortable and alert, he sat with hard pillows piled high behind him, hands on his lap and eyes half-closed. The fabric hospital walls let in every sound. He listened to his mother sigh, and then the nurse took a breath and let it out, and then the nurse asked his mother about her thoughts.

"My boys," Mom said. Glad for the topic, she told about when her oldest was ten and happy only when he was causing trouble. But nobody stays ten forever. The Army taught Matt to control his impulses, which was one good thing. "Every situation has its good," she said, almost believing it. The nurse made agreeable sounds and asked if Matt always wanted to be a soldier, and Mom admitted that he had. Then the nurse admitted that most military men were once that way. They liked playing army as boys, so much so they couldn't stop when they grew up.

"Does that ever happen?" Mom asked. "Do they actually grow up?"

The women laughed again, this time with heart. Mom kept it up longest and then confessed that she was worried about Bloch but it was Matt that she was thinking of, imagining that big alien ship crashing down on top of him. She gave out one sorry breath after another, and then with a flat, careful voice, she wondered what life was like on the Night Side.

That's what the other half of the world had been named. The Night Side was mysterious, wrong and lost. For the last few hours, refugees had been coming through town, trading stories for gasoline and working cars. And the stories didn't change. Bloch knew this because a group of soldiers were standing outside the hospital, gossiping. Every sound came through the fabric walls. Half a dozen men and one woman were talking about impossible things: the land squirming as if it was alive; alien trees black as coal sprouting until they were a mile high, and then the trees would spit out thick clouds that glowed purple and rode the hot winds into the Day Side, raining something that wasn't water, turning more swathes of the countryside into gelatin and black trees.

What was happening here was different. Everybody agreed about that. The ground shivered, but it was only ground. And people functioned well enough to talk with strained but otherwise normal voices. Concentrating, Bloch could make out every voice inside the hospital and every spoken word for a hundred yards in any direction, and that talent didn't feel even a little bit peculiar to him.

He heard boots walking. An officer approached the gossiping soldiers, and after the ritual greetings, one man dared ask, "Do we even stand a chance here, lieutenant?"

"A damned good chance," the lieutenant said loudly. "Our scientists are sitting in a classroom, building us weapons. Yeah, we're going to tear those aliens some new assholes, just as soon as they find enough glue guns and batteries to make us our death rays."

Everybody laughed.

One soldier said, "I'm waiting for earth viruses to hit."

"A computer bug," somebody said.

"Or AIDS," said a third.

The laughter ran a time and then faded.

Then the first soldier asked, "So this critter under us, sir . . . what is it, sir?"

There was a pause. Then the lieutenant said, "You want my opinion?"

"Please, sir."

"Like that zoo teacher says. The monster came from a different part of the sky, and it doesn't act the same. When you don't have enough firepower to kick the shit out of its enemy, you dig in. And that's what I think it is doing."

"This is some big galactic war, you mean?"

"You wanted my opinion. And that's my opinion for now."

One soldier chuckled and said, "Wild."

Nobody else laughed.

Then the woman soldier spoke. "So what's that make us?"

"Picture some field in Flanders," said the officer. "It's 1916, and the Germans and British are digging trenches and firing big guns. What are their shovels and shells churning up? Ant nests, of course. Which happens to be us. We're the ants in Flanders."

The soldiers quit talking.

Maybe Mom and the nurse were listening to the conversation. Or maybe they were just being quiet for a while. Either way, Mom broke the silence by saying, "I always worried about ordinary hazards. For Matt, I mean.

Bombs and bullets, and scars on the brain. Who worries about an invasion from outer space?"

Bloch pictured her sitting in the near-darkness, one hand under her heavy chin while the red eyes watched whatever was rolling inside her head.

"It's hard," said the nurse.

Mom made an agreeable sound.

Then with an important tone, the nurse said, "At least you can be sure that Matt's in a good place now."

Mom didn't say anything.

"If he's gone, I mean."

"I know what you meant," Mom said.

The nurse started to explain herself.

Mom cut her off, saying, "Except I don't believe in any of that."

"You don't believe in what?"

"The afterlife. Heaven and such."

The nurse had to breathe before saying, "But in times like this, darling? When everything is so awful, how can you not believe in the hereafter?"

"Well, let me tell you something," Mom said. Then she leaned forward her chair, her voice moving. "Long ago, when my husband was dying for no good reason, I realized that if a fancy god was in charge, then he was doing a pretty miserable job of running his corner of the universe."

The new friendship was finished. The two women sat uncomfortably close to each other for a few moments. Then one of them stood and walked over the rumbling floor, putting their head through the door to check on their patient. Bloch remained motionless, pretending to be asleep. The woman saw him sitting in the bed, lit only by battery-powered night-lights. Then to make sure that she was seeing what she thought she was seeing, she came all the way into the room, and with a high wild voice she began to scream.

The defender had landed far from open water, exhausted and exposed. Fuel was essential and hydrogen was the easy/best solution, but most of the local hydrogen was trapped in the subsurface water or chemically locked into the rock. Every atom had to be wrenched loose, wasting time and focus. Time and focus built a redoubt, but the vagaries of motion and fuel had dropped the defender too close to the great enemy, and there was nothing to be done about that, and there was nothing to work with but the drought and the sediments and genius and more genius.

Emotion helped. Rage was the first tool: a scorching hatred directed at a vast, uncaring enemy. Envy was nearly as powerful, the defender nurturing epic resentments aimed at its siblings sitting behind it in the ocean. Those lucky obscenities were blessed with more resources and considerably more time to prepare their redoubts, and did they appreciate how obscenely unfair this was? Fear was another fine implement. Too much work remained unfinished, grand palisades and serene weapons existing only as dream; absolute terror helped power the furious digging inside the half-born redoubt.

But good emotions always allowed the bad. That was how doubt emerged. The defender kept rethinking its landing. Easy fuel had been available, but there were rules and codes concerning how to treat life. Some of the local water happened to be self-aware. Frozen by taboos, the defender created a false body and appealing face. The scared little shreds of life were coaxed into helping it, but they were always doomed. It seemed like such a waste, holding sacred what was already dead. One piece of water that was ready to douse the defender with easy water. That first taste of fuel would have awakened every reactor, and the work would have commenced immediately. Yes, radiation would have poisoned the weak life, yes. But that would have given valuable minutes to fill with work and useful fear.

The mad rush was inevitable, and speed always brought mistakes. One minor error was to allow a creative-aspect to escape on the wind. The aspect eventually lodged on the paw of some living water, and then it was injected into a second piece of water, dissolving into the cool iron-infused blood, taking ten thousand voyages about that simple wet body. But this kind of mistake happened quite a lot. Hundreds, maybe thousands of aspects had been lost already. The largest blunder was leaving the aspect active—a totipotent agent able to interface with its environment, ready for that key moment when it was necessary to reshape water and minerals, weaving the best soldier possible from these miserable ingredients.

For every tiny mistake, the entity felt sorry. It nourished just enough shame to prove again that it was moral and right. Then it willfully ignored those obscure mistakes, bearing down on the wild useless sprint to the finish.

Soldiers ran into the hospital and found a monster. Spellbound and fearful, they stared at the creature sitting upright in the bed. Two prayed, the woman talking about Allah being the Protector of those who have faith. Another soldier summoned his anger, aiming at the gray human-shaped face.

"Fucking move and I'll kill you," he said.

Bloch wasn't sure that he could move, and he didn't try.

"Do you fucking hear me?" the soldier said.

Bloch's mouth could open, the tongue tasting hot air and his remade self. He tasted like dirty glass. A voice he didn't recognize said, "I hear you, yeah." Monsters should have important booming voices. His voice was quiet, crackly, and slow, reminding him of the artificial cackle riding on a doll's pulled string.

He laughed at the sound of himself.

His mother was kneeling beside his bed, weeping while saying his name again and again. "Simon, Simon."

"I'm all right," he said to her.

The nurse stood on the other side of him, trying to judge what she was seeing. The boy's skin looked like metal or a fancy ceramic, but that was only one piece of this very strange picture. Bloch was big before, but he was at least half a foot taller and maybe half again thicker, and the bed under him looked shriveled because it was. The metal frame and foam mattress were being absorbed by his growing body. Sheets and pillows were melting into him, harvested for their carbon. And the gray skin was hot as a furnace. Bloch was gone. Replacing him was a machine, human-faced but unconvincing, and the nurse felt well within her rights as a good person to turn to the soldiers, asking, "What are you waiting for? Shoot."

But even the angry soldier wouldn't. Bullets might not work. And if the gun was useless, then threats remained the best tactic.

"Go get the colonel," he said. "Go."

The Muslim soldier ran away.

Two minutes ago, Bloch had felt awake and alert but normal. Nothing was normal now. He saw his kneeling mother and everything else. There wasn't any darkness in this room, or anywhere. His new eyes found endless details—the weave of Mom's blouse and the dust in the air and a single fly with sense enough to hang away from the impossibility that was swelling as the fancy bed dissolved into his carapace.

"It's still me," he told his mother.

She looked up, wanting to believe but unable.

Then the colonel arrived, the physicist beside him, and the lieutenant came in with Mr. Rightly.

The colonel was gray and handsome and very scared, and he chuckled quietly, embarrassed by his fear.

Bloch liked the sound of that laugh.

"Can you hear me, boy?"

"No."

That won a second laugh, louder this time. "Do you know what's happening to you?"

Bloch said, "No."

Yet that wasn't true.

More soldiers were gathering outside the hospital, setting up weapons, debating lines of fire.

The physicist pointed at Bloch, looking sick and pleased in the same moment. "I was right," he boasted. "There is a contamination problem."

"Where did this happen?" the colonel asked.

"While people were carting the spaceman around, I'd guess," said the physicist.

Bloch slowly lifted his arms. The tube from the IV bottle had merged with him. His elbow still felt like an elbow except it wasn't sore, and the raking marks in his bicep had become permanent features.

"Don't move," the angry soldier repeated.

Mom climbed to her feet, reaching for him.

"Don't get near him," the nurse advised.

"I'm hot, be careful," Bloch said. But she insisted on touching the rebuilt arm, scorching each of her fingertips.

Mr. Rightly came forward, glasses dangling and forgotten on the tip of his moist little nose. "Is it really you?"

"Maybe," the boy said. "Or maybe not."

"How do you feel, Bloch?"

Bloch studied his hands with his fine new eyes. "Good," he said.

"Are you scared?"

"No."

The colonel whispered new orders to the lieutenant.

The lieutenant and a private pulled on leather gloves and came forward, grabbing the teacher under his arms.

"What is this?" Mr. Rightly asked.

"We're placing you under observation, as a precaution," the colonel explained.

"That's absurd," said Mr. Rightly, squirming hard.

On his own, the private decided that the situation demanded a small surgical punch—one blow to the kidneys, just to put the new patient to the floor.

The lieutenant cursed.

Bloch sat up, and the shriveled bed shattered beneath him.

"Don't move," the angry soldier repeated, drawing sloppy circles with the gun barrel.

"Leave him alone," Bloch said.

"I'm all right," Mr. Rightly said, lifting a shaking hand. "They just want to be cautious. Don't worry about it, son."

Bloch sat on the floor, watching every face.

Then the physicist turned to the colonel, whispering, "You know, the mother just touched him too."

The colonel nodded, and two more soldiers edged forward.

"No," Bloch said.

One man hesitated, and irritated by the perceived cowardice, his partner came faster, lifting a pistol, aiming at the woman who had a burnt hand and a monstrous child.

Thought and motion arrived in the same instant.

The pistol was crushed and the empty-handed soldier was on his back, sprawled out and unsure what could have put him there so fast, so neatly. Then Bloch leaped about the room, gracefully destroying weapons and setting bodies on their rumps before ending up in the middle of the chaos, seven feet tall and invulnerable. With the crackly new voice, he said, "I've touched all of you. And I don't think it means anything. And now leave my mother the hell alone."

"The monster's loose," the angry soldier screamed. "It's attacking us."

Three of the outside soldiers did nothing. But the fourth man had shot his first leopard in the morning, and he was still riding the adrenaline high. The hot target was visible with night goggles—a radiant giant looming over cowering bodies. The private sprayed the target with automatic weapons fire. Eleven bullets were absorbed by Bloch's chest, their mass and energy and sweet bits of metal feeding the body that ran through the shredded wall and ran into the open parking lot, carefully drawing fire away from those harmless sacks of living water.

A few people joined up with the refugee stream, abandoning the city for the Interstate and solid, trusted ground to the west. But most of the city remained close to home. People didn't know enough to be properly terrified. Some heard the same stories that the Army heard about the Night Side. But every truth had three rumors ready to beat it into submission. Besides, two hundred thousand bodies were difficult to move. Some cars still worked, but for how long? Sparks and odd magnetisms shared the air with a hundred comforting stories, and what scared people most was the idea that the family SUV would die on some dark stretch of road, in the cold and with hungry people streaming past.

No, it was better to stay inside your own house. People knew their homes. They had basements and favorite chairs and trusted blankets. Instinct and hope made it possible to sit in the dark, the ground rolling steadily but never hard enough to shake down the pictures on the wall. It was easy to shut tired eyes, entertaining the luscious idea that every light would soon pop on again, televisions and Google returning in force. Whatever the crisis was, it would be explained soon. Maybe the war would be won. Or an alien face would fill the plasma television—a brain-rich beast dressed in silver, its rumbling voice explaining why the world had been assimilated and what was demanded of the new slaves.

That was a very potent rumor. The world had been invaded, humanity enslaved. And slavery had its appeal. Citizens of all persuasions would chew on the notion until they tasted hope: property had value. Property needed to be cared for. Men and women sat in lounge chairs in their basements, making ready for what seemed like the worst fate short of death. But it wasn't death, and the aliens would want their bodies and minds for some important task, and every reading of history showed that conquerors always failed. Wasn't that common knowledge? Overlords grew sloppy and weak, and after a thousand years of making ready, the human slaves would rise up and defeat their hated enemies, acquiring starships and miracle weapons in the bargain.

That's what the woman was thinking. She was sitting beside the basement stove, burning the last of her Bradford pear. She was out of beer and cigarettes and sorry for that, but the tea was warm and not too bitter. She was reaching for the mug when someone forced the upstairs door open and came inside. She stopped in mid-reach, listening to a very big man moving across her living room, the floor boards complaining about the burden, and for the next mad moment she wondered if the visitor wasn't human. The zoo had ponies. The creature sounded as big as a horse. After everything else, was that so crazy? Then a portion of the oak turned to fire and soot, and something infinitely stranger than a Clydesdale dropped into the basement, landing gently beside her.

"Quiet," said the man-shaped demon, one finger set against the demon mouth.

She had never been so silent.

"They're chasing me," he said with a little laugh.

He was wearing nothing but a clumsy loincloth made from pink attic insulation. A buttery yellow light emerged from his face, and he was hotter than the stove. Studying his features, the woman saw that goofy neighbor boy who walked past her house every day. That was the boy who was standing outside just before the aliens crashed. Not even two days ago, incredible as that seemed.

"Don't worry," he said. "I'm no monster."

Unlikely though it was, she believed him.

A working spotlight swept through the upstairs of her house. She saw it through the hole and the basement windows. Then it was gone and there was just the two of them, and she was ready to be scared but she wasn't. This unexpected adventure was nothing but thrilling.

The boy-who-wasn't-a-monster knelt low, whispering, "I'm having this funny thought. Do you want to hear it?"

She nodded.

"Do you know why we put zoo animals behind bars?"

"Why?"

"The bars are the only things that keep us from shooting the poor stupid beasts."

WAR OF THE WORLDS

Whatever is inevitable becomes common.

Fire is inevitable. The universe is filled with fuel and with sparks. Chemicals create cold temporary fires and stars burn for luxurious spans, while annihilating matter and insulting deep reality, resulting in the most spectacular blazes.

Life is inevitable. Indeed, life is an elaborate, self-aware flame that begins cold but often becomes fiercely hot. Life is a fire that can think and then act on its passionate ideas. Life wants fuel and it wants reasons to burn, and this is why selfishness is the first right of the honest mind. But three hundred billion suns and a million trillion worlds are not enough fuel. Life emerges too often and too easily, and a galaxy full of wild suns and cold wet worlds is too tempting. What if one living fire consumed one little world, freely and without interference? Not much has been harmed, so where is the danger?

The danger, corrupting and remorseless, is that a second fire will notice that conquest and then leap toward another easy world, and a thousand more fires will do the same, and then no fire will want to be excluded, a singularly awful inferno igniting the galaxy.

Morality should be inevitable too. Every intelligence clings to an ethical code. Any two fires must have common assumptions about right and about evil. And first among the codes is the law that no solitary flame can claim the heavens, and if only to protect the peace, even the simplest and coldest examples of life must be held in safe places and declared sacred.

The city was exhausted, but it was far from quiet. The ground still rumbled, though the pitch was changing in subtle ways. Mice were squeaking and an owl told the world that she was brave, and endless human voices were talking in the darkness, discussing small matters and old regrets. Several couples were making spirited love. A few prayed, though without much hope behind the words. A senile woman spoke nonsense. And then her husband said that he was tired of her noise and was heading outside to wait for the sunrise.

Bloch was standing in the middle of Pender when the man emerged. This was the same old fellow who saw his brave oak stop the rolling spaceship. Cranes and a National Guard truck had carried away the useless egg case. Extra fragments and local dust had been swept into important buckets, waiting for studies that would never come about. But the human vehicles were left where they crashed, and Bloch saw every tire mark, every drop of vigorous blood, and he studied a blond Barbie, loved deeply by a little girl and now covered with dried, half-frozen pieces of her brother's brain.

The old man came out on his porch and looked at the apparition, and after taking careful stock of everything said, "Huh."

Nobody was hunting Bloch anymore. The initial panic and search for the monster had spread across the city and then dissolved, new and much larger panics taking hold. One monster was nothing compared to what was approaching, and the army had been dispatched to the east—Guard soldiers and policemen and a few self-appointed militia hunkering down in roadside ditches, ready to aim insults and useless guns at the coming onslaught.

The old man considered retreating into his house again. But he was too worn down to be afraid, and he didn't relish more time with his wife. So he came down the stairs and across the lawn, leaning his scrawny body against the gouged trunk. Pulling off a stocking cap, he rubbed his bald head a couple times, and using a dry slow voice explained, "I know about you. You were that kid who climbed inside first."

Bloch looked at him and looked East too. Dawn should be a smudged brightness pushing up from a point southeast. But there was no trace of the sun. The light was purple and steady, covering the eastern horizon.

"Do you know what's happening to you?" the old man asked.

"Maybe," Bloch said. Then he lifted one hand, a golden light brightening his entire arm. "A machine got inside me and shouldn't have. It started to rebuild me, but then it realized that I was alive and so it quit."

"Why did it quit?"

"Life is precious. The machine isn't supposed to build a weapon using a sentient organism."

"So you're what? Half-done?"

"More like three percent finished."

The old man moved to where Bloch's heat felt comfortable. Looking up at the gray face, he asked, "Are you just going to stand here?"

"This is a fine place to watch the battle, yes."

The man looked east and then back at Bloch. He seemed puzzled and a little curious, a thin smile showing more in his eyes than his mouth.

"But you won't be safe outside," the boy cautioned, new instincts using his mouth. "You'll survive longer if you get into your basement."

"How long is longer?"

"Twenty or thirty seconds, I would think."

The man tried to laugh, and then he tried to curse. Neither worked, which was when he looked down the hill, saying, "If it's all the same, I'll just stay outside and watch the show."

The purple line was taller and brighter, and the first trace of a new wind started nudging at the highest oak limbs.

"Here comes something," the man said.

There was quite a lot to see, yes. But following the man's eyes, Bloch found nothing but empty air.

"That soldier might be hunting you," the man said.

"What soldier?"

"Or maybe he's a deserter. I don't see a gun." This time the laugh worked—a sour giggle accompanied by some hard shaking of the head. "Of course you can't blame the fellow for running. All things considered."

"Who is he?" Bloch asked.

"You don't see him? The old grunt walking up the middle of the road?"

Nothing else was alive on Pender.

"Well, I'm not imagining this. And I wasn't crazy three minutes ago, so I doubt if I am now."

Bloch couldn't find anybody, but he felt movement, something massive and impressive that was suddenly close, and his next instinct touched him coldly, informing him that a cloaked warrior had him dead in its sights.

"What's our soldier look like?"

"A little like you," the old man said.

But there was no second gray monster, which made the moment deliciously peculiar.

"And now he's calling to you," the man said.

"Calling me what?"

"'Kid,' it sounds like."

And that was the moment when Bloch saw his brother standing in front of him.

M att always looked like their father, but never so much as now. He was suddenly grown. This wasn't the shaved-head, beer-belching boy who came home on leave last summer. This wasn't even the tough-talking soldier on Skype last week. Nothing about him was worn down or wrinkled, yet the apparition carried himself like their father did in the videos—a short thick fellow with stubby legs churning, shoulders squared up and ready to suffer any load. He was decked out in the uniform that he wore in Yemen, except it was too pressed and too clean. There was a sleepless, pained quality to the face, and that's where he most resembled Dad. But those big eyes had seen worse than what they were seeing now, and despite cares and burdens that a little brother could never measure, the man before him still knew how to smile.

"How you doing, kid?" Matt asked.

With the doll-voice, Bloch said, "You're not my brother."

"Think not?"

"I feel it. You're not human at all."

"So says the glowing monster decked out in his fancy fiberglass underwear." Matt laughed and the old man joined in. Then Matt winked, asking Bloch, "You scared of me?"

Bloch shook his head.

"You should be scared. I'm a very tough character now." He walked past both of the men, looking back to say, "March with me, monster. We got a pile of crap to discuss."

Long legs easily caught the short.

Turning the corner, Bloch asked where they were going. Matt said nothing. Bloch looked back. The old man had given up watching them, preferring to lean against the wrecked Buick, studying the purples in a long sky that was bewitched and exceptionally lovely.

"We're going to the zoo," Bloch guessed.

Matt started to nod and then didn't. He started to talk and then stopped himself. Then he gazed up at the giant beside him.

"What?" Bloch asked.

"Do you know what an adventure is?"

"Sure."

"No, you don't," Matt said. "When I was standing outside the barracks that night, texting you, I figured I was going to die. And that didn't seem too awful. A demon monster was dropping from the heavens and the world was finished, but what could I do? Nothing. This wasn't like a bomb hiding beside the road. This wasn't a bullet heading for me. There wasn't any gut-eating suspense to the show, and nothing was left to do but watch.

"Except that spaceship was just a beginning. Like the softest most wonderful blanket, it fell over me and over everything. An aspect found me and fell in love with my potential. Like you've been worked on, only more so. I learned tons of crazy shit. What I knew from my old life was still part of me, still holding my core, but with new meanings attached. It was the same for my unit and the Yemeni locals and even the worst bad guys. We were remade and put to work, which isn't the same as being drafted, since everybody understood the universe, and our work was the biggest best thing any of us could ever do."

They passed the house where Bloch spent the night, hiding in the basement. "What about the universe?" he asked.

"We're not alone, which you know. But we never have been alone. The Earth wasn't even born, and the galaxy was already full of bodies and brains and all sorts of plans for what could be done, and some of those projects were done but a lot of them were too scary, too big and fancy. There's too little energy to accomplish everything that can be dreamed up. Too many creatures want their little piece of the prize, and that's why a truce was put in place. A planet like the Earth is a tempting resource, but nobody is allowed to touch it. Not normally, they aren't. Earth has its own life, just like a hundred and six other planets and moons and big comets. And that's just inside our little solar system. Even the simplest life is protected by law and by machines—although 'machine' isn't the best word."

"We live in a zoo," Bloch said.

"And 'zoo' is a pretty lousy word too. But it works for now." Matt turned at the next intersection, taking a different route than Bloch usually walked to school. "Rules and regulations, that's how everything is put together. There's organizations older than the scum under our rocks. There's these systems that have kept the Earth safe from invaders, mostly. But not always. I'm telling you, this isn't the first time the Earth has been grabbed hard. You think the dinosaurs died from a meteor attack? Not possible. If a comet is going to be trouble, it's gently nudged and made safe again. Which is another blessing of living inside a zoo, and I guess we should have been thankful. If we knew about it before, that is."

"What killed them?"

"The T. rexes? Well, that depends on how you tell the story. A ship came out of deep space and got lucky enough to evade the defensive networks— networks that are never as fancy or new as is possible, by the way. Isn't that the way it always works? Dinosaurs got infected with aspects, and the aspects gave them big minds and new skills. But then defenders were sent down here to put up a fight. A worldwide battle went pretty well for the defenders, but not well enough. For a little while it looked as if maybe, just maybe the Earth could be rebuilt into something powerful enough to survive every one of the counterattacks."

"But the machines above us managed one hard cleansing attack. Cleansings are a miserable desperate tactic. Flares are woven on the sun and then focused on the planet, stripping its crust clean. But cleansing was the easy trick. Too much had to be rebuilt afterwards, and a believable scenario had to be impressed into the rock, and dinosaurs were compromised and unsafe. That's why the impact craters. That's why the iridium layer. And that's why a pack of little animals got their chance, which is you and me, and the next peace lasted for about sixty-five million years."

Small houses and leafless trees lined a road that ended with at tall chain-link fence topped with barbed wire.

"This war has two sides," said Matt. "Every kind of good is here, and there is no evil. Forget evil. A starship carrying possibilities struck the earth, and it claimed half of the planet in a matter of minutes. Not that that part of the war has been easy. There's a hundred trillion mines sitting in our dirt, hiding. Each one is a microscopic machine that waits, waits, waits for this kind of assault. I've been fighting booby traps ever since. In my new state, this war has gone on a hundred years. I've seen and done things and had things done to me, and I've met creatures you can't imagine, and machines that I can't comprehend, and nothing has been won easily for me, and now I'm back to my big question: Do you know what adventure is?"

"I think I know."

"You don't, kid. Not quite yet, you don't know."

The fence marked the zoo's eastern border. Guardsmen had cut through the chain-link, allowing equipment too big for the service entrance to be brought onto the grounds. Inside the nearest cage, a single Bactrian camel stood in the open, in the violet morning light, shaggy and calm and imbecilic.

Bloch stepped through the hole, but his brother remained outside.

The boy grew brighter and his voice sounded deeper. "So okay, tell me. What is an adventure?"

"You go through your life, and stuff happens. Some of that stuff is wild, but most of it is boring. That's the way it has to be. Like with me, for instance. The last hundred years of my life have been exciting and ordinary and treacherous and downright dull, depending on circumstances. I've given a lot to this fight, and I believe it's what I want to do. And we've got a lot of advantages on our side: surprise; an underfunded enemy; and invading a target that is the eighth or ninth best among the candidates."

"What is best?" Bloch asked.

"Jupiter is the prize. Because of its size, sure, but also because it's biosphere is a thousand times more interesting than ours." Matt stood before the gaping hole, hands on hips. "Yeah, my side has its advantages and the momentum, but it probably will fall short of its goal. We'll defeat the booby traps, sure, and beat the defenders inside their redoubts, but we probably won't be ready for the big cleansing attack. But what is happening, if you care . . . this is pretty much how the Permian came to an awful end. In four days, the Earth became something mighty, and then most everything went extinct. That's probably what happens here. And you know the worst of it? Humans will probably accept the villain's role in whatever the false fossil says. We killed our world from pollution and heat, and that's why the fence lizards and cockroaches are going to get their chance."

Bloch was crying.

"Adventure," said Matt. "No, that's not the crazy stupid heroic shit you do in your life. Adventure is the story you tell afterwards. It's those moments you pick out of everything that was boring and ordinary, and then put them on a string and give to another person as a gift. Your story."

Bloch felt sick inside.

"Feel scared, kid?"

"No."

"Good," his brother said, pulling a string necklace out of his shirt pocket and handing it to him. "Now go. You've got a job to do."

BLOCH'S ADVENTURE

The camel was chewing, except it wasn't. The mouth was frozen and the dark dumb eyes held half-closed, and a breath that began in some past age had ceased before the lungs were happy. The animal was a statue. The animal was some kind of dead, inert and without temperature, immune to rot and the tug of gravity while standing in the middle of a pen decorated with camel hoof prints and camel shit and the shit-colored feed that was destined for a camel's fine belly—the emperor resplendent in his great little realm.

Bloch turned back to his brother, wanting explanations. But Matt had vanished, or never was. So he completed one slow circle, discerning how the world was locked into a moment that seemed in no particular hurry to move to the next moment. But time must be moving, however slowly. Otherwise how could an eye see anything? The light reflected off every surface would be fixed in space, and frozen light was as good as no light, and wasn't it funny how quickly this new mind of his played with the possibilities?

The pale, broad hand of a boy came into his face, holding the white string of the necklace just given to him. Little candy beads looked real and felt real as his fingers made them dance. "Neat," he said, his newest voice flat and simple, like the tone from a cheap bell. But the hands and body were back where they began, just ten million times quicker, and the fiber-glass garb was replaced with the old jeans and Cornell sweatshirt. This is nuts, he thought. And fun. Then for no particular reason, he touched the greenest candy against his tongue, finding a sweetness that made it impossible not to shove all of the beads into his mouth, along with the thick rough string.

Each candy was an aspect, and the string was ten aspects woven together, and Bloch let them slide deep while waiting for whatever the magic would do to him next.

But nothing seemed to change, inside him or without.

The camel was a little deeper into its breath and its happiness when the boy moved on. He did not walk. He thought of moving and was immediately some distance down the concrete path, and he thought of moving faster and then stood at the zoo's west side. His school was a big steel building camouflaged behind a fake fire station and a half-sized red caboose. He knew where he needed to be, and he didn't go there. Instead he rose to the classroom where Mr. Rightly and his mother shared a lit-tle bed made of lost clothes. They were sitting up on the folded coats, a single camping lamp shining at their feet. Mom was talking and holding the teacher's hand. Mr. Rightly had always looked as old as his mother, but he wasn't. He was a young man who went gray young, sitting beside a careworn woman ten years his senior. Bloch leaned close to his mother and told her about seeing Matt just now. He said that his brother was alive and strong, and he explained a little something about what her youngest son was doing now, and finally enough time passed for that despairing face to change, maybe recognizing the face before, or at least startled by the shadow that Bloch cast.

Several people shared the dim room. The girl who had recently faced down the wild leopard was sitting across from Bloch's mother, bright tears frozen on the pretty face. In her lap were an old National Geographic and a half-page letter that began with "Dear Teddy" and ended with "Love" written several times with an increasingly unsteady hand. Bloch studied the girl's sorrow, wishing he could give her confidence. But none of the aspects inside could do that. Then he turned back to his mother's slow surprise and poor Mr. Rightly who hadn't slept in days and would never sleep again. That's what Bloch was thinking as he used his most delicate touch, one finger easing the sloppy glasses back up near the eyes.

He moved again, no time left to waste.

The penguin's new pond was empty of water but partly filled with machines, most of them dead and useless. A yellow crane was fixed in place, reaching to the treetops, and one steel cable dangled down to a point ten feet above the concrete deck. Flanking cherry pickers were filled with soldiers working furiously to arm what was tethered to the cable's end: a small atomic warhead designed to be flung against tank columns in the Fulda Gap. The soldiers were trying to make the bomb accept their commands. It was a useless activity; for endless reasons, the plutonium would never become angry. But Bloch was willing himself into the air, having a long penetrating look at what might be the most destructive cannonball the human species would ever devise.

At the edge of the pond, the terrified physicist and the equally traumatized colonel were arguing. The intricacies of their respective viewpoints were lost, but they were obviously exhausted, shouting wildly, cold fingers caught in mid-thrust and the chests pumped up, neither combatant noticing the boy who slipped between them before leaping into the waterless pond, tucking those big arms against his chest, pointing his toes as he fell into the deep, deep hole.

D amaged aspects returned to the nub on occasion, begging for repairs or death. Death was the standard solution, but sometimes the attached soldier could be healed and sent out again. There weren't enough soldiers, and the first assault hadn't begun. But the defender had to be relentlessly careful. Infiltrators moved among the wounded. Sabotage was licking at the edges and the soft places, at the less-than-pivotal functions, and worse were the lies and wild thoughts that would begin in one place and flow everywhere, doing their damage by cultivating confidence, by convincing some routine that it was strong—one little portion of the defender believing itself a bold rock-solid savior of the redoubt, shrugging aside ten microseconds of lucid doubt as it did what was less than ideal.

Among the mangled and failed was an aspect carried inside a sack of water. Tiny in endless ways, the aspect managed to escape notice until it had arrived—a dull fleck of material that would never accomplish any mission or accidentally hinder even the smallest task. Ignoring such debris was best, but some little reflex took charge eventually. The defender told that aspect to be still and wait, and it was very still and very patient while tools of considerable precision were brought to bear on what had never worked properly. The aspect was removed from its surroundings. The aspect was destroyed. And different tools reached for what seemed like common water, ready to harvest a drop or two of new fuel.

But then flourishes and little organs appeared on the wetness, or maybe they were always there, and one of the organs spoke.

I 'm not here to fight," Bloch said to the darkness.

It was his original voice, mostly. There was gravel at the edges, and it felt a little quick, but he liked how the words sounded in his head. And it was his head again, and his big old comfortable, clunky body. Time was again running at its proper speed, and the air was like a sauna, no oxygen to be found. "I'm not here to fight," he said, and then his head began to spin. One moment he was standing in some imprecise volume never intended to be a room, and then he was on his knees, gasping.

The uneven floor flattened. New air rushed in, and light came from everywhere while the floor rose around him, creating a bright bubble that isolated him from everything else.

The boy breathed until he could remember what felt normal, and he got up on his knees, wiping his mouth with the gray sleeve of his sweatshirt.

"Better," he said.

Then, "Thanks."

Nothing changed.

"I'm not here to fight," Bloch repeated. "I'm just delivering a message, and the other side went through a lot of trouble to put me here, which means maybe you should be careful and kill me now."

Then he paused, waiting.

Anticipating this moment, Bloch imagined a creature similar to what he found inside the spaceship. It would be larger and more menacing, but the monster of his daydreams always sported green eyes that glared down at the crafty little human. Except there were no eyes and nothing like a face, and the only presence inside the bubble room was Bloch.

He laughed and said, "I thought I might get scared. But nope, I'm not."

Then he sat, stretching his legs out before him.

"Maybe this sounds smug," he said. "But for the last half day or so, I've been telling myself that I was always part of some big plan. Your aspect gets loose. The leopard picks it up with his front paw. Some careful scheme puts the cat where he can find me, and he cuts me, and I get infected, and after running wild and getting strong, I find my brother. Then Matt gives me a heads-up and points me on my way.

"Except that's not how it works, is it?"

"If there was a fancy plan, it could be discovered. It could be fooled with or a million things could go wrong naturally, or maybe the gains wouldn't match the hope. And that's why real intelligence doesn't bother with plans. You don't, I bet. You've got a set of goals and principles and no end of complications, and everything changes from minute to second, and what the smart mind does is bury itself inside the possibilities and hope for the best."

Bloch paused, listening to nothing. Maybe the world outside was still shaking, but he felt nothing. Probably nobody was listening, but he had nothing else to do with his day. Pulling his legs in, he crossed them, Indian-style.

"I'm here because I'm here," he said. "Your enemy didn't go looking for a mentally defective human who couldn't feel fear. It's just chance that you're not facing down that blond girl or the leopard or maybe a little penguin. Any creature would have worked, and I shouldn't take this personally.

"But I bring something odd and maybe lucky to this table. I don't get scared, and that's an advantage. When everybody else charges around, hands high and voices screaming, I'm this clear-eyed animal watching everything with interest. When you bounced along Pender, I saw people wrestling with every kind of fear. You were dumped into the water, and I studied Mr. Rightly's face. Then there's my mother who gets scared on her happiest day, and the government people and the professors trying to deal with you and each other, and everybody and everything else too. I've been paying attention. I doubt if anybody else has. The world's never been this lost or this terrified, and during these last couple days, I've learned a great deal about the pissing of pants."

Bloch paused for a moment. Then he said. "I would make a lousy soldier. Matt told me that more than once. 'If you don't get scared, you get your head shot off,' he said. Which means, Mr. Monster, that you're probably sick with worry now, aren't you? A good soldier would have to have some fear. You're little more than nothing to your enemy. You're just one grunt-soldier, in his hole and facing down an army. Except that army isn't the real monster either. From what I've been told, the invader is pretty much sure to lose. No, the scary boy in this story is what turns the sun against its planet, scorching all this down to where everything is clean again. Clean but nearly dead. The monster is those laws and customs trying keep the galaxy from getting consumed by too much life trying to do everything at once. That's the real beast here. You know it and your enemy would admit as much, I bet, and that's not the only similarity you two have.

"Yeah, I think you must be shit-in-your-pants scared. Aren't you?"

Bloch stood again. The message had to be delivered, and he would do that on his feet. That felt best. He straightened and shook his arms, a heart indistinguishable from his original heart beating a little faster now. Then with the gravelly voice, he said, "Your enemy wants you to fight. It expects nothing but your best effort, using every trick and power to try to delay him. But your walls are going to collapse. He will absorb you and push to the Pacific and those next battles, and nothing will be won fast enough, and then the sun is going to wash this world with so much wild raw energy.

"Your enemy doesn't believe in plans," Bloch said. "But possibilities are everywhere, and I'm bringing you one of the best. Not that it's perfect, and maybe you won't approve. But the pain and terror are going to look a little more worthwhile in the end, if you accept what I am offering you.

"I have a set of aspects inside me. They're hiding other aspects, and I think they might be inside my stomach.

"You'll have to cut me open to find them, and sorry, I can't help you decipher them. But you're supposed to hold them until you're beaten, and then you can choose to accept your enemy's offer. Or refuse it. The decision is going to be yours. But talking for my sake and the survival of most everybody I know and love, I sure hope you can find the courage to push the fear aside.

"Shove the terror where it doesn't get in the way.

"And make your decision with those eyes open. Would you do that much for me, please?"

B loch stopped talking.

He wasn't standing in the bubble anymore. He was floating in a different place, and there was no telling how much time had passed, but the span felt large. Bloch floated at one end of an imprecise volume that was a little real but mostly just a projection—one enormous realm populated by tens of millions of earthly organisms.

Closest were the faces he knew. His mother and Mr. Rightly were there, and the scientists and that blond girl whose name he still didn't know. And the camel had been saved, and the rest of the surviving zoo animals, and two hundred thousand humans who in the end were pulled from their basements and off their front porches. The penguins hadn't made it to town in time, and the leopard was still dead, and Matt eventually died in the Pacific—an honored fighter doing what he loved.

Billions of people were lost. They had been gone for so long that the universe scarcely remembered them, and nobody ever marked their tragic passing. But inside this contrived, highly compressed volume, his species persisted. The adventure continued. Another passenger asked to hear Simon Bloch's story, and he told it from the beginning until now, stopping when he had nothing to add, enjoying the stares and the respectful silence.

Then he turned, throwing his gaze in a better direction.

Their starship was born while a great world died, and the chaos and rage of a solar flare had thrown it out into deepest space. Onboard were the survivors of many worlds, many tragedies, collected as a redoubt against the inevitable. The galaxy had finally fallen into that final war, but Bloch preferred to look ahead.

In the gloom and cold between galaxies, a little thread of gas and weak suns beckoned—an island where clever survivors could make a second stab at perfection.

It made a man think hard about his future, knowing that he was bound for such a place.

A different man might be scared.

But not Bloch, no.

Cixin Liu is a representative of the new generation of Chinese science fiction authors and recognized as a leading voice in Chinese science fiction. He has received the Yinhe (Chinese Galaxy) Award nine times, from 1999 to 2006, and again in 2010. His novel *The Three-Body Problem* won a 2015 Hugo Award and was the first translated work to receive that honor. *Ball Lightning*, his most recent translated novel, was published by Tor in August.

Taking Care of God

CIXIN LIU, TRANSLATED BY KEN LIU

1.

O nce again, God had upset Qiusheng's family.

This had begun as a very good morning. A thin layer of white fog floated at the height of a man over the fields around Xicen village like a sheet of rice paper that had just become blank: the quiet countryside being the painting that had fallen out of the paper. The first rays of morning fell on the scene, and the year's earliest dewdrops entered the most glorious period of their brief life . . . but God had ruined this beautiful morning.

God had gotten up extra early and gone into the kitchen to warm some milk for himself. Ever since the start of the Era of Support, the milk market had prospered. Qiusheng's family had bought a milk cow for a bit more than ten thousand yuan, and then, imitating others, mixed the milk with water to sell. The unadulterated milk had also become one of the staples for the family.

After the milk was warm, God took the bowl into the living room to watch TV without turning off the liquefied petroleum gas stove.

When Qiusheng's wife, Yulian, returned from cleaning the cowshed and the pigsty, she could smell gas all over the house. Covering her nose with a towel, she rushed into the kitchen to turn off the stove, opened the window, and turned on the fan.

"You old fool! You're going to get the whole family killed!" Yulian shouted into the living room. The family had switched to using liquefied petroleum gas for cooking only after they began supporting God. Qiusheng's father had always been opposed to it, saying that gas was not as good as honeycomb coal briquettes. Now he had even more ammunition for his argument.

As was his wont, God stood with his head lowered contritely, his broom-like white beard hanging past his knees, smiling like a kid who knew he had done something wrong. "I . . . I took down the pot for heating the milk. Why didn't it turn off by itself?"

"You think you're still on your spaceship?" Qiusheng said, coming down the stairs. "Everything here is dumb. We aren't like you, being waited on hand and foot by smart machines. We have to work hard with dumb tools. That's how we put rice in our bowls!"

"We also worked hard. Otherwise how did you come to be?" God said carefully.

"Enough with the 'how did you come to be?' Enough! I'm sick of hearing it. If you're so powerful, go and make other obedient children to support you!" Yulian threw her towel on the ground.

"Forget it. Just forget it," Qiusheng said. He was always the one who made peace. "Let's eat."

Bingbing got up. As he came down the stairs, he yawned. "Ma, Pa, God was coughing all night. I couldn't sleep."

"You don't know how good you have it," Yulian said. "Your dad and I were in the room next to his. You don't hear us complaining, do you?"

As though triggered, God began to cough again. He coughed like he was playing his favorite sport with great concentration.

Yulian stared at God for a few seconds before sighing. "I must have the worst luck in eight generations." Still angry, she left for the kitchen to cook breakfast.

God sat silently through breakfast with the rest of the family. He ate one bowl of porridge with pickled vegetables and half a *mantou* bun. During the entire time he had to endure Yulian's disdainful looks—maybe she was still mad about the liquefied petroleum gas, or maybe she thought he ate too much.

After breakfast, as usual, God got up quickly to clean the table and wash the dishes in the kitchen. Standing just outside the kitchen, Yulian shouted, "Don't use detergent if there's no grease on the bowl! Everything costs money. The pittance they pay for your support? Ha!"

God grunted nonstop to show that he understood.

Qiusheng and Yulian left for the fields. Bingbing left for school. Only now did Qiusheng's father get up. Still not fully awake, he came downstairs, ate two bowls of porridge, and filled his pipe with tobacco. At last he remembered God's existence.

"Hey, old geezer, stop the washing. Come out and play a game with me!" he shouted into the kitchen.

God came out of the kitchen, wiping his hands on his apron. He nodded ingratiatingly at Qiusheng's father. Playing Chinese Chess with the old man was a tough chore for God; winning and losing both had unpleasant consequences. If God won, Qiusheng's father would get mad: *You fucking old idiot! You trying to show me up? Shit! You're God! Beating me is no great accomplishment at all. Why can't you learn some manners? You've lived under this roof long enough!* But if God lost, Qiusheng's father would still get mad: *You fucking old idiot! I'm the best chess player for fifty kilometers. Beating you is easier than squishing a bedbug. You think I need you to let me win? You . . . to put it politely, you are insulting me!*

In any case, the final result was the same: the old man flipped the board, and the pieces flew everywhere. Qiusheng's father was infamous for his bad temper, and now he'd finally found a punching bag in God.

But the old man didn't hold a grudge. Every time after God picked up the board and put the pieces back quietly, he sat down and played with God again—and the whole process was repeated. After a few cycles of this, both of them were tired, and it was almost noon.

God then got up to wash the vegetables. Yulian didn't allow him to cook because she said God was a terrible cook. But he still had to wash the vegetables. Later, when Qiusheng and Yulian returned from the fields, if the vegetables hadn't been washed, she would be on him again with another round of bitter, sarcastic scolding.

While God washed the vegetables, Qiusheng's father left to visit the neighbors. This was the most peaceful part of God's day. The noon sun filled every crack in the brick-lined yard and illuminated the deep crevasses in his memory. During such periods God often forgot his work and stood quietly, lost in thought. Only when the noise of the villagers returning from the fields filled the air would he be startled awake and hurry to finish his washing.

He sighed. *How could life have turned out like this?*

This wasn't only God's sigh. It was also the sigh of Qiusheng, Yulian, and Qiusheng's father. It was the sigh of more than five billion people and two billion Gods on Earth.

2.

It all began with an autumn evening three years ago.

"Come quickly! There are toys in the sky!" Bingbing shouted in the yard. Qiusheng and Yulian raced out of the house, looked up, and saw that the sky really was filled with toys, or at least objects whose shapes could only belong to toys.

The objects spread out evenly across the dome of the sky. In the dusk, each reflected the light of the setting sun—already below the horizon—and each shone as bright as the full moon. The light turned Earth's surface as bright as it is at noon. But the light came from every direction and left no shadow, as though the whole world was illuminated by a giant surgical lamp.

At first, everyone thought the objects were within our atmosphere because they were so clear. But eventually, humans learned that these objects were just enormous. They were hovering about thirty thousand kilometers away in geostationary orbits.

There were a total of 21,530 spaceships. Spread out evenly across the sky, they formed a thin shell around Earth. This was the result of a complex set of maneuvers that brought all the ships to their final locations simultaneously. In this manner, the alien ships avoided causing life-threatening tides in the oceans due to their imbalanced mass. The gesture assured humans somewhat, as it was at least some evidence that the aliens did not bear ill will toward Earth.

During the next few days, all attempts at communicating with the aliens failed. The aliens maintained absolute silence in the face of repeated queries. At the same time, Earth became a nightless planet. Tens of thousands of spaceships reflected so much sunlight onto the night side of Earth that it was as bright as day, while on the day side, the ships cast giant shadows onto the ground. The horrible sight pushed the psychological endurance of the human race to the limit, so that most ignored yet another strange occurrence on the surface of the planet and did not connect it with the fleet of spaceships in the sky.

Across the great cities of the world, wandering old people had begun to appear. All of them had the same features: extreme old age, long white hair and beards, long white robes. At first, before the white robe, white beard, and white hair got dirty, they looked like a bunch of snowmen. The wanderers did not appear to belong to any particular race, as though all ethnicities were mixed in them. They had no documents to prove their citizenship or identity and could not explain their own history.

All they could do was to gently repeat, in heavily accented versions of various local languages, the same words to all passersby:

"We are God. Please, considering that we created this world, would you give us a bit of food?"

If only one or two old wanderers had said this, then they would have been sent to a shelter or nursing home, like the homeless with dementia.

But millions of old men and women all saying the same thing—that was an entirely different thing.

Within half a month, the number of old wanderers had increased to more than thirty million. All over the streets of New York, Beijing, London, Moscow . . . these old people could be seen everywhere, shuffling around in traffic-stopping crowds. Sometimes it seemed as if there were more of *them* than the original inhabitants of the cities.

The most horrible part of their presence was that they all repeated the same thing: "We are God. Please, considering that we created this world, would you give us a bit of food?"

Only now did humans turn their attention from the spaceships to the uninvited guests. Recently, large-scale meteor showers had been occurring over every continent. After every impressive display of streaking meteors, the number of old wanderers in the corresponding region greatly increased. After careful observation, the following incredible fact was discovered: the old wanderers came out of the sky, from those alien spaceships.

One by one, they leaped into the atmosphere as though diving into a swimming pool, each wearing a suit made from a special film. As the friction from the atmosphere burned away the surface of the suits, the film kept the heat away from the wearer and slowed their descent. Careful design ensured that the deceleration never exceeded 4G, well within the physical tolerance of the bodies of the old wanderers. Finally, at the moment of their arrival at the surface, their velocity was close to zero, as though they had just jumped down from a bench. Even so, many of them still managed to sprain their ankles. Simultaneously, the film around them had been completely burned away, leaving no trace.

The meteor showers continued without stopping. More wanderers fell to Earth. Their number rose to almost one hundred million.

The government of every country attempted to find one or more representatives among the wanderers. But the wanderers claimed that the "Gods" were absolutely equal, and any one of them could represent all of them. Thus, at the emergency session of the United Nations General Assembly, one random old wanderer, who was found in Times Square and who now spoke passable English, entered the General Assembly Hall.

He was clearly among the earliest to land: his robe was dirty and full of holes, and his white beard was covered with dirt, like a mop. There was no halo over his head, but a few loyal flies did hover there. With the help of a ratty bamboo walking stick, he shuffled his way to the round meeting table and lowered himself under the gaze of the leaders. He looked up at the

Secretary-General, and his face displayed the childlike smile particular to all the old wanderers.

"I . . . ha—I haven't had breakfast yet."

So breakfast was brought. All across the world, people stared as he ate like a starved man, choking a few times. Toast, sausages, and a salad were quickly gone, followed by a large glass of milk. Then he showed his innocent smile to the Secretary-General again.

"Haha . . . uh . . . is there any wine? Just a tiny cup will do."

So a glass of wine was brought. He sipped at it, nodding with satisfaction. "Last night, a bunch of new arrivals took over my favorite subway grille, one that blew out warm air. I had to find a new place to sleep in the Square. But now with a bit of wine, my joints are coming back to life . . . You, can you massage my back a little? Just a little."

The Secretary-General began to massage his back. The old wanderer shook his head, sighed, and said, "Sorry to be so much trouble to you."

"Where are you from?" asked the President of the United States.

The old wanderer shook his head. "A civilization only has a fixed location in her infancy. Planets and stars are unstable and change. The civilization must then move. By the time she becomes a young woman, she has already moved multiple times. Then they will make this discovery: no planetary environment is as stable as a sealed spaceship. So they'll make spaceships their home, and planets will just be places where they sojourn. Thus, any civilization that has reached adulthood will be a starfaring civilization, permanently wandering through the cosmos. The spaceship is her home. Where are we from? We come from the ships." He pointed up with a finger caked in dirt.

"How many of you are there?"

"Two billion."

"Who are you really?" The Secretary-General had cause to ask this. The old wanderers looked just like humans.

"We've told you many times." The old wanderer impatiently waved his hand. "We are God."

"Could you explain?"

"Our civilization—let's just call her the God Civilization—had existed long before Earth was born. When the God Civilization entered her senescence, we seeded the newly formed Earth with the beginnings of life. Then the God Civilization skipped across time by traveling close to the speed of light. When life on Earth had evolved to the appropriate stage, we came back, introduced a new species based on our ancestral genes, eliminated its enemies, and carefully guided its evolution until Earth was home to a new civilized species just like us."

"How do you expect us to believe you?"

"That's easy."

Thus began the half-year-long effort to verify these claims. Humans watched in astonishment as spaceships sent the original plans for life on Earth and images of the primitive Earth. Following the old wanderer's direction, humans dug up incredible machines from deep below Earth's crust, equipment that had through the long eons monitored and manipulated the biosphere on this planet.

Humans finally had to believe. At least with respect to life on Earth, the Gods really were God.

3.

At the third emergency session of the United Nations General Assembly, the Secretary-General, on behalf of the human race, finally asked God the key question: why did they come to Earth?

"Before I answer this question, you must have a correct understanding of the concept of civilization." God stroked his long beard. This was the same God who had been at the first emergency session half a year ago. "How do you think civilizations evolve over time?"

"Civilization on Earth is currently in a stage of rapid development. If we're not hit by natural disasters beyond our ability to resist, I think we will continue our development indefinitely," said the Secretary-General.

"Wrong. Think about it. Every person experiences childhood, youth, middle age, and old age, finally arriving at death. The stars are the same way. Indeed, everything in the universe goes through the same process. Even the universe itself will have to terminate one day. Why would civilization be an exception? No, a civilization will also grow old and die."

"How exactly does that happen?"

"Different civilizations grow old and die in different ways, just like different people die of different diseases or just plain old age. For the God Civilization, the first sign of her senescence was the extreme lengthening of each individual member's life span. By then, each individual in the God Civilization could expect a life as long as four thousand Earth years. By age two thousand, their thoughts had completely ossified, losing all creativity. Because individuals like these held the reins of power, new life had a hard time emerging and growing. That was when our civilization became old."

"And then?"

"The second sign of the civilization's senescence was the Age of the Machine Cradle."

"What?"

"By then our machines no longer relied on their creators. They operated independently, maintained themselves, and developed on their own. The smart machines gave us everything we needed: not just material needs, but also psychological ones. We didn't need to put any effort into survival. Taken care of by machines, we lived as though we were lying in comfortable cradles.

"Think about it; if the jungles of primitive Earth had been filled with inexhaustible supplies of fruits and tame creatures that desired to become food, how could apes evolve into humans? The Machine Cradle was just such a comfort-filled jungle. Gradually we forgot about our technology and science. Our civilization became lazy and empty, devoid of creativity and ambition, and that only sped up the aging process. What you see now is the God Civilization in her final dying gasps."

"Then . . . can you now tell us the goal for the God Civilization in coming to Earth?"

"We have no home now."

"But . . ." The Secretary-General pointed upward.

"The spaceships are old. It's true that the artificial environment on the ships is more stable than any natural environment, including Earth's. But the ships are so old, old beyond your imagination. Old components have broken down. Accumulated quantum effects over the eons have led to more and more software errors. The system's self-repair and self-maintenance functions have encountered more and more insurmountable obstacles. The living environment on the ships is deteriorating. The amount of life necessities that can be distributed to individuals is decreasing by the day. We can just about survive. In the twenty thousand cities on the various ships, the air is filled with pollution and despair."

"Are there no solutions? Perhaps new components for the ships? A software upgrade?"

God shook his head. "The God Civilization is in her final years. We are two billion dying men and women each more than three thousand years old. But before us, hundreds of generations had already lived in the comfort of the Machine Cradle. Long ago, we forgot all our technology. Now we have no way to repair these ships that have been operating for tens of millions of years on their own. Indeed, in terms of the ability to study and understand technology, we are even worse than you. We can't even connect a circuit for a lightbulb or solve a quadratic equation . . .

"One day, the ships told us that they were close to complete breakdown. The propulsion systems could no longer push the ships near the speed of light. The God Civilization could only drift along at a speed not even one-tenth the speed of light, and the ecological support systems were nearing collapse. The machines could no longer keep two billion of us alive. We had to find another way out."

"Did you ever think that this would happen?"

"Of course. Two thousand years ago, the ships already warned us. That was when we began the process of seeding life on Earth so that in our old age we would have support."

"Two thousand years ago?"

"Yes. Of course I'm talking about time on the ships. From your frame of reference, that was three-point-five billion years ago, when Earth first cooled down."

"We have a question: you say that you've lost your technology. But doesn't seeding life require technology?"

"Oh. To start the process of evolving life on a planet is a minor operation. Just scatter some seeds, and life will multiply and evolve on its own. We had this kind of software even before the Age of the Machine Cradle. Just start the program, and the machines can finish everything. To create a planet full of life, capable of developing civilization, the most basic requirement is time, a few billion years of time.

"By traveling close to the speed of light, we possess almost limitless time. But now, the God Civilization's ships can no longer approach the speed of light. Otherwise we'd still have the chance to create new civilizations and more life, and we would have more choices. We're trapped by slowness. Those dreams cannot be realized."

"So you want to spend your golden years on Earth."

"Yes, yes. We hope that you will feel a sense of filial duty toward your creators and take us in." God leaned on his walking stick and trembled as he tried to bow to the leaders of all the nations, and he almost fell on his face.

"But how do you plan to live here?"

"If we just gathered in one place by ourselves, then we might as well stay in space and die there. We'd like to be absorbed into your societies, your families. When the God Civilization was still in her childhood, we also had families. You know that childhood is the most precious time. Since your civilization is still in her childhood, if we can return to this era and spend the rest of our lives in the warmth of families, then that would be our greatest happiness."

"There are two billion of you. That means every family on Earth would have to take in one or two of you." After the Secretary-General spoke, the meeting hall sank into silence.

"Yes, yes, sorry to give you so much trouble . . ." God continued to bow while stealing glances at the Secretary-General and the leaders of all the nations. "Of course, we're willing to compensate you."

He waved his cane, and two more white-bearded Gods walked into the meeting hall, struggling under the weight of a silvery, metallic trunk they carried between them. "Look, these are high-density information storage devices. They systematically store the knowledge the God Civilization had acquired in every field of science and technology. With this, your civilization will advance by leaps and bounds. I think you will like this."

The Secretary-General, like the leaders of all the nations, looked at the metal trunk and tried to hide his elation. "Taking care of God is the responsibility of humankind. Of course this will require some consultation between the various nations, but I think in principle . . ."

"Sorry to be so much trouble. Sorry to be so much trouble . . ." God's eyes filled with tears, and he continued to bow.

After the Secretary-General and the leaders of all the nations left the meeting hall, they saw that tens of thousands of Gods had gathered outside the United Nations building. A white sea of bobbing heads filled the air with murmuring words. The Secretary-General listened carefully and realized that they were all speaking, in the various tongues of Earth, the same sentence:

"Sorry to be so much trouble. Sorry to be so much trouble . . ."

4.

Two billion Gods arrived on Earth. Enclosed in suits made of their special film, they fell through the atmosphere. During that time, one could see the bright, colorful streaks in the sky even during the day. After the Gods landed, they spread out into 1.5 billion families.

Having received the Gods' knowledge about science and technology, everyone was filled with hopes and dreams for the future, as though humankind was about to step into paradise overnight. Under the influence of such joy, every family welcomed the coming of God.

That morning, Qiusheng and his family and all the other villagers stood at the village entrance to receive the Gods allocated to Xicen.

"What a beautiful day," Yulian said.

Her comment wasn't motivated solely by her feelings. The spaceships had disappeared overnight, restoring the sky's wide open and limitless appearance. Humans had never been allowed to step onto any of the ships. The Gods did not really object to that particular request from the humans, but the ships themselves refused to grant permission. They did not acknowledge the various primitive probes which Earth sent and sealed their doors tightly. After the final group of Gods leaped into the atmosphere, all the spaceships, numbering more than twenty thousand, departed their orbit simultaneously. But they didn't go far, only drifting in the asteroid belt.

Although these ships were ancient, the old routines continued to function. Their only mission was to serve the Gods. Thus, they would not move too far. When the Gods needed them again, they would come.

Two buses arrived from the county seat, bringing the one hundred and six Gods allocated to Xicen. Qiusheng and Yulian met the God assigned to their family. The couple stood on each side of God, affectionately supported him by the arms, and walked home in the bright afternoon sun. Bingbing and Qiusheng's father followed behind, smiling.

"Gramps, um, Gramps God." Yulian leaned her face against God's shoulder, her smile as bright as the sun. "I hear that the technology you gave us will soon allow us to experience true Communism! When that happens, we'll all have things according to our needs. Things won't cost any money. You just go to the store and pick them up."

God smiled and nodded at her, his white hair bobbing. He spoke in heavily accented Chinese. "Yes. Actually, 'to each according to need' fulfills only the most basic needs of a civilization. The technology we gave you will bring you a life of prosperity and comfort surpassing your imagination."

Yulian's laughed so much her face opened up like a flower. "No, no! 'To each according to need' is more than enough for me!"

"Uh-huh," Qiusheng's father agreed emphatically.

"Can we live forever without aging like you?" Qiusheng asked.

"We can't live forever without aging. It's just that we can live longer than you. Look at how old I am! In my view, if a man lives longer than three thousand years, he might as well be dead. For a civilization, extreme longevity for the individual can be fatal."

"Oh, I don't need three thousand years. Just three hundred." Qiusheng's father was now laughing as much as Yulian. "In that case, I'd still be considered a young man right now. Maybe I can . . . hahahaha."

The village treated the day like it was Chinese New Year. Every family held a big banquet to welcome its God, and Qiusheng's family was no exception.

Qiusheng's father quickly became a little drunk with cups of vintage *huangjiu*. He gave God a thumbs-up. "You're really something! To be able to create so many living things—you're truly supernatural."

God drank a lot, too, but his head was still clear. He waved his hand. "No, not supernatural. It was just science. When biology has developed to a certain level, creating life is akin to building machines."

"You say that. But in our eyes, you're no different from immortals who have deigned to live among us."

God shook his head. "Supernatural beings would never make mistakes. But for us, we made mistake after mistake during your creation."

"You made mistakes when you created us?" Yulian's eyes were wide open. In her imagination, creating all those lives was a process similar to her giving birth to Bingbing eight years ago. No mistake was possible.

"There were many. I'll give a relatively recent example. The world-creation software made errors in the analysis of the environment on Earth, which resulted in the appearance of creatures like dinosaurs: huge bodies and low adaptability. Eventually, in order to facilitate your evolution, they had to be eliminated.

"Speaking of events that are even more recent, after the disappearance of the ancient Aegean civilizations, the world-creation software believed that civilization on Earth was successfully established. It ceased to perform further monitoring and microadjustments, like leaving a wound-up clock to run on its own. This resulted in further errors. For example, it should have allowed the civilization of ancient Greece to develop on her own and stopped the Macedonian conquest and the subsequent Roman conquest. Although both of these ended up as the inheritors of Greek civilization, the direction of Greek development was altered . . ."

No one in Qiusheng's family could understand this lecture, but all respectfully listened.

"And then two great powers appeared on Earth: Han China and the Roman Empire. In contrast to the earlier situation with ancient Greece, the two shouldn't have been kept apart and left to develop in isolation. They ought to have been allowed to come into full contact . . ."

"This 'Han China' you're talking about? Is that the Han Dynasty of Liu

Bang and Xiang Yu?" Finally Qiusheng's father heard something he knew. "And what is this 'Roman Empire'?"

"I think that was a foreigners' country at the time," Qiusheng said, trying to explain. "It was pretty big."

Qiusheng's father was confused. "Why? When the foreigners finally showed up during the Qing Dynasty, look how badly they beat us up. You want them to show up even earlier? During the Han Dynasty?"

God laughed at this. "No, no. Back then, Han China was just as powerful as the Roman Empire."

"That's still bad. If those two great powers had met, it would have been a great war. Blood would have flowed like a river."

God nodded. He reached out with his chopsticks for a piece of beef braised in soy sauce. "Could have been. But if those two great civilizations, the Occident and the Orient, had met, the encounter would have generated glorious sparks and greatly advanced human progress . . . Eh, if those errors could have been avoided, Earth would now probably be colonizing Mars, and your interstellar probes would have flown past Sirius."

Qiusheng's father raised his bowl of *huangjiu* and spoke admiringly. "Everyone says that the Gods have forgotten science in their cradle, but you are still so learned."

"To be comfortable in the cradle, it's important to know a bit about philosophy, art, history, etc.—just some common facts, not real learning. Many scholars on Earth right now have much deeper thoughts than our own."

For the Gods, the first few months after they entered human society were a golden age, when they lived very harmoniously with human families. It was as though they had returned to the childhood of the God Civilization, fully immersed in the long-forgotten warmth of family life. This seemed the best way to spend the final years of their extremely long lives.

Qiusheng's family's God enjoyed the peaceful life in this beautiful southern Chinese village. Every day he went to the pond surrounded by bamboo groves to fish, chat with other old folks from the village, play chess, and generally enjoy himself. But his greatest hobby was attending folk operas. Whenever a theatre troupe came to the village or the town, he made sure to go to every performance.

His favorite opera was *The Butterfly Lovers*. One performance was not enough. He followed one troupe around for more than fifty kilometers and attended several shows in a row. Finally Qiusheng went to town and bought him a VCD of the opera. God played it over and over until he could hum a few lines of *Huangmei* opera and sounded pretty good.

One day Yulian discovered a secret. She whispered to Qiusheng and her father-in-law, "Did you know that every time Gramps God finishes his opera, he always takes a little card out from his pocket? And while looking at the card, he hums lines from the opera. Just now I stole a glance. The card is a photo. There's a really pretty young woman on it."

That evening, God played *The Butterfly Lovers* again. He took out the photograph of the pretty young woman and started to hum. Qiusheng's father quietly moved in. "Gramps God, is that your . . . girlfriend from a long time ago?"

God was startled. He hid the photograph quickly and smiled like a kid at Qiusheng's father. "Haha. Yeah, yeah, I loved her two thousand years ago."

Yulian, who was eavesdropping, grimaced. *Two thousand years ago!* Considering his advanced age, this was a bit gag-inducing.

Qiusheng's father wanted to look at the photograph. But God was so protective of it that it would have been embarrassing to ask. So Qiusheng's father settled for listening to God reminisce.

"Back then we were all so young. She was one of the very few who wasn't completely absorbed by life in the Machine Cradle. She initiated a great voyage of exploration to sail to the end of the universe. Oh, you don't need to think too hard about that. It's very difficult to understand. Anyway, she hoped to use this voyage as an opportunity to awaken the God Civilization, sleeping so soundly in the Machine Cradle. Of course, that was nothing more than a beautiful dream. She wanted me to go with her, but I didn't have the courage. The endless desert of the universe frightened me. It would have been a journey of more than twenty billion light-years. So she went by herself. But in the two thousand years after that, I never stopped longing for her."

"Twenty billion light-years? So like you explained to me before, that's the distance that light would travel in twenty billion years? Oh my! That's way too far. That's basically good-bye for life. Gramps God, you have to forget about her. You'll never see her again."

God nodded and sighed.

"Well, isn't she now about your age, too?"

God was startled out of his reverie. He shook his head. "Oh, no. For such a long voyage, her explorer ship would have to fly at close to the speed of light. That means she would still be very young. The only one that has grown old is me. You don't understand how large the universe is. What you think of as 'eternity' is nothing but a grain of sand in space-time.

"Well, the fact that you can't understand and feel this is sometimes a blessing."

5.

The honeymoon between the Gods and humans quickly ended. People were initially ecstatic over the scientific material received from the Gods, thinking that it would allow mankind to realize its dreams overnight. Thanks to the interface equipment provided by the Gods, an enormous quantity of information was retrieved successfully from the storage devices. The information was translated into English, and in order to avoid disputes, a copy was distributed to every nation in the world.

But people soon discovered that realizing these God-given technologies was impossible, at least within the present century. Consider the situation of the ancient Egyptians if a time traveler had provided information on modern technology to them, and you will have some understanding of the awkward situation these humans faced.

As the exhaustion of petroleum supplies loomed over the human race, energy technology was at the top of everyone's minds. But scientists and engineers discovered that the God Civilization's energy technology was useless for humans at this time. The Gods' energy source was built upon the basis of matter-antimatter annihilation. Even if people could understand all the materials and finally create an annihilation engine and generator (a basically impossible task within this generation), it would still have been for naught. This was because the fuel for these engines, antimatter, had to be mined from deep space. According to the material provided by the Gods, the closest antimatter ore source was between the Milky Way and the Andromeda galaxy, about 550,000 light-years away.

The technology for interstellar travel at near the speed of light also involved every field of scientific knowledge, and the greater part of the theories and techniques revealed by the Gods were beyond human comprehension. Just to get a basic understanding of the foundations would require human scholars to work for perhaps half a century. Scientists, initially full of hope, had tried to search the material from the Gods for technical information concerning controlled nuclear fission, but there was nothing. This was easy to understand: our current literature on energy science contained no information on how to make fire from sticks, either.

In other scientific fields, such as information science and life sciences (including the secret of human longevity), it was the same. Even the most advanced scholars could make no sense of the Gods' knowledge. Between the Gods' science and human science, there was still a great abyss of understanding that could not be bridged.

The Gods who arrived on Earth could not help the scientists in any way. Like the God at the United Nations had said, among the Gods now there were few who could even solve quadratic equations. The spaceships adrift among the asteroids also ignored all hails from the humans. The human race was like a group of new elementary school students who were suddenly required to master the material of Ph.D. candidates, and were given no instructor.

On the other hand, Earth's population suddenly grew by two billion. These were all extremely aged individuals who could no longer be productive. Most of them were plagued by various diseases and put unprecedented pressure on human society. As a result, every government had to pay each family living with a God a considerable support stipend. Health care and other public infrastructures were strained beyond the breaking point. The world economy was pushed near the edge of collapse.

The harmonious relationship between God and Qiusheng's family was gone. Gradually the family began to see him as a burden that fell from the sky. They began to despise him, but each had a different reason.

Yulian's reason was the most practical and closest to the underlying problem: God made her family poor. Among all the members of the family God also worried the most about her; she had a tongue as sharp as a knife, and she scared him more than black holes and supernovas. After the death of her dream of true Communism, she unceasingly nagged God: *Before you came, our family had lived so prosperously and comfortably. Back then everything was good. Now everything is bad. All because of you. Being saddled with an old fool like you was such a great misfortune.* Every day, whenever she had the chance, she would prattle on like this in front of God.

God also suffered from chronic bronchitis. This was not a very expensive disease to treat, but it did require ongoing care and a constant outlay of money. Finally one day Yulian forbade Qiusheng from taking God to the town hospital to see doctors and stopped buying medicine for him. When the Secretary of the village branch of the Communist Party found out, he came to Qiusheng's house.

"You have to pay for the care of your family God," the Secretary said to Yulian. "The doctor at the town hospital already told me that if left untreated, the chronic bronchitis might develop into pulmonary emphysema."

"If you want him treated, then the village or the government can pay for it," Yulian shouted at the Secretary. "We're not made of money!"

"Yulian, according to the God Support Law, the family has to bear these kinds of minor medical expenses. The government's support fee already includes this component."

"That little bit of support fee is useless!"

"You can't talk like that. After you began getting the support fee, you bought a milk cow, switched to liquefied petroleum gas, and bought a big, new color TV! You're telling me now that you don't have money for God to see a doctor? Everyone knows that in your family, your word is law. I'm going to make it clear to you: right now I'm helping you save face, but don't push your luck. Next time, it won't be me standing here trying to persuade you. It will be the County God Support Committee. You'll be in real trouble then."

Yulian had no choice but to resume paying for God's medical care. But after that she became even meaner to him.

One time, God said to Yulian, "Don't be so anxious. Humans are very smart and learn fast. In only another century or so, the easiest aspects of the Gods' knowledge will become applicable to human society. Then your life will become better."

"Damn. *A whole century.* And you say 'only.' Are you even listening to yourself?" Yulian was washing the dishes and didn't even bother looking back at God.

"That's a very short period of time."

"For you! You think we can live as long as you? In another century, you won't even find my bones! But I want to ask you a question: how much longer do you think *you'll* be living?"

"Oh, I'm like a candle in the wind. If I can live another three or four hundred years, I'll be very satisfied."

Yulian dropped a whole stack of bowls on the ground. "This is not how 'support' is supposed to work! Ah, so you think not only I should spend my entire life taking care of you, but you have to have my son, my grandson, for ten generations and more!? Why won't you die?"

As for Qiusheng's father, he thought God was a fraud, and in fact, this view was pretty common. Since scientists couldn't understand the Gods' scientific papers, there was no way to prove their authenticity. Maybe the Gods were playing a giant trick on the human race. For Qiusheng's father, there was ample support for this view.

"You old swindler, you're way too outrageous," he said to God one day. "I'm too lazy to expose you. Your tricks are not worth my trouble. Heck, they're not even worth my grandson's trouble."

God asked him what he had discovered.

"I'll start with the simplest thing: our scientists know that humans evolved from monkeys, right?"

God nodded. "More accurately, you evolved from primitive apes."

"Then how can you say that you created us? If you were interested in creating humans, why not directly make us in our current form? Why bother first creating primitive apes and then go through the trouble of evolving? It makes no sense."

"A human begins as a baby, and then grows into an adult. A civilization also has to grow from a primitive state. The long path of experience cannot be avoided. Actually, humans began with the introduction of a much more primitive species. Even apes were already very evolved."

"I don't believe these made-up reasons. All right, here's something more obvious. This was actually first noticed by my grandson. Our scientists say that there was life on Earth even three billion years ago. Do you admit this?"

God nodded. "That estimate is basically right."

"So you're three billion years old?"

"In terms of your frame of reference, yes. But according to the frame of reference of our ships, I'm only thirty-five hundred years old. The ships flew close to the speed of light, and time passed much more slowly for us than for you. Of course, once in a while a few ships dropped out of their cruise and decelerated to come to Earth so that further adjustments to the evolution of life on Earth could be made. But this didn't require much time. Those ships would then return to cruise at close to the speed of light and continue skipping over the passage of time here."

"Bullshit," Qiusheng's father said contemptuously.

"Dad, this is the Theory of Relativity," Qiusheng interrupted. "Our scientists already proved it."

"Relativity, my ass! You're bullshitting me, too. That's impossible! How can time be like sesame oil, flowing at different speeds? I'm not so old that I've lost my mind. But you—reading all those books has made you stupid!"

"I can prove to you that time does indeed flow at different rates," God said, his face full of mystery. He took out that photograph of his beloved from two thousand years ago and handed it to Qiusheng. "Look at her carefully and memorize every detail."

The second Qiusheng looked at the photograph, he knew that he would be able to remember every detail. It would be impossible to forget. Like the other Gods, the woman in the picture had a blend of the features of all ethnicities. Her skin was like warm ivory, her two eyes were so alive that they seemed to sing, and she immediately captivated Qiusheng's soul. She was a woman among Gods, the God of women. The beauty of the Gods was like a second sun. Humans had never seen it and could not bear it.

"Look at you! You're practically drooling!" Yulian grabbed the photograph from the frozen Qiusheng. But before she could look at it, her father-in-law took it away from her.

"Let me see," Qiusheng's father said. He brought the photograph to his ancient eyes, as close as possible. For a long time he did not move, as though the photograph provided sustenance.

"Why are you looking so close?" Yulian said, her tone contemptuous.

"Shut it. I don't have my glasses," Qiusheng's father said, his face still practically on the photograph.

Yulian looked at her father-in-law disdainfully for a few seconds, curled her lips, and left for the kitchen.

God took the photograph out of the hands of Qiusheng's father, whose hands lingered on the photo for a long while, unwilling to let go. God said, "Remember all the details. I'll let you look at it again this time tomorrow."

The next day, father and son said little to each other. Both thought about the young woman, so there was nothing to say. Yulian's temper was far worse than usual.

Finally the time came. God had seemingly forgotten about it and had to be reminded by Qiusheng's father. He took out the photograph that the two men had been thinking about all day and handed it first to Qiusheng. "Look carefully. Do you see any change in her?"

"Nothing really," Qiusheng said, looking intently. After a while, he finally noticed something. "Aha! The opening between her lips seems slightly narrower. Not much, just a little bit. Look at the corner of the mouth here . . ."

"Have you no shame? To look at some other woman that closely?" Yulian grabbed the photo again, and again, her father-in-law took it away from her.

"Let me see—" Qiusheng's father put on his glasses and carefully examined the picture. "Yes, indeed the opening is narrower. But there's a much more obvious change that you didn't notice. Look at this wisp of hair. Compared to yesterday, it has drifted farther to the right."

God took the picture from Qiusheng's father. "This is not a photograph, but a television receiver."

"A . . . TV?"

"Yes. Right now it's receiving a live feed from that explorer spaceship heading for the end of the universe."

"Live? Like live broadcasts of football matches?"

"Yes."

"So . . . the woman in the picture, she's alive!" Qiusheng was so shocked that his mouth hung open. Even Yulian's eyes were now as big as walnuts.

"Yes, she's alive. But unlike a live broadcast on Earth, this feed is subject to a delay. The explorer spaceship is now about eighty million light-years away, so the delay is about eighty million years. What we see now is how she was eighty million years ago."

"This tiny thing can receive a signal from that far away?"

"This kind of super long-distance communication across space requires the use of neutrinos or gravitational waves. Our spaceships can receive the signal, magnify it, and then rebroadcast to this TV."

"Treasure, a real treasure!" Qiusheng's father praised sincerely. But it was unclear whether he was talking about the tiny TV or the young woman on the TV. Anyway, after hearing that she was still "alive," Qiusheng and his father both felt a deeper attachment to her. Qiusheng tried to take the tiny TV again, but God refused.

"Why does she move so slowly in the picture?"

"That's the result of time flowing at different speeds. From our frame of reference, time flows extremely slowly on a spaceship flying close to the speed of light."

"Then . . . can she still talk to you?" Yulian asked.

God nodded. He flipped a switch behind the TV. Immediately a sound came out of it. It was a woman's voice, but the sound didn't change, like a singer holding a note steady at the end of a song. God stared at the screen, his eyes full of love.

"She's talking right now. She's finishing three words: 'I love you.' Each word took more than a year. It's now been three and a half years, and right now she's just finishing 'you.' To completely finish the sentence will take another three months." God lifted his eyes from the TV to the domed sky above the yard. "She still has more to say. I'll spend the rest of my life listening to her."

Bingbing actually managed to maintain a pretty good relationship with God for a while. The Gods all had some childishness to them, and they enjoyed talking and playing with children. But one day, Bingbing wanted

God to give him the large watch he wore, and God steadfastly refused. He explained that the watch was a tool for communicating with the God Civilization. Without it, he would no longer be able to connect with his own people.

"Hmm, look at this. You're still thinking about your own civilization and race. You've never thought of us as your real family!" Yulian said angrily.

After that, Bingbing was no longer nice to God. Instead, he often played practical tricks on him.

The only one in the family who still had respect and feelings of filial piety toward God was Qiusheng. Qiusheng had graduated from high school and liked to read. Other than a few people who passed the college-entrance examination and went away for college, he was the most learned individual in the village. But at home, Qiusheng had no power. On practically everything he listened to the direction of his wife and followed the commands of his father. If somehow his wife and father had conflicting instructions, then all he could do was to sit in a corner and cry. Given that he was such a softy, he had no way to protect God at home.

6.

The relationship between the Gods and humans had finally deteriorated beyond repair.

The complete breakdown between God and Qiusheng's family occurred after the incident involving instant noodles. One day, before lunch, Yulian came out of the kitchen with a paper box and asked why half the box of instant noodles she had bought yesterday had already disappeared.

"I took them," God said in a small voice. "I gave them to those living by the river. They've almost run out of things to eat."

He was talking about the place where the Gods who had left their families were gathering. Recently there had been frequent incidents of abuse of the Gods in the village. One particularly savage couple had been beating and cursing out their God, and even withheld food from him. Eventually that God tried to commit suicide in the river that ran in front of the village, but luckily others were able to stop him.

This incident caused a great deal of publicity. It went beyond the county, and the city's police eventually came, along with a bunch of reporters from CCTV and the provincial TV station, and took the couple away in handcuffs. According to the God Support Law, they had committed God abuse and would be sentenced to at least ten years in jail. This was the only law that was universal among all the nations of the world, with uniform prison terms.

After that, the families in the village became more careful and stopped treating the Gods too poorly in front of other people. But at the same time, the incident worsened the relationship between the Gods and the villagers. Eventually, some of the Gods left their families, and other Gods followed. By now almost one-third of the Gods in Xicen had already left their assigned families. These wandering Gods set up camp in the field across the river and lived a primitive, difficult life.

In other parts of the country and across the world, the situation was the same. Once again, the streets of big cities were filled with crowds of wandering, homeless Gods. The number quickly increased like a repeat of the nightmare three years ago. The world, full of Gods and people, faced a gigantic crisis.

"Ha, you're very generous, you old fool! How dare you eat our food while giving it away?" Yulian began to curse loudly.

Qiusheng's father slammed the table and got up. "You idiot! Get out of here! You miss those Gods by the river? Why don't you go and join them?"

God sat silently for a while, thinking. Then he stood up, went to his tiny room, and packed up his few belongings. Leaning on his bamboo cane, he slowly made his way out the door, heading in the direction of the river.

Qiusheng didn't eat with the rest of his family. He squatted in a corner with his head lowered and not speaking.

"Hey, dummy! Come here and eat. We have to go into town to buy feed this afternoon," Yulian shouted at him. Since he refused to budge, she went over to yank his ear.

"Let go," Qiusheng said. His voice was not loud, but Yulian let him go as though she had been shocked. She had never seen her husband with such a gloomy expression on his face.

"Forget about him," Qiusheng's father said carelessly. "If he doesn't want to eat, then he's a fool."

"Ha, you miss your God? Why don't you go join him and his friends in that field by the river, too?" Yulian poked a finger at Qiusheng's head.

Qiusheng stood up and went upstairs to his bedroom. Like God, he packed a few things into a bundle and put it in a duffel bag he had once used when he had gone to the city to work. With the bag on his back, he headed outside.

"Where are you going?" Yulian yelled. But Qiusheng ignored her. She yelled again, but now there was fear in her voice. "How long are you going to be out?"

"I'm not coming back," Qiusheng said without looking back.

"What? Come back here! Is your head filled with shit?" Qiusheng's father followed him out of the house. "What's the matter with you? Even if you don't want your wife and kid, how dare you leave your father?"

Qiusheng stopped but still did not turn around. "Why should I care about you?"

"How can you talk like that? I'm your father! I raised you! Your mother died early. You think it was easy to raise you and your sister? Have you lost your mind?"

Qiusheng finally turned back to look at his father. "If you can kick the people who created our ancestors' ancestors' ancestors out of our house, then I don't think it's much of a sin for me not to support you in your old age."

He left, and Yulian and his father stood there, dumbfounded.

Qiusheng went over the ancient arched stone bridge and walked toward the tents of the Gods. He saw a few of the Gods had set up a pot to cook something in the grassy clearing strewn with golden leaves. Their white beards and the white steam coming out of the pot reflected the noon sunlight like a scene out of an ancient myth.

Qiusheng found his God and said stubbornly, "Gramps God, let's go."

"I'm not going back to that house."

"I'm not, either. Let's go together into town and stay with my sister for a while. Then I'll go into the city and find a job, and we'll rent a place together. I'll support you for the rest of my life."

"You're a good kid," God said, patting his shoulder lightly. "But it's time for us to go." He pointed to the watch on his wrist. Qiusheng now noticed that all the watches of all the Gods were blinking with a red light.

"Go? Where to?"

"Back to the ships," God said, pointing at the sky. Qiusheng lifted his head and saw that two spaceships were already hovering in the sky, standing out starkly against the blue. One of them was closer, and its shape and outline loomed huge. Behind it, another was much farther away and appeared smaller. But the most surprising sight was that the first spaceship had lowered a thread as thin as spider silk, extending from space down to Earth. As the spider silk slowly drifted, the bright sun glinted on different sections like lightning in the bright blue sky.

"A space elevator," God explained. "Already more than a hundred of these have been set up on every continent. We'll ride them back to the ships." Later Qiusheng would learn that when a spaceship dropped down a space elevator from a geostationary orbit, it needed a large mass on its other side, deep in space, to act as a counterweight. That was the purpose of the other ship he saw.

When Qiusheng's eyes adjusted to the brightness of the sky, he saw that there were many more silvery stars deep in the distance. Those stars were spread out very evenly, forming a huge matrix. Qiusheng understood that the twenty thousand ships of the God Civilization were coming back to Earth from the asteroid belt.

7.

Twenty thousand spaceships once again filled the sky above Earth. In the two months that followed, space capsules ascended and descended the various space elevators, taking away the two billion Gods who had briefly lived on Earth. The space capsules were silver spheres. From a distance, they looked like dewdrops hanging on spider threads.

The day that Xicen's Gods left, all the villagers showed up for the farewell. Everyone was affectionate toward the Gods, and it reminded everyone of the day a year ago when the Gods first came to Xicen. It was as though all the abuse and disdain the Gods had received had nothing to do with the villagers.

Two big buses were parked at the entrance to the village, the same two buses that had brought the Gods here a year ago. More than a hundred Gods would now be taken to the nearest space elevator and ride up in space capsules. The silver thread that could be seen in the distance was in reality hundreds of kilometers away.

Qiusheng's whole family went to send off their God. No one said anything along the way. As they neared the village entrance, God stopped, leaned against his cane, and bowed to the family. "Please stop here. Thank you for taking care of me this year. Really, thank you. No matter where I will be in this universe, I will always remember your family." Then he took off the large watch from his wrist and handed it to Bingbing. "A gift."

"But . . . how will you communicate with the other Gods in the future?" Bingbing asked.

"We'll all be on the spaceships. I have no more need for this," God said, laughing.

"Gramps God," Qiusheng's father said, his face sorrowful, "your ships are all ancient. They won't last much longer. Where can you go then?"

God stroked his beard and said calmly, "It doesn't matter. Space is limitless. Dying anywhere is the same."

Yulian suddenly began to cry. "Gramps God, I . . . I'm not a very nice person. I shouldn't have made you the target of all my complaints, which I'd saved up my whole life. It's just as Qiusheng said: I've behaved as if I don't have a conscience . . ." She pushed a bamboo basket into God's hands. "I boiled some eggs this morning. Please take them for your trip."

God picked up the basket. "Thank you." Then he took out an egg, peeled it, and began to eat, savoring the taste. Yellow flakes of egg yolk soon flaked his white beard. He continued to talk as he ate. "Actually, we came to Earth not only because we wanted to survive. Having already lived for two, three thousand years, what did we have to fear from death? We just wanted to be with you. We like and cherish your passion for life, your creativity, your imagination. These things have long disappeared from the God Civilization. We saw in you the childhood of our civilization. But we didn't realize we'd bring you so much trouble. We're really sorry."

"Please stay, Gramps," Bingbing said, crying. "I'll be better in the future."

God shook his head slowly. "We're leaving not because of how you treated us. The fact that you took us in and allowed us to stay was enough. But one thing made us unable to stay any longer: in your eyes, the Gods are pathetic. You pity us. Oh, you *pity* us."

God threw away the pieces of eggshell. He lifted his face, trailing a full head of white hair, and stared at the sky, as though through the blue he could see the bright sea of stars. "How can the God Civilization be pitied by man? You have no idea what a great civilization she was. You do not know what majestic epics she created, or how many imposing deeds she accomplished.

"It was 1857, during the Milky Way Era, when astronomers discovered a large number of stars was accelerating toward the center of the Milky Way. Once this flood of stars was consumed by the supermassive black hole found there, the resulting radiation would kill all life found in the galaxy.

"In response, our great ancestors built a nebula shield around the center of the galaxy with a diameter of ten thousand light-years so that life and civilization in the galaxy would continue. What a magnificent engineering project that was! It took us more than fourteen hundred years to complete . . .

"Immediately afterward, the Andromeda galaxy and the Large Magellanic Cloud united in an invasion of our galaxy. The interstellar fleet of the God Civilization leaped across hundreds of thousands of light-years and intercepted the invaders at the gravitational balance point between Andromeda and the Milky Way. When the battle entered into its climax, large numbers of ships from both sides mixed together, forming a spiraling nebula the size of the Solar System.

"During the final stages of the battle, the God Civilization made the bold decision to send all remaining warships and even the civilian fleet into the spiraling nebula. The great increase in mass caused gravity to exceed the centrifugal force, and this nebula, made of ships and people, collapsed under gravity and formed a star! Because the proportion of heavy elements in this star was so high, immediately after its birth, the star went supernova and illuminated the deep darkness between Andromeda and the Milky Way! Our ancestors thus destroyed the invaders with their courage and self-sacrifice, and left the Milky Way as a place where life could develop peacefully . . .

"Yes, now our civilization is old. But it is not our fault. No matter how hard one strives, a civilization must grow old one day. Everyone grows old, even you.

"We really do not need your pity."

"Compared to you," Qiusheng said, full of awe, "the human race is really nothing."

"Don't talk like that," God said. "Earth's civilization is still an infant. We hope you will grow up fast. We hope you will inherit and continue the glory of your creators." God threw down his cane. He put his hands on the shoulders of Bingbing and Qiusheng. "I have some final words for you."

"We may not understand everything you have to say," Qiusheng said, "but please speak. We will listen."

"First, you must get off this rock!" God spread out his arms toward space. His white robe danced in the autumn wind like a sail.

"Where will we go?" Qiusheng's father asked in confusion.

"Begin by flying to the other planets in the solar system, then to other stars. Don't ask why, but use all your energy toward the goal of flying away, the farther the better. In that process, you will spend a lot of money, and many people will die, but you must get away from here. Any civilization that stays on her birth world is committing suicide! You must go into the universe and find new worlds, new homes, and spread your descendants across the galaxy like drops of spring rain."

"We'll remember," Qiusheng said and nodded, even though neither he nor his wife nor father nor son really understood God's words.

"Good," God sighed, satisfied. "Next I will tell you a secret, a great secret." He stared at everyone in the family with his blue eyes. His stare was like a cold wind and caused everyone's heart to shudder. "You have brothers."

Qiusheng's family looked at God, utterly confused. But Qiusheng finally figured out what God meant. "You're saying that you created other Earths?"

God nodded slowly. "Yes, other Earths, other human civilizations. Other than you, there were three others. All are close to you, within two hundred light-years. You are Earth Number Four, the youngest."

"Have you been to the other Earths?" Bingbing asked.

God nodded again. "Before we came to you, we went first to the other three Earths and asked them to take us in. Earth Number One was the best among the bunch. After they obtained our scientific materials, they simply chased us away.

"Earth Number Two, on the other hand, kept one million of us as hostages and forced us to give them spaceships as ransom. After we gave them one thousand ships, they realized that they could not operate the ships. They then forced the hostages to teach them how, but the hostages didn't know how, either, since the ships were autonomous. So they killed all the hostages.

"Earth Number Three took three million of us as hostages and demanded that we ram Earth Number One and Earth Number Two with several spaceships each because they were in a prolonged state of war with the other two Earths. Of course, even a single hit from one of our antimatter-powered ships would destroy all life on a planet. We refused, and so they killed all the hostages."

"Unfilial children!" Qiusheng's father shouted in anger. "You should punish them!"

God shook his head. "We will never attack civilizations we created. You are the best of the four brothers. That's why I'm telling you all this. Your three brothers are drawn to invasion. They do not know what love is or what morality is. Their capacity for cruelty and bloodlust are impossible for you to imagine.

"Indeed, in the beginning we created six Earths. The other two were in the same solar systems as Earth Number One and Earth Number Three, respectively. Both were destroyed by their brothers. The fact that the other three Earths haven't yet destroyed one another is only due to the great distances separating their solar systems. By now, all three know of the existence of Earth Number Four and possess your precise coordinates. Thus, you must go and destroy them first before they destroy you."

"This is too frightening!" Yulian said.

"For now, it's not yet too frightening. Your three brothers are indeed more advanced than you, but they still cannot travel faster than one-tenth the speed of light, and cannot cruise more than thirty light-years from home. This is a race of life and death to see which one among you can achieve near-light-speed space travel first. It is the only way to break through the prison of time and space. Whoever can achieve this technology first will survive. Anyone slower will die a sure death. This is the struggle for survival in the universe. Children, you don't have much time. Work hard!"

"Do the most learned and most powerful people in our world know these things?" Qiusheng's father asked, trembling.

"Yes. But don't rely on them. A civilization's survival depends on the effort of every individual. Even the common people like you have a role to play."

"You hear that, Bingbing?" Qiusheng said to his son. "You must study hard."

"When you fly into the universe at close to the speed of light to resolve the threat of your brothers, you must perform another urgent task: find a few planets suitable for life and seed them with some simple, primitive life from here, like bacteria and algae. Let them evolve on their own."

Qiusheng wanted to ask more questions, but God picked up his cane and began to walk. The family accompanied him toward the bus. The other Gods were already aboard.

"Oh, Qiusheng." God stopped, remembering. "I took a few of your books with me. I hope you don't mind." He opened his bundle to show Qiusheng. "These are your high school textbooks on math, physics, chemistry."

"No problem. Take them. But why do you want these?"

God tied up the bundle again. "To study. I'll start with quadratic equations. In the long years ahead, I'll need some way to occupy myself. Who knows? Maybe one day, I'll try to repair our ships' antimatter engines and allow us to fly close to the speed of light again!"

"Right," Qiusheng said, excited. "That way, you'll be able to skip across time again. You can find another planet, create another civilization to support you in your old age!"

God shook his head. "No, no, no. We're no longer interested in being supported in our old age. If it's time for us to die, we die. I want to study because I have a final wish." He took out the small TV from his pocket. On the screen, his beloved from two thousand years ago was still slowly speaking the final word of that three-word sentence. "I want to see her again."

"It's a good wish, but it's only a fantasy," Qiusheng's father said. "Think about it. She left two thousand years ago at the speed of light. Who knows where she is now? Even if you repair your ship, how will you ever catch her? You told us that nothing can go faster than light."

God pointed at the sky with his cane. "In this universe, as long as you're patient, you can make any wish come true. Even though the possibility is minuscule, it is not nonexistent. I told you once that the universe was born out of a great explosion. Now gravity has gradually slowed down its expansion. Eventually the expansion will stop and turn into contraction. If our spaceship can really fly again at close to the speed of light, then we will endlessly accelerate and endlessly approach the speed of light. This way, we will skip over endless time until we near the final moments of the universe.

"By then, the universe will have shrunk to a very small size, smaller even than Bingbing's toy ball, as small as a point. Then everything in the entire universe will come together, and she and I will also be together."

A tear fell from God's eye and rolled onto his beard, glistening brightly in the morning sun. "The universe will then be the tomb at the end of *The Butterfly Lovers*. She and I will be the two butterflies emerging from the tomb . . ."

8.

A week later, the last spaceship left Earth. God left.

Xicen village resumed its quiet life.

On this evening, Qiusheng's family sat in the yard, looking at a sky full of stars. It was deep autumn, and insects had stopped making noises in the fields. A light breeze stirred the fallen leaves at their feet. The air was slightly chilly.

"They're flying so high. The wind must be so severe, so cold—" Yulian murmured to herself.

"There isn't any wind up there," Qiusheng said. "They're in space, where there isn't even air. But it is really cold. So cold that in the books they call it *absolute zero*. It's so dark out there, with no end in sight. It's a place that you can't even dream of in your nightmares."

Yulian began to cry again. But she tried to hide it with words. "Remember those last two things God told us? I understand the part about our three brothers. But then he told us that we had to spread bacteria onto other planets and so on. I still can't make sense of that."

"I figured it out," Qiusheng's father said. Under the brilliant, starry sky, his head, full of a lifetime of foolishness, finally opened up to insight. He looked up at the stars. He had lived with them above his head all his life, but only today did he discover what they really looked like. A feeling he had never had before suffused his blood, making him feel as if he had been touched by something greater. Even though it did not become a part of him, the feeling shook him to his core. He sighed at the sea of stars, and said,

"The human race needs to start thinking about who is going to support us in our old age."

Rich Larson was born in Galmi, Niger, has studied in Rhode Island and worked in the south of Spain, and now lives in Ottawa, Canada. His work appears in numerous Year's Best anthologies and has been translated into Chinese, Vietnamese, Polish, Czech, French, and Italian. He was the most prolific author of short science fiction in 2015, 2016, and possibly 2017 as well. His debut novel, *Annex*, comes out from Orbit Books in July 2018, and his debut collection, *Tomorrow Factory*, follows in October 2018 from Talos Press.

Water Scorpions

RICH LARSON

This is you," Noel says to his new brother, holding up a writhing water scorpion by its tail. Spindly legs churn and its pincers clack, but the tail is stingerless. It is thin and stiff and hollow like a straw, so the water scorpion can breathe through it when it clings to the rusty iron bar around the inside of the pool.

Danny rocks forward on his haunches and watches through his cluster of gleaming black eyes. His body is all slippery spars and gray angles. Noel hopes he sees the resemblance to the creature dangling between his fingers.

"This is you," Danny mimics, a warbling echo that doesn't require movement from his needle lined jaws, coming instead from the porous bulb underneath them.

Noel stands up from the pool's blue-tiled lip, keeping the water scorpion pinched between thumb and finger. He doesn't have to tell Danny to follow. Danny always follows, even when Noel stamps his feet and screams at him to go away.

He leads his brother along the concrete deck, slapping wet footprints. Danny's feet clop instead of slapping, like when their mother wears high heels. Now she sits barefoot in a dilapidated beach chair, wearing the stretchy black one-piece that hides her scar. Her eyes are on a work screen full of lab notes, but she sets down her stylus and waves and smiles when Noel and Danny pass by.

Noel lowers the water scorpion into the pocket of his trunks to shield it from view, still gripping the tail. It squirms and rasps against the fabric.

Nobody else looks up from their loungers. Nobody stares at Danny here, not even the cooks anymore. The private pool on the edge of Faya-Largeau, only hours from the Saharan crash site, was bought out by the UN specifically for its team of scientists, translators, engineers—all of them now used to seeing aliens.

Noel and Danny pass under a stucco arch, and the concrete becomes the courtyard's chipped mosaic tile, hot on Noel's feet. He does not know if it is hot on Danny's feet; Danny never jerks away from scalding sand or half-buried thorns. Not even when Noel has him walk over a spread of prickly goatheads.

Pungent eucalyptus overtakes the smell of chlorine and greasy samosas. The silvery-gray trees line a long open-air entryway. Noel leads Danny all the way to the end, into the red dust of the parking lot where the pool sounds of splashing and satellite radio and voices are muted. Danny's neck pops and swivels toward the family car where it gleams hot white in the sunlight.

"Look at this, Danny," Noel says, lifting the water scorpion from his pocket. "Watch this."

"Watch this," comes the wavery echo. He crouches obediently as Noel drops the creature into the warm sand. It makes a skittering circle, claws waving, then tries to dart away. Noel meets it with a wave of sand kicked up by the blade of his hand. The water scorpion flails and shies off, scuttles in the other direction. Noel tosses another fistful of sand.

Danny keeps watching, stone still, as Noel pours scoop after scoop of sand onto the panicking scorpion, sucking the moisture from the cracks in its keratin, battering down on its carapace, until the creature turns sluggish and can only slowly kick its legs in place.

"That's like you, if Mom didn't bring you to the pool all the time," Noel says softly. "You'd cook. You'd get all dried up and die, and after a while she'd forget you ever existed. Just like she forgot Maya."

Danny looks up at him with all of his black beetle eyes. Danny never blinks. He never smiles and never cries. He doesn't understand, not a single thing.

Noel covers the water scorpion over, heaping a burial mound. With his eyes on his work, he whispers, "I hate you."

"I hate you," Danny trills softly back.

The stork ship came down on the day Noel's sister died. He was sitting in the waiting room, watching red balloons in animated smartpaint drift across the peeling green walls, reminding him his tenth birthday wasn't far away, when the news feed sliced onto every screen in the hospital. A crumbling castle of pitted alloy and crystalline spars, falling from the sky. When the ship crash landed in the Sahara, an ocean away, an orderly gasped and bit the skin between her thumb and finger.

Noel understood it was something his xenobiologist mother would need to know about, something as important as the baby in her belly, so when she came from the examination room with her shoulders shaking, he rushed to show her the screen. She watched the crash calmly, nodded to herself as if it made perfect sense. Her eyes were shot through with pink.

Later, on the metro, she explained in her doctor voice that Maya's umbilical cord had shrunk too thin, and she'd starved, but they would still have to go back to the hospital the next day for induced labor.

"If she died, then how can you give birth to her?" Noel asked, feeling a wave of confusion, a panic aching his throat.

His mother wept then, a raw rusty sound that made other people watch her in the subway windows. Noel buried his face in the crook of her arm. The woman in front of them played the news feed at full volume on her tab, about the UN seeking to assemble a response party, to drown out the noise.

Back poolside, their mother has migrated back under the gazebo, rolling up her work screen. Noel and Danny join her in the straw shade for samosas. Iridescent green and purple swirls over Danny's body, as it always does around their mother. Noel leans back against a rust-flaking pole of the gazebo while Danny hurries to her. She strokes his jaws, an approved contact from the stork instructional transmissions, but can't resist giving a human squeeze at the end. When she motions the same for Noel he digs back against the pole, feeling it on the nodes of his spine.

"Have you been playing Marco Polo today?" she asks helplessly, trying to drop her open arms naturally to the tabletop.

"We're killing water scorpions," Noel says, just to watch her smile cloud over. "They're pests," he adds, because the clouding still hurts. "Jean says so. Says we can."

"Eat now," his mother says. "Stay in the shade for a while. You'll burn."

"Danny'll burn, you mean," Noel says. In the year since they came to Africa, leaving the flat in Montreal with the empty baby room, he's baked dark. He never burns anymore.

They eat the samosas without speaking. Noel hides the gristle with ketchup. Danny cakes them with the nutrient powder from their mother's

Tupperware, which is better than when he covers them in sand. Danny can eat anything. Once, he ate half the pages from Noel's favorite paperbook comic, slow and deliberate, back when Noel was scared to put his fingers near Danny's teeth. Their mother thought he confused it with the paper-wrapped spearmint gum she'd given him a day before.

"I have to go back on-site for a few hours," she says, zipping her swim bag. "Will the pair of you be all right until supper? Jean is in the clubhouse."

"Jean is in the clubhouse," Danny echoes, a high sweet distortion of their mother's voice. His bony head swivels toward the stucco entrance.

She smiles. "That's right. Noel, watch out for your brother."

She gives them francs so they can buy Fanta and credit for Noel's tab so he can play netgames. When she leaves, Danny's skin fades back to slippery gray.

They'd been in Chad for three months already when Noel's mother told him about Danny. He'd spent the day, like most, climbing trees, hurling a mangy tennis ball against the concrete wall of the house, and watching procedurally generated cartoons instead of doing Skype school.

The first weeks had been the exciting ones, with his mother coming home with stories each night about the team cleaving their way inside the ship to find the stork adults (Gliese-876s, back then, after their star system) dead and decaying, bonded by bone and neurocable to the ship's navigation equipment, rot seeping slowly outward. Noel had liked hearing about the low keening sound that made some of the other xenobiologists and one of the soldiers vomit, about the dissolving corpses in the dark swampy corridors.

He'd even liked hearing about the warm red amniotic pool where they found the babies who'd been remade, as best the storks' genelabs could achieve, in humanity's image, swapping vestigial wings and spiny shells for bipedalism and articulated necks. Babies who grew to child size with slender limbs and overlarge heads, features vaguely neotenized either by chance, a side-effect of the gene alterations that saved them from the ship-wide plague, or by design, like a cuckoo trying to slip its eggs in.

But now his mother wanted to bring one home.

"Danyal," she said, pulling herself up to the Formica countertop beside him. "The government still wants them all to have Arabic names. But we call him Danny."

Noel spooned yogurt into his ceramic bowl, listening to a breathless story about the one stork baby who wouldn't socialize with his siblings, who aced cognition tests and mimicked speech and followed her tirelessly through the lab.

"He's sort of imprinted," she said, with the fragile smile Noel had learned to cherish these past three months, learned to cup in his hands like a brittle bird. He felt the question coming before it reached her lips.

"What if he stays with us?" she asked. "He's not doing well at the center. And you always wanted a brother."

The word felt like a glass shard in his gut, but he kept his face blank, how he'd learned from watching her. Noel had wanted a brother. It was true. It gnawed at him. Maybe if he'd wanted a sister more, she wouldn't have died. They wouldn't have had to cut her out of his mother's belly. Maybe he hadn't wished hard enough.

"For just a little while," his mother said, smile already moving to slip away.

Noel couldn't say no.

Noel and Danny are swimming circles around the bobbing, plastic-coated lifeguard, making it spin in place like a sprinkler. No matter how hard Noel kicks, Danny is still quicker. They don't notice the weather turning until the stacks of rust-red cloud wall off the sun. Noel comes up for air in a sudden dusk and the smell of cool wet dirt itches inside his nose. The deserted pool deck is strangely still. Then all at once the trees frenzy, a ripple of whipping branches, and the dust storm the weather probes missed sweeps down over them.

Noel barely has time to pull up his goggles before the stinging sand slaps across his face. He throws out a hand for the lifeguard's orange floaters but finds Danny's slick hard skin instead and flinches away. But Danny's hands clamp to him, and then his legs, and Noel's chest seizes with a sudden panic: Danny is drowning him. Then Danny vanishes, slides past, and Noel thrashes blindly after him until he rams against the metal bar of the edge.

Someone heaves him up and out of the water; sand pelts his bare back and shoulders. "Inside, *vas-y*," Jean's voice booms in his ear. The big man has already draped a protective beach towel over Danny's head, and now grips Noel's arm.

"My tab," Noel says automatically, looking to where the table should have been visible, not looking at Danny.

"I have it. Dépêche-toi, hein?"

Jean ushers them back across the slippery deck, through a battering cloud of red dust, into the clubhouse. He puts his shoulder into the door to close it behind them. Noel claws sand out of his hair while Danny struggles out of the orange towel. The barrage has left small red welts on his gray skin.

"Wash out your eyes at the sink," Jean says, pointing to the concrete basin back behind the bar. The clubhouse is dark except for one flickering fluorescent tube in the ceiling and the glow of a plasma screen hooked to the wall. The few UN workers who didn't leave earlier now slouch to the sunken couches, mumbling bitterly about cell signals lost, windows left wide open, faulty weather probes.

"I had my goggles," Noel says, tapping one lens.

"Wash the rest of you," Jean says curtly. "Then help the stork."

Noel goes to the basin and splashes cold chemical-tanged water over his skinny arms, his chest, his face, rinsing away the dust stuck to his wet skin. When he straightens up, Danny is standing directly behind him. The sight jolts him.

"Don't do that," Noel hisses.

Danny says nothing, washing himself in silence. Someone brings two bottles of wine from the kitchen, and someone else finds a preset film on the television, something with arctic explorers on shifting glaciers, and everyone settles in to wait out the storm. Jean clears Noel a space on the far end of the couch, pulls his unharmed tab out of his pocket.

Noel keeps his head bent over the small screen when Danny slips away to the kitchen, but he still sees it happen.

D anny had lived with them for a week when Noel tried to show him Maya's picture. He took the Polaroid from his mother's closet, where she kept an album in case digital storage somehow disappeared, which to Noel sounded like the sun somehow going out. It showed Maya's small face in black-and-white, the face he remembered as scrunched and dead purple.

With the photo clutched to his chest, Noel went to the living room where Danny was playing. Their mother called it playing, but Danny mostly stared at the old die-cast Hot Wheels and Lego kits, except for the time Noel left and came back to find the plastic blocks built into a twisting Fibonacci spire. Now, Danny was crouched on the rug, holding a chewed yellow Mack truck in his spidery hands.

"This is the sister Mom lost," Noel said, extending the photo. "We lost. The one I told you about."

Danny gave him a gleaming black stare.

Noel had tried to teach him words, in English, in French, sometimes in the Arabic he picked up from the response center guard. *Car. Voiture. Sayara.* He'd guided Danny to the porch one morning to warble a near-indiscernible "I love you" to their mother. That had made her happy for an entire day.

"This is Maya," Noel said, shaking the photo slightly between his fingers.

Danny took it, gently, then eased upright, clicking and clacking, and walked away. Noel blinked. He followed Danny into the kitchen, past the fridge where he'd scrawled *Bienvenue Danyal* and then *Welcome Danny* the day Noel's mother brought him back from the response center, savoring the static crackle under his fingertip and the electricity of anticipation.

Danny opened the sink cupboard, looked back at him, and slipped the photo neatly into the garbage. As his new brother walked back out of the kitchen, Noel wanted desperately to hit him, to stop him, to make him understand, but he just stood digging crescents in his palms with the ragged edges of his nails.

He realized that he hated Danny. Danny, who was here because Noel's sister was *not*, who secreted his strange fluids on the concrete floor, who made a low keening screech in the night, who'd shredded Noel's book. Maybe his sister was *not* because Danny was *here*.

As soon as he'd fished Maya's photo out of the trash and put it back in its album, Noel went to his tab. It only took a simple question: *are storks bad*. The nets were inundated with vitriolic conspiracy rants and he read them now, one after another, even though he didn't understand some words. He read how the stork babies secreted a mind-altering pheromone like the ones that bonded pregnant mothers to their newborns.

"There is no pheromone, Noel," his mother told him that night, when he said, voice shaking, that they needed to wear masks around Danny. "Is that what's upset you? It's just a myth."

Noel knew better. Danny was making her forget.

On the screen, an explorer stuck in an ice crevasse takes the pickaxe to his trapped arm. The adults groan or stammer laughs, gesticulating with tumblers of sloshing wine. Noel makes himself watch the axe thwack, the blood trickle and steam, until the man's arm tears away. Then he slides from the couch into his chunky plastic flip-flops, and goes to the kitchen to find a Fanta.

He expects Danny to be there, because Danny doesn't like crowds of people unless their mother is nearby, but the kitchen is empty. A forgotten pot of coagulating spaghetti bubbles on the burner. The lime green radio built into the counter stutters static from the storm. Noel looks to the heavy back door and sees a wash of red sand around it.

Danny is outside. Noel finds a crate of lukewarm Fanta in the corner and tugs one free, replaces it with a handful of francs. He searches slowly for a bottle opener while he thinks of what might happen. Danny's skin is soft. Danny doesn't breathe well in Harmattan season. Stupid of him, to go out in the storm.

Noel knows in his hot angry gut that his mother will blame him if Danny is hurt. He could tell Jean to go look, but Jean would pick him up and bring him back without a flicker of irritation on his face. If Noel finds him alone, he can punish him for being so stupid, so selfish. Nobody will notice bruises among the welts.

Noel has never hit Danny before. The thought of it unsettles his stomach, but he loops it through his head as he sets the Fanta aside, pulls someone's track jacket from the hooks on the wall. By the time he wrestles his way out of the door, a brief shriek of wind that the adults won't notice with the volume up, he thinks he knows how it will feel.

Outside, the dust flies like shrapnel. Noel hides his face in the peaked hood of the jacket and wishes he'd brought his goggles. The transplanted eucalyptus trees are lurching with the wind, near cracking, as he battles his way into the courtyard. Sand peppers his exposed calves and feet like a thousand tiny wasps.

Through the maelstrom, Noel catches a flash of angular silhouette: Danny, hobbling away toward the parking lot, through the archway of thrashing trees. Noel opens his mouth to shout and ends up chewing sand. He pulls the hood tighter and follows Danny, eyes squeezed to slits, fists clenched inside the balled up ends of his sleeves.

By the time he fights his way to the end of the tile and scuttles down the worn steps into the lot, Danny is sitting where they buried the water scorpion. His head is bent against the wind and his overlong arms envelop his knees, compacting him. Waves of dust belt across him, rocking him back and forth.

"What are you doing?" Noel demands, fists still clenched, chest still scalding. The wind scours his words away, but Danny notices him. He looks up with all of his glittering black eyes. Then he reaches into the dirt and pours a handful over his head. The puff of dust is nothing in the storm, but Noel understands. He understands even before Danny's thin distorted voice slides under the windy howl.

"This is you," Danny says, shaking another handful of dust. "Watch this."

Noel's stomach plummets. He reaches for his anger. "Get up," he shouts. "You'll get us in trouble. You'll get me in trouble." He tries to kick at him and loses his flip flop. "Come back inside!" His eyes are stinging from sand and now tears, sliding thick down his grimy cheeks. "Come on," he pleads. He tries to haul Danny up by the shoulder, but his hand's shrugged off.

Noel feels a panic welling inside, panic for Danny's face crumpled purple, for a grave dug with one shovel. "Stay, then," he hollers. "Stay and get sand in your lungs and die."

Danny's head cocks up at the last word. He considers the sand trickling through his fingers. "This is Maya," he says.

Noel doesn't realize he's no longer standing until his kneecaps scrape the dirt. "I'm sorry," he says, crawling forward, face level with Danny's. "Danny. Sorry. It wasn't your fault. It's not your fault." He goes to drape his arms over Danny, but is shoved off. "Come inside," Noel begs.

Danny turns away. Another billow of dust blasts across them; Danny takes the brunt of it and every bit of him wilts. As the wind roars louder, Noel strips off his jacket and pulls it over their heads like a tarp. Danny stiffens, then allows it.

Their breath is hot underneath the nylon. Noel feels his skin press against Danny's clammy back. He feels the puckered marks left by flying sand.

"Not your fault," Noel mutters. The storm dances all around them.

He waits, and waits, for the echo.

Kelly Robson grew up in the foothills of the Canadian Rocky Mountains. In 2018, her story "A Human Stain" won the Nebula Award for Best Novelette, and in 2016, her novella "Waters of Versailles" won the Prix Aurora Award. She has also been a finalist for the Nebula, World Fantasy, Theodore Sturgeon, John W. Campbell, and Sunburst awards. In 2018, her time travel adventure "Gods, Monsters, and the Lucky Peach" debuted to high critical praise. After twenty-two years in Vancouver, she and her wife, fellow SF writer A.M. Dellamonica, now live in downtown Toronto.

The Three Resurrections of Jessica Churchill

KELLY ROBSON

"I rise today on this September 11th, the one-year anniversary of the greatest tragedy on American soil in our history, with a heavy heart . . ."

—Hon. Jim Turner

SEPTEMBER 9, 2001

Jessica slumped against the inside of the truck door. The girl behind the wheel and the other one squished between them on the bench seat kept stealing glances at her. Jessica ignored them, just like she tried to ignore the itchy pull and tug deep inside her, under her belly button, where the aliens were trying to knit her guts back together.

"You party pretty hard last night?" the driver asked.

Jessica rested her burning forehead on the window. The hum of the highway under the wheels buzzed through her skull. The truck cab stank of incense.

"You shouldn't hitchhike, it's not safe," the other girl said. "I sound like my mom saying it and I hate that but it's really true. So many dead girls. They haven't even found all the bodies."

"Highway of Tears," the driver said.

"Yeah, Highway of Tears," the other one repeated. "Bloody Sixteen."

"Nobody calls it that," the driver snapped.

Jessica pulled her hair up off her neck, trying to cool the sticky heat pulsing through her. The two girls looked like tree planters. She'd spent the summer working full time at the gas station and now she could smell a tree planter a mile away. They'd come in for smokes and mix, dirty, hairy, dressed in fleece and hemp just like these two. The driver had blond dreadlocks and the other had tattoos circling her wrists. Not that much older than her, lecturing her about staying safe just like somebody's mom.

Well, she's right, Jessica thought. A gush of blood flooded the crotch of her jeans.

Water. Jessica, we can do this but you've got to get some water. We need to replenish your fluids.

"You got any water?" Jessica asked. Her voice rasped, throat stripped raw from all the screaming.

The tattooed girl dug through the backpack at Jessica's feet and came up with a two-liter mason jar half-full of water. Hippies, Jessica thought as she fumbled with the lid. Like one stupid jar will save the world.

"Let me help." The tattooed girl unscrewed the lid and steadied the heavy jar as Jessica lifted it to her lips.

She gagged. Her throat was tight as a fist but she forced herself to swallow, wash down the dirt and puke coating her mouth.

Good. Drink more.

"I can't," Jessica said. The tattooed girl stared at her.

You need to. We can't do this alone. You have to help us.

"Are you okay?" the driver asked. "You look wrecked."

Jessica wiped her mouth with the back of her hand. "I'm fine. Just hot."

"Yeah, you're really flushed," said the tattooed girl. "You should take off your coat."

Jessica ignored her and gulped at the jar until it was empty.

Not so fast. Careful!

"Do you want to swing past the hospital when we get into town?" the driver asked.

A bolt of pain knifed through Jessica's guts. The empty jar slipped from her grip and rolled across the floor of the truck. The pain faded.

"I'm fine," she repeated. "I just got a bad period."

That did it. The lines of worry eased off both girls' faces.

"Do you have a pad? I'm gonna bleed all over your seat." Jessica's vision dimmed, like someone had put a shade over the morning sun.

"No problem." The tattooed girl fished through the backpack. "I bleed heavy too. It depletes my iron."

"That's just an excuse for you to eat meat," said the driver.

Jessica leaned her forehead on the window and waited for the light to come back into the world. The two girls were bickering now, caught up in their own private drama.

Another flood of blood. More this time. She curled her fists into her lap. Her insides twisted and jumped like a fish on a line.

Your lungs are fine. Breathe deeply, in and out, that's it. We need all the oxygen you can get.

The tattooed girl pulled a pink wrapped maxi pad out of her backpack and offered it to Jessica. The driver slowed down and turned the truck into a roadside campground.

"Hot," Jessica said. The girls didn't hear. Now they were bitching at each other about disposable pads and something called a keeper cup.

We know. You'll be okay. We can heal you.

"Don't wait for me," Jessica said as they pulled up to the campground outhouse. She flipped the door handle and nearly fell out of the truck. "I can catch another ride."

Cold air washed over her as she stumbled toward the outhouse. She unzipped her long coat and let the breeze play though—chill air on boiling skin. Still early September but they always got a cold snap at the start of fall. First snow only a few days ago. Didn't last. Never did.

The outhouse stench hit her like a slap. Jessica fumbled with the lock. Her fingers felt stiff and clumsy.

"Why am I so hot?" she said, leaning on the cold plywood wall. Her voice sounded strange, ripped apart and multiplied into echoes.

Your immune system is trying to fight us but we've got it under control. The fever isn't dangerous, just uncomfortable.

She shed her coat and let it fall to the floor. Unzipped her jeans, slipped them down her hips. No panties. She hadn't been able to find them.

No, Jessica. Don't look.

Pubic hair hacked away along with most of her skin. Two deep slices puckered angry down the inside of her right thigh. And blood. On her legs, on her jeans, inside her coat. Blood everywhere, dark and sticky.

Keep breathing!

An iron tang filled the outhouse as a gout of blood dribbled down her legs. Jessica fell back on the toilet seat. Deep within her chest something fluttered, like a bird beating its wings on her ribs, trying to get out. The light drained from the air.

If you die, we die too. Please give us a chance.

The flutters turned into fists pounding on her breastbone. She struggled to inhale, tried to drag the outhouse stink deep into her lungs but the air felt thick. Solid. Like a wall against her face.

Don't go. Please.

Breath escaped her like smoke from a fire burned down to coal and ash. She collapsed against the wall of the outhouse. Vision turned to pinpricks; she crumpled like paper and died.

E verything okay in there?"

The thumping on the door made the whole outhouse shake. Jessica lurched to her feet. Her chest burned like she'd been breathing acid.

You're okay.

"I'm fine. Gimme a second."

Jessica plucked the pad off the outhouse floor, ripped it open and stuck it on the crotch of her bloody jeans, zipped them up. She zipped her coat to her chin. She felt strong. Invincible. She unlocked the door.

The two girls were right there, eyes big and concerned and in her business.

"You didn't have to wait," Jessica said.

"How old are you, fifteen? We waited," the driver said as they climbed back into the truck.

"We're not going to let you hitchhike," said the tattooed girl. "Especially not you."

"Why not me?" Jessica slammed the truck door behind her.

"Most of the dead and missing girls are First Nations."

"You think I'm an Indian? Fuck you. Am I on a reserve?"

The driver glared at her friend as she turned the truck back onto the highway.

"Sorry," the tattooed girl said.

"Do I look like an Indian?"

"Well, kinda."

"Fuck you." Jessica leaned on the window, watching the highway signs peel by as they rolled toward Prince George. When they got to the city the invincible feeling was long gone. The driver insisted on taking her right to Gran's.

"Thanks," Jessica said as she slid out of the truck.

The driver waved. "Remember, no hitchhiking."

SEPTEMBER 8, 2001

Jessica never hitchhiked.

She wasn't stupid. But Prince George was spread out. Buses ran maybe once an hour weekdays and barely at all on weekends, and when the weather turned cold you could freeze to death trying to walk everywhere. So yeah, she took rides when she could, if she knew the driver.

After her Saturday shift she'd started walking down the highway. Mom didn't know she was coming. Jessica had tried to get through three times from the gas station phone, left voice mails. Mom didn't always pick up—usually didn't—and when she did it was some excuse about her phone battery or connection.

Mom was working as a cook at a retreat center out by Tabor Lake. A two-hour walk, but Mom would get someone to drive her back to Gran's.

Only seven o'clock but getting cold and the wind had come up. Semis bombed down the highway, stirring up the trash and making it dance at her feet and fly in her face as she walked along the ditch.

It wasn't even dark when the car pulled over to the side of the highway. "Are you Jessica?"

The man looked ordinary. Baseball cap, hoodie. Somebody's dad trying to look young.

"Yeah," Jessica said.

"Your mom sent me to pick you up."

A semi honked as it blasted past his car. A McDonald's wrapper flipped through the air and smacked her in the back of the head. She got in.

The car was skunky with pot smoke. She almost didn't notice when he passed the Tabor Lake turnoff.

"That was the turn," she said.

"Yeah, she's not there. She's out at the ski hill."

"At this time of year?"

"Some kind of event." He took a drag on his smoke and smiled.

Jessica hadn't even twigged. Mom had always wanted to work at the ski hill, where she could party all night and ski all day.

It was twenty minutes before Jessica started to clue in.

When he slowed to take a turn onto a gravel road she braced herself to roll out of the car. The door handle was broken. She went at him with her fingernails but he had the jump on her, hit her in the throat with his elbow. She gulped air and tried to roll down the window.

It was broken too. She battered the glass with her fists, then spun and lunged for the wheel. He hit her again, slammed her head against the dashboard three times. The world stuttered and swam.

Pain brought everything back into focus. Face down, her arms flailed, fingers clawed at the dirt. Spruce needles flew up her nose and coated her tongue. Her butt was jacked up over a log and every thrust pounded her face into the dirt. One part of her was screaming, screaming. The other part watched the pile of deer shit inches from her nose. It looked like a heap of candy. Chocolate-covered almonds.

She didn't listen to what he was telling her. She'd heard worse from boys at school. He couldn't make her listen. He didn't exist except as a medium for pain.

When he got off, Jessica felt ripped in half, split like firewood. She tried to roll off the log. She'd crawl into the bush, he'd drive away, and it would be over.

Then he showed her the knife.

When he rammed the knife up her she found a new kind of pain. It drove the breath from her lungs and sliced the struggle from her limbs. She listened to herself whimper, thinking it sounded like a newborn kitten, crying for its mother.

The pain didn't stop until the world had retreated to little flecks of light deep in her skull. The ground spun around her as he dragged her through the bush and rolled her into a ravine. She landed face down in a stream. Her head flopped, neck canted at a weird angle.

Jessica curled her fingers around something cold and round. A rock. It fit in her hand perfectly and if he came back she'd let him have it right in the teeth. And then her breath bubbled away and she died.

When she came back to life a bear corpse was lying beside her, furry and rank. She dug her fingers into its pelt and pulled herself up. It was still warm. And skinny—nothing but sinew and bone under the skin.

She stumbled through the stream, toes in wet socks stubbing against the rocks, but it didn't hurt. Nothing hurt. She was good. She could do anything.

She found her coat in the mud, her jeans too. One sneaker by the bear and then she looked and looked for the other one.

It's up the bank.

She climbed up. The shoe was by the log where it had happened. The toe was coated in blood. She wiped it in the dirt.

You need to drink some water.

A short dirt track led down to the road. The gravel glowed white in the dim light of early morning. No idea which way led to the highway. She picked a direction.

"How do you know what I need?"

We know. We're trying to heal you. The damage is extensive. You've lost a lot of blood and the internal injuries are catastrophic.

"No shit."

We can fix you. We just need time.

Her guts writhed. Snakes fought in her belly, biting and coiling.

Feel that? That's us working. Inside you.

"Why doesn't it hurt?"

We've established a colony in your thalamus. That's where we're blocking the pain. If we didn't, you'd die of shock.

"Again."

Yes, again.

"A colony. What the fuck are you? Aliens?"

Yes. We're also distributing a hormonal cocktail of adrenaline and testosterone to keep you moving, but we'll have to taper it off soon because it puts too much stress on your heart. Right now it's very important for you to drink some water.

"Shut up about the water." She wasn't thirsty. She felt great.

A few minutes later the fight drained out of her. Thirsty, exhausted, she ached as though the hinge of every moving part was crusted in rust, from her jaw to her toes. Her eyelids rasped like sandpaper. Her breath sucked and blew without reaching her lungs. Every rock in the road was a mountain and every pothole a canyon.

But she walked. Dragged her sneakers through the gravel, taking smaller and smaller steps until she just couldn't lift her feet anymore. She stood in the middle of the road and waited. Waited to fall over. Waited for the world to slip from her grasp and darkness to drown her in cold nothing.

When she heard the truck speeding toward her she didn't even look up. Didn't matter who it was, what it was. She stuck out her thumb.

SEPTEMBER 10, 2001

Jessica woke soaked. Covered in blood, she thought, struggling with the blankets. But it wasn't blood.

"What—"

Your urethra was damaged so we eliminated excess fluid through your pores. It's repaired now. You'll be able to urinate.

She pried herself out of the wet blankets.

No solid food, though. Your colon is shredded and your small intestine has multiple ruptures.

When the tree planters dropped her off, Gran had been sacked out on the couch. Jessica had stayed in the shower for a good half hour, watching the blood swirl down the drain with the spruce needles and the dirt, the blood clots and shreds of raw flesh.

And all the while she drank. Opened her mouth and let the cool spray fill her. Then she had stuffed her bloody clothes in a garbage bag and slept.

Jessica ran her fingertips over the gashes inside her thigh. The wounds puckered like wide toothless mouths, sliced edges pasted together and sunk deep within her flesh. The rest of the damage was hardened over with amber-colored scabs. She'd have to use a mirror to see it all. She didn't want to look.

"I should go to the hospital," she whispered.

That's not a good idea. It would take multiple interventions to repair the damage to your digestive tract. They'd never be able to save your uterus or reconstruct your vulva and clitoris. The damage to your cervix alone—

"My what?"

Do you want to have children someday?

"I don't know."

Trust us. We can fix this.

She hated the hospital anyway. Went to Emergency after she'd twisted her knee but the nurse had turned her away, said she wouldn't bother the on-call for something minor. Told her to go home and put a bag of peas on it.

And the cops were even worse than anyone at the hospital. Didn't give a shit. Not one of them.

Gran was on the couch, snoring. A deck of cards was scattered across the coffee table in between the empties—looked like she'd been playing solitaire all weekend.

Gran hadn't fed the cats, either. They had to be starving but they wouldn't come to her, not even when she was filling their dishes. Not even Gringo, who had hogged her bed every night since she was ten. He just hissed and ran.

Usually Jessica would wake up Gran before leaving for school, try to get her on her feet so she didn't sleep all day. Today she didn't have the strength. She shook Gran's shoulder.

"Night night, baby," Gran said, and turned over.

Jessica waited for the school bus. She felt cloudy, dispersed, her thoughts blowing away with the wind. And cold now, without her coat. The fever was gone.

"Could you fix Gran?"

Perhaps. What's wrong with her?

Jessica shrugged. "I don't know. Everything."

We can try. Eventually.

She sleepwalked through her classes. It wasn't a problem. The teachers were more bothered when she did well than when she slacked off. She stayed in the shadows, off everyone's radar.

After school she walked to the gas station. Usually when she got to work she'd buy some chips or a chocolate bar, get whoever was going off shift to ring it up so nobody could say she hadn't paid for it.

"How come I'm not hungry?" she asked when she had the place to herself.

You are; you just can't perceive it.

It was a quiet night. The gas station across the highway had posted a half cent lower so everyone was going there. Usually she'd go stir crazy from boredom but today she just zoned out. Badly photocopied faces stared at her from the posters taped to the cigarette cabinet overhead.

An SUV pulled up to pump number three. A bull elk was strapped to the hood, tongue lolling.

"What was the deal with the bear?" she said.

The bear's den was adjacent to our crash site. It was killed by the concussive wave.

"Crash site. A spaceship?"

Yes. Unfortunate for the bear, but very fortunate for us.

"You brought the bear back to life. Healed it."

Yes.

"And before finding me you were just riding around in the bear."

Yes. It was attracted by the scent of your blood.

"So you saw what happened to me. You watched." She should be upset, shouldn't she? But her mind felt dull, thoughts thudding inside an empty skull.

We have no access to the visual cortex.

"You're blind?"

Yes.

"What are you?"

A form of bacteria.

"Like an infection."

Yes.

The door chimed and the hunter handed over his credit card. She rang it through. When he was gone she opened her mouth to ask another question, but then her gut convulsed like she'd been hit. She doubled over the counter. Bile stung her throat.

He'd been here on Saturday.

Jessica had been on the phone, telling mom's voice mail that she'd walk out to Talbot Lake after work. While she was talking she'd rung up a purchase, $32.25 in gas and a pack of smokes. She'd punched it through automatically, cradling the phone on her shoulder. She'd given him change from fifty.

An ordinary man. Hoodie. Cap.

Jessica, breathe.

Her head whipped around, eyes wild, hands scrambling reflexively for a weapon. Nobody was at the pumps, nobody parked at the air pump. He could come back any moment. Bring his knife and finish the job.

Please breathe. There's no apparent danger.

She fell to her knees and crawled out from behind the counter. Nobody would stop him, nobody would save her. Just like they hadn't saved all those dead and missing girls whose posters had been staring at her all summer from up on the cigarette cabinet.

When she'd started the job they'd creeped her out, those posters. For a few weeks she'd thought twice about walking after dark. But then those dead and missing girls disappeared into the landscape. Forgotten.

You must calm down.

Now she was one of them.

We may not be able to bring you back again.

She scrambled to the bathroom on all fours, threw herself against the door, twisted the lock. Her hands were shuddering, teeth chattering like it was forty below. Her chest squeezed and bucked, throwing acid behind her teeth.

There was a frosted window high on the wall. He could get in, if he wanted. She could almost see the knife tick-tick-ticking on the glass.

No escape. Jessica plowed herself into the narrow gap between the wall and toilet, wedging herself there, fists clutching at her burning chest as she retched bile onto the floor. The light winked and flickered. A scream flushed out of her and she died.

A fist banged on the door.

"Jessica, what the hell!" Her boss's voice.

A key scraped in the lock. Jessica gripped the toilet and wrenched herself off the floor to face him. His face was flushed with anger and though he was a big guy, he couldn't scare her now. She felt bigger, taller, stronger, too. And she'd always been smarter than him.

"Jesus, what's wrong with you?"

"Nothing, I'm fine." Better than fine. She was butterfly-light, like if she opened her wings she could fly away.

"The station's wide open. Anybody could have waltzed in here and walked off with the till."

"Did they?"

His mouth hung open for a second. "Did they what?"

"Walk off with the fucking till?"

"Are you on drugs?"

She smiled. She didn't need him. She could do anything.

"That's it," he said. "You're gone. Don't come back."

A taxi was gassing up at pump number one. She got in the back and waited, watching her boss pace and yell into his phone. The invincible feeling faded before the tank was full. By the time she got home Jessica's joints had locked stiff and her thoughts had turned fuzzy.

All the lights were on. Gran was halfway into her second bottle of u-brew red so she was pretty out of it, too. Jessica sat with her at the kitchen table for a few minutes and was just thinking about crawling to bed when the phone rang.

It was Mom.

"Did you send someone to pick me up on the highway?" Jessica stole a glance at Gran. She was staring at her reflection in the kitchen window, maybe listening, maybe not.

"No, why would I do that?"

"I left you messages. On Saturday."

"I'm sorry, baby. This phone is so bad, you know that."

"Listen, I need to talk to you." Jessica kept her voice low.

"Is it your grandma?" Mom asked.

"Yeah. It's bad. She's not talking."

"She does this every time the residential school thing hits the news. Gets super excited, wants to go up north and see if any of her family are still alive. But she gives up after a couple of days. Shuts down. It's too much for her. She was only six when they took her away, you know."

"Yeah. When are you coming home?"

"I got a line on a great job, cooking for an oil rig crew. One month on, one month off."

Jessica didn't have the strength to argue. All she wanted to do was sleep.

"Don't worry about your Gran," Mom said. "She'll be okay in a week or two. Listen, I got to go."

"I know."

"Night night, baby," Mom said, and hung up.

SEPTEMBER 11, 2001

Jessica waited alone for the school bus. The street was deserted. When the bus pulled up the driver was chattering before she'd even climbed in.

"Can you believe it? Isn't it horrible?" The driver's eyes were puffy, mascara swiped to a gray stain under her eyes.

"Yeah," Jessica agreed automatically.

"When first I saw the news I thought it was so early, nobody would be at work. But it was nine in the morning in New York. Those towers were full of people." The driver wiped her nose.

The bus was nearly empty. Two little kids sat behind the driver, hugging their backpacks. The radio blared. Horror in New York. Attack on Washington. Jessica dropped into the shotgun seat and let the noise wash over her for a few minutes as they twisted slowly through the empty streets. Then she moved to the back of the bus.

When she'd gotten dressed that morning her jeans had nearly slipped off her hips. Something about that was important. She tried to concentrate, but the thoughts flitted from her grasp, darting away before she could pin them down.

She focused on the sensation within her, the buck and heave under her ribs and in front of her spine.

"What are you fixing right now?" she asked.

An ongoing challenge is the sequestration of the fecal and digestive matter that leaked into your abdominal cavity.

"What about the stuff you mentioned yesterday? The intestine and the . . . whatever it was."

Once we have repaired your digestive tract and restored gut motility we will begin reconstructive efforts on your reproductive organs.

"You like big words, don't you?"

We assure you the terminology is accurate.

There it was. That was the thing that had been bothering her, niggling at the back of her mind, trying to break through the fog.

"How do you know those words? How can you even speak English?"

We aren't communicating in language. The meaning is conveyed by socio-linguistic impulses interpreted by the brain's speech-processing loci. Because of the specifics of our biology, verbal communication is an irrelevant medium.

"You're not talking, you're just making me hallucinate," Jessica said.

That is essentially correct.

How could the terminology be accurate, then? She didn't know those words—cervix and whatever—so how could she hallucinate them?

"Were you watching the news when the towers collapsed?" the driver asked as she pulled into the high school parking lot. Jessica ignored her and slowly stepped off the bus.

The aliens were trying to baffle her with big words and science talk. For three days she'd had them inside her, their voice behind her eyes, their fingers deep in her guts, and she'd trusted them. Hadn't even thought twice. She had no choice.

If they could make her hallucinate, what else were they doing to her?

The hallways were quiet, the classrooms deserted except for one room at the end of the hall with 40 kids packed in. The teacher had wheeled in an AV cart. Some of the kids hadn't even taken off their coats.

Jessica stood in the doorway. The news flashed clips of smoking towers collapsing into ash clouds. The bottom third of the screen was overlaid with scrolling, flashing text, the sound layered with frantic voiceovers. People were jumping from the towers, hanging in the air like dancers. The clips replayed over and over again. The teacher passed around a box of Kleenex.

Jessica turned her back on the class and climbed upstairs, joints creaking, jeans threatening to slide off with every step. She hitched them up. The biology lab was empty. She leaned on the cork board and scanned the parasite diagrams. Ring worm. Tape worm. Liver fluke. Black wasp.

Some parasites can change their host's biology, the poster said, or even change their host's behavior.

Jessica took a push pin from the board and shoved it into her thumb. It didn't hurt. When she ripped it out a thin stream of blood trickled from the skin, followed by an ooze of clear amber from deep within the gash.

What are you doing?

None of your business, she thought.

Everything is going to be okay.

No it won't, she thought. She squeezed the amber ooze from her thumb, let it drip on the floor. The aliens were wrenching her around like a puppet, but without them she would be dead. Three times dead. Maybe she should feel grateful, but she didn't.

"Why didn't you want me to go to the hospital?" she asked as she slowly hinged down the stairs.

They couldn't have helped you, Jessica. You would have died.

Again, Jessica thought. Died again. And again.

"You said that if I die, you die too."

When your respiration stops, we can only survive for a limited time.

The mirror in the girls' bathroom wasn't real glass, just a sheet of polished aluminum, its shine pitted and worn. She leaned on the counter, rested her forehead on the cool metal. Her reflection warped and stretched.

"If I'd gone to the hospital, it would have been bad for you. Wouldn't it?"

That is likely.

"So you kept me from going. You kept me from doing a lot of things."

We assure you that is untrue. You may exercise your choices as you see fit. We will not interfere.

"You haven't left me any choices."

Jessica left the bathroom and walked down the hall. The news blared from the teacher's lounge. She looked in. At least a dozen teachers crowded in front of an AV cart, backs turned. Jessica slipped behind them and ducked into the teachers' washroom. She locked the door.

It was like a real bathroom. Air freshener, moisturizing lotion, floral soap. Real mirror on the wall and a makeup mirror propped on the toilet tank. Jessica put it on the floor.

"Since when do bacteria have spaceships?" She pulled her sweater over her head and dropped it over the mirror.

Jessica, you're not making sense. You're confused.

She put her heel on the sweater and stepped down hard. The mirror cracked.

Go to the hospital now, if you want.

"If I take you to the hospital, what will you do? Infect other people? How many?"

Jessica, please. Haven't we helped you?

"You've helped yourself."

The room pitched and flipped. Jessica fell to her knees. She reached for the broken mirror but it swam out of reach. Her vision telescoped and she batted at the glass with clumsy hands. A scream built behind her teeth, swelled and choked her. She swallowed it whole, gulped it, forced it down her throat like she was starving.

You don't have to do this. We aren't a threat.

She caught a mirror shard in one fist and swam along the floor as the room tilted and whirled. With one hand she pinned it to the yawning floor like a spike, windmilled her free arm and slammed her wrist down. The walls folded in, collapsing on her like the whole weight of the world, crushing in.

She felt another scream building. She forced her tongue between clenched teeth and bit down. Amber fluid oozed down her chin and pooled on the floor.

Please. We only want to help.

"Night night, baby," she said, and raked the mirror up her arm.

The fluorescent light flashed overhead. The room plunged into darkness as a world of pain dove into her for one hanging moment. Then it lifted. Jessica convulsed on the floor, watching the bars of light overhead stutter and compress to two tiny glimmers inside the thin parched shell of her skull. And she died, finally, at last.

James Patrick Kelly has won the Hugo, Nebula, and Locus awards; his fiction has been translated into twenty-one languages. His most recent book is the 2018 story collection *The Promise of Space* from Prime Books. His most recent novel was *Mother Go*, published in 2017 as an Audible original audiobook on Audible.com. He writes a column on the internet for *Asimov's Science Fiction Magazine* and is on the faculty of the Stonecoast Creative Writing MFA Program at the University of Southern Maine. Find him on the web at www.jimkelly.net.

Men Are Trouble

JAMES PATRICK KELLY

1.

I stared at my sidekick, willing it to chirp. I'd already tried watching the door, but no one had even breathed on it. I could've been writing up the Rashmi Jones case, but then I could've been dusting the office. It needed dusting. Or having a consult with Johnnie Walker, who had just that morning opened an office in the bottom drawer of my desk. Instead, I decided to open the window. Maybe a new case would arrive by carrier pigeon. Or wrapped around a brick.

Three stories below me, Market Street was as empty as the rest of the city. Just a couple of plain janes in walking shoes and a granny in a blanket and sandals. She was sitting on the curb in front of a dead Starbucks, strumming street guitar for pocket change, hoping to find a philanthropist in hell. Her singing was faint but sweet as peach ice cream. *My guy, talking 'bout my guy*. Poor old bitch, I thought. There are no guys—not yours, not anyone's. She stopped singing as a devil flapped over us, swooping for a landing on the next block. It had been a beautiful June morning until then, the moist promise of spring not yet broken by summer in our withered city. The granny struggled up, leaning on her guitar. She wrapped the blanket tight around her and trudged downtown.

My sidekick did chirp then, but it was Sharifa, my about-to-be ex-lover. She must have been calling from the hospital; she was wearing her light blue scrubs. Even on the little screen, I could see that she had been crying. "Hi, Fay."

I bit my lip.

"Come home tonight," she said. "Please."

"I don't know where home is."

"I'm sorry about what I said." She folded her arms tight across her chest. "It's your body. Your life."

I loved her. I was sick about being seeded, the abortion, everything that had happened between us in the last week. I said nothing.

Her voice was sandpaper on glass. "Have you had it done yet?" That made me angry all over again. She was wound so tight she couldn't even say the word.

"Let me guess, Doctor," I said, "Are we talking about me getting scrubbed?"

Her face twisted. "Don't."

"If you want the dirt," I said, "you could always hire me to shadow myself. I need the work."

"Make it a joke, why don't you?"

"Okey-doke, Doc," I said and clicked off. So my life was cocked—not exactly main menu news. Still, even with the window open, Sharifa's call had sucked all the air out of my office. I told myself that all I needed was coffee, although what I really wanted was a rich aunt, a vacation in Fiji, and a new girlfriend. I locked the door behind me, slogged down the hall and was about to press the down button when the elevator chimed. The doors slid open to reveal George, the bot in charge of our building, and a devil—no doubt the same one that had just flown by. I told myself this had nothing to do with me. The devil was probably seeing crazy Martha down the hall about a tax rebate or taking piano lessons from Abby upstairs. Sure, and drunks go to bars for the peanuts.

"Hello, Fay," said George. "This one had true hopes of finding you in your office."

I goggled, slack-jawed and stupefied, at the devil. Of course, I'd seen them on vids and in the sky and once I watched one waddle into City Hall but I'd never been close enough to slap one before. I hated the devils. The elevator doors shivered and began to close. George stuck an arm out to stop them.

"May this one borrow some of your time?" George said.

The devil was just over a meter tall. Its face was the color of an old bloodstain and its maw seemed to kiss the air as it breathed with a wet, sucking sound. The wings were wrapped tight around it; the membranes had a rusty translucence that only hinted at the sleek bullet of a body beneath. I could see my reflection in its flat compound eyes. I looked like I had just been hit in the head with a lighthouse.

"Something is regrettable, Fay?" said George.

That was my cue for a wisecrack to show them that no invincible mass-murdering alien was going to intimidate Fay Hardaway.

"No," I said. "This way."

If they could've sat in chairs, there would've been plenty of room for us in my office. But George announced that the devil needed to make itself comfortable before we began. I nodded as I settled behind my desk, grateful to have something between the two of them and me. George dragged both chairs out into the little reception room. The devil spread its wings and swooped up onto my file cabinet, ruffling the hardcopy on my desk. It filled the back wall of my office as it perched there, a span of almost twenty feet. George wedged himself into a corner and absorbed his legs and arms until he was just a head and a slab of gleaming blue bot stuff. The devil gazed at me as if it were wondering what kind of rug I would make. I brought up three new icons on my desktop. *New Case. Searchlet. Panic button.*

"Indulge this one to speak for Seeren?" said George. "Seeren has a bright desire to task you to an investigation."

The devils never spoke to us, never explained what they were doing. No one knew exactly how they communicated with the army of bots they had built to prop us up.

I opened the *New Case* folder and the green light blinked. "I'm recording this. If I decide to accept your case, I will record my entire investigation."

"A thoughtful gesture, Fay. This one needs to remark on your client Rashmi Jones."

"She's not my client." It took everything I had not to fall off my chair. "What about her?"

"Seeren conveys vast regret. All deaths diminish all."

I didn't like it that this devil knew anything at all about Rashmi, but especially that she was dead. I'd found the body in Room 103 of the Comfort Inn just twelve hours ago. "The cops already have the case." I didn't mind that there was a snarl in my voice. "Or what's left of it. There's nothing I can do for you."

"A permission, Fay?"

The icon was already flashing on my desktop. I opened it and saw a pix of Rashmi in the sleeveless taupe dress that she had died in. She had the blue ribbon in her hair. She was smiling, as carefree as a kid on the last day of school. The last thing she was thinking about was sucking on an inhaler filled with hydrogen cyanide. Holding her hand was some brunette dressed in a mannish chalk-stripe suit and a matching pillbox hat with a veil as fine as smoke. The couple preened under a garden arch that dripped with pink roses. They faced right, in the direction of the hand of some third party standing just off camera. It was an elegant hand, a hand that had never been in dishwater or changed a diaper. There was a wide silver ring on the fourth finger, engraved with a pattern or maybe some kind of fancy writing. I zoomed on the ring and briefly tormented pixels but couldn't get the pattern resolved.

I looked up at the devil and then at George. "So?"

"This one notices especially the digimark," said George. "Datestamped June 12, 2:52."

"You're saying it was taken yesterday afternoon?"

That didn't fit—except that it did. I had Rashmi downtown shopping for shoes late yesterday morning. At 11:46 she bought a thirteen-dollar pair of this season's Donya Durands and, now missing. At 1:23 she charged eighty-nine cents for a Waldorf salad and an iced tea at Maison Diana. She checked into the Comfort Inn at 6:40. She didn't have a reservation, so maybe this was a spur of the moment decision. The desk clerk remembered her as distraught. That was the word she used. A precise word, although a bit high-brow for the Comfort Inn. Who buys expensive shoes the day she intends to kill herself? Somebody who is distraught. I glanced again at my desktop. Distraught was precisely what Rashmi Jones was not in this pix. Then I noticed the shoes: ice and taupe Donya Durands.

"Where did you get this?" I said to the devil.

It stared through me like I was a dirty window.

I tried the bot. I wouldn't say that I liked George exactly, but he'd always been straight with me. "What's this about, George? Finding the tommy?"

"The tommy?"

"The woman holding Rashmi's hand."

"Seeren has made this one well aware of Kate Vermeil," said George. "Such Kate Vermeil takes work at 44 East Washington Avenue and takes home at 465 12th Avenue, Second Floor Left."

I liked that, I liked it a lot. Rashmi's mom had told me that her daughter had a Christer friend called Kate, but I didn't even have a last name, much less an address. I turned to the devil again. "You know this how?"

All that got me was another empty stare.

"Seeren," I said, pushing back out of my chair, "I'm afraid George has led you astray. I'm the private investigator." I stood to show them out. "The mind reader's office is across the street."

This time George didn't ask permission. My desktop chirped. I waved open a new icon. A certified bank transfer in the amount of a thousand dollars dragged me back onto my chair.

"A cordial inducement," said George. "With a like amount offered after the success of your investigation."

I thought of a thousand dinners in restaurants with linen tablecloths. "Tell me already." A thousand bottles of smoky scotch.

"This one draws attention to the hand of the unseen person," said the bot. "Seeren has the brightest desire to meeting such person for fruitful business discussions."

The job smelled like the dumpster at Fran's Fish Fry. Precious little money changed hands in the pretend economy. The bots kept everything running, but they did nothing to create wealth. That was supposed to be up to us, I guess, only we'd been sort of discouraged. In some parts of town, that kind of change could hire a Felony 1, with a handful of Misdemeanors thrown in for good luck.

"That's more than I'm worth," I said. "A hundred times more. If Seeren expects me to break the arm attached to that hand, it's talking to the wrong jane."

"Violence is to be deplored," said George. "However, Seeren tasks Fay to discretion throughout. Never police, never news, never even rumor if possible."

"Oh, discretion." I accepted the transfer. "For two large, I can be as discreet as the Queen's butler."

2.

I could've taken a cab, but they're almost all driven by bots now, and bots keep nobody's secrets. Besides, even though I had a thousand dollars in the bank, I thought I'd let it settle in for a while. Make itself at home. So I bicycled over to 12th Avenue. I started having doubts as I hit the 400 block. This part of the city had been kicked in the head and left bleeding on the sidewalk. Dark bars leaned against pawnshops. Board-ups turned their blank plywood faces to the street. There would be more bots than women in this neighborhood and more rats than bots.

The Adagio Spa squatted at 465 12th Avenue. It was a brick building with a reinforced luxar display window that was so scratched it looked like a thin slice of rainstorm. There were dusty plants behind it. The second floor windows were bricked over. I chained my bike to a dead car, set my sidekick to record and went in.

The rear wall of the little reception area was bright with pix of some Mediterranean seaside town. A clump of bad pixels made the empty beach flicker. A bot stepped through the door that led to the spa and took up a position at the front desk. "Good afternoon, Madam," he said. "It's most gratifying to welcome you. This one is called . . ."

"I'm looking for Kate Vermeil." I don't waste time on chitchat with bots. "Is she in?"

"It's regrettable that she no longer takes work here."

"She worked here?" I said. "I was told she lived here."

"You was told wrong." A granny filled the door, and then hobbled through, leaning on a metal cane. She was wearing a yellow flowered dress that was not quite as big as a circus tent and over it a blue smock with *Noreen* embroidered over the left breast. Her face was wide and pale as a hardboiled egg, her hair a ferment of tight gray curls. She had the biggest hands I had ever seen. "I'll take care of this, Barry. Go see to Helen Ritzi. She gets another needle at twelve, then turn down the heat to 101."

The bot bowed politely and left us.

"What's this about then?" The cane wobbled and she put a hand on the desk to steady herself.

I dug the sidekick out of my slacks, opened the PI license folder and showed it to her. She read it slowly, sniffed and handed it back. "Young fluffs working at play jobs. Do something useful, why don't you?"

"Like what?" I said. "Giving perms? Face peels?"

She was the woman of steel; sarcasm bounced off her. "If nobody does a real job, pretty soon the damn bots will replace us all."

"Might be an improvement." It was something to say, but as soon as I said it I wished I hadn't. My generation was doing better than the grannies ever had. Maybe someday our kids wouldn't need bots to survive.

Our kids. I swallowed a mouthful of ashes and called the pix Seeren had given me onto the sidekick's screen. "I'm looking for Kate Vermeil." I aimed it at her.

She peered at the pix and then at me. "You need a manicure."

"The hell I do."

"I work for a living, fluff. And my hip hurts if I stand up too long." She pointed her cane at the doorway behind the desk. "What did you say your name was?"

The battered manicure table was in an alcove decorated with fake grape-vines that didn't quite hide the water stains in the drop ceiling. Dust cov-ered the leaves, turning the plastic fruit from purple to gray.

Noreen rubbed a thumb over the tips of my fingers. "You bite your nails, or do you just cut them with a chainsaw?"

She wanted a laugh so I gave her one.

"So, nails square, round, or oval?" Her skin was dry and mottled with liver spots.

"Haven't a clue." I shrugged. "This was your idea."

Noreen perched on an adjustable stool that was cranked low so that her face was only a foot above my hands. There were a stack of stainless steel bowls, a jar of Vaseline, a round box of salt, a bowl filled with packets of sugar sto-len from McDonald's, and a liquid soap dispenser on the table beside her. She started filing each nail from the corner to the center, going from left to right and then back. At first she worked in silence. I decided not to push her.

"Kate was my masseuse up until last week," she said finally. "Gave her notice all of a sudden and left me in the lurch. I've had to pick up all her appointments and me with the bum hip. Some days I can't hardly get out of bed. Something happen to her?"

"Not as far as I know."

"But she's missing."

I shook my head. "I don't know where she is, but that doesn't mean she's missing."

Noreen poured hot water from an electric kettle into one of the stainless steel bowls, added cool water from a pitcher, squirted soap and swirled the mixture around. "You soak for five minutes." She gestured for me to dip my hands into the bowl. "I'll be back. I got to make sure that Barry doesn't burn Helen Ritzi's face off." She stood with a grunt.

"Wait," I said. "Did she say why she was quitting?"

Noreen reached for her cane. "Couldn't stop talking about it. You'd think she was the first ever."

"The first to what?"

The granny laughed. "You're one hell of a detective, fluff. She was sup-posed to get married yesterday. Tell me that pix you're flashing ain't her doing the deed."

She shuffled off, her white nursemate shoes scuffing against dirty lino-leum. From deeper in the spa, I heard her kettle drum voice and then the bot's snare. I was itching to take my sidekick out of my pocket, but I kept my hands in the soak. Besides, I'd looked at the pix enough times to know that she was right. A wedding. The hand with the ring would probably belong to a Christer priest. There would have been a witness and then the photographer, although maybe the photographer was the witness. Of course, I had tumbled to none of this in the two days I'd worked Rashmi Jones's disappearance. I was one hell of a detective, all right. And Rashmi's mom must not have known either. It didn't make sense that she would hire me to find her daughter and hold something like that back.

"I swear," said Noreen, leaning heavily on the cane as she creaked back to me, "that bot is scary. I sent down to City Hall for it just last week and already it knows my business left, right, up, and down. The thing is, if they're so smart, how come they talk funny?"

"The devils designed them to drive us crazy."

"They didn't need no bots to do that, fluff."

She settled back onto her stool, tore open five sugar packets and emptied their contents onto her palm. Then she reached for the salt box and poured salt onto the sugar. She squirted soap onto the pile and then rubbed her hands together. "I could buy some fancy exfoliating cream but this works just as good." She pointed with her chin at my hands. "Give them a shake and bring them here."

I wanted to ask her about Kate's marriage plans, but when she took my hands in hers, I forgot the question. I'd never felt anything quite like it; the irritating scratch of the grit was offset by the sensual slide of our soapy fingers. Pleasure with just the right touch of pain—something I'd certainly be telling Sharifa about, if Sharifa and I were talking. My hands tingled for almost an hour afterward.

Noreen poured another bowl of water and I rinsed. "Why would getting married make Kate want to quit?" I asked.

"I don't know. Something to do with her church?" Noreen patted me dry with a threadbare towel. "She went over to the Christers last year. Maybe Jesus don't like married women giving backrubs. Or maybe she got seeded." She gave a bitter laugh. "Everybody does eventually."

I let that pass. "Tell me about Kate. What was she like to work with?"

"Average for the kind of help you get these sorry days." Noreen pushed at my cuticles with an orangewood stick. "Showed up on time mostly; I could only afford to bring her in two days a week. No go-getter, but she could follow directions. Problem was she never really got close to the customers, always acting like this was just a pitstop. Kept to herself mostly, which was how I could tell she was excited about getting married. It wasn't like her to babble."

"And the bride?"

"Some Indian fluff—Rashy or something."

"Rashmi Jones."

She nodded. "Her I never met."

"Did she go to school?"

"Must have done high school, but damned if I know where. Didn't make much of an impression, I'd say. College, no way." She opened a drawer where a flock of colored vials was nesting. "You want polish or clear coat on the nails?"

"No color. It's bad for business."

She leered at me. "Business is good?"

"You say she did massage for you?" I said. "Where did she pick that up?"

"Hold still now." Noreen uncapped the vial; the milky liquid that clung to the brush smelled like super glue's evil twin. "This is fast dry." She painted the stuff onto my nails with short, confident strokes. "Kate claimed her mom taught her. Said she used to work at the health club at the Radisson before it closed down."

"Did the mom have a name?"

"Yeah." Noreen chewed her lower lip as she worked. "Mom. Give the other hand."

I extended my arm. "So if Kate didn't live here, where she did live?"

"Someplace. Was on her application." She kept her head down until she'd finished. "You're done. Wave them around a little—that's it."

After a moment, I let my arms drop to my side. We stared at each other. Then Noreen heaved herself off the stool and led me back out to the reception room.

"That'll be eighty cents for the manicure, fluff." She waved her desktop on. "You planning on leaving a tip?"

I pulled out the sidekick and beamed two dollars at the desk. Noreen opened the payment icon, grunted her approval and then opened another folder. "Says here she lives at 44 East Washington Avenue."

I groaned.

"Something wrong?"

"I already have that address."

"Got her call too? Kate@Washington.03284."

"No, that's good. Thanks." I went to the door and paused. I don't know why I needed to say anything else to her, but I did. "I help people, Noreen. Or at least I try. It's a real job, something bots can't do."

She just stood there, kneading the bad hip with a big, dry hand.

I unchained my bike, pedaled around the block, and then pulled over. I read Kate Vermeil's call into my sidekick. Her sidekick picked up on the sixth chirp. There was no pix.

"You haven't reached Kate yet, but your luck might change if you leave a message at the beep." She put on the kind of low, smoky voice that doesn't come out to play until dark. It was a nice act.

"Hi Kate," I said. "My name is Fay Hardaway and I'm a friend of Rashmi Jones. She asked me to give you a message about yesterday so please give me a call at Fay@Market.03284." I wasn't really expecting her to respond, but it didn't hurt to try.

I was on my way to 44 East Washington Avenue when my sidekick chirped in the pocket of my slacks. I picked up. Rashmi Jones's mom, Najma, stared at me from the screen with eyes as deep as wells.

"The police came," she said. "They said you were supposed to notify them first. They want to speak to you again."

They would. So I'd called the law after I called the mom—they'd get over it. You don't tell a mother that her daughter is dead and then ask her to act surprised when the cops come knocking. "I was working for you, not them."

"I want to see you."

"I understand."

"I hired you to find my daughter."

"I did," I said. "Twice." I was sorry as soon as I said it.

She glanced away; I could hear squeaky voices in the background. "I want to know everything," she said. "I want to know how close you came."

"I've started a report. Let me finish it and I'll bring it by later . . ."

"Now," she said. "I'm at school. My lunch starts at eleven-fifty and I have recess duty at twelve-fifteen." She clicked off.

I had nothing to feel guilty about, so why was I tempted to wriggle down a storm drain and find the deepest sewer in town? Because a mom believed that I hadn't worked fast enough or smart enough to save her daughter? Someone needed to remind these people that I didn't fix lost things, I just found them. But that someone wouldn't be me. My play now was simply to stroll into her school and let her beat me about the head with her grief. I could take it. I ate old Bogart movies for breakfast and spit out bullets. And at the end of this cocked day, I could just forget about Najma Jones, because there would be no Sharifa reminding me how much it cost me to do my job. I took out my sidekick, linked to my desktop and downloaded everything I had in the Jones file. Then I swung back onto my bike.

The mom had left a message three days ago, asking that I come out to her place on Ashbury. She and her daughter rattled around in an old Victorian with gingerbread gables and a front porch the size of Cuba. The place had been in the family for four generations. Theirs had been a big family—once. The mom said that Rashmi hadn't come home the previous night. She hadn't called and didn't answer messages. The mom had contacted the cops, but they weren't all that interested. Not enough time would have passed for them. Too much time had passed for the mom.

The mom taught fifth grade at Reagan Elementary. Rashmi was a twenty-six year-old-grad student, six credits away from an MFA in Creative Writing. The mom trusted her to draw money from the family account, so at first I thought I might be able to find her by chasing debits. But there was no activity in the account we could attribute to the missing girl. When I suggested that she might be hiding out with friends, the mom went prickly on me. Turned out that Rashmi's choice of friends was a cause of contention between them. Rashmi had dropped her old pals in the last few months and taken up with a new, religious crowd. Alix, Gratiana, Elaine, and Kate—the mom didn't know their last names—were members of the Church of Christ the Man. I'd had trouble with Christers before and wasn't all that eager to go up against them again, so instead I biked over to campus to see Rashmi's advisor. Zelda Manotti was a dithering old granny who would have loved to help except she had all the focus of paint spatter. She did let me copy Rashmi's novel-in-progress. And she did let me tag along to her advanced writing seminar, in case Rashmi showed up for it. She didn't. I talked to the three other students after class, but they either didn't know where she was or wouldn't say. None of them was Gratiana, Alix, or Elaine.

That night I skimmed *The Lost Heart*, Rashmi's novel. It was a nostalgic and sentimental weeper set back before the devils disappeared all the men. Young Brigit Bird was searching for her father, a famous architect who had been kidnapped by Colombian drug lords. If I was just a fluff doing a fantasy job in the pretend economy, then old Noreen would have crowned Rashmi Jones queen of fluffs.

I'd started day two back at the Joneses' home. The mom watched as I went through Rashmi's room. I think she was as worried about what I might find as she was that I would find nothing. Rashmi listened to the Creeps, had three different pairs of Kat sandals, owned everything Denise Pepper had ever written, preferred underwire bras and subscribed to *News for the Confused*. She had kicked about a week's worth of dirty clothes under her bed. Her wallpaper mix cycled through koalas, the World's Greatest Beaches, ruined castles, and *Playgirl* Centerfolds 2000–2010. She'd kept a handwritten diary starting in the sixth grade and ending in the eighth in which she often complained that her mother was strict and that school was boring. The only thing I found that rattled the mom was a Christer Bible tucked into the back of the bottom drawer of the nightstand. When I pulled it out, she flushed and stalked out of the room.

I found my lead on the Joneses' home network. Rashmi was not particularly diligent about backing up her sidekick files, and the last one I found was almost six months old, which was just about when she'd gotten religion. She'd used simple encryption, which wouldn't withstand a serious hack, but which would discourage the mom from snooping. I doglegged a key and opened the file. She had multiple calls. Her mother had been trying her at Rashmi@Ashbury.03284. But she also had an alternate: Brigitbird@Vincent.03284. I did a reverse lookup and that turned an address: The Church of Christ the Man, 348 Vincent Avenue. I wasn't keen for a personal visit to the church, so I tried her call.

"Hello," said a voice.

"Is this Rashmi Jones?"

The voice hesitated. "My name is Brigit. Leave me alone."

"Your mother is worried about you, Rashmi. She hired me to find you."

"I don't want to be found."

"I'm reading your novel, Rashmi." It was just something to say; I wanted to keep her on the line. "I was wondering, does she find her father at the end?"

"No." I could hear her breath caressing the microphone. "The devils come. That's the whole point."

Someone said something to her and she muted the speaker. But I knew she could still hear me. "That's sad, Rashmi. But I guess that's the way it had to be."

Then she hung up.

The mom was relieved that Rashmi was all right, furious that she was with Christers. So what? I'd found the girl: case closed. Only Najma Jones begged me to help her connect with her daughter. She was already into me for twenty bucks plus expenses, but for another five I said I'd try to get her away from the church long enough for them to talk. I was on my way over when the searchlet I'd attached to the Jones account turned up the hit at Grayle's Shoes. I was grateful for the reprieve, even more pleased when the salesbot identified Rashmi from her pix. As did the waitress at Maison Diana.

And the clerk at the Comfort Inn.

3.

Ronald Reagan Elementary had been recently renovated, no doubt by a squad of janitor bots. The brick facade had been cleaned and repointed; the long row of windows gleamed like teeth. The asphalt playground had been ripped up and resurfaced with safe-t-mat, the metal swingsets swapped for gaudy towers and crawl tubes and slides and balance beams and decks. The chain link fences had been replaced by redwood lattice through which twined honeysuckle and clematis. There was a boxwood maze next to the swimming pool that shimmered, blue as a dream. Nothing was too good for the little girls—our hope for the future.

There was no room in the rack jammed with bikes and scooters and goboards, so I leaned my bike against a nearby cherry tree. The very youngest girls had come out for first recess. I paused behind the tree for a moment to let their whoops and shrieks and laughter bubble over me. My business didn't take me to schools very often; I couldn't remember when I had last seen so many girls in one place. They were black and white and yellow and brown, mostly dressed like janes you might see anywhere. But there were more than a few whose clothes proclaimed their mothers' life-styles. Tommys in hunter camo and chaste Christers, twists in chains and spray-on, clumps of sisters wearing the uniforms of a group marriage, a couple of furries and one girl wearing a body suit that looked just like bot skin. As I lingered there, I felt a chill that had nothing to do with the shade of a tree. I had no idea who these tiny creatures were. They went to this well-kept school, led more or less normal lives. I grew up in the wild times, when everything was falling apart. At that moment, I realized that they were as far removed from me as I was from the grannies. I would always watch them from a distance.

Just inside the fence, two sisters in green-striped shirtwaists and green knee socks were turning a rope for a ponytailed jumper who was executing nimble criss-crosses. The turners chanted,

Down in the valley where the green grass grows,
there sits Stacy pretty as a rose! She sings, she sings, she sings so sweet,
Then along comes Chantall to kiss her on the cheek!

Another jumper joined her in the middle, matching her step for step, her dark hair flying. The chant continued,

How many kisses does she get?

One, two, three, four, five . . .

The two jumpers pecked at each other in the air to the count of ten without missing a beat. Then Ponytail skipped out and the turners began the chant over again for the dark-haired girl. Ponytail bent over for a moment to catch her breath; when she straightened, she noticed me.

"Hey you, behind the tree." She shaded her eyes with a hand. "You hiding?"

I stepped into the open. "No."

"This is our school, you know." The girl set one foot behind the other and then spun a hundred and eighty degrees to point at the door to the school. "You supposed to sign in at the office."

"I'd better take care of that then."

As I passed through the gate into the playground, a few of the girls stopped playing and stared. This was all the audience Ponytail needed. "You someone's mom?"

"No."

"Don't you have a job?" She fell into step beside me.

"I do."

"What is it?"

"I can't tell you."

She dashed ahead to block my path. "Probably because it's a pretend job."

Two of her sisters in green-striped shirtwaists scrambled to back her up.

"When we grow up," one of them announced, "we're going to have real jobs."

"Like a doctor," the other said. "Or a lion tamer."

Other girls were joining us. "I want to drive a truck," said a tommy. "Big, big truck." She specified the size of her rig with outstretched arms.

"That's not a real job. Any bot could do that."

"I want to be a teacher," said the dark-haired sister who had been jumping rope.

"Chantall loves school," said a furry. "She'd marry school if she could." Apparently this passed for brilliant wit in the third grade; some girls laughed so hard they had to cover their mouths with the backs of their hands. Me, I was flummoxed. Give me a spurned lover or a mean drunk or a hardcase cop and I could figure out some play, but just then I was trapped by this giggling mob of children.

"So why you here?" Ponytail put her fists on her hips.

A jane in khakis and a baggy plum sweater emerged from behind a blue tunnel that looked like a centipede. She pinned me with that penetrating but not unkind stare that teachers are born with, and began to trudge across the playground toward me. "I've come to see Ms. Jones," I said.

"Oh." A shadow passed over Ponytail's face and she rubbed her hands against the sides of her legs. "You better go then."

Someone called, "Are you the undertaker?"

A voice that squeaked with innocence asked, "What's an undertaker?"

I didn't hear the answer. The teacher in the plum sweater rescued me and we passed through the crowd.

I didn't understand why Najma Jones had come to school. She was either the most dedicated teacher on the planet or she was too numb to accept her daughter's death. I couldn't tell which. She had been reserved when we met the first time; now she was locked down and welded shut. She was a bird of a woman with a narrow face and thin lips. Her gray hair had a few lingering strands of black. She wore a long-sleeved white kameez tunic over shalwar trousers. I leaned against the door of her classroom and told her everything I had done the day before. She sat listening at her desk with a sandwich that she wasn't going to eat and a carton of milk that she wasn't going to drink and a napkin that she didn't need.

When I had finished, she asked me about cyanide inhalers.

"Hydrogen cyanide isn't hard to get in bulk," I said. "They use it for making plastic, engraving, tempering steel. The inhaler came from one of the underground suicide groups, probably Our Choice. The cops could tell you for sure."

She unfolded the napkin and spread it out on top of her desk. "I've heard it's a painful death."

"Not at all," I said. "They used to use hydrogen cyanide gas to execute criminals, back in the bad old days. It all depends on the first breath. Get it deep into your lungs and you're unconscious before you hit the floor. Dead in less than a minute."

"And if you don't get a large enough dose?"

"Ms. Jones . . ."

She cut me off hard. "If you don't?"

"Then it takes longer, but you still die. There are convulsions. The skin flushes and turns purple. Eyes bulge. They say it's something like having a heart attack."

"Rashmi?" She laid her daughter's name down gently, as if she were tucking it into bed. "How did she die?"

Had the cops shown her the crime scene pictures? I decided they hadn't. "I don't think she suffered," I said.

She tore a long strip off the napkin. "You don't think I'm a very good mother, do you?"

I don't know exactly what I expected her to say, but this wasn't it. "Ms. Jones, I don't know much about you and your daughter. But I do know that you cared enough about her to hire me. I'm sorry I let you down."

She shook her head wearily, as if I had just flunked the pop quiz. One third does not equal .033 and Los Angeles has never been the capital of California. "Is there anything else I should know?" she said.

"There is." I had to tell her what I'd found out that morning, but I wasn't going to tell her that I was working for a devil. "You mentioned before that Rashmi had a friend named Kate."

"The Christer?" She tore another strip off the napkin.

I nodded. "Her name is Kate Vermeil. I don't know this for sure yet, but there's reason to believe that Rashmi and Kate were married yesterday. Does that make any sense to you?"

"Maybe yesterday it might have." Her voice was flat. "It doesn't anymore."

I could hear stirring in the next classroom. Chairs scraped against linoleum. Girls were jabbering at each other.

"I know Rashmi became a Christer," she said. "It's a broken religion. But then everything is broken, isn't it? My daughter and I . . . I don't think we ever understood each other. We were strangers at the end." The napkin was in shreds. "How old were you when it happened?"

"I wasn't born yet." She didn't have to explain what it was. "I'm not as old as I look."

"I was nineteen. I remember men, my father, my uncles. And the boys. I actually slept with one." She gave me a bleak smile. "Does that shock you, Ms. Hardaway?"

I hated it when grannies talked about having sex, but I just shook my head.

"I didn't love Sunil, but I said I'd marry him just so I could get out of my mother's house. Maybe that was what was happening with Rashmi and this Kate person?"

"I wouldn't know."

The school bell rang.

"I'm wearing white today, Ms. Hardaway, to honor my darling daughter." She gathered up the strips of napkin and the sandwich and the carton of milk and dropped them in the trashcan. "White is the Hindu color of mourning. But it's also the color of knowledge. The goddess of learning,

Saraswati, is always shown wearing a white dress, sitting on a white lotus. There is something here I must learn." She fingered the gold embroidery at the neckline of her kameez. "But it's time for recess."

We walked to the door. "What will you do now?" She opened it. The fifth grade swarmed the hall, girls rummaging through their lockers.

"Find Kate Vermeil," I said.

She nodded. "Tell her I'm sorry."

4.

I tried Kate's call again, but when all I got was the sidekick I biked across town to 44 East Washington Avenue. The Poison Society turned out to be a jump joint; the sign said it opened at nine P.M. There was no bell on the front door, but I knocked hard enough to wake Marilyn Monroe. No answer. I went around to the back and tried again. If Kate was in there, she wasn't entertaining visitors.

A sidekick search turned up an open McDonald's on Wallingford, a ten-minute ride. The only other customers were a couple of twists with bound breasts and identical acid-green vinyl masks. One of them crouched on the floor beside the other, begging for chicken nuggets. A bot took my order for the twenty-nine-cent combo meal—it was all bots behind the counter. By law, there was supposed to be a human running the place, but if she was on the premises, she was nowhere to be seen. I thought about calling City Hall to complain, but the egg rolls arrived crispy and the McLatte was nicely scalded. Besides, I didn't need to watch the cops haul the poor jane in charge out of whatever hole she had fallen into.

A couple of hardcase tommys in army surplus fatigues had strutted in just after me. They ate with their heads bowed over their plastic trays so the fries didn't have too far to travel. Their collapsible titanium nightsticks lay on the table in plain sight. One of them was not quite as wide as a bus. The other was nothing special, except that when I glanced up from my sidekick, she was giving me a freeze-dried stare. I waggled my shiny fingernails at her and screwed my cutest smile onto my face. She scowled, said something to her partner and went back to the trough.

My sidekick chirped. It was my pal Julie Epstein, who worked Self-Endangerment/Missing Persons out of the second precinct.

"You busy, Fay?"

"Yeah, the Queen of Cleveland just lost her glass slipper and I'm on the case."

"Well, I'm about to roll through your neighborhood. Want to do lunch?"

I aimed the sidekick at the empties on my table. "Just finishing."

"Where are you?"

"McD's on Wallingford."

"Yeah? How are the ribs?"

"Couldn't say. But the egg rolls are triple dee."

"That the place where the owner is a junkliner? We've had complaints. Bots run everything?"

"No, I can see her now. She's shortchanging some beat cop."

She gave me the laugh. "Got the coroner's on the Rashmi Jones. Cyanide-induced hypoxia."

"You didn't by any chance show the mom pix of the scene?"

"Hell no. Talk about cruel and unusual." She frowned. "Why?"

"I was just with her. She seemed like maybe she suspected her kid wrestled with the reaper."

"We didn't tell her. By the way, we don't really care if you call your client, but next time how about trying us first?"

"That's cop law. Me, I follow PI law."

"Where did you steal that line from, *Chinatown*?"

"It's got better dialogue than *Dragnet*." I swirled the last of my latte in the cup. "You calling a motive on the Rashmi Jones?"

"Not yet. What do you like?" She ticked off the fingers of her left hand. "Family? School? Money? Broke a fingernail? Cloudy day?"

"Pregnancy? Just a hunch."

"You think she was seeded? We'll check that. But that's no reason to kill yourself."

"They've all got reasons. Only none of them makes sense."

She frowned. "Hey, don't get all invested on me here."

"Tell me, Julie, do you think I'm doing a pretend job?"

"Whoa, Fay." Her chuckle had a sharp edge. "Maybe it's time you and Sharifa took a vacation."

"Yeah." I let that pass. "It's just that some granny called me a fluff."

"Grannies." She snorted in disgust. "Well, you're no cop, that's for sure. But we do appreciate the help. Yeah, I'd say what you do is real. As real as anything in this cocked world."

"Thanks, flatfoot. Now that you've made things all better, I'll just click off. My latte is getting cold and you're missing so damn many persons."

"Think about that vacation, shamus. Bye."

As I put my sidekick away, I realized that the tommys were waiting for me. They'd been rattling ice in their cups and folding McWrappers for the past ten minutes. I probably didn't need their brand of trouble. The smart move would be to bolt for the door and leave my bike for now; I could lose them on foot. But then I hadn't made a smart move since April. The big one was talking into her sidekick when I sauntered over to them.

"What can I do for you ladies?" I said.

The big one pocketed the sidekick. Her partner started to come out of her seat but the big one stretched an arm like a telephone pole to restrain her.

"Do we know you?" The partner had close-set eyes and a beak nose; her black hair was short and stiff as a brush. She was wearing a black tee under her fatigue jacket and black leather combat boots. Probably had steel toes. "No," she continued, "I don't think we do."

"Then let's get introductions out of the way," I said. "I'm Fay Hardaway. And you are . . . ?"

They gave me less than nothing.

I sat down. "Thanks," I said. "Don't mind if I do."

The big one leaned back in her chair and eyed me as if I was dessert. "Sure you're not making a mistake, missy?"

"Why, because you're rough, tough, and take no guff?"

"You're funny." She smirked. "I like that. People who meet us are usually so very sad. My name is Alix." She held out her hand and we shook. "Pleased to know you."

The customary way to shake hands is to hold on for four, maybe five seconds, squeeze good-bye, then loosen the grip. Maybe big Alix wasn't familiar with our customs—she wasn't letting go.

I wasn't going to let a little thing like a missing hand intimidate me. "Oh, then I do know you," I said. We were in the McDonald's on Wallingford Street—a public place. I'd just been talking to my pal the cop. I was so damn sure that I was safe, I decided to take my shot. "That would make the girlfriend here Elaine. Or is it Gratiana?"

"Alix." The beak panicked. "Now we've got to take her."

Alix sighed, then yanked on my arm. She might have been pulling a tissue from a box for all the effort she expended. I slid halfway across the table as the beak whipped her nightstick to full extension. I lunged away from her and she caught me just a glancing blow above the ear but then Alix stuck a popper into my face and spattered me with knockout spray. I saw a billion stars and breathed the vacuum of deep space for maybe two seconds before everything went black.

B ig Ben chimed between my ears. I could feel it deep in my molars, in
the jelly of my eyes. It was the first thing I had felt since World War
II. Wait a minute, was I alive during World War II? No, but I had seen
the movie. When I wiggled my toes, Big Ben chimed again. I realized that
the reason it hurt so much was that the human head didn't really contain
enough space to hang a bell of that size. As I took inventory of body parts,
the chiming became less intense. By the time I knew I was all there, it was
just the sting of blood in my veins.

I was laid out on a surface that was hard but not cold. Wood. A bench.
The place I was in was huge and dim but not dark. The high ceiling was
in shadow. There was a hint of smoke in the air. Lights flickered. Candles.
That was a clue, but I was still too groggy to understand what the mystery
was. I knew I needed to remember something, but there was a hole where
the memory was supposed to be. I reached back and touched just above my
ear. The tip of my finger came away dark and sticky.

A voice solved the mystery for me. "I'm sorry that my people overre-
acted. If you want to press charges, I've instructed Gratiana and Alix to
surrender to the police."

It came back to me then. It always does. McDonald's. Big Alix. A long
handshake. That would make this a church. I sat up. When the world
stopped spinning, I saw a vast marble altar awash in light with a crucifix
the size of a Cessna hanging behind it.

"I hope you're not in too much pain, Miss Hardaway." The voice came
from the pew behind me. A fortyish woman in a black suit and a Roman
collar was on the kneeler. She was wearing a large silver ring on the fourth
finger of her left hand.

"I've felt worse."

"That's too bad. Do you make a habit of getting into trouble?" She
looked concerned that I might be making some bad life choices. She had
soft eyes and a kindly face. Her short hair was the color of ashes. She was
someone I could tell my guilty secrets to, so I could sleep at night. She
would speak to Christ the Man himself on my behalf, book me into the
penthouse suite in heaven.

"Am I in trouble?"

She nodded gravely. "We all are. The devils are destroying us, Miss
Hardaway. They plant their seed not only in our bodies, but our minds and
our souls."

"Please, call me Fay. I'm sure we're going to be just the very best of
friends." I leaned toward her. "I'm sorry, I can't read your name tag."

"I'm not wearing one." She smiled. "I'm Father Elaine Horváth."

We looked at each other.

"Have you ever considered suicide, Fay?" said Father Elaine.

"Not really. It's usually a bad career move."

"Very good. But you must know that since the devils came and changed everything, almost a billion women have despaired and taken their lives."

"You know, I think I did hear something about that. Come on, lady, what's this about?"

"It is the tragedy of our times that there are any number of good reasons to kill oneself. It takes courage to go on living with the world the way it is. Rashmi Jones was a troubled young woman. She lacked that courage. That doesn't make her a bad person, just a dead one."

I patted my pocket, looking for my sidekick. Still there. I pulled it out and pressed *record*. I didn't ask for permission. "So I should mind my own business?"

"That would be a bad career move in your profession. How old are you, Fay?"

"Thirty-three."

"Then you were born of a virgin." She leaned back, slid off the kneeler and onto the pew. "Seeded by the devils. I'm old enough to have had a father, Fay. I actually remember him a little. A very little."

"Don't start." I spun out of the pew into the aisle. I hated cock nostalgia. This granny had me chewing aluminum foil; I would have spat it at Christ himself if he had dared come down off his cross. "You want to know one reason why my generation jumps out of windows and sucks on cyanide? It's because twists like you make us feel guilty about how we came to be. You want to call me devil's spawn, go ahead. Enjoy yourself. Live it up. Because we're just waiting for you old bitches to die off. Someday this foolish church is going to dry up and blow away and you know what? We'll go dancing that night, because we'll be a hell of a lot happier without you to remind us of what you lost and who we can never be."

She seemed perversely pleased by my show of emotion. "You're an angry woman, Fay."

"Yeah," I said, "but I'm kind to children and small animals."

"What is that anger doing to your soul? Many young people find solace in Christ."

"Like Alix and Gratiana?"

She folded her hands; the silver ring shone dully. "As I said, they have offered to turn themselves . . ."

"Keep them. I'm done with them." I was cooling off fast. I paused, considering my next move. Then I sat down on the pew next to Father Elaine, showed her my sidekick and made sure she saw me pause the recording. Our eyes met. We understood each other. "Did you marry Kate Vermeil and Rashmi Jones yesterday?"

She didn't hesitate. "I performed the ceremony. I never filed the documents."

"Do you know why Rashmi killed herself?"

"Not exactly." She held my gaze. "I understand she left a note."

"Yeah, the note. I found it on her sidekick. She wrote, 'Life is too hard to handle and I can't handle it so I've got to go now. I love you Mom, sorry.' A little generic for a would-be writer, wouldn't you say? And the thing is there's nothing in the note about Kate. I didn't even know she existed until this morning. Now I have a problem with that. The cops would have the same problem if I gave it to them."

"But you haven't."

"Not yet."

She thought about that for a while.

"My understanding," said Father Elaine at last, "is that Kate and Rashmi had a disagreement shortly after the ceremony." She was tiptoeing around words as if one of them might wake up and start screaming. "I don't know exactly what it was about. Rashmi left, Kate stayed here. Someone was with her all yesterday afternoon and all last night."

"Because you thought she might need an alibi?"

She let that pass. "Kate was upset when she heard the news. She blames herself, although I am certain she is without blame."

"She's here now?"

"No." Father Elaine shrugged. "I sent her away when I learned you were looking for her."

"And you want me to stop."

"You are being needlessly cruel, you know. The poor girl is grieving."

"Another poor girl is dead." I reached into my pocket for my penlight. "Can I see your ring?"

That puzzled her. She extended her left hand and I shone the light on it. Her skin was freckled but soft, the nails flawless. She would not be getting them done at a dump like the Adagio Spa.

"What do these letters mean?" I asked. "IHS?"

"*In hoc signo vinces.* 'In this sign you will conquer.' The emperor Constantine had a vision of a cross in the sky with those words written in fire on it. This was just before a major battle. He had his soldiers paint the cross on their shields and then he won the day against a superior force."

"Cute." I snapped the light off. "What's it mean to you?"

"The Bride of God herself gave this to me." Her face lit up, as if she were listening to an angelic chorus chant her name. "In recognition of my special vocation. You see, Fay, our Church has no intention of drying up and blowing away. Long after my generation is gone, believers will continue to gather in Christ's name. And someday they'll finish the work we have begun. Someday they will exorcise the devils."

If she knew how loopy that sounded, she didn't show it. "Okay, here's the way it is," I said. "Forget Kate Vermeil. I only wanted to find her so she could lead me to you. A devil named Seeren hired me to look for a certain party wearing a ring like yours. It wants a meeting."

"With me?" Father Elaine went pale. "What for?"

"I just find them." I enjoyed watching her squirm. "I don't ask why."

She folded her hands as if to pray, then leaned her head against them and closed her eyes. She sat like that for almost a minute. I decided to let her brood, not that I had much choice. The fiery pit of hell could've opened up and she wouldn't have noticed.

Finally, she shivered and sat up. "I have to find out how much they know." She gazed up at the enormous crucifix. "I'll see this devil, but on one condition: you guarantee my safety."

"Sure." I couldn't help myself; I laughed. The sound echoed, profaning the silence. "Just how am I supposed to do that? They disappeared half the population of Earth without breaking a sweat."

"You have their confidence," she said. "And mine."

A vast and absurd peace had settled over her; she was seeing the world through the gauze of faith. She was a fool if she thought I could go up against the devils. Maybe she believed Christ the Man would swoop down from heaven to protect her, but then he hadn't been seen around the old neighborhood much of late. Or maybe she had projected herself into the mind of the martyrs who would embrace the sword, kiss the ax that would take their heads. I reminded myself that her delusions were none of my business.

Besides, I needed the money. And suddenly I just had to get out of that big, empty church.

"My office is at 35 Market," I said. "Third floor. I'll try to set something up for six tonight." I stood. "Look, if they want to take you, you're probably gone. But I'll record everything and squawk as loud as I can."

"I believe you will," she said, her face aglow.

5.

I didn't go to my office after I locked my bike to the rack on Market Street. Instead I went to find George. He was stripping varnish from the bead-board wainscoting in Donna Belasco's old office on the fifth floor. Donna's office had been vacant since last fall, when she had closed her law practice and gone south to count waves at Daytona Beach. At least, that's what I hoped she was doing; the last I'd heard from her was a Christmas card. I missed Donna; she was one of the few grannies who tried to understand what it was like to grow up the way we did. And she had been generous about steering work my way.

"Hey George," I said. "You can tell your boss that I found the ring."

"This one offers the congratulations." The arm holding the brush froze over the can of stripper as he swiveled his head to face me. "You have proved true superiority, Fay." George had done a good job maintaining our building since coming to us a year ago, although he had something against wood grain. We had to stop him from painting over the mahogany paneling in the foyer.

I hated to close the door, but this conversation needed some privacy. "So I've set up a meeting." The stink of the varnish stripper was barbed wire up my nose. "Father Elaine Horváth will be here at six."

George said nothing. Trying to read a bot is like trying to read a refrig-erator. I assumed that he was relaying this information to Seeren. Would the devil be displeased that I had booked its meeting into my office?

"Seeren is impressed by your speedy accomplishment," George said at last. "Credit has been allotted to this one for suggesting it task you."

"Great, take ten bucks a month off my rent. Just so you know, I promised Father Elaine she'd be safe here. Seeren is not going to make a liar out of me, is it?"

"Seeren rejects violence. It's a regrettable technique."

"Yeah, but if Seeren disappears her to wherever, does that count?"

George's head swiveled back toward the wainscoting. "Father Elaine Horváth will be invited to leave freely, if such is her intention." The brush dipped into the can. "Was Kate Vermeil also found?"

"No," I said. "I looked, but then Father Elaine found me. By the way, she didn't live at 465 12th Avenue."

"Seeren had otherwise information." The old varnish bubbled and sagged where George had applied stripper. "Such error makes a curiosity."

It was a little thing, but it pricked at me as I walked down to the third floor. Was I pleased to discover that the devils were neither omnipotent nor infallible? Not particularly. For all their crimes against humanity, the devils and their bots were pretty much running our world now. It had been a small if bitter comfort to imagine that they knew exactly what they were doing.

I passed crazy Martha's door, which was open, on the way to my office. "Yaga combany wading," she called.

I backtracked. My neighbor was at her desk, wearing her Technopro gas mask, which she claimed protected her from chlorine, hydrogen sulfide, sulfur dioxide, ammonia, bacteria, viruses, dust, pollen, cat dander, mold spores, nuclear fallout, and sexual harassment. Unfortunately, it also made her almost unintelligible.

"Try that again," I said.

"You've. Got. Company. Waiting."

"Who is it?"

She shook the mask and shrugged. The light of her desktop was reflected in the faceplate. I could see numbers swarming like black ants across the rows and columns of a spreadsheet.

"What's with the mask?"

"We. Had. A. Devil. In. The. Building."

"Really?" I said. "When?"

"Morning."

There was no reason why a devil shouldn't come into our building, no law against having one for a client. But there was an accusation in Martha's look that I couldn't deny. Had I betrayed us all by taking the case? She said, "Hate. Devils."

"Yeah," I said. "Me too."

I opened my door and saw that it was Sharifa who was waiting for me. She was trying on a smile that didn't fit. "Hi Fay," she said. She looked as elegant as always and as weary as I had ever seen her. She was wearing a peppered black linen dress and black dress sandals with thin crossover straps. Those weren't doctor shoes—they were pull down the shades and turn up the music shoes. They made me very sad.

As I turned to close the door, she must have spotted the patch of blood that had dried in my hair. "You're hurt!" I had almost forgotten about it— there was no percentage in remembering that I was in pain. She shot out of her chair. "What happened?"

"I slipped in the shower," I said.

"Let me look."

I tilted my head toward her and she probed the lump gently. "You could have a concussion."

"PIs don't get concussions. Says so right on the license."

"Sit," she said. "Let me clean this up. I'll just run to the bathroom for some water."

I sat and watched her go. I thought about locking the door behind her but I deserved whatever I had coming. I opened the bottom drawer of the desk, slipped two plastic cups off the stack and brought Johnnie Walker in for a consultation.

Sharifa bustled through the doorway with a cup of water in one hand and a fistful of paper towels in the other but caught herself when she saw the bottle. "When did this start?"

"Just now." I picked up my cup and slugged two fingers of Black Label Scotch. "Want some?"

"I don't know," she said. "Are we having fun or are we self-medicating?"

I let that pass. She dabbed at the lump with a damp paper towel. I could smell her perfume, lemon blossoms on a summer breeze and just the smallest bead of sweat. Her scent got along nicely with the liquid smoke of the scotch. She brushed against me and I could feel her body beneath her dress. At that moment I wanted her more than I wanted to breathe.

"Sit down," I said.

"I'm not done yet," she said.

I pointed at a chair. "Sit, damn it."

She dropped the paper towel in my trash as she went by.

"You asked me a question this morning," I said. "I should've given you the answer. I had the abortion last week."

She studied her hands. I don't know why; they weren't doing anything. They were just sitting in her lap, minding their own business.

"I told you when we first got together, that's what I'd do when I got seeded," I said.

"I know."

"I just didn't see any good choices," I said. "I know the world needs children, but I have a life to lead. Maybe it's a rude, pointless, dirty life but it's what I have. Being a mother . . . that's someone else's life."

"I understand," said Sharifa. Her voice was so small it could have crawled under a thimble. "It's just . . . it was all so sudden. You told me and then we were fighting and I didn't have time to think things through."

"I got tested in the morning. I told you that afternoon. I wasn't keeping anything a secret."

She folded her arms against her chest as if she were cold. "And when I get seeded, what then?"

"You'll do what's best for you."

She sighed. "Pour me some medication, would you?"

I poured scotch into both cups, came around the desk, and handed Sharifa hers. She drank, held the whiskey in her mouth for a moment and then swallowed.

"Fay, I . . ." The corners of her mouth were twitchy and she bit her lip. "Your mother told me once that when she realized she was pregnant with you, she was so happy. So happy. It was when everything was crashing around everyone. She said you were the gift she needed to . . . not to . . ."

"I got the gift lecture, Sharifa. Too many times. She made the devils sound like Santa Claus. Or the stork."

She glanced down as if surprised to discover that she was still holding the cup. She drained it at a gulp and set it on my desk. "I'm a doctor. I know they do this to us; I just wish I knew how. But it isn't a bad thing. Having you in the world can't be a bad thing."

I wasn't sure about that, but I kept my opinion to myself.

"Sometimes I feel like I'm trying to carry water in my hands but it's all leaking out and there's nothing I can do to stop it." She started rubbing her right hand up and down her left forearm. "People keep killing themselves. Maybe it's not as bad as it used to be, but still. The birth rate is barely at replacement levels. Maybe we're doomed. Did you ever think that? That we might go extinct?"

"No."

Sharifa was silent for a long time. She kept rubbing her arm. "It should've been me doing your abortion," she said at last. "Then we'd both have to live with it."

I was one tough PI. I kept a bottle of scotch in the bottom drawer and had a devil for a client. Tommys whacked me with nightsticks and pumped knockout spray into my face. But even I had a breaking point, and Dr. Sharifa Ramirez was pushing me up against it hard. I wanted to pull her into my arms and kiss her forehead, her cheeks, her graceful neck. But I couldn't give in to her that way—not now anyway. Maybe never again. I had a case, and I needed to hold the best part of myself in reserve until it was finished. "I'll be in charge of the guilt, Sharifa," I said. "You be in charge of saving lives." I came around the desk. "I've got work to do, so you go home now, sweetheart." I kissed her on the forehead. "I'll see you there."

Easier to say than to believe.

6.

S harifa was long gone by the time Father Elaine arrived at ten minutes
to six. She brought muscle with her; Gratiana loitered in the hallway
surveying my office with sullen calculation, as if estimating how long it
would take to break down the door, leap over the desk, and wring somebody's neck. I shouldn't have been surprised that Father Elaine's faith in
me had wavered—hell, I didn't have much faith in me either. However, I
thought she showed poor judgment in bringing this particular thug along.
I invited Gratiana to remove herself from my building. Perhaps she might
perform an autoerotic act in front of a speeding bus? Father Elaine dismissed her, and she slunk off.

Father Elaine appeared calm, but I could tell that she was as nervous
as two mice and a gerbil. I hadn't really had a good look at her in the dim
church, but now I studied her in case I had to write her up for the Missing
Persons Index. She was a tallish woman with round shoulders and a bit
of a stoop. Her eyes were the brown of wet sand; her cheeks were blood-
less. Her smile was not quite as convincing in good light as it had been in
gloom. She made some trifling small talk, which I did nothing to help with.
Then she stood at the window, watching. A wingtip loafer tapped against
bare floor.

It was about ten after when my desktop chirped. I waved open the icon
and accepted the transfer of a thousand dollars. Seeren had a hell of a
calling card. "I think they're coming," I said. I opened the door and stepped
into the hall to wait for them.

"It gives Seeren the bright pleasure to meet you, Father Elaine Horváth,"
said George as they shuffled into the office.

She focused everything she had on the devil. "Just Father, if you don't
mind." The bot was nothing but furniture to her.

"It's kind of crowded in here," I said. "If you want, I can wait outside . . ."

Father Elaine's facade cracked for an instant, but she patched it up nicely.
"I'm sure we can manage," she said.

"This one implores Fay to remain," said George.

We sorted ourselves out. Seeren assumed its perch on top of the file cabinet and George came around and compacted himself next to me. Father
Elaine pushed her chair next to the door. I think she was content to be
stationed nearest the exit. George looked at Father Elaine. She looked at
Seeren. Seeren looked out the window. I watched them all.

"Seeren offers sorrow over the regrettable death of Rashmi Jones," said
George. "Such Rashmi was of your church?"

"She was a member, yes."

"According to Fay Hardaway, a fact is that Father married Kate Vermeil and Rashmi Jones."

I didn't like that. I didn't like it at all.

Father Elaine hesitated only a beat. "Yes."

"Would Father permit Seeren to locate Kate Vermeil?"

"I know where she is, Seeren," said Father Elaine. "I don't think she needs to be brought into this."

"Indulge this one and reconsider, Father. Is such person pregnant?"

Her manner had been cool, but now it dropped forty degrees. "Why would you say that?"

"Perhaps such person is soon to become pregnant?"

"How would I know? If she is, it would be your doing, Seeren."

"Father well understands *in vitro* fertilization?"

"I've heard of it, yes." Father Elaine's shrug was far too elaborate. "I can't say I understand it."

"Father has heard then of transvaginal oocyte retrieval?"

She thrust out her chin. "No."

"Haploidisation of somatic cells?"

She froze.

"Has Father considered then growing artificial sperm from embryonic stem cells?"

"I'm a priest, Seeren." Only her lips moved. "Not a biologist."

"Does the Christer Church make further intentions to induce pregnancies in certain members? Such as Kate Vermeil?"

Father Elaine rose painfully from the chair. I thought she might try to run, but now martyr's fire burned through the shell of ice that had encased her. "We're doing Christ's work, Seeren. We reject your obscene seeding. We are saving ourselves from you and you can't stop us."

Seeren beat its wings, once, twice, and crowed. It was a dense, jarring sound, like steel scraping steel. I hadn't known that devils could make any sound at all, but hearing that hellish scream made me want to dive under my desk and curl up in a ball. I took it though, and so did Father Elaine. I gave her credit for that.

"Seeren makes no argument with the Christer Church," said George. "Seeren upholds only the brightest encouragement for such pregnancies."

Father Elaine's face twitched in disbelief and then a flicker of disappointment passed over her. Maybe she was upset to have been cheated of her glorious death. She was a granny after all, of the generation that had embraced the suicide culture. For the first time, she turned to the bot. "What?"

"Seeren tasks Father to help numerous Christers become pregnant. Christers who do such choosing will then give birth."

She sank back onto her chair.

"Too many humans now refuse the seeding," said the bot. "Not all then give birth. This was not foreseen. It is regrettable."

Without my noticing, my hands had become fists. My knuckles were white.

"Seeren will announce its true satisfaction with the accomplishment of the Christer Church. It offers a single caution. Christers must assure all to make no XY chromosome."

Father Elaine was impassive. "Will you continue to seed all nonbelievers?"

"It is prudent for the survival of humans."

She nodded and faced Seeren. "How will you know if we do try to bring men back into the world?"

The bot said nothing. The silence thickened as we waited. Maybe the devil thought it didn't need to make threats.

"Well, then." Father Elaine rose once again. Some of the stoop had gone out of her shoulders. She was trying to play it calm, but I knew she'd be skipping by the time she hit the sidewalk. Probably she thought she had won a great victory. In any event, she was done with this little party.

But it was my little party, and I wasn't about to let it break up with the devils holding hands with the Christers. "Wait," I said. "Father, you better get Gratiana up here. And if you've got any other muscle in the neighborhood, call them right now. You need backup fast."

Seeren glanced away from the window and at me.

"Why?" Father Elaine already had her sidekick out. "What is this?"

"There's a problem."

"Fay Hardaway," said George sharply. "Indulge this one and recall your task. Your employment has been accomplished."

"Then I'm on my own time now, George." I thought maybe Seeren would try to leave, but it remained on its perch. Maybe the devil didn't care what I did. Or else it found me amusing. I could be an amusing girl, in my own obtuse way.

Gratiana tore the door open. She held her nightstick high, as if expecting to dive into a bloodbath. When she saw our cool tableau, she let it drop to her side.

"Scooch over, Father," I said, "and let her in. Gratiana, you can leave the door open but keep that toothpick handy. I'm pretty sure you're going to be using it before long."

"The others are right behind me, Father," said Gratiana as she crowded into the room. "Two, maybe three minutes."

"Just enough time." I let my hand fall to the middle drawer of my desk. "I have a question for you, Father." I slid the drawer open. "How did Seeren know all that stuff about haploid this and *in vitro* that?"

"It's a devil." She watched me thoughtfully. "They come from two hundred light-years away. How do they know anything?"

"Fair enough. But they also knew that you married Kate and Rashmi. George here just said that I told them, except I never did. That was a mistake. It made me wonder whether they knew who you were all along. It's funny, I used to be convinced that the devils were infallible, but now I'm thinking that they can screw up any day of the week, just like the rest of us. They're almost human that way."

"A regrettable misstatement was made." The bot's neck extended until his head was level with mine. "Indulge this one and refrain from further humiliation."

"I've refrained for too long, George. I've had a bellyful of refraining." I was pretty sure that George could see the open drawer, which meant that the devil would know what was in it as well. I wondered how far they'd let me go. "The question is, Father, if the devils already knew who you were, why would Seeren hire me to find you?"

"Go on," she said.

My chest was tight. Nobody tried to stop me, so I went ahead and stuck my head into the lion's mouth. Like that little girl at school, I'd always wanted to have a real job when I grew up. "You've got a leak, Father. Your problem isn't devil super-science. It's the good old-fashioned Judas kiss. Seeren has an inside source, a mole among your congregation. When it decided the time had come to meet with you, it wanted to be sure that none of you would suspect where its information was actually coming from. It decided that the way to give the mole cover was to hire some gullible PI to pretend to find stuff out. I may be a little slow and a lot greedy but I do have a few shreds of pride. I can't let myself be played for an idiot." I thought I heard footsteps on the stairs, but maybe it was just my own blood pounding. "You see, Father, I don't think that Seeren really trusts you. I sure didn't hear you promise just now not to be making little boys. And yes, if they find out about the boy babies, the devils could just disappear them, but you and the Bride of God and all your batty friends would find ways to make that very public, very messy. I'm guessing that's part of your plan, isn't it? To remind us who the devils are, what they did? Maybe get people into the streets again. Since the devils still need to know what you're up to, the mole had to be protected."

Father Elaine flushed with anger. "Do you know who she is?"

"No," I said. "But you could probably narrow it down to a very few. You said you married Rashmi and Kate, but that you never filed the documents. But you needed someone to witness the ceremony. Someone who was taking pix and would send one to Seeren . . ."

Actually, my timing was a little off. Gratiana launched herself at me just as big Alix hurtled through the doorway. I had the air taser out of the drawer, but my plan had been for the Christers to clean up their own mess. I came out of my chair and raised the taser but even fifty thousand volts wasn't going to keep that snarling bitch off me.

I heard a huge wet pop, not so much an explosion as an implosion. There was a rush of air through the doorway but the room was preternaturally quiet, as if someone had just stopped screaming. We humans gaped at the void that had formerly been occupied by Gratiana. The familiar surroundings of my office seemed to warp and stretch to accommodate that vacancy. If she could vanish so completely, then maybe chairs could waltz on the ceiling and trashcans could sing *Carmen*. For the first time in my life I had a rough sense of what the grannies had felt when the devils disappeared their men. It would be one thing if Gratiana were merely dead, if there were blood and bone and flesh left behind. A body to be buried. But this was an offense against reality itself. It undermined our common belief that the world is indeed a fact, that we exist at all. I could understand how it could unhinge a billion minds. I was standing next to Father Elaine beside the open door to my office holding the taser and I couldn't remember how I had gotten there.

Seeren hopped down off the bookcase as if nothing important had happened and wrapped its translucent wings around its body. The devil didn't seem surprised at all that a woman had just disappeared. Maybe there was no surprising a devil.

And then it occurred to me that this probably wasn't the first time since they had taken all the men that the devils had disappeared someone. Maybe they did it all the time. I thought of all the missing persons whom I had never found. I could see the files in Julie Epstein's office bulging with unsolved cases. Had Seeren done this thing to teach us the fragility of being? Or had it just been a clumsy attempt to cover up its regrettable mistakes?

As the devil waddled toward the door, Alix made a move as if to block its exit. After what had just happened, I thought that was probably the most boneheaded, brave move I had ever seen.

"Let them go." Father Elaine's voice quavered. Her eyes were like wounds.

Alix stepped aside and the devil and the bot left us. We listened to the devil scrabble down the hall. I heard the elevator doors open and then close.

Then Father Elaine staggered and put a hand on my shoulder. She looked like a granny now.

"There are no boy babies," she said. "Not yet. You have to believe me."

"You know what?" I shook free of her. "I don't care." I wanted them gone. I wanted to sit alone at my desk and watch the room fill with night.

"You don't understand."

"And I don't want to." I had to set the taser on the desk or I might have used it on her.

"Kate Vermeil is pregnant with one of our babies," said Father Elaine. "It's a little girl, I swear it."

"So you've made Seeren proud. What's the problem?"

Alix spoke for the first time. "Gratiana was in charge of Kate."

7.

The Poison Society was lit brightly enough to give a camel a headache. If you forgot your sunglasses, there was a rack of freebies at the door. Set into the walls were terrariums where diamondback rattlers coiled in the sand, black neck cobras dangled from dead branches and brown scorpions basked on ceramic rocks. The hemlock was in bloom; clusters of small, white flowers opened like umbrellas. Upright stems of monkshood were interplanted with death cap mushrooms in wine casks cut in half. Curare vines climbed the pergola over the alcohol bar.

I counted maybe fifty customers in the main room, which was probably a good crowd for a Wednesday night. I had no idea yet how many might be lurking in the specialty shops that opened off this space, where a nice girl might arrange for a guaranteed-safe session of sexual asphyxia either by hanging or drowning, or else get her cerebrum toasted by various brain lightning generators. I was hoping Kate was out in the open with the relatively sane folks. I didn't really want to poke around in the shops, but I would if I had to. I thought I owed it to Rashmi Jones.

I strolled around, pretending to look at various animals and plants, carrying a tumbler filled with a little Johnnie Walker Black Label and a lot

of water. I knew Kate would be disguised but if I could narrow the field
of marks down to three or four, I might actually snoop her. Of course, she
might be on the other side of town, but this was my only play. My guess
was that she'd switch styles, so I wasn't necessarily looking for a tommy.
Her hair wouldn't be brunette, and her skin would probably be darker, and
contacts could give her cat's eyes or zebra eyes or American flags, if she
wanted. But even with padding and lifts she couldn't change her body type
enough to fool a good scan. And I had her data from the Christer medical
files loaded into my sidekick.

Father Elaine had tried Kate's call, but she wouldn't pick up. That made
perfect sense since just about anyone could put their hands on software
that could replicate voices. There were bots that could sing enough like
Velma Stone to fool her own mother. Kate and Gratiana would have agreed
on a safe word. Our problem was that Gratiana had taken it with her to
hell, or wherever the devil had consigned her.

The first mark my sidekick picked out was a redhead in silk pajamas and
lime green bunny slippers. A scan matched her to Kate's numbers to within
5 percent. I bumped into her just enough to plant the snoop, a sticky hom-
ing device the size of a baby tooth.

"'Scuse me, sorry." I said. "S-so sorry." I slopped some of my drink onto
the floor.

She gave me a glare that would have withered a cactus and I noodled off.
As soon as I was out of her sight, I hit the button on my sidekick to which
I'd assigned Kate's call. When Kate picked up, the snoop would know if
the call had come from me and signal my sidekick that I had found her. The
redhead wasn't Kate. Neither was the bald jane in distressed leather.

The problem with trying to locate her this way was that if I kept calling
her, she'd get suspicious and lose the sidekick.

I lingered by a pufferfish aquarium. Next to it was a safe, and in front
of that a tootsie fiddled with the combination lock. I scanned her and got
a match to within 2 percent. She was wearing a spangle wig and a stretch
lace dress with a ruffle front. When she opened the door of the safe, I saw
that it was made of clear luxar. She reached in, then slammed the door and
trotted off as if she were late for the last train of the night.

I peeked through the door of the safe. Inside was a stack of squat blue
inhalers like the one Rashmi had used to kill herself. On the wall above the
safe, the management of The Poison Society had spray-painted a mock
graffiti. *21L 4R 11L*. There was no time to plant a snoop. I pressed the call
button as I tailed her.

With a strangled cry, the tootsie yanked a sidekick from her clutch purse, dropped it to the floor, and stamped on it. She was wearing Donya Durand ice and taupe flat slingbacks.

As I moved toward her, Kate Vermeil saw me and ducked into one of the shops. She dodged past fifty-five-gallon drums of carbon tetrachloride and dimethyl sulfate and burst through the rear door of the shop into an alley. I saw her fumbling with the cap of the inhaler. I hurled myself at her and caught at her legs. Her right shoe came off in my hand, but I grabbed her left ankle and she went down. She still had the inhaler and was trying to bring it to her mouth. I leapt on top of her and wrenched it away.

"Do you really want to kill yourself?" I aimed the inhaler at her face and screamed at her. "Do you, Kate? Do you?" The air in the alley was thick with despair and I was choking on it. "Come on, Kate. Let's do it!"

"No." Her head thrashed back and forth. "No, please. Stop."

Her terror fed mine. "Then what the hell are you doing with this thing?" I was shaking so badly that when I tried to pitch the inhaler into the dumpster, it hit the pavement only six feet away. I had come so close to screwing up. I climbed off her and rolled on my back and soaked myself in the night sky. When I screwed up, people died. "Cyanide is awful bad for the baby," I said.

"How do you know about my baby?" Her face was rigid with fear. "Who are you?"

I could breathe again, although I wasn't sure I wanted to. "Fay Hardaway." I gasped. "I'm a PI; I left you a message this morning. Najma Jones hired me to find her daughter."

"Rashmi is dead."

"I know," I said. "So is Gratiana." I sat up and looked at her. "Father Elaine will be glad to see you."

Kate's eyes were wide, but I don't think she was seeing the alley. "Gratiana said the devils would come after me." She was still seeing the business end of the inhaler. "She said that if I didn't hear from her by tomorrow then we had lost everything and I should . . . do it. You know, to protect the church. And just now my sidekick picked up three times in ten minutes only there was nobody there and so I knew it was time."

"That was me, Kate. Sorry." I retrieved the Donya Durand slingback I'd stripped off her foot and gave it back to her. "Tell me where you got this?"

"It was Rashmi's. We bought them together at Grayles. Actually I picked them out. That was before . . . I loved her, you know, but she was crazy. I can see that now, although it's kind of too late. I mean, she was okay when she was taking her meds, but she would stop every so often. She called it taking a vacation from herself. Only it was no vacation for anyone else, especially not for me. She decided to go off on the day we got married and didn't tell me and all of a sudden after the ceremony we got into this huge fight about the baby and who loved who more and she stared throwing things at me—these shoes—and then ran out of the church barefoot. I don't think she ever really understood about . . . you know, what we were trying to do. I mean, I've talked to the Bride of God herself . . . but Rashmi." Kate rubbed her eye and her hand came away wet.

I sat her up and put my arm around her. "That's all right. Not really your fault. I think poor Rashmi must have been hanging by a thread. We all are. The whole human race, or what's left of it."

We sat there for a moment.

"I saw her mom this morning," I said. "She said to tell you she was sorry."

Kate sniffed. "Sorry? What for?"

I shrugged.

"I know she didn't have much use for me," said Kate. "At least that's what Rashmi always said. But as far as I'm concerned the woman was a saint to put up with Rashmi and her mood swings and all the acting out: She was always there for her. And the thing is, Rashmi hated her for it."

I got to my knees, then to my feet. I helped Kate up. The alley was dark, but that wasn't really the problem. Even in the light of day, I hadn't seen anything.

8.

I had no trouble finding space at the bike rack in front of Ronald Reagan Elementary. The building seemed to be drowsing in the heavy morning air, its brick wings enfolding the empty playground. A janitor bot was vacuuming the swimming pool, another was plucking spent blossoms from the clematis fence. The bots were headache yellow; the letters RRE in puffy orange slanted across their torsos. The gardening bot informed me that school wouldn't start for an hour. That was fine with me. This was just a courtesy call, part of the total service commitment I made to all the clients whom I had failed. I asked if I could see Najma Jones and he said he doubted that any of the teachers were in quite this early but he walked me to the office. He paged her; I signed the visitors' log. When her voice crackled over the intercom, I told the bot that I knew the way to her classroom.

I paused at the open door. Rashmi's mom had her back to me. She was wearing a sleeveless navy dress with cream-colored dupatta scarf draped over her shoulders. She passed down a row of empty desks, perching origami animals at the center of each. There were three kinds of elephants, ducks and ducklings, a blue giraffe, a pink cat that might have been a lion.

"Please come in, Ms. Hardaway," she said without turning around. She had teacher radar; she could see behind her back and around a corner.

"I stopped by your house." I slouched into the room like a kid who had lost her civics homework. "I thought I might catch you before you left for school." I leaned against a desk in the front row and picked up the purple crocodile on it. "You fold these yourself?"

"I couldn't sleep last night," she said, "so finally I gave up and went for a walk. I ended up here. I like coming to school early, especially when no one else is around. There is so much time." She had one origami swan left over that she set on her own desk. "Staying after is different. If you're always the last one out at night, you're admitting that you haven't got anything to rush home to. It's pathetic, actually." She settled behind her desk and began opening windows on her desktop. "I've been teaching the girls to fold the ducks. They seem to like it. It's a challenging grade, the fifth. They come to me as bright and happy children and I am supposed to teach them fractions and pack them off to middle school. I shudder to think what happens to them there."

"How old are they?"

"Ten when they start. Most of them have turned eleven already. They graduate next week." She peered at the files she had opened. "Some of them."

"I take it on faith that I was eleven once," I said, "but I just don't remember."

"Your generation grew up in unhappy times." Her face glowed in the phosphors. "You haven't had a daughter yet, have you, Ms. Hardaway?"

"No."

We contemplated my childlessness for a moment.

"Did Rashmi like origami?" I didn't mean anything by it. I just didn't want to listen to the silence anymore.

"Rashmi?" She frowned, as if her daughter were a not-very-interesting kid she had taught years ago. "No. Rashmi was a difficult child."

"I found Kate Vermeil last night," I said. "I told her what you said, that you were sorry. She wanted to know what for."

"What for?"

"She said that Rashmi was crazy. And that she hated you for having her."

"She never hated me," said Najma quickly. "Yes, Rashmi was a sad girl. Anxious. What is this about, Ms. Hardaway?"

"I think you were at the Comfort Inn that night. If you want to talk about that, I would like to hear what you have to say. If not, I'll leave now."

She stared at me for a moment, her expression unreadable. "You know, I actually wanted to have many children." She got up from the desk, crossed the room and shut the door as if it were made of handblown glass. "When the seeding first began, I went down to City Hall and volunteered. That just wasn't done. Most women were horrified to find themselves pregnant. I talked to a bot, who took my name and address and then told me to go home and wait. If I wanted more children after my first, I was certainly encouraged to make a request. It felt like I was joining one of those mail order music clubs." She smiled and tugged at her dupatta. "But when Rashmi was born, everything changed. Sometimes she was such a needy baby, fussing to be picked up, but then she would lie in her crib for hours, listless and withdrawn. She started antidepressants when she was five and they helped. And the Department of Youth Services issued me a full time bot helper when I started teaching. But Rashmi was always a handful. And since I was all by myself, I didn't feel like I had enough to give to another child."

"You never married?" I asked. "Found a partner?"

"Married who?" Her voice rose sharply. "Another woman?" Her cheeks colored. "No. I wasn't interested in that."

Najma returned to her desk but did not sit down. "The girls will be coming soon." She leaned toward me, fists on the desktop. "What is it that you want to hear, Ms. Hardaway?"

"You found Rashmi before I did. How?"

"She called me. She said that she had had a fight with her girlfriend who was involved in some secret experiment that she couldn't tell me about and they were splitting up and everything was shit, the world was shit. She was off her meds, crying, not making a whole lot of sense. But that was nothing new. She always called me when she broke up with someone. I'm her mother."

"And when you got there?"

"She was sitting on the bed." Najma's eyes focused on something I couldn't see. "She put the inhaler to her mouth when I opened the door." Najma was looking into Room 103 of the Comfort Inn. "And I thought to myself, what does this poor girl want? Does she want me to witness her death or stop it? I tried to talk to her, you know. She seemed to listen. But when I asked her to put the inhaler down, she wouldn't. I moved toward her, slowly. Slowly. I told her that she didn't have to do anything. That we could just go home. And then I was this close." She reached a hand across the desk. "And I couldn't help myself. I tried to swat it out of her mouth.

Either she pressed the button or I set it off." She sat down abruptly and put her head in her hands. "She didn't get the full dose. It took forever before it was over. She was in agony."

"I think she'd made up her mind, Ms. Jones." I was only trying to comfort her. "She wrote the note."

"I wrote the note." She glared at me. "I did."

There was nothing I could say. All the words in all the languages that had ever been spoken wouldn't come close to expressing this mother's grief. I thought the weight of it must surely crush her.

Through the open windows, I heard the snort of the first bus pulling into the turnaround in front of the school. Najma Jones glanced out at it, gathered herself and smiled. "Do you know what Rashmi means in Sanskrit?"

"No, ma'am."

"Ray of sunlight," she said. "The girls are here, Ms. Hardaway." She picked up the origami on her desk. "We have to be ready for them." She held it out to me. "Would you like a swan?"

By the time I came through the door of the school, the turnaround was filled with busses. Girls poured off them and swirled onto the playground: giggling girls, whispering girls, skipping girls, girls holding hands. And in the warm June sun, I could almost believe they were happy girls.

They paid no attention to me.

I tried Sharifa's call. "Hello?" Her voice was husky with sleep.

"Sorry I didn't make it home last night, sweetheart," I said. "Just wanted to let you know that I'm on my way."

Alaya Dawn Johnson is the author of six novels for adults and young
adults. Her novel *The Summer Prince* was longlisted for the National Book
Award for Young People's Literature. Her most recent, *Love Is the Drug*,
won the Andre Norton Award. Her short stories have appeared in many
magazines and anthologies, including *Asimov's, Fantasy & Science Fiction,
Interzone, Subterranean, Zombies vs. Unicorns,* and *Welcome to Bordertown.* In
addition to the Norton, she has won the Nebula and Cybils awards and
been nominated for the Indies Choice Award and Locus Award. She lives
in Mexico City, where she is getting her master's in Mesoamerican studies.

They Shall Salt the Earth
with Seeds of Glass

ALAYA DAWN JOHNSON

It's noon, the middle of wheat harvest, and Tris is standing on the edge of
the field while Bill and Harris and I drive three ancient combine threshers across the grain. It's dangerous to stand so close and Tris knows it.
Tris knows better than to get in the way during harvest, too. Not a good
idea if she wants to survive the winter. Fifteen days ago a cluster bomb
dropped on the east field, so no combines there. No harvest. Just a feast for
the crows.

Tris wrote the signs (with pictures for the ones who don't read) warning the kids to stay off the grass, stay out of the fields, don't pick up the
bright-colored glass jewels. So I raise my hand, wave my straw hat in the
sun—it's hot as hell out here, we could use a break, no problem—and the
deafening noise of eighty-year-old engines forced unwillingly into service
chokes, gasps, falls silent.

Bill stands and cups his hands over his mouth. "Something wrong with
Meshach, Libby?"

I shake my head, realize he can't see, and holler, "The old man's doing
fine. It's just hot. Give me ten?"

Harris, closer to me, takes a long drink from his bottle and climbs off
Abednego. I don't mind his silence. This is the sort of sticky day that
makes it hard to move, let alone bring in a harvest, and this sun is hot
enough to burn darker skin than his.

It's enough to burn Tris, standing without a hat and wearing a skinny

strappy dress of faded red that stands out against the wheat's dusty gold. I
hop off Meshach, check to make sure he's not leaking oil, and head over to
my sister. I'm a little worried. Tris wouldn't be here if it wasn't important.
Another cluster bomb? But I haven't heard the whining drone of any reapers. The sky is clear. But even though I'm too far to read her expression,
I can tell Tris is worried. That way she has of balancing on one leg, a red
stork in a wheat marsh. I hurry as I get closer, though my overalls stick
to the slick sweat on my thighs and I have to hitch them up like a skirt to
move quickly.

"Is it Dad?" I ask, when I'm close.

She frowns and shakes her head. "Told me this morning he's going fishing again."

"And you let him?"

She shrugs. "What do you want me to do, take away his cane? He's old,
Libs. A few toxic fish won't kill him any faster."

"They might," I grumble, but this is an old argument, one I'm not winning, and besides that's not why Tris is here.

"So what is it?"

She smiles, but it shakes at the edges. She's scared and I wonder if that
makes her look old or just reminds me of our age. Dad is eighty, but I'm
forty-two and we had a funeral for an eight-year-old last week. Every night
since I was ten I've gone to sleep thinking I might not wake up the next
morning. I don't know how you get to forty-two doing that.

Tris is thirty-eight, but she looks twenty-five—at least, when she isn't
scanning the skies for reapers, or walking behind a tiny coffin in a funeral
procession.

"Walk with me," she says, her voice low, as though Harris can hear us
from under that magnolia tree twenty feet away. I sigh and roll my eyes
and mutter under my breath, but she's my baby sister and she knows I'll
follow her anywhere. We climb to the top of the hill, so I can see the
muddy creek that irrigates the little postage stamp of our corn field, and
the big hill just north of town, with its wood tower and reassuring white
flag. Yolanda usually takes the morning shift, spending her hours watching the sky for that subtle disturbance, too smooth for a bird, too fast for a
cloud. Reapers. If she rings the bell, some of us might get to cover in time.

Sometimes I don't like to look at the sky, so I sprawl belly-down on the
ground, drink half of the warm water from my bottle and offer the rest to
Tris. She finishes it and grimaces.

"Don't know how you stand it," she says. "Aren't you hot?"

"You won't complain when you're eating cornbread tonight."

"You made some?"

"Who does everything around here, bookworm?" I nudge her in the ribs and she laughs reluctantly and smiles at me with our smile. I remember learning to comb her hair after Mom got sick; the careful part I would make while she squirmed and hollered at me, the two hair balls I would twist and fasten to each side of her head. I would make the bottom of her hair immaculate: brushed and gelled and fastened into glossy, thick homogeneity. But on top it would sprout like a bunch of curly kale, straight up and out and olive-oil shiny. She would parade around the house in this flouncy slip she thought was a dress and pose for photos with her hand on her hip. I'm in a few of those pictures, usually in overalls or a smock. I look awkward and drab as an old sock next to her, but maybe it doesn't matter, because we have the same slightly bucked front teeth, the same fat cheeks, the same wide eyes going wider. We have a nice smile, Tris and I.

Tris doesn't wear afro-puffs any more. She keeps her hair in a bun and I keep mine short.

"Libs, oh Libs, things aren't so bad, are they?"

I look up at Tris, startled. She's sitting in the grass with her hands beneath her thighs and tears are dripping off the tip of her nose. I was lulled by her laugh—we don't often talk about the shit we can't control. Our lives, for instance.

I think about the field that we're going to leave for crows so no one gets blown up for touching one of a thousand beautiful multicolored jewels. I think about funerals and Dad killing himself faster just so he can eat catfish with bellies full of white phosphorus.

"It's not that great, Tris."

"You think it's shit."

"No, not *shit*—"

"Close. You think it's close."

I sigh. "Some days. Tris. I have to get back to Meshach in a minute. What is going on?"

"I'm pregnant," she says.

I make myself meet her eyes, and see she's scared; almost as scared as I am.

"How do you know?"

"I suspected for a while. Yolanda finally got some test kits last night from a river trader."

Yolanda has done her best as the town midwife since she was drafted into service five years ago, when a glassman raid killed our last one. I'm surprised Tris managed to get a test at all.

"What are you going to do? Will you . . ." I can't even bring myself to say "keep it." But could Yolanda help her do anything else?

She reaches out, hugs me, buries her head in my shirt and sobs like a baby. Her muffled words sound like "Christ" and "Jesus" and "God," which ought to be funny since Tris is a capital-A atheist, but it isn't.

"No," she's saying, "Christ, no. I have to . . . someone has to . . . I need an abortion, Libby."

Relief like the first snow melt, like surviving another winter. Not someone else to worry about, to love, to feed.

But an abortion? There hasn't been a real doctor in this town since I was twelve.

Bill's mom used to be a registered nurse before the occupation, and she took care of everyone in town as best she could until glassman robots raided her house and called in reapers to bomb it five years ago. Bill left town after that. We never thought we'd see him again, but then two planting seasons ago, there he was with this green giant, a forty-year-old Deere combine—Shadrach, he called it, because it would make the third with our two older, smaller machines. He brought engine parts with him, too, and oil and enough seed for a poppy field. He had a bullet scar in his forearm and three strange, triangular burns on the back of his neck. You could see them because he'd been shaved bald and his hair was only starting to grow back, a patchy gray peach-fuzz.

He'd been in prison, that much was obvious. Whether the glassmen let him go or he escaped, he never said and we never asked. We harvested twice as much wheat from the field that season, and the money from the poppy paid for a new generator. If the bell on lookout hill rang more often than normal, if surveillance drones whirred through the grass and the water more than they used to, well, who was to say what the glassmen were doing? Killing us, that's all we knew, and Bill was one of our own.

So I ask Bill if his mother left anything behind that might help us—like a pill, or instructions for a procedure. He frowns.

"Aren't you a little old, Libby?" he says, and I tell him to fuck off. He puts a hand on my shoulder—conciliatory, regretful—and looks over to where Tris is trudging back home. "You saw what the reapers did to my Mom's house. I couldn't even find all of her *teeth*."

I'm not often on that side of town, but I can picture the ruin exactly. There's still a crater on Mill Street. I shuffle backward, contrite. "God, Bill. I'm sorry. I wasn't thinking."

He shrugs. "Sorry, Libs. Ask Yolanda, if you got to do something like that." I don't like the way he frowns at me; I can hear his judgment even when all he does is turn and climb back inside Shadrach.

"Fucking hot out here," I say, and walk back over to Meshach. I wish Bill wasn't so goddamn judgmental. I wish Tris hadn't messed up with whichever of her men provided the sperm donation. I wish we hadn't lost the east field to another cluster bomb.

But I can wish or I can drive, and the old man's engine coughs loud enough to drown even my thoughts.

Tris pukes right after dinner. That was some of my best cornbread, but I don't say anything. I just clean it up.

"How far along are you?" I ask. I feel like vomit entitles me to this much.

She pinches her lips together and I hope she isn't about to do it again. Instead, she stands up and walks out of the kitchen. I think that's her answer, but she returns a moment later with a box about the size of my hand. It's got a hole on one side and a dial like a gas gauge on the other. The gauge is marked with large glassman writing and regular letters in tiny print: "Fetal Progression," it reads, then on the far left "Not Pregnant," running through "Nine Months" on the far right. I can't imagine what the point of that last would be, but Tris's dial is still barely on the left hand side, settled neatly between three and four. A little late for morning sickness, but maybe it's terror as much as the baby that makes her queasy.

"There's a note on the side. It says 'All pregnant women will receive free rehabilitative healthcare in regional facilities.'" She says the last like she's spent a long day memorizing tiny print.

"Glassmen won't do abortions, Tris."

No one knows what they really look like. They only interact with us through their remote-controlled robots. Maybe they're made of glass themselves—they give us pregnancy kits, but won't bother with burn dressings. Dad says the glassmen are alien scientists studying our behavior, like a human would smash an anthill to see how they scatter. Reverend Beale always points to the pipeline a hundred miles west of us. They're just men stealing our resources, he says, like the white man stole the Africans', though even he can't say what those resources might be. It's a pipeline from nowhere, to nothing, as far as any of us know.

Tris leans against the exposed brick of our kitchen wall. "All fetuses are to be carried to full term," she whispers, and I turn the box over and see her words printed in plain English, in larger type than anything else on the box. Only one woman in our town ever took the glassmen up on their offer. I don't know how it went for her; she never came home.

"Three months!" I say, though I don't mean to.

Tris rubs her knuckles beneath her eyes, though she isn't crying. She looks fierce, daring me to ask her how the hell she waited this long. But I don't, because I know. Wishful thinking is a powerful curse, almost as bad as storytelling.

I don't go to church much these days, not after our old pastor died and Beale moved into town to take his place. Reverend Beale likes his fire and brimstone, week after week of too much punishment and too little brotherhood. I felt exhausted listening to him rant in that high collar, sweat pouring down his temples. But he's popular, and I wait on an old bench outside the red brick church for the congregation to let out. Main Street is quiet except for the faint echoes of the reverend's sonorous preaching. Mostly I hear the cicadas, the water lapping against a few old fishing boats and the long stretch of rotting pier. There used to be dozens of sailboats here, gleaming creations of white fiberglass and heavy canvas sails with names like "Bay Princess" and "Prospero's Dream." I know because Dad has pictures. Main Street was longer then, a stretch of brightly painted Tudors and Victorians with little shops and restaurants on the bottom floors and rooms above. A lot of those old buildings are boarded up now, and those that aren't look as patched-over and jury-rigged as our thresher combines. The church has held up the best of any of the town's buildings. Time has hardly worn its stately red brick and shingled steeples. It used to be Methodist, I think, but we don't have enough people to be overly concerned about denominations these days. I've heard of some towns where they make everyone go Baptist, or Lutheran, but we're lucky that no one's thought to do anything like that here. Though I'm sure Beale would try if he could get away with it. Maybe Tris was right to leave the whole thing behind. Now she sits the children while their parents go to church.

The sun tips past its zenith when the doors finally open and my neighbors walk out of the church in twos and threes. Beale shakes parishioners' hands as they leave, mopping his face with a handkerchief. His smile looks more like a grimace to me; three years in town and he still looks uncomfortable anywhere but behind a pulpit. Men like him think the glassmen are right to require "full gestation." Men like him think Tris is a damned sinner, just because she has a few men and won't settle down with one. He hates the glassmen as much as the rest of us, but his views help them just the same.

Bill comes out with Pam. The bones in her neck stand out like twigs, but she looks a hell of a lot better than the last time I saw her, at Georgia's funeral. Pam fainted when we laid her daughter in the earth, and Bill had to take her home before the ceremony ended. Pam is Bill's cousin, and Georgia was her only child—blown to bits after riding her bicycle over a hidden jewel in the fields outside town. To my surprise, Bill gives me a tired smile before walking Pam down the street.

Bill and I used to dig clams from the mud at low tide in the summers. We were in our twenties and my mother had just died of a cancer the glassmen could have cured if they gave a damn. Sometimes we would build fires of cedar and pine and whatever other tinder lay around and roast the clams right there by the water. We talked about anything in the world other than glassmen and dead friends while the moon arced above. We planned the cornfield eating those clams, and plotted all the ways we might get the threshers for the job. The cow dairy, the chicken coop, the extra garden plots—we schemed and dreamt of ways to help our town hurt a little less each winter. Bill had a girlfriend then, though she vanished not long after; we never did more than touch.

That was a long time ago, but I remember the taste of cedar ash and sea salt as I look at the back of him. I never once thought those moments would last forever, and yet here I am, regretful and old.

Yolanda is one of the last to leave, stately and elegant with her braided white hair and black church hat with netting. I catch up with her as she heads down the steps.

"Can we talk?" I ask.

Her shoulders slump a little when I ask, but she bids the reverend farewell and walks with me until we are out of earshot.

"Tris needs an abortion," I say.

Yolanda nods up and down like a sea bird, while she takes deep breaths. She became our midwife because she'd helped Bill's mother with some births, but I don't think she wants the job. There's just no one else.

"Libby, the glassmen don't like abortions."

"If the glassmen are paying us enough attention to notice, we have bigger problems."

"I don't have the proper equipment for a procedure. Even if I did, I couldn't."

"Don't tell me you agree with Beale."

She draws herself up and glares at me. "I don't know *how*, Libby! Do you want me to kill Tris to get rid of her baby? They say the midwife in Toddville can do them if it's early enough. How far along is she?"

I see the needle in my mind, far too close to the center line for comfort. "Three and a half months," I say.

She looks away, but she puts her arm around my shoulders. "I understand why she would, I do. But it's too late. We'll all help her."

Raise the child, she means. I know Yolanda is making sense, but I don't want to hear her. I don't want to think about Tris carrying a child she doesn't want to term. I don't want to think about that test kit needle pointing inexorably at *too fucking late*. So I thank Yolanda and head off in the other direction, down the cracked tarmac as familiar as a scar, to Pam's house. She lives in a small cottage Victorian with peeling gray paint that used to be blue. Sure enough, Bill sits in an old rocking chair on the porch, thumbing through a book. I loved to see him like that in our clam-digging days, just sitting and listening. I would dream of him after he disappeared.

"Libs?" he says. He leans forward.

"Help her, Bill. You've been outside, you know people. Help her find a doctor, someone who can do this after three months."

He sighs and the book thumps on the floor. "I'll see."

Three days later, Bill comes over after dinner.

"There's rumors of something closer to Annapolis," he says. "I couldn't find out more than that. None of my . . . I mean, I only know some dudes, Libby. And whoever runs this place only talks to women."

"Your mother didn't know?" Tris asks, braver than me.

Bill rubs the back of his head. "If she did, she sure didn't tell me."

"You've got to have more than that," she says. "Does this place even have a name? How near Annapolis? What do you want us to do, sail into the city and ask the nearest glassman which way to the abortion clinic?"

"What do I want you to do? Maybe I want you to count your goddamn blessings and not risk your life to murder a child. It's a *sin*, Tris, not like you'd care about that, but I'd've thought Libby would."

"God I know," I say, "but I've never had much use for sin. Now why don't you get your nose out of our business?"

"You invited me in, Libby."

"For *help*—"

He shakes his head. "If you could see what Pam's going through right now . . ."

Bill has dealt with as much grief as any of us. I can understand why he's moralizing in our kitchen, but that doesn't mean I have to tolerate it.

But Tris doesn't even give me time. She stands and shakes a wooden spatula under his nose. Bill's a big man, but he flinches. "So I should have this baby just so I can watch it get blown up later, is that it? Don't put Pam's grief on me, Bill. I'm sorrier than I can say about Georgia. I taught that girl to read! And I can't. I just can't."

Bill breathes ragged. His dark hands twist his muddy flannel shirt, his grip so tight his veins are stark against sun-baked skin. Tris is still holding that spatula.

Bill turns his head abruptly, stalks back to the kitchen door with a "Fuck," and he wipes his eyes. Tris leans against the sink.

"Esther," he says quietly, his back to us. "The name of a person, the name of a place, I don't know. But you ask for that, my buddy says you should find what you're after."

I follow him outside, barefoot and confused that I'd bother when he's so clearly had enough of us. I call his name, then start jogging and catch his elbow. He turns around.

"What, Libby?"

He's so angry. His hair didn't grow in very long or thick after he came back. He looks like someone mashed him up, stretched him out and then did a hasty job of putting him back together. Maybe I look like that, too.

"Thanks," I say. We don't touch.

"Don't die, Libs."

The air is thick with crickets chirping and fireflies glowing and the swampy, seaweed-and-salt air from the Chesapeake. He turns to walk away. I don't stop him.

We take Dad's boat. There's not enough gas left to visit Bishop's Head, the mouth of our estuary, let alone Annapolis. So we bring oars, along with enough supplies to keep the old dinghy low in the water.

"I hope we don't hit a storm," Tris says, squinting at the clear, indigo sky as though thunderheads might be hiding behind the stars.

"We're all right for now. Feel the air? Humidity's dropped at least 20 percent."

Tris has the right oar and I have the left. I don't want to use the gas unless we absolutely have to, and I'm hoping the low-tech approach will make us less noticeable to any patrolling glassmen. It's tough work, even in the relatively cool night air, and I check the stars to make sure we're heading in more or less the right direction. None of the towns on our estuary keep lights on at night. I only know when we pass Toddville because of the old lighthouse silhouetted against the stars. I lost sight of our home within five minutes of setting out, and God how a part of me wanted to turn the dinghy right around and go back. The rest of the world isn't safe. Home isn't either, but it's familiar.

Dad gave us a nautical chart of the Chesapeake Bay, with markers for towns long destroyed, lighthouses long abandoned, by people long dead. He marked our town and told us to get back safe. We promised him we would and we hugged like we might never see each other again.

"What if we hit a jewel?" Tris asks. In the dark, I can't tell if it's fear or exertion that aspirates her words. I've had that thought myself, but what can we do? The glassmen make sure their cluster bombs spread gifts everywhere.

"They don't detonate that well in water," I offer.

A shift in the dark; Tris rests her oar in the boat and stretches her arms. "Well enough to kill you slowly."

I'm not as tired, but I take the break. "We've got a gun. It ought to do the trick, if it comes to that."

"Promise?"

"To what? Mercy kill you?"

"Sure."

"Aren't you being a little melodramatic?"

"And we're just out here to do a little night fishing."

I laugh, though my belly aches like she's punched me. "Christ, Tris." I lean back in the boat, the canvas of our food sack rough and comforting on my slick skin, like Mom's gloves when she first taught me to plant seeds.

"Libs?"

"Yeah?"

"You really don't care who the father is?"

I snort. "If it were important, I'm sure you would have told me."

I look up at the sky: there's the Milky Way, the North Star, Orion's belt. I remember when I was six, before the occupation. There was so much light on the bay you could hardly see the moon.

"Reckon we'll get to Ohio, Jim?" Tris asks in a fake Southern drawl.

I grin. "Reckon we might. If'n we can figure out just how you got yerself pregnant, Huck."

Tris leans over the side of the boat, and a spray of brackish water hits my open mouth. I shriek and dump two handfuls on her head and she splutters and grabs me from behind so I can't do more than wiggle in her embrace.

"Promise," she says, breathing hard, still laughing.

The bay tastes like home to me, like everything I've ever loved. "Christ, Tris," I say, and I guess that's enough.

We round Bishop's Head at dawn. Tris is nearly asleep on her oar, though she hasn't complained. I'm worried about her, and it's dangerous to travel during the day until we can be sure the water is clear. We pull into Hopkins Cove, an Edenic horseshoe of brown sand and forest. It doesn't look like a human foot has touched this place since the invasion, which reassures me. Drones don't do much exploring. They care about people.

Tris falls asleep as soon as we pull the boat onto the sand. I wonder if I should feed her more—does she need extra for the baby? Then I wonder if that's irrational, since we're going all this way to kill it. But for now, at least, the fetus is part of her, which means we have to take it into consideration. I think about Bill with his big, dumb eyes and patchy bald head telling me that it's a *sin*, as though that has anything to do with your sister crying like her insides have been torn out.

I eat some cornbread and a peach, though I'm not hungry. I sit on the shore with my feet in the water and watch for other boats or drones or reapers overhead. I don't see anything but seagulls and ospreys and minnows that tickle my toes.

"Ain't nothing here, Libs," I say, in my mother's best imitation of *her* mother's voice. I never knew my grandmother, but Mom said she looked just like Tris, so I loved her on principle. She and Tris even share a name: Leatrice. I told Mom that I'd name my daughter Tamar, after her. I'd always sort of planned to, but when my monthlies stopped a year ago, I figured it was just as well. *Stupid Bill, and his stupid patchy hair,* I think.

I dream of giant combines made from black chrome and crystal, with headlights of wide, unblinking eyes. I take them to the fields, but something is wrong with the thresher. There's bonemeal dust on the wheat berries.

"Now, Libby," Bill says, but I can't hear the rest of what he's saying because the earth starts shaking and—

I scramble to my feet, kicking up sand with the dream still in my eyes.

There's lights in the afternoon sky and this awful thunder, like a thousand lightning bolts are striking the earth at once.

"Oh, Christ," I say. A murder of reapers swarm to the north, and even with the sun in the sky their bombs light the ground beneath like hellfire. It's easier to see reapers from far away, because they paint their underbellies light blue to blend with the sky.

Tris stands beside me and grips my wrist. "That's not . . . it has to be Toddville, right? Or Cedar Creek? They're not far enough away for home, right?"

I don't say anything. I don't know. I can only look.

Bill's hair is patchy because the glassmen arrested him and they tortured him. Bill asked his outside contacts if they knew anything about a place to get an illegal abortion. Bill brought back a hundred thousand dollars' worth of farm equipment and scars from wounds that would have killed someone without access to a doctor. But what kind of prisoner has access to a real doctor? Why did the glassmen arrest him? What if his contacts are exactly the type of men the glassmen like to bomb with their reapers? What if Bill is?

But I know it isn't that simple. No one knows why the glassmen bomb us. No one *really* knows the reason for the whole damn mess, their reapers and their drones and their arcane rules you're shot for not following.

"Should we go back?"

She says it like she's declared war on a cardinal direction, like she really will get on that boat and walk into a reaper wasteland and salvage what's left of our lives and have that baby.

I squeeze her hand. "It's too close," I say. "Toddville, I think you're right. Let's get going, though. Probably not safe here."

She nods. She doesn't look me in the eye. We paddle through the choppy water until sun sets. And then, without saying anything, we ship the oars and I turn on the engine.

Three nights later, we see lights on the shore. It's a glassmen military installation. Dad marked it on the map, but still I'm surprised by its size, its brightness, the brazen way it sits on the coastline, as though daring to attract attention.

"I'd never thought a building could be so . . ."

"Angry?" Tris says.

"Violent."

"It's like a giant middle finger up the ass of the Chesapeake."

I laugh despite myself. "You're ridiculous."

We're whispering, though we're on the far side of the bay and the water is smooth and quiet. After that reaper drone attack, I'm remembering more than I like of my childhood terror of the glassmen. Dad and Mom had to talk to security drones a few times after the occupation, and I remember the oddly modulated voices, distinctly male, and the bright unblinking eyes behind the glass masks of their robot heads. I don't know anyone who has met a real glassman, instead of one of their remote robots. It's a retaliatory offense to harm a drone because the connection between the drone and the glassman on the other side of the world (or up in some space station) is so tight that sudden violence can cause brain damage. I wonder how they can square *potential brain damage* with *dead children*, but I guess I'm not a glassman.

So we row carefully, but fast as we can, hoping to distance our little fishing boat from the towering building complex. Its lights pulse so brightly they leave spots behind my eyes.

And then, above us, we hear the chopping whirr of blades cutting the air, the whine of unmanned machinery readying for deployment. I look up and shade my eyes: a reaper.

Tris drops her oar. It slides straight into the bay, but neither of us bother to catch it. If we don't get away now, a lost oar won't matter anyway. She lunges into our supply bag, brings out a bag of apples. The noise of the reaper is close, almost deafening. I can't hear what she yells at me before she jumps into the bay. I hesitate in the boat, afraid to leave our supplies and afraid to be blown to pieces by a reaper. I look back up and see a panel slide open on its bright blue belly. The panel reveals dark glass; behind it, a single, unblinking eye.

I jump into the water, but my foot catches on the remaining oar. The boat rocks behind me, but panic won't let me think—I tug and tug until the boat capsizes and suddenly ten pounds of supplies are falling on my head, dragging me deeper into the dark water. I try to kick out, but my leg is tangled with the drawstring of a canvas bag, and I can't make myself focus enough to get it loose. All I can think of is that big glass eye waiting to kill me. My chest burns and my ears fill to bursting with pressure. I'd always thought I would die in fire, but water isn't much better. I don't even know if Tris made it, or if the eye caught her, too.

I try to look up, but I'm too deep; it's too dark to even know which way that is. *God*, I think, *save her. Let her get back home.* It's rude to demand things of God, but I figure dying ought to excuse the presumption.

Something tickles my back. I gasp and the water flows in, drowning my lungs, flooding out what air I had left. But the thing in the water with me has a light on its head and strange, shiny legs and it's using them to get under my arms and drag me up until we reach the surface and I cough and retch and *breathe, thank you God.* The thing takes me to shore, where Tris is waiting to hug me and kiss my forehead like I'm the little sister.

"Jesus," she says, and I wonder if God really does take kindly to demands until I turn my head and understand: my savior is a drone.

I will feed you," the glassman says. He looks like a spider with an oversized glassman head: eight chrome legs and two glass eyes. "The pregnant one should eat. Her daughter is growing."

I wonder if some glassman technology is translating his words into English. If in his language, whatever it is, *the pregnant one* is a kind of respectful address. Or maybe they taught him to speak to us that way.

I'm too busy appreciating the bounty of air in my lungs to notice the other thing he said.

"Daughter?" Tris says.

The glassman nods. "Yes. I have been equipped with a body-safe sonic scanning device. Your baby has not been harmed by your ordeal. I am here to help and reassure you."

Tris looks at me, carefully. I sit up. "You said something about food?"

"Yes!" It's hard to tell, his voice is so strange, but he sounds happy. As though rescuing two women threatened by one of his reaper fellows is the best piece of luck he's had all day. "I will be back," he says, and scuttles away, into the forest.

Tris hands me one of her rescued apples. "What the hell?" Her voice is low, but I'm afraid the glassman can hear us anyway.

"A trap?" I whisper, barely vocalizing into her left ear.

She shakes her head. "He seems awfully . . ."

"Eager?"

"Young."

The glassman comes back a minute later, walking on six legs and holding two boxes in the others. His robot must be a new model; the others I've seen look more human. "I have meals! A nearby convoy has provided them for you," he says, and places the boxes carefully in front of us. "The one with a red ribbon is for the pregnant one. It has nutrients."

Tris's hands shake as she opens it. The food doesn't look dangerous, though it resembles the strange pictures in Tris's old magazines more than the stuff I make at home. A perfectly rectangular steak, peas, corn mash. Mine is the same, except I have regular corn. We eat silently, while the glassman gives every impression of smiling upon us benevolently.

"Good news," he pipes, when I'm nearly done forcing the bland food down my raw throat. "I have been authorized to escort you both to a safe hospital facility."

"Hospital?" Tris asks, in a way that makes me sit up and put my arm around her.

"Yes," the glassman says. "To ensure the safe delivery of your daughter."

The next morning, the glassman takes us to an old highway a mile from the water's edge. A convoy waits for us, four armored tanks and two platform trucks. One of the platform beds is filled with mechanical supplies, including two dozen glass-and-chrome heads. The faces are blank, the heads unattached to any robot body, but the effect makes me nauseous. Tris digs her nails into my forearm. The other platform bed is mostly empty except for a few boxes and one man tied to the guardrails. He lies prone on the floor and doesn't move when we climb in after our glassman. At first I'm afraid that he's dead, but then he twitches and groans before falling silent again.

"Who is he?" Tris asks.

"Non-state actor," our glassman says, and pulls up the grate behind us.

"What?"

The convoy engines whirr to life—quiet compared to the three old men, but the noise shocks me after our days of silence on the bay.

The glassman swivels his head, his wide unblinking eyes fully focused on my sister. I'm afraid she's set him off and they'll tie us to the railings like that poor man. Instead, he clicks his two front legs together for no reason that I can see except maybe it gives him something to do.

"Terrorist," he says, quietly.

Tris looks at me and I widen my eyes: *don't you dare say another word.* She nods.

"The convoy will be moving now. You should sit for your safety."

He clacks away before we can respond. He hooks his hind legs through the side rail opposite us and settles down, looking like nothing so much as a contented cat.

The armored tanks get into formation around us and then we lurch forward, rattling over the broken road. Tris makes it for half an hour before she pukes over the side.

For two days, Tris and I barely speak. The other man in our truck wakes up about once every ten hours, just in time for one of the two-legged glassmen from the armored tanks to clomp over and give us all some food and water. The man gets less than we do, though none of it is very good. He eats in such perfect silence that I wonder if the glassmen have cut out his tongue. As soon as he finishes, one of the tank glassmen presses a glowing metal bar to the back of his neck. The mark it leaves is a perfect triangle, raw and red like a fresh burn. The prisoner doesn't struggle when the giant articulated metal hand grips his shoulders, he only stares, and soon after he slumps against the railing. I have lots of time to wonder about those marks; hour after slow hour with a rattling truck bruising my tailbone and regrets settling into my joints like dried tears. Sometimes Tris massages knots from my neck, and sometimes they come right back while I knead hers. I can't see any way to escape, so I try not to think about it. But there's no helping the sick, desperate knowledge that every hour we're closer to locking Tris in a hospital for six months so the glassmen can force her to have a baby.

During the third wake-up and feeding of the bound man, our glassman shakes out his legs and clacks over to the edge of the truck bed. The robots who drive the tanks are at least eight feet tall, with oversized arms and legs equipped with artillery rifles. They would be terrifying even if we weren't completely at their mercy. The two glassmen stare at each other, eerily silent and still.

The bound man, I'd guess Indian from his thick straight hair and dark skin, strains as far forward as he can. He nods at us.

"They're talking," he says. His words are slow and painstakingly formed. We crawl closer to hear him better. "In their real bodies."

I look back up, wondering how he knows. They're so still, but then glassmen are always uncanny.

Tris leans forward, so her lips are at my ear. "Their eyes," she whispers.

Glassman robot eyes never blink. But their pupils dilate and contract just like ours do. Only now both robots' eyes are pupil-blasted black despite the glaring noon sun. Talking in their real bodies? That must mean they've stopped paying us any attention.

"Could we leave?" I whisper. No one has tied us up. I think our glassman is under the impression he's doing us a favor.

Tris buries her face in the back of my short nappy hair and wraps her arms around me. I know it's a ploy, but it comforts me all the same. "The rest of the convoy."

Even as I nod, the two glassmen step away from each other, and our convoy is soon enough on its way. This time, though, the prisoner gets to pass his time awake and silent. No one tells us to move away from him.

"I have convinced the field soldier to allow me to watch the operative," our glassman says proudly.

"That's very nice," Tris says. She's hardly touched her food.

"I am glad you appreciate my efforts! It is my job to assess mission parameter achievables. Would you mind if I asked you questions?"

I frown at him and quickly look away. Tris, unfortunately, has decided she'd rather play with fire than her food.

"Of course," she says.

We spend the next few hours subjected to a tireless onslaught of questions. Things like, "How would you rate our society-building efforts in the Tidewater Region?" and "What issue would you most like to see addressed in the upcoming Societal Health Meeting?" and "Are you mostly satisfied or somewhat dissatisfied with the cleanliness of the estuary?"

"The fish are toxic," I say to this last question. My first honest answer. It seems to startle him. At least, that's how I interpret the way he clicks his front two legs together.

Tris pinches my arm, but I ignore her.

"Well," says the glassman. "That is potentially true. We have been monitoring the unusually high levels of radiation and heavy metal toxicity. But you can rest assured that we are addressing the problem and its potential harmful side-effects on Beneficial Societal Development."

"Like dying of mercury poisoning?" Tris pinches me again, but she smiles for the first time in days.

"I do not recommend it for the pregnant one! I have been serving you both nutritious foods well within the regulatory limits."

I have no idea what those regulatory limits might be, but I don't ask.

"In any case," he says. "Aside from that issue, the estuary is very clean."

"Thank you," Tris says, before I can respond.

"You're very welcome. We are here to help you."

"How far away is the hospital?" she asks.

I feel like a giant broom has swept the air from the convoy, like our glassman has tossed me back into the bay to drown. I knew Tris was desperate; I didn't realize how much.

"Oh," he says, and his pupils go very wide. I could kiss the prisoner for telling us what that means: no one's at home.

The man now leans toward us, noticing the same thing. "You pregnant?" he asks Tris.

She nods.

He whistles through a gap between his front teeth. "Some rotten luck," he says. "I never seen a baby leave one of their clinics. Fuck knows what they do to them."

"And the mothers?" I ask.

He doesn't answer, just lowers his eyes and looks sidelong at our dormant glassman. "Depends," he whispers, "on who they think you are."

That's all we have time for; the glassman's eyes contract again and his head tilts like a bird's. "There is a rehabilitative facility in the military installation to which we are bound. Twenty-three hours ETA."

"A prison?" Tris asks.

"A hospital," the glassman says firmly.

When we reach the pipeline, I know we're close. The truck bounces over fewer potholes and cracks; we even meet a convoy heading in the other direction. The pipeline is a perfect clear tube about sixteen feet high. It looks empty to me, a giant hollow tube that distorts the landscape on the other side like warped glass. It doesn't run near the bay, and no one from home knows enough to plot it on a map. Maybe this is the reason the glassmen are here. I wonder what could be so valuable in that hollow tube that Tris has to give birth in a cage, that little Georgia has to die, that a cluster bomb has to destroy half our wheat crop. What's so valuable that looks like nothing at all?

The man spends long hours staring out the railing of the truck, as though he's never seen anything more beautiful or more terrifying. Sometimes he talks to us, small nothings, pointing out a crane overhead or a derelict road with a speed limit sign—*55 miles per hour*, it says, *radar enforced.*

At first our glassman noses around these conversations, but he decides they're innocuous enough. He tells the man to "refrain from exerting a corrupting influence," and resumes his perch on the other side of the truck bed. The prisoner's name is Simon, he tells us, and he's on watch. For what, I wonder, but know well enough not to ask.

"What's in it?" I say instead, pointing to the towering pipeline.

"I heard it's a wormhole." He rests his chin on his hands, a gesture that draws careful, casual attention to the fact that his left hand has loosened the knots. He catches my eye for a blink and then looks away. My breath catches—Is he trying to escape? Do we dare?

"A wormhole? Like, in space?" Tris says, oblivious. Or maybe not. Looking at her, I realize she might just be a better actor.

I don't know what Tris means, but Simon nods. "A passage through space, that's what I heard."

"That is incorrect!"

The three of us snap our heads around, startled to see the glassman so close. His eyes whirr with excitement. "The Designated Area Project is not what you refer to as a wormhole, which are in fact impractical as transportation devices."

Simon shivers and looks down at his feet. My lips feel swollen with regret—what if he thinks we're corrupted? What if he notices Simon's left hand? But Tris raises her chin, stubborn and defiant at the worst possible time—I guess the threat of that glassman hospital is making her too crazy to feel anything as reasonable as fear.

"Then what is it?" she asks, so plainly that Simon's mouth opens, just a little.

Our glassman stutters forward on his delicate metallic legs. "I am not authorized to tell you," he says, clipped.

"Why not? It's the whole goddamned reason all your glassman reapers and drones and robots are swarming all over the place, isn't it? We don't even get to know what the hell it's all for?"

"Societal redevelopment is one of our highest mission priorities," he says, a little desperately.

I lean forward and grab Tris's hand as she takes a sharp, angry breath. "Honey," I say, "Tris, *please.*"

She pulls away from me, hard as a slap, but she stops talking. The glassman says nothing; just quietly urges us a few yards away from Simon. No more corruption on his watch.

Night falls, revealing artificial lights gleaming on the horizon. Our glassman doesn't sleep. Not even in his own place, I suppose, because whenever I check with a question his eyes stay the same and he answers without hesitation. Maybe they have drugs to keep themselves awake for a week at a time. Maybe he's not human. I don't ask—I'm still a little afraid he might shoot me for saying the wrong thing, and more afraid that he'll start talking about Ideal Societal Redevelopment.

At the first hint of dawn, Simon coughs and leans back against the railing, catching my eye. Tris is dozing on my shoulder, drool slowly soaking my shirt. Simon flexes his hands, now free. He can't speak, but our glassman isn't looking at him. He points to the floor of the truckbed, then lays himself out with his hands over his head. There's something urgent in his face. Something knowledgable. To the glassmen he's a terrorist, but what does that make him to us? I shake Tris awake.

"Libs?"

"Glassman," I say, "I have a question about societal redevelopment deliverables."

Tris sits straight up.

"I would be pleased to hear it!" the glassman says.

"I would like to know what you plan to do with my sister's baby."

"Oh," the glassman says. The movement of his pupils is hardly discernible in this low light, but I've been looking. I grab Tris by her shoulder and we scramble over to Simon.

"Duck!" he says. Tris goes down before I do, so only I can see the explosion light up the front of the convoy. Sparks and embers fly through the air like a starfall. The pipeline glows pink and purple and orange. Even the strafe of bullets seems beautiful until it blows out the tires of our truck. We crash and tumble. Tris holds onto me, because I've forgotten how to hold onto myself.

The glassmen are frozen. Some have tumbled from the overturned trucks, their glass and metal arms halfway to their guns. Their eyes don't move, not even when three men in muddy camouflage lob sticky black balls into the heart of the burning convoy.

Tris hauls me to my feet. Simon shouts something at one of the other men, who turns out to be a woman.

"What the hell was that?" I ask.

"EMP," Simon says. "Knocks them out for a minute or two. We have to haul ass."

The woman gives Simon a hard stare. "They're clean?"

"They were prisoners, too," he says.

The woman—light skinned, close-cropped hair—hoists an extra gun, unconvinced. Tris straightens up. "I'm pregnant," she says. "And ain't nothing going to convince me to stay here."

"Fair enough," the woman says, and hands Tris a gun. "We have ninety seconds. Just enough time to detonate."

Our glassman lies on his back, legs curled in the air. One of those sticky black balls has lodged a foot away from his blank glass face. It's a retaliatory offense to harm a drone. I remember what they say about brain damage when the glassmen are connected. Is he connected? Will this hurt him? I don't like the kid, but he's so young. Not unredeemable. He saved my life.

I don't know why I do it, but while Tris and the others are distracted, I use a broken piece of the guard rail to knock off the black ball. I watch it roll under the truck, yards away. I don't want to hurt him; I just want my sister and me safe and away.

"Libs!" It's Tris, looking too much like a terrorist with her big black gun. Dad taught us both to use them, but the difference between us is I wish that I didn't know how, and Tris is glad.

I run to catch up. A man idles a pickup ten yards down the road from the convoy.

"They're coming back on," he says.

"Detonating!" The woman's voice is a bird-call, a swoop from high to low. She presses a sequence of buttons on a remote and suddenly the light ahead is fiercer than the sun and it smells like gasoline and woodsmoke and tar. I've seen plenty enough bomb wreckage in my life; I feel like when it's *ours* it should look different. Better. It doesn't.

Tris pulls me into the back of the pickup and we're bouncing away before we can even shut the back door. We turn off the highway and drive down a long dirt road through the woods. I watch the back of the woman's head through the rear window. She has four triangular scars at the base of her neck, the same as Bill's.

Something breaks out of the underbrush on the side of the road. Something that moves unnaturally fast, even on the six legs he has left. Something that calls out, in that stupid, naive, inhuman voice:

"Stop the vehicle! Pregnant one, do not worry, I will—"

"Fuck!" Tris's terror cuts off the last of the speech. The car swerves, tossing me against the door. I must not have latched it properly, because next thing I know I'm tumbling to the dirt with a thud that jars my teeth. The glassman scrambles on top of me without any regard for the pricking pain of his long, metallic limbs.

"Kill that thing!" It's a man, I'm not sure who. I can't look, pinioned as I am.

"Pregnant one, step down from the terrorist vehicle and I will lead you to safety. There is a Reaper Support Flyer on its way."

He grips me between two metallic arms and hauls me up with surprising strength. The woman and Simon have guns trained on the glassman, but they hesitate—if they shoot him, they have to shoot me. Tris has her gun up as well, but she's shaking so hard she can't even get her finger on the trigger.

"Let go of me," I say to him. He presses his legs more firmly into my side.

"I will save the pregnant one," he repeats, as though to reassure both of us. He's young, but he's still a glassman. He knows enough to use me as a human shield.

Tris lowers the gun to her side. She slides from the truck bed and walks forward.

"Don't you dare, Tris!" I yell, but she just shakes her head. My sister, giving herself to a glassman? What would Dad say? I can't even free a hand to wipe my eyes. I hate this boy behind the glass face. I hate him because he's too young and ignorant to even understand what he's doing wrong. Evil is good to a glassman. Wrong is right. The pregnant one has to be saved.

I pray to God, then. I say, *God, please let her not be a fool. Please let her escape.*

And I guess God heard, because when she's just a couple of feet away she looks straight at me and smiles like she's about to cry. "I'm sorry, Libs," she whispers. "I love you. I just can't let him take me again."

"Pregnant one! Please drop your weapon and we will—"

And then she raises her gun and shoots.

My arm hurts. Goddamn it hurts, like there's some small, toothy animal burrowing inside. I groan and feel my sister's hands, cool on my forehead.

"They know the doctor," she says. "That Esther that Bill told us about, remember? She's a regular doctor, too, not just abortions. You'll be fine."

I squint up at her. The sun has moved since she shot me; I can hardly see her face for the light behind it. But even at the edges I can see her grief. Her tears drip on my hairline and down my forehead.

"I don't care," I say, with some effort. "I wanted you to do it."

"I was so afraid, Libs."

"I know."

"We'll get home now, won't we?"

"Sure," I say. *If it's there.*

The terrorists take us to a town fifty miles from Annapolis. Even though it's close to the city, the glassmen mostly leave it alone. It's far enough out from the pipeline, and there's not much here, otherwise: just a postage stamp of a barley field, thirty or so houses and one of those large, old, whitewashed barn-door churches. At night, the town is ghost empty.

Tris helps me down from the truck. Even that's an effort. My head feels half-filled with syrup. Simon and the others say their goodbyes and head out quickly. It's too dangerous for fighters to stay this close to the city. Depending on how much the glassmen know about Tris and me, it isn't safe for us either. But between a baby and a bullet, we don't have much choice.

Alone, now, we read the church's name above the door: *Esther Zion Congregation Church, Methodist.*

Tris and I look at each other. "Oh, Christ," she says. "Did Bill lie, Libby? Is he really so hung up on that sin bullshit that he sent me all the way out here, to a *church . . .*"

I lean against her and wonder how he ever survived to come back to us. It feels like a gift, now, with my life half bled out along the road behind. "Bill wouldn't lie, Tris. Maybe he got it wrong. But he wouldn't lie."

The pews are old but well-kept. The prayer books look like someone's been using them. The only person inside is a white lady, sweeping the altar.

"Simon and Sybil sent you," she says, not a question. Sybil—we never even asked the woman's name.

"My sister," we both say, and then, improbably, laugh.

A month later, Tris and I round Bishop's Head and face north. At the mouth of our estuary, we aren't close enough to see Toddville, let alone our home, but we can't see any drones either. The weather is chillier this time around, the water harder to navigate with the small boat. Tris looks healthy and happy; older and younger. No one will mistake her for twenty-five again, but there's nothing wrong with wisdom.

The doctor fixed up my arm and found us an old, leaky rowboat when it was clear we were determined to go back. Tris has had to do most of the work; her arms are starting to look like they belong to someone who doesn't spend all her time reading. I think about the harvest and hope the bombs didn't reap the grain before we could. If anyone could manage those fields without me, Bill can. We won't starve this winter, assuming reapers didn't destroy everything. Libby ships the oars and lets us float, staring at the deep gray sky and its reflection on the water that seems to stretch endlessly before us.

"Bill will have brought the harvest in just fine," I say.

"You love him, don't you?"

I think about his short, patchy hair. That giant green monster he brought back like a dowry. "He's good with the old engines. Better than me."

"I think he loves you. Maybe one of you could get around to doing something about it?"

"Maybe so."

Tris and I sit like that for a long time. The boat drifts toward shore, and neither of us stop it. A fish jumps in the water to my left; a heron circles overhead.

"Dad's probably out fishing," she says, maneuvering us around. "We might catch him on the way in."

"That'll be a surprise! Though he won't be happy about his boat."

"He might let it slide. Libby?"

"Yes?"

"I'm sorry—"

"You aren't sorry if you'd do it again," I say. "And I'm not sorry if I'd let you."

She holds my gaze. "Do you know how much I love you?"

We have the same smile, my sister and I. It's a nice smile, even when it's scared and a little sad.

Naomi Kritzer has been writing science fiction and fantasy for twenty years. Her short story "Cat Pictures Please" won the 2016 Hugo and Locus awards and was nominated for the Nebula Award. A collection of her short stories was released in 2017, and her YA novel, tentatively called *Welcome to Catnet*, is forthcoming from Tor Books. She lives in St. Paul, Minnesota, with her spouse, two kids, and four cats. The number of cats is subject to change without notice.

Bits

NAOMI KRITZER

So here is something a lot of people don't realize: most companies that make sex toys are really small. Even a successful sex-toy manufacturer like Squishies (tm) is still run out of a single office attached to a warehouse, and the staff consists of Julia (the owner), Juan (the guy who does all the warehouse stuff), and me (the person who does everything else).

(You are probably wondering right now if that includes product testing. I make it a habit not to talk about my sex life with strangers but Julia requires that everyone she hires take home a Squishie or a Firmie or one of the other IntelliFlesh products and try it out, either solo or with a partner. I pointed out that if she ever hired an alien—sorry, "extraterrestrial immigrant"—the neurology doesn't match up, and does she want to admit she discriminates in hiring? But I didn't argue that hard, because hey, free sex toy, why not? Frankly, I found it a kind of freaky experience, having this piece of sensate flesh that didn't really belong there, and after a little bit of experimentation I stuck it in a drawer and haven't touched it since.)

Anyway, we outsource the manufacturing and the boxes of Squishies and Firmies get shipped to us on shrink-wrapped pallets and Juan breaks them down to re-ship in more manageable quantities to the companies that resell our products.

The original product were the Squishies, and Julia is not at ALL shy about people knowing about her sex life (we have an instructional video, and she's IN it), so I don't mind telling you that she came up with it because her boyfriend at the time had a fetish for really large breasts, we're not talking "naturally gifted" or even "enhanced with silicone" but "truly impractical for all real-world purposes like breathing and using your arms," and conveniently at the time she was working at a company making top-of-the-line prosthetics with neural integration. She made herself a really enormous set of breasts and after a lot of futzing with the neural integration she got them to be sensate. Then the boyfriend dumped her and she didn't really need them anymore, but her friend who'd had a double mastectomy said, "why don't you make me a smaller set?" and that, supposedly, was when it occurred to her that maybe she could make this product to SELL. She found a manufacturing facility and office space, hired me and Juan, and went into the Fully Sensate Attachable Flesh business.

Depending on your predilections you may already be wondering why she started with boobs. IntelliFlesh is re-shapable, at least up to a point, and since I was the Customer Service department I started getting calls from people who wanted to reshape it into something longer, stiffer, and pointier.

"Julia," I said one day, taking off my headset, "you need to start making strap-on dicks."

"I can't call those Squishies," she said dismissively.

"So? Roll out a new line. Hardies. Dickies. Cockies. If you go with Cockies you can say 'like cookies, only better' in the ads." Maybe I should note that one of the few things Julia doesn't let me do is write the ad copy.

The Firmies were an even bigger seller than the Squishies. Between boobs and dicks, we had most users covered, but every now and then I got a call from someone who wanted something a little more customized.

"You've reached Afton Enterprises, home of Squishies and Firmies," I said. "How may I help you?" (In addition to not getting to write the ad copy, I don't get to decide how to answer the phone, judging from the fact that Julia shot down the greeting, "How may I improve your sex life today?")

"I'm thinking about buying either a Squishie or a Firmie, and I . . . had some questions," the woman said, her voice hesitant. "They're sort of expensive and I'm not sure which will meet my needs."

"Well, the Squishie is squishier," I said. "It's more malleable, but it also doesn't tend to hold alternate shapes for very long unless you refrigerate it for a while before you get started. The Firmie arrives long and narrow, but if you want it to have a different shape—say, a curve or even a hook—you can *gently* heat it up and mold it."

"What I want is a prosthetic vagina," the woman blurted out. "In a different spot."

You're not really supposed to say, "you want *what?*" to customers when you're doing customer support for a sex toy shop. We are pro-sex, pro-kink, and anti-shame: there is officially no wrong way to have sex. So: "Which spot?" I asked.

"Well, we're not exactly sure. Part of the advantage of your products is that we can move them around. What if I bought two Firmies? Could I reshape those into two halves of a vagina, like maybe one could be the top of the, um, tube, and the other could be the bottom . . . are your products compatible with lubricant?"

"There's a special lube that we sell," I said. "Other lubricants might void the warranty."

"That adds to the cost even more," the woman said, clearly frustrated. "Is there *any* way to find out before I put down all that money whether it's going to work for me? If they sold these at REI I would just *buy it* and figure I'd return it if I needed to, but nobody takes returns on sex toys."

"We do, under some circumstances," I said. "Can you give me a little more information about what your goal is with our product?"

"I want to have sex with my husband," she said, impatiently, "*real* sex, or as real as it can get. And he's a K'srillan male. Our God-given parts just don't match up."

The K'srillan—our "extraterrestrial immigrants"—made radio contact about a decade ago, and arrived on earth a year and three months ago. Juan periodically mutters about how no matter what they say, they might still be planning invasion and how would we even stop them? But they offered us suspended-animation technology in exchange for asylum (from *who?* was Juan's immediate question, but we've been assured that they were fleeing the death of their sun, not some second wave of dangerous aliens), and a dozen U.S. cities wound up taking settlements. (They're spread around. There are a bunch of others in other countries all over the world.) So far in the U.S. it was mostly okay, other than some anti-immigrant rioting in Kansas City. I hadn't actually met any K'srillan—there was a settlement in Minneapolis but I live in St. Paul and don't cross the river much— but from what I could tell they were all law-abiding and hard working and in general the sort of people you want to have come and settle in your city.

They also looked kind of like roadkilled giant squid. They don't have faces, as such. I mean, they have eyes, seven of them, which are on stalks, and they have a mouth, which they use to eat and speak, but they're not right next to each other the way you would expect in practically every earth species out there, from mammals to reptiles to fish. I mean, okay, we do have squids. But they don't walk around the shopping mall. On tentacles.

K'srillan do talk, but they aren't physically capable of making the same sounds as us, so they carry a voice synthesizer for communication.

The thought of sex with, or marriage to, a K'srillan was completely baffling to me.

Even, dare I say it, *gross*.

B ut we are pro-sex, pro-kink, and anti-shame, so I said, "Okay!" in as cheerful a voice as I could muster, and didn't add, "Husband? You sure moved fast." (I might not judge sex lives but I reserve the right to judge major life decisions.) "I don't actually know that much about K'srillan sexual anatomy. So, um. He has a penis?"

"Yes, we don't need a Firmie for *him*," the woman said, dismissively. "Your products don't interface with K'srillan neurology anyway or we'd consider buying him a Firmie and having him use that instead of his own penis. He has a penis, but it's eighteen inches long, and bifurcated."

"Bifurcated?"

"Branches into two, basically."

"You'd need at least four Firmies," I blurted out. "To make a vagina for eighteen inches of branched penis."

"That is a *lot* of money."

"Yeah, for that much you could practically get a custom order."

"Oh! You do custom orders?"

"No. We don't. But surely *someone* . . ."

"Do you think I haven't *checked*?" the woman asked, exasperated. "There has been a lot of discussion of this in the Full Integration community. *I am not the only woman looking.*"

"You aren't?"

"No!"

Well, that changed things, maybe. A custom order was one thing. A *prototype* was potentially a whole different matter.

N o."
      "No? Just no?"

"Would you rather I went with 'no, that's a repulsive idea'?"

I stared at Julia. "I thought we were pro-kink and anti-shame?" To be fair, I'd had a similar reaction at first, but I was actively trying to get past my emotional reaction. Everyone involved was a consenting adult— okay, so the K'srillans had a different life span and developmental arc from humans, but I'd checked, and since the K'srillan males didn't actually develop a penis until sexual maturity, clearly these *were* adults we were talking about. Anyway. "Did you know that there's already a sector of the porn industry devoted to sex between human women and K'srillan males? Apparently an eighteen-inch bifurcated—"

"*Stop*. I don't want to hear about it."

"Did I ever say that about your ex-boyfriend's fetish for massive boobs? *No*. Your kink is not my kink, and your kink is okay. Their kink is not our kink, but that doesn't mean we can't sell them stuff!"

Julia threw down the silicone butt plug she'd been examining. (We'd been thinking about new ways to extend our line *anyway*. It's not as if my suggestion had come completely out of the blue.) "Okay. Fine. You want to design something, we'll test the market. But *you* are going to have to take the measurements, *you* are going to have to build the prototype, and you are *certainly* going to have to do the focus group and interviews because *this is a repulsive idea*."

"Fine!" I said. "Fine. I will handle—" I cut myself off. "I will *deal with* all of it. And we'll see if enough people want this to make it viable."

The woman who'd called was named Liz, and her husband's name was Zmivla, and it turned out that Zmivla was part of the group that had settled in Minneapolis, so they lived less than five miles from my office. I drove to the high-rise apartment where so many of the new arrivals had moved in, and took an elevator to their apartment on the twelfth floor.

"Come in," Liz said when she answered the door. "I've made coffee." She laughed nervously. "Do you drink coffee?"

Zmivla was lounging in the recliner, tentacles draped over both the arm rests and the foot rest. Two of his eye stalks swiveled to look at me when I came in and his speech synthesizer said, "Hello, Ms. Marshall."

"Call me Renee," I said.

Liz handed me a cup of coffee and I studied Zmivla, wondering if I should just whip out the tape measure and ask him to whip out his penis, or if we should have some more preliminaries first. When Julia started making the Firmies, I think rather than measuring actual penises she bought the dozen or so top-selling models of dildo and measured *those*. But there aren't currently any K'srillan dildo models on the market, so we were going to have to go with some actual penises. I took a deep breath. "I should ask some sort of basic questions first, I think."

"Would you like to know how we met?" Liz asked, brightly.

Actually, I mostly wanted to know how K'srillan sex normally worked *with another K'srillan* but if she wanted to start with something a little less explicit I supposed that was a reasonable lead-in, so I nodded and drank my coffee while they told me their how-we-met story. I think it involved a conversation that started at the Powderhorn Art Fair but it's possible I'm misremembering and actually that's how my sister met her ex-husband. If you want to know the truth, all the cutesy "how we met" stories blur together for me. If you met your sweetie because he was third in line for the organized gang bang at the local dungeon and you really liked the shape of his dick, *that* I'll remember. If he offered to help you carry your pottery in his tentacles while you kept your dog from bolting, I just don't care enough to keep it in my head for more than fifteen minutes.

Liz worked in a boring office and Zmivla had a boring job that was clearly beneath his talents and after they told me that Liz's hobby was making still life paintings it was clear they were stalling, and I couldn't entirely blame them, given that I was there to measure the guy's penis.

"I know this is a somewhat uncomfortable situation for all of us," I said. "But we really probably should get down to business, okay?"

"I just want you to . . ." Liz hesitated.

Zmivla stroked the back of her hand with the tip of one of his tentacles, delicately. With one of the others, he brushed a strand of hair out of her face. "Liz and I appreciate your open-mindedness," he said. "But it's important to her that you see us as people first. As a couple who has a right to be together, to share the love that we do."

"You want me to think that you're normal," I said. I tried to keep the edge of sarcasm out of my voice, but I probably didn't entirely succeed. "Just another Minneapolis family."

"I know we're not like everyone else," Liz said. "But we love each other and take care of each other. And that's what's *important.*"

"Right," I said. "But you didn't call me to affirm your relationship. You called me to help you with your sex life. So let's talk about *that.*"

So, among actual K'srillans, the female folds herself around the male; she does have a short channel that's there all the time, but a decent amount of her sexual passageway is constructed on-the-fly. I took notes. The actual sex involved friction, but some of it was accomplished by the same muscles that were used to fold the extended vagina into place; I wasn't entirely sure whether the male K'srillan thrusted, or not.

"You realize," I said, "there is *no way* we can build an IntelliFlesh vagina that will do the folding thing. Or the rippling, or whatever. Maybe we could add a vibrator . . ."

"Older K'srillan females sometimes lose a certain amount of strength," Zmivla offered. "There is a procedure that allows the female to fasten her channel into place, and when having sex with a female who has had this procedure, the male thrusts. It should work." The tips of his tentacles turned pink and I wasn't sure whether he was embarrassed, sexually aroused, or something else entirely. "Though this vibration option you mention . . ."

I had brought the tape measure but I wound up having Liz do the measurements. I made a sketch and had her call out the measurements as I noted them down. Eighteen inches was a rough estimate, it turned out: one branch ran 18.25 inches stem to stern and the other branch was 17.8 inches. Girth of the trunk portion was comparable to a soda can; the branches were a lot more slender and tapered toward the tip, like extremely long carrots. The K'srillan penis is *blue*, I noticed, or at least it's blue when he's sexually aroused, sort of a dusky violet-blue that would indicate in a human that he's oxygen-deprived or possibly freezing to death. There are visible veins in the sides.

"I don't suppose you know how typical you are," I said. "I mean, for a K'srillan male, are you on the large side or the small side, are you more or less asymmetrical than most, how does your girth compare . . ."

"I don't know," he said. "But I don't think it would be too hard to find out. There are about a thousand K'srillans living in this apartment complex, after all, and I know two dozen others with human wives."

I spent two entire days measuring K'srillan penises.

The good news was that K'srillan penises turned out to be reasonably uniform. I mean, they ranged in length from sixteen inches all the way up to twenty, and they ranged in girth from pop can to coffee mug, and there were some penises where one branch was noticeably shorter, even by as much as six inches. But human penises *also* vary. I mean, the average length for an erect dick is about five inches, but the record holder was 13.5 inches long. (Not to overshare but that just sounds like it would be *painful.*)

The variety of sizing in human dicks has not prevented the successful marketing of any number of artificial vaginas (or "masturbation sleeves," to use the technical industry term). I mean, just like with dildos you can provide a set of different sizes but they are not all THAT customized, and given that IntelliFlesh is a lot more adaptable than silicone, I was pretty sure we'd be able to come up with something that would work.

Anyway, that was the good news. The bad news was that I had to spend *two entire days* measuring K'srillan penises.

Fortunately, K'srillan men seem to be pretty secure in their masculinity. I mean, imagine the reaction if you came at the average human male with a tape measure. My former brother-in-law actually measured his *own* dick at some point and it was 4.5 inches long, so a whopping half-inch shorter than the average. My sister told absolutely everyone, after the divorce, but the problem wasn't really his very-slightly-runty dick, it was the ways in which he compensated and the fact that he was a complete loser in the sack, one of those men who thinks that his penis is *magic* and if you can't climax in two minutes just from him sticking it in you, you must be broken. One-half-inch-less than average length: not a problem. Complete boredom in the sack: definite problem.

(Sorry. Very few people in my life seem to embrace my no-overshares policy.)

Anyway. There was one K'srillan who shrank at the sight of the tape measure, but then he laughed (K'srillans actually have a physical response to humor, I found out, but the voice synthesizers are programmed to pick up on it and translate it into a ha-ha-ha sound) and said, "Give me just one moment" and swelled back up to full size within a few seconds. K'srillans all grew up in K'srillan society, which has its own set of gender roles and expectations that are absolutely nothing whatsoever like human gender stereotypes, and then they were plunged into human society and forced to adapt. One of the men noted, as I wrapped the tape measure around the trunk portion at the bottom, that in K'srillan society it is the *woman* who is expected to make the first move; a man who propositions a woman is shameless and forward, and he thinks human women like that, once we get used to the idea.

"Maybe," I said, and measured his length on the left-hand side: 17.85. "How'd you meet *your* wife, anyway?"

"I thought they told you?" he said, a little mournfully. "I have not been so fortunate yet, but I volunteered for this exciting project because it will perhaps raise interest in our kind."

"Wouldn't you honestly prefer to marry someone of your own *species?*" I said.

"Among my own kind I am considered unattractive," he said.

I stepped back and took a look at him. Over the two days, K'srillans had stopped looking like roadkilled squid to me, but I still wouldn't call any individual *attractive* as such. I finished the last measurement, wrote it down, and tossed my gloves into his kitchen trash can. "Thanks for your help," I said.

I was back in the office, finishing up my prototype design, when my phone rang.

"You do us an injustice," said a synthesized voice on the other end of the line.

"I'm sorry," I said. "Who's calling, please?"

"For *days* you come to our settlement and measure the male organs," the voice said, distressed. "And now I find out it is so that you can make *false female organs* for *human women*."

I scratched my head, wondering how I'd gotten myself into this. "Look. You do realize that we specialize in false organs of all varieties for humans—both women *and* men."

"Yes!" the voice said, furious. "And *I* am a K'srillan *female* married to a human *male*. Why are you not going to make false K'srillan *male* organs? What is *my* husband supposed to do to please me?"

So in the end, I'm sure you'll be shocked to hear, we made both. We made K'srillan vaginas: as I warned Liz, they're not capable of the K'srillan pre-sex vaginal origami action, but they do simulate the muscle movements with the addition of an adjustable vibrator. We also made K'srillan penises, though due to limited market penetration at this point we have only one size and shape (pop-bottle girth at the bottom, 17.85 on the left-hand size, 18.1 on the right-hand side).

What I find the weirdest these days are not the human/K'srillan couples. It's the human/human couples that buy one from each set and have sex with the detachable genitals instead of the compatible set they already had. Or maybe it's the porn of humans having sex with the K'srillan artificial genitalia. Or possibly the *gay* porn of humans having sex with K'srillan artificial genitalia. Or possibly the absolute weirdest is the porn of K'srillans having sex with artificial human genitalia—they can't do that with IntelliFlesh (years of research into their neurology remain to be done) but there's always the good old-fashioned strap-on option on one side, and an artificial vagina on the other.

Because really, there are two immutable laws of nature at work here: number one, love will find a way; and number two, if a sexual act can be conceived of, someone will pay money to watch it.

I've been thinking a lot about that first rule, lately. Because I told my sister about the "unattractive" K'srillan and jokingly—I swear I was joking!—pointed out that at least she'd never be bored in bed. She jokingly—she claims she was joking—asked me for his number. I told her she could have it if she promised to *never* tell me the details of their sex life, and she pointed out that I already knew this guy's penis size down to the quarter-inch . . .

Yeah, they're dating. They're not rushing into anything, so this story doesn't end with, "And the wedding's next week!" But I have to say—you do get used to the seven eyes looking at you over the after-dinner drinks and I've learned to spot the physical cues of the laugh even before the synthesizer goes "ha ha ha." And Gintika (that's his name) definitely doesn't make me think of roadkilled squid anymore. He makes me think about how sometimes we have more in common with people than we realize; he makes me think about all the ways to form a connection. He makes me think about the look on my sister's face when she talks about him. He makes me think, *love finds a way*, and *hey, sometimes finding a way, finds you love.*

Keffy R. M. Kehrli is a science fiction and fantasy writer currently living on Long Island in New York. When not writing, he's busy working on his PhD, editing *GlitterShip* (www.glittership.com), or petting dogs. His own fiction has previously appeared in publications such as *Uncanny Magazine*, *Apex Magazine*, *Lightspeed Magazine*, and *Clockwork Phoenix 5*, among others.

And Never Mind the Watching Ones

KEFFY R. M. KEHRLI

AARON

He is lying on the splintered, faded-gray wood of the dock, the fingers of one hand dangling in the slough and glitter frogs in his hair. His breath catches and he cups the back of Christian's head. An airplane is flying far, far overhead. It sounds like the purring exhale of the frogs. Aaron wonders where it's going.

When he comes, his abdominal muscles tense, pulling his shoulders off the planking. The frogs in his hair go tumbling nubbly ass over nose, their creaking noises gone silent. The orgasm is an adrenaline rush that outlines his body in nervous fire before fading, leaving a ringing in his ears.

Aaron stares up at the broadening remains of the jet contrail, sucking air like he's been running rather than getting head. He thinks, like every time, that he should have liked it more. He wonders if there's something wrong with his dick. Christian crawls across the dock and flops beside him, one arm draped carelessly over the baseball logo on Aaron's T-shirt.

One of the frogs has come back. It puts a clammy little hand on Aaron's cheek before letting out a croak. The others are scattered across the dock and they answer in identical voices.

"God, they're so creepy," Christian says. He picks up the frog. It kicks out its back legs and inflates its neck. It doesn't ribbit; it freezes as though holding its breath. The two boys can see the delicate iridescent shading on the frog's belly, the flecks of "glitter"—sensors of some kind, probably alien nanotech. They can see circuitry, visible under thin layers of skin.

"I like them," Aaron says, reaching out to touch the frog's nose with a fingertip. It opens its mouth slightly.

Christian holds the frog closer to his face, eyes narrowed in mock anger. "If you're going to watch, the least you could do is pay us, frogface."

"We still don't know if they're individuals, or like a hive mind or something," Aaron offers.

Christian drops the frog into the slough and it hits the muddy water with a disconsolate plunk. "Holy shit, I hope not."

"Is there really a difference between one super smart alien frog brain or a thousand of them, if they're always watching?"

"Is that like, if a tree falls in the forest?"

Aaron doesn't answer. The contrail overhead is starting to dissipate. The clouds around it have turned pink at the edges.

Christian rolls onto his side, propping his head up on one elbow. "Well, I've got something to tell you," he says.

"Yeah?"

Christian brushes hair out of Aaron's face, and then tucks his own long, dark brown hair behind his left ear. It falls forward over his shoulder and across his neck. There's a mole near where his clavicle peeks out from the collar of his yellow-and-green shirt. Aaron watches his lips as he says, "I got into Dartmouth."

He says something else, but Aaron doesn't hear it. And then Christian is looking at him expectantly. And Aaron knows that what he's supposed to say is, "Congratulations," or "Oh wow," or "I knew you'd get in."

But what comes out is, "I thought we were going to U of O!"

Christian puts his head down on his arm and sighs. "You're going to U of O. I told you I was applying to better schools."

Aaron only vaguely remembers those conversations, whispered to him in the back of the band room while waiting for the conductor to drill the flute section on a difficult part of the song. He *does* remember hiding in Christian's attic room, with stolen bottles of hard lemonade, talking about how they could be roommates. Was that all bullshit then?

"I didn't think you'd actually apply to them," Aaron says. "We had plans."

Aaron thinks he can sense Christian rolling his eyes. "*You* had plans."

"But you can't just . . . I mean, what about . . ."

Christian picks his head up to look at Aaron, and then all he says is, "Well, I guess either we'll spend a lot of time on Skype or you'll get over it."

"Fine," Aaron says, and he gets up. Once he's standing, his head is above the shadow of the slough's bank, and he has to shade his eyes to look down at Christian. But he doesn't. His huffy attempt to stomp off is made less dramatic and more comical by his need to tuck his underwhelmed penis back into his pants and zip his fly. So he's already less angry and more embarrassed, cheeks burning, as he hunts around the grass for his sneakers. But it would be worse to back down and face Christian now, so he musters what anger he can and storms off.

"Whatever," Christian shouts after him, as he struggles through the tall grass at the edge of the field, glitter frogs hopping up and away from his stomping feet, their bulging eyes watching him. "Text me when you feel like talking about this like an adult!"

Aaron rides home, stuffs his bike in the garage, heads for his room. There are frogs all up and down the stairs. Even though he likes the stupid aliens, he wants to kick them out of spite. He wonders if he drop-kicked one down the hall if it'd bounce off the back wall or splat horribly. The frogs hop away from him, as if they can tell what he's thinking, and he feels awful. "Sorry," he whispers, a roiling sickness in his guts. He can't get the image of a splatted glitter frog dripping off the wall out of his head.

There are about a hundred of them in his bedroom when he gets the door open. Unlike the glitter frogs in the hall, these ones don't scatter when they see him. He wonders how they get through closed doors and what they've been doing in here alone all day.

He swipes his tablet on and tries to distract himself with Facebook, which mostly works. Well, until Christian's status changes to single.

Aaron stares at the notification. The thick feeling in his throat is the same one he gets right before he cries. "I didn't mean *that*," he says to nobody in particular, though of course the frogs are listening.

One of the glitter frogs jumps up onto Aaron's shoulder. Its back is such a dark and stormy blue, speckled with metallic flecks, that it looks like the night sky. Aaron picks it up and holds it in his hands, feeling the cold fluttering of its heart and breath. It smells odd, like a spice barely remembered from childhood. He wonders if the frogs are alive, or if they're robots, or if it's just a grand, mass hallucination. "Well, you were there, some of you." Aaron says, "Tell me why he did it."

The frog doesn't say anything, even after Aaron lifts its face to the screen, showing it his Twitter feed. The feed is full of tweets by Christian that are definitely about him, though they don't mention him by name. The glitter frogs never say anything.

Aaron puts the frog down on his desk. He lowers his face so their eyes are on the same level. Another frog, this one striped red and black, jumps onto his computer tower without displacing the rejection letters piled on top. From underneath, looking up, Aaron can see the Harvard crest. That response? No. Princeton: no. Yale: no, not even. Don't even think about it. And Dartmouth? Ha.

The night sky frog ribbits. It sounds disgruntled. Aaron sighs; the puff of his breath makes the frog blink. Here is the pain of his future collapsing on itself and the realization that no, he's not that great. He's not great at all. He's completely, devastatingly average. Seventeen years of denial couldn't change that.

"I wish for once I could be the one leaving, not the one being left behind," he says.

The frog stares at him; its wet eyes reflect the cloud-studded sky out the window.

Tumblr gif set, eight images: Rescue Dog "Saves" Frog. Taken from a YouTube video of the same name, filmed on a smartphone in portrait mode.

One: A mottled green and purple glitter frog swimming in someone's backyard pool.

Two: A golden retriever paces left on the pool deck. Barking.

Three: Glitter frog is still swimming, minding its own business.

Four: Retriever leaps into the pool, and the splash repeats incessantly in the browser window until you tap over to the next gif.

Five: Retriever paddling toward the pool stairs, glitter frog held in its soft jaws.

Six: Retriever puts down frog and backs two steps away. The frog blinks and its throat expands with a mighty, pissed-off croak.

Seven: Retriever lying next to the frog on the pool deck, wagging its wet tail.

Eight: Retriever licks frog. Frog retracts its eyes to escape the overeager tongue.

CHRISTIAN

The last time he ever sees Aaron is when he watches the other boy walk away from their fight. He'll come to think of it as the stupidest fight that he's ever had. He'll spend years wondering if Aaron would have still run away if they hadn't broken up with each other on Facebook.

Aaron's parents come to Christian's house two days later, looking as though they've been crying, or not sleeping, or both.

"Have you seen him?" "Did he say anything about where he was going?" "If you hear anything, will you tell us?" "Does he have any other accounts online that we don't know about?" "Did he say he was meeting anyone you don't know?"

And Christian has no answers for them, sitting in the dining room with his own parents nearby, their faces also drawn and worried, as though running away might be contagious.

He's still no help later, when it's the cops come to ask almost the exact same questions, or when the school counselor asks him how he feels about it, or when mutual friends, voices low and quavering with awe, ask what *exactly* he said to Aaron?

"Nothing. I told him I got into Dartmouth, that's all. I didn't think it was a big deal. I don't know where he went, he didn't say anything about leaving. I don't know why he left. I don't know. I don't know. I don't remember."

Christian isn't sure what he expects, but he knows that people can't vanish without a trace, especially if they don't have that much money and extra especially if they still expect to graduate from high school.

Everyone is so nice to him.

Except that the frogs are starting to avoid him, a scattering cloud of various colors every time he steps into a room. They're still watching him, the way they watch everyone, but from a distance now. From under the bed, not from his desk. From the shower curtain rod, not from beside the sink. From behind the Xbox, not from the arm of the couch. When he can catch them out, hiding behind a cup of pencils or a pillow or the venetian blinds, Christian thinks they look strangely content. Like they know something.

There's a SoundCloud user who records the glitter frog songs almost nightly and puts them up raw. This is unusual, as most users remix their recordings into songs. On one track, a flurry of comments at the four minute mark:

Whoa, is it just me or does this sound like a code?

FROG CODE!!!!1

Dont b fukin stupid

No, it kinda does.

Y WOULD ALIENS USE MORSE CODE!?

its just u

TRISTAN

He's looking for somewhere to sleep that doesn't smell like pee. Before he left home, he wouldn't have thought it'd be this hard, but he learned better pretty quickly. Timing is also important. You don't want to wait until it's too late, because then all the really good places to sleep are taken. You don't want to go too early, though, because if you're too early, there's a much higher chance that a janitor or someone will notice and kick you out.

So far, every place that he's checked smells like pee. Usually he can smell it before he even gets under the awning. It's the spots that don't get rained on that smell the worst. They get pissed on and then forgotten, and the piss bakes into the concrete when the weather gets hotter, drier.

It's not hot or dry right now. The air has that heavy, waiting feel. It's cold enough to make people complain about May being too late in the year for chill, northern winds. Occasionally a single raindrop falls.

The frogs don't seem to mind. When the rain falls to the stained concrete, the frogs rush to it, a wave of glittering color that bunches and scatters. Tristan used to like the frogs, when he was younger. He used to fall asleep listening to them outside his window, in the house, sitting on the edge of his pillow, their voices not-quite harmonizing. That was before stepfather number three dragged the family into the kind of turmoil Tristan thought was restricted to TV movies until it happened to him. But after Tristan ran away, nobody paid much attention to him, including, and perhaps especially, the frogs.

Past the abandoned theater, there's an awning for a stage door. There's a half-wall that blocks view of the door from the alley. Great. Three walls and a crappy roof. Tristan pulls his sleeping bag and backpack down the stairs, lays out the sleeping bag. He rips open a half-melted granola bar for dinner as the sky opens up and rain pounds the awning overhead. There's a leak near the door, but Tristan finds an old coffee can, a few long-dead cigarette butts in the bottom of it, and uses that to catch the water.

While he eats, some of the glitter frogs, slick with rain, seem to grow tired of the weather. They come down the stairs in butt-bumping hops, surrounding him. One climbs up onto his knee.

He pulls out his old cell phone, the SIM card deactivated long ago. He's still got some juice, but there's no WiFi near enough, so he saves the power. He thinks about offering the frog on his knee some of the granola bar, but he isn't sure if the frogs eat.

He remembers a news article that went the social media rounds a few months ago:

Question: Alien "Glitter" Frogs: CO_2-Eating Terraforming Technology?

Answer: Nobody knows, but they do seem to exhale oxygen, despite looking like animals. However, it's not enough oxygen to reliably light them on fire.

Tristan is putting the phone away when another boy comes around the corner of the half-wall, drenched from the rainstorm, his hair plastered to his face and his T-shirt stuck to his torso.

The boy stops, staring, his hand on the half-wall. His fingers leave little damp marks on the painted concrete. He picks at the edges, dislodging crumbling bits of stone. There are glitter frogs all over him, of all sizes. Large ones sit on his shoulders, cling to the wet fabric of his clothing. His hair seems to move of its own accord, but it's just small frogs climbing between the strands.

Tristan has never seen anyone with that many frogs on them before.

"It's raining," the boy says.

"Yeah," Tristan answers. He wonders if the boy is high. If he is, that's fine unless it's meth or something and he's going to flip out. Tristan wonders what the frogs would do if the boy flipped out. Probably leave.

Tristan shifts his sleeping bag, crumpling it up so that there's bare concrete for the boy to stand or sit on. He doesn't want his bed to get wet. "Come in," he says. "What's your name?"

The boy steps out of the rain, dripping on the dusty concrete. Tracks of rainwater run down his face and arms. "Aaron," he says. He crouches, his back against the wall, watching Tristan. The frogs also follow him in, too many.

Tristan tries to keep them off the sleeping bag, but eventually gives up. Most of them don't climb on him, but the entire space is quickly covered in a shifting mass of the glitter frogs, all colors and sizes hopping, shifting, trying to stay close to Aaron. This makes Tristan nervous.

"Do you have somewhere to stay?"

Aaron blinks rapidly, wipes the rainwater off his face. "No," he says, and then he laughs. "I didn't plan this very well, I guess." He pulls off his T-shirt, scattering the frogs. He shakes it out gently to make sure there are no frogs inside, and then he leans over the wall to wring it out into the rain.

He must have run away recently, Tristan thinks. Or been kicked out in the past few days. But it's strange for him to be so calm about it. Maybe this isn't the first time. "I can help you find somewhere to go tomorrow," he says. "If you need it."

Aaron drapes the shirt over the wall, and even though he got a lot of the water out, it trickles down to pool on the floor. "I don't," he says. "I'm not planning on sticking around very long. I've decided to go away with the frogs."

He looks slightly surprised when he says it. Like he's just now put the thought into words. But he doesn't take it back.

They are glitter frogs, and they are aliens, but nobody has ever gone away with them. There are so many frogs that Tristan has to be careful if he shifts his legs, otherwise he'll squish them.

"Running away to join the alien circus," Tristan says.

Aaron shrugs.

A YouTube video that persisted for six months before someone reported it for terms of service violations:

The camera is fixed on the ground, bouncing with every step. Glitter frogs dive out of the way. The person behind the camera knows better than to tilt the camera back and show their face.

There's a clearing in the tall grass, glistening where it's been wetted down with a hose. Just in case. There's a flat piece of particle board on the ground, dented, scratched, splattered with paint of various colors. The camera gets especially haphazard as something is put on the wet piece of particle board. It's one of the glitter frogs, but it doesn't look quite right. Something is wrong with its legs.

And there are fire crackers next to it.

You can guess the rest. You don't need to see it. Don't go looking. The video was taken down. There are no torrents.

NICKIE

Nickie's high school doesn't do dissections any more. It hasn't for years. Her parents once asked if she was going to be dissecting worms in biology class and then looked dismayed when she said, "Uh, no. Duh."

Duh. You can't cut up unassuming animals for fun. And there's no way that the school would want to court more controversy after firing their biology teacher for being too aggressive in his teaching of evolutionary theory.

Nickie saw him in the grocery store afterward. He looked drunk, or like he'd been drunk, or maybe he wanted to be drunk. She waved at him, after shifting the box of Coke to her left arm. He stared through her like she wasn't even there, picking up glitter frogs from where they sat among the kumquats. In retrospect, Nickie didn't think that she'd want to be reminded she'd been fired, either.

Even though the equipment never gets used anymore, the school never throws anything out. After class, Nickie steals one dissecting tray, two scalpels (in case the first one isn't sharp enough), ten pins, and a pair of rusty surgical scissors. She has her own scissors, but the idea of using them on dead animal guts and then putting them back in her desk drawer is gross.

At home, the frogs are everywhere, so they're not hard to catch. Nickie holds the frog while others hop around her feet in the living room. Her parents have tried to keep the frogs out, but they always get back in.

Whenever Nickie types a question into a search engine that starts with "How," the autofill gives her variations on "How do I keep frogs out of my house?" She clicked a link once, and the suggestions horrified her. But that was then. Now, she's watched an old instructional video about Earth frog dissections, taken careful notes. All of the Google results for dissections of the *glitter* frogs come up broken. Her other searches weren't much better.

What are the frogs?

What are they doing here?

What are they made of?

Nickie carries the frog into the kitchen and puts it down on the counter. There are so many others—almost as though they know what she's about to do and are coming to watch. She hopes not. Psychic alien frogs are even worse than regular alien frogs.

She drops the frog into a canning jar. It puts its brilliant green hands up against the side of the glass, its purple-blue throat pulsing more rapidly than the frogs on the counter. Nickie drops in three cotton balls covered in acetone and tightens the lid.

She watches the glitter frog suffocate.

Nickie takes the frog and supplies into the garage and sets up on the concrete floor. There are more frogs in the garage than she expected, hundreds of them sitting on every surface. Nickie has to nudge them out of the way with her sneakers.

The frog doesn't move when she takes it out of the jar. She hopes it's completely dead. To make sure, she waits a few minutes, the frog resting motionless in the center of the dissecting tray. She cautiously pokes it in the back with her set of tweezers. Then she flips it over onto its back like she saw in the video. She uses the pins to stick it to the pad underneath, trying not to gag at how hard it is to push pins through the stringy flesh of its legs.

She makes the cuts with the stolen scalpel, wishing it was sharper, trying not to break anything that could be interesting. The skin of the glitter frog parts easily, though it rips in places and she has trouble cutting through the sections that appear to be circuits.

The dissection video hasn't prepared her for the blood. It wells out of every cut; it oozes from the pinholes. This is nothing like the nice, neat dissection she had planned. It's worse. Messier. There is *so much* blood. She pulls back the layer of skin from the torso, pins it to the side, and looks down at the smooth, peeled wall of the glitter frog's abdominal cavity. There's a thin circuit embedded in the muscle. Nickie takes her tweezers and carefully, gently, extracts it from the bloody mess. The thin metal wire keeps coming until she pulls it free. There's a square bit at the end that looks more like an RF chip than anything else. She holds it up to the light, frowning because it doesn't look all that alien.

Next, Nickie cuts through the muscle itself even though her scalpel slides around on the wet tissue. She can see the glitter frog's organs, and she realizes that they look nothing like the ones she saw on the video. These organs are shaped differently and of course, they're not dyed.

The other glitter frogs around her are staring; their eyes are huge in the dim light of the garage. The frogs crowd so close that she can feel them pressing up against her legs, against her arms. There's an army of them, a nation of them, and she thinks she can feel them climbing up her back.

The cold, wet sensation of a frog on the back of her neck jars her into motion. Nickie stands suddenly, accidentally kicking the dissection tray so that it clatters across the concrete floor. The frogs fall from her, and she hears soft thuds as they hit the ground.

She bags the dead glitter frog in a Ziploc sandwich bag to carry it out to the woods behind her house—a stand of tragic cedars and vine maples between her house and the neighbors. She hides the body under a rotting log and hopes something out here will eat it.

She hoses off the dissection tray in the backyard, her golden retriever snuffling around the sullen red puddle at her feet, the bloody water flecked with tufts of shed hair and tiny bits of frog guts. When the dog laps up the bloodied water, she turns the hose on him, and he dances away. He stares at her from a few feet away, head cocked to the side, pink tongue dripping.

Nickie washes the RF chip in the sink, dries it on a paper towel, and brings it with her to school the next morning.

She finds her chem lab partner before class. Christian has been doing the same thing every morning since his boyfriend—ex-boyfriend—ran away from home. He's sitting out on the picnic table that nobody ever uses, picking at flecks of lichen and peeling paint, moping. Nickie had a crush on him, once, in like elementary school. She'd held out hope he was bi until sophomore year, when they had the most awkward conversation ever.

Nickie brushes some frogs off the table and sits next to him. "Hey," she says.

He frowns at her through that missing-someone-plus-senioritis haze. "We don't have anything due today, do we?"

"No. Remember how I was telling you that I couldn't find anything online about what the glitter frogs are made of?" She pulls off her backpack and swings it around onto her lap. It's warm for being so early. There are other students out, though most of them are walking to the lunchroom or heading toward class.

"Yeah?"

She pulls out the plastic baggie, hands it to him. "This was under its skin."

Christian frowns at the piece of metal, frowns at her, holds it up to the light. He slides the plastic baggie around with his fingers, as though the clear plastic is obstructing his view. Nickie's about to tell him that he can take it out of the bag if he wants when he asks, "Are you sure?"

"What do you mean, 'am I sure?'" Nickie takes the RF chip back, stuffs it in her backpack. "I took it out of the frog myself."

Christian looks at the glitter frogs surrounding them on the grass. They are watching. He pitches his voice low, almost a whisper. "You cut one of them up?"

Nickie zips her bag with more force than she intended. "Yes. I did. I thought that it was weird that they're apparently such a big fucking secret. But look at that. It doesn't look very alien, does it?"

Christian closes his eyes and exhales, but before she can ask him what he thinks about it, he says, "I didn't see anything. You didn't show me anything, I don't know anything."

"What?"

When he opens his eyes, all she can see is fear. "I don't want to know," he says, as a glitter frog lands between them.

O f course, if someone were systematically scrubbing the internet of all references to the glitter frogs, then how do you explain the Tumblr gif sets? The audio recordings? The videos that don't involve illegal firecrackers and animal cruelty?

Surely someone would have taken down the space frog conspiracy theory site designed by a person with only a very cursory understanding of HTML?

The site has a star field background with red, white, and blue text. The

only thing less systematic than the wildly varying font size is the capital-
ization, which seems to occur at random.

tHe FRogS ArE NOT alIeNS, ThEY are GOveRnmENT sPiES!

DO NoT leT TheM FOOL yOU!

i HaVE THE uLTiMatE PrOoF thAt THE sHIp iN oRbIT iS FAkE

tHeRE ARE NO aLiENs

tHAt iS whAt THEY WanT YOu tO BeLiEVE

cIA and FbI haVE bEEN tRYinG tO ShUT Me uP FoR YEARS

NsA iS UsInG FROGs tO ImPLAnt TheIR InSTRUctiOnS In YoUR
ChilDRenS MInDS

We MuST RISE UP BeFoRE iT iS TOo LaTE!!!

And so on . . .

This site has been up for at least a year now. If these sites were under
surveillance, don't you think it'd be down already?

KAREN

She is really surprised how easy it is to get drinks at this show. She's
got three years to go before she can drink legally, but the show is 21+
and the bartender is assuming the door guys did their job. The door guys
checked out her boobs with about ten times more attention than they did
her fake ID.

Her friends, Trisha and Moira, are drinking whatever they want, ordering drinks that sound funny and then snickering behind their hands when
the bartender, harried and over-busy with the number of drink orders
during the shitty opener's set, just nods. It seems that he's completely lost
the ability to find "sex on the beach" funny. Karen doesn't blame him.

She orders her fourth rum and coke and wonders if she should be feeling
drunk yet.

Trisha has ordered a drink that is a horrifying shade of blue, and she's
trying to get Moira to bet on whether or not it's going to make her tongue
change colors. Karen is still watching them when one of the glitter frogs
on the counter walks over with its halting, I-should-be-jumping frog walk.
She thinks that it might be planning to climb up the side of her glass—
yuck. The last thing she wants is a frog in her drink.

The frog stops a few inches short, staring at her with its incomprehen-
sible gaze. Then it crawls to the other side of the bar, where it stares at a
fallen slice of lime in a puddle of tepid water.

"I guess there's so much heavy breathing going on that there's enough

CO2 for you all," Karen says, flicking a piece of ice at the frog. She misses, and the ice skitters away over the bar. The alien turns its long-suffering eyes on her again. She sips her rum and coke and stares back until she starts to feel distinctly uncomfortable. She leans left, and the frog's eyes follow her. Then she leeeaaans left, and the frog is still staring. She leans so far that she loses balance and falls against Trisha.

Trisha laughs and pushes her back upright on her barstool. "Hoo boy, Karen's smashed already."

"No, I'm not," Karen says, hoping that the bartender didn't see her fall. Luckily, he's busy, slinging limp white napkins and pouring cheap beer.

It's easier to hear now, and it takes a moment for Karen to step outside of her drink-tunneled attention and realize that the opener has stopped playing. In the silence between sets, the bar gets so busy that she can feel the press of people against her back as they crowd forward to order drinks over her head. A guy stumbles against her, grabbing her boob for balance, and then he slides away down the bar before she can respond. Trisha and Moira either didn't see or don't care. Karen bites her lip, hunches her shoulders, and wishes she'd stayed home. She doesn't even like the headliner much, it's Moira's favorite. She wishes she'd responded faster and punched the guy in the kidney, or something.

The glitter frog is gone. Karen wonders if they can walk on the floor in this crush of people, and then she imagines the floor coated with the remains of glitter frogs like stomped grapes.

The benefit of going to a show in another city is that it means the chances of running into someone you know, or worse, someone who knows your parents, are much slimmer. Still, Karen thinks she recognizes one of the young men on the other side of the bar. She squints in the dim light and can make out his features.

It's the missing boy from her high school, she realizes. He has glitter frogs on both his shoulders and he's buying a drink for the boy next to him. People thought he was dead. He's been gone for months.

She's about to go over to him and tell him that he should call his parents and at least tell them that he's alive when Trisha says, "Oh my god, can we dance already?"

Karen realizes that she hadn't noticed the headliner beginning to play.

Moira throws back the rest of her drink, and then she grabs Trisha by the arm, pulling her off the stool. "Come on," she says, "I love this song!"

Karen chugs the rum and coke, which is a mistake because she realizes that she isn't quite sure how many drinks she's had so far.

She follows her friends out into the mass of people, shoving her way past sweaty arms and glowsticks, past people dancing so close that she wants to scream "Get a room!" but doesn't because she figures they wouldn't hear her anyway. Moira is extremely good at working the crowd, and it doesn't take long before they're only a few people from the front. And then they are in the crush of humanity, everything smelling hot and damp-slick with sweat.

Karen feels like she should be repulsed by the warm sweat of strangers, but instead she lifts her arms over her head, lets the stage lights strobe between her fingers and the thrumming bass fill her head.

For the first two songs, she hopes that the night lasts forever, that the set will go on and on until she dies of old age here in this dark room. There are no frogs on the floor, but there are some on the stage. One is even clinging to the microphone stand.

But then the first few songs turn into a few more, and a few more, and suddenly Karen realizes four things:

a) She isn't sure where her friends even are anymore.

b) She would rather the show be over sooner rather than later because she's not sure she can keep up with this pace much longer.

c) Most of the guys on the floor seem to have the same balance problems as that one man did by the bar.

d) She's going to need to puke soon.

Her feeling of malaise turns into an even stronger need to puke as the slower song she'd been swaying to segues into something faster, hotter, and with more thumping in it. And then she's dodging elbows on her way to the edge of the crowd. The world consists of nothing anymore but the sour smell of other humans, the bruising force of their bodies against hers every single time she misjudges the tempo of their terrible fucking dancing.

Karen thinks she's going to start screaming, crying, or maybe just pass out, but then she's miraculously outside the crowd, stumbling toward the can. There's a man near the door checking her out, and she barely manages to flip him off before stumbling through the bathroom door.

The women's restroom is full of glitter frogs. They're everywhere—on the floor, clinging to the stalls, on the sinks, in the sinks, by the sinks. On the paper towel dispenser.

She stumbles into one of the stalls—of course none of them have doors—and hovers over the painted-black toilet with the cracked seat, trying to puke so that the bathroom will stop spinning. She tries to stick her finger down her throat as if that might help. It should have, since her finger tasted grosser than anything, but it didn't.

After a few minutes of fighting to give in to the nausea, she gives up, sits on the toilet with her pants still up, breathing heavily and trying not to cry. The sickness encompasses everything. She is in a building with several hundred people, here with friends, and she's alone.

The glitter frogs are watching her.

Air, she thinks, and even though the room is still spinning, she climbs to her feet and stumbles out of the bathroom, following the wall to the front door, and then she's out on the street.

It's raining, cold fat drops are landing on her hair, soaking through her shirt. The door guys watch her like the glitter frogs as she stumbles around the corner and leans back against the jagged bricks of the wall. The street keeps tilting clockwise.

"Are you okay?"

Karen blinks. Standing at the corner is the boy she recognized earlier. He is covered in frogs. He doesn't seem to mind the rain.

"Are you Aaron?" she asks. *Missing* Aaron.

He smiles. "Kind of."

She squeezes her eyes shut to make the spinning stop. This makes her more dizzy, so she opens them again.

He asks, "Do you need help getting back inside?"

"Not yet." Karen can hear the music. She can feel it against her back, the vibrations working their way through the wall.

"I'll wait with you," he says. He doesn't add, "Because you're way too drunk."

Minutes pass. Karen asks, "Why'd you run away?"

Aaron's voice is so soft that she almost can't hear him over the music and the sound of rain. "The frogs," he says. "I want to go away with them. Me and Tristan are going away with them."

Karen laughs. "Oh my god," she says. "Are you serious?"

He lifts a glitter frog off his left shoulder. This one is dark blue, and it glistens in the streetlight. She can't tell if that's from the metallic flecks in its skin, or from rainwater. Aaron holds it out to her. "Haven't you ever felt like you didn't belong here?"

Karen takes the glitter frog, holds it in the palm of her hand.

Aaron says, "Neither do they."

For Sale Listing: GLITTER FROG CLOTHING—COTTON— SHIRTS, PANTS, SUITS, SUN DRESSES—$20-$75

All glitter frog clothing hand sewn by ME! Are there alien frogs in your life that you're starting to get attached to? Are you having trouble telling them apart? Price varies depending on the amount of fabric needed! When you order, send a photo of the frog next to a ruler or something so I can figure out the measurements.

AVERY

She's sitting on a bench outside the bus station in Baker City, feeling the dust and the heat seep through her skin. Regrets are crawling around her veins like one hit too many of a cheap upper. It's already late afternoon, but the next bus won't be leaving for hours. She watches the cars pass on the interstate to the east. The rolling foothills to the west bake golden in the hundred-and-ten-degree air.

It's probably too hot for the glitter frogs and she's glad. She doesn't think she could handle their disappointment on top of her own.

"Should've just stayed in the car," she tells herself, but when she thinks about Aaron's wide eyes and mumbling, of wandering the western states without a single fucking clue where they're going, feeling less and less connected to the world . . . she doesn't really regret leaving them.

There's no shame in getting scared and buying a ticket back to Centralia, she tells herself. Her mom cried on the phone when she said she was coming home. It's been more than a year.

A car pulls into the parking lot, kicking up a plume of orange dust that obscures the semis behind it. It's red, an old, kinda boxy car, probably one from the '90s or something. The windows are up, so it's got air conditioning.

The man who gets out of the car is tall, and he's got long brown hair that he hasn't bothered to tie back. He's wearing tight jeans and a green Dartmouth T-shirt. His sneakers look new, even from halfway across the lot. He leans on the driver's side door, looking at the building, at her. He's frowning like he's looking for someone. He checks his iPhone before slipping it into the pocket of his jeans.

The only sounds are the thud of the car door shutting, the interstate beside them, and the scuff of his feet on the faded asphalt. Avery puts a hand on her ratty old backpack, but she doesn't move it off the bench. He comes so close that she can see her wind-burnt, sun-scorched face reflected in his shades. Strands of his hair drift in the breeze like spider silk.

"Hey," he says. "You wouldn't have happened to see a car or a van or something here recently? Maybe an older one. There's probably be a couple people in it about our age."

"You got a cigarette?" Avery asks. There's this sick feeling in the pit of her stomach, because she already knows who he's asking about. And she doesn't know if she should play stupid or what.

He glances over his shoulder at the car and then shakes his head. "I don't have any tobacco, sorry."

"Weed's fine," she says, but she already knows he's not going to give her any.

He puts his sunglasses on his forehead and digs his phone back out of his pocket. He swipes past some screens and then holds it out to her. Avery has a brief impulse to grab the phone and run, but there's really nowhere to go from here and it's too fucking hot for that kind of shit.

"I'm looking for this guy," he says. "I was supposed to meet him here, but my flight home from school was late and I couldn't get here any earlier."

Of course it's a picture of Aaron. It's Aaron and the boy standing in front of her. They're sitting on the edge of a fountain, holding hands, heads bent, foreheads touching.

Avery feels something rising inside. Fear, anger, self-loathing. She'd be down that road already, in a car full of frogs, going to meet the aliens, finally, if she hadn't been so fucking afraid. Because what if they turn us inside out, and what if they get tired of us and shove us out the airlock, and what if it means leaving everyone we know behind, coming back in four hundred years. She wants to scream at this guy to fuck off and leave her alone, and she almost does.

But there's such a sad look on his face. She pulls her backpack off the bench to the ground next to her feet. "You just missed them," she says.

"You know him? Oh, god, how long ago did they leave?"

Avery shrugs, "Like an hour ago."

"Do you have his number? I mean, to whatever phone he's got now? I tried to call him back but the number didn't work. Maybe if I can call him . . ."

Avery hates him a little bit for his assumption that he can show up at the last minute in all his Ivy League glory and be welcomed. "He's not going to come back, you know," she says. She flips the phone to his address book and puts the newest number in under Aaron's name. There are four old numbers there, all defunct.

"Thanks," he says, and he dials immediately, pacing in the dust, in and out of the shade. When he says, "Fuck," Avery knows that the phone has gone to voice mail. If this surprises him, it makes Avery think that he must not have known Aaron all that well.

"Aaron," he says, and then there's a pause before he continues. "It's Christian. I made it to Baker City and there's a guy here who says I just missed you, but I meant to be here, really. I want to see you. Your parents have been crazy for the past year and a half, absolutely batshit. I'll be waiting here. Call me back."

Then he sends a text, and another, and finally slumps on the bench beside her.

"He's not coming back," she says. "And I'm not a dude."

"Oh, *oh*, I'm so—"

"Don't worry about it," she says, waving his apology away like a cloud of gnats.

They sit together on that bench while the sun crosses the sky and slips behind the hills, barely talking. Christian's got questions, of course. He wants to know where they've been, where they were going, how Aaron's been doing. Avery shuts him down. She's marking time until she can get on the bus and head back to the real world. It kills her that he doesn't seem to have figured out that they've both missed their chance. Some people you can't explain this shit to. They've got to figure it out on their own.

When the bus comes, she flips her hair out of her face and says goodbye to Christian, who's checking his phone again. She slides into a stained fabric bus seat that smells a lot like spilled coffee and a little like piss. He's sitting alone when the bus drives off, waiting in the night for a phone call that's never going to come.

ALIEN BABIES

The car is full of four teenagers and too many glitter frogs, sitting on laps, on feet, on the floor, in the back window. The car rattles down a dirt road somewhere in Utah, a ranch exit fifty or eighty or a hundred miles from civilization.

They're driving with no lights, leaving the freeway far behind. It's a full moon so they can see the road anyway, their eyes adjusted to night. Tristan is driving. Aaron is drumming his hands on the dashboard, making up for the radio that he turned off once I-84 turned south, way back in Idaho.

In the back seat, J is staring out the window at nothing. Karen's sitting on the driver's side, head pressed against the back of Tristan's seat. She keeps thinking that she should have stayed in Baker City with Avery, but she doesn't say a single word.

The car hits a bump so hard that their asses all leave the seats. Aaron stops drumming. "Here," he says. "STOP HERE."

Tristan stomps the brakes, and there's an exhalation of breath from slamming into the chest straps of their seatbelts, and then Tristan kills the motor. Silence.

Aaron climbs out of the car first, the dust of the road under his boots soft and dry. The air has gone cold, but he imagines he can still feel the warmth of the rocks underfoot. The others, human and glitter frog, follow him out of the car.

"Now what?" Tristan asks, the words strange in a place so quiet. Behind them is the buzzing rattle of someone's phone left in the car.

Aaron skids down the embankment, dislodging dirt and gravel in a rush, and he starts walking away from the road. He doesn't think he's ever seen so many stars.

At first he thinks that the glitter frogs are catching up with him as he walks, but then he realizes that these are new frogs. More frogs. He can't see where they're coming from, but there are more, and more, until the ground is a shifting mass of glittering sparks.

He stops, waits for the others to catch up with him, waits for Tristan to be close so he can grip the other boy's hand tight in his. They are barely breathing for the anticipation. Karen takes Aaron's other hand, and J takes Tristan's. Together, they wonder what the ship will be like, the stars, the swiftly receding earth.

All around them, spread out for miles as dense as carpet, the glitter frogs begin to sing.

Gregory Benford is a professor of physics and astronomy at the University of California, Irvine. He is a Woodrow Wilson Fellow, was Visiting Fellow at Cambridge University, and in 1995 received the Lord Prize for contributions to science. In 2007 he won the Asimov Award for science writing. His fiction has won many awards, including the Nebula Award for his novel *Timescape*. He has published forty-two books, mostly novels.

Dark Heaven

GREGORY BENFORD

The body was bloated and puckered. The man looked to be in his thirties maybe, but with the bulging face and goggle eyes it was hard to tell. His pants and shirt were gone so he was down to his skivvies. They were grimy on the mud beach.

That wasn't unusual at all. Often the Gulf currents pulled the clothes off. Inquisitive fish or sharks came to visit, and indeed there was a chunk out of the left calf and thigh. Someone had come for a snack. Along the chest and belly were long raised red marks, and that was odd. McKenna hadn't seen anything like that before.

McKenna looked around but the muddy beach and stands of reeds held nothing of interest. As the first homicide detective there it was his case, and they were spread so thin he got no backup beyond a few uniforms. Those were mostly just standing around. The photo/video guy was just finishing with his systematic sweep of the area.

The body didn't smell. It had been in the salt water at least a day, the medical examiner had said, judging from the swelling. McKenna listened to the drone of the ME's summary as he circled around the body, his boots scrunching on the beach.

Outside Mobile and the coastal towns, most bodies get found by a game warden or fisherman or by somebody on a beach party who wanders off into the cattails. This one was apparently a wash-up, left by the tide for a cast fisherman to find. A kid had called it in. There was no sign of a boating accident and no record of men missing off a fishing boat; McKenna had checked before leaving his office.

The sallow-faced ME pointed up to a pine limb. "Buzzards get the news first." There were three up there in the cypress.

"What are those long scars?" McKenna asked, ignoring the buzzards.

"Not a propeller, not knife wounds. Looks swole up." A shrug. "I dunno for now."

"Once you get him on the table, let me know."

The ME was sliding the corpse's hands into a metal box with a battery pack on the end. He punched in a command and a flash of light lit the hand for an instant.

"What's that?" McKenna pointed.

The ME grinned up at him as he fitted the left hand in, dropping the right. "I thought the perfessor was up on all the new tech."

McKenna grimaced. Back at the beginning of his career he had been the first in the department to use the internet very much, when he had just been promoted into the ranks that could wear a suit to work. He read books too, so for years everybody called him the "perfessor." He never corrected their pronunciation and they never stopped calling him that. So for going on plenty years now he was the "perfessor" because he liked to read and listen to music in the evenings rather than hang out in bars or go fishing. Not that he didn't like fishing. It gave a body time to think.

The ME took his silence as a mild rebuke and said finally, as the light flashed again, "New gadget, reads fingerprints. Back in the car I connect it and it goes wireless to the FBI database, finds out who this guy is. Maybe."

McKenna was impressed but decided to stay silent. It was better to be known as a guy who didn't talk much. It increased the odds that when you did say something, people listened. He turned and asked a uniform, "Who called it in?"

It turned out to be one of the three kids standing by a prowl car. The kid had used a cell phone, of course, and knew nothing more. He and his buddies were just out here looking, he said. For what, he didn't say.

The ME said, "I'd say we wait for the autopsy before we do more." He finished up. Homicide got called in on accidental deaths, suicides, even deaths by natural causes, if there was any doubt. "How come you got no partner?" the ME asked.

"He's on vacation. We're shorthanded."

McKenna turned back to the beach for a last look. So the case was a man in his thirties, brown hair cropped close, a moustache, no scars. A tattoo of a dragon adorned the left shoulder. Except for the raised red stripes wrapped around the barrel chest, nothing unusual that McKenna could spot. But those red ridges made it a possible homicide, so here he was.

Anything more? The camera guy took some more shots and some uniforms were searching up and down the muddy beach but they weren't turning up anything. McKenna started to walk away along the long curve of the narrow beach and then turned back. The ME was already supervising two attendants, the three of them hauling the body onto a carry tarp toward the morgue ambulance. "Was it a floater?" McKenna called.

The ME turned and shouted back, "Not in long enough, I'd say."

So maybe in the Gulf for a day, tops, McKenna figured as his boots squished through the mud back to his car. Without air in the lungs, bodies sank unless a nylon jacket or shirt held a bubble and kept them on the surface. More often a body went straight down to the sand and mud until bacteria in the gut did its work and the gas gave lift, bringing the dead soul back into sunshine and more decay. But that took days here so this one was fresh. He didn't have to wait on the ME to tell him that, and except for fingerprints and the teeth that was probably all the physical evidence they would ever get from the poor bastard back there.

The ME caught up to him and said, "He's real stiff, too, so I'd say he struggled in the water a while."

McKenna nodded. A drowning guy burns up his stored sugar and the muscles go rigid quickly.

Two uniforms were leaning against his car, picking their teeth, and he answered their nods but said nothing. This far from Mobile McKenna was technically working beyond his legal limits, but nobody stood on procedure this far into the woods. Not on the coast. The body might be from Mississippi or even Louisiana or Florida, given the Gulf currents, so jurisdiction was uncertain, and might never be decided. A body was a body was a body, as an old New Orleans cop had told him once. Gone to rest. It belongs to no one anymore.

People started out in life looking different. But they ended up a lot alike. Except this one had some interesting ridges.

McKenna recalled being called out for bodies that turned out to be parts of long-drowned deer, the hair gone missing from decay. People sometimes mistook big dogs and even cows for people. But he had never seen any body with those long ridges of reddened, puckering flesh on anything. At least those made this case interesting.

He paused in the morning mist that gathered up from the bayou nearby and watched the impromptu funeral cortège escort the body away, prowl cars going first, crunching along the narrow oyster shell road. The kids were staring at the body, the uniforms, eyeing every move.

Routine, really, probably leading to nothing at all. But something about this bothered him and he could not say what.

He drove back toward Mobile with the window open to the pine-scented spring breezes. To get back from Bayou La Batre, you turn north toward U.S. 90. But he kept going east on two-lane blacktop. At a Citgo station a huge plastic chicken reared up from the bed of a rusted-out El Camino, pointing to a Sit 'n Rest Restaurant that featured shrimp and oysters and fresh catch, the proceeds of the Gulf that had long defined Bayou La Batre.

The book that turned into the movie *Forrest Gump* was set partly around there and the whole place looked it. But Katrina and the hurricanes that came after, pounding the coast like an angry Climate God, had changed the terms of discussion. As if the aliens hadn't, too.

He watched people walking into the Sit 'n Rest and wondered if he should stop and eat. The sunset brimmed the empty sky with rosy fingers, but he didn't feel like eating yet. There was a bottle of Pinot Grigio waiting at home and he somehow didn't want to see people tonight. But he did want to swing by the Centauri Center. The ones around here regarded everybody else as "farmers," as locals along the coast refer to anyone who lives inland. Tough and hard-working people, really, and he respected them. They could handle shrimp, hurricanes, civil rights, Federal drug agents, so why should aliens from another star be any more trouble? At least the aliens didn't want to raise taxes.

And he had taken this case off the board right away, back in Mobile, because it gave him a chance to go by the Centauri Center. He kept going across the long flat land toward the bay, looking for the high building he had read about but never seen. The Feds kept people away from here, but he was on official business.

There were boats in the trees. Two shrimpers, eighty feet long at least, lying tilted on their hulls in scrub oak and pine, at least half a mile from their bayou. Bows shoved into the green, their white masts and rigging rose like bleached treetops. Still not pulled out, nine months since the last hurricane had howled through here. The Feds had other things to do, like hosting amphibians from another star.

That, and discounting insurance for new construction along the Gulf Coast. Never mind that the glossy apartments and condos were in harm's way just by being there.

Just barely off-road, a trawler had its bow planting a hard kiss on a pine.

He drove through a swarm of yellow flies, rolling up the windows though he liked the aroma of the marsh grass.

He had heard the usual story, a Federal acronym agency turned into a swear word. A county health officer had the boats declared a public hazard, so the Coast Guard removed the fuel and batteries, which prompted FEMA to say it no longer had reason to spend public money on retrieving private property, and it followed as the night the day that the state and the city submitted applications to "rescue" the boats. Sometime real soon now.

Wind dimpled the bays beside the causeway leading to Mobile Bay. Willow flats and drowned cypress up the far inlets gave way to cattails, which blunted the marching whitetops of the bay's hard chop. They were like endless regiments that had defeated oil platforms and shipping fleets but broke and churned against the final fortress of the land.

He drove toward Mobile Bay and soon he could see what was left of the beach-front.

The sun sparkled on the bay and heat waves rose from the beaches so the new houses there seemed to flap in the air like flags of gaudy paper.

They were pricey, with slanted roofs and big screened porches, rafts supported meters above the sand on tall stilts. They reminded him of ladies with their skirts hoisted to step over something disagreeable.

He smiled at the thought and then felt a jolt as he saw for the first time the alien bunker near the bay. It loomed over the center of Dauphin Island, where Fed money had put it up with round-the-clock labor, to Centauri specs. The big dun-colored stucco frame sloped down toward the south. Ramps led onto the sand where waves broke a few meters away. Amphibian access, he guessed. It had just been finished, though the papers said the Centauri delegation to this part of the Gulf Coast had been living in parts of it for over a year.

He slowed as the highway curved past and nosed into a roadblock. A woman Fed officer in all black fatigues came over to the window. McKenna handed out his ID and the narrow-faced woman asked, "You have business here?"

"Just following a lead on a case."

"Going to need more than that to let you get closer."

"I know." She kept her stiff face and he said, "Y'know, these wrinkles I got at least show that I smiled once upon a time."

Still the flat look. He backed away and turned along a curve taking him inland. He was a bit irked with himself, blundering in like that, led only by curiosity, when his cell phone chimed with the opening bars of "Johnny B. Goode." He wondered why he'd said that to her, and recalled an article he had read this week. Was he a dopamine-rich nervous system pining for its serotonin heartthrob? Could be, but what use was knowing that?

He thumbed the phone on and the ME's voice said, "You might like to look at this."

"Or maybe not. Seen plenty."

"Got him on the table, IDed and everything. But there's something else."

The white tile running up to the ceiling reminded him that this place got hosed down every day. You did that in damp climates because little life forms you could barely see came through even the best air conditioning and did awful things to dead matter. Otherwise it was like all other autopsy rooms. Two stainless steel tables, overhead spray hoses on auto, counters of gleaming stainless, cabinets and gear on three walls. The air conditioning hummed hard but the body smell layered the room in a damp musk. The ME was working and barely glanced up. The county couldn't afford many specialists so the ME did several jobs.

Under the relentless ceramic lights the body seemed younger. Naked, tanned legs and arms and face, the odd raised welts. The ME was at home with bodies, touching and probing and squeezing. Gloved fingers combing the fine brown hair. Fingers in the mouth and throat, doubtless after probing the other five openings with finer tools. The ME used a magnifying glass to look carefully at the throat, shook his head as if at another idea gone sour, then picked up a camera.

He studied the extremities, feet and hands and genitalia. The magnifier swept over the palms and fingers and he took pictures, the flash startling McKenna, adding a sudden whiteness to the ceramic room.

The ME looked up as if noticing McKenna for the first time. "Wanna help?"

They turned the body after McKenna pulled on rubber gloves. A head-to-foot search, careful attention to the tracery of raised yellow-white marks that now had deep purple edges. The bruises lay under the skin and were spreading like oozing ink. The ME took notes and samples and then stepped back and sighed.

"Gotta say I just dunno. He has two clear signatures. Drowning in the lungs, but his heart stopped before that."

"From what?"

"Electrocution. And there's these—" He showed five small puncture wounds on both arms. Puckered and red. "Funny, not like other bites I've seen. So I got to do the whole menu, then."

The county had been going easy on full autopsies. They cost and budgets were tight. "At least you have his name."

"Ethan Anselmo. No priors, FBI says. Married, got the address."

"Wounds?"

"The big welts, I dunno. Never seen such. I'll send samples to the lab. Those punctures on the hands, like he was warding something off. That sure didn't work."

"Torture?"

"Not any kind I know."

"Anybody phone the widow?"

He looked up from his notes, blinking back sweat though the air conditioning was running full blast. "Thought that was your job."

I t was. McKenna knocked on the door of the low-rent apartment and it swung open to reveal a woman in her thirties with worried eyes. He took a deep breath and went into the ritual. Soon enough he saw again the thousand-yard stare of the new widow. It came over her after he got only a few sentences into his description. Ordinary people do not expect death's messenger to be on the other side of the knock. Marcie Anselmo got a look at the abyss and would never be the same.

McKenna never wanted to be the intruder into others' pain. He didn't like asking the shell-shocked widow details about their life, his job, where he'd been lately. All she knew was he hadn't come home last night. He did some night jobs but he had never stayed out all night like this before.

He spent a long hour with her. She said he sometimes hung out at The Right Spot. McKenna nodded, recognizing the name. Then they talked some more and he let the tensions rise and fall in her, concluding that maybe it was time to call their relatives. Start the process. Claim the body, the rest. Someone would be calling with details.

He left his card. This part went with the job. It was the price you paid to get to do what came next. Figure out. Find out.

E than Anselmo had worked as a pickup deck man on shrimpers out of Bayou La Batre. She hadn't asked which one he went out on lately. They came and went, after all.

McKenna knew The Right Spot, an ancient bar that had once sported decent food and that knew him, too. He forgot about the Pinot Grigio chilling at home and drove through the soft night air over to the long line of run-down docks and sheds that had avoided the worst of the last hurricane. The Right Spot had seen better days but then so had he.

He changed in the darkness to his down-home outfit. Dirty jeans, blue work shirt with snaps instead of buttons, baseball cap with salt stains. Last time he had been here he had sported a moustache, so maybe clean-shaven he would look different. Older, too, by half of a pretty tough year. Showtime . . .

Insects shrilled in the high grass of the wiped-out lot next door and frogs brayed from the swampy pond beyond. There was even a sort-of front yard to it, since it had once been a big rambling house, now canted to the left by decay. Night creeper and cat's claw smothered the flowerbeds and flavored the thick air.

There was a separate bar to the side of the restaurant and he hesitated. The juke joint music was pump and wail and crash, sonic oblivion for a few hours. Food first, he decided. Mercifully, there were two rooms and he got away from the noise into the restaurant, a room bleached out by the flat ceramic light. A sharp smell of disinfectant hiding behind the fried food aroma. New South, all right. A sign on the wall in crude type said FRIENDS DON'T LET FRIENDS EAT FOREIGN SHRIMP.

The joint had changed. He sat at a table and ordered jambalaya. When it came, too fast, he knew what to expect before the first mouthful.

It was a far, forlorn cry from the semi-Cajun coast food he knew as a boy, spicy if you wanted and not just to cover the taste of the ingredients. The shrimp and okra and oysters were fresh then, caught or picked that day. That was a richer time, when people ate at home and grew or caught much of what they ate. Paradise, and as usual, nobody had much noticed it at the time.

He looked around and caught the old flavor. Despite his disguise, he saw that some people notice you're a cop. After a few minutes their eyes slide away and they go back to living their lives whether he was watching them or not. Their talk followed the meandering logic of real talk or the even more wayward path of stoned talk. Half-lowered eyelids, gossip, beer smells mingling with fried fish and nose-crinkling popcorn shrimp. Life.

He finished eating, letting the place get used to him. Nobody paid him much attention. The Right Spot was now an odd combination, a restaurant in steep decline with a sleazy bar one thin wall away. Maybe people only ate after they'd guzzled enough that the taste didn't matter anyway.

When he cut through the side door two Cajun women at the end of the bar gave him one glance that instantly said cop at the same time his eyes registered hookers. But they weren't full-on pros. They looked like locals in flutty blouses and skinny pants who made a little extra on the side and told themselves they were trying out the talent for the bigger game, a sort of modern style of courtship, free of hypocrisy. Just over the line. He had seen plenty of them when he worked vice. It was important to know the difference, the passing tide of women versus the real hard core who made up the true business. These were just true locals. Fair enough.

The woman bartender leaned over to give him a look at the small but nicely shaped breasts down the top of her gold lame vest. She had a rose tattoo on one.

"Whiskey rocks, right?" She gave him a thin smile.

"Red wine." She had made him as a cop, too. Maybe he had even ordered whiskey last time he was here.

"You been gone a while."

Best to take the polite, formal mode, southern Cary Grant. "I'm sure you haven't lacked for attention." Now that he thought about it, he had gotten some good information here about six months back, and she had pointed out the source.

"I could sure use some." A smile and a slow wink.

"Not from me. Too old. I can remember when the air was clean and sex was dirty."

She laughed, showing a lot of bright teeth, even though it was an old line, maybe as ancient as the era it referred to. But this wasn't what he was here for, no. He took the wine, paid, and turned casually to case the room.

Most of the trade here was beer. Big TVs showed talking heads with thick necks against a backdrop of a football field. Guys in jeans and work shirts watched, rapt eyes above the bottles pressed to their mouths. He headed for the back with the glass of indifferent wine, where an old juke strummed with Springsteen singing "There's a darkness on the edge of town."

The fishermen sat along the back. He could tell by the work boots, worn hands, and salt-rimmed cuffs of their jeans and by something more, a squinty look from working in the sea glare. He walked over and sat down at the only open table, at the edge of maybe a dozen of the men sipping on beers.

It took a quarter of an hour before he could get into their conversation. It helped that he had spent years working on his family's boat. He knew the rhythms and lingo, the subtle lurch of consonants and soft vowels that told them he was from around here. He bought the next table over a round of Jax beers and that did it. Only gradually did it dawn on him that they already knew about Ethan Anselmo's death. The kids on the beach had spread the story, naturally.

But most of them here probably didn't know he was a cop, not yet. He sidled along and sat in a squeaky oak chair. Several of the guys were tired and loaded up with beer, stalling before going home to the missus. Others were brighter and on a guess he asked one, "Goin' out tonight?"

"Yeah, night dredgin'. All I can get lately."

The man looked like he had, in his time, quite probably eaten dinner in lot of poolrooms, or out of vending machines, and washed off using a garden hose. Working a dredger at night was mean work. Also, the easiest way to avoid the rules about damaging the sea bottom. Getting caught at that was risky and most men wouldn't take it.

McKenna leaned back and said in slow syllables, "This guy Ethan, the dead guy, know him?"

A nod, eyes crinkling with memory. "He worked the good boat. That one the Centauris hired, double money."

"I hadn't heard they hired anybody other than on Dauphin Island."

"This was some special work. Not dredgin'. Hell, he'd be here right now gettin' ready if he hadn't fell off that boat."

"He fell?" McKenna leaned forward a little and then remembered to look casual.

"They say."

"Who says?" Try not to seem too urgent.

A slow blink, sideways glance, a decision made. "Merv Pitscomb, runs the Busted Flush. Now and then they went out together on night charter."

"Really? Damn." He let it ride a little, then asked, "They go out last night?"

"I dunno."

"What they usually go for? Night fishin'?"

Raised eyebrows, shrug. "No bidness of mine."

"Pitscomb works for the Centauris?"

"Not d'rectly. They got a foreman kinda, big guy named Durrer. He books work for the Centauris when they need it."

"Regular work?"

A long tug at his beer. "Comes an' goes. Top dollar, I hear."

McKenna had to go slow here. The man's face was closing in, suspicion written in the tight mouth. McKenna always had a problem pressing people for information, and that got around, but apparently not to The Right Spot just yet. One suspect had once named him, Man Who Ax Questions

More'n He Should. True, but the suspect got ten to twenty upstate just the same.

McKenna backed off and talked football until the guy told him his name, Fred Godwin. Just then, by pure luck that at first didn't look like it, a woman named Irene came over to tell them both that she'd all heard about the body and all, and to impart her own philosophy on the matter.

The trouble with teasing information out of people was you get interrupted. It felt like losing a fish from a line, knowing it would never fall for the hook again. Irene went on about how it was a tragedy of course and she knew it weighed upon everybody. That went without saying, only she said it. She looked to be about forty going on fifty pretty hard, and unsteady on her shimmering gold high heels.

"Look at it this way," she said profoundly, eyes crinkling up above her soulful down-turned lips, "Ethan was young, so that as he was taken up on an angel's wing to the Alabaster City, he will be still brimming with what he could be. See? Set down at the Lord's Table, he will have no true regret. There will be no time for that. Another life will beckon to him while he is still full of energy, without memories of old age. No fussing with medicine and fear and failed organs, none. No such stations of duress on the way to Glory."

He could hear the capitals. Godwin looked like he was waiting for the right moment to escape. Which meant it was the right moment to buy him a beer, which McKenna did. To keep control of the conversation, maybe hinting at an invitation to sit with them, Irene volunteered that she'd heard Ethan had been working on the Busted Flush the night before his body washed up. Bingo.

McKenna bought Godwin the beer anyway.

Up toward the high end districts of Mobile the liquor stores stocked decades-old single malt Scotch and groceries had goat yoghurt and five kinds of oregano and coffee from nations you never heard of since high school. You could sip it while you listened to Haydn in their coffee shops and maybe scan the latest *New Yorker* for an indie film review.

But down by the coast the stores had Jim Beam if you asked right and the only seasoning on their shelves was salt and pepper, usually lots of pepper for Cajun tastes, and coffee came in cans. There was no music at all where he shopped and he was grateful. Considering what it might have been.

He got a bottle of a good California red to wash away the taste of the stuff he'd had earlier and made his way to the dock near the Busted Flush mooring. From his trunk he got out his rod and tackle and bait and soon enough was flipping his lure toward the lily pads in the nearby bayou. He pulled it lazily back, letting the dark water savor it. In a fit of professional rigor he had left the good California red in the car.

The clapboard shack beside the mooring was gray, the nail holes trailing rust and the front porch sagging despite the cinder blocks loyally holding it up from the damp sand. There was a big aluminum boathouse just beyond but no lights were on. He guessed it was too austere and indeed the only murmur of talk came from the shack. A burst of cackling laughter from the fishing crew leaked out of the walls.

He sat in the shadows. An old Dr Pepper sign was almost gone but you could still see the holes from buckshot. Teenagers love targets.

It made no real good sense to fish at night but the moon was coming up like a cat's yellow smile over the shimmering gulf and some thought that drew the fish out. Like a false dawn, an old fisherman had said to him long ago, and maybe it was true. All he needed was the excuse anyway so he sat and waited. He always kept worms in a moist loam pail in the car trunk and maybe they would work tonight even if this stakeout didn't.

The Busted Flush crew was hauling out the supplies for a night run. There was always something to do on a boat, as McKenna knew from working them as a teenager, but these guys were taking longer than it should.

He had learned long ago the virtues of waiting. At his distance of about a hundred meters simple binoculars told him all he needed, and they had an IR filter to bring out the detail if he needed it. The amber moonlight glanced off the tin-roofed shotgun shacks down along the curve of the bay. Night-blooming flowers perfumed the night air and bamboo rattled in the distance like a whisper in his ear.

Then a big van rumbled up. Two guys got out, then a woman. They wore black and moved with crisp efficiency, getting gear out of the back. This didn't fit.

The team went to the dock and Merv Pitscomb ambled along to greet them. McKenna recognized him as skipper of the Busted Flush from a car fax he had gotten from the Mobile Main library, after leaving the restaurant. His car was more his office now than the desk he manned; electronics had changed everything.

The team and Pitscomb went together back to the van, talking. Pitscomb slid open the side door and everyone stepped back. A dark shape came out— large, moving slowly and in a silence from the Feds that was like reverence.

McKenna froze. He knew immediately it was a Centauri. Its arms swung slowly, as if heavily muscled. The oddly jointed elbow swung freely like a pendulum, going backward. In water that would be useful, McKenna imagined. The arm tapered down to a flat four-fingered hand that he knew could be shaped to work like the blade of an oar.

The amphibians were slow and heavy, built for a life spent moving from water to land. It walked solidly behind the two guys in black, who were forming a screen of what had to be Federal officers. No talk. Centauris' palates could not manage the shaped human sounds, so all communication was written.

It shuffled toward Busted Flush on thick legs that had large, circular feet. With help at the elbows from the Feds it mounted the gangplank. This was the first he had seen for real, not on TV, and it struck him that it waddled more than walked. It was slow here, in a slightly stronger gravity. Centauris had evolved from a being that moved on sand, seldom saw rock, and felt more at home in the warm waters of a world that was mostly sea.

He realized as it reached the boat that he had been holding his breath. It was strange in a way he could not define. The breeze blew his way. He sniffed and wondered if that rank flavoring was the alien.

It went aboard, the Federal officers' eyes swiveling in all directions. McKenna was under a cypress and hard to spot and their eyes slid right over him. He wondered why they didn't use infrared goggles.

Busted Flush started up with a hammering turbo engine. It turned away from the dock and headed straight out into the gulf. McKenna watched it go but he could not see the alien. The shrimp nets hung swaying on their high rocker arms and Busted Flush looked like any other dredge shrimper going out for the night. That was the point, McKenna guessed.

When he finally got home down the oyster-shell road and parked under the low pines, he walked out onto his dock to look at the stars above the gulf. It always helped. He did not want to go right away into the house where he and his lost wife had lived. He had not moved away, because he loved this place, and though she was not here at least the memories were.

He let the calm come over him and then lugged his briefcase up onto the porch and was slipping a key into the lock when he heard a scraping. He turned toward the glider where he had swung so many happy times and someone was getting up from it. A spike of alarm shot through him, the one you always have once you work the hard criminals, and then he saw it was a woman in a pale yellow dress. Yellow hair, too, blond with a ribbon in it. Last time it had been red.

"John! Now, you did promise you'd call."

At first he could not tell who she was, but he reached inside the door and flipped on the porch light and her face leaped out of the darkness. "Ah, uh, Denise?"

"Why yes, did you forget me already?" Humorous reproach, coquettish and a little strained.

She swayed toward him, her hair bouncing as if just washed. Which it probably was. He felt his spirits sinking. If the average woman would rather have beauty than brains, it's because the average man can see better than he can think. Denise believed that and so was even more dolled up than on their first date. Also, last date.

"I figured out where you lived, so stopped by." Her broad smile was wise and enticing. "You didn't call, you know."

The vowels rolled off her tongue like sugar and he remembered why he had found her so intriguing.

"I've been awful busy."

"So've I, but you cain't just let life go by, y'know."

What to say to that? She was here for a clear purpose, her large red handbag on a shoulder strap and probably packed with cosmetics and a change of underwear. Yet he had no easy counter to it.

"Denise, I'm . . . seeing someone else." Easy, reasoned.

Her expression shifted subtly, the smile still in place but now glassy. "I . . . I didn't know that."

"It didn't make the papers."

No, that was wrong, humor wouldn't work here. He decided on the physical instead and held out a hand, edge on, thumb straight up, for a shake. A long moment passed while her eyelashes batted beneath the yellow porch light and he could hear frogs croaking in the night marsh.

She looked at his hand and blinked and the smile collapsed. "I . . . I thought . . ."

It was his duty to make this as easy as possible so he took her half-offered hand and put an arm around her shoulders. He turned her delicately, murmuring something that made sense at the time but that he could not remember ten seconds later. With a sweeping arm he ushered her down the wooden stairs, across the sandy lawn in the moist sea air. Without more than soft words they both got to the car he had not even seen parked far back under the big oak tree aside the house. He said nothing that meant anything and she did the same and they got through the moment with something resembling their dignity.

He helped her into her car and turned back toward his house. A year ago, in a momentary fit, one member of the sorority of such ladies of a certain age had tried to run him down. This time, though, her Chevy started right off, growling like a late model, and turned toward the oyster driveway that shimmered in the silvery moon glow. He walked away from it, the noise pushing him.

The lie about seeing someone settled in him. His social graces were rusty. He mounted the steps as her headlights swept across the porch, spotlighting him momentarily, like an angry glare. To jerk open the front door and finally get inside felt like a forgiveness.

McKenna got into work early. It had bothered him to usher Denise off like that and he had stayed up too late thinking about it. Also, there was that good California red. Not that he had failed to enjoy Denise and the others in their mutual nonjudgmental rejection of middle class values. Not at all.

But that style wasn't working for him anymore. He had set out vaguely searching for someone who could bring that light back into his life, the oblivious glow he had basked in for decades of a happy marriage. He had thought that if it happened once it could happen again. But since Linda's death nothing had that magic to it. Not dating—a term he hated, preferring "courtship"—and most of the time not even sex, his old standby.

So Denise's sad approach, the stuff of every teenage boy's dream, had been too little, too late.

He was still musing about this when he got to his desk. Homicide was a big squad room in worn green industrial carpet. The work pods had five desks each and he walked past these because he at last had gained a sheltered cubicle. The sergeant's desk was nearby his lieutenant's cubicle and framing the whole array was a rank of file cabinets. No paperless office here, no. Maybe never. At least there was no smoking anymore, but the carpet remembered those days. Especially after a rain, which meant usually.

The morning squad room buzzed with movement, talk, caffeine energy. Homicide detectives always run because it's a timed event. You close in on the perp inside two weeks or it's over.

And here was the ME folder on Ethan Anselmo. Once you've studied a few hundred autopsy reports you know you can skip the endless pages of organs, glands, general chemistry, and just go to the conclusions. Forensic analysis had a subreport labeled GSR, which meant gunshot residue, that was blank.

The ME was confused. Heart stopped, lungs full, much like a drowning victim who had fought the ocean to his last. But the strange ridges on his skin looked like nerve damage, seared as if in an electrocution. The punctures McKenna had seen just obscured the case further.

McKenna hated muddy cases. Now he had to assign cause, focusing the ME report and the background he had gotten last night. He didn't hesitate. Probable homicide, he wrote.

The usual notices had gone through, assigning case and ME numbers, letting the Squad and Precinct Captains know, asking if there seemed any link to other cases—all routine. Section Command and District Office heard, all by standard e-mail heads-up forms, as did Photo and Latent and Lab.

He took out a brown loose-leaf binder and made up a murder book. First came the Homicide Occurrence Report with Mobile Main as the address in the right upper corner. Then the basics. A door that opened wide with no sure destination beyond.

McKenna sat back and let his mind rove. Nothing. Sometimes an idea lurked there after he had reviewed the case; not now.

He knew he had to finish up a report on a domestic slaying from two days back, so he set to it. Most murders were by guys driven crazy by screeching kids and long-term debt and bipolar wives. Alcohol helped. They had figured out their method about ten seconds before doing it and had no alibi, no plausible response to physical evidence, and no story that didn't come apart under a two-minute grilling. When you took them out to the car in cuffs the neighbors just nodded at each other and said they'd always figured on this, hadn't they said so?

This was a no-brainer case. He finished the paperwork, longing for that paperless office, and dispatched it to the prosecutor's office. They would cut the deal and McKenna would never hear of it again. Unless the perp showed up in fifteen years on his front porch, demanding vengeance. That had happened, too. Now McKenna went armed, even on Sundays to church.

Then he sat and figured.

The ME thought the odd marks on Ethan Anselmo might be electrocution. Torture? Yet the guy was no lowlife. He had no history of drug-running using shrimp boats, the default easy way for a fisherman to bring in extra income all along the Gulf. For a moment McKenna idly wondered when the War on Drugs would end, as so many failed American adventures had, with admission that the war was clearly lost. It would certainly be easier to legalize, tax, and control most drugs than it was to chase after them. He had at first figured Anselmo for a drug gang killing. There were plenty of them along the Gulf shore. But now that felt wrong.

His desktop computer told him that the Anselmo case was now online in the can't-crack site Mobile used to coordinate police work now. There were some additions from the autopsy and a background report on Anselmo, but nothing that led anywhere.

He sighed. Time to do some shoe-leather work.

The Busted Flush was back at its dock. McKenna had changed into a beat-up work shirt and oil-stained jeans. Sporting a baseball cap, he found the crew hosing off a net rig inside the big aluminum boathouse nearby. "Pitscomb around?" he asked them, rounding the vowels to fit the local accent.

A thirty-something man walked over to McKenna. One cheek had a long, ugly scar now gone to dirty pink. His hair was blond and ratty, straight and cut mercifully short. But the body was taut and muscular and ready; the scrollwork tattoos of jailhouse vintage showed he had needed for much of his life. He wore a snap-button blue work shirt with a stuck-on nameplate that said Buddy Johnson. Completing the outfit was a hand-tooled belt with carry hooks hanging and half-topped boots that needed a polish pretty bad.

"Who wants to know?"

The stern, gravel voice closed a switch in McKenna's head. He had seen this guy a decade before when he helped make an arrest. Two men tried to pull the front off a cash machine by running a chain from the machine to the bumper of their pickup truck. Instead of pulling the front panel off the machine, though, they yanked the bumper off the truck. They panicked and fled, leaving the chain still attached to the machine, their bumper still attached to the chain, and their license plate still attached to the bumper.

"Lookin' for work," McKenna said. This guy couldn't be heading up the operation, so he needed to go higher.

"We got none." The eyes crinkled as if Buddy was trying to dredge up a memory.

McKenna shifted his own tone from soft to medium. "I need to see your boss."

Still puzzling over the memory, Johnson waved toward the boathouse. McKenna walked away, feeling Johnson's eyes on his back.

Pitscomb was at the back of the building, eating hog cracklings from a greasy bag, brushing the crumbs into the lagoon. Carrion birds eyed him as they drifted by on the soft slurring wind, keeping just above the gnarled tops of the dead cypress, just in case they saw some business below that needed doing.

Pitscomb was another matter. Lean, angular, intelligent blue eyes. McKenna judged that he might as well come clean. He showed his badge and said with a drawl, "Need to talk about Ethan Anselmo."

Pitscomb said, "Already heard. He didn't come to work that night."

"Your crew, they'll verify that?"

He grinned. "They'd better."

"Why you have an ex-con working your boat?"

"I don't judge people, I just hire 'em. Buddy's worked out fine."

"What do you do for the Centauris?"

"That's a Federal matter, I was told to say."

McKenna leaned against a pier stay. "Why do they use you, then? Why not take the Centauri out on their own boat?"

Pitscomb brushed his hands together, sending the last of the cracklings into the water. "You'd have to ask them. Way I see it, the Feds want to give the Centauris a feel for our culture. And spread the money around good an' local, too."

"What's the Centauri do out there?"

"Just looks, swims. A kind of night off, I guess."

"They live right next to the water."

"Swimming out so far must be a lot of work, even for an amphibian." By now Pitscomb had dropped the slow-South accent and was eyeing McKenna.

"How far out?"

"A few hours."

"Just to swim?"

"The Feds don't want me to spread gossip."

"This is a murder investigation."

"Just gossip, far as I'm concerned."

"I can take this to the Feds."

Again the sunny smile, as sincere as a postage stamp. "You do that. They're not backwoods coon-asses, those guys."

Meaning, pretty clearly, that McKenna was. He turned and walked out through the machine oil smells of the boathouse. Buddy Johnson was waiting in the moist heat. He glowered but didn't say anything.

As he walked past McKenna said, using hard vowels, "Don't worry, now. I haven't chewed off anybody's arm in nearly a week."

Buddy still didn't say anything, just smiled slyly. When McKenna got to his car he saw the reason.

A tire was flat, seeming to ooze into the blacktop. McKenna glanced back at Buddy, who waved and went back inside. McKenna thought about following him but it was getting warm and he was sticking to his shirt. Buddy would wait until he knew more, he figured.

He got his gloves from the trunk, then lifted out the jack, lug wrench, and spare. He squatted down and started spinning the nuts off, clattering them into the hubcap. By the time he fitted the spare on the axle and tightened the wheel nuts with the jack, then lowered it, he had worked up a sweat and smelled himself sour and fragrant.

The work had let him put his mind on cruise and as he drove away he felt some connections link up.

The Pizottis. One of them was a real professor, the kind he needed. Was that family fish fry tonight? He could just about make it.

Since Linda died he had seen little of the Pizotti family. Their shared grief seemed to drive them apart. The Pizottis always kept somewhat distant anyway, an old country instinct.

He drove over the causeway to the eastern shore of the bay and then down through Fairhope to the long reaches south of the Grand Hotel. He had grown up not far away, spending summers on the Fish River at Grammaw McKenzie's farm. To even reach the fish fry, on an isolated beach, he decided to take a skiff out across Weeks Bay.

The Pizottis had invited him weeks ago, going through the motions of pretending he was family. They weren't the reason, of course. He let himself forget about all that as he poled along amid the odors of reeds and sour mud, standing in the skiff. In among the cattails lurked alligators, one with three babies a foot and a half long. They scattered away from the skiff, nosing into the muddy fragrant water, the mother snuffing as she sank behind the young ones. He knew the big legendary seventeen-footers always lay back in the reeds, biding their time. As he coasted forward on a few oar strokes, he saw plenty of lesser lengths lounging in the late sun like metallic sculptures. A big one ignored the red-tailed hawk on a log nearby, knowing it was too slow to ever snare the bird. By a cypress tree, deep in a thick tangle of matted saw grass, a gray possum was picking at something and sniffing like it couldn't decide whether to dine or not. The phosphorus-loving cattails had moved in further up the bay, stealing away the skiff's glide so he came to a stop. He didn't like the cattails and felt insulted by their presence. Cattails robbed sunlight from the paddies and fish below, making life harder for the water-feeding birds.

He cut toward Mobile Bay where the fish fry should be and looked in among the reeds. There were lounging gators like logs sleeping in the sun. One rolled over in the luxury of the warm mud and gave off a moaning grunt, an umph-umph-umph with mouth closed. Then it opened in a yawn and achieved a throaty, bellowing roar. He had seen alligators like that before in Weeks Bay where the Fish River eased in, just below the old arched bridge. Gators seemed to like bridges. They would lie in the moist heat and sleep, the top predators here, unafraid. He admired their easy assurance that nothing could touch them, their unthinking arrogance.

Until people came along, only a few centuries before, with their rifles. He suddenly wondered if the Centauris were like this at all. They were amphibians, not reptiles. What would they make of gators?

A gator turned and looked up at him for a long moment. It held the gaze, as if figuring him out. It snuffed and waddled a little in the mud to get more comfortable and closed its big eyes. McKenna felt an odd chill. He paddled faster.

The other wing of the Pizotti family was on the long sand bar at the end of Weeks Bay, holding forth in full cry. He came ashore, dragged the skiff up to ground it, and tried to mix. The Pizottis' perfunctory greetings faded and they got back to their social games.

He had loved Linda dearly but these were not truly his kind of people. She had been serene, savoring life while she had it. The rest of the Pizottis were on the move. Nowadays the Gulf's Golden Coast abounded with Masters of the Universe. They sported excellently cut hair and kept themselves slim, casually elegant, and carefully muscled. Don't want to look like a laborer, after all, never mind what their grandfathers did for a living. The women ran from platinum blond through strawberry, quite up to the minute. Their plastic surgery was tasteful: eye-smoothings and maybe a discreet wattle tuck. They carried themselves with that look not so much of energetic youth but rather of expert maintenance, like a Rolls with the oil religiously changed every 1500 miles. Walking in their wake made most working stiffs feel just a touch shabby.

One of them eyed him and professed fascination with a real detective. He countered with enthusiasm for the fried flounder and perch a cousin had brought. Food was a good dodge, though these were fried in too much oil. He held out for a polite ten minutes and then went to get one of the crab just coming off the grill. And there, waiting for the next crab to come sizzling off, was Herb. Just in time. McKenna could have kissed him.

It didn't take too long to work around to the point of coming here. Herb was an older second cousin of Linda, and had always seemed to McKenna like the only other Pizotti who didn't fit in with the rest. He had become an automatic friend as soon as McKenna started courting her.

"It's a water world," Herb said, taking the bit immediately. He had been a general science teacher at Faulkner State in Fairhope, handling the chemistry and biology courses. "You're dead on, I've been reading all I could get about them."

"So they don't have much land?" McKenna waved to the woman who loved detectives and shrugged comically to be diplomatic. He got Herb and himself a glass of red, a Chianti.

"I figure that's why they're amphibians. Best to use what there's plenty of. Their planet's a moon, right?—orbiting around a gas giant like Jupiter. It gets sunlight from both Centauri stars, plus infrared from the gas giant. So it's always warm and they don't seem to have plate tectonics, so their world is real, real different."

McKenna knew enough from questioning witnesses to nod and look interested. Herb was already going beyond what he'd gotten from TV and newspapers and Scientific American. McKenna tried to keep up. As near as he could tell, plate tectonics was something like the grand unified theory of geology. Everything from the deep plains of the ocean to Mount Everest came from the waltz of continents, butting together and churning down into the deep mantle. Their dance rewrote climates and geographies, opening up new possibilities for life and at times closing down old ones. But that was here, on Earth.

The other small planets of our solar system didn't work that way. Mars had been rigid for billions of years. Venus upchucked its mantle and buried its crust often enough to leave it barren.

So planets didn't have to work like Earth, and the Centauri water world was another example. It rotated slowly, taking eight days to get around its giant neighbor. It had no continents, only strings of islands. And it was old—more than a billion years older than Earth. Life arose there from nothing more than chemicals meeting in a warm sea while sunlight boomed through a blanket of gas.

"So they got no idea about continents?" McKenna put in.

Herb said he sure seemed to miss lecturing, ever since he retired, and it made him a dinner companion not exactly sought after here among the Pizottis. McKenna had never thought he could be useful, like now. "They took one up in an airplane, with window blinds all closed, headphones on its ears. Turns out it liked Bach! Great, huh?"

McKenna nodded, kept quiet. None of the other Pizottis was paying any attention to Herb. They seemed to be moving away, even.

"The blindfold was so it wouldn't get scared, I guess. They took off the blindfold and showed it mountains, river valleys, all that. Centauris got no real continents, just strings of islands. It could hardly believe its clamshell eyes."

"But they must've seen those from space, coming in. Continents and all."

"Not the same, close up."

"So maybe they're thinking to move inland, explore?"

"I doubt it. They got to stick close to warm, salty water."

McKenna wondered if they had any global warming there and then said, "They got no oil, I guess. No place for all those ferns to grow, so long ago."

Herb blinked. "Hadn't figured that. S'pose so. But they say they got hurricanes alla time, just the way we do now."

McKenna poked a finger up and got them another glass of the Chianti. Herb needed fueling.

"It's cloudy alla time there, the astro boys say. They can never see through the clouds. Imagine, not knowing for thousands of years that there are stars."

McKenna imagined never having a sunny day. "So how'd they ever get a space program going?"

"Slow and steady. Their civilization is way old, y'know, millions of years. They say their spaceships are electric, somehow."

McKenna couldn't imagine electric rockets. "And they've got our kind of DNA."

Herb brightened. "Yeah, what a surprise. Spores brought it here, *Scientific American* figures."

"Amazing. What sort of biology do amphibians have?"

Herb shrugged and pushed a hush puppy into his mouth, then chewed thoughtfully. The fish fry was a babble all around them and McKenna had to concentrate. "Dunno. There's nothing in the science press about that. Y'know, Centauris are mighty private about that stuff."

"They give away plenty of technology, the financial pages say."

"You bet, whole new products. Funny electrical gadgets, easy to market."

"So why are they here? Not to give us gifts." Might as well come out and say it.

"Just like Carl Sagan said, right? Exchange cultures and all. A great adventure, and we get it without spending for starships or anything."

"So they're tourists? Who pay with gadgets?"

Herb knocked back the rest of his Chianti. "Way I see it, they're lonely. They heard our radio a century back and started working on a ship to get here."

"Just like us, you think about it. Why else do we make up ghosts and angels and the like? Somebody to talk to."

"Only they can't talk."

"At least they write."

"Translation's hard, though. The Feds are releasing a little of it, but there'll be more later. You see those Centauri poems?"

He vaguely recalled some on the front page of the paper. "I couldn't make sense of it."

Herb grinned brightly. "Me either, but it's fascinating. All about the twin suns. Imagine!"

When he got home he showered, letting the steam envelop him and ease away the day. His mind had too much in it, tired from the day. Thinking about sleep, when he often got his best ideas, he toweled off.

The shock came when he wiped the steam from the mirror and saw a smeary old man, blotchy skin, gray hair pasted to the skull, ashen whiskers sprouting from deep pores. He had apparently gone a decade or two without paying attention to mirrors.

Fair enough, if they insult you this deeply. He slapped some cream on the wrinkles hemming in his eyes, dressed, sucked in his belly, and refused to check himself out in the mirror again. Insults enough, for one day. Growing older he couldn't do much about, but Buddy Johnson was another matter.

At dawn he quite deliberately went fishing. He needed to think.

He sat on his own wharf and sipped orange juice. He had to wash off the reels with the hose from the freshwater tank as waves came rolling in and burst in sprays against the creaking pilings. He smelled the salty tang of bait fish in his bucket and, as if to tantalize him, a speckled fish broke from a curling wave, plunging headfirst into the foam. He had never seen a fish do that and it proved yet again that the world was big and strange and always changing. Other worlds, too.

He sat at his desk and shuffled paper for the first hour of the morning shift. He knew he didn't have long before the Ethan Anselmo case hit a dead end. Usually a homicide not wrapped up in two weeks had a less-than-even chance of ever getting solved at all. After two weeks the case became an unclaimed corpse in the files, sitting there in the dark chill of neglect.

Beyond the autopsy you go to the evidence analysis reports. Computer printouts, since most detectives still worked with paper. Tech addenda and photos. All this under a time and cost constraint, the clock and budget always ticking along. "Investigative prioritizing," the memos called it. Don't do anything expensive without your supe's nod.

So he went to see his supe, a black guy two months in from Vice, still learning the ropes. And got nothing back.

"The Feds, you let them know about the Centauri connection, right?" the supe asked.

"Sure. There's a funnel to them through the Mobile FBI office."

Raised eyebrows. "And?"

"Nothing so far."

"Then we wait. They want to investigate, they will."

"Not like they don't know the Centauris are going out on civilian boats." McKenna was fishing to see if his supe knew anything more but the man's eyes betrayed nothing.

The supe said, "Maybe the Centauris want it this way. But why?"

"Could be they want to see how ordinary people work the sea?"

"We gotta remember they're aliens. Can't think of them as like people."

McKenna couldn't think of how that idea could help so he sat and waited. When the supe said nothing more, McKenna put in, "I'm gonna get a call from the Anselmo widow."

"Just tell her we're working on it. When's your partner get back?"

"Next week. But I don't want a stand-in."

A shrug. "Okay, fine. Just don't wait for the Feds to tell you anything. They're just like the damn FBI over there."

M cKenna was in a meeting about new arrest procedures when the watch officer came into the room and looked at him significantly.

The guy droning on in front was a city government lawyer and most of his audience was nodding off. It was midafternoon and the coffee had long run out but not the lawyer.

McKenna ducked outside and the watch officer said, "You got another, looks like. Down in autopsy."

It had washed up on Orange Beach near the Florida line, so Baldwin County Homicide had done the honors. Nobody knew who it was and the fingerprints went nowhere. It had on jeans and no underwear, McKenna read in the Baldwin County report.

When the Baldwin County sheriff saw on the Internet cross-correlation index that it was similar to McKenna's case they sent it over for the Mobile ME. That had taken a day, so the corpse was a bit more rotted. It was already gutted and probed, and the ME had been expecting him.

"Same as your guy," the ME said. "More of those raised marks, all over the body."

Suited up and wearing masks, they went over the swollen carcass. The rot and swarming stink caught in McKenna's throat but he forced down the impulse to vomit. He had never been good at this clinical stuff. He made himself focus on what the ME was pointing out, oblivious to McKenna's rigidity.

Long ridges of reddened, puckering flesh laced around the trunk and down the right leg. A foot was missing. The leg was drained white, and the ME said it looked like a shark bite. Something had nibbled at the genitals. "Most likely a turtle," the ME said. "They go for the delicacies."

McKenna let this remark pass by and studied the face. Black eyes, broad nose, weathered brown skin. "Any punctures?"

"Five, on top of the ridges. Not made by teeth or anything I know."

"Any dental ID?"

"Not yet."

"I need pictures," McKenna said. "Cases like this cool off fast."

"Use my digital, I'll e-mail them to you. He looks like a Latino," the ME said. "Maybe that's why no known fingerprints or dental. Illegal."

Ever since the first big hurricanes, Katrina and Rita, swarms of Mexicans had poured in to do the grunt work. Most stayed, irritating the working class who then competed for the construction and restaurant and fishing jobs. The ME prepared his instruments for further opening the swollen body and McKenna knew he could not take that. "Where . . . where's the clothes?"

The ME looked carefully at McKenna's eyes. "Over there. Say, maybe you should sit down."

"I'm okay." It came out as a croak. McKenna went over to the evidence bag and pulled out the jeans. Nothing in the pockets. He was stuffing them back in when he felt something solid in the fabric. There was a little inner pocket at the back, sewed in by hand. He fished out a key ring with a crab-shaped ornament and one key on it.

"They log this in?" He went through the paperwork lying on the steel table. The ME was cutting but came over. Nothing in the log.

"Just a cheap plastic thingy," the ME said, holding it up to the light. "Door key, maybe. Not a car."

"Guy with one key on his ring. Maybe worked boats, like Anselmo."

"That's the first guy, the one who had those same kinda marks?"

McKenna nodded. "Any idea what they are?"

The ME studied the crab ornament. "Not really. Both bodies had pretty rough hands, too. Manual labor."

"Workin' stiffs. You figure he drowned?"

"Prob'ly. Got all the usual signs. Stick around, I'll know soon."

McKenna very carefully did not look back at the body. The smell was getting to him even over the air conditioning sucking air out of the room with a loud hum. "I'll pick up the report later." He left right away.

H is supe sipped coffee, considered the sound-absorbing ceiling, and said, "You might see if VICAP got anything like this."

The Violent Criminal Apprehension Program computer would cross-filter the wounds and tell him if anything like that turned up in other floaters. "Okay. Thought I'd try to track that crab thing on the key chain."

The supe leaned back and crossed his arms, showing scars on both like scratches on ebony. "Kinda unlikely."

"I want to see if anybody recognizes it. Otherwise this guy's a John Doe."

"It's a big gulf. The ME think it could've floated from Mexico?"

"No. Local, from the wear and tear."

"Still a lot of coastline."

McKenna nodded. The body had washed up about forty miles to the east of Bayou La Batre, but the currents could have brought it from anywhere. "I got to follow my hunches on this."

The supe studied McKenna's face like it was a map. He studied the ceiling again and sighed. "Don't burn a lot of time, okay?"

T here were assorted types working in homicide but he broke them into two different sorts.

Most saw the work as a craft, a skill they learned. He counted himself in those, though wondered lately if he was sliding into the second group: those who thought it was a mission in life, the only thing worth doing. Speakers for the dead, he called them.

At the crime scene a bond formed, a promise from the decaying corpse to the homicide detective: that this would be avenged. It went with the job.

The job was all about death, of course. He had shot only two perps in his career. Killed one in a messy attempt at an arrest, back when he was just getting started. A second when a smart guy whose strategy had gone way wrong decided he could still shoot his way out of his confusion. All he had done was put a hole through McKenna's car.

But nowadays he felt more like an avenging angel than he had when young. Closer to the edge. Teetering above the abyss.

Maybe it had something to do with his own wife's death, wasting away, but he didn't go there anymore. Maybe it was just about death itself, the eternal human problem without solution. If you can't solve it you might as well work at it anyway.

Murderers were driven, sometimes just for a crazed moment that shaped all the rest of their lives. McKenna was a cool professional, calm and sure—or so he told himself.

But something about the Anselmo body—drowned and electrocuted both—got to him. And now the anonymous illegal, apparently known to nobody, silent in his doom.

Yet he, the seasoned professional, saw no place to go next. No leads. This was the worse part of any case, where most of them went cold and stayed that way. Another murder file, buried just like the bodies.

McKenna started in the west, at the Mississippi state line. The Gulf towns were much worse off after getting slammed with Katrina and Rita and the one nobody could pronounce right several years after. The towns never got off the ropes. The Gulf kept punching them hard, maybe fed by global warming and maybe just out of some kind of natural rage. Mother Earth Kicks Ass, part umpty-million.

He had the tech guy Photoshop the photos of the Latino's face, taking away the swelling and water bleaching. With eyes open he looked alive. Then he started showing it around.

He talked to them all—landlords and labor in-between men, Mexicans who worked the fields, labor center types. Nothing. So he went to the small-time boosters, hookers, creeps in alleys, button men, strong-arm types slow and low of word, addicts galore, those who thrived on the dark suffering around them—the underlife of the decaying coast. He saw plenty of thick-bodied, smoldering anger that would be bad news someday for someone, of vascular crew-cut slick boys, stained jeans, arms ridged with muscle that needed to be working. Some had done time in the bucket and would again.

Still, nothing. The Latino face rang no bells.

He was coming out of a gardening shop that used a lot of Latinos when the two suits walked up. One wore a Marine-style bare-skull haircut and the other had on dark glasses and both those told him Federal.

"You're local law?" the Marine type said.

Without a word McKenna showed them his badge. Dark Glasses and Marine both showed theirs, FBI, and Dark Glasses said, "Aren't you a long way beyond Mobile city lines?"

"We're allowed to follow cases out into the county," McKenna said levelly.

"May we see the fellow you're looking for?" Mr. Marine asked, voice just as flat.

McKenna showed the photo. "What did he do?" Mr. Marine asked.

"Died. I'm Homicide."

"We had a report you were looking in this community for someone who worked boats," Dark Glasses said casually.

"Why would that interest the FBI?"

"We're looking for a similar man," Mr. Marine said. "On a Federal issue."

"So this is the clue that I should let you know if I see him? Got a picture?"

Dark Glasses started a smile and thought better of it. "Since there's no overlap, I think not."

"But you have enough sources around here that as soon as I show up, you get word." McKenna said it flatly and let it lie there in the sun.

"We have our ways," Dark Glasses said. "How'd this guy die?"

"Drowned."

"Why think it's homicide?" Mr. Marine came in.

"Just a hunch."

"Something tells me you have more than that," Mr. Marine shot back.

"You show me yours, I'll show you mine."

They looked at each other and McKenna wondered if they got the joke. They turned and walked away without a word.

His bravado with them made him feel good but it didn't advance his case. His mind spun with speculations about the FBI and then he put them away. The perpetual rivalry between local and federal always simmered, since the Feds could step in and capture a case when they thought they could profit from it. Or solve it better. Sometimes they were even right.

He prowled the Latino quarters. Hurricane damage was still common all along the Gulf Coast, years after the unpronounceable hurricane that had made Katrina and Rita look like mere overtures. He worked his way east and saw his fill of wrecked piers, abandoned houses blown out when the windows gave in, groves of pines snapped off halfway up, roofs ripped away, homes turned to flooded swamps. Weathered signs on damaged walls brought back to mind the aftermath: LOOTERS SHOT; on a roof: HELP;

a plaintive WE'RE HERE; an amusing FOR SALE: SOME WATER DAMAGE on a condo completely gutted. Historical documents, now.

Hurricanes had hammered the coast so hard that in the aftermath businesses got pillaged by perfectly respectable people trying to hang on, and most of those stores were still closed. Trucks filled with scrap rumbled along the pitted roads. Red-shirted crews wheelbarrowed dark debris out of good brick homes. Blue tarp covered breached roofs, a promise that eventually they would get fixed. Near the beaches, waterline marks of scummy yellow remained, head high.

Arrival of aliens from another star had seemed less important to the coast people. Even though the Centauris had chosen the similar shores in Thailand, Africa, and India to inhabit, the Gulf was their focus, nearest an advanced nation. McKenna wondered what they thought of all the wreckage.

The surge of illegal Mexicans into the Gulf Coast brought a migration of some tough gangs from California. They used the illegal worker infrastructure as shelter, and occupied the drug business niches. Killings along the Mobile coast dropped from an average of three or four a day before to nearly zero, then rose in the next two years. Those were mostly turf wars between the druggies and immigrant heist artists of the type who prey on small stores.

So he moved among them in jeans, dog-eared hat, and an old shirt, listening. Maybe the Centauris were making people think about the stars and all, but he worked among a galaxy of losers: beat-up faces, hangdog scowls, low-hanging pants, and scuffed brown shoes. They would tell you a tearful life story in return for just looking at them. Every calamity that might befall a man had landed on them: turncoat friends, deadbeat buddies, barren poverty, cold fathers, huge bad luck, random inexplicable diseases, prison, car crashes, and of course the eternal forlorn song: treacherous women. It was a seminar in the great themes of Johnny Cash.

Then a droopy-eyed guy at a taco stand said he had seen the man in the picture over in a trailer park. McKenna approached it warily. If he got figured for a cop the lead would go dead.

Nearby were Spanish-language graffiti splashed on the minimart walls, and he passed Hispanic mothers and toddlers crowding into the county's health clinic. But the shabby mobile homes were not a wholly Hispanic enclave. There was a lot of genteel poverty making do here. Pensioners ate in decrepit diners that gave seniors a free glass of anonymous domestic wine with the special. Workers packed into nearby damaged walk-ups with no air conditioning. On the corners clumps of men lounged, rough-handed types who never answered questions, maybe because they knew no English.

McKenna worked his way down the rows of shabby trailers. Welfare mothers blinked at him and he reassured them he was not from the county office. It was hard to read whether anybody was lying because they seemed dazed by the afternoon heat. Partway through the trailer park a narrow-chested guy in greasy shorts came up and demanded, "Why you bothering my tenants?"

"Just looking for a friend."

"What for?"

"I owe him money."

A sarcastic leer snaked across the narrow face. "Yeah, right."

"Okay, I got a job for him." McKenna showed the photo.

A flicker in the man's eyes came and went. "Huh."

"Know him?"

"Don't think so."

"You don't lie worth a damn."

The mouth tightened. "You ax me an I tole you."

McKenna sighed and showed the badge. After a big storm a lot of fake badges sprouted on the chests of guys on the make, so this guy's caution was warranted. County sheriffs and state police tried to enforce the law and in byways like this they gave up. Time would sort it out, they figured. Some of the fakes became hated, then dead.

To his surprise, the man just stiffened and jutted his chin out. "Got nothin' to say."

McKenna leaned closer and said very fast, "You up to code here? Anybody in this trailer park got an outstanding warrant? How 'bout illegals? Safety code violations? I saw that extension cord three units back, running out of a door and into a side shed. You charge extra for the illegals under that tent with power but no toilet? Bet you do. Or do you just let it happen on the side and pick up some extra for being blind?"

The man didn't even blink.

McKenna was enjoying this. "So suppose we deport some of these illiterates, say. Maybe call in some others here, who violated their parole, uh? So real quick your receivables drop, right? Maybe a lot. Child support could come in here, too, right? One phone call would do it. There's usually a few in a trailer park who don't want to split their check with the bitch that keeps hounding them with lawyers, right? So with them gone, you got open units, buddy. Which means no income, so you're lookin' worse to the absentee landlord who cuts your check, you get me?"

McKenna could hear the gears grind and the eyes got worried. "Okay, look, he left a week back."

"Where to?"

"You know that bayou east about two miles, just before Angel Point? He went to an island just off there, some kind of boat work."

Floating lilies with lotus flowers dotted the willow swamp. Tupelo gums hung over the brown water as he passed, flavoring the twilight. The rented skiff sent its bow wash lapping at half-sunken logs with hides like dead manatees.

His neck felt sunburned from the sour day and his throat was raspy-dry. He cut the purring outboard and did some oar work for the last half mile. The skiff drifted silently up to the stilt house. It leaned a little on slender pilings, beneath a vast canopy of live oaks that seemed centuries old. The bow thumped at the tiny gray-wood dock, wood piling brushing past as he stepped softly off, lashing the stay rope with his left hand while he pulled his 9mm out and forward. No point in being careless.

Dusk settled in. A purple storm hung on the southern horizon and sheet lighting worked yellow magic at its edges. A string of lights hung along the wharf, glowing dimly in the murk, and insects batted at them. Two low pirogues drifted on the tide and clanked rusty chains.

The lock was antique and took him ten seconds.

The room smelled of damp dogs. He searched it systematically but there was nothing personal beyond worn clothes and some letters in Spanish. The postmarks were blurred by the moisture that never left the old wooden drawers. But in another drawer one came through sharp, three weeks old from Veracruz. That was a port town down the long curve of the eastern Mexican coast. From his knowledge of the Civil War era, which was virtually a requirement of a Southern man when he grew up, Veracruz was where Grant and Lee nearly got killed. Together they went out in a small boat to survey the shore in the Mexican war and artillery fire splashed within ten yards of them.

Lots of fishing in Veracruz. A guy from there would know how to work nets.

He kept the letters and looked in the more crafty places. No plastic bag in the commode water closet. Nothing under the filthy pine floor. No hollow legs on the flimsy wooden chairs. In his experience, basically no perp hid anything in smart-ass places or even planned their murders. No months of pondering, of painstaking detail work, alibi prep, escape route, weapon disposal. Brilliant murders were the stuff of television, where the cop played dumb and tripped up the canny murderer, ha ha.

The storm came in off the Gulf and rattled the shack's tin roof. In the musty two-roomer he thought as mist curled up from great steaming sheets of rain. Drops tapped on leaves outside the window and the air mixed with sharp, moist smells of bird droppings. He stood in the scrappy kitchen and wondered if this was a phony lead. The Spanish letters probably wouldn't help but they were consistent at least with the Latino body. Still, he was getting nowhere.

His intuition was fuzzy with associations, a fog that would not condense. The battering shower made him think of the oceans rising and warming from the greenhouse gases and how the world might come to be more like the Centauris' moon, more tropical sea and the land hammered with storms. Out the streaked front window he wondered if aliens swam among the quilted waves, living part of their lives among the schools of fishes.

This thinking went nowhere and his ankle had acquired red dots of flea bites. He looked out the back window. The rain tapered off and he saw now the gray of a FEMA trailer back in the woods. A breeze came from it. Frying peppers and onions flavored the air with pungent promise.

He knocked on the front door and a scrawny white man wearing jeans and nothing else answered. "Hello, sir," plus the badge got him inside.

In a FEMA trailer even words take up room. You have to stand at a conversational distance in light-metal boxes that even a tropical storm could flip like playing cards. His initial urge was to hunch, then to make a joke about it. Mr. Fredson, a gangly six foot two, stretched out his arms to show how he could at the same time touch the ceiling with one hand and the floor with the other. Hangers in the small closet were tilted sideways to fit and beside them stood a short bronze-skinned woman who was trying not to look at him.

"I was wondering if you knew who lived up front there."

"He been gone more'n a week."

"Did he look like this?" McKenna showed the picture.

"Yeah, that's Jorge."

"Jorge what?"

"Castan," the woman said in a small, thin voice. Her hands twisted at the pale pink fabric of the shift she wore. "You la migra?"

"No ma'am. Afraid I got some bad news about Jorge though."

"He dead?" Mr. Fredson said, eyes downcast.

"'Fraid so. He washed up on a beach east of here."

"He worked boats," Fredson said, shaking his head. "Lot of night work, fillin' in."

"Mexican, right? Wife in Veracruz?"

"Yeah, he said. Sent money home. Had two other guys livin' up there for a while, nice fellas, all worked the boats. They gone now."

McKenna looked around, thinking. The Latino woman went stiffly into the kitchen and rearranged paper plates and plastic cups from Wal-Mart, cleaned a Reed & Barton silver coffeepot. Fredson sighed and sat on a small, hard couch. The woman didn't look like a good candidate to translate the Veracruz letter, judging from her rigid back. To unlock her he had to ask the right question

"Jorge seem okay? Anything bother him?"

Fredson thought, shrugged. "I'd look in over there sometimes when he was out on the Gulf for a few days. He axed me to. Lately his baidclose all tangled up come mornin'."

"Maybe afraid of la migra?" McKenna glanced at the woman. She had stopped pretending to polish the coffeepot and was staring at them.

"Lotsa people are." Fredson jutted his chin out. "They come for the work, we make out they be criminals."

"We do have a justice system." McKenna didn't know how to work this so he stalled.

"Jorge, he get no justice in the nex' world either." Fredson looked defiantly at him. "I'm not religious, like some."

"I'm not sayin' Jorge was doin' anything dishonest." McKenna was dropping into the coast accent, an old strategy to elicit trust. "Just want to see if he died accidentally of drowning."

Fredson said flatly, knotting his hands, "Dishonest ain't same as dishonorable."

He was getting nowhere here. "I'll need to report his death to his wife. Do you have any papers on him, so I can send them?"

The woman said abruptly, "Documento."

Fredson stared at her and nodded slowly. "Guess we ought to."

He got up and reached back into the packed closet. How they had gotten a FEMA trailer would be an interesting story, but McKenna knew not to press his luck. Fredson withdrew a soiled manila envelope and handed it to McKenna. "I kept this for him. He weren't too sure about those other two guys he was renting floor space to, I guess."

McKenna opened it and saw inside a jumble of odd-sized papers. "I sure thank you. I'll see this gets to her."

"How you know where she is?" Fredson asked.

"Got the address."

"Searched his place, did ya?"

"Of course. I'll be leaving—"

"Have a warrant?"

McKenna smiled slowly. "Have a law degree, do you?" His eyes slid toward the woman and he winked. Fredson's mouth stiffened and McKenna left without another word.

He crunched down his oyster-shell road in the dark. Coming around the bend he barely saw against the yard light two people sitting in the glider swing on his porch. He swung his car off into the trees. He wanted to get inside and study the papers he had from Fredson, but he had learned caution and so put his hand on his 9mm as he walked toward them. The gulf salt tang hung under the mimosa tree. A breeze stirred the smell of salt and fish and things dead, others spawning. Sugarcane near the house rattled in the breeze as he worked around to the back.

He let himself silently into his back door. When he snapped on the porch light the two figures jumped. It was Denise and his distant relative, Herb. Unlikely they knew each other.

McKenna opened the front door and let them in, a bit embarrassed at his creeping around. Denise made great fun of it and Herb's confused scowl said he had been rather puzzled by why this woman was here. McKenna wondered, too. He thought he had been pretty clear last time Denise showed up. He didn't like pushy women, many with one eye on his badge and the other on his pension. Even coming to his front door, like they were selling something. Well, maybe they were. He grew up when women didn't ask for dates. Whatever happened to courtship?

Not that he was all that great with women. In his twenties he had been turned down more times than an old blanket. He got them drinks and let the question of why Denise was here lie.

They traded pleasantries and McKenna saw maybe a way to work this. Herb said he'd been in the neighborhood and just stopped by to say hello. Fine. He asked Herb if he knew anything new about the Centauris, since the Pizotti fish fry, and that was enough. Herb shifted into lecture mode and McKenna sat back and watched Denise's reaction.

"There's all kinda talk on the internet 'bout this," Herb said with relish.

"Seems the Centauris deliberately suppressed their radio stations, once they picked up Marconi's broadcasts. They'd already spotted Earth as a biological planet centuries ago, see?—from studying the atmosphere. They'd already spent more centuries building those electric starships."

"My, my," Denise said softly.

Herb beamed at her, liking the audience. "Some think they're the origin of UFOs!"

Denise blinked, mouth making a surprised O. "The UFOs are theirs?"

"The UFOs we see, they're not solid, see? The Centauris sent them as a kind of signaling device. Pumped some kind of energy beams into our atmosphere, see, made these UFO images. Radar could pick them up 'cause they ionized the gas. That's why we never found anything solid."

McKenna was enjoying this. "Beams?"

Herb nodded, eyes dancing. "They excited some sorta atmospheric resonance effects. They projected the beams from our own asteroid belt."

Denise frowned. "But they got here only a few years back."

"They sent robot probes that got here in the 1940s. They'd already planned to send a one here and land to take samples. So they used the beams somehow to, I dunno, maybe let us know somethin' was up."

"Seems odd," Denise said. "And what about all those people the UFOs kidnapped? They did all kinds of experiments on 'em!"

Herb's mouth turned down scornfully. "That's just *National Enquirer* stuff, Denise."

McKenna smiled so he could control the laugh bubbling up in his throat. "Learn any biology?"

Herb said, "We've got plenty land-dwelling reptiles, plenty fish. Not many species use both land and sea."

Herb took a breath to launch into a lecture and Denise put in, "How about gators?"

Herb blinked, gave a quick polite smile and said, "The bio guys figure the Centauris had some reptile predators on the islands, gave what they call selection pressure. Centauris developed intelligence to beat them down when they came ashore, could be. Maybe like frogs, start out as larvae in the water."

Denise said wonderingly, eyeing Herb, "So they're like tadpoles at first?"

"Could be, could be." Herb liked feedback and McKenna guessed he didn't get a lot from women. Maybe they were too polite to interrupt. "They grow and develop lungs, legs, those funny hand-like fins, big opposable thumbs. Then big brains to deal with the reptiles when they go ashore."

McKenna asked, "So they're going to hate our gators."

"S'pose so," Herb allowed. "They sure seem hostile to 'em around Dauphin Island. Could be they're like frogs, put out lots of offspring. Most tadpoles don't survive, y'know, even after they get ashore."

Denise said brightly, "But once one does crawl ashore, the adults would have to help it out a lot. Defend it against reptiles. Teach it how to make tools, maybe. Cooperation, but social competition, too."

Both men looked at her and she read their meaning. "I majored in sociology, minor in biology."

Herb nodded respectfully, looking at her with fresh eyes. "Hard to think that something like frogs maybe could bring down big reptiles, eh?"

Denise tittered at the very thought, eyes glistening eagerly, and McKenna got up to get them more drinks. By the time he came back out, though, they were getting up. Herb said he had to get home and they discovered that they didn't live all that far from each other, what a surprise then to meet out here at this distance, and barely noticed McKenna's good-byes.

He watched them stand beside Denise's car and exchange phone numbers. Now if only he could be as good a matchmaker for himself. But something in him wasn't ready for that yet.

And what else have you got in your life? the unwelcome thought came.

Work. Oh yes, the Jorge papers from the FEMA people.

Jorge had stuffed all sorts of things into the envelope. Receipts, check stubs, unreadables, some telephone numbers, a Mexican passport with a picture that looked a lot like the corpse.

He was stacking these when a thin slip fell out. A note written on a rubberstamped sheet from Bayside Boats.

I t wasn't that far to Bayside Boats. He went there at dawn and watched a shrimp boat come in. When he showed every man in the place Jorge's photo, nobody recognized it. But the manager and owner, a grizzled type named Rundorf, hesitated just a heartbeat before answering. Then shook his head.

Driving away, he passed by the Busted Flush mooring. It was just coming in from a run and Merv Pitscomb stood at the prow.

H is supervisor said, "You get anything from SIU on these cases?"

"Nope." The Special Investigations Unit was notoriously jammed up and in love with the FBI.

"Any statewide CAPs?"

CAPs, Crimes Against Persons, was the latest correct acronym that shielded the mind from the bloody reality, kept you from thinking about the abyss. "Nope."

"So you got two drowned guys who worked boats out of the same town. Seems like a stretch."

McKenna tried to look judicious. "I want a warrant to look at their pay records. Nail when these two worked, and work from there."

The supervisor shook his head. "Seems pretty thin."

"I doubt I'll get much more."

"You've been workin' this one pretty hard. Your partner LeBouc, he's due back tomorrow."

"So?"

A level gaze. "Maybe you should work it with him. This FBI angle, these guys coming up to you like that. Maybe this really should be their game."

"They're playing close to their vest. No help there for sure. And waiting for LeBouc won't help, not without more substance."

"Ummm." The supervisor disliked the FBI, of course, but he didn't want to step on their toes. "Lessee. This would have to go through Judge Preston. He's been pretty easy on us lately, must be gettin' laid again . . ."

"Let me put it in the batch going up to him later this morning."

"Okay, but then you got to get onto some more cases. They're piling up."

He had boilerplate for the warrant application. He called it up and pasted in I respectfully request that the Court issue a Warrant and Order of Seizure in the form annexed, authorizing a search of premises at . . . And such as is found shall be brought before the Court, together with such other and further relief that the Court may deem proper. The lawyers loved such stuff.

Merv Pitscomb's face knotted with red rage. The slow-witted Buddy Johnson, ex-con and tire deflator, stood beside Pitscomb and wore a smirk. Neither liked the warrant and they liked it still less when he took their pay company records.

Ethan Anselmo was there, of course, and had gone out on the Busted Flush, a night job two days before the body washed up. No entry for Jorge Castan. But some initials from the bookkeeper a week before the last Anselmo entry, and two days after it, had a total, $178. One initial was GB and the other JC.

Bookkeepers have to write things down, even if they're supposed to keep quiet. Illegals were off the books, of course, usually with no Social Security numbers. But you had to balance your books, didn't you? McKenna loved bookkeepers.

"Okay," his supervisor said, "we got reasonable grounds to bring in this Pitscomb and the other one—"

"Rundorf."

"—to bring them in and work them a little. Maybe they're not wits, maybe these are just accidents the skippers don't want to own up to. But we got probable cause here. Bring them in tomorrow morning. It's near end of our shift."

There was always some paperwork confusion at quitting time. McKenna made up the necessaries and was getting some other, minor cases straightened out, thinking of heading home.

Then he had an idea.

He had learned a good trick a decade back, from a sergeant who had busted a lot of lowlife cases open.

If you had two different suspects for a murder, book them both. Hold them overnight. Let the system work on them.

In TV lawyer shows the law was a smart, orderly machine that eventually—usually about an hour—punished the guilty.

But the system was not about that at all. The minute you stepped into its grinder you lost control of your life and became a unit. You sat in holding cells thinking your own fevered thoughts. Nobody knew you. You stared at the drain hole in the gray concrete floor where recent stains got through even the bleaching disinfectant sprayed over them. On the walls you saw poorly scrawled drawings of organs and acts starkly illuminated by the actinic, buzzing lights that never went out. You heard echoing yells and cops rapping their batons on the bars to get some peace. Which never came. So you sat some more with your own fevered thoughts.

You had to ask permission to go to the toilet rather than piss down that hole. There was the phone call you could make and a lawyer you chose out of the phone book, and the fuzzed voice said he'd be down tomorrow. Maybe he would come and maybe not. It was not like you had a whole lot of money.

The cops referred to you by your last name and moved you like walking furniture to your larger stinking cell with more guys in it. None of them looked at you except the ones you didn't like the look of at all. Then it was night and the lights dimmed, but not much.

That was where the difference between the two suspects came in. One would sleep, the other wouldn't.

Anybody who kills someone doesn't walk away clean. Those movies and TV lawyer shows made out that murderers were smart, twisted people. Maybe twisted was right but not smart, and for sure they were not beasts. Some even dressed better than anyone he had ever seen.

But like it or not, they were people. Murderers saw all the same movies as ordinary folk, and a lot more TV. They sat around daytime making drug deals or waiting for nighttime to do second-story jobs. Plenty of time to think about their business. Most of them could quote from *The Godfather*. The movie, of course. None of them read novels or anything else. They were emotion machines running all the time and after a job they blew their energy right away. Drank, went out cruising for pussy, shot up.

Then, if you timed it right, they got arrested.

So then the pressure came off. The hard weight of tension, the slow-building stress fidgeting at the back of the mind—all that came home to roost. They flopped down on the thin pad of their bunk and pulled the rough wool blanket over their faces and fell like the coming of heaven into a deep sleep. Many of them barely made it to the bunk before the energy bled out of them.

But now think about the guy who didn't do it. He knows he didn't do it even if the goddamn world doesn't. He is scared, sure, because he is far enough into the downstreet culture to know that justice is a whore and lawyers run the whorehouse. And so he is in real danger here. But he also for sure knows that he has to fight hard now, think, pay attention. And he is mad too because he didn't do it and shouldn't that matter?

So he frets and sits and doesn't sleep. He is ragged-eyed and slurring his words when he tries to tell the other guys in the cell—who have rolled over and gone to sleep—that he didn't do it. It would be smart to be some kind of Zen samurai and sleep on this, he knows that, but he can't. Because he didn't do it.

On a cell surveillance camera you can see the difference immediately. Get the cell assignments and go to the room where a bored overweight uniform watched too many screens. Check out the numbers on the screens, find the cells, watch the enhanced-light picture. The sleepers faced away from the lights, coiled up in their blankets. The ones who wouldn't or couldn't—it didn't matter much which—ignored the lights and you could see their eyes clicking around as they thought all this through.

Next morning, he leaned on the sleeper and released the guy who had stayed up all night. Sometimes the innocent ones could barely walk. But at least they were out in the sun.

The sleepers sometimes took days to break. Some of them had the smarts or the clout lawyers, to lawyer up. But he had them and that was the point.

He had learned all this, more years back than he wanted to think about, and it would still be true when he was long gone from this Earth.

He brought in Pitscomb and Rundorf at sunset. Got them booked, photoed, fingerprinted. They gave him plenty of mouth and he just stayed silent, doing his job.

Into the overnight holding cell they went.

He had a bottle of Zinfandel and slept well that night.

Back in at sunup, Pitscomb and Rundorf were red-eyed and irritated.

His supervisor was irritated, too. "I didn't tell you to bring them in late."

"You didn't? I must have misheard." McKenna kept his face absolutely still while he said it. He had practiced that in the mirror when he first made detective and it was a valuable skill.

He made the best of interrogating Pitscomb and Rundorf but the simple fact that they had stayed awake most of the night took McKenna's confidence away. The two gave up nothing. He booked them out and had some uniforms drive them home.

His partner came in that afternoon. LeBouc was a burly man who liked detail, so McKenna handed off some stickup shootings to him. They had been waiting for attention and McKenna knew they would get no leads. The perps were the same black gang that had hit the minimarkets for years and they knew their stuff. The videotapes showed only rangy guys in animal masks. LeBouc didn't seem to mind. McKenna filled him in on the drowned cases but he couldn't make an argument for where to go next. The cases were cooling off by the minute now, headed for the storage file.

McKenna had never been as systematic as LeBouc, who was orderly even when he was fishing. So when LeBouc said, "How'd those phone numbers from the illegal turn out?" McKenna felt even worse. He had noticed them in the stack of paper at Castan's shack, just before he found the Bayside Boats notepaper. Like a hound dog, he chased that lead down and forgot the telephone numbers.

He got right on them. One was the Mexican consulate in New Orleans, probably for use if Jorge got picked up.

One number answered in a stony voice saying only, "Punch in your code." The rest answered in Spanish and he got nowhere with them. He thought of getting a Spanish speaker but they were in high demand and he would have to wait for days. Nobody in Homicide knew more than restaurant Spanish. He went back to the stony voice, a Mobile number.

Usually, to break a number you use a reverse directory of published numbers. McKenna found nothing there. There were lesser-known electronic directories of unpublished numbers that link phone numbers to people and addresses. He found those in the Mobile Police database. They were built up nationally, working from anyone who used the number to place a phone order. So he considered pretexting. To pretext, you call the phone company repair department, saying there's a problem on the line and getting them to divulge the address associated with the account. But you needed a warrant to do that and his credit had run out with Judge Preston.

If he couldn't pretend to be someone else, maybe he could pretend that his phone was someone else's. That would be caller-ID spoofing—making it seem as if a phone call is coming from another phone, rather than his Homicide number. That made it more likely that the target person would answer the call, even if they had the new software that back-tracked the caller in less than a second. McKenna's office number was not in the phone book but for sure it was in any sophisticated database software. And the stony voice sounded professional, smart.

Spoofing used to require special equipment, but now with internet phone calling and other Web services it was relatively easy to do. So easy, in fact, that just about anyone can do it. But McKenna hadn't. It took an hour of asking guys and gals in the office to get it straight. Everybody had a fine time making fun of "the Perfesser" coming to them for help, of course. He developed a fixed grin.

Once you burned an hour to know how, it took less than a minute.

The site even had a code breakdown for the number, too. When stony voice answered, McKenna typed in the last four digits of the number again and in a few more seconds he got a ring. "Hello?"

McKenna said nothing. "Hello?" the voice of Dark Glasses said.

It took a while for his supervisor to go through channels and pin a name on Dark Glasses. The next morning Dark Glasses was in Federal court, the FBI office said. So McKenna found him, waiting to testify.

"May I have a word in the hallway?" McKenna sat down in the chair at the back of the court. Somebody was droning on in front and the judge looked asleep.

"Who are you?" Dark Glasses said, nose up in the air. He wasn't wearing the glasses now and it was no improvement.

McKenna showed the badge. "Remember me? You were with Mr. Marine."

"Who?"

"You didn't say you were a lawyer, too."

"Who told you that?"

"Your office. The FBI, remember?"

The lawyer inched away but kept his chin out, first line of defense. "I'm waiting to testify on a Federal case."

"Murder crosses boundaries."

The bailiff was looking at them. He jerked a thumb toward the doors. In the hallway Dark Glasses had revived his lawyerly presence. "Make it quick."

"This is about one of your cases, Jorge Castan."

"I don't discuss my cases."

He moved to go past and McKenna casually put a hand on his chest.

"You have no right to touch me. Move away."

McKenna just shook his head. "You know what's up. Your case got himself murdered, looks like. The second one like that in a week. And the Bar Association Web site says that before you got hired into the FBI you were an immigration lawyer. And you must know that your case was an illegal or else you're dumber than you look."

"I do not take a liking to insult. You touch me—"

"You're in serious trouble if you know what's really up. See, murder is a local crime unless you can show it has a proper Federal issue that trumps local. Do you?"

"I do not have to—"

"Yes you do."

"There is not one scintilla of evidence—"

"Save it for the judge. Wrong attitude, counselor."

"I don't know what—"

"What I'm talking about, yeah. I hear it all the time. You guys must all watch the same movies."

"I am an attorney." He drew himself up.

"Yeah, and I know the number of the Bar Association. Being FBI won't protect you."

"I demand to know—"

Dark Glasses went on but little by little McKenna had been backing him up against the marble walls until the man's shoulder blades felt it. Then his expression changed. McKenna could see in the lawyer's face the schoolboy threatened by bullies. So he had gone into the law, which meant good ol' safe words and paper, to escape the real world where the old primate signals held sway. Dark Glasses held his briefcase in front of his body in defense, but the shield wasn't thick enough to stop McKenna from poking a finger into the surprisingly soft Dark Glasses bicep. "You're up at bat now, lawyer."

"As an attorney—"

"You're assumed to be a liar. For hire. Almost rhymes, don't it?"

"I do not respond to insults." He was repeating his material and he tilted his chin up again. McKenna felt his right hand come halfway up, balling into a fist, wanting so much to hit this clown hard on the point of that chin.

"You knew to go looking for Jorge in jig time. Or maybe for the people who knew him. Why's that?"

"I—I'm going to walk away now."

"Not if you're smart. One of those who knew him is an illegal, too. Maybe you wanted to use that to shut her up?"

"That's speculative—"

"Not really, considering your expression. No, you're working for somebody else. Somebody who has influence."

"My clients and cases are Bureau—"

"Confidential, I know."

"I have every assurance that my actions will prove victorious in this matter."

McKenna grinned and slapped an open palm against the briefcase, a hard smack. The lawyer jumped, eyebrows shooting up, back on the playground during recess. "I—I have an attorney-client relationship that by the constitution—"

"How 'bout the Bible?"

"—demands that you respect his . . . protection."

"The next one who dies is on you, counselor."

In a shaky voice the lawyer pulled his briefcase even closer and nodded, looking at the floor as if he had never seen it before. A small sigh came from him, filled with gray despair.

It was a method McKenna had worked out years ago, once he understood that lawyers were all talk and no muscle. Good cop/bad cop is a cliché, only the lawyer keeps looking for the good cop to show up and the good cop doesn't. Bluff is always skin deep.

The lawyer backed away once McKenna let him. "You better think about who you choose to represent. And who might that be, really?"

"My client is—"

"No, I mean who, really? Whose interest?"

"I . . . I don't know what you mean. I—"

"You know more than you've said. I expect that. But you still have to think about what you do." A rogue smile. "We all do."

"Look, we can handle this issue in a nice way—"

"I'll try being nicer if you'll try being smarter."

McKenna slid a business card into the suit handkerchief pocket of Dark Glasses Lawyer. "Call me. I find out the same stuff before you do, and that you knew it—well, I'll be without mercy, Counselor. No quarter."

McKenna stepped aside and let the lawyer flee from the playground. Dark Glasses didn't look back.

M cKenna's supervisor leaned back and scowled. "And you did this because? . . ."

"Because two drowned men with strange scars don't draw FBI without a reason, for starters."

"Not much to go on."

"The ME says he can't identify the small puncture marks. Or what made those funny welts."

His supervisor made a sour grin. "You know how much physical evidence is worth. It has to fit a filled-in story."

"And I don't have enough story."

He spread his hands, the cuff sliding up to expose part of his arm tattoo, rosy barbed wire.

M cKenna had read somewhere that an expert is one who has made all the possible mistakes in a narrow field. A wise man is one who has made them widely. It was supposed to be funny but it was too true for that.

So he followed his good ole friend Buddy Johnson home from work that evening. Buddy liked his pleasures and spent the first hour of his night in a bar. Then he went out back to smoke a joint. It was dark and Buddy jumped a foot when McKenna shined the flashlight straight into his eyes.

"Gee, that cigarette sure smells funny."

"What? Who you?"

"The glare must be too much for you. Can't you recognize my voice?"

"What the—Look, I—"

McKenna slipped behind him, dropping the flashlight to distract him, and got the cuffs on. "We're gonna take a little ride."

McKenna took him in cuffs down a scruffy side alley and got him into Buddy's own convertible. Puffing, feeling great, he strapped Buddy in with the seat belt, passenger side. Then McKenna drove two quick miles and turned into a car wash. The staff was out front finishing up and when they came out McKenna showed them the badge and they turned white. All illegals, of course, no English. But they knew the badge. They vanished like the dew after the dawn.

Game time, down south.

Even with cuffs behind his back, Buddy kept trying to say something.

"Remember letting the air out of my tires?" McKenna hit him hard in the nose, popped some blood loose and Buddy shut up. McKenna drove the convertible onto the ratchet conveyor and went back to the control panel. It was in English and the buttons were well-thumbed, some of the words gone in the worn plastic. McKenna ran up a SUPER CLEAN and HOT WAX and LIGHT BUFF. Then he gave a little laugh and sent Buddy on his way.

Hissing pressure hoses came alive. Big black brushes lowered into the open seats and whirred up to speed. They ripped Buddy full on. He started yelling and the slapping black plastic sheets slammed into him hard and he stopped screaming. McKenna hit the override and the brushes lifted away. Silence, only the dripping water on the convertible's leather seats.

McKenna shouted a question and waited. No answer. He could see the head lolling back and wondered if the man was conscious.

McKenna thought about the two drowned men and hit the buttons again.

The brushes hardly got started before a shrill cry came echoing back. McKenna stopped the machine. The brushes rose. He walked forward into the puddles, splashing and taking his time.

"You're nearly clean for the first time in your life, Buddy. Now I'm gonna give you a chance to come full clean with me."

"I . . . They ain't gonna like . . ." His mouth opened expectantly, rimmed with drool. The eyes flickered, much too white.

"Just tell me."

"They really ain't gonna like—"

McKenna turned and started back toward the control board. The thin, plaintive sobbing told him to turn around again. You could always tell when a man was broke clean through.

"Where'd they go?"

"Nearly to Chandeleur."

"The islands?"

"Yeah . . . long way out . . . takes near all night. Oil rigs . . . the wrecked ones."

"What'd you take out?"

"Centauris. Usually one, sometimes two."

"The same one?"

"Who can tell? They all look alike to me. Pitscomb, he bowed and scraped to the Centauri and the Feds with him, but he don't know them apart either."

"Pitscomb have anything to do with Ethan's death?"

"Man, I weren't workin' that night."

"Damn. What'd the rest of the crew say about it?"

"Nothin'. All I know is that Ethan was on the boat one night and he didn't come back to work next day."

"Who else was with the Centauri?"

"Just Feds."

"What was the point of going out?"

"I dunno. We carried stuff in big plastic bags. Crew went inside for 'bout an hour while we circled round the messed-up oil rigs. FBI and Centauri were out there. Dunno what they did. Then we come back."

McKenna took the cuffs off Buddy and helped him out of the car. To his surprise, Buddy could walk just fine. "You know Jorge?"

"Huh? Yeah, that wetback?"

"Yeah. You're a wetback too now."

"Huh? Oh." Buddy got the joke and to his credit, grinned. "Look, you don't nail me on the dope, it's even, okay?"

"You're a gentleman and a scholar, Buddy."

"Huh?"

"It's fine. Keep your nose clean from here on out or I'll bring you back here to clean it myself."

He hung his head. "Y'know, you're right. I got to straighten up."

"You're straight with me right now."

They even shook hands.

A take-charge raccoon was working the trash when he hauled in on the oyster shell road. He shooed it away and then tossed it a watermelon that had gone old anyway.

Then he sat on the porch and sipped a Cabernet and worked himself over about the car wash stunt. His wife had once told him, after he had worked up through being a uniform, then Vice and then bunko and finally Homicide, that the process had condensed him into a hard man. He had never said to her that maybe it was her long illness that had made him quiet around the house, wary and suspicious . . . but in the end maybe it was both. He had never been interested in small talk but had picked up the skill for getting witnesses to open up.

Now he felt very little after working Buddy over. He had done it with a vague intuition that the kid needed a wake up call, sure, but mostly because he was blocked in this case. And he couldn't let it go. Maybe it helped fill the emptiness in him, one he felt without shame or loss, as not a lack but as a blank space—an openness that made him hear the wind sigh and waves slosh not as mere background but as life passing while most people ignored it, talked over it, trying to pin life down with their words. He listened at nightfall, sitting out here on the warped planking of his wharf, to the planet breathing in its sleep. A world never fully revealed, a planet with strangeness at its core.

The next day he and LeBouc worked some ordinary gang-related cases. And planned. LeBouc was a fisherman and would go out for just about any reason. Not a hard sell. And neither of them could think of anything else to do. The FBI had called up their supervisor and bad-mouthed McKenna, of course. But they wouldn't reveal anything more and tried to pry loose what McKenna knew. The supe stonewalled. A Mexican standoff.

Just before twilight McKenna sprayed on exercise shorts plus shirt. This was a semi-new techie product, snug and light, and he wanted to try them. The shorts were black, the cheapest spray-on, with spaced breather holes to respire sweat through. His belly was a bit thick and his calves stringy, but nobody was going to see him anyway if he could help it. The smart fibers itched as they linked up to form the hems, contouring to his body, the warmth from their combining getting him in the mood. He drove to the boat ramp just west of Bayou La Batre, huffing the salty sunset breeze into his lungs with a liberating zest.

LeBouc was there with an aluminum boat and electric motor and extra batteries, rented from a Mobile fishing company. Great for quiet night work, spotlights and radiophone, the works. LeBouc was pumped, grinning and stowing gear.

"Thought I'd do some line trawling on the way," he said, bringing on a big pole and a tackle box. He carried a whole kit of cleaning knives and an ice chest. "Never know when you might bag a big one."

McKenna's shoes grated on the concrete boat ramp as the water lapped against the pilings. The boat rose on the slow, lumbering tide. A dead nutria floated by, glassy-eyed and with a blue crab gouging at it. Business as usual at the Darwin Café.

They used a gas outboard to reach the estimated rendezvous point, to save on the batteries. McKenna had planted a directional beeper on the Busted Flush in late afternoon, using a black guy he hired in Bayou La Batre to pretend to be looking for work. Right away they picked up the microwave beeper, using their tracking gear. With GPS geared into the tracker they could hang back a mile away and follow them easily. LeBouc was a total non-tech type and had never once called McKenna "the Perfesser."

LeBouc flipped on the Raytheon acoustic radar and saw the sandy bottom sliding away into deeper vaults of mud. Velvet air slid by. The night swallowed them.

It was exciting at first, but as they plowed through the slapping swells the rhythm got to McKenna. He hadn't been sleeping all that well lately, so LeBouc took the first watch, checking his trailing line eagerly. LeBouc had spent his vacation deep-sea fishing off Fort Lauderdale and was happy to be back on the water again.

LeBouc shook McKenna awake three hours later. "Thought you were gonna wake me for a watch," McKenna mumbled.

"Nemmine, I was watchin' my line. Almost got one too."

"What's up?"

"They hove to, looks like from the tracker."

They quietly approached the Busted Flush using the electric motor. The tracker picked up a fixed warning beacon. "Maybe an oil platform," McKenna said. LeBouc diverted slightly toward it.

Out of the murk rose a twisted skeleton. Above the waterline the main platform canted at an angle on its four pylons. A smashed carcass of a drilling housing lay scattered across its steel plates. Three forlorn rotating beacons winked into the seethe of the sea.

LeBouc asked, "How far's the shrimper?"

McKenna studied the tracker screen, checked the scale. "About three hundred yards. Not moving."

LeBouc said, "Let's tuck in under that platform. Make us hard to see."

"Don't know if I can see much in IR at this range."

"Try now."

The IR goggles LeBouc had wangled out of Special Operations Stores fit on McKenna's head like a fat parasite. In them he could see small dots moving, the infrared signature blobs of people on the shrimper deck. "Barely," McKenna said.

"Lemme try it."

They carefully slid in under the steel twenty feet above. LeBouc secured them with two lines to the pylon cleats and the boat did not rock with the swell so much. McKenna could make out the Busted Flush better here in the deeper dark. He studied it and said, "They're moving this way. Slow, though."

"Good we're under here. Wonder why they chose a platform area."

Many of the steel bones had wrenched away down on the shoreward side of the platform and now hung down beneath the waves. The enviros made the best of it, calling these wrecks fish breeders, and maybe they were.

"Fish like it here, maybe."

"Too far offshore to fish reg'lar."

McKenna looked up at the ripped and rusted steel plates above, underpinned by skewed girders. His father had died on one of these twelve years back, in the first onslaught of a hurricane. When oil derricks got raked in a big storm and started to get worked, you hooked your belt to a Geronimo wire and bailed out from the top—straight into the dark sea, sliding into hope and kersplash. He had tried to envision it, to see what his father had confronted.

When you hit the deck of the relief hauler it was awash. Your steel-toed boots hammered down while you pitched forward, face down, with your hard hat to save the day, or at least some memories. But his father's relief hauler had caught a big one broadside and the composite line had snapped and his father went into the chop. They tried to get to him but somehow he didn't have his life jacket on and they lost him.

With his inheritance from his father McKenna bought their house on the water. He recalled how it felt getting the news, the strange sensation that he had dropped away into an abyss. How his father had always hated life jackets and didn't wear them to do serious work.

McKenna realized abruptly that he didn't have his own life jacket on. Maybe it was genetic. He found some in the rear locker and pulled one on, tossing another to LeBouc, who was fooling with his tackle and rod.

LeBouc said, "You watch, I'll try a bait line."

McKenna opened his mouth and heard a faint rumble in the distance. The boat shuttled back and forth on its cleat lines. Waves smacked against steel and shed a faint luminous glow. He could see nothing in the distance though and sat to pull down the IR goggles. A hazy shimmer image. The Busted Flush was coming closer, on a course that angled to the left. "They're moving."

There was a lot of splashing nearby as currents stirred among the pylons. The three figures on the deck of the shrimper were easier to see now.

The IR blobs were right at the edge of definition. Then one of them turned into the illumination cone of a pale running light, making a jabbing gesture to another blob. He couldn't quite resolve the face, but McKenna recognized the man instantly.

Dark Glasses stood out like a clown at a funeral.

The man next to him must be Pitscomb, McKenna figured. The third form was fainter and taller and with a jolt McKenna knew it was a Centauri. It moved more gracefully at sea than on land as it walked along the railing. Its sliding gait rocked with the ship, better than the men. It held a big dark lump and seemed to be throwing something from the lump over the side.

McKenna focused to make sense of the image. The Centauri had a bag, yes—

A grunt from nearby told him LeBouc was casting and an odd splash came and then thumping. The boat shifted and jerked as he tried to focus on the IR images and another big splash came.

He jerked off the goggles. His eyes took a few seconds to adjust. There was fitful radiance from the surf. LeBouc was not in the boat.

A leg jerked up in the water, arms flailed in a white churn. Long swift things like ropes whipped around the leg. McKenna reached for the oars secured along the boatline. A sudden pain lurched up in his right calf and he looked down. A furred cord was swiftly wrapping itself up his leg, over his knee, starting on his calf. Needles of pain shot into his leg. The sting of it ran up his spine and provoked a shudder through his torso. His leg twitched, out of his control.

The wrapping rope stopped at his thigh and yanked. He fell over and his knee slammed hard on the bottom of the boat. Another cord came over and hit his shoulder. It clung tight and snarled around him. The shoulder muscles thrashed wildly as the thing bit through his plastic all-weather jacket and his shirt. Pain jabbed into his chest.

Other wriggling strands came snaking across the bowed deck. He wrenched around and hit his head on LeBouc's tackle box. He thought one of the things had grabbed his ear but it was the latch on the box, caught in his hair. A hollering came and he realized it was his own ragged voice.

His hands beat at the cord but prickly spines jutting out of it stung him. That jolted him badly and he tried to pull himself up to get a tool. The tackle box. He grabbed a gutting knife. With both hands he forced it under the edge of the cord across his chest. The ropy thing was strong and fought against the blade. He got some leverage and pulled up and the blade bit. The pink cord suddenly gave way. It flailed around and the main body lashed back at him. He caught it on the point of the knife and drove it into the side of the boat. That gave him a cutting surface and he worked the knife down the length of the thing. He sawed with all his strength. It split into two splices that went still. Stroking along it he sliced it in two, clear up to the housing at the stern.

The shooting pain in his calf he had made himself ignore and now he turned to it. The cord had sunk into his jeans. He pried it up as before and turned the blade. This one popped open and drooled milky fluid. He hacked away at it, free of the lancing pain. It took a moment to cut away chunks. They writhed on the boat bottom. With stinging hands he reached into the tackle box and found the workman's gloves. That made it easier to pick up and toss the long strands into the sea. They struggled weakly.

Numbness crept up his leg and across his chest. He felt elated and sleepy and wanted to rest. His eyes flickered and he realized that his face was numb too. Everything was moving too fast. He needed a rest. Then he could think about this. Figure it out.

Then another pink rope came sliding over the gunnel. It felt around and snaked toward him as if it could sense his heat or smell. He felt the tip of it touch his deck shoe. Sharp fear cleared his mind.

The knife came down on it and he pounded the point along its length.

Without cutting it into pieces he lurched toward the gunwale. With a swipe the tie line popped away from its cleat. He leaped over a section of pink rope and cut the second line. He could barely see. With his hands he felt along the stern and found the starter button and helm. The outboard caught right away. With a strum the engines turned over and he slid the throttles forward to rev the engines into a quick-start warmup.

He veered among the pylons. With a click the flashlight glare made the scene jump out at him. There were pink strands in the water.

No sign at all of LeBouc.

He hit the throttle and shot out into open water and reached for the radiophone.

The worst of it was the wait.

He stung in running sheets of fire all over the right leg and chest. The thing had wrapped around his calf like a bracelet. He wondered why the ME never said anything about the corpses being pumped full of venom and only then realized that he had felt electrical shocks, not stings. His leg and arm had been jerking on their own. He fingered the trembling muscles, remembering through a fog.

He got away from there into the darkness, not caring any more about the Busted Flush. Eventually he thought that they might be following the sound of the outboard. He shut it off and drifted. Then he called the shore and said he was headed in on the electric. By then he was flopping on the deck as debilitating cramps swept through him. Breath came hard and he passed out several times.

Then a chopper came out of the murk. It hovered over him like an angel with spotlights and an unfurling ladder. Men in wet suits dropped onto the deck. They harnessed him up and he spun away into the black sky. On the hard floor of the chopper a woman stood over him with a big needle of epinephrine, her face lined with concern. He could not get his thick tongue to tell her that this case was something else. She shot him full of it and his heart pounded. That did clear his sluggish mind but it did not stop the shooting jolts that would come up suddenly in his leg and chest and in other places he had no memory of the pink rope being at all.

She gave him other injections though and those made the whole clattering chopper back away. It was like a scene on late night television, mildly interesting and a plot you could vaguely remember seeing somewhere. She barked into her helmet mike and asked him questions but it was all theory now, not really his concern.

The next few hours went by like a movie you can't recall the next day. A cascading warm shower lined in gray hospital tile, McKenna lying on the tiles. A doctor in white explaining how they had to denature something, going on and on, just about as interesting as high school chemistry. They said they needed his consent for some procedure and he was happy to give it so long as they agreed to leave him alone.

He slowly realized the ER whitecoats were not giving him painkillers because of the War on Drugs and its procedural requirements. A distant part of him considered how it would be for a lawman to die of an excess of law. Doctors X and then Y and finally Z had to sign off. Time equaled pain and dragged on tick by tick.

Then there was Demerol, which settled the arguments nicely.

The next day he found a striping of tiny holes along his leg. More across his chest. He guessed the corpses had sealed up most of these when they swelled, so they showed only a few tiny holes.

The ME came by and talked to McKenna as though he were an unusually fascinating museum exhibit. At least he brought some cortisone cream to see if it would help and it did. He recalled distantly that the ME was actually a doctor of some sort. Somehow he had always thought of the ME as a cop.

Two days later a team of Fed guys led him out of the hospital and into a big black van. They had preempted local law, of course, so McKenna barely got to see his supervisor or the Mobile Chief of Police, who was there mostly for a photo op anyway.

In the van a figure in front turned and gave him a smile without an ounce of friendliness in it. Mr. Marine.

"Where's Dark Glasses?" McKenna asked but Mr. Marine looked puzzled and then turned away and watched the road. Nobody said anything until they got to Dauphin Island.

They took him up a ramp and down a corridor and then through some sloping walkways and odd globular rooms and finally to a little cell with pale glow coming from the walls. It smelled dank and salty and they left him there.

A door he hadn't known was there slid open in the far wall. A man all in white stepped in carrying a big, awkward laptop and behind him shuffled a Centauri.

McKenna didn't know how he knew it, but this was the same Centauri he had seen getting onto the Busted Flush. It looked at him with the famous slitted eyes and he caught a strange scent that wrinkled his nose.

The man in white sat down in one of two folding chairs he had brought and gestured for McKenna to sit in the other. The Centauri did not sit. It carefully put a small device on the floor, a bulb and nozzle. Then it stood beside the man and put its flipper-hands on the large keyboard of the laptop. McKenna had heard about these devices shaped to the Centauri movements.

"It will reply to questions," the man in white said. "Then it types a reply. This computer will translate on-screen."

"It can't pronounce our words, right?" McKenna had read that.

"It has audio pickups that transduce our speech into its own sounds. But it can't speak our words, no. This is the best we've been able to get so far." The man seemed nervous.

The Centauri held up one flipper-hand and with the device sprayed itself, carefully covering its entire skin. Or at least it seemed more like skin now, and not the reptile armor McKenna had first thought it might be.

"It's getting itself wetted down," the man said. "This is a dry room, easier for us to take."

"The wet rooms have—"

"Ceiling sprays, yeah. They gotta stay moist 'cause they're amphibians. That's why they didn't like California. It's too dry, even at the beach."

The Centauri was finished with its spraying. McKenna thought furiously and began. "So, uh, why were you going out on the shrimp boat?" Its jointed flippers were covered in a mesh hide. They moved in circular passes over pads on the keyboard. The man had to lift the awkward computer a bit to the alien, who was shorter than an average man. On the screen appeared:

<<Feed our young.>>

"Is that what attacked me?"

<<Yes. Friend died.>>

"Your young are feeding?"

<<Must. Soon come to land.>>

"Why don't we know of this?"

<<Reproducing private for you also.>>

He could not look away from those eyes. The scaly skin covered its entire head. The crusty deep green did not stop at the big spherical eyes, but enclosed nearly all of it, leaving only the pupil open in a clamshell slit. He gazed into the unreadable glittering black depths of it. The eyes swiveled to follow him as he fidgeted. McKenna couldn't think of anything to say.

"I, I can't read your expression. Like *Star Trek* and that stuff, we expect aliens to be like humans, really."

The alien wrote:

<<I know of your vision programs. The *Trek* drama we studied. To discern how you would think of us.>>

"You don't have our facial expressions."

<<We have our own.>>

"Of course. So I can't tell if you care whether your young killed two men on fishing boats."

<<They were close to water. Young. Hungry. Your kind stay away is best.>>

"We don't know! Our government has not told us. Why?"

The man holding the computer opened his mouth to say something and thought better of it. The alien wrote:

<<Change is hard for both our kinds. Ideas should come slowly to be understood.>>

"People are okay with your visit. They might not like your seeding our oceans and moving in. Plus killing us."

This time it took a while to answer:

<<Those you call dead live on now in the dark heaven.>>

McKenna blinked. "Is that a religious idea?"

<<No. It arises from our skystorians.>>

"Uh, sky? . . ."

The computer guy said, "Mistranslation. I saw that one with the astro guys last week. The software combines two concepts, see. Sky—means astronomy, 'cause their world is always cloudy, so the night sky is above that—and history. Closest word is cosmology, astronomy of the past."

McKenna looked at the alien's flat, unreadable gaze. "So it's . . . science."

<<Your term for this bedrock of the universe is the dark energy. I modify these words to show the nature of your dark energy. It forces open the universe.>>

McKenna could not see where this was going. He had read some pop science about something called dark energy, sure. It supposedly was making the whole universe expand faster and faster. "So what's it . . . this dark heaven . . . do?"

<<It is the . . . substrate. Entangled information propagates as waves in it. Organized minds of high level emit probability waves in packets of great complexity. These persist long after the original emitter is dead.>>

McKenna blinked. "You mean we . . . our minds . . . send out their . . ."

<<Their presence, that is a better term. Minds emit presence. This persists as waves in the dark heaven that is everywhere in the universe. All minds join it.>>

"This sounds like religion."

<<Your distinction between fears for your fate and the larger category of science is not one we share. This required long study by us to understand since you are a far younger life-form. You have not yet had the time and experience to study the universe for long.>>

McKenna was getting in over his head. He felt light-headed, taking shallow breaths, clenching his hands. "You don't regret that those men died?"

<<Our emotions do not fit in your categories, either. We sorrow, yes. While also knowing that the loss is only a transition, as when our young come to shore. One gives up one form for another. Beyond the dark heaven perhaps there is something more but we do not know. Probably that is a question beyond our categories. We have limits just as do you, though not so great. You are young. There is time.>>

"Around here murder is a crime."

<<We are not from here.>>

"Look, even if spirits or whatever go someplace else, that doesn't excuse murder."

<<Our young do not murder. They hunt and eat and grow. Again, a category difference between our kinds.>>

"Being dead matters to us."

<<Our young that you attacked. By your own terms you murdered them.>>

The Centauri blinked slowly at McKenna with its clamshell opening in the leathery, round eyes. Then it stooped to get its sprayer. From its wheezing spout moisture swirled around all of them.

The giddy swirl of this was getting to him. "I, I don't know where to go with this. Your young have committed a crime."

<<The coming together between stars of intelligence has a cost. We all pay it.>>

McKenna stood up. The damp scent of the alien swarmed around him. "Some more than others."

He barely made it to LeBouc's funeral. It was a real one, with a burial plot. At the church he murmured soft words to the widow, who clung to him, sobbing. He knew that she would later ask how her husband had died. It was in her pleading eyes. He would not know what to say. Or what he would be allowed to say. So he sat in the back of the whitewashed Baptist church and tried to pay attention to the service. As LeBouc's partner he had to say something in the eulogies. A moment after he sat down again he had no idea what he had said. People looked oddly at him. In the graveyard, as protocol demanded, he stood beside the phalanx of uniforms, who fired a popping salute.

At least LeBouc got buried. He had washed up on a beach while McKenna was in the hospital. McKenna had never liked the other ways, especially after his wife went away into cremation. One dealt with death, he felt, by dealing with the dead. Now bodies did not go into the earth but rather the air through cremation or then the ashes into the sea. People were less grounded, more scattered. With the body seldom present, the wheel working the churn between the living and dead could not truly spin.

God had gone out of it, too. LeBouc's fishing friends got up and talked about that. For years McKenna had noticed how his friends in their last profile became not dead Muslims or Methodists but dead bikers, golfers, surfers. That said, a minister inserted talk about the afterlife at the grave site and then the party, a respectable several hundred, went to the reception. There the tone shifted pretty abruptly. McKenna heard some guy in a seersucker suit declare "closure" just before the Chardonnay ran out.

On his sunset drive back down by the Bay he rolled down the windows to catch the sea breeze tang. He tried to think about the alien.

It had said they wanted privacy in their reproductive cycle. But was that it? Privacy was a human concept. The Centauris knew that because they had been translating human radio and TV dramas for a century. Privacy might not be a Centauri category at all, though. Maybe they were using humans' own preconceptions to get some maneuvering room?

He needed to rest and think. There would for sure come a ton of questions about what happened out there in the dark Gulf. He did not know what he would or could say to LeBouc's widow. Or what negotiations would come between Mobile PD and the Feds. Nothing was simple, except maybe his slow-witted self.

What he needed was some Zinfandel and an hour on his wharf.

A black Ford sedan was parked on the highway a hundred yards from his driveway. It looked somehow official, deliberately anonymous. Nobody around here drove such a dull car, one without blemish or rust. Such details probably meant nothing, but he had learned what one of the desk sergeants called "street sense" and he never ignored it.

He swung onto the oyster drive, headed toward home, and then braked. He cut his lights and engine, shifting into neutral, and eased the car down the sloping driveway, gliding along behind a grove of pines.

In the damp night air rushing by he heard the crunching of the tires and wondered if anybody up ahead heard them too. Around the bend before the house he stopped and let the motor tick, cooling, while he just listened. Breeze whispered through the pines and he was upwind from the house. He eased open the car door and pulled his 9mm from the glove compartment, not closing it, letting the silence settle.

No bird calls, none of the rustle and scurry of early night.

He slid out of the car, keeping low under the window of the door. No moon yet. Clouds scudded off the Gulf, masking the stars.

He circled around behind the house. On the Gulf side a man stood in shadows just around the corner from the porch. He wore jeans and a dark shirt and cradled a rifle. McKenna eased up on him, trying to ID the profile from the dim porch light. At the edge of the pines he surveyed the rest of his yard and saw no one.

Nobody carries a rifle to make an arrest. The smart way to kill an approaching target was to bracket him, so if there was a second guy he would be on the other side of the house, under the oak tree.

McKenna faded back into the pines and circled left to see the other side of his house. He was halfway around when he saw the head of another man stick around the corner. There was something odd about the head as it turned to survey the backyard but in the dim light he could not make it out.

McKenna decided to walk out to the road and call for backup. He stepped away. This caught the man's attention and brought up another rifle and aimed straight at him. McKenna brought his pistol up.

The recoil rocked his hand back and high as the 9mm snapped away, two shots. Brass casings curled back past his vision, time in slow-mo. The man went down and McKenna saw he was wearing IR goggles.

McKenna turned to his right in time to see the other man moving. McKenna threw himself to the side and down and a loud report barked from the darkness. McKenna rolled into a low bush and lay there looking out through the pines. The man was gone. McKenna used both hands to steady his pistol, elbows on the sandy ground, knowing that with a rifle the other man had the advantage at this distance, maybe twenty yards.

He caught a flicker of movement at his right. The second man was well away from the wall now, range maybe thirty yards, bracing his rifle against the old cypress trunk. McKenna fired fast, knowing the first shot was off but following it with four more. He could tell he was close but the hammering rounds threw off his judgment. He stopped, the breech locking open on the last one. He popped the clip and slid in another, a stinging smell in his widened nostrils.

The flashes had made him night blind. He lay still, listening, but his ears hummed from the shooting. This was the hardest moment, when he did not know what had happened. Carefully he rolled to his left and behind a thick pine tree. No sounds, as near as he could tell.

He wondered if the neighbors had heard this, called some uniforms.

He should do the same, he realized. Quietly he moved further left.

The clouds had cleared and he could see better. He looked toward the second guy's area and saw a shape lying to the left of the tree. Now he could make out both the guys, down.

He called the area dispatcher on his cell phone, whispering.

Gingerly he worked around to the bodies. One was Dark Glasses, the other Mr. Marine. They were long gone.

They both carried M-1A rifles, the semiauto version for civilians of the old M-14. Silenced and scoped, fast and sure, the twenty-round magazines were packed firm with snub-nosed .308s. A perfectly deniable, non-Federal weapon.

So the Feds wanted knowledge of the aliens tightly contained. And Dark

Glasses had a grudge, no doubt. The man had been a stack of anxieties walking around in a suit.

He walked out onto the wharf, nerves jumping in the salty air, and looked up at the glimmering stars. So beautiful.

Did some dark heaven lurk out there? As nearly as he could tell, the alien meant that it filled the universe. If it carried some strange wave packets that minds emitted, did that matter?

That Centauri had seemed to say that murder didn't matter so much because it was just a transition, not an ending.

So was his long-lost wife still in this universe, somehow? Were all the minds that had ever lived?

Minds that had lived beneath distant suns? Mingled somehow with Dark Glasses and Mr. Marine?

This might be the greatest of all possible revelations. A final confirmation of the essence of religion, of the deepest human hopes.

Or it might be just an alien theology, expressed in an alien way.

A heron flapped overhead and the night air sang with the chirps and scurries of the woods. Nature was getting back to business, after all the noise and death.

Business as usual.

But he knew that this night sky would never look the same again.

Molly Tanzer is the author of *Creatures of Will and Temper, Creatures of Want and Ruin* (November 2018), and the weird western *Vermilion*. For more information about her critically acclaimed novels and short fiction, sign up for her newsletter at mollytanzer.com, or follow her @molly_the_tanz on Twitter.

Nine-Tenths of the Law

MOLLY TANZER

Donna had picked up Jared's favorite—Romano's to go, he liked the rosemary bread and the penne rustica—and was just putting it in the oven to keep warm when they brought him in. *They* being EMTs, after pounding urgently on the door, and *brought him in* meaning he was on a stretcher. He had an IV in his arm and his eyes were bandaged with thick layers of gauze.

Donna felt a flash of annoyance as the EMTs wheeled him toward their bedroom, sending their cat Skimbleshanks hissing and skittering nervously out of the way. She had planned to propose they separate that night, over the tiramisu she'd put in the fridge. Then Jared moaned, and she chided herself. She was still his wife . . . for now, at least. She ought to be beside herself with worry, not annoyed over having to put off an awkward conversation.

"What happened?" she asked, hovering in the doorway while they got him into his pajamas and between the sheets, fumbling in the darkness of the room. Jared seemed pretty out of it. Doped up on painkillers, maybe? "Why didn't someone call me?"

"Workplace accident," the woman replied, answering only the first of Donna's questions. "He'll be fine, he just needs to rest. Please don't turn on those lights. His eyes are very sensitive right now."

Jared worked in administration at Denver International Airport. "What sort of workplace accident?"

"Someone will be by to talk to you," the woman assured her, her eyes flickering to the other EMT, a buff young man with tattoos and one of those man-buns.

"What sort of someone?" Donna did not have to fake the concern in her voice, as it was due to the oddness of the situation rather than her husband's condition.

As if on cue, there was a knock at the front door. Donna left the EMTs to let in a man in a gray suit. His hair was short; his shoulders, broad. Donna thought he looked vaguely military, but the pin on his lapel was the new DIA logo, the white peaks of the airport's distinctive roof against a dark blue background.

"Mrs. Crane?"

For now. She pushed away the thought, and nodded.

"My name is Mr. Smoot. I'm sorry to meet you under these circumstances, but it's a pleasure." He did not try to shake her hand. "How is he?"

"He's in bed," she said. She suddenly smelled the food, and rushed into the kitchen to turn down the oven temperature. Mr. Smoot followed her. "That's all I know at this point," she said, over her shoulder. "What happened to him?"

"Nothing a few days of rest won't cure."

She frowned. "That he needs rest is all anyone's told me."

"There's not much to tell. Just a workplace accident." Donna was becoming annoyed; given how everyone was putting her off, she suspected something might really be wrong. Her face must have betrayed this, as Mr. Smoot set his briefcase on the table and opened it, withdrawing a single sheet of paper from one of the files. He handed it to her—it was a photocopy of an incident report.

She began to skim it as Mr. Smoot spoke; he and the document said basically the same thing: "He was riding in the employee train. They were testing a new sort of lighting system down there, and a bulb flared and burst. He was looking in the wrong place at the wrong time. We had him rushed to the hospital. They did a quick surgery—with a laser, nothing to worry about. Really, he will be *fine.* He'll have to wear the bandages for a few days. When they come off, he'll have two black eyes, but that should be it."

"I see." Donna set the paper on the table. She was relieved to finally have an answer, and understood why they'd wanted a DIA rep to tell her. Damage control; lawsuit avoidance. "I'm glad it's not serious."

Mr. Smoot smiled. "We are, too. Now, as to the logistics, you work as a dental hygienist, correct?"

Donna frowned. "Um, yes." Creepy that he knew, but it must be in Jared's file somewhere . . . ? And yet, every time a new acquaintance learned her husband worked at Denver International Airport, they inevitably asked about one or more of the *X-Files*-style rumors that floated around the place like cottonwood fluff in the springtime. Was DIA where they'd take the President in the event of a global crisis? Did its murals predict the rapture? Were the delays and budget increases that had plagued its construction due to the secret alien research facility beneath the tunnels? The truth is out there . . . except it wasn't. She'd been on tours of the facility with Jared. It was just an airport.

"We'll make sure you get all the paid time off you need to take care of your husband. Or would you prefer a nurse be assigned? One will stop by, of course, to check in on him until the bandages come off, but without being able to see, he'll need someone here to help him. We'll of course cover any and all costs of home health care if you choose the second option, but we thought you might like a little mini-break."

"Sure . . ." Donna may have gotten her GED, but she was no dummy. This was *definitely* lawsuit avoidance. "Thanks."

"Excellent. Well, I'm sure you'd prefer to be in there with him than out here with me." Mr. Smoot sniffed the air. "Smells like you had dinner ready for him . . . so sorry."

"It's just takeout," she assured him. "Would you . . . like some?" Jared wasn't going to want the penne rustica that she'd driven twenty minutes into Aurora to get. Someone ought to enjoy it, and Mr. Smoot wasn't bad looking, actually. It might be nice to have dinner with someone different, just for a change. What might they talk about? The possibilities were endless! "I got wine. He probably can't have any of it."

"I'm sure once the painkillers wear off he'll be hungry. Thank you though, very kind of you to offer."

The EMT showed up in the kitchen doorway. "Mrs. Crane, he's as comfortable as we can make him, and awake. He's asking for you. And we'd like to go over some aftercare."

"Thank you," she said automatically.

"I should get going," said Mr. Smoot, closing his briefcase. "Here's my card," he said, handing her one. "Call me if you need *anything*."

"Okay," she agreed.

Just as they'd promised, all Jared needed was rest and darkness. A little help getting to the bathroom and back, or to the kitchen table for meals. After five days, the bandages came off, and for better or for worse he was back to his usual self.

Donna forced herself to put off bringing up a possible separation until at least his black eyes faded; tried to focus on the positive within their relationship. Jared had a good job, as did she. They lived in a nice house a reasonable commute away from the airport and the dental office where she worked, and had nice friends whom they saw regularly.

Turning these facts and others into a sort of litany, Donna began to doubt herself. Her life was good, so why did she feel so on edge all the time? Her feelings of dissatisfaction made no sense. Why did she feel relief instead of regret when Jared called to say he'd be working late? She shouldn't feel that flash of annoyance when she heard his key in the lock; shouldn't find it so irritating when she asked how his day was and he said, literally every afternoon or evening, "Good. Busy." Shouldn't resent the way he never asked about *her* day, or his perpetually preoccupied, predictable "Oh?" when she prompted him with an "I had a long day" or similar. That and a million other things ought not to make her nerves sing with tension and her heart flutter with frustration and resentment.

But they did.

Jared was *exactly* the same after he recovered. That's what confirmed for Donna that the oddness surrounding his accident was simply DIA attempting to avoid going to court. Jared worked the same amount, said the same damn things, ate with the same hand. Nothing was different about him. Sadly.

At least so she thought . . .

Just like every other part of their marriage, sex had become a routine. To be fair, *that* monotony was pleasant enough, not like his responses to her attempts at conversation. Always shy about such matters, Jared would turn off his light and pretend to sleep, waiting for her to tire of reading. Once she turned off her lamp, he would grope for her under the covers in the darkness of their bedroom, first finding a breast, then drifting down to her sex, which he would caress until she was wet enough to accommodate him. Usually she came, either while he was inside her, or after, squeezing her thighs together after he rolled off.

About a week after the accident, when the purple bruises around his eyes had faded to mustard yellow and a soft, pea-soup green, Jared reached for her. She was ready. As far as she was concerned, Jared's ability to sexually satisfy her, however inadvertently, was the only thing he had going for him. Responding more eagerly than usual to his touch, she was pleased when, instead of anxiously stroking her over her panties, he pulled them aside and slid a finger gently but deeply inside her—and gasped in surprise when he inserted a second.

All too soon he withdrew them both, to snap on his bedside light. She blinked, and when her eyes adjusted she saw he was sucking his fingers as he gazed at her exposed body. She shuddered, half-alarmed, half-aroused, and covered her breasts with her hands, unaccountably shy. He pulled them away almost roughly.

"I want to see," he said.

His voice was the same, but something *was* different. His eyes. They glinted queerly in the light, like Skimbleshanks's did when he was hiding under the bed. Were they a slightly different color now? Or was it just the low wattage of the bedside lamp and the sickly bruises?

She didn't think long on it. How could she, while he was peeling down her undies and pushing her knees apart to inspect her sex? She was unable to interpret his expression—all she could come up with was *wonder*, but that wasn't possible, not after ten years. And yet, how else could she explain the way his eyes widened and breath quickened as he spread her open before tasting her, which he'd never previously been particularly inclined to do. His attentions inspired her to respond with equal enthusiasm and soon she was suckling his hard cock. His delight inspired her, and she actually whined a little when he took it away from her—but her complaints turned to moans when he plunged it inside her and proceeded apace with more than his usual vigor.

He came before her, with an unexpected yelp much different from his usual relieved exhalation of breath; more aroused than she could ever remember being, she came as he slowed his thrusting. He said nothing after, just smiled and pushed her sweaty bangs away from her forehead before turning off the light. She was left in darkness, confused but far too happy to worry much about it as she drifted off.

The next morning she felt like a housewife in an old movie when she caught herself humming as she toasted her English muffin. Amazing, the power of excellent sex . . . she was actually in a good mood. Sliding into the chair beside him instead of across from him, she grinned at him.

"Have a nice time last night?"

"Hm?" He looked up from the paper. His awful bruised eyes no longer shone with that same intense, interested light.

"Last night," she said, faltering.

"Oh," he said vaguely. "Yes."

Donna no longer had any appetite for her cooling English muffin, margarine coagulating in all the nooks and crannies. Feeling disappointed— even a bit betrayed—she said nothing as he folded the paper, gave her a quick peck on the cheek, and left for work without putting his cereal bowl in the sink, as usual.

Things went back to normal, and Donna cooled down enough that when Jared next feigned sleep she didn't keep reading until he *really* fell asleep, as she sometimes did when feeling particularly resentful. Indeed, she put her book down early, as she was curious to see if she'd be treated to another display of genuine interest in her needs and her body. Hell, if the shift proved permanent, she might be able to deal with their marriage. For a little while longer, at least.

He reached for her in the darkness, to her mild disappointment. As tired as she had become of her husband's face, she had enjoyed watching him grimace and wince during their lovemaking last time. His lip had curled and his eyes had closed when he came; it had almost looked like it pained him, which had been very hot to watch. So, while she usually kept quiet during sex, that night she asked, "Want me to turn the light on?" as he fiddled with her nipple.

"What?" Jared's surprise was genuine.

"The light," she said. "Like last time."

He paused, then reached over and snapped it on. "*Definitely*," he said, as his eyes gleamed.

While she was tempted to pay more attention to the fact that he was already hard, she placed a hand on his chest.

"What's going on?" She said it calmly.

Jared froze. She waited.

"What do you mean?" he asked.

"Something's going on, and I want to know what it is. And I want to know badly enough that I'm putting off ... *things* ... which, let me tell you, is difficult after last time."

Jared laughed. "You did seem to like it. I did, too."

"Oh, *now* you want to talk about it?"

"I wanted to talk about it before, but ..." He looked worried for a moment. "I couldn't."

"Why not?"

"Because ..." He shrugged. "Because I'm not your husband."

This shocked her less than she thought it should. Then again, she was tired of her husband. Whoever he was now, he had the advantage of not being Jared.

"All right," she said. "Who are you, then?"

"That's hard to explain ..."

"Try."

Jared—well, *Not*-Jared—nodded. "I thought it was strange, when I found out, that you don't know. But your husband, he isn't an . . ." Not-Jared squinted, as if thinking hard, "*administrator*. I mean, he *is*, but not for the airport. For what's under the airport."

She felt a frisson of fear and pleasure. The truth *had* been out there! All those times she'd scoffed at friends or strangers . . . "What's under the airport?"

"A research facility. Around twenty of your Earth years ago, we made contact with you. Ever since, we—our two species—have been working to facilitate an *experimental collaborative co-consciousness*. Jared is hosting my mind in his body."

Donna held up a hand. "Our two species? What sort of species are you?" It—it was now an *it* to her mind—opened its mouth, but before it responded, she added, "And what is your name?"

"My name is," it sounded like *Glreerak*, and when Donna repeated it, Not-Jared—Glreerak—smiled and nodded. "Close enough. My world is—"

"You're an alien." Donna, again, felt minimal surprise.

"I am. But we are not so different. Neither of our species has achieved faster-than-light travel, and yet we wished to know more of who else might be living in our galaxy. My people are naturally able to separate our consciousness from our physical forms, so we developed the technology to send out a psychic beacon. You—humanity—were the first to respond."

Donna finally felt upset. "And Jared? He knew? All this time?"

"Yes. He has been the . . . *accountant* for the program since before you were married, but his selection as my host was more recent. They ran tests on everyone who worked there, from the top scientists to the janitors, and he was the most naturally receptive to the process." Glreerak stared at her. "This dismays you."

"He never told me."

"He could not. He was forbidden. But," it was studying her face, "perhaps he ought to have trusted you? You are . . . *married*. It is the sort of relationship where confidences are exchanged, according to my understanding." Donna nodded. She felt furious, miserable. "We have a similar pair-bonding—my species, I mean—where intimacy is encouraged."

Donna dashed a tear from her eye. It felt ridiculous, crying about such a small thing, when she had been ready to leave Jared anyway. "Are you . . . pair-bonded?" she asked.

Glreerak nodded. "I am."

"But the other night . . ."

It shrugged. "I am not in my own body. And I have been instructed by my government to find out as much as I can about human ways and lives. My mate knows sex is a part of that."

Donna looked sidelong at it; met its eyes that were not her husband's eyes. Jared wasn't unattractive. She'd been very eager for his attentions when they began dating, set up by a mutual friend. Then, his reticence had seemed manly, his steady, government job a sign of maturity.

"So, does that mean you want to . . ."

"*Definitely*," it replied. "I am supposed to learn all I can about you, after all."

"But for now," it said, once it had her writhing, three fingers inside her, "let's just keep this, ah, *educational session* between us?"

"Of course," she gasped.

Jared's eyes healed up enough that he agreed to go to a party at a friend's house. It was a nice time, for a bit, at least. Donna was with her girlfriends in the grass, giggling over a joint and drinking Mang-o-Ritas when her husband broke off from the pack of men standing around the grill to take her aside. He was grumpy after two scotch and sodas, and wanted to go home.

It was just so goddamn typical. She felt cute in her nice dress, the weather was finally good after several late spring snows, and she hadn't seen Vicky or Marissa in a while. Of course he would be a pill.

"Just a bit longer," she said, feeling like a child pleading with her parents to be allowed to stay in the pool.

"I didn't want to come anyway," he snapped. "We've stayed long enough."

"But . . ."

"Donna, I have to work tomorrow." She felt her expression sour at his condescending words in that exasperated tone. Work! Indeed he did, at his secret job, living his secret life. Well, she had to work, too, at her decidedly not-clandestine dentist's office, her back aching as she picked things out of people's teeth.

"Please?" she asked.

He shook his head, but then paused; looked back at her. "Well . . . all right," he said, with a slow smile that was not Jared's smile. "We haven't been out in so long. You go spend time with your friends. I'll get another drink."

It was Glreerak speaking. She was sure of it. The alien was talking to her, here, in front of all these people. It was actually kind of a turn-on, the secret. Maybe she *did* want to go home . . .

"We can't stay *too* late," it cautioned her, waggling its finger. "But a bit longer. You're having a nice time. Later, you can thank me," it said, and winked.

They stayed until the sun set. Donna couldn't remember the last time she felt so happy, alternating between chatting with her friends and sneaking kisses with Glreerak. When she climbed into the passenger's side, she favored Jared—she was pretty sure he was Jared again—with a smile. He didn't see it, however, sitting there with the key in the ignition.

"It got so late," he said, sounding confused. "How did it get so late? I was ready to go hours ago."

Donna froze. Of course, Jared didn't recall when the alien took over. It had seemed so harmless in bed. But in public, among friends . . .

Then she recalled his tone, earlier, when he'd insisted they leave. Recalled that he had kept secrets from her—secrets bigger than how a pleasant afternoon had been passed.

"You had another drink," she said as casually as she could, buckling her seatbelt as cover. "Maybe you got a little drunker than you realized. Sure you're okay to drive?"

"I feel totally sober," he said. "Huh." He waited for another moment, then turned the key. "Better keep it to two next time, I suppose."

Donna said nothing. Eventually, her heart slowed down.

B*efore going into the induced sleep that allowed its mind to live within Jared's, Glreerak dwelt beneath the waves, in a vast city of coral skyscrapers grown and maintained by bioarchitects to harvest and emit the faint light of the planet's sun. Millions lived in that phosphorescently illuminated gloaming, lived and worked and loved and died in ways similar and different to humans in their cities on Earth.*

Glreerak lived with its mate in a flat high above the ocean floor. It was comfortable—luxurious even, with a good view of the surrounding towers and parks and even the farmland beyond the city limits. They had been assigned such a wonderful home because while Glreerak's mate was one of the scientists working on the project to make contact with Earth, Glreerak held a much higher-status job: sanitation.

As with all civilizations, waste removal was an issue. Burying garbage beneath the ocean bed poisoned the food supply; allowing it to drift away created problems for other cities. So, there was only one place it could go.

While all of Glreerak's people were telepathic, only the most powerful communicators were able to pass the rigorous tests to become sanitation workers. Those who did were trained to develop their mental aptitude from a young age, until they were able to throw their minds into the bodies of simpler creatures, such as the mammal-like bipeds that lived on land. Teams of sanitation workers could combine their efforts to mobilize whole packs of them to haul waste out of the sea and inland, away from rivers and other tributaries, to minimize seepage back into the water. Glreerak was particularly talented; in fact, it could control these creatures for miles, and had seen more of its planet's land masses than any other, such as the astonishing—

"Wait," said Donna.

"What's that?" said Glreerak.

It had been an intense evening. Donna had been overwhelmed by the menu at Linger, a trendy eatery with a spectacular view of Denver that Jared had never been willing to brave due to its world cuisine-inspired menu. Indeed, Jared would have hated it—would hate it tomorrow, given how spicy everything had been. Then again, maybe he wouldn't notice anything even as fundamental as altered digestion. He'd been withdrawn and preoccupied of late, even for him, and had become nervous as well, startling at loud noises, rubbing his eyes.

To be fair, Linger's menu had been a little weird for Donna, too, but she'd done all right with red wine, an order of sweet potato waffle fries, and the kofta, which turned out to essentially be meatballs dressed up for a night out.

Glreerak had liked everything, and the drinks along with the view of the city skyline had made it a bit homesick for its watery world.

"You can control other creatures with your mind?"

Glreerak didn't answer; it just sipped on its cocktail, some weird thing called "Streets of Puebla" that Donna hadn't liked *at all.*

"Well," it said after swallowing, "yes. My telepathic prowess is why they chose me."

Whatever she'd eaten for dinner felt like a cold and leaden lump inside her.

"So you knew."

"Knew what?"

"That you'd be able to control . . . *us.*"

"No!" Glreerak pursed its lips. "We wondered—*hypothesized*, as my mate would say. But we didn't *know*. I mean, it was a week before I felt comfortable enough to try, just to see. And it was you who inspired me, Donna. Your body was so soft—you seemed so receptive to pleasure. I had to see you! The shape of you, all of you. The way you responded to him, I couldn't let my time on Earth go by without taking advantage of the endless possibilities you suggested to me . . ."

Was it wooing her with sweet talk to distract her from the idea of a mass invasion? Were Glreerak's people testing the waters, so to speak, to turn humanity into their next generation of garbage-hauling slaves?

"You know, Donna," it said, reaching its hand across the table to take hers, "when your husband takes his turn living in *my* head, we will be revealing our planet's secrets to your species."

More than thoughts of their lovemaking, this distracted Donna from her worries of a future invasion. "What?"

"Eventually he will return with me. I am to spend a year with him, then he will spend a year with me." Glreerak looked upset. "I know he has been concerned about how to tell you—how to explain his absence. I thought you should know, though."

"He agreed to all this without . . ." Donna shook her head. She was so unimportant to him. What a fool she had been!

"Are you upset about the idea of losing him for so long?"

Donna looked up from her wine, saw the gleam of the ocular implants as it tilted its head at her like a quizzical puppy. She was upset—but she was upset about losing Glreerak; jealous that Jared, who had all the sense of wonder of a sack of potatoes, would get to live with it on its planet. Would get to see how it made love to its mate.

She laughed. It was the only thing she could do, really. "Well, maybe he'll come back with a few new tricks to try on me after watching you with your mate."

"Perhaps. At home, I would be the one to be fertilized."

Donna blinked at it. "You're a woman?"

"No, *you're* a woman. I'm barely female! It's rather a bit more complicated, at home. If we were interested in reproducing, my mate would fertilize me. Once the egg developed to its solid jelly form, I would pass it back to be incubated in my partner's pouch. Eventually we would give it over to the city, where it would be implanted into a host along with the rest of the eggs around its stage. Once fully mature, it would hatch, and eat its way out of—well," it trailed off, seeing her face. "The point is, when we fuck for pleasure, it's a bit different."

"Sounds like it will definitely broaden his mind." Donna smiled. "Glreerak . . ."

"Yes?"

"Even if we only have a year, we have a year. Together. Let's make it a fun one."

"It has been already!"

"Sure, the past few weeks have been great, but still—you didn't come all the way to Earth just to go to work under DIA every day and live in Aurora."

"Well, a month from now, Jared's going on a tour of world heritage sites . . ." Glreerak paused. "Don't be upset . . . you were to come on that one. Mr. Smoot has been arranging it with your job. It was to be a surprise. That's why I didn't tell you, either. You know *I* would have, don't you, Donna?"

"Well then let's at least go away for a weekend. To the mountains, maybe. Together. Just the two of us, I mean. When we go abroad, I'm sure we'll have all kinds of handlers and such. If you—if Jared could get a half-day some Friday . . ."

Glreerak nodded, smiling in that way Jared never smiled at her. "Sounds delightful," it agreed. "I'll ask for the . . ." its eyes went a bit dim as they did when it was searching through Jared's mind for the correct turn of phrase, "*time off.*"

"Good." She reached for the small menu beside her elbow. "But first, how about dessert?"

She decided on Steamboat Springs. It was inexpensive now that the snowpack was mostly gone, she knew no one who lived in the area, and there was a legendary hot spring up there, Strawberry Park, that was supposed to be gorgeous. Plus, the drive up would show Glreerak the mountains, where the aspens were still the pale gold-green of springtime against the dark pines.

It was exhilarating. The whole drive, Donna felt like she was going on a dirty weekend, even though it was her husband was in the passenger's seat. Well, sort of.

Glreerak was pleased with everything—pointed out gorgeous vistas, gasped as they crested various passes. Jared would only have remarked on the traffic; worried whether they should have made dinner reservations.

Saturday, they took a picnic lunch up to the springs, sandwiches and chips and a can of the kale-flavored soda that Donna had only ever seen Glreerak buy. By late in the afternoon, they'd had enough of dipping in the various pools, heating up and cooling down by turns. But that was fine, they had urgent business in the hotel room.

Donna's googling had told her Café Diva was a hot spot even in the warmer weather, but when they walked in the door, she saw something she didn't like one bit. Vicky and her husband Mark were there, and before

Donna could suggest ought to go elsewhere to avoid being spotted, they were.

"Donna!" cried Vicky. "I didn't know you and Jared would be here this weekend. You sly dogs, are you on a lovers' getaway?"

"Haha," said Donna, just like that—not a laugh, but a statement. "Yeah, we are, you caught us."

"We are, too! Come on, join us for dinner! It'll be fun, you can go back to your place after." She winked outrageously at Donna. "We've only just ordered starters."

"Oh, we wouldn't want to . . ."

"To what? Have fun? Come on, you won't be bothering us."

Donna looked to Glreerak. It shrugged.

They actually had a really nice dinner. Glreerak did well with Vicky and Mark, even if sometimes it had to think, scanning through Jared's brain, before responding. Donna ordered a second bottle of wine to keep them from noticing too much. It seemed to work.

Back at the hotel, Donna collapsed onto the bed.

"That was close," she said. "I'm so glad we're free of them. I could barely eat, I was so worried."

Glreerak pushed her skirt up over her thighs. "Your species' constant need for nourishment isn't unpleasant, but it's a shame we have to leave the hotel to do it."

"We can order room service tomorrow morning."

"Good. No more distractions from what *really* matters."

It was the longest amount of time they'd spent together without letting Jared surface. Donna felt bad—a little bit, at least—but she hadn't wanted to argue with her husband about the drive, where to stay, what to do, where to eat. She'd wanted to enjoy some time with Glreerak without distractions, just for once.

When they cruised back into town that Sunday, after grabbing a late lunch in Denver, she felt a bit low to have to return to her marriage; her life. Even the idea of their upcoming around-the-world trip couldn't cheer her. Glreerak had said they'd see the Library of Celsus—the Parthenon—the Pyramids—the Great Wall—the Tower of London—Machu Picchu . . . but she'd be seeing it all with Jared. She would know Gleerak was there, just beyond Jared's eyes, but they wouldn't be *together*. Not really.

They'd agreed on a cover story: A stomach virus had knocked Jared out all weekend. As Donna unpacked the last of their things, Glreerak changed into pajamas and got into bed.

"Wow, it must have really knocked me out," remarked Jared, as Donna brought him a glass of watered-down Gatorade. "Well, I'm feeling better now."

"I'm so glad," said Donna. "You were really miserable. Probably best you don't remember it."

"Would you bring me my laptop? I ought to see if any work emails came in while I was so out of it . . ."

Yeah, maybe some new alien species made contact with the secret research facility where you work, she thought, but all she said was, "Sure."

She took a long shower; took her time drying off. She'd brought her pajamas with her into the bathroom—it was silly, but she felt less comfortable changing in front of Jared of late. When she re-emerged, he was in bed, laptop open. He was staring intently at the screen.

"Hungry at all?" she asked, putting a little hopefulness into her voice, as if urging him.

He said nothing; didn't look up at her.

"Well . . . let me know if you need anything," she said. "I'm going to watch a little TV."

"No," he said. "*Wait.*"

When he looked up at her, finally, his expression was not a friendly one.

"More Gatorade?" she asked.

"I don't want any goddamn Gatorade," he said, throwing off the covers and advancing on her. Donna shrank against the wall. Jared was really upset; he didn't usually swear . . .

"What's wrong?"

"*What's wrong?* What's wrong is that I was in Steamboat Springs this weekend," he said. "Apparently I had a lovely dinner with Vicky and Mark in some restaurant up there. But how could that be, if my wife assures me I was sick in bed?"

Donna didn't know what to do. She hadn't anticipated this; hadn't thought she would ever be caught. Oh, she'd been such a fool!

"Nothing to say?"

She shrugged; shook her head.

"How long have you known?"

"Known . . . about Glreerak?"

"*Who?*"

Donna felt faint. "Your . . . your experimental collaborative co-consciousness."

Jared's eyes went wide. He grabbed his phone; dialed quickly. "I need someone here, *now*. To bring me in," he said. "Yes. *Yes*. Yes!" He hung up the phone.

"Bring you in?"

"You think I'm going to drive, knowing it could take me over at any moment?" he snarled, almost yanking out a dresser drawer in his haste to grab a shirt. "Oh god, what am I going to tell them? None of us knew it even had a name, much less that it could make a puppet of me without my consent of my knowledge! None of us . . . except *you*."

"I can explain . . ."

"Oh, please do!" he said, struggling into a pair of sweatpants. "I'm eager to hear you *explain* going out of town for a weekend with it." His eyes snapped back to hers. "You fucked it, didn't you? You fucking fucked it!"

Donna wished Glreerak could intervene, but it had told her it was more difficult to take over Jared when he was emotionally agitated. She would just have to deal with this on her own. "Well . . ." she began.

"Never mind! I don't want to hear it, actually. I'm leaving," he said unnecessarily, "and I don't know when I'll be back."

"What's going to happen?" she asked.

"It's not up to me," he snapped. "But I have my doubts they'll be pleased. This was not part of our agreement! Jesus, they can take us over! No wonder they were so eager for this partnership . . . this is not good, this is really not good. Where *are* they?" he said, stomping out of the bedroom.

Donna felt a chill as she followed him into the living room, and not in regards to Jared's fears of planetary domination. "Can't we talk about this?" she said, pleading with him.

"Talk? Talk about what?"

"Are they going to terminate the . . . the co-habitation?"

"Probably! Donna, I was supposed to be reporting anything strange. This is new technology—new law—new everything!" He shook his head. "I'm such an idiot. I knew something was wrong, but I believed your excuses. How stupid of me, to trust my own wife!"

Now Donna was furious; all her rage came bubbling up like lava, hot and toxic. "Trust! You want to talk about trust? If Glreerak hadn't told me, how would I have known? You never even told me where you worked, what you did!"

"It's top secret!"

"Top secret!" She scoffed at him. "*You* reached for *me* that first night, you know. Did it excite you, the idea of it watching us?"

He blushed. She'd never seen him blush, not in a decade of marriage.

"It was here to learn about us! That includes how married couples . . . um, *behave* with each other!"

"I guess it learned a hell of a lot, didn't it? Mission accomplished." Something occurred to Donna, contemplating the way she and Jared had behaved with one another, before Glreerak. She really didn't want to go back to that. Couldn't go back to that. "Maybe . . . maybe you won't have to terminate the relationship. Maybe there's a way . . ."

"What?" Jared's face crumpled. "*A way?* You're more worried about losing your lover than my mental health! It was taking me over, Donna! It pushed me out of my own mind, my own body! My own marriage!"

"No. We pushed ourselves out of that."

There was a knock at the door. Donna answered it. There stood Mr. Smoot; behind him were several military men brandishing weapons. Mr. Smoot was the only one who appeared unarmed, but given everything, it wouldn't surprise her if he had something concealed on his person.

"Come in," she said, as if this were the most typical of social calls.

"I'm afraid I can't," said he, equally pleasant. "Jared? Is that you?"

"Yes, it's *me*," he said, not exactly elbowing his way past Donna, but not waiting for her to move out of the doorway, either. "Let's go."

They walked to the black car parked in the driveway, Donna barefoot and following at a bit of a distance. She felt embarrassed to be seen with her damp hair and worn cotton pajamas, but she couldn't help but tag along. She would likely never speak to Glreerak again. She had no idea if she would ever see Jared, either. He had to come back at some point . . . didn't he?

Who could say? He'd never told her anything about any of it.

There was no time to ask. Mr. Smoot got in the driver's side, and Jared slammed the car door shut in her face as she approached. He had clearly not calmed down at all, but maybe Glreerak would peek through, one last time. She looked into her husband's eyes, hoping to see the familiar gleam . . . but as Mr. Smoot put the car in reverse, late afternoon sunlight glinted off the passenger window. It was impossible for Donna to tell who it was who mouthed "good-bye."

Hugo and three-time Nebula award finalist Caroline M. Yoachim is the author of over a hundred short stories, appearing in *Asimov's*, *Fantasy & Science Fiction*, *Clarkesworld*, and *Lightspeed*, among other places. Her work has been reprinted in multiple year's best anthologies and translated into Chinese, Spanish, and Czech. Yoachim's debut short story collection, *Seven Wonders of a Once and Future World & Other Stories*, came out in 2016. For more, check out her website at carolineyoachim.com

Five Stages of Grief After the Alien Invasion

CAROLINE M. YOACHIM

DENIAL

Ellie huddled in the corner of her daughter's room. She sang a quiet lullaby and cradled her swaddled infant in her arms. Lexi was four months old, or maybe thirteen months? Ellie shook her head. There hadn't been a birthday party, and thirteen-month-olds didn't need swaddling. She tried to rearrange the swaddling blankets so they didn't cover Lexi's face, but every time she moved the blankets, all she saw underneath was another layer of blankets.

"Oskar?" she called. "Come and hold the baby for a bit, I need to go out and buy formula."

Oskar came in and gave her the same sad look he'd worn all week. Work, she decided, must be going poorly. She wished he would confide in her about it, but he didn't like to burden her with his problems. Lexi's room was dark, and the light switch wasn't working. Ellie opened the blinds, but the window was covered in white paint, making it impossible to see outside.

"Did you paint the windows?" she asked. Their apartment was on the third floor, and it had a lovely view of the treetops. "Lexi will want to see the birds."

"Sporefall killed all the birds," Oskar said, his voice bitter, "and we don't need formula. It's been months, Ellie. I know how hard this is, but I can't do this anymore. The pain is bad enough without reliving it with you every day."

Ellie frowned. "If you're too busy to watch the baby you should say so."

Oskar leaned down and kissed the top of her head. "I'm going, Ellie. There's a caravan heading down to L.A., and I haven't heard a thing from Jessica since sporefall. She didn't even answer the letter I sent about Lexi. I've hired a caretaker to help you get by without me, her name is Marybeth. She lost her wife to the sporefall, so maybe you two can help each other get through your grief."

"A little extra help around the house will be nice," Ellie said. "Tell your sister hello."

Ellie smiled. Jessica was a good influence on Oskar. She'd cheer him right up.

Oskar's eyes were teary when he turned to leave the room. She wondered if his allergies were acting up. He'd said something about spores. When she went to get the formula, she could pick up an antihistamine for him.

Ellie put Lexi in the high chair, still swaddled in blankets, and tried to spoon-feed her pureed peas. It wasn't working very well. Four months was too early for solids and the entire jar ended up on the blankets rather than in the baby. Ellie put the empty jar in the sink.

Someone knocked on the door, unlocked it, and came inside. It wasn't Oskar.

"Your husband gave me a key," the woman said, "I'm Marybeth. You must be Ellie."

Ellie nodded, "And this is Lexi. She's a bit of a mess right now." Ellie dabbed at the blankets with a napkin, then added, embarrassed, "She's a bit young for it, but I tried to feed her."

Marybeth smiled sadly. "Lexi died, Ellie. Nine months ago the Eridani seeded the planet with spores. Once they realized the planet was inhabited, they undid the damage as best they could, but they came too late for the elderly and the very young."

"Well, I'm glad they came nine months ago and not now," Ellie said, wiping the tray of the highchair with the food-smeared napkin. "Oskar hired you to watch Lexi? Do you do laundry, too? Her blankets are a mess."

Marybeth carefully unwound Lexi's outermost blanket and put it in the laundry hamper. "It would be better if you could move on, Ellie. This isn't healthy."

Satisfied that Marybeth could take care of Lexi, Ellie went to the bathroom and took a shower. Cold water poured down around her skin, and she scrubbed until she was red to be sure she got rid of all the spores. Oskar was allergic to spores, and she didn't want to make his symptoms any worse. Oh, but the babysitter—she came from outside, she must have been covered in spores.

Ellie ran out from the bathroom, dripping wet and wrapped in a towel. "You came from outside! You've exposed poor Lexi to spores!"

Marybeth put one hand on Ellie's shoulder and gently guided her back to the bathroom. "Hush now, the spores are gone, all grown into plants. We don't have to worry about spores."

Marybeth returned the next day with an old man. Ellie hoped he wasn't sick. He was dressed too warmly for the weather: clunky black boots, several layers of baggy clothes, and a fleece hat with flaps that covered his ears. He was short and stout with ashen skin and a grin too broad for his face. It made him look like a toad, Ellie thought, then pushed the uncharitable thought from her head.

"Come in, come in," Ellie said, then realized that her welcome was too late and Marybeth and her—was the man her father? Maybe her grandfather—were already in the entryway of her apartment.

"I thought it'd be good for you to meet one of the Eridani," Marybeth said. "It might help you come to grips with what happened."

"Nice to meet you, Mr. Eridani," Ellie said. It was time for Lexi's nap. The apartment was warm, good for sleeping, but Ellie could use some fresh air. "Do you sing, Marybeth?"

"Sing?" Marybeth asked. "No, not really."

"What about you, Mr. Eridani?" Ellie turned to the old man. "Will you sing my daughter lullabies? I'd like to go for a walk."

"It might be good for her to get out of the house," Marybeth told her grandfather. "I think Oskar made a mistake in painting the windows." She went over to the kitchen window and pried it open, sending flecks of dried paint flying everywhere.

Ellie turned her back on the kitchen, trying to protect Lexi from the nasty paint dust. "Don't let her breathe the dust, she just got over a terrible cough."

The old man nodded, then held out his arms to take Lexi. He held her gently, and while his mouth was fixed in the same broad smile, his bulging black eyes seemed sad. Ellie wondered if he was longing for grandchildren of his own.

"Don't be sad. Lexi clearly likes you. She didn't even cry." Ellie put on a sweater and opened her apartment door. "I won't be gone long."

The trees along the edge of the sidewalk had oddly purple leaves, and the people that passed looked far too weary for a sunny Saturday afternoon, but as she walked beneath the open windows of her apartment, she could hear the low hum of a lullaby, slow and sweet, sure to soothe her daughter straight to sleep.

ANGER

Amelia was twelve the night the spores fell, and she remembered it vividly. Thousands of meteors burned bright as they fell through the atmosphere. Charred black pods burst open when they crashed to the ground. By dawn, the air was filled with swirling clouds of orange mist, like pollen blowing from the trees. Every person and creature on the planet breathed the spores. The birds were the first to die, but not the last.

"Come away from the window, Sis." Brayden tried to tousle her hair like she was six years old or something. "Dad will be home soon, and you haven't done your homework yet."

"I didn't do my homework because it's stupid to pretend that nothing has changed," Amelia said. "Everyone in my class lost people to the spore. Friends, grandparents . . . siblings. Tia's parents got killed in the riots. Zach's older brother died in one of the fires. Then the way they healed us—"

She shuddered. She still had nightmares about the croaker that thinned into some kind of fog and poured itself down her throat, picking the spores out of her lungs and healing the damage the sprouting plants had done. It was that or die when the spores grew, but she'd still thrashed so much that Dad had to hold her down to keep her from hurting herself.

"It was eleven months ago," Brayden said. He stared at the sky for a moment, lost in his own thoughts. "What's the alternative to going back to normal? If you didn't have school, you'd sit home and sulk all day like that guy that came down from Portland."

Their neighbor's brother had showed up on the caravan last week, looking for Jessica, but she'd already left for the space station. She was one of the scientists chosen to help negotiate a treaty with the aliens. The only treaty Amelia wanted to see was 'get off our planet and take your damned purple plants with you.'

"Oskar sits around and sulks all day," Amelia said, "but I would go out and kill croakers."

Brayden shook his head. "You can't kill croakers. People have tried. They can't be poisoned, stabbed, or shot. No matter what you do to them, they reco- here, they heal. If you did more of your homework, you might know that."

Unlike the rest of her classes, which she'd given up on, Amelia had paid careful attention to all the details of croaker biology. Despite their sol- id-seeming forms, croakers were essentially sentient fog. The squat frog- like body they used on Earth was a dense gray cloud, thick enough to hold up the clothes they wore, but little else. Projectiles and blades passed right through and did little harm, and poison passed through unabsorbed.

Amelia had a different plan. She would trap a croaker bit by bit in a hun- dred glass jars. Then she'd throw the jars into a fire, one by one. Would the pain of that death be as bad as the last desperate gasps of her little brother? Gavin was four, and screamed all his last night in pain and fear. Spores made his lungs burn, the doctor said.

Amelia would make a croaker burn.

C roakers wandered the streets like ghosts, occasionally stopping to eat leaves from the purple plants that had grown from the spores. According to the news, the croakers were observing, collecting data so they could repair more of the damage they did at sporefall, but as near as Amelia could tell, the big gray frogs were just making themselves right at home. Amelia waited behind one of their licorice-smelling plants with a cardboard box full of glass jars.

A croaker came to nibble at the leaves, and she jumped out from behind the bush, jar in hand. She scooped out a big section of the croaker's ugly frogface. The croaker was thicker than she expected, like gelatin or pudding, rather than air. The gray goo in the jar was repulsively flesh-like, and her stomach churned as she screwed the lid into place. The croaker let out a high pitched whine. Its face appeared unchanged, despite her jarful of gray goo.

She couldn't do it. She had a boxful of jars, and she wanted the croaker to burn, but she couldn't bring herself to take another scoop of its ashen flesh. It stared at her with round black eyes, still making a high-pitched sound, though softer now, a sad keening sound.

"You killed Gavin!" she screamed. "You messed up my whole world and now you stay here like you own it! You should burn for it!"

She hurled the jar of gray goo at the sidewalk. It shattered against the concrete and shards of glass flew everywhere. A cloud of gray swirled up from the shimmering fragments of the jar before drifting back onto the croaker. Into the croaker.

She grabbed another jar from her box and threw it at the croaker. It bounced off the alien's face, and the froglike grin didn't even flinch. "Go back to where you came from!" she shouted and flung jar after jar at the croaker, until her cardboard box was empty and the sidewalk was buried beneath a pile of shattered glass.

The croaker scooped up the broken glass in big webbed hands, mounding it and sculpting it into its own image. Amelia watched, fascinated despite herself. The croaker smoothed the bits of glass as easily as a sculptor might shape clay. It made a statue of a croaker, and in the statue's broad glass hands there was a human child with indistinct features. Not her brother, but a child like him. Perhaps all children like him. Unlike every croaker Amelia had ever seen, there was no froglike grin on the statue's face.

Brayden ran over. "I heard all the noise, and—" He stared at the statue.

"I wanted to set a croaker on fire, but I couldn't do it." Amelia said. "Not even after everything they did."

Perhaps it was a trick of the light, but the statue didn't look empty. Delicate orange flames danced inside the statue of the croaker, complete with thin wisps of gray smoke that reminded her of the swirling cloud when she broke the jar and let the croaker go. It had left a piece of itself inside the statue, to burn inside the glass.

She thought her mind was playing tricks on her, but Brayden saw it too. "They already burn for what they did."

The croaker bowed its head, then turned and walked away.

BARGAINING

The alien standing in front of Jessica was four feet tall, slate gray, and shaped like an oversized toad. It smelled like chalk and made a quiet wheezing noise, barely audible over the hum of the orbital stabilizers. The temperature onboard the station was comfortable for humans, but the alien wore a thick sweater, knitted by one of Jessica's former graduate students as a gesture of goodwill from all humankind. A large round button with the number 17 was pinned to the purple wool. Eridani didn't use names.

Eridani 17 extended a webbed hand. The flesh of its fingers thinned, creating the illusion of wisps of smoke curling up from its palm. The smoke shaped itself into North America, and then a city skyline.

"Toronto?" Jessica asked. The city had a distinctive tower. Eridani 17 shook its head.

Negotiating with the Eridani was like a game of Pictionary, except that

Jessica was sober and—thank god—didn't have to actually draw anything. Her brother Oskar had always been the artist in the family, excelling at Pictionary even when he was half her age. If his most recent message was any indication, all he ever drew now was pictures of his estranged wife, who lost her mind after sporefall killed their baby.

"Seattle," Jessica said.

The Eridani understood spoken language, but not by translating individual words. According to the best available translation, the Eridani heard ideas in the spaces between the words.

She hoped that this was true. She was not authorized to ask for what she truly wanted, and the sessions were recorded.

Eridani 17 transformed its speaking hand into an image of several Eridani standing between two skyscrapers. As Jessica watched, a giant web appeared between the two buildings, soon followed by several pods filled with what she guessed were baby Eridani.

"Seattle has a substantial human population, but I'm sure we can find an abandoned region that suits your needs," Jessica said. Atlanta, perhaps. It was warmer there, and the sporefall had been particularly dense.

Eridani 17 made no response, and its hand solidified. This meant that an alternate site was acceptable. Jessica would get a list of abandoned and near-abandoned cities to propose in tomorrow's negotiations.

Next on her agenda was a request for additional technology to assist in maintaining and rebuilding the human population in the regions hardest hit by sporefall. Negotiations happened in parallel, with dozens of humans in one-on-one sessions with the Eridani at any given time. She checked her tablet to make sure that nothing from the other sessions had altered her agenda.

"Like many of my people, I lost family members to the spore," Jessica began. She concentrated on her memories of her niece, a tiny baby that she had held only once. "We struggle to rebuild what we once had."

She was supposed to be asking for technological advances in transportation and communications, for new methods of agriculture to help human crops coexist with the invasive purple weeds that grew from the Eridani spores. She was supposed to infuse her spoken words with a plea for these things, so that the aliens would hear their needs in the spaces between her words. Instead, she thought of all the people she had lost in the sporefall and the chaos afterwards—relatives, coworkers, neighbors, friends.

Give them back, she pleaded. The Eridani were so advanced; there had to be something they could do. "Surely there is some technology you have that can help us."

Eridani 17 thinned itself entirely into cloud, leaving the purple sweater in a puddle on the floor. It reformed itself into the shape of Gavin, her neighbor's four-year-old son who had died from the spore. The boy sat cross-legged on the floor and in his lap was a tightly swaddled baby with a drooly grin and dimpled cheeks. Lexi.

The alien had somehow called the children from her mind, but the scene that it created was not a remembered image. Gavin had never met Lexi. And yet, if he had, this was exactly how it might have looked. The boy's expression was a mix of curiosity and wariness, and Lexi—

She very nearly said what she was thinking, that she would give anything to have her back. Her death, and Ellie's breakdown, was destroying Oskar. Each death from the spore cascaded into a thousand unwanted consequences, and all the world was broken now. There must be some way the Eridani could undo time or reshape space and reverse the deaths they'd caused. There had to be a way.

Gavin held Lexi with one arm and raised the other up in front of him. He thinned his fingers, which was disconcerting. Jessica knew the ghosts were really just Eridani 17, but human fingers shouldn't thin the way that Gavin's were thinning.

"You will give us back the ones we've lost in exchange for," Jessica paused to study the map that hovered where Gavin's hand should have been. "The entire West Coast?"

It snapped Jessica back to reality. The Eridani had always shown remorse for what they'd done. They'd claimed to be unaware that the planet was inhabited, that they would not have sent their spore and, later, their colony ships, if they had known otherwise. She hadn't expected them to use her grief to their advantage in negotiations. She could not trade that much territory, not for mere ghosts.

"Not for shadows and memories," Jessica said.

Gavin leaned forward and kissed baby Lexi on the forehead. It was so close to what she wanted, they were almost real. Better than Ellie's empty bundle of blankets. Close enough, perhaps, to pull her sister-in-law back to reality. So close to what she wanted, and yet so far. And she couldn't trade that much territory even if the Eridani offered to pull the actual children from the past. "I am not authorized to negotiate concessions of this magnitude."

Gavin and Lexi melted right before her eyes, merged into a puddle, and reformed into the default frogform of Eridani 17. The entire session was recorded, and back on Earth it was undoubtedly already being analyzed. They would see the tears in her eyes, and she would be sent back to the planet in disgrace. Back to Earth, but not back home. Home was a place that still had those children in it.

DEPRESSION

Oskar got home from a long shift of weeding alien foodplants out of the avocado grove. His hands were stained purple and smelled of licorice. He set a 10 pound bag of avocadoes on the counter. He should trade some avocadoes to the neighbor kids for one of the trout they farmed in the courtyard fountain, but he didn't want to eat. He shut himself into his sister's guest bedroom and stared at the ceiling, crushed beneath the weight of his bad choices.

He shouldn't have left Ellie.

The walls were covered in sketches of his wife. Her smile, her eyes, her slender hands. Cheeks dotted with pale brown freckles. Hair tied back with a few loose strands to frame her face. She was the one who left him. She left reality behind and spent all day pretending a bundle of blankets was their baby girl. No one could blame him for not wanting to relive that kind of pain, day after day. He'd tried for months. Marybeth was a family friend, and he'd given her everything they had to take care of his wife.

All of that so Oskar could go and find his sister, Jessica. He'd been worried that she might need help, but she wasn't sitting helpless in her apartment. No, she'd gone off to the space station to be one of Earth's ambassadors. This was supposed to be his big chance to not be the baby brother anymore, to swoop in and save Jessica from the post-invasion chaos, and she hadn't needed him at all. She never did. He had no idea if she'd even gotten the message he'd tried to send.

Someone pounded on the door. Probably the neighbor kids. Brayden liked avocadoes, and trading with him was a better deal than trying to buy them somewhere.

He opened the door. "Jessica."

"I can't believe you changed my locks." Jessica faked a scowl, then grinned and gave him a big hug. "You look like crap."

Oskar retreated to Jessica's guestroom. His sister hadn't understood how he could come down here and leave Ellie behind, no matter how he tried to explain.

People started pouring in from the east. They moved into abandoned apartments, office buildings, malls. Los Angeles turned back into a bustling city. Jessica said that the government had traded Arizona and New Mexico to the frogs. All the extra people made it harder to get work. His heavy heart made it harder to wake up and face the day.

On his second straight day of refusing to get out of bed, Jessica marched into his room like she was twenty and he was ten, and she could boss him around. "Draw me a bird."

"Go away," he said. There were no birds, and he could see right through his sister's scheme. Birds were from happier times. She thought sketching a picture would pull him out of this funk. She was wrong. Remembering the way things were would only make it worse. "There are no birds. Sporefall killed them all."

"Think of it as rent. It'll do you good to draw something other than Ellie, over and over again. All I'm asking for is one really good picture of a bird." Jessica left without waiting for him to answer.

He only had a few sheets of good thick paper left, he'd used most of it to draw his pictures of Ellie. He got one out. He closed his eyes and tried to picture the stellar jays that had eaten peanuts from the feeder outside his window, back before the sporefall. He remembered blue and black feathers, and the general shape of the head, but the details were fuzzy. There were pictures of birds in books, but he shouldn't need that. He should be able to do this. It had only been a year.

For the first time in weeks, he opened the guestroom blinds. The apartment was on the fourth floor, and the window looked across the alley at a near-identical brick building. He tried to imagine birds flying in the alley, landing on the concrete below to hunt for bugs or seeds, but thoughts of flying set his mind to thinking about soaring out through the window and falling into oblivion.

He closed the blinds.

Two days later Oskar had only one sheet of good paper left, and he had not yet managed a picture of a bird. He ate when Jessica forced him to, and he slept until Jessica made him get out of bed. There was no point to pictures of birds. There was no point to anything, not anymore.

Jessica came in with half an avocado. Did he really have to eat, again? But no, she started eating it herself, spooning the mushy green into her mouth and smiling as though it actually tasted good to eat a plain avocado, again. "This is the last one from the bag, and food rations have been short at the community center, so we can't count on that. We need to decide what to do next. There's a caravan going north, right through Portland."

He didn't want to go back. What if Marybeth had abandoned Ellie, despite all her promises? He couldn't face the chance. "I'm staying here."

Jessica shook her head. "You're not. I'm trading the apartment for passage on the caravan and food for the trip. If you want to stay in L.A., you're on your own."

She left him to consider his options, and his gaze drifted to the window. It would be so easy, so quick. If he never went back to Ellie, he could believe that she was okay, maybe even happy. He wouldn't have to face a world that could never possibly be right again.

He opened the blinds. An alien was walking in the alley, smiling the same damn frog-smile that the aliens always smiled. It saw him in the window, and thinned into a cloud. When it came back together, it was a flock of birds. Not the stellar jays he'd been trying to draw, but pigeons, plump and gray. They fluttered up and landed on windowsills and power lines outside the window. They weren't real, but they were enough to evoke a clear memory in his mind.

Oskar could soar out the window, or he could draw this memory of birds for Jessica and go with her back to Portland.

He calmed his shaking hands and sketched the birds.

ACCEPTANCE

Marybeth walked with Ellie to the clinic. Ellie insisted on bringing 'Lexi,' a bundle of filthy blankets that she refused to believe wasn't actually her dead baby. Marybeth hoped the new treatment would help. Ellie was an amazing woman, able to find joy in all the smallest things. Even now, as they walked along abandoned streets with Eridani food-plants, Ellie chattered to her blanket-bundle baby about how beautiful the orange blossoms were on the lovely purple trees.

Marybeth couldn't appreciate the beauty of the 'blossoms.' They weren't flowers at all, but clusters of tiny spheres, each one full of orange spores. The trees would release spores soon, and despite Eridani assurances that there would be no harm to humans this time, she could not put aside her memories of the last sporefall, and all the death it caused. Yolanda's death.

Very few healthy adults had died in the sporefall, but her wife hadn't been healthy. She'd had alpha-1-antitrypsin deficiency emphysema—a genetic disease that left her with the lungs of a sixty-year-old smoker when she was only thirty-two. Even without the sporefall, her condition had been deteriorating. She'd had a complex daily routine of inhalers and pills to try to keep the coughing fits and wheezing in check, and a tank of supplemental oxygen for her worst days.

Yolanda would have seen the beauty in the alien plants, just as Ellie did. Looking at Ellie was like looking into Yolanda's past, back to the early days of their relationship, before her illness sapped away her strength.

Was falling in love with a straight woman any better than carrying around a bundle of filthy blankets?

The clinic was an Eridani clinic, one of several that were part of the treaty that had been negotiated with the aliens. They were greeted by a man in a white coat when they entered, and left to wait in a small room with black plastic chairs and battered magazines from before the sporefall.

"Will Oskar meet us here?" Ellie asked. Much as she refused to accept the death of her baby, she continued to believe that Oskar would return.

"He's not here, El. We're going to see one of the Eridani," Marybeth explained. "They have a treatment that might help you."

An alien appeared in the doorway, wearing what looked like a down comforter tied like a toga. It studied them with beady black eyes, then beckoned to Ellie, recognizing that she was the one more in need of treatment.

"I'd like to come too." Marybeth said.

The Eridani doctor nodded its assent.

The treatment was painful to watch. The alien thinned itself into a gray fog, then reformed into images drawn from Ellie's mind—not mindreading, exactly. If Ellie said nothing, the alien could not hear her thoughts. It was only when Ellie spoke about her daughter that the memories came through. Then it was like watching a moving slideshow all in shades of gray:

Oskar holding Lexi in the hospital, the day she was born.

Ellie's struggles with breastfeeding when Lexi wouldn't latch.

Bottles of formula, carefully mixed and warmed at all hours of the night.

So many things that Marybeth had never seen, memories that haunted poor Ellie and made her break from reality. Then came the worst, the sporefall.

Ellie going out to find formula for Lexi, and coming back covered in fine orange dust.

Lexi's pitiful coughing and weak cries.

The days on end where she only slept upright, leaning on Ellie's chest.

Finally, the end, the moment when there were no more breaths, and

Oskar took Lexi away. Marybeth cried as the baby disappeared from the three-dimensional scene the Eridani recreated from the particles of its own body. She glanced at her friend, hopeful that the therapy had helped. Ellie was crying, but she continued talking. Her baby was dead, but Ellie wasn't finished.

More images appeared, of a Lexi that never was, in a world that no longer existed. Lexi toddling across the living room, Lexi putting on a ridiculously big backpack and going off to kindergarten, Lexi at the park feeding ducks. There were no ducks, and Lexi would never be six, but the Eridani doctor showed the impossible futures right along with the horrifying past.

Lexi's senior prom, her wedding, the birth of Ellie's first grandchild. The scenes skimmed through time and Marybeth could no longer watch, no longer listen to Ellie's words. She simply watched Ellie stare into the images that poured out, and held Ellie's hand as she cried. Since she had turned away from the doctor, it took her a moment to realize that the Eridani had resumed its default frogform. Ellie was no longer speaking, only sobbing softly.

She met Marybeth's eyes, and there was a depth to her gaze that was missing before.

"My Lexi," Ellie said. "My Lexi is gone."

After the treatment, Ellie didn't need a caretaker, but Marybeth had long since abandoned her apartment and they enjoyed each other's company. Ellie often wore the same grim smile that so often graced Yolanda's face when she was sick, and it tugged at Marybeth's heart. She tried to remind herself that Ellie was a different woman, a *straight* woman, but she could not help but hope that somehow, if enough time passed, things could be different.

Ellie made good progress in embracing reality. Together they dismantled Lexi's crib and set it out on the curb in front of the apartment. It wasn't long before a woman who looked like she might be expecting came and carried it away.

Oskar came back from L.A. Marybeth greeted him at the door, and had no choice but to let him in, for all that he abandoned Ellie when she needed him most.

"I'm so glad you're both okay," he said. Marybeth shrugged. He could say what he wanted, it wouldn't change what he had done. She only hoped that she wouldn't lose Ellie, now that he was back.

"Hi, Oskar," Ellie said. The sight of him brought her to tears, but Marybeth couldn't tell whether they were tears of joy or pain or anger.

"I'm so sorry," Oskar said. "I didn't want to leave you, but I couldn't stay. I was hurting too."

"I forgive you," Ellie said. "I know it must have been hard."

He smiled and went to embrace her, but she stepped back. "I forgive you, but we can't go back to how things were. I saw what might have been, if the Eridani had never come, and Lexi had lived, and it was beautiful. We could have had an amazing life. But those are impossible futures, and I have to let them go and come back to what is real."

"Is it another man?" Oskar asked, then realized that Marybeth was standing there. "Or another woman?"

Ellie shook her head. "There's no one else. Certainly not Marybeth, though she's a dear friend."

It was nothing that Marybeth did not already know. She had always known that Ellie was straight; there had never been any sign that she was interested. Ellie would never be Yolanda.

Marybeth grabbed her coat and made polite excuses. Ellie and Oskar had a lot to talk about, and Marybeth didn't want to hear it. She went outside and started walking, not caring where she went.

The wind picked up, and an orange cloud blew down from the Eridani foodtrees. The second sporefall had begun, a new cycle of alien life. According to the translators, the initial sporefall had been a different strain, modified to be more aggressive for terraforming, so that the Eridani would be sure to have foodplants when they arrived at their new home. This second sporefall should be as harmless to humans as ordinary pollen.

Marybeth sneezed at the orange air, but she refused to go back inside.

She would not hide from this new world.

A.M. Dellamonica's first novel, *Indigo Springs*, won the Sunburst Award for Canadian Literature of the Fantastic. Her fourth, *A Daughter of No Nation*, has won the 2016 Prix Aurora. She has published over forty short stories in *Tor.com, Strange Horizons, Lightspeed*, and numerous print magazines and anthologies. She was the co-editor of *Heiresses of Russ 2016.* She teaches writing at two universities and is pursuing an MFA in creative writing at a third.

Alyx is married to fellow Aurora winner Kelly Robson; the two made their outlaw wedding of 1989 legal in 2003, when the Canadian Supreme Court conferred equality on same-sex couples.

Time of the Snake

A.M. DELLAMONICA

My offworlder allies don't trust me.

Squid, we call them, though their home planet is named Kabuva. They're twelve feet in length from top to tip, see, with bullet-shaped caps that pull tight over a spaghetti of tentacles. When they bell out these caps, they look less like calamari and more like giant umbrellas. The Brits used to call them "brollies," as a matter of fact, back before England was annihilated.

All the players in this game have nicknames. The other human army wrangling for control of Earth calls itself the Friends of Liberation. Pompous, right? We've shortened it to Fiends.

As for us, the squid-sponsored Democratic Army, we're the Dems. "It's either Dems or us," the Fiends say. Bad pun; they end up taking over the world, they'll probably outlaw laughing.

It's just after dawn on a sunny July morning and I'm humping through East Los Angeles with a squad of ten heavily armed and overtired squid fry. Squid-squad, get it? Hence the song. *How many Fiends can a squid-squad squash?*

It doesn't help that squid armor is silly looking—essentially an upside-down mussel shell that hooks to their bullet-shaped caps. When the going gets hot, they yank in their tentacles and seal the carapace tight, firing weapons from inside the all-but-impregnable canister. Once sealed in, though, they can barely move.

The newest fry teedle along on the tips of their tentacles, shell all but shut. Vets tend to leave it half open, on the grounds that the carapace sensors don't work for shit.

We're here today because Intelligence has designated this neighborhood so thoroughly infiltrated by Fiends that there's no way to tell the bad guys from noncombatants. An evac order's gone out, and now we're one of the squads going block to block ensuring each house, shop, and low-rise is empty. Behind us floats a demolition ship, hanging just over the rooftops like a big blimpy starfish. Every time we give the all-clear on a building, the ship glides in and starts dusting the structure to nothingness.

Once this whole area is flattened, the squid will compile a few dozen skyscrapers for the humans who lived here. These buildings will be wired, so that any Fiendish conversations go straight to Kabuva Intelligence. The general idea is neighborhood Fiends will have to move elsewhere . . . those that do will be tagged as probable hostiles and rounded up for interrogation.

Bluto, on point, goes rigid and the squad snaps to alertness. He rips an apartment door off its hinges.

"Cantil?" The unit commander, Loot, caresses the back of my neck; this is his idea of a nudge.

"Anyone in there?" I call, first in American and then in Spanish. The amplifier built into my face mask makes my voice come out officious and strident, anything but reassuring. "It's okay. Come out and you won't be harmed."

The response is a pepper of bullets from antique machine guns, and the squad barges in happily. I wait in the hall. Loot's a good guy, as squid go; he doesn't expect me to pitch in when they're beating on probable civilians.

Screams, thumps, punches. The firing stops. I inhale a dense reek of gunpowder. Ah, the good old days.

Soon enough they're hauling out the troublemakers: a mother and son maybe, both netted like trout. The boy is unconscious; livid sucker marks show he's been throttled. The woman is shrieking.

Loot asks: "What is she saying?"

I tilt up my mask, taking the opportunity to poke a stick of gum into my mouth, and kneel beside her. "Ma'am? Nobody's going to hurt you. We need to evacuate—"

"We ain't leaving!" she yells.

I turn to Loot. "She doesn't want to leave her home. I doubt she's a Fiend."

"We'll see." A bloom of mildew-pink within his cap betrays irritation. "We are falling behind the other teams."

The others are probably doing cursory checks. Plenty of squid are fed up with being unable to tell Fiends from allies. If a few stubborn humans get dusted with their houses, they probably figure it's a bonus. Loot's more conscientious . . . and his family connections mean he can get away with it.

Now the woman bellows in sudden rage, glaring past my legs at a squid I've dubbed Gollum. He's lingering over the trussed-up son, poking a tentacle into the boy's mouth, getting a taste of him.

I vault over her, shoving the offworlder's carapace. "Cut it out."

Loot kills the fight before it can begin, bringing Gollum to heel. Then he orders Squiggly to haul the prisoners back to the evacuation team, effectively reducing our strength by ten percent. More, really—Squiggly's worth three of Gollum.

"Your son'll be okay," I tell the woman. "I can see he's breathing."

Her reply doesn't require translation; every squid in California knows "Fuck you, traitor," when they hear it. I let the words glide over my skin, light as the rush of sweat raining down my face.

"Building is empty," Loot reports. We pull out, and the floater drifts in to demolish the low-rise.

"The strip mall next?" I ask.

"Yes," he says, and we move out. "Tell me something, Cantil?"

"Sure."

"This city lies on a major fault line, does it not? Wouldn't it make sense to take the population inland?"

"You saying your fancy nano-built condos can't handle the occasional earthquake, Lieutenant?"

Gollum smacks me, accidentally-on-purpose, for dissing Kabuva architecture. Loot flicks him back into line.

"Of course they can. But if the land's unstable—"

"You can't just uproot all of L.A."

"You could build somewhere tectonically stable—house everyone in a tenth of the land area," throws in Bluto.

It's a fight not to sigh. You wouldn't believe how offworlders can go on and fucking on about urban sprawl. "People like to live near the beach."

That gets a ripple of amusement from the platoon. As far as these guys are concerned, humans can't swim. Take a squid to a dive shop, he'd probably laugh himself into a stroke.

Mmmm, interesting thought. I file it away, cracking out a fresh stick of gum before I close up my mask.

At the strip mall we check a liquor store and a magazine shop. Both are empty, eminently dustable. Troops poke into a third, bored. All routine until there's a flash and a series of whumps—modified car airbags, from the sound. Three squid race out of the shop. A black cloud follows: toner from photocopiers, almost certainly. The stuff gets everywhere, burns their skin, infiltrates their delicate gills.

"Why didn't you say there was a print shop?" Loot, furious, hitches two tentacles into my armpits and takes a full taste of me.

"I didn't know!" My pulse goes haywire as he hoists me to my tiptoes. "It says Office Furnishings."

He runs a tentacle around my forearm, checking blood pressure, suspicious. I wait, chewing my gum furiously and trying to get my breath under control. When they're calm they're decent lie detectors, but you never know when a squid might decide you're stringing him along, not because you are but just because he's upset.

Calm. Focus on concrete things. I watch the remainder of the squad heading back into the shop. They come out a minute later carrying what's left of Harpo, webbing up the dead fry in grim silence. My runaway heart slows as the wounded lift him gently and start limping to the rear.

"Down to half strength now," Kramer grumbles.

"Pull back." Loot still hasn't let go. "We'll dust the retail block."

Bluto asks: "We're moving on to the single-family dwellings?"

"Perhaps." He shakes me. "Are there signs, Cantil? What do they say?"

"People don't put signs on their houses. Numbers, names, sometimes, but—" I glance ahead. The other squads' demolition ships are fifteen to twenty blocks ahead of us.

"What about that?" He unfurls an anger-white tentacle, pointing. Definitely worked up now, not so keen to believe the copy shop thing's not my fault.

I swallow. "It's an old 'For Sale' sign—the owners tried to sell the house."

"And that?"

"Beware of dog," I translate. "Look, pick any house. Any street. I'll go in first."

"And lead us into a trap?"

"You've seen my file, Loot." I press my face mask against his armor, glaring into his cap. Sweat flows off me, soaking the sticky tentacles holding me up. "You know I hate everything Fiendish."

Gollum scoffs. "Easy to say."

"You want me to take point? I'll take point. Fuck, you can take my vest off. Pick the house, Loot, send me in."

No response. I let fury take over, popping catches on my protective vest. "I'll go naked, how's that?"

"Wait." Finally releasing me, Loot knots a couple tentacles in a ritual gesture of apology and presses them against my shoulder.

"Cantil in front works for me," Gollum snarls.

Ignoring him, Loot says: "Let's move on."

Five houses into the next block, we find a family chained to the pipes in their basement.

There are four of them: mama, papa, grandma, and a daughter who's maybe twelve. They're white, old Euro from the looks of them. This probably isn't the first time they've been displaced.

The old woman shrieks in a foreign tongue.

"What is she saying?"

"Not sure—I think they might be Greek."

"You don't speak Greek?" Bluto asks accusingly. As if, you know, I'm a moron.

"American, Spanish, Mandarin, French, and Kabuva."

This gets me the usual response. "But Greek's just another Euro dialect, isn't it?"

Sighing, I try the girl. "Come on, honey, you must've been born here. Speak American? ¿Habla Español?"

She does a burrow into Mama's leg.

"We'll cut them free," decides Loot. "Apply taser patches." Gollum gleefully presses the patches against the back of each human's neck.

"One wrong move, we zap you into a coma," he warns. I make gestures, trying to get the idea across via charades. Granny waves her evil-eye pendant oh so theatrically. The squid, forced to crowd together in the low-ceilinged basement, are nevertheless relaxing their guard. It's cooler out here than in the sun.

Only Loot remains sharp.

Toady shoves Papa away from the end of the pipe, brandishing a mini-saw. Meanwhile, Bluto unrolls the first body restraint, his tentacles roiling fluidly as he flaps the net out like a rug.

The mini-saw bites into the pipe, sending up a stream of sparks. The whole family starts wailing and shrieking; you'd think they were being murdered.

Loot turns to me in exasperation.

"Sorry," I say. "It's all Greek to me."

Just then Toady's saw breaks through the pipes. Gas belches out. Loot reacts quickly, jerking Bluto and Gollum away from the billow of white fog.

The gas is high-end stuff, no improvised booby trap this time. Toady and Kramer collapse like punctured balloons. Granny and the girl fall atop them as Loot hits the tasers.

Mama and Papa Fiend must have ditched the taser patches somehow. They're loose, armed and firing.

Quarters are close. Bodies, human and offworlder, are surging everywhere. I'm drawing a bead on Papa when four Fiends in sensor-clouding capes drop out of the T-bar ceiling. Gollum clamps his shell shut, a hair too late. The caped human drives a firespike into the carapace before it locks. A whoosh of heat—the smell of grilled seafood fills the air.

Nerve gas and flame spikes, I think. This little operation is well funded.

I'm aiming at a caped Fiend when I feel a flamespike against the nape of my neck.

"Guns down." It's Mama Fiend, speaking American.

"She's telling us to surrender," I say.

Loot and Bluto grope at each other, tentacles twining in the squid equivalent of nonverbal communication.

"Now," Mama says. "Or I burn your head off."

"Come on, they're going to waste me." I stare across the room at Loot. He's a good-enough guy, in his way, but we're not the same species. He'll clamp his armor and take his chances. It's what they do, every time.

But no. Flesh darkening with frustration and fear, they surrender.

"What now?" I ask, feeling oddly giddy. She thumps me upside the head, just a warning, no real damage. Loot, bless his weird offworlder heart, fluffs his cap protectively.

"It'll be all right," he tells me. "Tell her she has three minutes before our backup takes the roof off this dwelling."

Before I can translate, we hear the whump of surface-to-air packets. A high-pitched shriek and a thunderclap follow; a few seconds later, the ground shakes. Upstairs, windows shatter.

"That'd be your air support biting dirt," explains Mama Fiend unnecessarily.

Loot's strange, moist skin mottles in an unreadable roil of emotions. "Tell her we'll send missiles."

"He says they'll bomb you from orbit."

"They aren't going to dust their own people," Mama Fiend says. Her pals are gleefully using the squad's own restraints to bind the surviving squid onto wheeled palettes. One of them is setting up a webcam, pointing it at Loot's face as they wrench off his mussel shell and the hydrator that keeps his skin moist.

"It seems Intel was right for a change," he says calmly.

"Sir?"

"A new-hatched fry could see this neighborhood really is Fiendish. What do you suppose their plan is?"

I shrug. "We're alive, so Command can't bomb."

"We're bait," he agrees. "They'll draw the other squads back to rescue us."

"Into a trap." I nod. This street lies at the bottom of a gently rising wave of cookie-cutter houses. If Fiends are dug in all along the hill, the slaughter will be unthinkable. "It'll be kill at will."

Flashes of blue-white fury bloom across his translucent, helpless body, but what can he do? It's all been very neatly planned.

"It won't work," he says finally. "We'll lose a few squads here, but you'll all die."

You. A bit of a chill.

"Tell them," he says, and I realize he just wants me to pass the word along.

"What's he saying?" asks Mama Fiend.

I let out a long breath. "Basically? They rock, we suck, we're all gonna die."

Mama laughs. "Let him know we don't need a traitor on-hand to translate his bullshit."

Loot fluffs again—probably caught the word "traitor." "Tell them you're a prisoner, Cantil. Say we forced you to help us."

Poor guy. Impulsively, I knot my bony fingers into a sign of friendship, then press both hands into the flesh of his webbed-up tentacle, giving him a last taste of my damp palms and dirty fingers. "Thanks for everything, Loot."

"Come on." Mama Fiend drags me toward the door, leaving her minions to watch the hostages.

He bellows in fractured American as we disappear down the hall. "Don't hurt! Not hurt! Cantil!"

But Cantil is flaking away, all but gone. He was never more than a false skin, and it is good to finally shed him.

Mama Fiend, whose name is Debra Notting, hits a remote on an antique iPod. The basement fills with the sound of me shrieking in agony. We pass through an old bedroom, where a redheaded girl is pouring two pints of blood—mine, donated a couple months back—onto a stained mattress.

Deb points at my shoes. I slip them off, along with my sweat-stained socks, and kick them into a corner. There won't be a body, but there's a lot of my DNA in here now. Given the way Dust can obliterate a person from existence, you can never know for sure if someone's alive or dead.

"Spit your gum onto the floor?" the girl suggests.

"Can't—it's laced with drugs," I reply, undertone.

Beyond the bedroom is a squalid john whose tub is full of broken tile. A crude tunnel has been hacked into its wall; we head down and then east for two hundred feet, coming up in another basement. The battle wranglers are here, crouched in a sensor-proof tent, peering into portable datascreens and murmuring orders into headsets. The others are tracking the incoming squid squads that are heading back to rescue Loot and his fry.

"Demolition ships are clearing off," reports one old man.

"Told you, Deb," I say. "They're too pricey to risk when we've got surface-to-air."

"What happened with the ship we hit?" she asks.

"Four survivors, pinned down in the Hamiltons' backyard," a wrangler answers.

"The squid receiving video of their captured platoon?"

"Affirmative." He tilts a screen and we see Loot and the others, bound tightly onto the pallets, taser-patched and already drying out. I make myself smile. It's always important at this point to look solid, loyal.

The mental shift of gears is harder this time.

"One squad's almost back to Sycamore Drive," a wrangler reports. "Permission to fire?"

"No," Deb says. "Wait until they're closer. We're wasting five hundred troops here. To make it worth the blood, we need to draw in and kill as many as we can. I want lots of bait, well-placed bait."

"They'll deploy," I say. It took me months of careful maneuvering to get onto Loot's squad. Months of minty chewing gum that made me sweat like a pig and smell ever so faintly sweet. Months of shooting Fiends and telling dumb Dem jokes and worrying that Kabuva Intel would figure out I'd been behind the bloodbath last year in Atlanta. "The lieutenant's mother will throw half the West Coast Command in here if she thinks it'll get Loot back."

"You sez," Debra replies, but she's smiling.

"Been right so far, haven't I?"

"No," she says.

"No? I brought him right here, on time."

"Yeah." She taps the screen. "You also said he'd sell you out."

It's true. Loot came through, unlike all the other squid I've so carefully betrayed. My voice, when I answer, is steady: "Kid's an idealist, the real deal. Had to happen eventually, I guess."

"Almost a shame we're gonna kill him, huh?"

She's watching me carefully.

"Almost," I agree. If I do feel a pang, if the game is suddenly less fun than it used to be, how's she going to know? I'm a serpent. I lie.

"Okay." She smiles. "Time you scrambled. I'm sure you've got a hot date with a new identity."

"I'm going after the spaceport in Tulsa," I say. There's no harm in telling. Everyone in the room took slow poison as soon as my squad passed the copy shop. The squid will overrun this position eventually—there's no avoiding that. But they won't be interrogating anyone but grunts.

She draws back the cover on another tunnel. "This one leads to the sewers. There's a truck waiting."

"Thanks." Still barefoot, I ease onto the ladder.

To my surprise, Deb gives me a hug before I can go. "Thanks for setting the stage."

"Make a good show of it," I reply, squeezing back. For a second, the hard tissue of her muscles feel strange. Almost alien.

Letting me go, she salutes.

Then she turns back to her work and I start down the ladder, leaving my friends and enemies together, locked in the endless dance of mutual annihilation.

Judith Berman is a writer, anthropologist, and long-time aikido practitioner. Her fiction, which has been shortlisted for the Nebula and Sturgeon awards, has appeared in *Asimov's*, *Black Gate*, *Interzone*, *Realms of Fantasy*, *Lightspeed*, and the chapbook *Lord Stink and Other Stories*. Her novel *Bear Daughter* was a finalist for the Crawford Award, and her influential essay "Science Fiction Without the Future" received the Science Fiction Research Association's Pioneer Award. She has lived in Philadelphia, Dubai, and northern Idaho, and currently resides on a hilltop on Vancouver Island, BC, in sight of the ocean.

The Fear Gun

JUDITH BERMAN

1.

The dawn found Harvey Gundersen on the deck of his house, as it had nearly every morning since the eetee ship had crashed on Cortez Mountain. There he stood a nightly watch for the fear storms. On this last watch, though, the eetees had worn him out—an incursion at the Carlson's farm *and* the lone raider at his own well, where the black sky had rained pure terror—and fatigue had overcome him just as the sky began to lighten. When Susan shook him awake, he jerked upright in his lawn chair, heart a-gallop.

She gripped red plastic in her hand. For an instant, Harvey was sure that his worst suspicions had proved true, and his wife had learned how to bring on the bad weather. But even as he swung up his shotgun, finger on the trigger, he saw that what Susan pointed at him was not a weather-maker, not even an eetee gun about to blast him to splat, but the receiver of their landline phone. The cord trailed behind her.

Susan's gaze riveted on the shotgun. Harvey took a deep breath and lowered the barrel. Only then did Susan say, flatly, "Your brother's calling."

"What does *he* want?"

She shrugged, two shades too casual. Harvey knew Susan and Ben plotted about him in secret. His pulse still racing, he carried the phone into the house and slid the glass door closed so Susan could not overhear. He stood where he could keep his eye on both Susan and the eetee-infested mountains.

As he slurped last night's mormon tea from his thermos, liquid spilled onto the arm of his coat. Strange that his hands never shook while he held a gun.

"Hello, Ben," he said into the receiver.

"Nice work last night, Harve," said Ben. "Good spotting. You saved some lives there, buddy."

Although Harvey knew better than to trust his brother's sincerity, he could not repress a surge of pride. "I watch the weather, Ben. I can see it coming five miles off. And I look for the coyotes. They track the eetees. They keep a *watch* on them. The coyotes—"

"Sure, Harve," Ben said. "Sure. I've never doubted it. You're the best spotter we have."

"Well, thanks, Ben." Harvey seized the moment to describe how, two days ago, the coyotes had used telepathy to trick a van-load of eetees over the edge of the road to their deaths. As long as Ben was de facto dictator of Lewis County, for everyone's good Harvey had to *try* to warn him what was happening out there in the parched mountains.

But Ben cut him off before he'd even reached the part about the eetee heads. "Harvey, Harvey, you sound pretty stressed. What about you come in and let Dr. King give you something for your jitters? You tell me all the time how jittery you get, keeping watch day and night. I'll tell you honestly I'm worried, Harve. Come in before you mistake Susan for an eetee, or do something else we'll all regret."

What a lying fuck Ben was. Ben just wanted Dr. King to trank him stupid with Ativan. If Ben were truly worried, he wouldn't force Harvey and Susan to stay out here in this horribly vulnerable spot, where Harvey was exposed to bad weather two or three times a week. *That* was what made him so jittery. But it was always, "Sorry, Harve, you can't expect anyone in town to just *give* you food or gasoline or Clorox, or repair your phone line when the eetees cut it, not when supplies are dwindling by the day. We all have to contribute to the defense of Lewisville. Manning your observation post—the closest we have now to the ship—is the contribution we need from *you*."

What Ben really wanted was for the eetees to rid him of his trouble-maker brother. And on the day the weather finally killed Harvey, Ben would send a whole platoon of deputies out to De Soto Hill to take over Harvey's house and deck. Ben would equip *them* with the eetee weapons and tools he kept confiscating from Harvey. Can't hoard these, Harve, my men need them. *Lewisville* needs 'em.

Ben's invitation to visit Dr. King, though: Harvey couldn't afford to pass that up. Although the timing of the offer was a little too perfect . . .

"Ben, I'd rather have a couple of deputies to spell me than a pass for a doctor visit. What about it?"

"You know how short I am of manpower." Ben sighed. "I'll work on it, but in the meantime why don't you come on in?"

"Okay," Harvey said. "Okay, Ben, I'll stop by Dr. King's. If I can get Susan to stand watch for me. You know how she is these days. I don't think it's a good idea to leave the observation post that long, do you? How can you be *sure* eetees won't come in daytime?"

There was a moment of silence at the other end. Then Ben said goodbye and hung up.

Harvey swallowed a few more gulps of mormon tea, feeling the ephedrine buzz now, and returned outside for recon. First he checked the weather. No fear-clouds on the horizon that he could detect. But lingering jumpiness from last night's raid, and the scare Susan had given him on waking, might obscure an approaching front.

His video monitors showed him the view toward Lewisville, from the north and front side of the house. At this distance the town was a tiny life raft of houses, trees and grain elevators adrift on the rolling sea of golden wheat. The deck itself gave him a 270-degree view west, south, and east: over the highway and the sweep of fields below De Soto Hill, and of course toward the pine-forested mountains and that immense wreck.

Harvey cast around for the Nikons, only to discover that Susan had usurped his most powerful binoculars and was gazing through them toward the mountains. Anger stirring in him, he picked up the little Minoltas. Through *them*, the world looked quiet enough. The only movement was a hawk floating across the immaculate blue sky. But Harvey never trusted the quiet. The eetees might avoid the desiccating heat of daytime, but they were always stirring around up there. Plotting the next raid. And the coyotes—

If only he could spy into those mountains as easily as the eetees' fear-storms roared into his own head.

The nape of Harvey's neck began to twitch. "Do you *see* something?" he demanded. "Are the coyotes—"

"I'm looking for Fred," Susan said coldly, without lowering the binoculars.

"Fred is gone." Now the anger boiled in Harvey's gut. "You should be watching for eetees, not pining after your lost dog."

"*Fuck* your eetees! Fred is out there somewhere. He wouldn't leave us and never come back!"

Her voice had turned flat and uncompromising, and Harvey knew one of her rages was coming on. But he could not rein in his own fury.

"If you care so much," he said, "why did you let him loose?"

Susan finally turned to stare at Harvey. She was breathing hard. "*I* didn't let Fred out."

"Oh, so the *coyotes* unbuckled his collar?"

Deep red suffused Susan's face. "Fuck you," she screamed, "and fuck your coyotes!" She slammed the binoculars onto the deck, she reached toward the rifle—

Harvey grabbed his shotgun and aimed. How *stupid* to leave his rifle propped against the railing, out of reach—

Susan threw the rifle onto the deck, and then the tray holding the remains of his midnight snack; she kicked over his lawn chair and the tripod for his rifle, and upended the box of shotgun cartridges he'd been packing with rock salt. "Shoot me, Harvey!" she screamed. "*Shoot me!* I *know* you want to!"

Harvey snatched up his rifle but did not shoot. At last Susan stopped her rampage. She stared with fierce hatred through her tangled, greasy hair, panting. "I didn't let Fred out, you moron. You did." Then she flung herself in her own lawn chair and picked up a tattered and yellowing issue of last summer's *Lewisville Tribune*.

The shakes took Harvey. While he waited for the waves of fever cold to recede, he gritted his teeth and said to her, "I'm going to do my rounds now. Just keep an eye out, okay, Susan? That's all I ask? Watch for *eetees*, who want to kill us and steal our water, and not for your *dead dog*?"

When she did not answer, he heaved open the glass door again and stalked into the house. Susan might as well be using a weather-maker, the way she kept terrifying him. Harvey was jumpy enough today. He just had been lucky that last night's raider had probably stolen its weather-maker from a higher-ranking eetee and wasn't skilled in its use. And by now Harvey had learned to keep his distance and rely on his rifle and sniper's night-scope. So the lightning strike of blind terror had fallen short. Harvey had caught only the peripheral shockwave—although that that had been horrible enough.

Weather-maker was what Harvey called the weapon. Other people called it a fear gun. Dr. King and Joe Hansen, putting their heads together, had suggested that the gun produced (as quoted in a bulletin distributed by the sheriff's office) "wireless stimulation of the amygdala, mimicking the neurochemical signature of paralytic terror." But no one had yet been able to figure out the insides of those whorled red pendants, and no one could do with them what the eetees did, not even Harvey, who was so hypersensitive from repeated exposure that the weapon affected him even when he wasn't its target. Even when they weren't being used. (When Dr. King told him that human researchers had for years been able to produce a similar if weaker effect with a simple electrode, Harvey had, next time he was alone, checked his scalp for unfamiliar scar tissue. But if Susan or Ben had had such an electrode implanted, they had also concealed the traces well.)

Harvey unbolted the connecting door that led from the kitchen into the garage. As angry as Susan's abdication of responsibility made him, this was the opportunity he needed. She would read and re-read her *Tribune* for hours, trying to pretend that the entire last year hadn't happened.

In the garage he quickly donned his rubber gloves and plastic raincoat. He raised the lid of the big chest freezer, long emptied of anything edible, and heaved out the large tarpaulin-wrapped bundle, humping it into the pickup bed. The raider's corpse hadn't frozen yet; Harvey just hoped it had chilled sufficiently to last until he reached Dr. King.

Then he stripped off his protective gear and gave it a swift rinse with Clorox in the utility sink. On the cement floor beside the sink, still at the end of its chain, lay Fred's unbuckled collar of blue nylon webbing—a testament to Susan's lies.

Harvey fetched last night's newly scavenged eetee gun from the wheel well of his pickup, where he hoped this time to keep it hidden from Susan and Ben. Next, after checking the yard through the front door peephole, he bore the ladder outside to begin his daily inspection of the video cameras, the locks and chains, the plywood boarding up their windows, the eetee cell that powered the house (one of the few perks Ben allowed them).

It hurt Harvey to think about Fred, happy Fred, the only one of them unchanged since the days before the eetees had come to Earth. When he and Susan had been happy, too, in their dream house with the panoramic view atop De Soto Hill. Fred was just one dumb, happy golden retriever with no notion of the dangers out there in the mountains. More likely the coyotes had gotten Fred than the eetees—not that it made any difference.

Sweating, his scalp twitching, Harvey made his way downhill through dry grass and buzzing grasshoppers. He righted the black power cell (how he'd had to argue with Ben to keep two), slipped on a spare adapter to re-connect the cell to his well pump, and refilled the salt-loaded booby traps the raider had sprung. All the while he searched the trampled ground for the raider's missing weather-maker, but still without success.

Had the coyotes taken it? There couldn't have been bad weather without a weather-maker . . .

Finally he was climbing the hill again, eager to return to his deck. On his deck he was king—at least, on the deck he had a chance of seeing death before it peered at *him* with its yellow, slime-covered eyeball.

He had nearly reached the house when a new sound stopped him in his tracks. A shape thrashed through the tall thistles along the driveway. Adrenaline and ephedrine together surged in Harvey's veins, making his hands tremble like grass in the breeze.

But even as he pulled the eetee gun from his waistband and clutched at his rifle with his other hand, he saw that what rustled onto the driveway was not an eetee. It was not even a demented coyote come to grin mockingly at him and then zigzag wildly away into the fields, tongue flapping, while Harvey tried in vain to ventilate its diseased hide.

"Fred!" Harvey whispered in horror. Fred dropped what he was carrying and wagged his tail.

Dust, burrs, and thistledown clung to Fred's copper-colored rump, and he smelled like rotten raw chicken. As he approached Harvey, his tail-wagging increased in frequency and amplitude until his entire hind end swung rapidly from side to side. Fred tried to nose Harvey's hand, but Harvey shoved him away with the point of the rifle.

The swellings and bare patches in the fur were unmistakable. The biggest swelling rose at the base of Fred's skull.

Just like the coyotes.

Eetee cancer, Harvey called it. Ben said that was just more of Harvey's paranoia. No other spotters had seen it.

But *their* posts—the ones still manned, anyway—lay miles further from the shipwreck.

Harvey had only one choice. It was pure self-defense.

Fred lay down and smacked his tail on the ground. His eyes pleaded as if he knew what Harvey intended. But Harvey remembered the coyotes and their gleeful eetee hunts, and he hardened his thoughts as if pummeled by stormy weather. He slipped off the safety. His finger tightened on the trigger—

Footsteps rasped behind him. He spun and found himself staring into the short, ugly red bore of another eetee gun.

"Don't you *dare* shoot Fred, you fuck," Susan hissed.

Oh, Harvey, stupid, *stupid*—the video monitors on the deck—Ben must have given her a gun, *knowing* she would someday use it—

They stood there aiming at each other. Harvey could see in her face that this time she really would do it. She was going to splatter him over Fred, and Ben would get his way at last.

The blazing July sun heated his skull like a roast in an oven. Susan's gun did not waver. Harvey willed himself to breathe.

Fred thwacked his tail another couple of times, then pawed playfully at Harvey's foot. A lump pushed up suddenly in Harvey's throat and he had to blink several times to clear his vision. In a thick voice he said, "Look at Fred, Susan! He's sick! You don't want *us* to catch it, do you? You don't want *us* to get all freaky like the coyotes, do you?"

"You," Susan said, "already have."

Bleak inspiration came to Harvey. He forced himself to drop his rifle and eetee gun, slip the shotgun from his shoulder to the ground, raise his hands. "I could take Fred to Dr. King. Maybe she would look at him."

"She's not a vet and he's not sick."

"Yes, he is! Susan, look at those tumors!"

Her gaze did flick toward Fred, growing the slightest bit uncertain. "Abscesses."

"Then he needs to have them cleaned. At least."

Something broke in Susan then. Her lip trembled. She blinked. She looked at Fred. Fred crawled toward her and wagged his tail some more. Tears began to roll down Susan's cheeks. Suddenly, unexpectedly, a wave of sympathy rushed through Harvey. He had loved Fred, too.

"What do we have," Susan said in despair, "what do we have that *she* would take in trade?"

And there it was: the first acknowledgement in months that their world had changed forever. Harvey's hands were shaking again, but he managed to gesture at the garage. Susan looked at him askance, then, gun still trained on Harvey, backed toward it. Harvey followed, though he hated leaving his guns behind. Fred lay beside them, thumping his tail.

When Susan pulled back the tarpaulin in his pickup bed, she gasped and jerked her hand back as if bitten. "Harvey, Ben will *kill* you! And me, too, you asshole!" Which was probably not just a figure of speech.

Susan said, wiping at her tears with a filthy hand, "Promise me, *promise me*, Harvey, that you aren't going to hurt Fred. That you won't let *her* hurt him."

"I won't," Harvey lied, trying again to swallow the lump in his throat. "Promise *me* that while I'm gone, you'll keep watch?"

Susan said nothing, but this time Harvey felt as if she might actually do it. Donning his raincoat and gloves and now rubber waders as well, Harvey took Fred's collar out into the yard to buckle it around the dog's neck. As he urged Fred into the back of the pickup and chained him there, Fred tried to lick him in the face. Up close, the stench of carrion was enough to make Harvey gag.

Two presents for Dr. King, just sitting in the back of his pickup for anyone to discover. What risks he was taking today! Harvey had survived this long by trusting his fears and keeping a close eye on the weather. By being infinitely careful. Today he was throwing all caution to the winds.

But he couldn't afford to nod off the way he had this morning. He needed Dr. King's little pills. And he couldn't let Susan keep Fred *here.*

Harvey wondered whether on his return he should just shoot Susan before she learned he'd had Fred put down. She *would* try to kill him again when she found out.

He didn't want to shoot her.

Maybe, he thought, looking at the happily panting Fred, just maybe he would turn out to be wrong about Fred's tumors. Maybe Dr. King would tell him they weren't contagious. The coyotes' fur had grown back, after all, and most of the swellings had vanished.

Or maybe that notion was just Fred trying, the way the coyotes did, to control Harvey's thoughts.

One last task before departing: Harvey picked up the thing Fred had brought home. He dropped it in his Weber. Up close, the lump of rotting eetee flesh looked like raw hamburger, had the consistency of custard, and smelled like the bottom of a Dumpster. Golden retrievers had such delicate mouths; Fred hadn't left so much as a tooth mark in it.

Sweltering in his raincoat and waders, Harvey poured on the gasoline provided by the sheriff's office. As he dropped in the match, and flames sheeted up from the charcoal bed, Fred began to bark in agitation. So he did not hear Susan's shouts until she rushed up to him waving the Nikons. "Look, Harvey! Look!"

He dropped the lid on the grill to char Fred's little present to a cinder. Then he pulled off his befouled rubber gloves, took the binocs, and peered in the direction she pointed.

The highway had been dust-blown and empty for a year. Now, vehicles climbed over a rise three miles away, popping into view one after the other like an endless chain of ants: trucks, fuel tankers, humvees, and Bradleys carrying helmeted men and women. The convoy ground steadily along, heading toward Lewisville.

Susan said, almost sobbing, "It's the Army. Oh, God, Harvey, they've come to save us at last."

"Save us?" Harvey said. "*What* Army?"

2.

Colonel Jason Fikes could see right away that something was fishy about the town. Since the liberation of Earth he had been traveling what was left of America—the devastated cities, the suburban wastelands dotted with grim encampments of refugees, the endless reaches of fallow farmland. The trip from Spokane, chasing the rumor of another downed ship, had been no different. They had passed mile after mile of fields grown up into weeds. At scattered houses and small towns, women stooped in gardens and men, shotguns in hand, sullenly eyed the convoy. Or sometimes they ran after the convoy, begging for gasoline, for medicine, for food, for rescue.

The locals' plight ought to have grown more desperate the closer he got to the mountains and the starship. Fikes had seen the classified reports from Yosemite: starving refugees reduced to eating eetees, then each other.

But when the convoy came over a rise and Lewisville itself came into view, everything changed. Weeds gave way to neat furrows of golden wheat. Cattle grazed along the streamside meadows. And in the town itself, healthy children clustered in front of well-kept houses, staring at the convoy until adults rushed to herd them inside. Yes, most of the lawns had been dug into gardens, and only a handful of vehicles seemed to be working, and the grass in front of the county courthouse was dry and yellow now; but it had been *mowed*.

You could suppose they had carefully rationed supplies since the war, that they had their own hydro dam or windmill farm. Or you could glance eastward to that mile-long wreck atop the ridge, and you could draw another conclusion.

"They've been scavenging," said young Lieutenant Briggs beside him, eager as a preacher pouncing upon evidence of fornication. "We'll have to search house-to-house."

Briggs had not seen the Yosemite reports and did not yet know the enormity of their orders. Fikes nodded wearily. "They'll try to hide as much as they can."

During the approach to Lewisville he had spotted a feral cat crouched in the roadside weeds, a pair of crows pecking at a dead owl. But no eetees had showed themselves. On this brilliant summer morning, the distant shipwreck looked no more menacing than a junked car. In Fikes's experience, though, the eetees didn't surrender and they didn't admit defeat. If even a single one had survived, sooner or later it would test his soldiers. Still, they would have to wait on more urgent tasks.

Fikes gave the order to halt in front of the courthouse. There waited a knot of local men bedecked with an arsenal of rifles, shotguns, and semi-automatic small arms. Neatly dressed and clean-shaven, they looked like Norman Rockwell banditos who'd just staged their own revolution.

Or rather, Norman Rockwell meets the Sci-Fi Channel: half of them bore red splatterguns. Eetee weapons. That would make Briggs happy. A weight descended onto Fikes's shoulders.

As Fikes climbed out of his humvee, one of the locals stepped forward. This was a lean man in a sheriff's khaki uniform and badge, with cowboy boots, a straw cowboy hat, and mirror shades to complete the ensemble. The only weapon the sheriff carried in plain view was a holstered .45.

"Howdy, folks," he drawled. "Welcome to Lewisville. I'm Ben Gundersen, Lewis County sheriff."

Fikes held out his hand. "Colonel Fikes," he said. "U.S. Army."

Sheriff Gundersen put out his own hand, and the two of them shook. "What brings you fellows to Lewisville?"

Under the circumstances, the question was an odd one. Fikes said, "Your community is in proximity to a downed enemy vessel, Mr. Gundersen. Assessing that threat and mounting an appropriate response is our immediate priority. But our long-term mission is to restore services and connect you to the outside world again."

"No offense," said the sheriff, "but with all the satellites gone, we haven't heard much news since last summer. Who's the U.S. Army taking orders from these days?"

"The President has installed a Provisional Congress until new elections can be held," Fikes said. "Meanwhile, the Army is authorized under the Public Safety Act to take charge here."

"You're talking about the U.S. President. The U.S. Congress."

"That's right," said Fikes.

One of the other banditos called out, smirking, "Didn't they nuke Washington? I thought that was one good thing come out of all this."

"Yes," Fikes said. "Washington was destroyed. Now, may I ask if you have spotted survivors from the wreck? Has your town come under attack?"

"Survivors?" Gundersen tipped his hat back and scratched his forehead. "Well, now. We shot us a few last winter. They come down near town and found we weren't easy pickings. If there're any of 'em left, they pretty much leave us alone. They'd be camped out in the mountains, I guess."

"Have you seen enemy aircraft at all? Any other vehicles?"

"I guess most of their fighters crashed with the ship," Gundersen said. "Lost their guidance systems or something. Haven't seen any recently, anyway."

"But you think they still have some?"

The sheriff shrugged, inscrutable behind mirror shades. "Could be."

Since his childhood in Baltimore, Fikes had learned there were large swaths of the U.S. where well-scrubbed white people said "gosh," "shucks," and "you bet" without irony. But this sheriff wasn't just a folksy good ol' boy.

He was plain bullshitting.

Fikes had already noted that Gundersen hadn't addressed him as "sir" or "colonel," and that the pole on the courthouse lawn bore no flag.

Reluctant to take the inevitable next step, Fikes bent to read the plaque on a nearby statue of buckskin-clad men. *Explorers Meriwether Lewis and William Clark, openers of the American West, passed through Lewis County on October 3, 1806.*

If the sheriff and his gang had been just your *posse comitatus* militia types hoping to secede from the federal government in its time of weakness, Fikes's task would have been simple. Sooner or later he'd have won over the townsfolk with liberal bribes of booze, chocolate, condoms, antibiotics, disposable diapers, toilet paper. The sheriff he would have defanged first of all; in Fikes's experience, those with a taste for power were easily seduced by another helping of the same.

But the solution to the problem this town presented would not be so easy to accomplish.

Not that Fikes's orders weren't clear or that he shrank from enforcing them. From what he had read in the Yosemite reports, from the panic still electrifying headquarters in Colorado, the rule he must now impose could not be too draconian. It was up to him, he had been told, to ensure that nothing like the Yosemite massacres ever became necessary again.

Fikes knew, however, that he could end up as lost in a repeat of Yosemite as that hapless colonel had been. In the slaughter at Upper Pines, the Yosemite rebels had demonstrated unequivocally that human beings could wield that most dreaded of eetee weapons, the handarm of the eetee elite, the *fearmonger*. The Army, on the other hand, had never learned how to operate the weapon—had no defense against it. The rebels who had understood the weapon had all been killed. Army scientists, such as they were now, had offered only useless speculation: perhaps the ordinary silent communication of eetees was a form of telepathy; perhaps eetees operated their terrible weapon, too, with some kind of thought wave.

No one understood how eetees used the guns. How could *he* anticipate by what means human beings would acquire the skill?

But he had to anticipate it. He had to prevent it. If possible, he had to acquire the power for the Army.

At least his first items of business were clear: separating the townspeople from their eetee toys, disrupting their lines of communication, bringing them firmly under Army control.

Fikes straightened. "Mr. Gundersen, may I ask how you dispose of enemy remains?"

He thought he had pegged Gundersen, but the pride that lit up the sheriff's face surprised him. "We're real strict about that, Colonel. I'll show you our health ordinances. Can't risk some kind of strange disease, I tell people. We built a special crematorium to incinerate the bodies. We use bleach to clean up anything we take from them." He nodded toward a splattergun in the waistband of one of his deputies. "We could use more Clorox, now that you mention it."

Fikes nodded. "That's all very well, Mr. Gundersen, but our scientists can't yet say what potential disease vectors would look like, how they might spread, or how they could be destroyed. I must stress that anyone in your town who's had contact with the enemy, living or dead, is required to report to us. Any items of wreckage that people have picked up *must* be turned over. That includes your weapons, I regret to say. The Army will assume the burden of protecting the town from this point onward. I have strict orders on this matter. And I do have the authority to search every house. It's a vital matter of public health."

The sheriff opened his mouth to reply. Before he could speak, Fikes said, "After you hand over your splatterguns, I believe I'd like to start by taking a look at those pickup trucks over there. Is it possible you're still running them on gasoline?"

3.

The Army had kept Reggie Forrester awake all the first night with the roar of tanks and trucks and the stink of diesel exhaust, which over the last year had become unfamiliar and offensive. In the morning, he dragged himself two blocks over to the highway and discovered that, just as he feared, the soldiers had moved into his warehouses. Armed sentries already surrounded them. "Move along, sir," the sentries had said. Chasing him—the mayor!—off his own property. Probably Ben had suggested the location, stone bastard that he was.

Reggie headed out to learn what else was befalling his town. His dismay only compounded. Searches and detentions had started before breakfast. "Quarantine," the Army called it, but they did not name the disease they feared.

From Bob Fisher's distraught wife, Reggie learned that soldiers had "quarantined" Bob, stolid city engineer, when he'd showed up for work. And they had abruptly confiscated the networked eetee power cells that since last winter had supplied the town with electricity and pumped its artesian wells. Municipal power shut off in mid-morning, and tap water would cease flowing once the water tower emptied.

They hadn't consulted Reggie or anyone else at City Hall, or warned the townspeople what was coming.

From Estelle Gordon, administrative secretary at the community college, Reggie heard that the Army was cleaning out Joe Hansen's lab. Everyone brought their salvage to Joe, and it sat around while he and his students figured out what it was supposed to do. That morning the Army confiscated all of it, and all of Joe's notes, and they hauled away Joe, too. But so far as Estelle had been able to determine, they hadn't taken Joe to the so-called "quarantine facility" in the junior high school. No one knew where Joe was now.

Joe's students protested his detention. Angry townspeople joined them, demanding restoration of water and power. Shockingly, the Army tear-gassed them and hauled the lot off to quarantine.

By afternoon, when Reggie went to lodge an official protest with Colonel Fikes, unease had rooted deep in his belly. He told himself, though, that if he didn't try *something*, he would only prove his irrelevance. Ben might be the Big Man now, savior of Lewisville, but Reggie Forrester wasn't going to allow anyone to outdo him when it came to looking after the *everyday* needs of Lewisville's citizens.

When Reggie pulled up in front of the courthouse, the soldiers first evicted him from his Ford Excursion, then confiscated it. "Contamination," they said, when they found the black disk where the engine block had been. They refused to tell him what kind, but by now Reggie was certain that the disease issue was entirely fiction. No one in Lewisville had contracted an inexplicable illness, had they? Moreover, that morning, through the fence surrounding his warehouses, Reggie had spotted soldiers *installing* eetee power cells in their humvees. He now realized these must have been the ones confiscated from the town.

At least the soldiers did not march Reggie away at gunpoint. In fact, when he indignantly identified himself as Lewisville's mayor, they led him inside to their colonel. Reggie enjoyed a moment's relief at this belated acknowledgement of his importance. The fact that the colonel now occupied Ben's office also tickled him. Ben would not like that *at all.*

But then the interview, if that was the word for it, started. The colonel threatened Reggie with the ridiculous quarantine, stressing its indefinite nature. He then cited Reggie's warehouses, filled with wrecked fighters and heavy weaponry that had not yet been stripped or adapted to human use. Sweating, Reggie denied having anything to do with the contents of his warehouses. He had never touched any of it. He just rented space to people. But the colonel showed no interest in his protests.

Then Fikes suggested that detention was not inevitable. He offered Reggie an incentive for cooperation, an unspecified place in the new administration. The sort of position, Colonel Fikes said, that Reggie deserved.

Flattering. But Reggie was not naïve. The world was piss or be pissed on, and right now Reggie Forrester, sad to say, was not in a position to piss on anyone. His status had been on a dizzying downward slide since the start of the war, and now he would have to wiggle hard to avoid the hot yellow stream that gravity was pulling his way. To escape it, he'd have to make himself not just useful but *indispensable* to the new regime.

Which was fraught with its own dangers. He wondered if the colonel had interviewed Ben yet, and what incentives he might have offered Ben.

That evening, Reggie slipped through backyards to Paula's house. He was shocked to see how few people had evaded the Army's tightening net. Those who'd made it to the meeting perched on Paula's sofas and chairs and shared their news. The Army had rounded up the network of spotters guarding Lewisville, including Ben's own brother, and replaced them with their own people. The colonel had posted new rules at the county courthouse. Electricity would be down until the town was reconnected to the national grid. Drinking water would be distributed between 8 and 11 a.m. at the corner of Main and Third, no other uses of water except as authorized for agricultural production. A blanket curfew would be enforced between 9 p.m. and 7 a.m.; no civilian was allowed on the streets during those hours for any reason at all. No assembly of more than eight civilians except under Army auspices. Reggie counted: including himself, this meeting numbered nine.

"The right to assembly," Jim Hanover fumed, "is guaranteed by the U.S. Constitution!" Jim had been a lawyer.

Flora Bucholter was distraught. "Just how long will it take to hook us up to the grid? How do they think they'll be able to protect the lines? What's the *point* of taking away our electricity?"

"That salvage doesn't *belong* to the Army," said Dave Sutton, whom Ben often used to float ideas. "It belongs to the people who risked their lives bringing it back—who've fought to keep the town safe!"

That predictably set off the ever-volatile Otis Redinger. "Dave's right! We've worked hard just to survive! We've been listening to other folks on the shortwave, we know what it's like in the rest of the country. It's totally lawless. Now these people show up and say, 'We're from the government and we're here to help you—'" (that drew a chuckle) "—but they've brought their lawlessness with them. All they've done is destroy or steal everything we've fought to preserve. This is an illegal military occupation by an illegal government. We've managed to protect our community from *aliens*. Now we have to protect it from dangerous *human beings* as well!"

Several people applauded this impassioned speech, and Otis's face grew red from embarrassment. But then Todd Myklebust, always a wiseass, said, "Ah, sedition. Is that right enshrined in the Constitution, too?"

For a moment the meeting lapsed into nervous silence. Otis and Todd had spoken out loud what the others had only come up to the edge of saying. Then everyone started talking at once.

Up to this point in the discussion Ben had stayed silent. That was his style: remain above the fray, the calm militia commander. Now he put down the footrest of Paula's plush blue recliner and rocked into an upright position. The uproar stopped as suddenly as it had begun. Everyone turned to look at him.

"George," Ben said, "you've been doing some reconnaissance. Why don't you tell us what you've learned?"

Although no one would guess it to look at him, unshaven, shambling George Brainerd had once been an Army Ranger. His skills had immeasurably aided both Lewisville and Ben's wartime ascent to the top of the town's chicken-coop ladder. He was not, however, one of Ben's acolytes. (Although George had not gotten up to offer that easy chair to the *mayor*, either! Reggie was squeezed between Dave and Flora on the sectional sofa.)

Now Ben's question made George look unhappy. "Their communications equipment isn't much better than ours. I didn't see anything fancier than off-the-shelf shortwave. No cell phones and they haven't set up any dishes, so my guess is that the military hasn't launched new satellites yet. No indication of aircraft, not even a recon balloon. They may patch the lines out of Lewisville for landline service, but that'll take time."

"Until then," Ben said, "we take away their radios and they're completely isolated."

"Sure," said George, looking unhappier. "If we take away *all* of them."

"Then we eliminate them," Otis said.

"You mean *kill* them?" Flora said. "Otis, you are a bloodthirsty son-of-a-bitch."

Otis shifted uncomfortably. "Well, probably they'd surrender long before that."

"What do we do with them when they do surrender?" George asked. "Or if they don't? What will the *Army* do when an entire battalion disappears after going to look for a downed eetee ship?"

"We could get the enemy to do the job for us," said Otis. "We could send them into a trap. Then no one would know we were involved."

"So," George said, "you want to set up your fellow human beings so aliens can kill them for you?"

Silence fell on the room. Apparently even Otis felt that sounded nasty.

Then George said, "What do you think, Mr. Mayor?"

That was, Reggie knew, an appeal for his help. Reggie was flattered. And usually persuading people to a course of action was something he liked to do, something he was good at. But tonight the power of his words was far less important than their real-world consequences. When one boat was going to sink, and you didn't know whether it would be Ben's or the Army's, you needed to make very certain you had a place on both boats.

He sighed audibly and rubbed his forehead. "I agree with George that you have to think about *the long term*. Unless we have weapons that provide a *decisive* advantage over the Army—that would allow us to keep the Army and everyone else out of Lewisville for the foreseeable future—all an attempt at secession will accomplish is make our situation worse."

So far, so good. No one could accuse him either of pushing for Otis's little revolt, or of siding with the evil invading Army. People were turning from Ben to Reggie. Ben looked sour but not yet angry.

"You want to hand them a petition?" Jim said. "We, the undersigned, protest your wholesale abuses of civil rights, the U.S. Constitution, and common decency?"

"Oh, sure," Reggie said. "As a first step. But we need something that will make it worthwhile for them to *negotiate*—in earnest—instead of rounding us all up. *I've* been wondering, why is the Army spending all its resources to gather up not just every last piece of eetee salvage, but nearly *every person* who's worked with it? Does anyone here believe this disease nonsense? I think instead they're *looking* for something, but they don't yet know *what it is.*"

George had leaned forward and was listening intently. Flora said, "And you think that if we could figure out what that thing was, if we could find it first, it would give us an advantage in negotiations?"

"Maybe they're searching for a key that activates the fear guns," said Dave.

Jim objected, "We've been looking for it for a year and turned up squat. How do you propose we find it *now?*"

His ploy was at least half working, Reggie thought. They were listening. They were beginning to think twice. Reggie the voice of reason, Reggie the idea man. When he saw George opening his mouth to add to the discussion, he even began to hope they two could convince the others to forego the uprising altogether.

But then George abruptly shut his mouth. And Otis burst out, "Reggie's right! We *force* them to negotiate! We do it right away, while we still have *some* weapons. If we get back what they've taken, they're at a disadvantage. Look: a few hundred of them, fifteen thousand of us. Ben, they can't keep control if we don't let them—"

"No, no," Reggie said, "that isn't what I was saying—" But like Otis, Jim, Dave, Todd and even Flora had turned back toward Ben. They looked to *Ben* to decide the fate of Lewisville.

Oh, how that burned Reggie.

And now Ben spoke. "I've heard some good points. We can't throw away the lives of our men. We do have to think about the long term. But we can't let things go on the way they're heading. We take our weapons back, we force new terms on the Army, but no big battles. That's not a winning proposition."

So that was the decision. They fell to planning how they were going to break into Reggie's warehouses. Reggie had a physical sensation of sliding uncontrollably down the hen house ladder toward the guano at the bottom. And here he had thought the Army's arrival might make Ben a little circumspect.

To ensure his own survival, he had to get rid of Ben one way or the other. But how to do so safely? He couldn't simply go to Colonel Fikes and report tonight's meeting. For one thing, Reggie had made no secret of his afternoon visit to the colonel. Ben would be keeping a close eye on Reggie now.

It was amusing to imagine Ben sweating at hard labor in "indefinite quarantine," somewhere deep in a government reservation with nothing but sagebrush and jackrabbits for a hundred miles in every direction. It was considerably less amusing to contemplate what Ben might do to avoid such a fate. A bullet, say, speeding into Reggie's back from out of the shadows. Such things had happened in the last year.

At last Ben concluded the meeting by saying, "Now, folks, we've got to be off the streets before curfew. Be careful going home."

Reggie left with George through the back door. Jim Hanover followed them. They skulked along the shadows between Paula's raspberry patch and the Fortescues' pole beans. Far away, a coyote yipped into the chill of evening.

"Good try," George said to Reggie in a low voice.

Wondering why George had suddenly dropped his opposition to the ridiculous plan, Reggie glanced back at him. That was why, framed in Paula's candlelit kitchen window, he saw Ben and Otis talking. Otis appeared to be very excited. So Ben had a second, *secret* plan, one catering to Otis' enthusiasms.

"It wasn't good enough," said Reggie.

George went his own way, but Jim followed Reggie silently home, saying goodbye only at Reggie's front door. Jim's own darkened house stood across the street. Jim would now, Reggie thought, keep watch through his windows. Another of Ben's deputies was no doubt already guarding Reggie's back door.

4.

Annoyed, but not wanting to argue in the hearing of the security guard, Anna King buzzed George Brainerd into the morgue corridor. George was discreet and sympathetic to her work. But she preferred no witnesses, and no interruptions.

She waited to finish the last careful slice exposing the *corpus minutalis*—so she had named the organ, in honor of its resemblance to hamburger—before she buzzed George through the door of the autopsy room as well.

"Pee-yoo!" said George, and then, shambling closer to peer over her shoulder, "Holy shit, doc, that's fresh kill."

The sight of him kindled anticipatory warmth on Anna's skin. Pavlovian conditioning. She firmly ignored it and turned away to pick up her digital camera. "Yes," she said, snapping photographs of the *minutalis*, "and I want to keep working on it while it still *is* fresh. You know how fast they deteriorate. Now, what's so important that it can't wait until morning? Haven't our Army friends instituted a curfew, and doesn't it start in about five minutes?"

"I was kinda hoping I could stay here." He grinned at her.

"You'll be cold."

"Not my idea of romance, either," said George. "The drawers are a bit small for two people."

He almost made her smile. At the same time—it must be fatigue that rendered her so vulnerable—his words caused her throat to constrict. Did he really think their trysts in empty hospital rooms, never the same one twice, deserved the term *romance*?

The glass partition on the far side of the table reflected its own judgement: herself, brown-haired and petite, neat in her spotless lab coat and face mask; him in unkempt flannel shirt and baggy jeans, face unshaven, hair uncombed. At least today he wasn't sporting his usual assortment of firearms.

They had nothing in common outside of bed. She still felt awkward saying his given name. Her sleeping pill, was how she thought of him. Since the starship had crashed on Cortez Mountain, it was either George, Ambien, or a long wakeful night in the morgue.

"Doc," he said, staring down at her prize specimen. He rocked back and forth on his heels. "This isn't the best time to have an eetee in your morgue."

She picked up her scalpel again. "What, is the sheriff on the warpath?"

"Ben—fuck no, it's the Army you should worry about."

"They've been here already," she said, beginning to sever the major nerves leading from the *minutalis* to the brain proper.

"*Here*? In the *morgue*?"

"We gave them a tour of the hospital today. Don't look so horrified. They didn't unzip any body bags, and they were kind enough to give us diesel to run our generators. Is that all you came here about?"

George was still rocking on his toes. Usually he stayed relaxed, even irreverent, under the worst of circumstances. "Ben wants to know if we can have some kind of strong narcotic, like in a hypodermic or something."

"What are you boys up to now?" she asked, but she didn't expect an answer. She knew such little favors were the quid pro quo that enabled George to keep Ben from shutting down her research altogether. Still, she wondered if the timing of this particular request should give her cause for hesitation. Even she had noticed the discontent abroad in Lewisville.

"I can give you some Fentanyl. But I'll have to get it from upstairs. Is tomorrow morning soon enough?"

"Sure," said George. "I guess."

But he showed no sign of leaving. She thought she had made it clear that she had no time for him tonight. Unfortunately, she could not rely on the eetee itself, sliced open from sagittal crest to cloacal canal, to drive him away. Such sights and smells did not disturb George.

Anna leaned over the table for better access to the left posterior pseudo-thalamic nerve. It required concentration to sever cleanly, running as it did through a layer of tough and slimy dura. Naturally George chose that moment to pick up one of her scalpels and prod at the section of skin and skull she had sawed out for access to the creature's brain stem. The mucous that protected a live and healthy eetee's skin had dried to a hard, yellowish crust. As George poked at it, a flake of the crust dropped onto the table.

"Get your hands away!" Anna said. "You aren't even wearing gloves!"

He pressed on the flake with the scalpel, crumbling it, and frowned. "Doc, I've handled a lot of dead ones in the last year. I've been covered in splat. I've had 'em keel over on top of me and vomit in my face. If they were going to make me sick, wouldn't it have happened already?"

They had discussed this topic before, but today there was a new, speculative tone in George's voice. "You're wondering about the Army's quarantine regulations?" she asked. Again George did not answer. "Well, perhaps they're justified—in principle. There are plenty of diseases with a long incubation period, and if you didn't know what to look for, you couldn't spot the infection."

"As you've said. AIDS. And mad cow disease."

"Creutzfeldt-Jakob," she corrected.

"And kuru."

Surprised he had heard of an obscure disease of New Guinea cannibals, Anna glanced up. George had been doing a little research on his own? She knew George wasn't stupid, despite his unkempt, sometimes goofy persona. In his own way, he was one of the smartest people in Lewisville.

"But those are hard to catch," George said. "A quarantine wouldn't have much effect. And no one here has been eating any eetee brains." Then he reverted to form. He poked at the *minutalis*, making it quiver like Jell-O, and grinned again. "Sure looks like it would cook up good on a grill, though."

Anna had not eaten dinner. The image was unfortunate. Her mouth watered and her stomach grumbled. She sliced away the last of the dura, and at last was able to slip her gloved hand beneath the *minutalis* and lift it onto the scale.

One-point-five-four kilos. A middling weight. From the accounts of Ben's deputies and her own labors here, she had become convinced that variation in the size of this particular organ correlated with social or military rank. The eetees with the very largest *minutalis* were always the ones carrying the fear guns and directing the others. Her first theory had been that the *minutalis* manufactured dominance pheromones, but then she had begun to wonder about the magnetic anomalies, and the odd rabbit-ear deposits of metallic compounds in the sagittal crest—

George tapped his scalpel on the metal table. "Doc, we haven't talked about it in a long time—have you or Joe Hansen made any progress on how the eetees use the fear guns?"

"Oh, sure," she said, removing the *minutalis* to a tray under the hood. She started to wash it down with ethanol. "Molecular microwave transmitters. Proteins with encapsulated crystalline segments, manufactured inside specialized neural tissue. That's how the eetees communicate with each other, too."

"What?" The stark astonishment in his voice made her turn. "Have you said anything about this to *anyone else*?"

"I'm being sarcastic, George," she said crossly.

"But you have a theory."

"Guesses. Flights of fancy. I'm not a neurochemist or a molecular biologist, or, for that matter, a physicist, and I don't have the resources—"

"But you have evidence—"

"Nothing worth the name."

George gazed down at the eetee. "Too bad we couldn't ever bring you a live one and do the CAT scan thing. See what lights up when they do different things."

"No, on that particular idea I'm in complete agreement with the sheriff."

The last thing in the world Anna wanted was a live eetee to experiment on. She did not even like George in her morgue. She wanted it cold, silent, and stark, filled only with her well-tended garden of the dead. She wanted to keep dissecting her specimen, taking it apart organ by organ, slice by tiny slice, protein by protein. Over the dead she had total control.

But she also wanted George to stay. She wanted to touch his warm flesh and feel his hands on her own skin. It was the only thing these days that made her feel like a human being.

"What's really on your mind, George?" she asked.

"Doc," he said, "I know you aren't going to like this. You need to clean out your lab. Tonight. Get rid of your friend here. Destroy all your samples and slides. Remove all your files. Hide them—incinerate them."

"Don't be ridiculous," Anna said.

"It's not Ben you're dealing with anymore. The Army is confiscating everything that came out of that ship—"

"So I've heard. They want the goodies for themselves."

"They are also quarantining anyone who's worked with eetee goodies, and anyone who's had contact with eetees dead or alive."

"Not to mention anyone who protests the policy," Anna said. "It's not a real quarantine, George. If the Army was serious about an outbreak, the first people they would isolate would be those with the greatest exposure. And that's you deputies."

"I disagree that they're not serious," George said. "They are extremely serious. And very soon someone will tell them about Dr. Anna King and how she trades pharmaceuticals for eetee corpses in good condition. How you have a whole fucking eetee *research project* down here."

"I keep a very clean lab," Anna said. "They can check it if they want. I can't believe the Army could be *less* sensible than the sheriff on the subject of basic research."

"Oh, yes, they could be," said George. "You know, don't you, that Joe *and* all of his files have disappeared?"

Anna had heard, but she'd dismissed it as a wild rumor. The thought of ignorant soldiers ransacking her lab, her refuge, her life—destroying a year of work—terrified and enraged her. She tried to push the thought away. "I'm happy to share everything I've learned, though I'm sure people elsewhere with better equipment have found out a whole lot more than I have."

"Suppose," George said, "sharing is not the goal. Suppose they want to know everything you've learned, and then make sure *no one else* ever sees that information."

"But what could they possibly want to conceal? It's not as if the eetees are a secret!"

"Look," said George, "the Army comes here, to an enemy crash site, but instead of going after the eetees, they devote all their manpower and attention to *this*—whatever it is. It's important, a real disease, a—a real *something*. Maybe they don't know exactly. Maybe they know the symptoms but not the cause—maybe they don't know whether it's a disease or an effect of eetee technology. But whatever this quarantine is about, for them it is taking precedence over everything else. They are serious about it."

Anna tried once more to dismiss George's arguments. She found she could not. She gazed wistfully at the *minutalis* and her waiting culture plates. "Well, then," she said, at last, "I suppose I should take a look at Harvey Gundersen's dog."

"His dog?!"

"Harvey claims the dog has an eetee disease." Anna grimaced. "That the coyotes have it, too, and they have developed not just dementia but telepathic powers. Yes, I know what it sounds like—but today he brought in the dog, and it does have some odd lumps. I said I'd do biopsies and what blood work I have the facilities for."

"You have it *here*? Jesus, Anna, get rid of the dog, get rid of the eetee. *Now!* I'll help you. They *will* come here. Your only hope is to make sure they aren't ever able to pin this on you. Trading drugs is only a nasty rumor. You have never dissected an eetee."

"No, George. If the dog really has an eetee disease, it needs studying and *I* need to tell the colonel whatever I can find out. If people are in danger from it, I'd be criminally irresponsible not to!"

"You are not listening to me," George said. "They will take your notes and your little jars and they will take you away, too, and if I'm right they'll take you so far away I will never see you again."

"That's melodramatic."

"Anna," he said, taking hold of her shoulders. "Please." It was a violation of their unspoken protocol. He never touched her when she was working. The warmth of his hands percolated all the way through her lab coat and sweater. She held her own messy hands away from him.

The thing about George, the thing that had made the whatever-it-was between them possible, was that he never seemed scared. Now he was showing his fear. She didn't like it. She certainly didn't want George to know what *she* felt: how terrified she had been since the eetees had come. How, maybe, she loved him. That would be making the emotions real. That would be letting a live monster into the morgue.

She said, coolly, "Suppose Harvey Gundersen is even halfway right? You'd be asking me to trade the health of perhaps everyone on Earth for my personal safety."

"Yes," George said. "Let someone else figure it out."

She shook her head and glanced one last time at her beautiful, doomed specimen. "Help me with the dog. Then I'll clean everything out of my lab, as you want."

5.

The four humvees wound upward through the hills. Up on the mountain, about eight miles away now, the wreck sprawled like a giant trash-can lid someone had hammered onto the ridgetop. Corporal Denise Wyrzbowski watched it as best she could while wrestling her humvee along the unpaved road. No sign of activity at this distance. She distrusted the quiet, though; eetees were always busy with something.

The rolling terrain blocked the line of sight beyond the nearer slopes, but at least here it was grassland, dry and scant. Up ahead, pine trees accumulated with altitude until deep forest blanketed the highest ridges. Too much cover for the enemy.

She didn't feel comfortable here. She wasn't a country girl. She had fought house to house in the San Bernadino Valley with seized eetee firearms and makeshift body armor, but that was familiar freeway-and-subdivision country. You recognized what belonged and what didn't. Up there in the forest, she wouldn't know whether a sudden flight of birds was a nature show or an eetee ambush.

Not that she hadn't seen new sights in the Valley: eetees roaring along Figueroa Avenue in a Lincoln Navigator; eetee muckamucks cavorting in a swimming pool full of yellow slime; eetee grunts dead and bloated in an alleyway, lunch for a pack of feral dogs.

Movement in the sky. She tensed, then recognized it as a vulture rising on an updraft. Roadkill nearby? "What's that?" she asked the guide, a prim Nordic-looking local named Otis Redinger.

He turned to cast a disinterested glance in the direction she pointed. "Probably a dead gook," he said. "Or maybe a jackrabbit."

"A dead eetee?" Adrenaline stirred in her blood. "What could kill them out here? In the middle of nowhere?"

Redinger shrugged. "They lose their body suits, get a puncture, they're pretty vulnerable."

"Vulnerable, my gold-plated ass!" Wyrzbowski remembered how two of the mucousy little freaks had ripped apart Lieutenant Atherton with their bare talons while hopping up and down with glee. Silently: that was the really freaky part. Everyone knew they had some kind of mind talk.

Redinger said, "A ruptured body suit, and they're only good for a few days in the heat. Sheriff thinks they're short of water and fighting over it. We had a dry winter, no rain at all since May—and there's only a few small lakes up there. In town, we get our water from 300 feet underground."

"How often do you get expeditions coming after your water?"

He shrugged again and pointed. "Turn left up here."

A narrower gravel road led away through the hills. Wyrzbowski swung the humvee onto it, the others followed, and they began to bounce along in earnest, raising a column of dust visible to any eetee on the mountain. She glanced back. At this distance, the town had almost disappeared. A line of trees followed the course of a single winding stream. Yesterday, she had glanced over a bridge and seen that streambed almost dry. Lucky Lewisville: a year of drought, a moat of waterless grassland ten miles deep.

She thought about the water jugs they carried with them, about a shipload of eetees dying of thirst, and despite the blazing heat she took a hand from the wheel to pull on the helmet of her body armor.

A fence had been running along the right-hand side of the road. Up ahead, it bent right again and marched away across the hills, dividing fallow farmland from patchy brush. The bushes looked green. Further on, she could see the silvery foliage of cottonwoods and willows. She wasn't a Campfire Girl, but she could guess what trees meant out here.

Water.

She braked, and the line of hummers behind them did the same. In the back seat, Lieutenant Briggs glanced around nervously.

"What's the deal, Redinger?" she snapped at the guide. "Your sheriff claimed there was a big cache of eetee machinery abandoned here. Unguarded. But there's water here, right? And you still say there's no eetees camped out?"

Redinger looked offended. He was pulling out a Ruger Mini-14 that the colonel had given him leave to carry today. "We poisoned it," he said.

"Poison?" Briggs said, leaning forward.

"That's right. We dumped fertilizer in the pond. They can't take it. We saw 'em die when they tried to drink or swim in the creek, too much farm runoff. One of our doctors said it must be their, ah, electrolyte balance."

Well, gee, that could explain what had puzzled idiots like Atherton: why the downed eetees hadn't spread out into the California farmland. They'd stayed in the suburbs for treated water fresh from the tap.

"So if it's safe," she asked Redinger, "why do you suddenly need the gun?"

"Eh?" He looked at his firearm. "Oh. Sometimes one of 'em gets desperate. You get some sick gooks hanging around, waiting to die."

Wyrzbowski glanced into the back seat. "Sir?"

Briggs leaned back, nodded. "We go in. Be careful."

She put the hummer in motion again, slowly. Soon the road dead-ended in a dirt turnaround. Beyond that lay cattails and a sheet of greenish scum about fifty yards across, hemmed in by leafy brush and cottonwoods. Way, way too much cover.

Along the shoreline at different points, she could see the hardware the locals had mentioned, gargoyle surfaces peeking through the foliage. From here she couldn't recognize anything, but it was enough to give the colonel a real hard-on.

She personally wished he'd worry less about a few power cells falling into civilian hands than the vicious castaways on the mountain, every one of them as eager as the Terminix man to commit mass destruction on *H. sapiens*. Sure, the Army desperately needed all it could gather up, both to fight eetees and to keep control of restive civilians (and they did always seem to be restive). Everyone had heard about the hushed-up disaster at Yosemite: refugees so hungry they were eating eetees, who'd used some never-specified but terrifying eetee gewgaws to slaughter soldiers and loot their supplies.

Still, the colonel wasn't the one who had to drive his ass around right under eetee sights.

One day, Wyrzbowski thought, the so-called liberation of Earth would become a reality. She would never again have to inhale the stink of eetee splatter on a hot day. She would never again have to wonder when the next fearmonger would flatline her brain. She would never again have to worry about restive civilians shooting her in the back, or about participating in sleazy deceptions like this quarantine scam of the colonel's. She would go back to being a citizen of a goddamn democracy, all *Homo sapiens* are created equal, all eetees are vulture food.

She would lay in the shade, pop a cold beer, eat a hamburger.

"Let's go," said Briggs. Wyrzbowski pulled down her visor and rolled out of the hummer into low crouch, and the other five followed her. At least Briggs had enough sense to put on his helmet.

A trail led along the shore in both directions. Briggs sent one group right, another left; she got the left-hand job. Some soldiers stayed with the hummers to guard them; others headed away from the pond altogether, up the slope.

Her six worked slowly along the grassy trail. She sweltered inside her armor. The sun raised a sewage-y stench off the stagnant pond, and horse-flies the size of mice dive-bombed their heads. Insects in the grass fell silent as they approached and buzzed loudly again after they passed.

They reached the first pile of hardware without incident. Wyrzbowski took off a glove and gingerly touched the squat, lobed central piece. It was cool to the touch and, on the shady side, sweated condensation. Still working, whatever it was. She duck-walked around it. On the far side, a tube four inches in diameter snaked through the grass toward the pond. Her guess: some kind of purification unit.

Further along the trail, other globby Tinkertoys shone inscrutably in the sun. A lot of working hardware here. It didn't look all that abandoned, whatever the locals claimed.

Shouts. She twisted around. They came from the hummers, but she couldn't see well through the foliage. A plasma rifle opened up, setting a tree ablaze. And then eetee fire caught a hummer and blew it apart like the Fourth of July.

Wyrzbowski dropped on her belly and elbowed swiftly back to the others. "Back!" she hissed.

Her soldiers spread out among the trees, belly-crawling through the grass. Now the whole pond side was jumping with eetees in body suits. No, the gooks hadn't left their little water-treatment plant unguarded.

More fire from the soldiers at the turnaround, but not as much as there should be. She reached a rotting stump, balanced her rifle, whistled the signal over her mike. While Preston and Weinberg played rear-guard, the rest chose their targets deliberately. She sighted on the nearest of the eetees hopping toward Briggs, who stood as motionless as a department-store mannequin. She pressed the trigger. Got the hopper—whoops, a little splatter on the lieutenant. Other soldiers near Briggs had turned deer-in-the-headlights, too, perfect targets. Just like Atherton. There must be a mind-bender in this crew.

Wyrzbowski tried to sort out the pattern as she picked off a second hopper. Eetees descended the hillside beyond the humvees; more had popped up on the other side of the pond—but those soldiers were returning fire, so no mind control over there. A whistle from Weinberg to the rear. Enemy on *their* tail, too, but her group wasn't pissing their pants in cold terror.

Up there, then. On the hillside. She whistled another signal as she splattered a third eetee.

The other five came crawling to her. She raised her visor and whispered, in case the eetees were listening to radio. "There's an officer up there. We're going to get it."

The six of them spread out again, creeping through grass and brush away from the pond. The eetees attacking them from the rear didn't figure out what they'd done and joined the action at the humvees. Now Wyrzbowski could see the muckamuck, resplendent in the egg-sack slime of its body suit, wielding its red fearmonger while flunkies covered its spindle-shanked ass. Poor freak: A year ago it had been one of the exterminator kings of the galaxy, and now here it was on guard duty at a polluted frog pond. She wondered if the eetee mind-benders could hear human minds, if they took pleasure in the terror they caused.

She wriggled forward, hoping she wasn't already too close to the muckamuck. One of the hopper flunkies must have sensed something. It turned toward her soldiers. Silent communication and a rush of excited hopping. A bush in Phillips's direction burst into a flutter of shredded leaves. Someone, she thought Merlino, fired back, burning two of the hoppers.

The flunkies had left their muckamuck exposed, but it had also turned its glistening head in their direction. Searching. Not much time, Wyrzbowski thought, and right then the terror boiled out of the back of her skull.

It spilled like ice into her guts, congealed her limbs into stone. Time stopped. The hillside sharpened into impossibly sharp focus, cutting itself into her consciousness: light and shadow on a patch of wild rose; the gymsocks smell inside her helmet; a horsefly crawling across the visor.

She knew she just had to focus. Sight on the chest. Press the trigger. That's all she had to do.

An eetee landed on her back, then exploded drippily onto her armor. Concrete encased her hands, her arms. She heard someone whimpering and knew, from experience, that it was herself. Your buddies cover your back, but you have to face down your fear by yourself. Just focus. Breathe. Press the trigger, press press *press*. And her finger *moved*—

The weight dropped from her limbs. The ice melted from her body and left her, gasping, in the hot sunlight. She managed to raise her head. The muckamuck was nowhere to be seen, though its fearmonger had come to rest in a rosebush. She grabbed a handful of grass to wipe the viscous blobs clinging to her visor, and then scooped up the fearmonger for her collection. Four officers and counting.

The grunt eetees fled the hillside. She whistled. One by one, Weinberg, Preston, and Bernard appeared. Then Merlino dragged toward her through the brush. He'd taken a burn on the shoulder plate of his armor. "Phillips?" she asked. He shook his head.

She couldn't think about that now. She pointed down the hill, toward the single remaining humvee. As they ran at a crouch, Weinberg supporting Merlino, she took stock. It looked better than she'd expected. The party on the far side of the pond was still kicking, targeting the eetees trying to pick off survivors at the turnaround. The hoppers must have known their grand

and mighty mind-bender was now only a nasty spray of goobers, because as soon as her party came up behind, they turned and fled altogether.

Briggs was gone. It was Sergeant Libnitz who gave the orders: the wounded in the humvee, others to jog behind.

Redinger appeared out of nowhere to lope beside her. He didn't have so much as a singe-mark on him despite not being armored, but he was stinking wet from pond water. She raised her visor; she needed the air. She was soaked inside her armor, too, but from sweat.

"How come *you're* still alive?" she asked.

"Jumped in the pond and swam to your side," he gasped.

"Clever," she said. Redinger didn't fool her. The Lewisville militia had sent them into the ambush. When the reckoning came, she would make sure to splatter *this* prick for Phillips. She wished, not for the first time, that she knew how to use her red souvenir. She would make this little fuckhead shit himself, she would make him weep, she would feed him suffering and degradation. *Then* she would splatter him.

Adrenaline and the rush of hatred kept her moving until they reached the junction. And then the humvee in front of her stopped. "Fuck, fuck, fuck!" Libnitz was shouting.

She stopped, panting and dizzy from the heat. Then saw what he swore at.

Back in town, five miles away, black smoke coiled into the flawless blue sky. She made her way to Libnitz. "Can't raise anybody on the radio," he said.

6.

Out the café's back window, Alexandra Gundersen could see the Neanderthals coming out of their caves to beat their chests. It was the Big Noisy Machines the Army had driven into town; now Ben and his boys worried that their dicks were too small. So now they had to kill something, or make a big explosion. Nothing made your little dick feel bigger.

"I'm so sorry, Colonel," she said to the Army man. "They're all lent out right now. It's been such a popular book. I'll try to get one for you by tonight. In the meantime, let me check those other books out for you."

The colonel responded to her warm tone with a slight relaxation of posture. The lightening of his expression was not yet sufficient to call a smile. While Alexandra stamped his books, she glanced through her lashes at the window again. Ben and his *unter*-cavemen had separated and now walked in different directions. Her twin James aimed straight toward the café's back door. It was, unfortunately, too late to escape.

She handed Colonel Fikes his books and smiled again, and this time he did smile in return. He would be back. She knew her customers, and, for better or worse, she knew men.

The colonel headed through the adjoining bookshop toward the front door, even as brother James pushed through the back into the café.

"Good morning, Sandy," James said cheerfully.

Her twin used her childhood nickname only to annoy her. Since these days he preferred the proletarian *Jim*, she paid him back in kind. "Hello, James."

James stared at her customers significantly. Despite the Army's prohibition on civilian assembly, and the loss of power that made it impossible to open her café (only locally grown herbal or mormon tea anyway, alas), she could still let up to seven civilians and any number of soldiers into the bookshop. She no longer *sold* books or videos these days, with no new stock arriving in the foreseeable future, but she did lend them out, and since the demise of TV and radio, her store had always been busy. "Can we talk?" said James.

Alexandra waved at her assistant, deep in conversation with a soldier, to signal her departure. "Come on," she said to James. She led him through the door marked *Private*, into her stockroom's little office. "What do you want, James?"

"We need your help," he said.

We meant *Ben*, of course. How flattering that when Biggest Dick caveman needed a woman's help, he still thought of his ex-wife—though he was too cowardly to show up in person.

"I can't imagine what use I could be to you deputies."

"The Army stole some things from us," James said, "and we need to get them back."

"You mean your weapons."

"Sandy," James said, "we've been protecting you with those weapons."

"Isn't the Army going to take over that job?"

"Are they acting as if they came here to fight eetees?" James's foot jittered suddenly as Alexandra fixed him with a frown. "And what will you do when you need protection *from the Army*?"

The soldiers had come yesterday: hard men, and a few women, too, in desert camo and heavy boots, laden with guns. She hadn't liked them. But they hadn't dragged *her* off to "quarantine." When the very first tanks rolled into Lewisville, Alexandra had undertaken serious thinking on the subject of boss cavemen and the very biggest rocks. By the time the soldiers showed up at her door, her shop and house had been cleared of all eetee artifacts. She had smiled and offered them tea.

They had frightened her nevertheless.

"I don't particularly like this . . . occupation," she said. "But the soldiers are acting under orders from our government."

"*Our* government?" said James. "The eetees nuked *our* government. These folks are enforcers for a military dictatorship."

"And just what is Sheriff wonderful Ben Gundersen setting up? How much has *he* been promoting your precious civil rights and rule of law?"

James's foot jittered again. Poor James. He fancied himself such an independent thinker. But when the other cavemen start heaving around rocks and grunting, you have to join in. Otherwise they might think you have a *really* little dick.

Okay, so it wasn't the actual, physical dick (*obviously,* in Ben's case!) that determined where you stood in Neanderthal hierarchy. It was all the subtle, almost imperceptible inflections of display, of action and reaction, dominance and deference, intimidation and submission, and meanwhile the metaphorical dick grows bigger and bigger. Fear, manipulation, and mind control. The boss caveman is created by *attitude,* his, theirs. Hers— although she had at last won free.

"I grant you," James said, "Ben's gone overboard sometimes. But he's kept the town together in difficult times, he's really done a tremendous job. He's preserved . . . *civilization* here, when the war turned the rest of our country into rubble."

Alexandra knew there was some truth in what her brother said. Behavior that was bad for a marriage might be less bad for a town. Because of Ben's diligent ruthlessness, she could sleep at night, she could still open up her store and serve customers. But it wasn't the whole story, was it?

"Order," she said, "is not the same as civilization. Order is about the strong controlling the weak. *Civilization* is about *protecting* the weaker from the stronger, about us all living *together* in empathy, cultivating the connections between us—"

"Sandy," said James, "empathy *is* what we're after. We want the Army folks to *empathize* with our point of view."

"With the aid of weapons," she said sharply. James made no reply, but he jiggled his foot again. "I don't want part of it. I'm a civilized person. I won't participate in violence against fellow human beings, moreover against people who are serving my country. And I thought I had made myself clear. I have no interest in doing anything for or because of Ben, ever, I want to have no connection with him *at all*, *ever again*, and this is *his* plan. Don't tell me it isn't."

"Don't make this personal—"

"It *is* personal. It's all personal. You want to belong to a cause that's bigger than you and, and—then you don't have to think about your actions. *Your* violence is good, *theirs* is bad. And then it's a big flashy Hollywood story, small-town heroes fight off aliens *and* the bad Army guys at the same time. But it all begins with *you*, James, and me, and Ben. Good and evil begin in each person's heart and mind. *That's* the story."

James began to laugh. "You and Ben were a Hollywood story, all right. The problem was, you both wanted top billing." Alexandra flushed, enraged at his mockery, yet another betrayal of *her*, his *twin sister*. He ducked his head and said, hastily, waving his hands, "No, no, forget about Ben, okay?"

"How can I? This *is* all about him, and his ego. He just can't stand not being the one on top!"

"It's only about Ben for you, Sandy. And doesn't that mean you're making it all about *you*?" That stopped her. James went on: "It's the *town* that needs your help. Your *neighbors*. Individuals. It's *your* choice to do good and not evil to them."

"And you," she said coldly, "are so sure this is for their own good."

"What good has the Army done for Lewisville so far? What happens to *your* business when they've locked away half the town? Do you think they'll go on differently than they've begun?"

No, that did seem unlikely. Alexandra looked away.

After the divorce, exhausted and alone, she had convinced herself that what she had most wanted was the opposite of her life with Ben. She wanted to live quietly. She wanted a loving world founded on empathy, not conquest. Starting up her café-bookstore had been part of it, a microcosm of her ideal of civilization, bringing people together for the exchange of ideas and fellowship. And hadn't she been successful at that, at least in a small way?

But, to tell the truth, it was boring. And while she dwindled into a mousy spinster, the bookstore lady, the war came along and metamorphosed Ben into gun-toting action hero. Not that she could ever have fought the eetees the way he had. She had no physical courage and would sooner pick up a poisonous viper than a gun. But—admit it, James was right—she *hated* being out of the spotlight. She hated *Ben* hogging the stage.

And now, wriggling up from the dark depths of her psyche, came this self-destructive impulse to prove herself to Ben. To the town. To prove she was useful in this new caveman world of fear and guns, and not just in the sad, lost world of civilization, where she had known she was Ben's superior.

Had Ben known she would feel such an impulse? Had he known she would be more afraid of the strange cavemen, the Army soldiers, than the cavemen she knew?

Fear, manipulation, and mind control. Good old Ben. Once she had admired that will toward dominance.

Then, James said, "Maybe you're afraid you won't measure up." Reading her mind, too—he was her twin, after all.

Strange how knowing what was in someone else's mind ought to give you empathy for that person. Instead it seemed as if only the weak could sustain empathy. The strong couldn't resist the temptation to use their knowledge to get what they wanted.

Defeated by James and Ben, by her own *attitude*, Alexandra said, "All right. Tell me what you want me to do."

And so that afternoon, clad in a clingy flowered sundress and straw hat, her long blond hair spilling over her shoulders, Alexandra walked up to a pair of beefy soldiers and smiled. "Excuse me? Officers? I wonder if I could get into the warehouse."

One of the soldiers swiveled his head toward her, so she could see her reflection in his sunglasses. She still looked pretty damn good. The soldiers' guns turned her stomach queasy and her hands cold, but, she told herself firmly, what was in their minds mattered more.

"We're not officers, ma'am—" the soldier began, politely.

"Oh!" she said. "Of course! How silly of me! You're not the *police*!"

"—but no," he went on, "we can't let you into the warehouses."

"But you see," she said, "I rent space in one. For some of my overflow." He was staring politely but blankly at her. "I own a bookstore, you see? The only one in town. And your colonel, Mr. Fikes, came in today and we started talking about Lewis and Clark, and whether they should be admired as brave explorers, or whether they were just the vanguard of genocide and colonial oppression, and he asked for a book about them."

She smiled again at them. Their body language was changing subtly but unmistakably: shoulders relaxing, faces turning towards her. Excitement mixed with terror rose in her. They were falling for it . . .

"I recommended *Undaunted Courage* to start with, but, as you can imagine, it's a popular book around here, at least since there hasn't been any TV. I didn't have any copies left in the store, but I know there are some out here in the warehouse. So I came out here to pick up a copy for the colonel. You can check with him if you like."

Part of her still hoped the soldiers would send her away, and she would be able to tell James she had done her best. But she was also fiercely willing them to submit.

He nodded. "All right, Ms.—?"

"Alexandra Hanover," she said, using her maiden name.

"I'll have to accompany you."

"Oh, that's fine!" she said, and smiled her most glorious smile at him. And she followed him across the parking lot between the tanker trucks, and through the big roll-up door.

The space inside was cavernous, dark and cool. The soldiers had shoved aside quite a few of the pallets and shelving units to make room for their equipment, and the smells of diesel oil and sweat mingled with the older dusty scent of dried peas. The guard accompanying her paused to explain their mission to a man leaning over a trestle table—probably a genuine officer.

The man at the table looked her up and down with a hard, suspicious stare, but Alexandra smiled at him, too, with just the right mixture of hopeful inquiry, submission to his authority, and winning, wholesome cheerfulness. (Oh, it *was* going to work. All those years with Ben had been good for something after all.) Then he, too, nodded.

She and her guard threaded their way around pallets laden with sacks of dried peas, heading toward the back of the warehouse. The shelving units that she rented stood against the wall at the back, next to a locked metal door that led outside.

Next came a part that depended on her own physical quickness, something she had never had to rely upon before. But excitement propelled her now. She no longer wanted to turn back.

"Could you help me?" she asked the guard. "I have a bad back." The guard glanced at her. She pointed. He still wore his sunglasses, so he wouldn't be able to see the nervous tremor in her hands. "It's in that box there, on the second shelf."

He bent over, reaching for the box. Alexandra opened her purse and took out the vet's tranquilizer dart that James had given her. The guard started to pull the box off the shelf. She reached over and stabbed his neck with the dart.

"Hey!" he yelled, turning swiftly toward her. She backed up, but before he could take a single step, his knees buckled and he pitched face forward onto the concrete floor.

That looked as if it hurt. But she could not help smiling. She had done it!

She reached in her purse again and took out the key that James had given her, doubtless Reggie Forrester's. She slid back the deadbolts and opened the door.

The gravel lane behind the warehouse was deserted except for a skittering stray cat. For a moment she thought the soldiers must already have arrested Ben's deputies. Then behind her, inside the warehouse, a commotion erupted: people yelling, booted feet clomping at a run across concrete.

And then brother James rose out of the brush on the far side of the lane and ran toward the back door. A line of Lewisville deputies followed him. Two tremendous explosions detonated at the front of the warehouse, one right after the other. A blast of heat and smoke and a rain of debris rattled across the interior of the warehouse. Alexandra jumped outside through the doorway.

Alexandra thought: People were being shot, even killed. She had helped it happen. It was a betrayal of everything she thought she stood for. Why was she so excited?

But then, at that same moment, moving so unbelievably fast that she barely had time to register what happened, a dark shape roared across the sky, shrank into a distant speck. Another deafening explosion—

The deputies all ducked belatedly. "Raid! Raid! Eetees!" James shouted. Now gunfire and screams echoed from inside the warehouse.

Then a band of eetees, all thin heads and long froggy legs, came around the corner of the warehouse and started shooting.

She had never seen them in the flesh. They weren't supposed to come out in daylight! Terrified, she flung herself back inside, crawled away among the pallets into the darkest corner she could find, and wedged herself behind a row of fiberboard barrels, arms over her head. Smoke filled her nose and mouth. Explosions echoed through the warehouse, more yelling and screaming, the crash of metal shelves overturning.

Then she heard a sound right nearby.

She looked up. One of the aliens squatted atop a stack of barrels. It apparently hadn't seen her yet. It gazed out from its high vantage point into the chaos of the warehouse. The alien wasn't any larger, really, than a Great Dane or a teenage boy. It had long legs and arms and wore some kind of glistening translucent all-over covering like a wetsuit, and its taloned glove held a long-barreled red pistol. It smelled like slightly rancid raw chicken. Alexandra looked at its narrow chest for one of those red whorled pendants James had once shown her, carried by the high-ranking eetees, that could paralyze this entire warehouse full of men. She did not see one.

She must have made a sound—whimpered, perhaps—because the eetee turned and glanced down at her. Its narrow face was unreadable behind the slimy protective sac. Its pistol was aimed at her negligently, as if she were no threat at all, but she *really* did *not* like guns.

As angry as if it were Ben, Alexandra threw her weight into the stack of barrels. The eetee toppled to the floor along with all the rolling, tumbling sections of its unstable perch. The pistol flew from its hand, fell and struck Alexandra's hip. Her first instinctive reaction was to bat the horrible object away from her; then, fumbling, she grabbed for it and caught the wrong end.

The eetee scrabbled to its feet, heaving barrels aside. Alexandra reoriented the pistol with two clumsy, shaking hands, and took aim. She clearly did not inspire fear: Instead of ducking behind a barrel or throwing itself to one side, the eetee fixed Alexandra with its egg-yolk gaze.

Icy blackness swept her mind, it stopped her breath and froze her limbs— But the eetee didn't, it *surely* . . .

The overwhelming weight of her terror crushed the half-finished thought toward nothingness, and all that Alexandra could grab hold of was her desperate rage. She was so tired of being on the sidelines, the one *not in control.* She realized she had squeezed her eyes shut. She forced herself to open them. There was no blackness except on the backs of her eyelids.

Mind control she understood.

She pressed the button on the red pistol and the eetee *exploded,* showering the wall above her with great gobs and ropy drips of what looked like snot.

"Take *that, Ben,*" she whispered.

Civilization is a wonderful thing, but survival trumps it every time.

Then a human soldier, a black woman, pushed through the barrels toward her to offer a hand. "The warehouse is burning! Come on!"

The soldier took the red pistol from Alexandra's now nerveless hands and tugged her through an obstacle course of tumbled communications equipment, pooled blood, dead human and alien bodies, and furiously burning sacks of dried peas. At last they burst onto the smoke-filled parking lot. The remains of the Army's fuel trucks still blazed brightly. Soldiers pushed her down behind a tank.

"This the one who let the militia in?" one of them said.

"She splattered the froggy with the fearmonger," her rescuer told them. "Lucky for you."

But there had been no fearmonger.

As the flood of paralytic terror receded, dragging cold shakiness in its wake, Alexandra's last thought but one rose back into sight. The eetee hadn't carried a fear gun. It hadn't needed one to shoot her full of abject terror.

Noise and commotion went on for a long time after that: the burning diesel, eetee aircraft sweeping overhead, explosions, missiles screaming into the sky, shouts, rattling gunfire. Alexandra knew Ben's plan had gone entirely wrong, and she was, plainly and simply, screwed. Ben and his deputies were even more screwed, if they weren't already dead. Now Lewisville really would suffer a military occupation. They would *all* be herded into camps.

Still, right at the moment she felt like God looking down on creation. She had killed an eetee.

Her brain could not leave alone the image of that clouded alien face at the moment she had pressed the trigger.

All this time she'd been hearing about Ben and his deputies—so brave to venture out, over and over, against such a terrible weapon—and it turned out there was *no such thing* as a fear gun.

The red pendants must be just some kind of officer's insignia. It said you were *authorized*, you had the *ability* or the *training* to wield terror. But as for the fear itself—

It all begins and ends in the mind.

7.

Fred crossed the dry, thistly lawn and stopped in front of the old brick building with the flagpoles that Harvey would never let him piss on. In hot weather the children stayed away and the building usually sat empty, but now the strangers had brought grownup people there. Fred hoped Harvey might be one of them.

Fred dropped his burden to sample the air for Harvey's scent. The air was still heavy with the acrid taste of yesterday's conflagration. He reared on hind legs to put his nose to the windows. No one had opened the mesh coverings, but the sashes had been raised so he could smell all the guests packed inside. There were even more than at the big barbecues Harvey and Susan used to hold. The people were not enjoying this party, though.

Many stood in line in front of a table. The rest sat around on cots or folded blankets, glum, angry, or fearful.

Fred recognized some of the people. Mister Mayor drifted along the line of people, talking. Fred could tell that Mister Mayor felt glum and fearful, too, but he soothed the others with his warm smooth voice that had always reminded Fred of cow fat.

At the table at the head of the line sat the woman vet who had kept Fred tied up in the cold hard room. With her was the otherwise nice man who had helped with the big, long, nasty needle. Now the vet-woman had a lot more needles with her, and the nice man—as well as some of the strangers—were helping her, sticking needles in each person and writing things down.

Near the table Fred noticed Alexandra, who had stopped coming out to Harvey's a long time ago. Alexandra hadn't liked Fred's nose, even when he'd sniffed her crotch in the friendliest way. Alexandra had already gone through the line and now *she* was smiling and being friendly to some of the strangers.

Ben was not talking to the strangers or to Alexandra. Ben had a leash between his feet and hands and he could only shuffle along. Several strangers led him forward to get stuck with a needle. Fred hoped Ben would be okay. The night before, he had smelled Ben, angry and afraid, through a basement window in the building with the big statue.

At last, in the far corner, Fred located Susan, and nearby, Harvey. Harvey sat on a cot and stared miserably at the wall.

Fred remembered the old days when he and Harvey had romped for hours in the cool of the evening, when the two of them had been joyously happy together. Then Harvey had grown afraid: so afraid of the world and of Fred, he thought he should kill Fred, even though he didn't want to.

Fred so much wanted Harvey and Susan to be happy again. When Harvey got the present Fred was trying to give him, he would quit being so miserable and alone. He would know that he didn't have to be afraid of Fred.

Fred picked up the present in his jaws again and loped around the corner of the brick building. A couple of the strangers' trucks pulled out of the driveway. Their occupants paid no attention to him.

Toward the back of the brick building it was cooler and shady. A cat turd lay under a bush. For a moment, he thrust his nose against it, intrigued. Then he recalled his mission. He would not be able to go home if he failed, not while Harvey and the vet-woman wanted to kill him.

He continued to the back door of the place where the children used to eat. The sweet odor of old garbage lingered here, but there were also fresh smells where cans of oil, bags of potatoes, and crates of stale crackers and raisins had rested on the cement for a few moments. Most interesting was the delirious scent of raw meat. Someone had recently killed a cow.

From inside the building, Fred could smell boiling potatoes. He trotted up to the door itself. Two sweaty strangers guarded it. Fred put down the present and wagged his tail.

Hello, he said to them, in the new way he had learned.

They glanced down. "Hey, boy," said one of the strangers. Fred wagged his tail some more and the stranger patted him on the head. The stranger liked him. Most people liked Fred.

I like you, too, Fred told him, wagging some more. *Will you open the door, please?*

The stranger pulled open the door. He didn't look down as Fred picked up his present and trotted inside. It was just the way it had worked with Harvey and Susan, and at the big building that was kind of like the vet's. The nice man hadn't noticed he was letting Fred out. It was because he had wanted Fred to be happy, even though he was afraid Fred was sick.

None of them would be afraid of Fred anymore if they understood that Fred wasn't sick, he had just learned to do some new things.

They would learn new things, too. They would all be happy once they understood each other. They would stop being afraid of each other, and hating each other, and trying to make each other do things. Like him, they would take off their leashes and run joyously, rapturously free.

At least, that's what he hoped they would do. But people were sometimes unaccountable.

Fred followed the scent of raw meat into a big kitchen where there was a lot of stainless steel. Men and women chopped potatoes and onions, and big pots of water steamed on the burners. More strangers with guns stood around, making sure the men and women didn't go outside. The strangers were looking forward to the meat, too.

Don't bother about me, Fred told them, and no one did, because they didn't want to. It was a little sneaky, a coyote trick.

Off to one side, one of the men was spilling a bowl of stinky chopped onions into a big vat of ground-up raw meat, ruining its smell. *Why don't you stop and talk to your friend?* Fred asked him, knowing, because of the new way, that it was what the man really wanted to do.

He couldn't do this to the coyotes. They would have caught on right away. But, except for Harvey, the humans didn't know yet that Fred was talking to them, or that he was trying to get them to do things, just for their own good. Until then he could be a little sneaky.

Fred trotted over to the vat of ground-up cow and dropped in the present he had carried all the way from the vet's.

"Hey!" the man yelled, suddenly noticing him. "Get away from there! How'd you get in?" But he wasn't really mad.

Fred backed away and lay down, wagging his tail. The man began mixing the pungent onions in with Fred's present. By the grill, a woman shouted, "You almost done with that hamburger?"

Ian McDonald is an SFF writer living in Northern Ireland, just outside
Belfast, by the sea. He's a multiple-award winning writer, and his most
recent writings are *Luna: New Moon* and *Luna: Wolf Moon* (Tor, Gollancz)
and novella *Time Was*, from Tor.com. Forthcoming is *Luna: Moon Rising*.

Tendeléo's Story

IAN MCDONALD

I shall start my story with my name. I am Tendeléo. I was born here, in
Gichichi. Does that surprise you? The village has changed so much that
no one born then could recognize it now, but the name is still the same.
That is why names are important. They remain.

I was born in 1995, shortly after the evening meal and before dusk. That
is what Tendeléo means in my language, Kalenjin: early-evening-short-
ly-after-dinner. I am the oldest daughter of the pastor of St. John's
Church. My younger sister was born in 1998, after my mother had two
miscarriages, and my father asked the congregation to lay hands on her.
We called her Little Egg. That is all there are of us, two. My father felt
that a pastor should be an example to his people, and at that time the government was calling for smaller families.

My father had cure of five churches. He visited them on a red scrambler bike the bishop at Nakuru had given him. It was good motorbike, a
Yamaha. Japanese. My father loved riding it. He practiced skids and jumps
on the back roads because he thought a clergyman should not be seen
stunt-riding. Of course, people did, but they never said to him. My father
built St. John's. Before him, people sat on benches under trees. The church
he made was sturdy and rendered in white concrete. The roof was red
tin, trumpet vine climbed over it. In the season flowers would hang down
outside the window. It was like being inside a garden. When I hear the
story of Adam and Eve, that is how I think of Eden, a place among the
flowers. Inside there were benches for the people, a lectern for the sermon
and a high chair for when the bishop came to confirm children. Behind the
altar rail was the holy table covered with a white cloth and an alcove in the
wall for the cup and holy communion plate. We didn't have a font. We took
people to the river and put them under. I and my mother sang in the choir.

The services were long and, as I see them now, quite boring, but the music was wonderful. The women sang, the men played instruments. The best was played by a tall Luo, a teacher in the village school we called, rather blasphemously, Most High. It was a simple instrument: a piston ring from an old Peugeot engine which he hit with a heavy steel bolt. It made a great, ringing rhythm.

What was left over from the church went into the pastor's house. It had poured concrete floors and louvre windows, a separate kitchen and a good charcoal stove a parishioner who could weld had made from a diesel drum. We had electric light, two power sockets and a radio/cassette player, but no television. It was inviting the devil to dinner, my father told us. Kitchen, living room, our bedroom, my mother's bedroom, and my father's study. Five rooms. We were people of some distinction in Gichichi; for Kalenjin.

Gichichi was a thin, straggly sort of village; shops, school, post-office, matatu office, petrol station and mandazi shop up on the main road, with most of the houses set off the footpaths that followed the valley terraces. On one of them was our shamba, half a kilometer down the valley. The path to it went past the front door of the Ukerewe family. They had seven children who hated us. They threw dung or stones and called us see-what-we-thought-of-ourselves-Kalenjin and hated-of-God-Episcopalians. They were African Inland Church Kikuyu, and they had no respect for the discipline of the bishop.

If the church was my father's Eden, the shamba was my mother's. The air was cool in the valley and you could hear the river over the stones down below. We grew maize and gourds and some sugar-cane, which the local rummers bought from my father and he pretended not to know. Beans and chillis. Onions and potatoes. Two trees of finger bananas, though M'zee Kipchobe maintained that they sucked the life out of the soil. The maize grew right over my head, and I would run into the sugar-cane and pretend that two steps had taken me out of this world into another. There was always music there; the solar radio, or the women singing together when they helped each other turn the soil or hoe the weeds. I would sing with them, for I was considered good at harmonies. The shamba too had a place where the holy things were kept. Among the thick, winding tendrils of an old tree killed by strangling fig the women left little wooden figures gifts of money, Indian-trader jewelry, and beer.

You are wondering, what about the Chaga? You've worked out from the dates that I was nine when the first package came down on Kilimanjaro. How could such tremendous events, a thing like another world taking over our own, have made so little impression on my life? It is easy, when it is no nearer to you than another world. We were not ignorant in Gichichi. We had seen the pictures from Kilimanjaro on the television, read the articles in the *Nation* about the thing that is like a coral reef and a rainforest that came out of the object from the sky. We had heard the discussions on the radio about how fast it was growing—fifty meters every day, it was ingrained on our minds—and what it might be and where it might come from. Every morning the vapor trails of the big UN jets scored our sky as they brought more men and machines to study it, but it was another world. It was not our world. Our world was church, home, shamba, school. Service on Sunday, Bible Study on Monday. Singing lessons, homework club. Sewing, weeding, stirring the ugali. Shooing the goats out of the maize. Playing with Little Egg and Grace and Ruth from next door in the compound: not too loud, Father's working. Once a week, the mobile bank. Once a fortnight, the mobile library. Mad little matatus dashing down, overtaking everything they could see, people hanging off every door and window. Big dirty country buses winding up the steep road like oxen. Gikombe, the town fool, if we could have afforded one, wrapped in dung-colored cloth sitting down in front of the country buses to stop them moving. Rains and hot seasons and cold fogs. People being born, people getting married, people running out on each other, or getting sick, or dying in accidents. Kilimanjaro, the Chaga? Another picture in a world where all pictures come from the same distance.

I was thirteen and just a woman when the Chaga came to my world and destroyed it. That night I was at Grace Muthiga's where she and I had a homework club. It was an excuse to listen to the radio. One of the great things about the United Nations taking over your country is the radio is very good. I would sing with it. They played the kind of music that wasn't approved of in our house.

We were listening to trip hop. Suddenly the record started to go all pha-sey, like the radio was tuning itself on and off the station. At first we thought the disc was slipping or something, then Grace got up to fiddle with the tuning button. That only made it worse. Grace's mother came in from the next room and said she couldn't get a picture on the battery television. It was full of wavy lines. Then we heard the first boom. It was far away and hollow and it rolled like thunder. Most nights up in the Highlands we get thunder. We know very well what it sounds like. This was something else. *Boom!* Again. Closer now. Voices outside, and lights. We took torches and went out to the voices. The road was full of people;

men, women, children. There were torch beams weaving all over the place. *Boom!* Close now, loud enough to rattle the windows. All the people shone their torches straight up into the sky, like spears of light. Now the children were crying and I was afraid. Most High had the answer: "Sonic booms! There's something up there." As he said those words, we saw it. It was so slow. That was the amazing thing about it. It was like a child drawing a chalk line across a board. It came in from the south east, across the hills east of Kiriani, straight as an arrow, a little to the south of us. The night was such as we often get in late May, clear after evening rains, and very full of stars. We all saw a glowing dot cut across the face of the stars. It seemed to float and dance, like illusions in the eye if you look into the sun. It left a line behind it like the trails of the big UN jets, only pure, glowing blue, drawn on the night. Double-boom now, so close and loud it hurt my ears. At that, one of the old women began wailing. The fear caught, and soon whole families were looking at the line of light in the sky with tears running down their faces, men as well as women. Many sat down and put their torches in their laps, not knowing what they should do. Some of the old people covered their heads with jackets, shawls, newspapers. Others saw what they were doing, and soon everyone was sitting on the ground with their heads covered. Not Most High. He stood looking up at the line of light as it cut his night in half. "Beautiful!" he said. "That I should see such things, with these own eyes!"

He stood watching until the object vanished in the dark of the mountains to the west. I saw its light reflected in his eyes. It took a long time to fade.

For a few moments after the thing went over, no one knew what to do. Everyone was scared, but they were relieved at the same time because, like the angel of death, it had passed over Gichichi. People were still crying, but tears of relief have a different sound. Someone got a radio from a house. Others fetched theirs, and soon we were all sitting in the middle of the road in the dark, grouped around our radios. An announcer interrupted the evening music show to bring a news flash. At twenty twenty eight a new biological package had struck in Central Province. At those words, a low keen went up from each group.

"Be quiet!" someone shouted, and there was quiet. Though the words would be terrible, they were better than the voices coming out of the dark.

The announcer said that the biological package had come down on the eastern slopes of the Nyandarua near to Tusha, a small Kikuyu village. Tusha was a name we knew. Some of us had relatives in Tusha. The country bus to Nyeri went through Tusha. From Gichichi to Tusha was twenty kilometers. There were cries. There were prayers. Most said nothing. But we all knew time had run out. In four years the Chaga had swallowed up Kilimanjaro, and Amboseli, and the border country of Namanga, and was advancing up the A104 on Kajiado and Nairobi. We had ignored it and gone on with our lives, believing that when it finally came, we would know what to do. Now it had dropped out of the sky twenty kilometers north of us and said, Twenty kilometers, four hundred days: that's how long you've got to decide what you're going to do.

Then Jackson who ran the Peugeot Service Office stood up. He cocked his head to one side. He held up a finger. Everyone fell silent. He looked to the sky. "Listen!" I could hear nothing. He pointed to the south, and we all heard it: aircraft engines. Flashing lights lifted out of the dark tree-line on the far side of the valley. Behind it came others, then others, then ten, twenty, thirty, more. Helicopters swarmed over Gichichi like locusts. The sound of their engines filled the whole world. I wrapped my school shawl around my head and put my hands over my ears and yelled over the noise but it still felt like it would shatter my skull like a clay pot. Thirty-five helicopters: They flew so low their down-wash rattled our tin roofs and sent dust swirling up around our faces. Some of the teenagers cheered and waved their torches and white school shirts to the pilots. They cheered the helicopters on, right over the ridge. They cheered until the noise of their engines was lost among the night-insects. Where the Chaga goes, the United Nations comes close behind, like a dog after a bitch.

A few hours later the trucks came through. The grinding of engines as they toiled up the winding road woke all Gichichi. "It's three o'clock in the morning!" Mrs. Kuria shouted at the dusty white trucks with the blue symbol of UNECTA on the doors, but no one would sleep again. We lined the main road to watch them go through our village. I wonder what the drivers thought of all those faces and eyes suddenly appearing in their headlights as they rounded the bend. Some waved. The children waved back. They were still coming through as we went down to the shamba at dawn to milk the goats. They were a white snake coiling up and down the valley road as far as I could see. As they reached the top of the pass the low light from the east caught them and burned them to gold.

The trucks went up the road for two days. Then they stopped and the refugees started to come the other way, down the road. First the ones with the vehicles: matatus piled high with bedding and tools and animals, trucks with the family balanced in the back on top of all the things they had saved. A Toyota microbus, bursting with what looked like bolts of colored cloth but which were women, jammed in next to each other. Ancient cars, motorbikes, and mopeds vanishing beneath sagging bales of possessions. It was a race of poverty; the rich ones with machines took the lead. After motors came animals; donkey carts and ox-wagons, pedal-rickshaws. Most came in the last wave, the ones on foot. They pushed handcarts laden with pots and bedding rolls and boxes lashed with twine, or dragged trolleys on ropes or shoved frightened-faced old women in wheelbarrows. They struggled their burdens down the steep valley road. Some broke free and bounced over the edge down across the terraces, strewing clothes and tools and cooking things over the fields. Last of all came hands and heads. These people carried their possessions on their heads and backs and children's shoulders.

My father opened the church to the refugees. There they could have rest, warm chai, some ugali, some beans. I helped stir the great pots of ugali over the open fire. The village doctor set up a treatment center. Most of the cases were for damaged feet and hands, and dehydrated children. Not everyone in Gichichi agreed with my father's charity. Some thought it would encourage the refugees to stay and take food from our mouths. The shopkeepers said he was ruining their trade by giving away what they should be selling. My father told them he was just trying to do what he thought Jesus would have done. They could not answer that, but I know he had another reason. He wanted to hear the refugees' stories. They would be his story, soon enough.

What about Tusha?

The package missed us by a couple of kilometers. It hit a place called Kombé; two Kikuyu farms and some shit-caked cows. There was a big bang. Some of us from Tusha took a matatu to see what had happened to Kombé. They tell us there is nothing left. There they are, go, ask them.

This nothing, my brothers, what was it like? A hole?

No, it was something, but nothing we could recognize. The photographs? They only show the thing. They do not show how it happens. The houses, the fields, the fields and the track, they run like fat in a pan. We saw the soil itself melt and new things reach out of it like drowning men's fingers.

What kind of things?

We do not have the words to describe them. Things like you see in the television programs about the reefs on the coast, only the size of houses, and striped like zebras. Things like fists punching out of the ground, reaching up to the sky and opening like fingers. Things like fans, and springs, and balloons, and footballs.

So fast?

Oh yes. So fast that even as we watched, it took our matatu. It came up the tires and over the bumper and across the paintwork like a lizard up a wall and the whole thing came out in thousands of tiny yellow buds.

What did you do?

What do you think we did? We ran for our lives.

The people of Kombé?

When we brought back help from Tusha, we were stopped by helicopters. Soldiers, everywhere. Everyone must leave, this is a quarantine area. You have twenty-four hours.

Twenty-four hours!

Yes, they order you to pack up a life in twenty-four hours. The Blue Berets brought in all these engineers who started building some great construction, all tracks and engines. The night was like day with welding torches. They plowed Kiyamba under with bulldozers to make a new airstrip. They were going to bring in jets there. And before they let us go they made everyone take medical tests. We lined up and went past these men in white coats and masks at tables.

Why?

I think they were testing to see if the Chaga-stuff had got into us.

What did they do, that you think that?

Pastor, some they would tap on the shoulder, just like this. Like Judas and the Lord, so gentle. Then a soldier would take them to the side.

What then?

I do not know, pastor. I have not seen them since. No one has.

These stories troubled my father greatly. They troubled the people he told them to, even Most High, who had been so thrilled by the coming of the alien to our land. They especially troubled the United Nations. Two days later a team came up from Nairobi in five army hummers. The first thing they did was tell my father and the doctor to close down their aid station. The official UNHCR refugee center was Muranga. No one could stay here in Gichichi, everyone must go.

In private they told my father that a man of his standing should not be sowing rumors and half-truths in vulnerable communities. To make sure that we knew the real truth, UNECTA called a meeting in the church. Everyone packed onto the benches, even the Muslims. People stood all the way around the walls; others outside lifted out the louvres to listen in at the windows. My father sat with the doctor and our local chief at a table. With them was a government man, a white soldier, and an Asian woman in civilian dress who looked scared. She was a scientist, a xenologist. She did most of the talking; the government man from Nairobi twirled his pencil between his fingers and tapped it on the table until he broke the point. The soldier, a French general with experience of humanitarian crises, sat motionless.

The xenologist told us that the Chaga was humanity's first contact with life from beyond the Earth. The nature of this contact was unclear; it did not follow any of the communication programs we had predicted. This contact was the physical transformation of our native landscape and vegetation. But what was in the package was not seeds and spores. The things that had consumed Kombé and were now consuming Tusha were more like tiny machines, breaking down the things of this world to pieces and rebuilding them in strange new forms. The Chaga responded to stimuli and adapted to counterattacks on itself. UNECTA had tried fire, poison, radioactive dusting, genetically modified diseases. Each had been quickly routed by the Chaga. However, it was not apparent if it was intelligent, or the tool of an as-yet unseen intelligence.

"And Gichichi?" Ismail the barber asked.

The French general spoke now.

"You will all be evacuated in plenty of time."

"But what if we do not want to be evacuated?" Most High asked. "What if we decide we want to stay here and take our chances with the Chaga?"

"You will all be evacuated," the general said again.

"This is our village, this is our country. Who are you to tell us what we must do in our own country?" Most High was indignant now. We all applauded, even my father up there with the UNECTA people. The Nairobi political looked vexed.

"UNECTA, UNHCR, and the UN East Africa Protection Force operate with the informed consent of the Kenyan government. The Chaga has been deemed a threat to human life. We're doing this for your own good."

Most High drove on. "A threat? Who 'deems' it so? UNECTA? An organization that is eighty percent funded by the United States of America? I have heard different, that it doesn't harm people or animals. There are people living inside the Chaga; it's true, isn't it?"

The politician looked at the French general, who shrugged. The Asian scientist answered.

"Officially, we have no data."

Then my father stood up and cut her short.

"What about the people who are being taken away?"

"I don't know anything . . ." the UNECTA scientist began but my father would not be stopped.

"What about the people from Kombé? What are these tests you are carrying out?"

The woman scientist looked flustered. The French general spoke.

"I'm a soldier, not a scientist. I've served in Kosovo and Iraq and East Timor. I can only answer your questions as a soldier. On the fourteenth of June next year, it will come down that road. At about seven thirty in the evening, it will come through this church. By Tuesday night, there will be no sign that a place called Gichichi ever existed."

And that was the end of the meeting. As the UNECTA people left the church, the Christians of Gichichi crowded around my father. What should they believe? Was Jesus come again, or was it anti-Christ? These aliens, were they angels, or fallen creatures like ourselves? Did they know Jesus? What was God's plan in this? Question after question after question.

My father's voice was tired and thin and driven, like a leopard harried by beaters toward guns. Like that leopard, he turned on his hunters.

"I don't know!" he shouted. "You think I have answers to all these things? No. I have no answers. I have no authority to speak on these things. No one does. Why are you asking these silly silly questions? Do you think a country pastor has the answers that will stop the Chaga in its tracks and drive it back where it came from? No. I am making them up as I go along, like everyone else."

For a moment the whole congregation was silent. I remember feeling that I must die from embarrassment. My mother touched my father's arm. He had been shaking. He excused himself to his people. They stood back to let us out of the church. We stopped on the lintel, amazed. A rapture had indeed come. All the refugees were gone from the church compound. Their goods, their bundles, their carts and animals. Even their excrement had been swept away.

As we walked back to the house, I saw the woman scientist brush past Most High as she went to the UNECTA hummer. I heard her whisper, "About the people. It's true. But they're changed."

"How?" Most High asked but the door was closed. Two blue berets lifted mad Gikombe from in front of the hummer and it drove off slowly through the throng of people. I remembered that the UNECTA woman looked frightened.

That afternoon my father rode off on the red Yamaha and did not come back for almost a week.

I learned something about my father's faith that day. It was that it was strong in the small, local questions because it was weak in the great ones. It believed in singing and teaching the people and the disciplines of personal prayer and meditation, because you could see them in the lives of others. In the big beliefs, the ones you could not see, it fell.

That meeting was the wound through which Gichichi slowly bled to death. "This is our village, this is our country," Most High had declared, but before the end of the week the first family had tied their things onto the back of their pickup and joined the flow of refugees down the road to the south. After that a week did not pass that someone from our village would not close their doors a last time and leave Gichichi. The abandoned homes soon went to ruin. Water got in, roofs collapsed, then rude boys set fire to them. The dead houses were like empty skulls. Dogs fell into toilet pits and drowned. One day when we went down to the shamba there were no names and stones from the Ukerewe house. Within a month its windows were empty, smoke-stained sockets.

With no one to tend them, the shambas went to wild and weeds. Goats and cows grazed where they would, the terrace walls crumbled, the rains washed the soil down the valley in great red tears. Fields that had fed families for generations vanished in a night. No one cared for the women's tree anymore, to give the images their cups of beer. Hope stopped working in Gichichi. Always in the minds of the ones who remained was the day when we would look up the road and see the spines and fans and twisted spires of the Chaga standing along the ridge-line like warriors.

I remember the morning I was woken by the sound of voices from the Muthiga house. Men's voices, speaking softly so as not to waken anyone, for it was still dark, but they woke me. I put on my things and went out into the compound. Grace and Ruth were carrying cardboard boxes from the house, their father and a couple of other men from the village were loading them onto a Nissan pick-up. They had started early, and the pick-up was well laden. The children were gathering up the last few things.

"Ah, Tendeléo," Mr. Muthiga said, sadly. "We had hoped to get away before anyone was around."

"Can I talk to Grace?" I asked.

I did not talk to her. I shouted at her. I would be all alone when she went. I would be abandoned. She asked me a question. She said, "You say we must not go. Tell me, Tendeléo, why must you stay?"

I did not have an answer to that. I had always presumed that it was because a pastor must stay with his people, but the bishop had made several offers to my father to relocate us to a new parish in Eldoret.

Grace and her family left as it was getting light. Their red tail lights swung into the slow stream of refugees. I heard the horn hooting to warn stragglers and animals all the way down the valley. I tried to keep the house good and safe but two weeks later a gang of rude boys from another village broke in, took what they could and burned the rest. They were a new thing in what the radio called the "sub-terminum," gangs of raiders and looters stripping the corpses of the dead towns.

"Vultures, is what they are," my mother said.

Grace's question was a dark parting gift to me. The more I thought about it, the more I became convinced that I must see this thing that had forced such decisions on us. The television and newspaper pictures were not enough. I had to see it with my own eyes. I had to look at its face and ask it its reasons. Little Egg became my lieutenant. We slipped money from the collection plate, and we gathered up secret bundles of food. A schoolday was the best to go. We did not go straight up the road, where we would have been noticed. We caught a matatu to Kinangop in the Nyandarua valley where nobody knew us. There was still a lively traffic; the matatu was full of country people with goods to sell and chickens tied together by the feet stowed under the bench. We sat in the back and ate nuts from a paper cone folded from a page of the Bible. Everywhere were dirty white United Nations vehicles. One by one the people got out and were not replaced. By Ndunyu there was only me and Little Egg, jolting around in the back of the car.

The driver's mate turned around and said, "So, where for, girls?"

I said, "We want to look at the Chaga."

"Sure, won't the Chaga be coming to look at you soon enough?"

"Can you take us there?" I showed him Church shillings.

"It would take a lot more than that." He talked to the driver a moment. "We can drop you at Njeru. You can walk from there, it's under seven kilometers."

Njeru was what awaited Gichichi, when only the weak and poor and mad remained. I was glad to leave it. The road to the Chaga was easy to find, it was the direction no one else was going in. We set off up the red dirt road toward the mountains. We must have looked very strange, two girls walking through a ruined land with their lunches wrapped in kangas. If anyone had been there to watch.

The soldiers caught us within two kilometers of Njeru. I had heard the sound of their engine for some minutes, behind us. It was a big eight-wheeled troop carrier of the South African army.

The officer was angry, but I think a little impressed. What did we think we were doing? There were vultures everywhere. Only last week an entire bus had been massacred, five kilometers from here. Not one escaped alive. Two girls alone, they would rob us and rape us, hang us up by our heels and cut our throats like pigs. All the time he was preaching, a soldier in the turret swept the countryside with a big heavy machine gun.

"So, what the hell are you doing here?"

I told him. He went to talk on the radio. When he came back, he said, "In the back."

The carrier was horribly hot and smelled of men and guns and diesel. When the door clanged shut on us I thought we were going to suffocate.

"Where are you taking us?" I asked, afraid.

"You came to see the Chaga," the commander said. We ate our lunch meekly and tried not to stare at the soldiers. They gave us water from their canteens and tried to make us laugh. The ride was short but uncomfortable. The door clanged open. The officer helped me out and I almost fell over with shock.

I stood in a hillside clearing. Around me were tree stumps, fresh cut, sticky with sap. From behind came the noise of chain saws. The clearing was full of military vehicles and tents. People hurried every way. Most of them were white. At the center of this activity was what I can only call a city on wheels. I had not yet been to Nairobi, but I knew it from photographs, a forest of beautiful towers rising out of a circle of townships. That was how the base seemed to me when I first saw it. Looking closer, I saw that the buildings were portable cabins stacked up on big tracked flat-beds, like the heavy log-carriers up in Eldoret. The tractors and towers were joined together with walkways and loops of cable. I saw people running along the high walkways. I would not have done that, not for a million shillings.

I tell you my first impressions, of a beautiful white city—and you may laugh because you know it was only a UNECTA mobile base—that they put together as fast and cheap as they could. But there is a truth here; seeing is magical. Looking kills. The longer I looked, the more the magic faded.

The air in the clearing smelled as badly of diesel smoke as it had in the troop carrier. Everywhere was engine-noise. A path had been slashed through the forest, as if the base had come down it. I looked at the tracks. The big cog wheels were turning. The base was moving, slowly and heavily, like the hands of a clock, creaking backward on its tracks in pace with the advance of the Chaga. Little Egg took my hand. I think my mouth must have been open in wonder for some time.

"Come on then," said the officer. He was smiling now. "You wanted to see the Chaga."

He gave us over to a tall American man with red hair and a red beard and blue eyes. His name was Byron and he spoke such bad Swahili that he did not understand when Little Egg said to me, "he looks like a vampire."

"I speak English," I told him and he looked relieved.

He took us through the tractors to the tower in the middle, the tallest. It was painted white, with the word UNECTA big in blue on the side, and beneath it, the name, Nyandarua Station. We got into a small metal cage. Byron closed the door and pressed a button. The cage went straight up the side of the building. I tell you this, that freight elevator was more frightening than any stories about murdering gangs of vultures. I gripped the handrail and closed my eyes. I could feel the whole base swaying below me.

"Open your eyes," Byron said. "You wouldn't want to come all this way and miss it."

As we rose over the tops of the trees the land opened before me. Nyandarua Station was moving down the eastern slopes of the Aberdare range: the Chaga was spread before me like a wedding kanga laid out on a bed.

It was as though someone had cut a series of circles of colored paper and let them fall on the side of the mountains. The Chaga followed the ridges and the valleys, but that was all it had to do with our geography. It was completely something else. The colors were so bright and silly I almost laughed: purples, oranges, lots of pink and deep red. Veins of bright yellow. Real things, living things were not these colors. This was a Hollywood trick, done with computers for a film. I guessed we were a kilometer from the edge. It was not a very big Chaga, not like the Kilimanjaro Chaga that had swallowed Moshi and Arusha and all the big Tanzanian towns at the foot of the mountain and was now halfway to Nairobi. Byron said this Chaga was about five kilometers across and beginning to show the classic form, a series of circles. I tried to make out the details. I thought details would make it real to me. I saw jumbles of reef-stuff the color of wiring. I saw a wall of dark crimson trees rise straight for a tremendous height. The trunks were as straight and smooth as spears. The leaves joined together like umbrellas. Beyond them, I saw things like icebergs tilted at an angle, things like open hands, praying to the sky, things like oil refineries made out of fungus, things like brains and fans and domes and footballs. Things like other things. Nothing that seemed a thing in itself. And all this was reaching toward me. But, I realized, it would never catch me. Not while I remained here, on this building that was retreating from it down the foothills of the Aberdares, fifty meters every day.

We were close to the top of the building. The cage swayed in the wind. I felt sick and scared and grabbed the rail and that was when it became real for me. I caught the scent of the Chaga on the wind. False things have no scent. The Chaga smelled of cinnamon and sweat and soil new turned up. It smelled of rotting fruit and diesel and concrete after rain. It smelled like my mother when she had The Visit. It smelled like the milk that babies spit out of their mouths. It smelled like televisions and the stuff the Barber Under the Tree put on my father's hair and the women's holy place in the shamba. With each of these came a memory of Gichichi and my life and people. The scent stirred the things I had recently learned as a woman. The Chaga became real for me there, and I understood that it would eat my world.

While I was standing, putting all these things that were and would be into circles within circles inside my head, a white man in faded jeans and Timberland boots rushed out of a sliding door onto the elevator.

"Byron," he said, then noticed that there were two little Kenyan girls there with him. "Who're these?"

"I'm Tendeléo and this is my sister," I said. "We call her Little Egg. We've come to see the Chaga."

This answer seemed to please him.

"I'm called Shepard." He shook our hands. He also was American. "I'm a Peripatetic Executive Director. That means I rush around the world finding solutions to the Chaga."

"And have you?"

For a moment he was taken aback, and I felt bold and rude. Then he said, "Come on, let's see."

"Shepard," Byron the vampire said. "It'll wait."

He took us in to the base. In one room were more white people than I had seen in the whole of my life. Each desk had a computer but the people—most of them were men dressed very badly in shorts, with beards—did not use them. They preferred to sit on each other's desks and talk very fast with much gesturing.

"Are African people not allowed in here?" I asked.

The man Shepard laughed. Everything I said that tour he treated as if it had come from the lips of a wise old m'zee. He took us down into the Projection Room where computers drew huge plans on circular tables: of the Chaga now, the Chaga in five years' time, and the Chaga when it met with its brother from the south and both of them swallowed Nairobi like two old men arguing over a stick of sugar cane.

"And after Nairobi is gone?" I asked. The maps showed the names of all the old towns and villages, under the Chaga. Of course. The names do not change. I reached out to touch the place that Gichichi would become.

"We can't project that far," he said. But I was thinking of an entire city, vanished beneath the bright colors of the Chaga like dirt trodden into carpet. All those lives and histories and stories. I realized that some names can be lost, the names of big things, like cities, and nations, and histories.

Next we went down several flights of steep steel stairs to the "lab levels." Here samples taken from the Chaga were stored inside sealed environments. A test tube might hold a bouquet of delicate fungi, a cylindrical jar a fistful of blue spongy fingers, a tank a square meter of Chaga, growing up the walls and across the ceiling. Some of the containers were so big people could walk around inside. They were dressed in bulky white suits that covered every part of them and were connected to the wall with pipes and tubes so that it was hard to tell where they ended and alien Chaga began. The weird striped and patterned leaves looked more natural than the UNECTA people in their white suits. The alien growing things were at least in their right world.

"Everything has to be isolated." Mr. Shepard said.

"Is that because even out here, it will start to attack and grow?" I asked.

"You got it."

"But I heard it doesn't attack people or animals," I said.

"Where did you hear that?" this man Shepard asked.

"My father told me," I said mildly.

We went on down to Terrestrial Cartography, which was video-pictures the size of a wall of the world seen looking down from satellites. It is a view that is familiar to everyone of our years, though there were people of my parents' generation who laughed when they heard that the world is a ball, with no string to hold it up. I looked for a long time—it is the one thing that does not pale for looking—before I saw that the face of the world was scarred, like a Giriama woman's. Beneath the clouds, South America and South Asia and mother Africa were spotted with dots of lighter color than the brown-green land. Some were large, some were specks, all were precise circles. One, on the eastern side of Africa, identified this disease of continents to me. Chagas. For the first time I understood that this was not a Kenyan thing, not even an African thing, but a whole world thing.

"They are all in the south," I said. "There is not one in the north."

"None of the biological packages have seeded in the northern hemisphere. This is what makes us believe that there are limits to the Chaga. That it won't cover our whole world, pole to pole. That it might confine itself only to the southern hemisphere."

"Why do you think that?"

"No reason at all."

"You just hope."

"Yeah. We hope."

"Mr. Shepard," I said. "Why should the Chaga take away our lands here in the south and leave you rich people in the north untouched? It does not seem fair."

"The universe is not fair, kid. Which you probably know better than me."

We went down then to Stellar Cartography, another dark room, with walls full of stars. They formed a belt around the middle of the room, in places so dense that individual stars blurred into masses of solid white.

"This is the Silver River," I said. I had seen this on Grace's family's television, which they had taken with them.

"Silver river. It is that. Good name."

"Where are we?" I asked.

Shepard went over to the wall near the door and touched a small star down near his waist. It had a red circle around it. Otherwise I do not think even he could have picked it out of all the other small white stars. I did not like it that our sun was so small and common. I asked, "And where are they from?"

The UNECTA man drew a line with his finger along the wall. He walked down one side of the room, halfway along the other, before he stopped. His finger stopped in a swirl of rainbow colors, like a flame.

"Rho Ophiuchi. It's just a name, it doesn't matter. What's important is that it's a long long way from us . . . so far it takes light—and that's as fast as anything can go—eight hundred years to get there, and it's not a planet, or even a star. It's what we call a nebula, a huge cloud of glowing gas."

"How can people live in a cloud?" I asked. "Are they angels?"

The man laughed at that.

"Not people," he said. "Not angels either. Machines. But not like you or I think of machines. Machines more like living things, and very very much smaller. Smaller even than the smallest cell in your body. Machines the size of chains of atoms, that can move other atoms around and so build copies of themselves, or copies of anything else they want. And we think those gas clouds are trillions upon trillions of those tiny, living machines."

"Not plants and animals," I said.

"Not plants and animals, no."

"I have not heard this theory before." It was huge and thrilling, but like the sun, it hurt if you looked at it too closely. I looked again at the swirl of color, colored like the Chaga scars on Earth's face, and back at the little dot by the door that was my light and heat. Compared to the rest of the room, they both looked very small. "Why should things like this, from so far away, want to come to my Kenya?"

"That's indeed the question."

That was all of the science that the UNECTA man was allowed to show us, so he took us down through the areas where people lived and ate and slept, where they watched television and films and drank alcohol and coffee, the places where they exercised, which they liked to do a lot, in immodest costumes. The corridors were full of them, immature and loosely put together, like leggy puppies.

"This place stinks of wazungu," Little Egg said, not thinking that maybe this m'zungu knew more Swahili than the other one. Mr. Shepard smiled.

"Mr. Shepard," I said. "You still haven't answered my question."

He looked puzzled a moment, then remembered.

"Solutions. Oh yes. Well, what do you think?"

Several questions came into my head but none as good, or important to me, as the one I did ask.

"I suppose the only question that matters, really, is can people live in the Chaga?"

Shepard pushed open a door and we were on a metal platform just above one of the big track sets.

"That, my friend, is the one question we aren't even allowed to consider," Shepard said as he escorted us onto a staircase.

The tour was over. We had seen the Chaga. We had seen our world and our future and our place among the stars; things too big for country church children, but which even they must consider, for unlike most of the wazungu here, they would have to find answers.

Down on the red dirt with the diesel stink and roar of chain-saws, we thanked Dr. Shepard. He seemed touched. He was clearly a person of

power in this place. A word, and there was a UNECTA Landcruiser to take
us home. We were so filled up with what we had seen that we did not think
to tell the driver to let us off at the next village down so we could walk.
Instead we went landcruising right up the main road, past Haran's shop
and the Peugeot Service Station and all the Men Who Read Newspapers
under the trees.

Then we faced my mother and father. It was bad. My father took me
into his study. I stood. He sat. He took his Kalenjin Bible, that the Bishop
gave him on his ordination so that he might always have God's word in his
own tongue, and set it on the desk between himself and me. He told me
that I had deceived my mother and him, that I had led Little Egg astray,
that I had lied, that I had stolen, not God's money, for God had no need
of money, but the money that people I saw every day, people I sang and
prayed next to every Sunday, gave in their faith. He said all this in a very
straightforward, very calm way, without ever raising his voice. I wanted to
tell him all the things I said seen, offer them in trade, yes, I have cheated, I
have lied, I have stolen from the Christians of Gichichi, but I have learned.
I have seen. I have seen our sun lost among a million other suns. I have
seen this world, that God is supposed to have made most special of all
worlds, so small it cannot even be seen. I have seen men, that God is supposed to have loved so much that he died for their evils, try to understand
living machines, each smaller than the smallest living thing, but together,
so huge it takes light years to cross their community. I know how different
things are from what we believe, I wanted to say, but I said nothing, for my
father did an unbelievable thing. He stood up. Without sign or word or any
display of strength, he hit me across the face. I fell to the ground, more
from the unexpectedness than the hurt. Then he did another unbelievable
thing. He sat down. He put his head in his hand. He began to cry. Now I
was very scared, and I ran to my mother.

"He is a frightened man," she said. "Frightened men often strike out at
the thing they fear."

"He has his church, he has his collar, he has his Bible, what can frighten
him?"

"You," she said. This answer was as stunning as my father hitting me.
My mother asked me if I remembered the time, after the argument outside
the church, when my father had disappeared on the red Yamaha for a week.
I said I did, yes.

"He went down south, to Nairobi, and beyond. He went to look at the thing he feared, and he saw that, with all his faith, he could not beat the Chaga."

My father stayed in his study a long time. Then he came to me and went down on his knees and asked me to forgive him. It was a Biblical principle, he said. Do not let the sun go down on your anger. But though Bible principles lived, my father died a little to me that day. This is life: a series of dyings and being born into new things and understandings.

Life by life, Gichichi died too. There were only twenty families left on the morning when the spines of the alien coral finally reached over the tree-tops up on the pass. Soon after dawn the UNECTA trucks arrived. They were dirty old Sudanese Army things, third-hand Russian, badly painted and billowing black smoke. When we saw the black soldiers get out we were alarmed because we had heard bad things about Africans at the hands of other Africans. I did not trust their officer; he was too thin and had an odd hollow on the side of his shaved head, like a crater on the moon. We gathered in the open space in front of the church with our things piled around us. Ours came to twelve bundles wrapped up in kangas. I took the radio and a clatter of pots. My father's books were tied with string and balanced on the petrol tank of his red scrambler.

The moon-headed officer waved and the first truck backed up and let down its tail. A soldier jumped out, set up a folding beach-chair by the tail-gate and sat with a clip-board and a pencil. First went the Kurias, who had been strong in the church. They threw their children up into the truck, then passed up their bundles of belongings. The soldier in the beach-chair watched for a time, then shook his head.

"Too much, too much," he said in bad Swahili. "You must leave something."

Mr. Kuria frowned, measuring all the space in the back of the truck with his eyes. He lifted off a bundle of clothes.

"No no no," the soldier said, and stood up and tapped their television with his pencil. Another soldier came and took it out of Mr. Kuria's arms to a truck at the side of the road, the tithe truck.

"Now you get on," the soldier said, and made a check on his clip-board.

It was as bold as that. Wide-open crime under the blue sky. No one to see. No one to care. No one to say a word.

Our family's tax was the motorbike. My father's face had gone tight with anger and offense to God's laws, but he gave it up without a whisper. The officer wheeled it away to a group of soldiers squatting on their heels by a smudge-fire. They were very pleased with it, poking and teasing its engine with their long fingers. Every time since that I have heard a Yamaha engine I have looked to see if it is a red scrambler, and what thief is riding it.

"On, on," said the tithe-collector.

"My church," my father said and jumped off the truck. Immediately there were a dozen Kalashnikovs pointing at him. He raised his hands, then looked back at us.

"Tendeléo, you should see this."

The officer nodded. The guns were put down and I jumped to the ground. I walked with my father to the church. We proceeded up the aisle. The prayer books were on the bench seats, the woven kneelers set square in front of the pews. We went into the little vestry, where I had stolen the money from the collection. There were other dark secrets here. My father took a battered red petrol can from his robing cupboard and carried it to the communion table. He took the chalice, offered it to God, then filled it with petrol from the can. He turned to face the holy table.

"The blood of Christ keep you in eternal life," he said, raising the cup high. The he poured it out onto the white altar cloth. A gesture too fast for me to see; he struck fire. There was an explosion of yellow flame. I cried out. I thought my father had gone up in the gush of fire. He turned to me. Flames billowed behind him.

"Now do you understand?" he said.

I did. Sometimes it is better to destroy a thing you love than have it taken from you and made alien. Smoke was pouring from under the roof by the time we climbed back onto the truck. The Sudanese soldiers were only interested in that it was fire, and destruction excites soldiers. Ours was the church of an alien god.

Old Gikombe, too old and stupid to run away, did his "sitting in front of the trucks" trick. Every time the soldiers moved him, he scuttled back to his place. He did it once too often. The truck behind us had started to roll, and the driver did not see the dirty, rag-wrapped thing dart in under his wing. With a cry, Gikombe fell under the wheels and was crushed.

A wind from off the Chaga carried the smoke from the burning church over us as we went down the valley road. The communion at Gichichi was broken.

I think time changes everything into its opposite. Youth into age, innocence into experience, certainty into uncertainty. Life into death. Long before the end, time was changing Nairobi into the Chaga. Ten million people were crowded into the shanties that ringed the towers of downtown.

Every hour of every day, more came. They came from north and south, from Rift Valley and Central Province, from Ilbisil and Naivasha, from Makindu and Gichichi.

Once Nairobi was a fine city. Now it was a refugee camp. Once it had great green parks. Now they were trampled dust between packing-case homes. The trees had all been hacked down for firewood. Villages grew up on road roundabouts, like castaways on coral islands, and in the football stadiums and sports grounds. Armed patrols daily cleared squatters from the two airport runways. The railway had been abandoned, cut south and north. Ten thousand people now lived in abandoned carriages and train sheds and between the tracks. The National Park was a dust bowl, ravaged for fuel and building material, its wildlife fled or slaughtered for food. Nairobi air was a smog of wood smoke, diesel and sewage. The slums spread for twenty kilometers on every side. It was an hour's walk to fetch water, and that was stinking and filthy. Like the Chaga, the shanties grew, hour by hour, family by family. String up a few plastic sheets here, shove together some cardboard boxes there, set up home where a matatu dies, pile some stolen bricks and sacking and tin. City and Chaga reached out to each other, and came to resemble each other.

I remember very little of those first days in Nairobi. It was too much, too fast—it numbed my sense of reality. The men who took our names, the squatting people watching us as we walked up the rows of white tents looking for our number, were things done to us that we went along with without thinking. Most of the time I had that high-pitched sound in my ear when you want to cry but cannot.

Here is an irony: we came from St. John's, we went to St. John's. It was a new camp, in the south close by the main airport. One eight three two. One number, one tent, one oil lamp, one plastic water bucket, one rice scoop. Every hundred tents there was a water pipe. Every hundred tents there was a shit pit. A river of sewage ran past our door. The stench would have stopped us sleeping, had the cold not done that first. The tent was thin and cheap and gave no protection from the night. We huddled together under blankets. No one wanted to be the first to cry, so no one did. Between the big aircraft and people crying and fighting, there was no quiet, ever. The first night, I heard shots. I had never heard them before but I knew exactly what they were.

In this St. John's we were no longer people of consequence. We were no longer anything. We were one eight three two. My father's collar earned no respect. The first day he went to the pipe for water he was beaten by young men, who stole his plastic water pail. The collar was a symbol of God's treachery. My father stopped wearing his collar; soon after, he stopped going out at all. He sat in the back room listening to the radio and looking at his books, which were still in their tied-up bundles. St. John's destroyed the rest of the things that had bound his life together. I think that if we had not been rescued, he would have gone under. In a place like St. John's, that means you die. When you went to the food truck you saw the ones on the way to death, sitting in front of their tents, holding their toes, rocking, looking at the soil.

We had been fifteen days in the camp—I kept a tally on the tent wall with a burned-out match—when we heard the vehicle pull up and the voice call out, "Jonathan Bi. Does anyone know Pastor Jonathan Bi?" I do not think my father could have looked anymore surprised if Jesus had called his name. Our savior was the Pastor Stephen Elezeke, who ran the Church Army Centre on Jogoo Road. He and my father had been in theological college together; they had been great footballing friends. My father was godfather to Pastor Elezeke's children; Pastor Elezeke, it seemed, was my godfather. He piled us all in the back of a white Nissan minibus with Praise Him on the Trumpet written on one side and Praise Him with the Psaltery and Harp, rather squashed up, on the other. He drove off hooting at the crowds of young men, who looked angrily at church men in a church van. He explained that he had found us through the net. The big churches were flagging certain clergy names. Bi was one of them.

So we came to Jogoo Road. Church Army had once been an old, pre-Independence teaching center with a modern, two-level accommodation block. These had overflowed long ago; now every open space was crowded with tents and wooden shanties. We had two rooms beside the metal working shop. They were comfortable but cramped, and when the metal workers started, noisy. There was no privacy.

The heart of Church Army was a little white chapel, shaped like a drum, with a thatched roof. The tents and lean-tos crowded close to the chapel but left a respectful distance. It was sacred. Many went there to pray. Many went to cry away from others, where it would not infect them like dirty water. I often saw my father go into the chapel. I thought about listening at the door to hear if he was praying or crying, but I did not. Whatever he looked for there, it did not seem to make him a whole man again.

My mother tried to make Jogoo Road Gichichi. Behind the accommodation block was a field of dry grass with an open drain running down the far side. Beyond the drain was a fence and a road, then the Jogoo Road market with its name painted on its rusting tin roof, then the shanties began again. But this field was untouched and open. My mother joined a group of women who wanted to turn the field into shambas. Pastor Elezeke agreed and they made mattocks in the workshops from bits of old car, broke up the soil, and planted maize and cane. That summer we watched the crops grow as the shanties crowded in around the Jogoo Road market, and stifled it, and took it apart for roofs and walls. But they never touched the shambas. It was as if they were protected. The women hoed and sang to the radio and laughed and talked women-talk, and Little Egg and the Chole girls chased enormous sewer rats with sticks. One day I saw little cups of beer and dishes of maize and salt in a corner of the field and understood how it was protected.

My mother pretended it was Gichichi but I could see it was not. In Gichichi, the men did not stand by the fence wire and stare so nakedly. In Gichichi the helicopter gunships did not wheel overhead like vultures. In Gichichi the brightly painted matatus that roared up and down did not have heavy machine guns bolted to the roof and boys in sports fashion in the back looking at everything as if they owned it. They were a new thing in Nairobi, these gun-gangs; the Tacticals. Men, usually young, organized into gangs, with vehicles and guns, dressed in anything they could make a uniform. Some were as young as twelve. They gave themselves names like the Black Simbas and the Black Rhinos and the Ebonettes and the United Christian Front and the Black Taliban. They liked the word black. They thought it sounded threatening. These Tacticals had as many philosophies and beliefs as names, but they all owned territory, patrolled their streets, and told their people they were the law. They enforced their law with kneecappings and burning car tires, they defended their streets with AK47s. We all knew that when the Chaga came, they would fight like hyenas over the corpse of Nairobi. The Soca Boys was our local army. They wore sports fashion and knee-length manager's coats and had football team logos painted in the sides of their picknis, as the armed matatus were called. On their banners they had a black-and-white patterned ball on a green field. Despite their name, it was not a football. It was a buckyball, a carbon fullerene molecule, the half-living, half-machine building-brick of the Chaga. Their leader, a rat-faced boy in a Manchester United coat and shades that kept sliding down his nose, did not like Christians, so on Sundays he would send his picknis up and down Jogoo Road, roaring their engines and shooting into the air, but because they could.

The Church Army had its own plans for the coming time of changes. A few nights later, as I went to the choo, I overheard Pastor Elezeke and my father talking in the Pastor's study. I put my torch out and listened at the louvres.

"We need people like you, Jonathan," Elezeke was saying. "It is a work of God, I think. We have a chance to build a true Christian society."

"You cannot be certain."

"There are Tacticals . . ."

"They are filth. They are vultures."

"Hear me out, Jonathan. Some of them go into the Chaga. They bring things out—for all their quarantine, there are things the Americans want very much from the Chaga. It is different from what we are told is in there. Very very different. Plants that are like machines, that generate electricity, clean water, fabric, shelter, medicines. Knowledge. There are devices, the size of this thumb, that transmit information directly into the brain. And more; there are people living in there, not like primitives, not, forgive me, like refugees. It shapes itself to them, they have learned to make it work for them. There are whole towns—towns, I tell you—down there under Kilimanjaro. A great society is rising."

"It shapes itself to them," my father said. "And it shapes them to itself."

There was a pause.

"Yes. That is true. Different ways of being human."

"I cannot help you with this, my brother."

"Will you tell me why?"

"I will," my father said, so softly I had to press close to the window to hear. "Because I am afraid, Stephen. The Chaga has taken everything from me, but that is still not enough for it. It will only be satisfied when it has taken me, and changed me, and made me alien to myself."

"Your faith, Jonathan. What about your faith?"

"It took that first of all."

"Ah," Pastor Elezeke sighed. Then, after a time, "You understand you are always welcome here?"

"Yes, I do. Thank you, but I cannot help you."

That same night I went to the white chapel—my first and last time—to force issues with God. It was a very beautiful building, with a curving inner wall that made you walk halfway around the inside before you could enter. I suppose you could say it was spiritual, but the cross above the table angered me. It was straight and true and did not care for anyone or any-thing. I sat glaring at it some time before I found the courage to say, "You say you are the answer."

I am the answer, said the cross.

"My father is destroyed by fear. Fear of the Chaga, fear of the future, fear of death, fear of living. What is your answer?"

I am the answer.

"We are refugees, we live on wazungus' charity, my mother hoes corn, my sister roasts it at the roadside; tell me your answer."

I am the answer.

"An alien life has taken everything we ever owned. Even now, it wants more, and nothing can stop it. Tell me, what is your answer?"

I am the answer.

"You tell me you are the answer to every human need and question, but what does that mean? What is the answer to your answer?"

I am the answer, the silent, hanging cross said.

"That is no answer!" I screamed at the cross. "You do not even understand the questions, how can you be the answer? What power do you have? None. You can do nothing! They need me, not you. I am going to do what you can't."

I did not run from the chapel. You do not run from gods you no longer believe in. I walked, and took no notice of the people who stared at me.

The next morning, I went into Nairobi to get a job. To save money I went on foot. There were men everywhere, walking with friends, sitting by the roadside selling sheet metal charcoal burners or battery lamps, or making things from scrap metal and old tires, squatting together outside their huts with their hands draped over their knees. There must have been women, but they kept themselves hidden. I did not like the way the men worked me over with their eyes. They had shanty-town eyes, that see only what they can use in a thing. I must have appeared too poor to rob and too hungry to sexually harass, but I did not feel safe until the downtown towers rose around me and the vehicles on the streets were diesel-stained green and yellow buses and quick white UN cars.

I went first to the back door of one of the big tourist hotels.

"I can peel and clean and serve people," I said to an undercook in dirty whites. "I work hard and I am honest. My father is a pastor."

"You and ten million others," the cook said. "Get out of here."

Then I went to the CNN building. It was a big, bold idea. I slipped in behind a motorbike courier and went up to a good-looking Luo on the desk.

"I'm looking for work," I said. "Any work, I can do anything. I can make chai, I can photocopy, I can do basic accounts. I speak good English and a little French. I'm a fast learner."

"No work here today," the Luo on the desk said. "Or any other day. Learn that, fast."

I went to the Asian shops along Moi Avenue.

"Work?" the shopkeepers said. "We can't even sell enough to keep ourselves, let alone some up-country refugee."

I went to the wholesalers on Kimathi Street and the City Market and the stall traders and I got the same answer from each of them: no economy, no market, no work. I tried the street hawkers, selling liquidated stock from tarpaulins on the pavement, but their bad mouths and lewdness sickened me. I walked the five kilometers along Uhuru Highway to the UN East Africa Headquarters on Chiromo Road. The soldier on the gate would not even look at me. Cars and hummers he could see. His own people, he could not. After an hour I went away.

I took a wrong turn on the way back and ended up in a district I did not know, of dirty-looking two-story buildings that once held shops, now burned out or shuttered with heavy steel. Cables dipped across the street, loop upon loop upon loop, sagging and heavy. I could hear voices but see no one around. The voices came from an alley behind a row of shops. An entire district was crammed into this alley. Not even in St. John's camp have I seen so many people in one place. The alley was solid with bodies, jammed together, moving like one thing, like a rain cloud. The noise was incredible. At the end of the alley I glimpsed a big black foreign car, very shiny, and a man standing on the roof. He was surrounded by reaching hands, as if they were worshipping him.

"What's going on?" I shouted to whoever would hear. The crowd surged. I stood firm.

"Hiring," a shaved-headed boy as thin as famine shouted back. He saw I was puzzled. "Watekni. Day jobs in data processing. The UN treats us like shit in our own country, but we're good enough to do their tax returns."

"Good money?"

"Money." The crowd surged again, and made me part of it. A new car arrived behind me. The crowd turned like a flock of birds on the wing and pushed me toward the open doors. Big men with dark glasses got out and made a space around the watekni broker. He was a small Luhya in a long white jellaba and the uniform shades. He had a mean mouth. He fanned a fistful of paper slips. My hand went out by instinct and I found a slip in it. A single word was printed on it: Nimepata.

"Password of the day," my thin friend said. "Gets you into the system."

"Over there, over there," one of the big men said, pointing to an old bus at the end of the alley. I ran to the bus. I could feel a hundred people on my heels. There was another big man at the bus door.

"What're your languages?" the big man demanded.

"English and a bit of French," I told him.

"You waste my fucking time, kid," the man shouted. He tore the password slip from my hand, pushed me so hard, with two hands, I fell. I saw feet, crushing feet, and I rolled underneath the bus and out the other side. I did not stop running until I was out of the district of the watekni and into streets with people on them. I did not see if the famine-boy got a slip. I hope he did.

Singers wanted, said the sign by the flight of street stairs to an upper floor. So, my skills had no value in the information technology market. There were other markets. I climbed the stairs. They led to a room so dark I could not at first make out its dimensions. It smelled of beer, cigarettes, and poppers. I sensed a number of men.

"Your sign says you want singers," I called into the dark.

"Come in then." The man's voice was low and dark, smoky, like an old hut. I ventured in. As my eyes grew used to the dark, I saw tables, chairs upturned on them, a bar, a raised stage area. I saw a number of dark figures at a table, and the glow of cigarettes.

"Let's have you."

"Where?"

"There."

I got up on the stage. A light stabbed out and blinded me.

"Take your top off."

I hesitated, then unbuttoned my blouse. I slipped it off, stood with my arms loosely folded over my breasts. I could not see the men, but I felt the shanty-eyes.

"You stand like a Christian child," smoky voice said. "Let's see the goods."

I unfolded my arms. I stood in the silver light for what seemed like hours.

"Don't you want to hear me sing?"

"Girl, you could sing like an angel, but if you don't have the architecture . . ."

I picked up my blouse and rebuttoned it. It was much more shaming putting it on than taking it off. I climbed down off the stage. The men began to talk and laugh. As I reached the door, the dark voice called me.

"Can you do a message?"

"What do you want?"

"Run this down the street for me right quick."

I saw fingers hold up a small glass vial. It glittered in the light from the open door.

"Down the street."

"To the American Embassy."

"I can find that."

"That's good. You give it to a man."

"What man?"

"You tell the guard on the gate. He'll know."

"How will he know me?"

"Say you're from Brother Dust."

"And how much will Brother Dust pay me?"

The men laughed.

"Enough."

"In my hand?"

"Only way to do business."

"We have a deal."

"Good girl. Hey."

"What?"

"Don't you want to know what it is?"

"Do you want to tell me?"

"They're fullerenes. They're from the Chaga. Do you understand that? They are alien spores. The Americans want them. They can use them to build things, from nothing up. Do you understand any of this?"

"A little."

"So be it. One last thing."

"What?"

"You don't carry it in your hand. You don't carry it anywhere on you. You get my meaning?"

"I think I do."

"There are changing rooms for the girls back of the stage. You can use one of them."

"Okay. Can I ask a question?"

"You can ask anything you like."

"These . . . fullerenes. These Chaga things . . . What if they—go off, inside?"

"You trust the stories that they never touch human flesh. Here. You may need this." An object flipped through the air toward me. I caught it . . . a tube of KY jelly. "A little lubrication."

I had one more question before I went backstage area.

"Can I ask, why me?"

"For a Christian child, you've a decent amount of dark," the voice said. "So, you've a name?"

"Tendeléo."

Ten minutes later I was walking across town, past all the UN check-points and security points, with a vial of Chaga fullerenes slid into my vagina. I walked up to the gate of the American Embassy. There were two guards with white helmets and white gaiters. I picked the big black one with the very good teeth.

"I'm from Brother Dust," I said.

"One moment please," the marine said. He made a call on his PDU. One minute later the gates swung open and a small white man with sticking-up hair came out.

"Come with me," he said, and took me to the guard unit toilets, where I extracted the consignment. In exchange he gave me a playing card with a portrait of a President of the United States on the back. The President was Nixon.

"You ever go back without one of these, you die," he told me. I gave the Nixon card to the man who called himself Brother Dust. He gave me a roll of shillings and told me to come back on Tuesday.

I gave two thirds of the roll to my mother.

"Where did you get this?" she asked, holding the notes in her hands like blessings.

"I have a job," I said, challenging her to ask. She never did ask. She bought clothes for Little Egg and fruit from the market. On the Tuesday, I went back to the upstairs club that smelled of beer and smoke and come and took another load inside me to the spikey-haired man at the Embassy.

So I became a runner. I became a link in a chain that ran from legend-ary cities under the clouds of Kilimanjaro across terminum, past the UN Interdiction Force, to an upstairs club in Nairobi, into my body, to the US Embassy. No, I do not have that right. I was a link in a chain that started eight hundred years ago, as light flies, in a gas cloud called Rho Ophiuchi, that ran from US Embassy to US Government, and on to a man whose face was on the back on one of my safe-conduct cards and from him into a future no one could guess.

"It scares them, that's why they want it," Brother Dust told me. "Americans are always drawn to things that terrify them. They think these fullerenes will give the edge to their industries, make the economy inde-structible. Truth is, they'll destroy their industries, wreck their economy.

With these, anyone can make anything they want. Their free market can't stand up to that."

I did not stay a runner long. Brother Dust liked my refusal to be impressed by what the world said should impress me. I became his personal assistant. I made appointments, kept records. I accompanied him when he called on brother Sheriffs. The Chaga was coming closer, the Tacticals were on the streets; old enemies were needed as allies now.

One such day, Brother Dust gave me a present wrapped in a piece of silk. I unwrapped it; inside was a gun. My first reaction was fear; that a sixteen-year-old girl should have the gift of life or death in her hand. Would I, could I, ever use it on living flesh? Then a sense of power crept through me. For the first time in my life, I had authority.

"Don't love it too much," Brother Dust warned. "Guns don't make you safe. Nowhere in this world is safe, not for you, not for anyone."

It felt like a sin, like a burn on my body as I carried it next to my skin back to Jogoo Road. It was impossible to keep it in our rooms, but Simeon in the metal shop had been stashing my roll for some time now and he was happy to hide the gun behind the loose block. He wanted to handle it. I would not let him, though I think he did when I was not around. Every morning I took it out, some cash for lunch and bribes, and went to work.

With a gun and money in my pocket, Brother Dust's warning seemed old and full of fear. I was young and fast and clever. I could make the world as safe or as dangerous as I liked. Two days after my seventeenth birthday, the truth of what he said arrived at my door.

It was late, it was dark, and I was coming off the matatu outside Church Army. It was a sign of how far things had gone with my mother and father that they no longer asked where I was until so late, or how the money kept coming. At once I could tell something was wrong; a sense you develop when you work on the street. People were milling around in the compound, needing to do something, not knowing what they could do. Elsewhere, women's voices were shouting. I found Simeon.

"What's happening, where is my mother?"

"The shambas. They have broken through into the shambas."

I pushed my way through the silly, mobbing Christians. The season was late, the corn over my head, the cane dark and whispering. I strayed off the shamba paths in moments. The moon ghosted behind clouds, the air-glow of the city surrounded me but cast no light. The voices steered me until I saw lights gleaming through the stalks: torches and yellow naphtha flares. The voices were loud now, close. There were now men, loud men. Loud men have always frightened me. Not caring for the crop, I charged through the maize, felling rich, ripe heads.

The women of Church Army stood at the edge of the crushed crop. Maize, potatoes, cane, beans had been trodden down, ripped out, torn up. Facing them was a mob of shanty-town people. The men had torches and cutting tools. The women's kangas bulged with stolen food. The children's baskets and sacks were stuffed with bean pods and maize cobs. They faced us shamelessly. Beyond the flattened wire fence, a larger crowd was waiting in front of the market; the hyenas, who if the mob won, would go with them, and if it lost, would sneak back to their homes. They outnumbered the women twenty to one. But I was bold. I had the authority of a gun.

"Get out of here," I shouted at them. "This is not your land."

"And neither is it yours," their leader said, a man thin as a skeleton, barefoot, dressed in cut-off jeans and a rag of a fertilizer company T-shirt. He held a tincan oil-lamp in his left hand, in his right a machete. "It is all borrowed from the Chaga. It will take it away, and none of us will have it. We want what we can take, before it is lost to all of us."

"Go to the United Nations," I shouted.

The leader shook his head. The men stepped forward. The women murmured, gripped their mattocks and hoes firmly.

"The United Nations? Have you not heard? They are scaling down the relief effort. We are to be left to the mercy of the Chaga."

"This is our food. We grew it, we need it. Get off our land!"

"Who are you?" the leader laughed. The men hefted their pangas and stepped forward. The laughter lit the dark inside me that Brother Dust had recognized, that made me a warrior. Light-headed with rage and power, I pulled out my gun. I held it over my head. One, two, three shots cracked the night. The silence after was more shocking than the shots.

"So. The child has a gun," the hungry man said.

"The child can use it too. And you will be first to die."

"Perhaps." the leader said. "But you have three bullets. We have three hundred hands."

My mother pulled me to one side as the shanty men came through. Their pangas caught the yellow light as they cut their way through our maize and cane. After them came the women and the children, picking, sifting, gleaning. The three hundred hands stripped our fields like locusts. The gun pulled my arm down like an iron weight. I remember I cried with frustration and shame. There were too many of them. My power, my resolve, my weapon, were nothing. False bravery. Boasting. Show.

By morning the field was a trampled mess of stalks, stems, and shredded leaves. Not a grain worth eating remained. By morning I was waiting on the Jogoo Road, my thumb held out for a matatu, my possessions in a sports bag on my back. A refugee again. The fight had been brief and muted.

"What is this thing?" My mother could not touch the gun. She pointed at it on the bed. My father could not even look. He sat hunched up in a deep, old armchair, staring at his knees. "Where did you get such a thing?"

The dark thing was still strong in me. It had failed against the mob, but it was more than enough for my parents.

"From a Sheriff," I said. "You know what a sheriff is? He is a big man. For him I stick Chaga-spores up my crack. I give them to Americans, Europeans, Chinese, anyone who will pay."

"Do not speak to us like that!"

"Why shouldn't I? What have you done, but sit here and wait for something to happen? I'll tell the only thing that is going to happen. The Chaga is going to come and destroy everything. At least I have taken some responsibility for this family, at least I have kept us out of the sewer! At least we have not had to steal other people's food!"

"Filth money! Dirt money, sin money!"

"You took that money readily enough."

"If we had known . . ."

"Did you ever ask?"

"You should have told us."

"You were afraid to know."

My mother could not answer that. She pointed at the gun again, as if it were the proof of all depravity.

"Have you ever used it?"

"No," I said, challenging her to call me a liar.

"Would you have used it, tonight?"

"Yes," I said. "I would, if I thought it would have worked."

"What has happened to you?" my mother said. "What have we done?"

"You have done nothing," I said. "That's what's wrong with you. You give up. You sit there, like him." My father had not yet said a word. "You sit there, and you do nothing. God will not help you. If God could, would he have sent the Chaga? God has made you beggars."

Now my father got up out of his deep chair.

"Leave this house," he said in a very quiet voice. I stared. "Take your things. Go on. Go now. You are no longer of this family. You will not come here again."

So I walked out with my things in my bag and my gun in my pants and my roll in my shoe and I felt the eyes in every room and lean-to and shack and I learned Christians can have shanty-eyes too. Brother Dust found me a room in the back of the club. I think he hoped it would give him a chance to have sex with me. It smelled and it was noisy at night and I often had to quit it to let the prostitutes do their business, but it was mine, and I believed I was free and happy. But his words were a curse on me. Like Evil Eye, I knew no peace. You do nothing, I had accused my parents, but what had I done? What was my plan for when the Chaga came? As the months passed and the terminum was now at Muranga, now at Ghania Falls, now at Thika, Brother Dust's curse accused me. I watched the Government pull out for Mombasa in a convoy of trucks and cars that took an hour and a half to go past the Haile Selassie Avenue cafe where I bought my runners morning coffee. I saw the gangs of picknis race through the avenues, loosing off tracer-like firecrackers, until the big UN troop carriers drove them before them like beggars. I crouched in roadside ditches from terrible firefights over hijacked oil tankers. I went up to the observation deck of the Moi Telecom Tower and saw the smoke from battles out in the suburbs, and beyond, on the edge of the heat-haze, to south and north, beyond the mottled duns and dusts of the squatter towns, the patterned colors of the Chaga. I saw the newspapers announce that on July 18th, 2013, the walls of the Chaga would meet and Nairobi cease to exist. Where is safe? Brother Dust said in my spirit. What are you going to do?

A man dies, and it is easy to say when the dying ends. The breath goes out and does not come in again. The heart stills. The blood cools and congeals. The last thought fades from the brain. It is not so easy to say when a dying begins. Is it, for example, when the body goes into the terminal decline? When the first cell turns black and cancerous? When we pass our DNA to a new human generation, and become genetically redundant? When we are born? A civil servant once told me that when they make out your birth certificate, they also prepare your death certificate.

It was the same for the big death of Nairobi. The world saw the end of the end from spy satellites and camera-blimps. When the end for a city begins is less clear. Some say it was when the United Nations pulled out and left Nairobi open. Others, when the power plants at Embakasi went down and the fuel and telephone lines to the coast were cut. Some trace it to the first Hatching Tower appearing over the avenues of Westlands; some to the pictures on the television news of the hexagon pattern of Chaga-moss slowly obliterating a "Welcome to Nairobi" road sign. For me it was when I slept with Brother Dust in the back room of the upstairs club.

I told him I was a virgin.

"I always pegged you for a Christian child," he said, and though my virginity excited him, he did not try and take it from me forcefully or disrespectfully. I was fumbling and dry and did not know what to do and pretended to enjoy it more than I did. The truth was that I did not see what all the fuss was about. Why did I do it? It was the seal that I had become a fine young criminal, and tied my life to my city.

Though he was kind and gentle, we did not sleep together again.

They were bad times, those last months in Nairobi. Some times, I think, are so bad that we can only deal them with by remembering what is good, or bright. I will try and look at the end days straight and honestly. I was now eighteen, it was over a year since I left Jogoo Road, and I had not seen my parents or Little Egg since. I was proud and angry and afraid. But a day had not passed that I had not thought about them and the duty I owed them. The Chaga was advancing on two fronts, marching up from the south and sweeping down from the north through the once-wealthy suburbs of Westlands and Garden Grove. The Kenyan Army was up there, firing mortars into the cliff of vegetation called the Great Wall, taking out the Hatching Towers with artillery. As futile as shelling the sea. In the south the United Nations was holding the international airport open at every cost. Between them, the Tacticals tore at each other like street dogs. Alliances formed and were broken in the same day. Neighbor turned on neighbor, brother killed brother. The boulevards of downtown Nairobi were littered with bullet casings and burned out picknis. There was not one pane of glass whole on all of Moi Avenue, nor one shop that was not looted. Between them were twelve million civilians, and the posses.

We too made and dissolved our alliances. We had an arrangement with Mombi, who had just bloodily ended an agreement with Haran, one of the big sheriffs, to make a secret deal with the Black Simbas, who intended to be a power in the new order after the Chaga. The silly, vain Soca Boys had been swept away in one night by the Simbas East Starehe Division. Custom matatus and football managers' coats were no match for Russian APCs and light-scatter combat-suits. Brother Dust's associations were precarious: the posses had wealth and influence but no power. Despite our AK47s and street cool uniforms—in the last days, everyone had a uniform—even the Soca Boys could have taken us out. We were criminals, not warriors.

Limuru, Tigani, Kiambu, in the north. Athi River, Matathia, Embakasi to the south. The Chaga advanced a house here, a school there, half a church, a quarter of a street. Fifty meters every day. Never slower, never faster. When the Supreme Commander East African Protection Force announced terminum at Ngara, I made my move. In my Dust Girl uniform of street-length, zebra-stripe PVC coat over short-shorts, I took a taxi to the Embassy of the United States of America. The driver detoured through Riverside.

"Glider come down on Limuru Road," the driver explained. The gliders scared me, hanging like great plastic bats from the hatching towers, waiting to drop, spread their wings and sail across the city sowing Chaga spores. To me they were dark death on wings. I have too many Old Testament images still in me. The army took out many on the towers, the helicopters the ones in the air, but some always made it down. Nairobi was being eaten away from within.

Riverside had been rich once. I saw a tank up-ended in a swimming pool, a tennis court strewn with swollen bodies in purple combats. Chaga camouflage. Beyond the trees I saw fans of lilac land-coral.

I told the driver to wait outside the Embassy. The grounds were jammed with trucks. Chains of soldiers and staff were loading them with crates and machinery. The black marine knew me by now.

"You're going?" I asked.

"Certainly are, ma'am," the marine said. I handed him my gun. He nodded me through. People pushed through the corridors under piles of paper and boxes marked Property of the United States Government. Everywhere I heard shredders. I found the right office. The spikey-haired man, whose name was Knutson, was piling cardboard boxes on his desk.

"We're not open for business."

"I'm not here to trade," I said. I told him what I was here for. He looked at me as if I had said that the world was made of wool, or the Chaga had reversed direction. So I cleared a space on his desk and laid out the photographs I had brought.

"Please tell me, because I don't understand this attraction," I said. "Is it that, when they are that young, you cannot tell the boys from the girls? Or is it the tightness?"

"Fuck you. You'll never get these public."

"They already are. If the Diplomatic Corps Personnel Section does not receive a password every week, the file will download."

If there had been a weapon to hand, I think Knutson would have killed me where I stood.

"I shouldn't have expected any more from a woman who sells her cunt to aliens."

"We are all prostitutes, Mr. Knutson. So?"

"Wait there. To get out you need to be chipped." In the few moments he was out of the room I studied the face of the President on the wall. I was familiar with Presidential features; is it something in the nature of the office, I wondered, that gives them all the same look? Knutson returned with a metal and plastic device like a large hypodermic. "Name, address, Social Security Number." I gave them to him. He tapped tiny keys on the side of the device, then he seized my wrist, pressed the nozzle against my forearm. There was click; I felt a sharp pain but I did not cry out.

"Congratulations, you're an employee of US Military Intelligence. I hope that fucking hurt."

"Yes it did." Blood oozed down my wrist. "I need three more. These are the names."

Beside the grainy snaps of Knutson on the bed with the naked children, I laid out my family. Knutson thrust the chip gun at me.

"Here. Take it. Take the fucking thing. They'll never miss it, not in all this. It's easy to use, just dial it in there. And those."

I scooped up the photographs and slid them with the chip gun into my inside pocket. The freedom chip throbbed under my skin as I walked through the corridors full of people and paper into the light.

Back at the club I paid the driver in gold. It and cocaine were the only universally acceptable street currencies. I had been converting my roll to Krugerrands for some months now. The rate was not good. I jogged up the stairs to the club, and into slaughter.

Bullets had been poured into the dark room. The bar was shattered glass, stinking of alcohol. The tables were spilled and splintered. The chairs were overturned, smashed. Bodies lay among them, the club men, sprawled inelegantly. The carpet was sticky with blood. Flies buzzed over the dead. I saw the Dust Girls, my sisters, scattered across the floor, hair and bare skin and animal prints drenched with blood. I moved among them. I thought of zebras on the high plains, hunted down by lions, limbs and muscle and skin torn apart. The stench of blood is an awful thing. You never get it out of you. I saw Brother Dust on his back against the stage. Someone had emptied a clip of automatic fire into his face.

Our alliances were ended.

A noise; I turned. I drew my gun. I saw it in my hand, and the dead lying with their guns in their hands. I ran from the club. I ran down the stairs onto the street. I was a mad thing, screaming at the people in the street, my gun in hand, my coat flying out behind me. I ran as fast as I could. I ran for home, I ran for Jogoo Road. I ran for the people I had left there. Nothing could stop me. Nothing dared, with my gun in my hand. I would go home and I would take them away from this insanity. The last thing the United Nations will ever do for us is fly us out of here, I would tell them. We will fly somewhere we do not need guns or camps or charity, where we will again be what we were. In my coat and stupid boots, I ran, past the plastic city at the old country bus terminal, around the metal barricades on Landhies Road, across the waste ground past the Lusaka Road roundabout where two buses were burning. I ran out into Jogoo Road.

There were people right across the road. Many many people, with vehicles, white UN vehicles. And soldiers, a lot of soldiers. I could not see Church Army. I slammed into the back of the crowd, I threw people out of my way, hammered at them with the side of my gun.

"Get out of my way, I have to get to my family!"

Hands seized me, spun me around. A Kenyan Army soldier held me by the shoulders.

"You cannot get through."

"My family lives here. The Church Army Centre, I need to see them."

"No one goes through. There is no Church Army."

"What do you mean? What are you saying?"

"A glider came down."

I tore away from him, fought my way through the crowd until I came to the cordon of soldiers. A hundred meters down the road was a line of hummers and APCs. A hundred yards beyond them, the alien infection. The glider had crashed into the accommodation block. I could still make out the vile bat-shape among the crust of fungus and sponge spreading across the white plaster. Ribs of Chagacoral had burst the tin roof of the teaching hall, the shacks were a stew of dissolving plastic and translucent bubbles that burst in a cloud of brown dust. Where the dust touched, fresh bubbles grew. The chapel had vanished under a web of red veins. Even Jogoo Road was blistered by yellow flowers and blue barrel-like objects. Fingers of the hexagonal Chaga moss were reaching toward the road block. As I watched, one of the thorn trees outside the center collapsed into the sewer and sent up a cloud of buzzing silver mites.

"Where are the people?" I asked a soldier.

"Decontamination," he said.

"My family was in there!" I screamed at him. He looked away. I shouted at the crowd. I shouted my father's name, my mother's name, Little Egg's, my own name. I pushed through the people, trying to look at the faces. Too many people, too many faces. The soldiers were looking at me. They were talking on radios, I was disturbing them. At any moment they might arrest me. More likely, they would take me to a quiet place and put a bullet in the back of my skull. Too many people, too many faces. I put the gun away, ducked down, slipped between the legs to the back of the crowd. Decontamination. A UN word, that. Headquarters would have records of the contaminated. Chiromo Road. I would need transport. I came out of the crowd and started to run again. I ran up Jogoo Road, past the sports stadium, around the roundabout onto Landhies Road. There were still a few civilian cars on the street. I ran up the middle of the road, pointing my gun at every car that came toward me.

"Take me to Chiromo Road!" I shouted. The drivers would veer away, or hoot and swear. Some even aimed at me. I sidestepped them, I was too fast for them. "Chiromo Road, or I will kill you!" Tacticals laughed and yelled as they swept past in their picknis. Not one stopped. Everyone had seen too many guns.

There was a Kenyan Army convoy on Pumwani Road, so I cut up through the cardboard cities into Kariokor. As long as I kept the Nairobi River, a swamp of refuse and sewage, to my left, I would eventually come out onto Ngara Road. The shanty people fled from the striped demon with the big gun.

"Get out of my way!" I shouted. And then, all at once, the alley people disobeyed me. They stood stock still. They looked up.

I felt it before I saw it. Its shadow was cold on my skin. I stopped running. I too looked up and it swooped down on me. That is what I thought, how I felt—this thing had been sent from the heart of the Chaga to me alone. The glider was bigger than I had imagined, and much much darker. It swept over me. I was paralyzed with dread, then I remembered what I held in my hand. I lifted my gun and fired at the dark bat-thing. I fired and fired and fired until all I heard was a stiff click. I stood, shaking, as the glider vanished behind the plastic shanty roofs. I stood, staring at my hand holding the gun. Then the tiniest yellow buds appeared around the edge of the cylinder. The buds unfolded into crystals, and the crystals spread across the black, oiled metal like scale. More buds came out of the muzzle and grew back down the barrel. Crystals swelled up and choked the cocked hammer.

I dropped the gun like a snake. I tore at my hair, my clothes, I scrubbed at my skin. My clothes were already beginning to change. My zebra-striped coat was blistering. I pulled out the chip injector. It was a mess of yellow crystals and flowers. I could not hope to save them now. I threw it away from me. The photographs of Knutson with the children fell to the earth. They bubbled up and went to dust. I tore at my coat; it came apart in my fingers into tatters of plastic and spores. I ran. The heel of one knee-boot gave way. I fell, rolled, recovered, and stripped the foolish things off me. All around me, the people of Kariokor were running, ripping at their skin and their clothes with their fingers. I ran with them, crying with fear. I let them lead me. My finery came apart around me. I ran naked, I did not care. I had nothing now. Everything had been taken from me, everything but the chip in my arm. On every side the plastic and wood shanties sent up shoots and stalks of Chaga.

We crashed up against the UN emergency cordon at Kariokor Market. Wicker shields pushed us back; rungu clubs went up, came down. People fell, clutching smashed skulls. I threw myself at the army line.

"Let me through!"

I thrust my arm between the riot shields.

"I'm chipped! I'm chipped!"

Rungus rose before my face.

"UN pass! I'm chipped!"

The rungus came down, and something whirled them away. A white man's voice shouted.

"Jesus fuck, she is! Get her out of there! Quick!"

The shield wall parted, hands seized me, pulled me through.

"Get something on her!"

A combat jacket fell on my shoulders. I was taken away very fast through the lines of soldiers to a white hummer with a red cross on the side. A white man with a red cross vest sat me on the back step and ran a scanner over my forearm. The wound was livid now, throbbing.

"Tendeléo Bi. US Embassy Intelligence Liaison. Okay, Tendeléo Bi, I've no idea what you were doing in there, but it's decontam for you."

A second soldier—an officer, I guessed—had come back to the hummer.

"No time. Civs have to be out by twenty three hundred."

The medic puffed his cheeks.

"This is not procedure . . ."

"Procedure?" the officer said. "With a whole fucking city coming apart around us? But I guarantee you this, the Americans will go fucking ballistic if we fuck with one of their spooks. A surface scrub'll do . . ."

They took me over to a big boxy truck with a biohazard symbol on the side. It was parked well away from the other vehicles. I was shivering from shock. I made no complaint as they shaved all hair from my body. Someone gently took away the army jacket and showed me where to stand. Three men unrolled high-pressure hoses from the side of the truck and worked me from top to bottom. The water was cold, and hard enough to be painful. My skin burned. I twisted and turned to try to keep it away from my nipples and the tender parts of my body. On the third scrub, I realized what they were doing, and remembered.

"Take me to decontam!" I shouted. "I want to go to decontam! My family's there, don't you realize?" The men would not listen to me. I do not think they even knew it was a young woman's body they were hosing down. No one listened to me. I was dried with hot air guns, given some loose fatigues to wear, then put in the back of a diplomatic hummer that drove very fast through the streets to the airport. We did not go to the terminal building. There, I might have broken and run. We went through the wire gates, and straight to the open back of a big Russian transport plane. A line of people was going up the ramp into the cavern of its belly. Most of them were white, many had children, and all were laden with bags and goods. All were refugees, too . . . like me.

"My family is back there, I have to get them," I told the man with the security scanner at the foot of the ramp.

"We'll find them," he said as he checked off my Judas chip against the official database. "That's you. Good luck." I went up the metal ramp into the plane. A Russian woman in uniform found me a seat in the middle block, far from any window. Once I was belted in I sat trembling until I heard the ramp close and the engines start up. Then I knew I could do nothing, and the shaking stopped. I felt the plane bounce over the concrete and turn onto the runway. I hoped a terrible hope: that something would go wrong and the plane would crash and I would die. Because I needed to die. I had destroyed the thing I meant to save and saved the thing that was worthless. Then the engines powered up and we made our run and though I could see only the backs of seats and the gray metal curve of the big cabin, I knew when we left the ground because I felt my bond with Kenya break and my home fall away beneath me as the plane took me into exile.

I pause now in my story now, for where it goes now is best told by another voice.

My name is Sean. It's an Irish name. I'm not Irish. No bit of Irish in me, as you can probably see. My mum liked the name. Irish stuff was fashionable, thirty years ago. My telling probably won't do justice to Tendeléo's story; I apologize. My gift's numbers. Allegedly. I'm a reluctant accountant. I do what I do well, I just don't have a gut feel for it. That's why my company gave me all the odd jobs. One of them was this African-Caribbean-World restaurant just off Canal Street. It was called I-Nation—the menu changed every week, the ambience was great, and the music was mighty. The first time I wore a suit there, Wynton the owner took the piss so much I never dressed up for them again. I'd sit at a table and poke at his VAT returns and find myself nodding to the drum and bass. Wynton would try out new grooves on me and I'd give them thumbs up or thumbs down. Then he'd fix me coffee with this liqueur he imported from Jamaica and that was the afternoon gone. It seemed a shame to invoice him.

One day Wynton said to me, "You should come to our evening sessions. Good music. Not this fucking bang bang bang. Not fucking deejays. Real music. Live music."

However, my mates liked fucking deejays and bang bang bang so I went to I-Nation on my own. There was a queue but the door staff nodded me right in. I got a seat at the bar and a Special Coffee, compliments of the house. The set had already begun, the floor was heaving. That band knew how to get a place moving. After the dance set ended, the lead guitarist gestured offstage. A girl got up behind the mic. I recognized her—she waitressed in the afternoons. She was a small, quiet girl, kind of unnoticeable, apart from her hair which stuck out in spikes like it was growing back after a Number Nought cut with the razor.

She got up behind that mic and smiled apologetically. Then she began to sing, and I wondered how I had never thought her unnoticeable. It was a slow, quiet song. I couldn't understand the language. I didn't need to, her voice said it all: loss and hurt and lost love. Bass and rhythm felt out the depth and damage in every syllable. She was five foot nothing and looked like she would break in half if you blew on her, but her voice had a stone edge that said, I've been where I'm singing about. Time stopped; she held a note then gently let it go. I-Nation was silent for a moment. Then it exploded. The girl bobbed shyly and went down through the cheering and whistling. Two minutes later she was back at work, clearing glasses. I could not take my eyes off her. You can fall in love in five minutes. It's not hard at all.

When she came to take my glass, all I could say was, "That was . . . great."

"Thank you."

And that was it. How I met Ten, said three shit words to her, and fell in love.

I never could pronounce her name. On the afternoons when the bar was quiet and we talked over my table she would shake her head at my mangling the vowel sounds.

"Eh-yo."

"Ay-oh?"

The soft spikes of hair would shake again. Then, she never could pronounce my name either. Shan, she would say.

"No, Shawn."

"Shone . . ."

So I called her Ten, which for me meant Il Primo, Top of the Heap, King of the Hill, A-Number-One. And she called me Shone. Like the sun. One afternoon when she was off shift, I asked Boss Wynton what kind of name Tendeléo was.

"I mean, I know it's African, I can tell by the accent, but it's a big continent."

"It is that. She not told you?"

"Not yet."

"She will when she's ready. And Mr. Accountant, you fucking respect her."

Two weeks later she came to my table and laid a series of forms before me like tarot cards. They were Social Security applications, Income Support, Housing Benefit.

"They say you're good with numbers."

"This isn't really my thing, but I'll take a look." I flipped through the forms. "You're working too many hours . . . they're trying to cut your benefits. It's the classic welfare trap. It doesn't pay you to work."

"I need to work," Ten said.

Last in line was a Home Office Asylum Seeker's form. She watched me pick it up and open it. She must have seen my eyes widen.

"Gichichi, in Kenya."

"Yes."

I read more.

"God. You got out of Nairobi."

"I got out of Nairobi, yes."

I hesitated before asking, "Was it bad?"

"Yes," she said. "I was very bad."

"I?" I said.

"What?"

"You said 'I.' I was very bad."

"I meant it, it was very bad."

The silence could have been uncomfortable, fatal even. The thing I had wanted to say for weeks rushed into the vacuum.

"Can I take you somewhere? Now? Today? When you finish? Would you like to eat?"

"I'd like that very much," she said.

Wynton sent her off early. I took her to a great restaurant in Chinatown where the waiters ask you before you go in how much you'd like to spend.

"I don't know what this is," she said as the first of the courses arrived.

"Eat it. You'll like it."

She toyed with her wontons and chopsticks.

"Is something wrong with it?"

"I will tell you about Nairobi now," she said. The food was expensive and lavish and exquisitely presented and we hardly touched it. Course after course went back to the kitchen barely picked over as Ten told me the story of her life, the church in Gichichi, the camps in Nairobi, the career as a posse girl, and of the Chaga that destroyed her family, her career, her hopes, her home, and almost her life. I had seen the coming of the Chaga on the television. Like most people, I had tuned it down to background muzak in my life; oh, wow, there's an alien life-form taking over the southern hemisphere. Well, it's bad for the safari holidays and carnival in Rio is fucked and you won't be getting the Brazilians in the next World Cup, but the Cooperage account's due next week and we're pitching for the Maine Road job and interest rates have gone up again. Aliens schmaliens. Another humanitarian crisis. I had followed the fall of Nairobi, the first of the really big cities to go, trying to make myself believe that this was not Hollywood, this was not Bruce Willis versus the CGI. This was twelve million people being swallowed by the dark. Unlike most of my friends and work mates. I had felt something move painfully inside me when I saw the walls of the Chaga close on the towers of downtown Nairobi. It was like a kick in my heart. For a moment I had gone behind the pictures that are all we are allowed to know of our world, to the true lives. And now the dark had spat one of these true lives up onto the streets of Manchester. We were on the last candle at the last table by the time Ten got around to telling me how she had been dumped out with the other Kenyans at Charles de Gaulle and shuffled for months through EU refugee quotas until she arrived, jet-lagged, culture-shocked, and poor as shit, in the gray and damp of an English summer.

Afterward, I was quiet for some time. Nothing I could have said was adequate to what I had heard. Then I said, "Would you like to come home with me for a drink, or a coffee, or something?"

"Yes," she said. Her voice was husky from much talking, and low, and unbearably attractive. "I would, very much."

I left the staff a big tip for above-and-beyondness.

Ten loved my house. The space astonished her. I left her curled up on my sofa savoring the space as I went to open wine.

"This is nice," she said. "Warm. Big. Nice. Yours."

"Yes," I said and leaned forward and kissed her. Then, before I could think about what I had done, I took her arm and kissed the round red blemish of her chip. Ten slept with me that night, but we did not make love. She lay, curled and chaste, in the hollow of my belly until morning. She cried out in her sleep often. Her skin smelled of Africa.

The bastards cut her housing benefit. Ten was distraught. Home was everything to her. Her life had been one long search for a place of her own; safe, secure, stable.

"You have two options," I said. "One, give up working here."

"Never," she said. "I work. I like to work." I saw Wynton smile, polishing the glasses behind the bar.

"Option two, then."

"What's that?"

"Move in with me."

It took her a week to decide. I understood her hesitation. It was a place, safe, secure, stable, but not her own. On the Saturday I got a phone call from her. Could I help her move? I went around to her flat in Salford. The rooms were tatty and cold, the furniture charity-shop fare, and the decor ugly. The place stank of dope. The television blared, unwatched; three different boomboxes competed with each other. While Ten fetched her stuff, her flatmates stared at me as if I were something come out of the Chaga. She had two bags—one of clothes, one of music and books. They went in the back of the car and she came home with me.

Life with Ten. She put her books on a shelf and her clothes in a drawer. She improvised harmonies to my music. She would light candles on any excuse. She spent hours in the bathroom and used toilet paper by the roll. She was meticulously tidy. She took great care of her little money. She would not borrow from me. She kept working at I-Nation, she sang every Friday. She still killed me every time she got up on that stage.

She said little, but it told. She was dark and intensely beautiful to me. She didn't smile much. When she did it was a knife through the heart of me. It was a sharp joy. Sex was a sharpness of a different kind—it always seemed difficult for her. She didn't lose herself in sex. I think she took a great pleasure from it, but it was controlled . . . it was owned, it was hers. She never let herself make any sound. She was a little afraid of the animal inside. She seemed much older than she was; on the times we went dancing, that same energy that lit her up in singing and sex burned out of her. It was then that she surprised me by being a bright, energetic, sociable eighteen-year-old. She loved me. I loved her so hard it felt like sickness. I would watch her, unaware I was doing it . . . watch the way she moved her hands when she talked on the phone, how she curled her legs under her when she watched television, how she brushed her teeth in the morning. I would wake up in the night just to watch her sleep. I would check she was still breathing. I dreaded something insane, something out of nowhere, taking her away.

She stuck a satellite photograph of Africa on the fridge. She showed me how to trace the circles of the Chaga through the clouds. Every week she updated it. Week by week, the circles merging. That was how I measured our life together, by the circles, merging. Week by week, her home was taken away. Her parents and sister were down there, under those blue and white bars of cloud; week by week the circles were running them out of choices.

She never let herself forget she had failed them. She never let herself forget she was a refugee. That was what made her older, in ways, than me. That was what all her tidiness and orderliness around the house were about. She was only here for a little time. It could all be lifted at a moment's notice.

She liked to cook for me on Sundays, though the kitchen smelled of it for a week afterward. I never told her her cooking gave me the shits. She was chopping something she had got from the Caribbean stores and singing to herself. I was watching from the hall, as I loved to watch her without being watched. I saw her bring the knife down, heard a Kalenjin curse, saw her lift her hand to her mouth. I was in like a shot.

"Shit shit shit shit," she swore. It was a deep cut, and blood ran freely down her forefinger. I rushed her to the tap, stuck it under the cold, then went for the medical bag. I returned with gauze, plasters, and a heal-the-world attitude.

"It's okay," she said, holding the finger up. "It's better."

The cut had vanished. No blood, no scab. All that remained was a slightly raised red weal. As I watched, even that faded.

"How?"

"I don't know," Ten said. "But it's better."

I didn't ask. I didn't want to ask. I didn't want there to be anything more difficult or complex in Ten's life. I wanted what she had from her past to be enough, to be all. I knew this was something alien; no one healed like that. I thought that if I let it go, it would never trouble us again. I had not calculated on the bomb.

Some fucking Nazis or other had been blast-bombing gay bars. London, Edinburgh, Dublin so far, always a Friday afternoon, work over, week- end starting. Manchester was on the alert. So were the bombers. Tuesday, lunch time, half a kilo of Semtex with nails and razor blades packed around it went off under a table outside a Canal Street bar. No one died, but a woman at the next table lost both legs from the knees down and there were over fifty casualties. Ten had been going in for the afternoon shift. She was twenty meters away when the bomb went off. I got the call from the hospital same time as the news broke on the radio.

"Get the fuck over there," Willy the boss ordered. I didn't need ordering. Manchester Royal Infirmary casualty was bedlam. I saw the doctors going around in a slow rush and the people looking up at everyone who came in, very very afraid and the police taking statements and the trolleys in the aisles and I thought: It must have been something like this in Nairobi, at the end. The receptionist showed me to a room where I was to wait for a doctor. I met her in the corridor, a small, harassed-looking Chinese girl.

"Ah, Mr. Giddens. You're with Ms. Bi, that's right?"

"That's right, how is she?"

"Well, she was brought in with multiple lacerations, upper body, left side of face, left upper arm and shoulder . . ."

"Oh Jesus God. And now?"

"See for yourself."

Ten walked down the corridor. If she had not been wearing a hospital robe, I would have sworn she was unchanged from how I had left her that morning.

"Shone."

The weals were already fading from her face and hands. A terrible pre- science came over me, so strong and cold I almost threw up.

"We want to keep her in for further tests, Mr. Giddens," the doctor said. "As you can imagine, we've never seen anything quite like this before."

"Shone, I'm fine, I want to go home."

"Just to be sure, Mr. Giddens."

When I brought Ten back a bag of stuff, the receptionist directed me to

Intensive Care. I ran the six flights of stairs to ICU, burning with dread. Ten was in a sealed room full of white equipment. When she saw me, she ran from her bed to the window, pressed her hands against it.

"Shone!" Her words came through a speaker grille. "They won't let me out!"

Another doctor led to me a side room. There were two policemen there, and a man in a suit.

"What the hell is this?"

"Mr. Giddens. Ms. Bi, she is a Kenyan refugee?"

"You fucking know that."

"Easy, Mr. Giddens. We've been running some tests on Ms. Bi, and we've discovered the presence in her bloodstream of fullerene nanoprocessors."

"Nanowhat?"

"What are commonly know as Chaga spores."

Ten, Dust Girl, firing and firing and firing at the glider, the gun blossoming in her hand, the shanty town melting behind her as her clothes fell apart, her arm sticking through the shield wall as she shouted, I'm chipped, I'm chipped! The soldiers shaving her head, hosing her down. Those things she had carried inside her. All those runs for the Americans.

"Oh my God."

There was a window in the little room. Through it I saw Ten sitting on a plastic chair by the bed, hands on her thighs, head bowed.

"Mr. Giddens." The man in the suit flashed a little plastic wallet. "Robert McGlennon, Home Office Immigration. Your, ah . . ." He nodded at the window.

"Partner."

"Partner. Mr. Giddens, I have to tell you, we cannot be certain that Ms. Bi's continued presence is not a public health risk. Her refugee status is dependent on a number of conditions, one of which is that . . ."

"You're fucking deporting her . . ."

The two policemen stirred. I realized then that they were not there for Ten. There were there for me.

"It's a public health issue, Mr. Giddens. She should never have been allowed in in the first place. We have no idea of the possible environmental impact. You, of all people, should be aware what these things can do. Have done. Are still doing. I have to think of public safety."

"Public safety, fuck!"

"Mr. Giddens . . ."

I went to the window. I beat my fists on the wired glass.

"Ten! Ten! They're trying to deport you! They want to send you back!"

The policemen prised me away from the window. On the far side, Ten yelled silently.

"Look, I don't like having to do this," the man in the suit said.

"When?"

"Mr. Giddens."

"When? Tell me, how long has she got?"

"Usually there'd be a detention period, with limited rights of appeal. But as this is a public health issue . . ."

"You're going to do it right now."

"The order is effective immediately, Mr. Giddens. I'm sorry. These officers will go with you back to your home. If you could gather up the rest of her things . . ."

"At least let me say goodbye, Jesus, you owe me that!"

"I can't allow that, Mr. Giddens. There's a contamination risk."

"Contamination? I've only been fucking her for the past six months."

As the cops marched me out, the doctor came up for a word.

"Mr. Giddens, these nanoprocessors in her bloodstream . . ."

"That are fucking getting her thrown out of the country."

"The fullerenes . . ."

"She heals quick. I saw it."

"They do much more than that, Mr. Giddens. She'll probably never get sick again. And there's some evidence that they prevent telomere depletion in cell division."

"What does that mean?"

"It means, she ages very much more slowly than we do. Her life expectancy may be, I don't know, two, three hundred years."

I stared. The policemen stared.

"There's more. We observed unfamiliar structures in her brain; the best I can describe them is, the nanoprocessors seem to be reengineering dead neurons into a complementary neural network."

"A spare brain?"

"An auxiliary brain."

"What would you do with that?"

"What wouldn't you do with that, Mr. Giddens." He wiped his hand across his mouth. "This bit is pure speculation, but . . ."

"But."

"But in some way, she's in control of it all. I think—this is just a theory—that through this auxiliary brain she's able to interact with the nanoprocessors. She might be able to make them do what she wants. Program them."

"Thank you for telling me that," I said bitterly. "That makes it all so much easier."

I took the policemen back to my house. I told them to make themselves tea. I took Ten's neatly arranged books and CDs off my shelves and her neatly folded clothes out of my drawers and her toilet things out of my bathroom and put them back in the two bags in which she had brought them. I gave the bags to the policemen; they took them away in their car. I never got to say goodbye. I never learned what flight she was on, where she flew from, when she left this country. A face behind glass. That was my last memory. The thing I feared—insane, out of nowhere—had taken her away.

After Ten went, I was sick for a long time. There was no sunshine, no rain, no wind. No days or time, just a constant, high-pitched, quiet whine in my head. People at work played out a slightly amplified normality for my benefit. Alone, they would ask, very gently, How do you feel?

"How do I feel?" I told them. "Like I've been shot with a single, high-velocity round, and I'm dead, and I don't know it."

I asked for someone else to take over the I-Nation account. Wynton called me but I could not speak with him. He sent around a bottle of that good Jamaican import liqueur, and a note, "Come and see us, any time." Willy arranged me a career break and a therapist.

His name was Greg, he was a client-centered therapist, which meant I could talk for as long as I liked about whatever I liked and he had to listen. I talked very little, those first few sessions. Partly I felt stupid, partly I didn't want to talk, even to a stranger. But it worked, little by little, without my knowing. I think I only began to be aware of that the day I realized that Ten was gone, but not dead. Her last photo of Africa was still on the fridge and I looked at it and saw something new: down there, in there, somewhere, was Ten. The realization was vast and subtle at the same time. I think of it like a man who finds himself in darkness. He imagines he's in a room, no doors, no windows, and that he'll never find the way out. But then he hears noises, feels a touch on his face, smells a subtle smell, and he realizes that he is not in a room at all—he is outside: the touch on his face is the wind, the noises are night birds, the smell is from night-blooming flowers, and above him, somewhere, are stars.

Greg said nothing when I told him this—they never do, these client-centered boys, but after that session I went to the net and started the hunt for

Tendeléo Bi. The Freedom of Information Act got me into the Immigration Service's databases. Ten had been flown out on a secure military transport to Mombasa. UNHCR in Mombasa had assigned her to Likoni Twelve, a new camp to the south of the city. She was transferred out on November Twelfth. It took two days' searching to pick up a Tendeléo Bi logged into a place called Samburu North three months later. Medical records said she was suffering from exhaustion and dehydration, but responding to sugar and salt treatment. She was alive.

On the first Monday of winter, I went back to work. I had lost a whole season. On the first Friday, Willy gave me print-out from an on-line recruitment agency.

"I think you need a change of scene," he said. "These people are looking for a stock accountant."

These people were Medecins Sans Frontiers. Where they needed a stock accountant was their East African theater.

Eight months after the night the two policemen took away Ten's things, I stepped off the plane in Mombasa. I think hell must be like Mombasa in its final days as capital of the Republic of Kenya, infrastructure unravelling, economy disintegrating, the harbor a solid mass of boat people and a million more in the camps in Likoni and Shimba Hills, Islam and Christianity fighting a new Crusade for control of this chaos and the Chaga advancing from the west and now the south, after the new impact at Tanga. And in the middle of it all, Sean Giddens, accounting for stock. It was good, hard, solid work in MSF Sector Headquarters, buying drugs where, when, and how we could; haggling down truck drivers and Sibirsk jet-jockeys; negotiating service contracts as spare parts for the Landcruisers gradually ran out, every day juggling budgets always too small against needs too big. I loved it more than any work I've ever done. I was so busy I sometimes forgot why I was there. Then I would go in the safe bus back to the compound and see the smoke going up from the other side of the harbor, hear the gunfire echo off the old Arab houses, and the memory of her behind that green wired glass would gut me.

My boss was a big bastard Frenchman, Jean-Paul Gastineau. He had survived wars and disasters on every continent except Antarctica. He liked Cuban cigars and wine from the valley where he was born and opera, and made sure he had them, never mind distance or expense. He took absolutely no shit. I liked him immensely. I was a fucking thin-blooded number-pushing black rosbif, but he enjoyed my creative accounting. He was wasted in Mombasa. He was a true frontline medic. He was itching for action.

One lunchtime, as he was opening his red wine, I asked him how easy it would to find someone in the camps. He looked at me shrewdly, then asked, "Who is she?"

He poured two glasses, his invitation to me. I told him my history and her history over the bottle. It was very good.

"So, how do I find her?"

"You'll never get anything through channels," Jean Paul said. "Easiest thing to do is go there yourself. You have leave due."

"No I don't."

"Yes you do. About three weeks of it. Ah. Yes." He poked about in his desk drawers. He threw me a black plastic object like a large cell-phone.

"What is it?"

"US ID chips have a GPS transponder. They like to know where their people are. Take it. If she is chipped, this will find her."

"Thanks."

He shrugged.

"I come from a nation of romantics. Also, you're the only one in this fucking place appreciates a good Beaune."

I flew up north on a Sibirsk charter. Through the window I could see the edge of the Chaga. It was too huge to be a feature of the landscape, or even a geographical entity. It was like a dark sea. It looked like what it was . . . another world, that had pushed up against our own. Like it, some ideas are too huge to fit into our everyday worlds. They push up through it, they take it over, and they change it beyond recognition. If what the doctor at Manchester Royal Infirmary had said about the things in Ten's blood were true, then this was not just a new world. This was a new humanity. This was every rule about how we make our livings, how we deal with each other, how we lead our lives, all overturned.

The camps, also, are too big to take in. There is too much there for the world we've made for ourselves. They change everything you believe. Mombasa was no preparation. It was like the end of the world up there on the front line.

"So, you're looking for someone," Heino Rautavana said. He had worked with Jean-Paul through the fall of Nairobi; I could trust him, Jay-Pee said, but I think he thought I was a fool, or, all at best, a romantic. "No shortage of people here."

Jean-Paul had warned the records wouldn't be accurate. But you hope. I went to Samburu North, where my search in England had last recorded Ten. No trace of her. The UNHCR warden, a grim little American woman, took me up and down the rows of tents. I looked at the faces and my tracker sat silent on my hip. I saw those faces that night in the ceiling, and for many nights after.

"You expect to hit the prize first time?" Heino said as we bounced along the dirt track in an MSF Landcruiser to Don Dul.

I had better luck in Don Dul, if you can call it that. Ten had definitely been here two months ago. But she had left eight days later. I saw the log in, the log out, but there was no record of where she had gone.

"No shortage of camps either," Heino said. He was a dour bastard. He couldn't take me any further but he squared me an authorization to travel on Red Cross/ Crescent convoys, who did a five hundred mile run through the camps along the northern terminum. In two weeks I saw more misery than I ever thought humanity could take. I saw the faces and the hands and the bundles of scavenged things and I thought, why hold them here? What are they saving them from? Is it so bad in the Chaga? What is so terrible about people living long lives, being immune from sickness, growing extra layers in their brains? What is so frightening about people being able to go into that alien place, and take control of it, and make it into what they want?

I couldn't see the Chaga, it lay just below the southern horizon, but I was constantly aware of its presence, like they say people who have plates in their skulls always feel a slight pressure. Sometimes, when the faces let me sleep, I would be woken instead by a strange smell, not strong, but distinct; musky and fruity and sweaty, sexy, warm. It was the smell of the Chaga, down there, blowing up from the south.

Tent to truck to camp to tent. My three weeks were running out and I had to arrange a lift back along the front line to Samburu and the flight to Mombasa. With three days left, I arrived in Eldoret, UNECTA's Lake Victoria regional center. It gave an impression of bustle, the shops and hotels and cafés were busy, but the white faces and American accents and dress sense said Eldoret was a company town. The Rift Valley Hotel looked like heaven after eighteen days on the front line. I spent an hour in the pool trying to beam myself into the sky. A sudden rain-storm drove everyone from the water but me. I floated there, luxuriating in the raindrops splashing around me. At sunset I went down to the camps. They lay to the south of the town, like a line of cannon-fodder against the Chaga. I checked the records, a matter of form. No Tendeléo Bi. I went in anyway. And it was another camp, and after a time, anyone can become insulated to suffering. You have to. You have to book into the big hotel and swim in the pool and eat a good dinner when you get back; in the camps you have to look at the faces just as faces and refuse to make any connection with the stories behind them. The hardest people I know work in the compassion business. So I went up and down the faces and somewhere halfway down some row I remembered this toy Jean-Paul had given me. I took it out. The display was flashing green. There was a single word: lock.

I almost dropped it.

I thought my heart had stopped. I felt shot between the eyes. I forgot to breathe. The world reeled sideways. My fucking stupid fingers couldn't get a precise reading. I ran down the row of tents, watching the figures. The digits told me how many meters I was to north and east. Wrong way. I doubled back, ducked right at the next opening and headed east. Both sets of figures were decreasing. I overshot, the cast reading went up. Back again. This row. This row. I peered through the twilight. At the far end was a group of people talking outside a tent lit by a yellow petrol lamp. I started to run, one eye on the tracker. I stumbled over guy-ropes, kicked cans, hurdled children, apologized to old women. The numbers clicked down, thirty five, thirty, twenty five meters . . . I could see this one figure in the group, back to me, dressed in purple combat gear. East zero, North twenty, eighteen . . . Short, female, Twelve, ten. Wore its hair in great soft spikes. Eight, six. I couldn't make it past four. I couldn't move. I couldn't speak. I was shaking.

Sensing me, the figure turned. The yellow light caught her.

"Ten," I said. I saw fifty emotions on that face. Then she ran at me and I dropped the scanner and I lifted her and held her to me and no words of mine, or anyone else's, I think, can say how I felt then.

N ow our lives and stories and places come together, and my tale moves to its conclusion.

I believe that people and their feelings write themselves on space and time. That is the only way I can explain how I knew, even before I turned and saw him there in that camp, that it was Sean, that he had searched for me, and found me. I tell you, that is something to know that another person has done for you. I saw him, and it was like the world had set laws about how it was to work for me, and then suddenly it said, no. I break them now, for you, Tendeléo, because it pleases me. He was impossible, he changed everything I knew, he was there.

Too much joy weeps. Too much sorrow laughs.

He took me back to his hotel. The staff looked hard at me as he picked up his keycard from the lobby. They knew what I was. They did not dare say anything. The white men in the bar also turned to stare. They too knew the meaning of the colors I wore.

He took me to his room. We sat on the verandah with beer. There was a storm that night—there is a storm most nights, up in the high country— but it kept itself in the west among the Nandi Hills. Lightning crawled between the clouds, the distant thunder rattled our beer bottles on the iron table. I told Sean where I had been, what I had done, how I had lived. It was a story long in the telling. The sky had cleared, a new day was breaking by the time I finished it. We have always told each other stories, and each other's stories.

He kept his questions until the end. He had many, many of them.

"Yes, I suppose, it is like the old slave underground railroads," I answered one.

"I still don't understand why they try to stop people going in."

"Because we scare them. We can build a society in there that needs nothing from them. We challenge everything they believe. This is the first century we have gone into where we have no ideas, no philosophies, no beliefs. Buy stuff, look at stuff. That's it. We are supposed to build a thousand years on that? Well, now we do. I tell you, I've been reading, learning stuff, ideas, politics. Philosophy. It's all in there. There are information storage banks the size of skyscrapers, Sean. And not just our history. Other people, other races. You can go into them, you can become them, live their lives, see things through their senses. We are not the first. We are part of a long, long chain, and we are not the end of it. The world will belong to us; we will control physical reality as easily as computers control information."

"Hell, never mind the UN . . . you scare me, Ten!"

I always loved it when he called me Ten. Il Primo, Top of the Heap, King of the Hill, A-Number-One.

Then he said, "And your family?"

"Little Egg is in a place called Kilandui. It's full of weavers, she's a weaver. She makes beautiful brocades. I see her quite often."

"And your mother and father?"

"I'll find them."

But to most of his questions, there was only one answer: "Come, and I will show you." I left it to last. It rocked him as if he had been struck.

"You are serious."

"Why not? You took me to your home once. Let me take you to mine. But first, it's a year . . . And so so much . . ."

He picked me up.

"I like you in this combat stuff," he said.

We laughed a lot and remembered old things we had forgotten. We slowly shook off the rust and the dust, and it was good, and I remember the room maid opening the door and letting out a little shriek and going off giggling.

Sean once told me that one of his nation's greatest ages was built on those words, why not? For a thousand years Christianity had ruled England with the question: "Why?" Build a cathedral, invent a science, write a play, discover a new land, start a business: "why?" Then came the Elizabethans with the answer: "Why not?"

I knew the old Elizabethan was thinking, why not? There are only numbers to go back to, and benefit traps, and an old, gray city, and an old, gray dying world, a safe world with few promises. Here there's a world to be made. Here there's a future of a million years to be shaped. Here there are a thousand different ways of living together to be designed, and if they don't work, roll them up like clay and start again.

I did not hurry Sean for his answer. He knew as well as I that it was not a clean decision. It was lose a world, or lose each other. These are not choices you make in a day. So, I enjoyed the hotel. One day I was having a long bath. The hotel had a great bathroom and there was a lot of free stuff you could play with, so I abused it. I heard Sean pick up the phone. I could not make out what he was saying, but he was talking for some time. When I came out he was sitting on the edge of the bed with the telephone beside him. He sat very straight and formal.

"I called Jean-Paul," he said. "I gave him my resignation."

Two days later, we set out for the Chaga. We went by matatu. It was a school holiday, the Peugeot Services were busy with children on their way back to their families. They made a lot of noise and energy. They looked out the corners of their eyes at us and bent together to whisper. Sean noticed this.

"They're talking about you," Sean said.

"They know what I am, what I do."

One of the schoolgirls, in a black and white uniform, understood our English. She fixed Sean a look. "She is a warrior," she told him. "She is giving us our nation back."

We left most of the children in Kapsabet to change onto other matatus; ours drove on into the heart of the Nandi Hills. It was a high, green, rolling country, in some ways like Sean's England. I asked the driver to stop just past a metal cross that marked some old road death.

"What now?" Sean said. He sat on the small pack I had told him was all he could take.

"Now, we wait. They won't be long."

Twenty cars went up the muddy red road, two trucks, a country bus and medical convoy went down. Then they came out of the darkness between the trees on the other side of the road like dreams out of sleep: Meji, Naomi and Hamid. They beckoned; behind them came men, women, children . . . entire families, from babes in arms to old men; twenty citizens, appearing one by one out of the dark, looking nervously up and down the straight red road, then crossing to the other side.

I fived with Meji; he looked Sean up and down.

"This is the one?"

"This is Sean."

"I had expected something, um . . ."

"Whiter?"

He laughed. He shook hands with Sean and introduced himself. Then Meji took a tube out of his pocket and covered Sean in spray. Sean jumped back, choking.

"Stay there, unless you want your clothes to fall off you when you get inside," I said.

Naomi translated this for the others. They found it very funny. When he had immunized Sean's clothes, Meji sprayed his bag.

"Now, we walk," I told Sean.

We spent the night in the Chief's house in the village of Senghalo. He was the last station on our railroad. I know from my Dust Girl days you need as good people on the outside as the inside. Folk came from all around to see the black Englishman. Although he found being looked at intimidating, Sean managed to tell his story. I translated. At the end the crowd outside the Chief's house burst into spontaneous applause and finger-clicks.

"Aye, Tendeléo, how can I compete?" Meji half-joked with me.

I slept fitfully that night, troubled by the sound of aircraft moving under the edge of the storm.

"Is it me?" Sean said.

"No, not you. Go back to sleep."

Sunlight through the bamboo wall woke us. While Sean washed outside in the bright, cold morning, watched by children curious to see if the black went all the way down, Chief and I tuned his shortwave to the UN frequencies. There was a lot of chatter in Klingon. You Americans think we don't understand *Star Trek?*

"They've been tipped off," Chief said. We fetched the equipment from his souterrain. Sean watched Hamid, Naomi, Meri and I put on the communicators. He said nothing as the black-green knob of cha-plastic grew around the back of my head, into my ear, and sent a tendril to my lips. He picked up my staff.

"Can I?"

"It won't bite you."

He looked closely at the fist-sized ball of amber at its head, and the skeleton outline of a sphere embedded in it.

"It's a buckyball," I said. "The symbol of our power."

He passed it to me without comment. We unwrapped our guns, cleaned them, checked them, and set off. We walked east that day along the ridges of the Nandi Hills, through ruined fields and abandoned villages. Helicopter engines were our constant companions. Sometimes we glimpsed them through the leaf cover, tiny in the sky like black mosquitoes. The old people and the mothers looked afraid. I did not want them to see how nervous they were making me. I called my colleagues apart.

"They're getting closer."

Hamid nodded. He was a quiet, thin twenty-two year old . . . Ethiopian skin, goatee, a political science graduate from the university of Nairobi.

"We choose a different path every time," he said. "They can't know this."

"Someone's selling us," Meji said.

"Wouldn't matter. We pick one at random."

"Unless they're covering them all."

In the afternoon we began to dip down toward the Rift Valley and terminum. As we wound our way down the old hunters' paths, muddy and slippery from recent rain, the helicopter came swooping in across the hillside. We scrambled for cover. It turned and made another pass, so low I could see the light glint from the pilot's heads-up visor.

"They're playing with us," Hamid said. "They can blow us right off this hill any time they want."

"How?" Naomi asked. She said only what was necessary, and when.

"I think I know," Sean said. He had been listening a little away. He slithered down to join us as the helicopter beat over the hillside again, flailing the leaves, showering us with dirt and twigs. "This." He tapped my forearm. "If I could find you, they can find you."

I pulled up my sleeve. The Judas chip seemed to throb under my skin, like poison.

"Hold my wrist," I said to Sean. "Whatever happens, don't let it slip."

Before he could say a word, I pulled my knife. These things must be done fast. If you once stop to think, you will never do it. Make sure you have it straight. You won't get another go. A stab down with the tip, a short pull, a twist, and the traitor thing was on the ground, greasy with my blood. It hurt. It hurt very much, but the blood had staunched, the wound was already closing.

"I'll just have to make sure not to lose you again," Sean said.

Very quietly, very silently, we formed up the team and one by one slipped down the hillside, out from under the eyes of the helicopter. For all I know, the stupid thing is up there still, keeping vigil over a dead chip. We slept under the sky that night, close together for warmth, and on the third day we came to Tinderet and the edge of the Chaga.

Ten had been leading us a cracking pace, as if she were impatient to put Kenya behind us. Since mid-morning, we had been making our way up a long, slow hill. I'd done some hill-walking, I was fit for it, but the young ones and the women with babies found it tough going. When I called for a halt, I saw a moment of anger cross Ten's face. As soon as she could, we upped packs and moved on. I tried to catch up with her, but Ten moved steadily ahead of me until, just below the summit, she was almost running.

"Shone!" she shouted back. "Come with me!"

She ran up through the thinning trees to the summit. I followed, went bounding down a slight dip, and suddenly, the trees opened and I was on the edge.

The ground fell away at my feet into the Rift Valley, green on green on green, sweeping to the valley floor where the patterns of the abandoned fields could still be made out in the patchwork of yellows and buffs and earth tones. Perspective blurred the colors—I could see at least fifty miles—until, suddenly, breathtakingly, they changed. Browns and dryland beiges blended into burgundies and rust reds, were shot through with veins of purple and white, then exploded into chaos, like a bed of flowers of every conceivable color, a jumble of shapes and colors like a mad coral reef, like a box of kiddie's plastic toys spilled out on a Chinese rug. It strained the eyes, it hurt the brain. I followed it back, trying to make sense of what I was seeing. A sheer wall, deep red, rose abruptly out of the chaotic landscape, straight up, almost as high as the escarpment I was standing on. It was not a solid wall; it looked to me to be made up of pillars or, I thought, tree trunks. They must have been of titanic size to be visible from this distance. They opened into an unbroken, flat, crimson canopy.

In the further distance, the flat roof became a jumble of dark greens, broken by what I can only describe as small mesas, like the Devil's Tower in Wyoming or the old volcanoes in Puy de Dome. But these glittered in the sun like glass. Beyond them, the landscape was striped like a tiger, yellow and dark brown, and formations like capsizing icebergs, pure white, lifted out of it. And beyond that, I lost the detail, but the colors went on and on, all the way to the horizon.

I don't know how long I stood, looking at the Chaga. I lost all sense of time. I became aware at some point that Ten was standing beside me. She did not try to move me on, or speak. She knew that the Chaga was one of these things that must just be experienced before it can be interpreted. One by one the others joined us. We stood in a row along the bluffs, looking at our new home.

Then we started down the path to the valley below.

Half an hour down the escarpment, Meji up front called a halt.

"What is it?" I asked Ten. She touched her fingers to her communicator; a half-eggshell of living plastic unfolded from the headset and pressed itself to her right eye.

"This is not good," she said. "Smoke, from Menengai."

"Menengai?"

"Where we're going. Meji is trying to raise them on the radio."

I looked over Ten's head to Meji, one hand held to his ear, looking around him. He looked worried.

"And?"

"Nothing."

"And what do we do?"

"We go on."

We descended through microclimates. The valley floor was fifteen degrees hotter than the cool, damp Nandi Hills. We toiled across brush and overgrown scrub, along abandoned roads, through deserted villages. The warriors held their weapons at the slope. Ten regularly scanned the sky with her all-seeing eye. Now even I could see the smoke, blowing toward us on a wind from the east, and smell it. It smelled like burned spices. I could make out Meji trying to call up Menengai. Radio silence.

In the early afternoon, we crossed terminum. You can see these things clearly from a distance. At ground level, they creep up on you. I was walking through tough valley grasses and thorn scrub when I noticed lines of blue moss between the roots. Oddly regular lines of moss, that bent and forked at exactly one hundred and twenty degrees, and joined up into

hexagons. I froze. Twenty meters ahead of me, Ten stood in one world . . .
I stood in another.

"Even if you do nothing, it will still come to you," she said. I looked
down. The blue lines were inching toward my toes. "Come on." Ten
reached out her hand. I took it, and she led me across. Within two minutes'
walk, the scrub and grass had given way entirely to Chaga vegetation. For
the rest of the afternoon we moved through the destroying zone. Trees
crashed around us, shrubs were devoured from the roots down, grasses fell
apart and dissolved; fungus fingers and coral fans pushed up on either side,
bubbles blew around my head. I walked through it untouched like a man
in a furnace.

Meji called a halt under an arch of Chaga-growth like a vault in a medieval cathedral. He had a report on his earjack.

"Menengai has been attacked."

Everyone started talking, asking questions, jabbering. Meji held up his
hand. "They were Africans. Someone had provided them with Chaga-proof
equipment, and weapons. They had badges on their uniforms: KLA."

"Kenyan Liberation Army," the quiet one, Naomi, said.

"We have enemies," the clever one, Hamid, said. "The Kenyan Government
still claims jurisdiction over the Chaga. Every so often, they remind us
who's in charge. They want to keep us on the run, stop us getting established. They're nothing but contras with western money and guns and
advisers."

"And Menengai?" I asked. Meji shook his head.

"Most High is bringing the survivors to Ol Punyata."

I looked at Ten.

"Most High?"

She nodded.

We met up with Most High under the dark canopy of the Great Wall.
It was an appropriately somber place for the meeting: the smooth soaring
trunks of the trees; the canopy of leaves, held out like hands, a kilometer
over our heads; the splashes of light that fell through the gaps to the forest
floor; survivors and travelers, dwarfed by it all. Medieval peasants must
have felt like this, awestruck in their own cathedrals.

It's an odd experience, meeting someone you've heard of in a story. You
want to say, I've heard about you, you haven't heard about me, you're nothing like I imagined. You check them out to make sure they're playing true
to their character. His story was simple and grim.

A village, waking, going about its normal business, people meeting and greeting, walking and talking, gossiping and idling, talking the news, taking coffee. Then, voices; strange voices, and shots, and people looking up wondering, What is going on here? and while they are caught wondering, strangers running at them, running through, strangers with guns, shooting at anything in front of them, not asking questions, not looking or listening, shooting and running on. Shooting, and burning. Bodies left where they lay, homes like blossoming flowers going up in gobs of flame. Through, back, and out. Gone. As fast, as off-hand as that. Ten minutes, and Menengai was a morgue. Most High told it as casually as it had been committed, but I saw his knuckles whiten as he gripped his staff.

To people like me, who come from a peaceful, ordered society, violence like that is unimaginable.

I've seen fights and they scared me, but I've never experienced the kind of violence Most High was describing, where people's pure intent is to kill other people. I could see the survivors—dirty, tired, scared, very quiet—but I couldn't see what had been done to them. So I couldn't really believe it. And though I'd hidden up there on the hill from the helicopter, I couldn't believe it would have opened up those big gatlings on me, and I couldn't believe now that the people who attacked Menengai, this Kenyan Liberation Army, whose only purpose was to kill Chaga-folk and destroy their lives, were out there somewhere, probably being resupplied by airdrop, reloading, and going in search of new targets. It seemed wrong in a place as silent and holy as this . . . like a snake in the garden.

Meji and Ten believed it. As soon as we could, they moved us on and out.

"Where now?" I asked Ten.

She looked uncertain.

"East. The Black Simbas have a number of settlements on Kirinyaga. They'll defend them."

"How far?"

"Three days?"

"That woman back there, Hope. She won't be able to go on very much longer." I had been speaking to her; she was heavily pregnant. Eight months, I reckoned. She had no English, and I had Aid-Agency Swahili, but she appreciated my company, and I found her big belly a confirmation that life was strong, life went on.

"I know," Ten said. She might wear the gear and carry the staff and have a gun at her hip, but she was facing decisions that told her, forcefully, You're still in your teens, little warrior.

We wound between the colossal buttressed roots of the roof-trees. The globes on the tops of the staffs gave off a soft yellow light—bioluminescence, Ten told me.

We followed the bobbing lights through the dark, dripping wall-forest. The land rose, slowly and steadily. I fell back to walk with Hope. We talked. It passed the time. The Great Wall gave way abruptly to an ecosystem of fungi. Red toadstools towered over my head, puff-balls dusted me with yellow spores, trumpetlike chanterelles dripped water from their cups, clusters of pin-head mushrooms glowed white like corpses. I saw monkeys, watching from the canopy.

We were high now, climbing up ridges like the fingers of a splayed out hand. Hope told me how her husband had been killed in the raid on Menengai. I did not know what to say. Then she asked me my story. I told it in my bad Swahili. The staffs led us higher.

"Ten."

We were taking an evening meal break. That was one thing about the Chaga: you could never go hungry. Reach out, and anything you touched would be edible. Ten had taught me that if you buried your shit, a good-tasting tuber would have grown in the morning. I hadn't had the courage yet to try it. For an alien invasion, the Chaga seemed remarkably considerate of human needs.

"I think Hope's a lot further on than we thought."

Ten shook her head.

"Ten, if she starts, will you stop?"

She hesitated a moment.

"Okay. We will stop."

She struggled for two days, down into a valley, through terribly tough terrain of great spheres of giraffe-patterned moss, then up, into higher country than any we had attempted before.

"Ten, where are we?" I asked. The Chaga had changed our geography, made all our maps obsolete. We navigated by compass, and major, geophysical landmarks.

"We've passed through the Nyandarua Valley, now we're going up the east side of the Aberdares."

The line of survivors became strung out. Naomi and I struggled at the rear with the old and the women with children, and Hope. We fought our way up that hillside, but Hope was flagging, failing.

"I think . . . I feel . . ." she said, hand on her belly.

"Call Ten on that thing," I ordered Naomi. She spoke into her mouthpiece.

"No reply."

"She what?"

"There is no reply."

I ran. Hands, knees, belly, whatever way I could, I made it up that ridge, as fast as I could. Over the summit the terrain changed, as suddenly as Chaga landscapes do, from the moss maze to a plantation of regularly spaced trees shaped like enormous ears of wheat.

Ten was a hundred meters downslope. She stood like a statue among the wheat-trees. Her staff was planted firmly on the ground. She did not acknowledge me when I called her name. I ran down through the trees to her.

"Ten, Hope can't go on. We have to stop."

"No!" Ten shouted. She did not look at me, she stared down through the rows of trees.

"Ten!" I seized her, spun her round. Her face was frantic, terrified, tear-ful, joyful, as if in this grove of alien plants was something familiar and absolutely agonizing. "Ten! You promised!"

"Shone! Shone! I know where I am! I know where this is! That is the pass, and that is where the road went, this is the valley, that is the river, and down there, is Gichichi!" She looked back up to the pass, called to the figures on the tree-line. "Most High! Gichichi! This is Gichichi! We are home!"

She took off. She held her staff in her hand like a hunter's spear, she leaped rocks and fallen trunks, she hurdled streams and run-offs; bounding down through the trees. I was after her like a shot but I couldn't hope to keep up. I found Ten standing in an open space where a falling wheat tree had brought others down like dominoes. Her staff was thrust deep into the earth. I didn't interrupt. I didn't say a word. I knew I was witnessing something holy.

She went down on her knees. She closed her eyes. She pressed her hands to the soil. And I saw dark lines, like slow, black lightning, go out from her fingertips across the Chaga-cover. The lines arced and intersected, sparked out fresh paths.

The carpet of moss began to resemble a crackle-glazed Japanese bowl. But they all focused on Ten. She was the source of the pattern. And the Chaga-cover began to flow toward the lines of force. Shapes appeared under the moving moss, like ribs under skin. They formed grids and squares, slowly pushing up the Chaga-cover. I understood what I was seeing. The lines of buried walls and buildings were being exhumed. Molecule by mol-ecule, centimeter by centimeter, Gichichi was being drawn out of the soil.

By the time the others had made it down from the ridge, the walls stood waist-high and service units were rising out of the earth, electricity generators, water pumps, heat-exchangers, nanofacturing cells. Refugees and warriors walked in amazement among the slowly rising porcelain walls.

Then Ten chose to recognize me.

She looked up. Her teeth were clenched, her hair was matted, sweat dripped from her chin and cheekbones. Her face was gaunt, she was burning her own body-mass, ramming it through that mind/Chaga interface in her brain to program nanoprocessors on a massive scale.

"We control it, Shone," she whispered. "We can make the world any shape we want it to be. We can make a home for ourselves."

Most High laid his hand on her shoulder.

"Enough, child. Enough. It can make itself now."

Ten nodded. She broke the spell. Ten rolled onto her side, gasping, shivering.

"It's finished," she whispered. "Shone . . ."

She still could not say my name right. I went to her, I took her in my arms while around us Gichichi rose, unfolded roofs like petals, grew gardens and tiny, tangled lanes. No words. No need for words. She had done all her saying, but close at hand, I heard the delighted, apprehensive cry of a woman entering labor.

We begin with a village, and we end with a village. Different villages, a different world, but the name remains the same. Did I not tell you that names are important? Ojok, Hope's child, is our first citizen. He is now two, but every day people come over the pass or up from the valley, to stay, to make their homes here. Gichichi is now two thousand souls strong. Five hundred houses straggle up and down the valley side, each with its own garden-shamba and nanofactory, where we can make whatever we require. Gichichi is famous for its nanoprocessor programmers. We earn much credit hiring them to the towns and villages that are growing up like mushrooms down in the valley of Nyeri and along the foothills of Mt. Kenya. A great city is growing there, I have heard, and a mighty culture developing; but that is for the far future. Here in Gichichi, we are wealthy in our own way; we have a community center, three bars, a mandazi shop, even a small theater. There is no church, yet. If Christians come, they may build one. If they do, I hope they call it St. John's. The vine-flowers will grow down over the roof again.

Life is not safe. The KLA have been joined by other contra groups, and we have heard through the net that the West is tightening its quarantine of the Chaga zones. There are attacks all along the northern edge. I do not imagine Gichichi is immune. We must scare their powerful ones very much, now. But the packages keep coming down, and the world keeps changing. And life is never safe. Brother Dust's lesson is the truest I ever learned, and I have been taught it better than many. But I trust in the future. Soon there will be a new name among the citizens of Gichichi, this fine, fertile town in the valleys of the Aberdares. Of course, Sean and I cannot agree what it should be. He wants to call her after the time of day she is born, I want something Irish.

"But you won't be able to pronounce it!" he says. We will think of something. That is the way we do things here. Whatever her name, she will have a story to tell, I am sure, but that is not for me to say. My story ends here, and our lives go on. I take up mine again, as you lift yours. We have a long road before us.

Paul McAuley worked as a research biologist and university lecturer before becoming a full-time writer. He is the author of more than twenty novels, several collections of short stories, a Doctor Who novella, and a BFI Film Classic monograph on Terry Gilliam's film *Brazil*. His fiction has won the Philip K. Dick Memorial Award, the Arthur C. Clarke Award, the John W. Campbell Memorial Award, the Sidewise Award, the British Fantasy Award and the Theodore Sturgeon Memorial Award. His latest novel, *Austral*, set in post-global warming Antarctica, was published in 2017.

The Choice

PAUL MCAULEY

In the night, tides and a brisk wind drove a raft of bubbleweed across the Flood and piled it up along the north side of the island. Soon after first light, Lucas started raking it up, ferrying load after load to one of the compost pits, where it would rot down into a nutrient-rich liquid fertiliser. He was trundling his wheelbarrow down the steep path to the shore for about the thirtieth or fortieth time when he spotted someone walking across the water: Damian, moving like a cross-country skier as he crossed the channel between the island and the stilt huts and floating tanks of his father's shrimp farm. It was still early in the morning, already hot. A perfect September day, the sky's blue dome untroubled by cloud. Shifting points of sunlight starred the water, flashed from the blades of the farm's wind turbine. Lucas waved to his friend and Damian waved back and nearly overbalanced, windmilling his arms and recovering, slogging on.

They met at the water's edge. Damian, picking his way between floating slicks of red weed, called out breathlessly, "Did you hear?"

"Hear what?"

"A dragon got itself stranded close to Martham."

"You're kidding."

"I'm not kidding. An honest-to-God sea dragon."

Damian stepped onto an apron of broken brick at the edge of the water and sat down and eased off the fat flippers of his Jesus shoes, explaining that he'd heard about it from Ritchy, the foreman of the shrimp farm, who'd got it off the skipper of a supply barge who'd been listening to chatter on the common band.

"It beached not half an hour ago. People reckon it came in through the cut at Horsey and couldn't get back over the bar when the tide turned. So it went on up the channel of the old riverbed until it ran ashore."

Lucas thought for a moment. "There's a sand bar that hooks into the channel south of Martham. I went past it any number of times when I worked on Grant Higgins's boat last summer, ferrying oysters to Norwich."

"It's almost on our doorstep," Damian said. He pulled his phone from the pocket of his shorts and angled it towards Lucas. "Right about here. See it?"

"I know where Martham is. Let me guess—you want me to take you."

"What's the point of building a boat if you don't use it? Come on, L. It isn't every day an alien machine washes up."

Lucas took off his broad-brimmed straw hat and blotted his forehead with his wrist and set his hat on his head again. He was a wiry boy not quite sixteen, bare-chested in baggy shorts, and wearing sandals he'd cut from an old car tire. "I was planning to go crabbing. After I finish clearing this weed, water the vegetable patch, fix lunch for my mother . . ."

"I'll give you a hand with all that when we get back."

"Right."

"If you really don't want to go I could maybe borrow your boat."

"Or you could take one of your dad's."

"After what he did to me last time? I'd rather row there in that leaky old clunker of your mother's. Or walk."

"That would be a sight."

Damian smiled. He was just two months older than Lucas, tall and sturdy, his cropped blond hair bleached by salt and summer sun, his nose and the rims of his ears pink and peeling. The two had been friends for as long as they could remember.

He said, "I reckon I can sail as well as you."

"You're sure this dragon is still there? You have pictures?"

"Not exactly. It knocked out the town's broadband, and everything else. According to the guy who talked to Ritchy, nothing electronic works within a klick of it. Phones, slates, radios, nothing. The tide turns in a couple of hours, but I reckon we can get there if we start right away."

"Maybe. I should tell my mother," Lucas said. "In the unlikely event that she wonders where I am."

"How is she?"

"No better, no worse. Does your dad know you're skipping out?"

"Don't worry about it. I'll tell him I went crabbing with you."

"Fill a couple of jugs at the still," Lucas said. "And pull up some carrots, too. But first, hand me your phone."

"The GPS coordinates are flagged up right there. You ask it, it'll plot a course."

Lucas took the phone, holding it with his fingertips—he didn't like the way it squirmed as it shaped itself to fit in his hand. "How do you switch it off?"

"What do you mean?"

"If we go, we won't be taking the phone. Your dad could track us."

"How will we find our way there?"

"I don't need your phone to find Martham."

"You and your off-the-grid horse shit," Damian said.

"You wanted an adventure," Lucas said. "This is it."

When Lucas started to tell his mother that he'd be out for the rest of the day with Damian, she said, "Chasing after that so-called dragon I suppose. No need to look surprised—it's all over the news. Not the official news, of course. No mention of it there. But it's leaking out everywhere that counts."

His mother was propped against the headboard of the double bed under the caravan's big end window. Julia Wittsruck, fifty-two, skinny as a refugee, dressed in a striped Berber robe and half-covered in a patchwork of quilts and thin orange blankets stamped with the Oxfam logo. The ropes of her dreadlocks tied back with a red bandana; her tablet resting in her lap.

She gave Lucas her best inscrutable look and said, "I suppose this is Damian's idea. You be careful. His ideas usually work out badly."

"That's why I'm going along. To make sure he doesn't get into trouble. He's set on seeing it, one way or another."

"And you aren't?"

Lucas smiled. "I suppose I'm curious. Just a little."

"I wish I could go. Take a rattle can or two, spray the old slogans on the damned thing's hide."

"I could put some cushions in the boat. Make you as comfortable as you like."

Lucas knew that his mother wouldn't take up his offer. She rarely left the caravan, hadn't been off the island for more than three years. A multi-locus immunotoxic syndrome, basically an allergic reaction to the myriad products and pollutants of the anthropocene age, had left her more or less completely bedridden. She'd refused all offers of treatment or help by the local social agencies, relying instead on the services of a local witchwoman who visited once a week, and spent her days in bed, working at her tab let. She trawled government sites and stealthnets, made podcasts, advised zero-impact communities, composed critiques and manifestos. She kept a public journal, wrote essays and opinion pieces (at the moment, she was especially exercised by attempts by multinational companies to move in on the Antarctic Peninsula, and a utopian group that was using alien technology to build a floating community on a drowned coral reef in the Midway Islands), and maintained friendships, alliances, and several rancorous feuds with former colleagues whose origins had long been forgotten by both sides. In short, hers was a way of life that would have been familiar to scholars from any time in the past couple of millennia.

She'd been a lecturer in philosophy at Birkbeck College before the nuclear strikes, riots, revolutions, and netwar skirmishes of the so-called Spasm, which had ended when the floppy ships of the Jackaroo had appeared in the skies over Earth. In exchange for rights to the outer solar system, the aliens had given the human race technology to clean up the Earth, and access to a wormhole network that linked a dozen M-class red dwarf stars. Soon enough, other alien species showed up, making various deals with various nations and power blocs, bartering advanced technologies for works of art, fauna and flora, the secret formula of Coca-Cola, and other unique items.

Most believed that the aliens were kindly and benevolent saviours, members of a loose alliance that had traced ancient broadcasts of *I Love Lucy* to their origin and arrived just in time to save the human species from the consequences of its monkey cleverness. But a vocal minority wanted nothing to do with them, doubting that their motives were in any way altruistic, elaborating all kinds of theories about their true motivations. We should choose to reject the help of the aliens, they said. We should reject easy fixes and the magic of advanced technologies we don't understand, and choose the harder thing: to keep control of our own destiny.

Julia Wittstruck had become a leading light in this movement. When its brief but fierce round of global protests and politicking had fallen apart in a mess of mutual recriminations and internecine warfare, she'd moved to Scotland and joined a group of green radicals who'd been building a self-sufficient settlement on a trio of ancient oil rigs in the Firth of Forth. But they'd become compromised too, according to Julia, so she'd left them and taken up with Lucas's father (Lucas knew almost nothing about him— his mother said that the past was the past, that she was all that counted in his life because she had given birth to him and raised and taught him), and they'd lived the gypsy life for a few years until she'd split up with him and, pregnant with her son, had settled in a smallholding in Norfolk, living off the grid, supported by a small legacy left to her by one of her devoted supporters from the glory days of the anti-alien protests.

When she'd first moved there, the coast had been more than ten kilometres to the east, but a steady rise in sea level had flooded the northern and eastern coasts of Britain and Europe. East Anglia had been sliced in two by levees built to protect precious farmland from the encroaching sea, and most people caught on the wrong side had taken resettlement grants and moved on. But Julia had stayed put. She'd paid a contractor to extend a small rise, all that was left of her smallholding, with rubble from a wrecked twentieth-century housing estate, and made her home on the resulting island. It had once been much larger, and a succession of people had camped there, attracted by her kudos, driven away after a few weeks or a few months by her scorn and impatience. Then most of Greenland's remaining ice cap collapsed into the Arctic Ocean, sending a surge of water across the North Sea.

Lucas had only been six, but he still remembered everything about that day. The water had risen past the high tide mark that afternoon and had kept rising. At first it had been fun to mark the stealthy progress of the water with a series of sticks driven into the ground, but by evening it was clear that it was not going to stop anytime soon and then in a sudden smooth rush it rose more than a hundred centimetres, flooding the vegetable plots and lapping at the timber baulks on which the caravan rested. All that evening, Julia had moved their possessions out of the caravan, with Lucas trotting to and fro at her heels, helping her as best he could until, some time after midnight, she'd given up and they'd fallen asleep under a tent rigged from chairs and a blanket. And had woken to discover that their island had shrunk to half its previous size, and the caravan had floated off and lay canted and half-drowned in muddy water littered with every kind of debris.

Julia had bought a replacement caravan and set it on the highest point of what was left of the island, and despite ineffectual attempts to remove them by various local government officials, she and Lucas had stayed on. She'd taught him the basics of numeracy and literacy, and the long and intricate secret history of the world, and he'd learned field- and wood- and watercraft from their neighbours. He snared rabbits in the woods that ran alongside the levee, foraged for hedgerow fruits and edible weeds and fungi, bagged squirrels with small stones shot from his catapult. He grubbed mussels from the rusting car-reef that protected the seaward side of the levee, set wicker traps for eels and trotlines for mitten crabs. He fished for mackerel and dogfish and weaverfish on the wide brown waters of the Flood. When he could, he worked shifts on the shrimp farm owned by Damian's father, or on the market gardens, farms, and willow and bamboo plantations on the other side of the levee.

In spring, he watched long vees of geese fly north above the floodwater that stretched out to the horizon. In autumn, he watched them fly south.

He'd inherited a great deal of his mother's restlessness and fierce independence, but although he longed to strike out beyond his little world, he didn't know how to begin. And besides, he had to look after Julia. She would never admit it, but she depended on him, utterly.

She said now, dismissing his offer to take her along, "You know I have too much to do here. The day is never long enough. There is something you can do for me, though. Take my phone with you."

"Damian says phones don't work around the dragon."

"I'm sure it will work fine. Take some pictures of that thing. As many as you can. I'll write up your story when you come back, and pictures will help attract traffic."

"Okay."

Lucas knew that there was no point in arguing. Besides, his mother's phone was an ancient model that predated the Spasm: it lacked any kind of cloud connectivity and was as dumb as a box of rocks. As long as he only used it to take pictures, it wouldn't compromise his idea of an off-the-grid adventure.

His mother smiled. "'ET go home.'"

"'ET go home?'"

"We put that up everywhere, back in the day. We put it on the main runway of Luton Airport, in letters twenty metres tall. Also dug trenches in the shape of the words up on the South Downs and filled them with diesel fuel and set them alight. You could see it from space. Let the unhuman know that they were not welcome here. That we did not need them. Check the toolbox. I'm sure there's a rattlecan in there. Take it along, just in case."

"I'll take my catapult, in case I spot any ducks. I'll try to be back before it gets dark. If I don't, there are MREs in the store cupboard. And I picked some tomatoes and carrots."

"'ET go home,'" his mother said. "Don't forget that. And be careful, in that little boat."

Lucas had started to build his sailboat late last summer, and had worked at it all through the winter. It was just four metres from bow to stern, its plywood hull glued with epoxy and braced with ribs shaped from branches of a young poplar tree that had fallen in the autumn gales. He'd used an adze and a homemade plane to fashion the mast and boom from the poplar's trunk, knocked up the knees, gunwale, outboard support and bow cap from oak, and persuaded Ritchy, the shrimp farm's foreman, to print off the cleats, oarlocks, bow eye and grommets for lacing the sails on the farm's maker. Ritchy had given him some half-empty tins of blue paint and varnish to seal the hull, and he'd bought a set of secondhand laminate sails from the shipyard in Halvergate, and spliced the halyards and sheet from scrap lengths of rope.

He loved his boat more than he was ready to admit to himself. That spring he'd tacked back and forth beyond the shrimp farm, had sailed north along the coast to Halvergate and Acle, and south and west around Reedham Point as far as Brundall, and had crossed the channel of the river and navigated the mazy mudflats to Chedgrave. If the sea dragon was stuck where Damian said it was, he'd have to travel further than ever before, navigating uncharted and ever-shifting sand and mudbanks, dodging clippers and barge strings in the shipping channel, but Lucas reckoned he had the measure of his little boat now and it was a fine day and a steady wind blowing from the west drove them straight along, with the jib cocked as far as it would go in the stay and the mainsail bellying full and the boat heeling sharply as it ploughed a white furrow in the light chop.

At first, all Lucas had to do was sit in the stern with the tiller snug in his right armpit and the main sheet coiled loosely in his left hand, and keep a straight course north past the pens and catwalks of the shrimp farm. Damian sat beside him, leaning out to port to counterbalance the boat's tilt, his left hand keeping the jib sheet taut, his right holding a plastic cup he would now and then use to scoop water from the bottom of the boat and fling in a sparkling arc that was caught and twisted by the wind.

The sun stood high in a tall blue sky empty of cloud save for a thin rim at the horizon to the northeast. Fret, most likely, mist forming where moisture condensed out of air that had cooled as it passed over the sea. But the fret was kilometres away, and all around sunlight flashed from every wave top and burned on the white sails and beat down on the two boys. Damian's face and bare torso shone with sunblock; although Lucas was about as dark as he got, he'd rubbed sunblock on his face too, and tied his straw hat under his chin and put on a shirt that flapped about his chest. The tiller juddered minutely and constantly as the boat slapped through an endless succession of catspaw waves and Lucas measured the flex of the sail by the tug of the sheet wrapped around his left hand, kept an eye the foxtail streamer that flew from the top of the mast. Judging by landmarks on the levee that ran along the shore to port, they were making around fifteen kilometres per hour, about as fast as Lucas had ever gotten out of his boat, and he and Damian grinned at each other and squinted off into the glare of the sunstruck water, happy and exhilarated to be skimming across the face of the Flood, two bold adventurers off to confront a monster.

"We'll be there in an hour easy," Damian said.

"A bit less than two, maybe. As long as the fret stays where it is."

"The sun'll burn it off."

"Hasn't managed it yet."

"Don't let your natural caution spoil a perfect day."

Lucas swung wide of a raft of bubbleweed that glistened like a slick of fresh blood in the sun. Some called it Martian weed, though it had nothing to do with any of the aliens; it was an engineered species designed to mop up nitrogen and phosphorous released by drowned farmland, prospering beyond all measure or control.

Dead ahead, a long line of whitecaps marked the reef of the old railway embankment. Lucas swung the tiller into the wind and he and Damian ducked as the boom swung across and the boat gybed around. The sails slackened, then filled with wind again as the boat turned towards one of the gaps blown in the embankment, cutting so close to the buoy that marked it that Damian could reach out and slap the rusty steel plate of its flank as they went by. And then they were heading out across a broad reach, with the little town of Acle strung along a low promontory to port. A slateless church steeple stood up from the water like a skeletal light-house. The polished cross at its top burned like a flame in the sunlight. A file of old pylons stepped away, most canted at steep angles, the twiggy platforms of heron nests built in angles of their girder work, whitened everywhere with droppings. One of the few still standing straight had been colonised by fisherfolk, with shacks built from driftwood lashed to its struts and a wave-powered generator made from oil drums strung out beyond. Washing flew like festive flags inside the web of rusted steel, and a naked small child of indeterminate sex clung to the unshuttered doorway of a shack just above the waterline, pushing a tangle of hair from its eyes as it watched the little boat sail by.

They passed small islands fringed with young mangrove trees, an engi-neered species that was rapidly spreading from areas in the south where they'd been planted to replace the levee. Lucas spotted a marsh harrier patrolling mudflats in the lee of one island, scrying for water voles and mitten crabs. They passed a long building sunk to the tops of its second-storey windows in the flood, with brightly coloured plastic bubbles pitched on its flat roof amongst the notched and spinning wheels of windmill generators, and small boats bobbing alongside. Someone standing at the edge of the roof waved to them, and Damian stood up and waved back and the boat shifted so that he had to catch at the jib leech and sit down hard.

"You want us to capsize, go ahead," Lucas told him.

"There are worse places to be shipwrecked. You know they're all married to each other over there."

"I heard."

"They like visitors too."

"I know you aren't talking from experience or you'd have told me all about it. At least a dozen times."

"I met a couple of them in Halvergate. They said I should stop by some time," Damian said, grinning sideways at Lucas. "We could maybe think about doing that on the way back."

"And get stripped of everything we own, and thrown in the water."

"You have a trusting nature, don't you?"

"If you mean, I'm not silly enough to think they'll welcome us in and let us take our pick of their women, then I guess I do."

"She was awful pretty, the woman. And not much older than me."

"And the rest of them are seahags older than your great-grandmother."

"That one time with my father . . . She was easily twice my age and I didn't mind a bit."

A couple of months ago, Damian's sixteenth birthday, his father had taken him to a pub in Norwich where women stripped at the bar and afterwards walked around bare naked, collecting tips from the customers. Damian's father had paid one of them to look after his son, and Damian hadn't stopped talking about it ever since, making plans to go back on his own or to take Lucas with him that so far hadn't amounted to anything.

He watched the half-drowned building dwindle into the glare striking off the water and said, "If we ever ran away we could live in a place like that."

"You could, maybe," Lucas said. "I'd want to keep moving. But I suppose I could come back and visit now and then."

"I don't mean *that* place. I mean a place like it. Must be plenty of them, on those alien worlds up in the sky. There's oceans on one of them. First Foot."

"I know."

"And alien ruins on all of them. There are people walking about up there right now. On all those new worlds. And most people sit around like . . . like bloody stumps. Old tree stumps stuck in mud."

"I'm not counting on winning the ticket lottery," Lucas said. "Sailing south, that would be pretty fine. To Africa, or Brazil, or these islands people are building in the Pacific. Or even all the way to Antarctica."

"Soon as you stepped ashore, L, you'd be eaten by a polar bear."

"Polar bears lived in the north when there were polar bears."

"Killer penguins then. Giant penguins with razors in their flippers and lasers for eyes."

"No such thing."

"The !Cha made sea dragons, didn't they? So why not giant robot killer penguins? Your mother should look into it."

"That's not funny."

"Didn't mean anything by it. Just joking, is all."

"You go too far sometimes."

They sailed in silence for a little while, heading west across the deepwater channel. A clipper moved far off to starboard, cylinder sails spinning slowly, white as salt in the middle of a flat vastness that shimmered like shot silk under the hot blue sky. Some way beyond it, a tug was dragging a string of barges south. The shoreline of Thurne Point emerged from the heat haze, standing up from mudbanks cut by a web of narrow channels, and they turned east, skirting stands of seagrass that spread out into the open water. It was a little colder now, and the wind was blowing more from the northwest than the west. Lucas thought that the bank of fret looked closer, too. When he pointed it out, Damian said it was still klicks and klicks off, and besides, they were headed straight to their prize now.

"If it's still there," Lucas said.

"It isn't going anywhere, not with the tide all the way out."

"You really are an expert on this alien stuff, aren't you?"

"Just keep heading north, L."

"That's exactly what I'm doing."

"I'm sorry about that crack about your mother. I didn't mean anything by it. Okay?"

"Okay."

"I like to kid around," Damian said. "But I'm serious about getting out of here. Remember that time two years ago, we hiked into Norwich, found the army offices?"

"I remember the sergeant there gave us cups of tea and biscuits and told us to come back when we were old enough."

"He's still there. That sergeant. Same bloody biscuits too."

"Wait. You went to join up without telling me?"

"I went to find out if I could. After my birthday. Turns out the army takes people our age, but you need the permission of your parents. So that was that."

"You didn't even try to talk to your father about it?"

"He has me working for him, L. Why would he sign away good cheap labour? I *did* try, once. He was half-cut and in a good mood. What passes for a good mood as far as he's concerned, any rate. Mellowed out on beer and superfine skunk. But he wouldn't hear anything about it. And then he got all the way flat-out drunk and he beat on me. Told me to never mention it again."

Lucas looked over at his friend and said, "Why didn't you tell me this before?"

"I can join under my own signature when I'm eighteen, not before," Damian said. "No way out of here until then, unless I run away or win the lottery."

"So are you thinking of running away?"

"I'm damned sure not counting on winning the lottery. And even if I do, you have to be eighteen before they let you ship out. Just like the fucking army." Damian looked at Lucas, looked away. "He'll probably bash all kinds of shit out of me, for taking off like this."

"You can stay over tonight. He'll be calmer, tomorrow."

Damian shook his head. "He'll only come looking for me. And I don't want to cause trouble for you and your mother."

"It wouldn't be any trouble."

"Yeah, it would. But thanks anyway." Damian paused, then said, "I don't care what he does to me anymore. You know? All I think is, one day I'll be able to beat up on him."

"You say that but you don't mean it."

"Longer I stay here, the more I become like him."

"I don't see it ever happening."

Damian shrugged.

"I really don't," Lucas said.

"Fuck him," Damian said. "I'm not going to let him spoil this fine day."

"Our grand adventure."

"The wind's changing again."

"I think the fret's moving in too."

"Maybe it is, a little. But we can't turn back, L. Not now."

The bank of cloud across the horizon was about a klick away, reaching up so high that it blurred and dimmed the sun. The air was colder and the wind was shifting minute by minute. Damian put on his shirt, holding the jib sheet in his teeth as he punched his arms into the sleeves. They tacked to swing around a long reach of grass, and as they came about saw a white wall sitting across the water, dead ahead.

Lucas pushed the tiller to leeward. The boat slowed at once and swung around to face the wind.

"What's the problem?" Damian said. "It's just a bit of mist."

Lucas caught the boom as it swung, held it steady. "We'll sit tight for a spell. See if the fret burns off."

"And meanwhile the tide'll turn and lift off the fucking dragon."

"Not for awhile."

"We're almost there."

"You don't like it, you can swim."

"I might." Damian peered at the advancing fret. "Think the dragon has something to do with this?"

"I think it's just fret."

"Maybe it's hiding from something looking for it. We're drifting backwards," Damian said. "Is that part of your plan?"

"We're over the river channel, in the main current. Too deep for my anchor. See those dead trees at the edge of the grass? That's where I'm aiming. We can sit it out there."

"I hear something," Damian said.

Lucas heard it too. The ripping roar of a motor driven at full speed, coming closer. He looked over his shoulder, saw a shadow condense inside the mist and gain shape and solidity: a cabin cruiser shouldering through windblown tendrils at the base of the bank of mist, driving straight down the main channel at full speed, its wake spreading wide on either side.

In a moment of chill clarity Lucas saw what was going to happen. He shouted to Damian, telling him to duck, and let the boom go and shoved the tiller to starboard. The boom banged around as the sail bellied and the boat started to turn, but the cruiser was already on them, roaring past just ten metres away, and the broad smooth wave of its wake hit the boat broadside and lifted it and shoved it sideways towards a stand of dead trees. Lucas gave up any attempt to steer and unwound the main halyard from its cleat. Damian grabbed an oar and used it to push the boat away from the first of the trees, but their momentum swung them into two more. The wet black stump of a branch scraped along the side and the boat heeled and water poured in over the thwart. For a moment Lucas thought they would capsize; then something thumped into the mast and the boat sat up again. Shards of rotten wood dropped down with a dry clatter and they were suddenly still, caught amongst dead and half-drowned trees.

The damage wasn't as bad as it might have been—a rip close to the top of the jib, long splintery scrapes in the blue paintwork on the port side—but it kindled a black spark of anger in Lucas's heart. At the cruiser's criminal indifference; at his failure to evade trouble.

"Unhook the halyard and let it down," he told Damian. "We'll have to do without the jib."

"*Abode Two.* That's the name of the bugger nearly ran us down. Registered in Norwich. We should find him and get him to pay for this mess," Damian said as he folded the torn jib sail.

"I wonder why he was going so damned fast."

"Maybe he went to take a look at the dragon, and something scared him off."

"Or maybe he just wanted to get out of the fret." Lucas looked all around, judging angles and clearances. The trees stood close together in water scummed with every kind of debris, stark and white above the tide line, black and clad with mussels and barnacles below. He said, "Let's try pushing backwards. But be careful. I don't want any more scrapes."

By the time they had freed themselves from the dead trees the fret had advanced around them. A cold streaming whiteness that moved just above the water, deepening in every direction.

"Now we're caught up in it, it's as easy to go forward as to go back. So we might as well press on," Lucas said.

"That's the spirit. Just don't hit any more trees."

"I'll do my best."

"Think we should put up the sail?"

"There's hardly any wind, and the tide's still going out. We'll just go with the current."

"Dragon weather," Damian said.

"Listen," Lucas said.

After a moment's silence, Damian said, "Is it another boat?"

"Thought I heard wings."

Lucas had taken out his catapult. He fitted a ball-bearing in the centre of its fat rubber band as he looked all around. There was a splash amongst the dead trees to starboard and he brought up the catapult and pulled back the rubber band as something dropped onto a dead branch. A heron, grey as a ghost, turning its head to look at him.

Lucas lowered the catapult, and Damian whispered, "You could take that easy."

"I was hoping for a duck or two."

"Let me try a shot."

Lucas stuck the catapult in his belt. "You kill it, you eat it."

The heron straightened its crooked neck and raised up and opened its wings and with a lazy flap launched itself across the water, sailing past the stern of the boat and vanishing into the mist.

"Ritchy cooked one once," Damian said. "With about a ton of aniseed. Said it was how the Romans did them."

"How was it?"

'Pretty fucking awful you want to know the truth."

"Pass me one of the oars," Lucas said. "We can row a while."

They rowed through mist into mist. The small noises they made seemed magnified, intimate. Now and again Lucas put his hand over the side and dipped up a palmful of water and tasted it, telling Damian that fresh water was slow to mix with salt, so as long as it stayed sweet it meant they were in the old river channel and shouldn't run into anything. Damian was sceptical, but shrugged when Lucas challenged him to come up with a better way of finding their way through the fret without stranding themselves on some mudbank

They'd been rowing for ten minutes or so when a long, low mournful note boomed out far ahead of them. It shivered Lucas to the marrow of his bones. He and Damian stopped rowing and looked at each other.

"I'd say that was a foghorn, if I didn't know what one sounded like," Damian said.

"Maybe it's a boat. A big one."

"Or maybe you-know-what. Calling for its dragon-mummy."

"Or warning people away."

"I think it came from over there," Damian said, pointing off to starboard.

"I think so too. But it's hard to be sure of anything in this stuff."

They rowed aslant the current. A dim and low palisade appeared, resolving into a bed of sea grass that spread along the edge of the old river channel. Lucas, believing that he knew where they were, felt a clear measure of relief. They sculled into a narrow cut that led through the grass. Tall stems bent and showered them with drops of condensed mist as they brushed past. Then they were out into open water on the far side. A beach loomed out of the mist and sand suddenly gripped and grated along the length of the little boat's keel. Damian dropped his oar and vaulted over the side and splashed away, running up the beach and vanishing into granular whiteness. Lucas shipped his own oar and slid into knee-deep water and hauled the boat through purling ripples, then lifted from the bow the bucket filled with concrete he used as an anchor and dropped it onto hard wet sand, where it keeled sideways in a dint that immediately filled with water.

He followed Damian's footprints up the beach, climbed a low ridge grown over with marram grass and descended to the other side of the sand bar. Boats lay at anchor in shallow water, their outlines blurred by mist. Two dayfishers with small wheelhouses at their bows. Several sail-boats not much bigger than his. A cabin cruiser with trim white super-structure, much like the one that had almost run him down.

A figure materialised out of the whiteness, a chubby boy of five or six in dungarees who ran right around Lucas, laughing, and chased away. He followed the boy toward a blurred eye of light far down the beach. Raised voices. Laughter. A metallic screeching. As he drew close, the blurred light condensed and separated into two sources: a bonfire burning above the tide line; a rack of spotlights mounted on a police speedboat anchored a dozen metres off the beach, long fingers of light lancing through mist and blur-rily illuminating the long sleek shape stranded at the edge of the water.

It was big, the sea dragon, easily fifteen metres from stem to stern and about three metres across at its waist, tapering to blunt and shovel-shaped points at either end, coated in close-fitting and darkly tinted scales. An alien machine, solid and obdurate. One of thousands spawned by sealed mother ships the UN had purchased from the !Cha.

Lucas thought that it looked like a leech, or one of the parasitic flukes that lived in the bellies of sticklebacks. A big segmented shape, vaguely streamlined, helplessly prostate. People stood here and there on the curve of its back. A couple of kids were whacking away at its flank with chunks of driftwood. A group of men and women stood at its nose, heads bowed as if in prayer. A woman was walking along its length, pointing a wand-like instrument at different places. A cluster of people were conferring amongst a scatter of toolboxes and a portable generator, and one of them stepped forward and applied an angle grinder to the dragon's hide. There was a ragged screech and a fan of orange sparks sprayed out and the man stepped back and turned to his companions and shook his head. Beyond the dragon, dozens more people could be glimpsed through the blur of the fret: everyone from the little town of Martham must have walked out along the sand bar to see the marvel that had cast itself up at their doorstep.

According to the UN, dragons cruised the oceans and swept up and digested the vast rafts of floating garbage that were part of the legacy of the wasteful oil-dependent world before the Spasm. According to rumours propagated on the stealth nets, a UN black lab had long ago cracked open a dragon and reverse-engineered its technology for fell purposes, or they were a cover for an alien plot to infiltrate Earth and construct secret bases in the ocean deeps, or geoengineer the world in some radical and inimical fashion. And so on, and so on. One of his mother's ongoing disputes was with the Midway Island Utopians, who were using modified dragons to sweep plastic particulates from the North Pacific Gyre and spin the polymer soup into construction materials: true Utopians shouldn't use any kind of alien technology, according to her.

Lucas remembered his mother's request to take photos of the dragon and fished out her phone; when he switched it on, it emitted a lone and plaintive beep and its screen flashed and went dark. He switched it off, switched it on again. This time it did nothing. So it was true: the dragon was somehow suppressing electronic equipment. Lucas felt a shiver of apprehension, wondering what else it could do, wondering if it was watching him and everyone around it.

As he pushed the dead phone into his pocket, someone called his name. Lucas turned, saw an old man dressed in a yellow slicker and a peaked corduroy cap bustling towards him. Bill Danvers, one of the people who tended the oyster beds east of Martham, asking him now if he'd come over with Grant Higgins.

"I came in my own boat," Lucas said.

"You worked for Grant though," Bill Danvers said, and held out a flat quarter-litre bottle.

"Once upon a time. That's kind, but I'll pass."

"Vodka and ginger root. It'll keep out the cold." The old man unscrewed the cap and took a sip and held out the bottle again.

Lucas shook his head.

Bill Danvers took another sip and capped the bottle, saying, "You came over from Halvergate?"

"A little south of Halvergate. Sailed all the way." It felt good to say it.

"People been coming in from every place, past couple of hours. Including those science boys you see trying to break into her. But I was here first. Followed the damn thing in after it went past me. I was fishing for pollack, and it went past like an island on the move. Like to have had me in the water, I was rocking so much. I fired up the outboard and swung around but I couldn't keep pace with it. I saw it hit the bar, though. It didn't slow down a bit, must have been travelling at twenty knots. I heard it," Bill Danvers said, and clapped his hands. "Bang! It ran straight up, just like you see. When I caught up with it, it was wriggling like an eel. Trying to move forward, you know? And it did, for a little bit. And then it stuck, right where it is now. Must be something wrong with it, I reckon, or it wouldn't have grounded itself. Maybe it's dying, eh?"

"Can they die, dragons?"

"You live long enough, boy, you'll know everything has its time. Even unnatural things like this. Those science people, they've been trying to cut into it all morning. They used a thermal lance, and some kind of fancy drill. Didn't even scratch it. Now they're trying this saw thing with a blade tougher than diamond. Or so they say. Whatever it is, it won't do any good. Nothing on Earth can touch a dragon. Why'd you come all this way?"

"Just to take a look."

"Long as that's all you do I won't have any quarrel with you. You might want to pay the fee now."

"Fee?"

"Five pounds. Or five euros, if that's what you use."

"I don't have any money," Lucas said.

Bill Danvers studied him. "I was here first. Anyone says different they're a goddamned liar. I'm the only one can legitimately claim salvage rights. The man what found the dragon," he said, and turned and walked towards two women, starting to talk long before he reached them.

Lucas went on down the beach. A man sat tailorwise on the sand, sketching on a paper pad with a stick of charcoal. A small group of women were chanting some kind of incantation and brushing the dragon's flank with handfuls of ivy, and all down its length people stood close, touching its scales with the palms of their hands or leaning against it, peering into it, like penitents at a holy relic. Its scales were easily a metre across and each was a slightly different shape, six- or seven-sided, dark yet grainily translucent. Clumps of barnacles and knots of hair-like weed clung here and there.

Lucas took a step into cold, ankle-deep water, and another. Reached out, the tips of his fingers tingling, and brushed the surface of one of the plates. It was the same temperature as the air and covered in small dimples, like hammered metal. He pressed the palm of his hand flat against it and felt a steady vibration, like touching the throat of a purring cat. A shiver shot through the marrow of him, a delicious mix of fear and exhilaration. Suppose his mother and her friends were right? Suppose there was an alien inside there? A Jackaroo or a !Cha riding inside the dragon because it was the only way, thanks to the agreement with the UN, they could visit the Earth. An actual alien lodged in the heart of the machine, watching everything going on around it, trapped and helpless, unable to call for help because it wasn't supposed to be there.

No one knew what any of the aliens looked like—whether they looked more or less like people, or were unimaginable monsters, or clouds of gas, or swift cool thoughts schooling inside some vast computer. They had shown themselves only as avatars, plastic man-shaped shells with the pleasant, bland but somehow creepy faces of old-fashioned shop dummies, and after the treaty had been negotiated only a few of those were left on Earth, at the UN headquarters in Geneva. Suppose, Lucas thought, the scientists broke in and pulled its passenger out. He imagined some kind of squid, saucer eyes and a clacking beak in a knot of thrashing tentacles, helpless in Earth's gravity. Or suppose something came to rescue it? Not the UN, but an actual alien ship. His heart beat fast and strong at the thought.

Walking a wide circle around the blunt, eyeless prow of the dragon, he found Damian on the other side, talking to a slender, dark-haired girl dressed in a shorts and a heavy sweater. She turned to look at Lucas as he walked up, and said to Damian, "Is this your friend?"

"Lisbeth was just telling me about the helicopter that crashed," Damian said. "Its engine cut out when it got too close and it dropped straight into the sea. Her father helped to rescue the pilot."

"She broke her hip," the girl, Lisbeth, said. "She's at our house now. I'm supposed to be looking after her, but Doctor Naja gave her something that put her to sleep."

"Lisbeth's father is the mayor," Damian said. "He's in charge of all this."

"He thinks he is," the girl said, "but no one is really. Police and everyone arguing amongst themselves. Do you have a phone, Lucas? Mine doesn't work. This is the best thing to ever happen here and I can't even tell my friends about it."

"I could row you out to where your phone started working," Damian said.

"I don't think so," Lisbeth said with a coy little smile, twisting the toes of her bare right foot in the wet sand.

Lucas had thought that she was around his and Damian's age; now he realised that she was at least two years younger.

"It'll be absolutely safe," Damian said. "Word of honour."

Lisbeth shook her head. "I want to stick around here and see what happens next."

"That's a good idea too," Damian said. "We can sit up by the fire and keep warm. I can tell you all about our adventures. How we found our way through the mist. How we were nearly run down—"

"I have to go and find my friends," Lisbeth said, and flashed a dazzling smile at Lucas and said that it was nice to meet him and turned away. Damian caught at her arm and Lucas stepped in and told him to let her go, and Lisbeth smiled at Lucas again and walked off, bare feet leaving dainty prints in the wet sand.

"Thanks for that," Damian said.

"She's a kid. And she's also the mayor's daughter."

"So? We were just talking."

"So he could have you locked up if he wanted to. Me too."

"You don't have to worry about that, do you? Because you scared her off," Damian said.

"She walked away because she wanted to," Lucas said.

He would have said more, would have asked Damian why they were arguing, but at that moment the dragon emitted its mournful wail. A great honking blare, more or less B-flat, so loud it was like a physical force, shocking every square centimetre of Lucas's body. He clapped his hands over his ears, but the sound was right inside the box of his skull, shivering deep in his chest and his bones. Damian had pressed his hands over his ears too, and all along the dragon's length people stepped back or ducked away. Then the noise abruptly cut off, and everyone stepped forward again. The women flailed even harder, their chant sounding muffled to Lucas; the dragon's call had been so loud it had left a buzz in his ears, and he had to lean close to hear Damian say, "Isn't this something?"

"It's definitely a dragon," Lucas said, his voice sounding flat and mostly inside his head. "Are we done arguing?"

"I didn't realise we were," Damian said. "Did you see those guys trying to cut it open?"

"Around the other side? I was surprised the police are letting them to do whatever it is they're doing."

"Lisbeth said they're scientists from the marine labs at Swatham. They work for the government, just like the police. She said they think this is a plastic eater. It sucks up plastic and digests it, turns it into carbon dioxide and water."

"That's what the UN wants people to think it does, anyhow."

"Sometimes you sound just like your mother."

"There you go again."

Damian put his hand on Lucas's shoulder. "I'm just ragging on you. Come on, why don't we go over by the fire and get warm?"

"If you want to talk to that girl again, just say so."

"Now who's spoiling for an argument? I thought we could get warm, find something to eat. People are selling stuff."

"I want to take a good close look at the dragon. That's why we came here, isn't it?"

"You do that, and I'll be right back."

"You get into trouble, you can find your own way home," Lucas said, but Damian was already walking away, fading into the mist without once looking back.

Lucas watched him fade into the mist, expecting him to turn around. He didn't.

Irritated by the silly spat, Lucas drifted back around the dragon's prow, watched the scientists attack with a jackhammer the joint between two large scales. They were putting everything they had into it, but didn't seem to be getting anywhere. A gang of farmers from a collective arrived on two tractors that left neat tracks on the wet sand and put out the smell of frying oil, which reminded Lucas that he hadn't eaten since breakfast. He was damned cold too. He trudged up the sand and bought a cup of fish soup from a woman who poured it straight from the iron pot she hooked out of the edge of the big bonfire, handing him a crust of bread to go with it. Lucas sipped the scalding stuff and felt his blood warm, soaked up the last of the soup with the crust and dredged the plastic cup in the sand to clean it and handed it back to the woman. Plenty of people were standing around the fire, but there was no sign of Damian. Maybe he was chasing that girl. Maybe he'd been arrested. Most likely, he'd turn up with that stupid smile of his, shrugging off their argument, claiming he'd only been joking. The way he did.

The skirts of the fret drifted apart and revealed the dim shapes of

Martham's buildings at the far end of the sandbar; then the fret closed up and the little town vanished. The dragon sounded its distress or alarm call again. In the ringing silence afterwards a man said to no one in particular, with the satisfaction of someone who has discovered the solution to one of the universe's perennial mysteries, "Twenty-eight minutes on the dot."

At last, there was the sound of an engine and a shadowy shape gained definition in the fret that hung offshore: a boxy, old-fashioned landing craft that drove past the police boat and beached in the shallows close to the dragon. Its bow door splashed down and soldiers trotted out and the police and several civilians and scientists went down the beach to meet them. After a brief discussion, one of the soldiers stepped forward and raised a bullhorn to his mouth and announced that for the sake of public safety a two-hundred-metre exclusion zone was going to be established.

Several soldiers began to unload plastic crates. The rest chivvied the people around the dragon, ordering them to move back, driving them up the beach past the bonfire. Lucas spotted the old man, Bill Danvers, arguing with two soldiers. One suddenly grabbed the old man's arm and spun him around and twisted something around his wrists; the other looked at Lucas as he came towards them, telling him to stay back or he'd be arrested too.

"He's my uncle," Lucas said. "If you let him go I'll make sure he doesn't cause any more trouble."

"Your uncle?" The soldier wasn't much older than Lucas, with cropped ginger hair and a ruddy complexion.

"Yes, sir. He doesn't mean any harm. He's just upset because no one cares that he was the first to find it."

"Like I said," the old man said.

The two soldiers looked at each other, and the ginger-haired one told Lucas, "You're responsible for him. If he starts up again, you'll both be sorry."

"I'll look after him."

The soldier stared at Lucas for a moment, then flourished a small-bladed knife and cut the plasticuffs that bound the old man's wrists and shoved him towards Lucas. "Stay out of our way, grandpa. All right?"

"Sons of bitches," Bill Danvers said as the soldiers had walked off. He raised his voice and called out, "I found it first. Someone owes me for that."

"I think everyone knows you saw it come ashore," Lucas said. "But they're in charge now."

"They're going to blow it open," a man said.

He held a satchel in one hand and a folded chair in the other; when he shook the chair open and sat down Lucas recognised him: the man who'd been sitting at the head of the dragon, sketching it.

"They can't," Bill Danvers said.

"They're going to try," the man said.

Lucas looked back at the dragon. Its streamlined shape dim in the steaming fret, the activity around its head (if that was its head) a vague shifting of shadows. Soldiers and scientists conferring in a tight knot. Then the police boat and the landing craft started their motors and reversed through the wash of the incoming tide, fading into the fret, and the scientists followed the soldiers up the beach, walking past the bonfire, and there was a stir and rustle amongst the people strung out along the ridge.

"No damn right," Bill Danvers said.

The soldier with the bullhorn announced that there would be a small controlled explosion. A moment later, the dragon blared out its loud, long call and in the shocking silence afterwards laughter broke out amongst the crowd on the ridge. The soldier with the bullhorn began to count backwards from ten. Some of the crowd took up the chant. There was a brief silence at zero, and then a red light flared at the base of the dragon's midpoint and a flat crack rolled out across the ridge and was swallowed by the mist. People whistled and clapped, and Bill Danvers stepped around Lucas and ran down the slope towards the dragon. Falling to his knees and getting up and running on as soldiers chased after him, closing in from either side.

People cheered and hooted, and some ran after Bill Danvers, young men mostly, leaping down the slope and swarming across the beach. Lucas saw Damian amongst the runners and chased after him, heart pounding, flooded with a heedless exhilaration. Soldiers blocked random individuals, catching hold of them or knocking them down as others dodged past. Lucas heard the clatter of the bullhorn but couldn't make out any words, and then there was a terrific flare of white light and a hot wind struck him so hard he lost his balance and fell to his knees.

The dragon had split in half and things were glowing with hot light inside and the waves breaking around its rear hissed and exploded into steam. A terrific heat scorched Lucas's face. He pushed to his feet. All around, people were picking themselves up and soldiers were moving amongst them, shoving them away from the dragon. Some complied; others stood, squinting into the light that beat out of the broken dragon, blindingly bright waves and wings of white light flapping across the beach, burning away the mist.

Blinking back tears and blocky afterimages, Lucas saw two soldiers dragging Bill Danvers away from the dragon. The old man hung limp and helpless in their grasp, splayed feet furrowing the sand. His head was bloody, something sticking out of it at an angle.

Lucas started towards them, and there was another flare that left him stunned and half-blind. Things fell all around and a translucent shard suddenly jutted up by his foot. The two soldiers had dropped Bill Danvers. Lucas stepped towards him, picking his way through a field of debris, and saw that he was beyond help. His head had been knocked out of shape by the shard that stuck in his temple, and blood was soaking into the sand around it.

The dragon had completely broken apart now. Incandescent stuff dripped and hissed into steaming water and the burning light was growing brighter.

Like almost everyone else, Lucas turned and ran. Heat clawed at his back as he slogged to the top of the ridge. He saw Damian sitting on the sand, right hand clamped on the upper part of his left arm, and he jogged over and helped his friend up. Leaning against each other, they stumbled across the ridge. Small fires crackled here and there, where hot debris had kindled clumps of marram grass. Everything was drenched in a pulsing diamond brilliance. They went down the slope of the far side, angling towards the little blue boat, splashing into the water that had risen around it. Damian clambered unhandily over thwart and Lucas hauled up the concrete-filled bucket and boosted it over the side, then put his shoulder to the boat's prow and shoved it the low breakers and tumbled in.

The boat drifted sideways on the rising tide as Lucas hauled up the sail. Dragon-light beat beyond the crest of the sandbar, brighter than the sun. Lucas heeled his little boat into the wind, ploughing through stands of sea grass into the channel beyond, chasing after the small fleet fleeing the scene. Damian sat in the bottom of the boat, hunched into himself, his back against the stem of the mast. Lucas asked him if he was okay; he opened his fingers to show a translucent spike embedded in the meat of his biceps. It was about the size of his little finger.

"Dumb bad luck," he said, his voice tight and wincing.

"I'll fix you up," Lucas said, but Damian shook his head.

"Just keep going. I think—"

Everything went white for a moment. Lucas ducked down and wrapped his arms around his head and for a moment saw shadowy bones through red curtains of flesh. When he dared look around, he saw a narrow column of pure white light rising straight up, seeming to lean over as it climbed into the sky, aimed at the very apex of heaven.

A hot wind struck the boat and filled the sail, and Lucas sat up and grabbed the tiller and the sheet as the boat crabbed sideways. By the time he had it under control again the column of light had dimmed, fading inside drifting curtains of fret, rooted in a pale fire flickering beyond the sandbar.

D amian's father, Jason Playne, paid Lucas and his mother a visit the next morning. A burly man in his late forties with a shaven head and a blunt and forthright manner, dressed in workboots and denim overalls, he made the caravan seem small and frail. Standing over Julia's bed, telling her that he would like to ask Lucas about the scrape he and his Damian had gotten into.

"Ask away," Julia said. She was propped amongst her pillows, her gaze bright and amused. Her tablet lay beside her, images and blocks of text glimmering above it.

Jason Playne looked at her from beneath the thick hedge of his eyebrows. A strong odour of saltwater and sweated booze clung to him. He said, "I was hoping for a private word."

"My son and I have no secrets."

"This is about *my* son," Jason Playne said.

"They didn't do anything wrong, if that's what you're worried about," Julia said.

Lucas felt a knot of embarrassment and anger in his chest. He said, "I'm right here."

"Well, you didn't," his mother said.

Jason Playne looked at Lucas. "How did Damian get hurt?"

"He fell and cut himself," Lucas said, as steadily as he could. That was what he and Damian had agreed to say, as they'd sailed back home with their prize. Lucas had pulled the shard of dragon stuff from Damian's arm and staunched the bleeding with a bandage made from a strip ripped from the hem of Damian's shirt. There hadn't been much blood; the hot sliver had more or less cauterised the wound.

Jason Playne said, "He fell."

"Yes sir."

"Are you sure? Because I reckon that cut in my son's arm was done by a knife. I reckon he got himself in some kind of fight."

Julia said, "That sounds more like an accusation than a question."

Lucas said, "We didn't get into a fight with anyone."

Jason Playne said, "Are you certain that Damian didn't steal something?"

"Yes sir."

Which was the truth, as far as it went.

"Because if he did steal something, if he still has it, he's in a lot of trouble. You too."

"I like to think my son knows a little more about alien stuff than most," Julia said.

"I'm don't mean fairy stories," Jason Playne said. "I'm talking about the army ordering people to give back anything to do with that dragon thing. You stole something and you don't give it back and they find out? They'll arrest you. And if you try to sell it? Well, I can tell you for a fact that the people in that trade are mad and bad. I should know. I've met one or two of them in my time."

"I'm sure Lucas will take that to heart," Julia said.

And that was that, except after Jason Playne had gone she told Lucas that he'd been right about one thing: the people who tried to reverse-engineer alien technology were dangerous and should at all costs be avoided. "If I happened to come into possession of anything like that," she said, "I would get rid of it at once. Before anyone found out."

But Lucas couldn't get rid of the shard because he'd promised Damian that he'd keep it safe until they could figure out what to do with it. He spent the next two days in a haze of guilt and indecision, struggling with the temptation to check that the thing was safe in its hiding place, wondering what Damian's father knew, wondering what his mother knew, wondering if he should sail out to a deep part of the Flood and throw it into the water, until at last Damian came over to the island.

It was early in the evening, just after sunset. Lucas was watering the vegetable garden when Damian called to him from the shadows inside a clump of buddleia bushes. He smiled at Lucas, saying, "If you think I look bad, you should see him."

"I can't think he could look much worse."

"I got in a few licks," Damian said. His upper lip was split and both his eyes were blackened and there was a discoloured knot on the hinge of his jaw.

"He came here," Lucas said. "Gave me and Julia a hard time."

"How much does she know?"

"I told her what happened."

"Everything?"

There was an edge in Damian's voice.

"Except about how you were hit with the shard," Lucas said.

"Oh. Your mother's cool, you know? I wish . . ."

When it was clear that his friend wasn't going to finish his thought, Lucas said, "Is it okay? You coming here so soon."

"Oh, Dad's over at Halvergate on what he calls business. Don't worry about him. Did you keep it safe?"

"I said I would."

"Why I'm here, L, I think I might have a line on someone who wants to buy our little treasure."

"Your father said we should keep away from people like that."

"He would."

"Julia thinks so too."

"If you don't want anything to do with it, just say so. Tell me where it is, and I'll take care of everything."

"Right."

"So is it here, or do we have to go somewhere?"

"I'll show you," Lucas said, and led his friend through the buddleias and along the low ridge to the northern end of the tiny island where an apple tree stood, hunched and gnarled and mostly dead, crippled by years of salt spray and saltwater seep. Lucas knelt and pulled up a hinge of turf and took out a small bundle of oilcloth. As he unwrapped it, Damian dropped to his knees beside him and reached out and touched an edge of the shard.

"Is it dead?"

"It wasn't ever alive," Lucas said.

"You know what I mean. What did you do to it?"

"Nothing. It just turned itself off."

When Lucas had pulled the shard from Damian's arm, its translucence had been veined with a network of shimmering threads. Now it was a dull reddish black, like an old scab.

"Maybe it uses sunlight, like phones," Damian said.

"I thought of that, but I also thought it would be best to keep it hidden."

"It still has to be worth something," Damian said, and began to fold the oilcloth around the shard.

Lucas was gripped by a sudden apprehension, as if he was falling while kneeling there in the dark. He said, "We don't have to do this right now."

"Yes we do. I do."

"Your father—he isn't in Halvergate, is he?"

Damian looked straight at Lucas. "I didn't kill him, if that's what you're worried about. He tried to knock me down when I went to leave, but I knocked him down instead. Pounded on him good. Put him down and put him out. Tied him up too, to give me some time to get away."

"He'll come after you."

"Remember when we were kids? We used to lie up here, in summer. We'd look up at the stars and talk about what it would be like to go to one of the worlds the Jackaroo gave us. Well, I plan to find out. The UN lets you buy tickets off lottery winners who don't want to go. It's legal and everything. All you need is money. I reckon this will give us a good start."

"You know I can't come with you."

"If you want your share, you'll have to come to Norwich. Because there's no way I'm coming back here," Damian said, and stood with a smooth, swift motion.

Lucas stood too. They were standing toe to toe under the apple tree, the island and the Flood around it quiet and dark. As if they were the last people on Earth.

"Don't try to stop me," Damian said. "My father tried, and I fucked him up good and proper."

"Let's talk about this."

"There's nothing to talk about," Damian said. "It is what it is."

He tried to step past Lucas, and Lucas grabbed at his arm and Damian swung him around and lifted him off his feet and ran him against the trunk of the tree. Lucas tried to wrench free but Damian bore down with unexpected strength, pressing him against rough bark, leaning into him. Pinpricks of light in the dark wells of his eyes. His voice soft and hoarse in Lucas's ear, his breath hot against Lucas's cheek.

"You always used to be able to beat me, L. At running, swimming, you name it. Not any more. I've changed. Want to know why?"

"We don't have to fight about this."

"No, we don't," Damian said, and let Lucas go and stepped back.

Lucas pushed away from the tree, a little unsteady on his feet. "What's got into you?"

Damian laughed. "That's good, that is. Can't you guess?"

"You need the money because you're running away. All right, you can have my share, if that's what you want. But it won't get you very far."

"Not by itself. But like I said, I've changed. Look," Damian said, and yanked up the sleeve of his shirt, showing the place on his upper arm where the shard had punched into him.

There was only a trace of a scar, pink and smooth. Damian pulled the skin taut, and Lucas saw the outline of a kind of ridged or fibrous sheath underneath.

"It grew," Damian said.

"Jesus."

"I'm stronger. And faster too. I feel, I don't know. Better than I ever have. Like I could run all the way around the world without stopping, if I had to."

"What if it doesn't stop growing? You should see a doctor, D. Seriously."

"I'm going to. The kind that can make money for me, from what happened. You still think that little bit of dragon isn't worth anything? It changed me. It could change anyone. I really don't want to fight," Damian said, "but I will if you get in my way. Because there's there's no way I'm stopping here. If I do, my dad will come after me. And if he does, I'll have to kill him. *And I know I can.*"

The two friends stared at each other in the failing light. Lucas was the first to look away.

"You can come with me," Damian said. "To Norwich. Then wherever we want to go. To infinity and beyond. Think about it. You still got my phone?"

"Do you want it back? It's in the caravan."

"Keep it. I'll call you. Tell you were to meet up. Come or don't come, it's up to you."

And then he ran, crashing through the buddleia bushes that grew along the slope of the ridge. Lucas went after him, but by the time he reached the edge of the water, Damian had started the motor of the boat he'd stolen from his father's shrimp farm, and was dwindling away into the thickening twilight.

The next day, Lucas was out on the Flood, checking baited cages he'd set for eels, when an inflatable pulled away from the shrimp farm and drew a curving line of white across the water, hooking towards him. Jason Playne sat in the inflatable's stern, cutting the motor and drifting neatly alongside Lucas's boat and catching hold of the thwart. His left wrist was bandaged and he wore a baseball cap pulled low over sunglasses that darkly reflected Lucas and Lucas's boat and the waterscape all around. He asked without greeting or preamble where Damian was, and Lucas said that he didn't know.

"You saw him last night. Don't lie. What did he tell you?"

"That he was going away. That he wanted me to go with him."

"But you didn't."

"Well, no. I'm still here."

"Don't try to be clever, boy." Jason Playne stared at Lucas for a long moment, then sighed and took off his baseball cap and ran the palm of his hand over his shaven head. "I talked to your mother. I know he isn't with you. But he could be somewhere close by. In the woods, maybe. Camping out like you two used to do when you were smaller."

"All I know is that he's gone, Mr. Payne. Far away from here."

Jason Playne's smile didn't quite work. "You're his friend, Lucas. I know you want to do the right thing by him. As friends should. So maybe you can tell him, if you see him, that I'm not angry. That he should come home and it won't be a problem. You could also tell him to be careful. And you should be careful, too. I think you know what I mean. It could get you both into a lot of trouble if you talk to the wrong people. Or even if you talk to the right people. You think about that," Jason Playne said, and pushed away from Lucas's boat and opened the throttle of his inflatable's motor and zoomed away, bouncing over the slight swell, dwindling into the glare of the sun off the water.

Lucas went back to hauling up the cages, telling himself that he was glad that Damian was gone, that he'd escaped. When he finished, he took up the oars and began to row towards the island, back to his mother, and the little circle of his life.

D amian didn't call that day, or the next, or the day after that. Lucas was angry at first, then heartsick, convinced that Damian was in trouble. That he'd squandered or lost the money he'd made from selling the shard, or that he'd been cheated, or worse. After a week, Lucas sailed to Norwich and spent half a day tramping around the city in a futile attempt to find his friend. Jason Playne didn't trouble him again, but several times Lucas spotted him standing at the end of the shrimp farm's chain of tanks, studying the island.

September's Indian summer broke in a squall of storms. It rained every day. Hard, cold rain blowing in swaying curtains across the face of the waters. Endless racks of low clouds driving eastward. Atlantic weather. The Flood was muddier and less salty than usual. The eel traps stayed empty and storm surges drove the mackerel shoals and other fish into deep water. Lucas harvested everything he could from the vegetable garden, and from the ancient pear tree and wild, forgotten hedgerows in the ribbon of woods behind the levee, counted and recounted the store of cans and

MREs. He set rabbit snares in the woods, and spent hours tracking squirrels from tree to tree, waiting for a moment when he could take a shot with his catapult. He caught sticklebacks in the weedy tide pools that fringed the broken brickwork shore of the island and used them to bait trotlines for crabs, and if he failed to catch any squirrels or crabs he collected mussels from the car reef at the foot of the levee.

It rained through the rest of September and on into October. Julia developed a racking and persistent cough. She enabled the long-disused keyboard function of her tablet and typed her essays, opinion pieces, and journal entries instead of giving them straight to camera. She was helping settlers on the Antarctic Peninsula to petition the International Court in Johannesburg to grant them statehood, so that they could prevent exploitation of oil and mineral reserves by multinationals. She was arguing with the Midway Island utopians about whether or not the sea dragons they were using to harvest plastic particulates were also sucking up precious phytoplankton, and destabilising the oceanic ecosystem. And so on, and so forth.

The witchwoman visited and treated her with infusions and poultices, but the cough grew worse and because they had no money for medicine, Lucas tried to find work at the algae farm at Halvergate. Every morning, he set out before dawn and stood at the gates in a crowd of men and women as one of the supervisors pointed to this or that person and told them to step forward, told the rest to come back and try their luck tomorrow. After his fifth unsuccessful cattle call, Lucas was walking along the shoulder of the road towards town and the jetty where his boat was tied up when a battered van pulled up beside him and the driver called to him. It was Ritchy, the stoop-shouldered, one-eyed foreman of the shrimp farm. Saying, "Need a lift, lad?"

"You can tell him there's no point in following me because I don't have any idea where Damian is," Lucas said, and kept walking.

"He doesn't know I'm here." Ritchy leaned at the window, edging the van along, matching Lucas's pace. Its tyres left wakes in the flooded road. Rain danced on its roof. "I got some news about Damian. Hop in. I know a place does a good breakfast, and you look like you could use some food."

They drove past patchworks of shallow lagoons behind mesh fences, past the steel tanks and piping of the cracking plant that turned algal lipids into biofuel. Ritchy talked about the goddamned weather, asked Lucas how his boat was handling, asked after his mother, said he was sorry to hear that she was ill and maybe he should pay a visit, he always liked talking to her because she made you look at things in a different way, a stream of inconsequential chatter he kept up all the way to the café.

It was in one corner of a layby where two lines of trucks were parked nose to tail. A pair of shipping containers welded together and painted bright pink. Red and white chequered curtains behind windows cut in the ribbed walls. Formica tables and plastic chairs crowded inside, all occupied and a line of people waiting, but Ritchy knew the Portuguese family who ran the place and he and Lucas were given a small table in the back, between a fridge and the service counter, and without asking were served mugs of strong tea, and shrimp and green pepper omelets with baked beans and chips.

"You know what I miss most?" Ritchy said. "Pigs. Bacon and sausage. Ham. They say the Germans are trying to clone flu-resistant pigs. If they are, I hope they get a move on. Eat up, lad. You'll feel better with something inside you."

"You said you had some news about Damian. Where is he? Is he all right?"

Ritchy squinted at Lucas. His left eye, the one that had been lost when he'd been a soldier, glimmered blankly. It had been grown from a sliver of tooth and didn't have much in the way of resolution, but allowed him to see both infrared and ultraviolet light.

He said, "Know what collateral damage is?"

Fear hollowed Lucas's stomach. "Damian is in trouble, isn't he? What happened?"

"Used to be, long ago, wars were fought on a battlefield chosen by both sides. Two armies meeting by appointment. Squaring up to each other. Slogging it out. Then wars became so big the countries fighting them became one huge battlefield. Civilians found themselves on the front line. Or rather, there was no front line. Total war, they called it. And then you got wars that weren't wars. Asymmetrical wars. Netwars. Where war gets mixed up with crime and terrorism. Your mother was on the edge of a netwar at one time. Against the Jackaroo and those others. Still thinks she's fighting it, although it long ago evolved into something else. There aren't any armies or battlefields in a netwar. Just a series of nodes in distributed organisation. Collateral damage," Ritchy said, forking omelet into his mouth, "is the inevitable consequence of taking out one of those nodes, because all of them are embedded inside ordinary society. It could be a flat in an apartment block in a city. Or a little island where someone thinks something useful is hidden."

"I don't—"

"You don't know anything," Ritchy said. "I believe you. Damian ran off with whatever it was you two found or stole, and left you in the lurch. But the people Damian got himself involved with don't know you don't know. That's why we've been looking out for you. Making sure you and your mother don't become collateral damage."

"Wait. What people? What did Damian do?"

"I'm trying to tell you, only it's harder than I thought it would be." Ritchy set his knife and fork together on his plate and said, "Maybe telling it straight is the best way. The day after Damian left, he tried to do some business with some people in Norwich. Bad people. The lad wanted to sell them a fragment of that dragon that stranded itself, but they decided to take it from him without paying. There was a scuffle and the lad got away and left a man with a bad knife wound. He died from it, a few weeks later. Those are the kind of people who look after their own, if you know what I mean. Anyone involved in that trade is bad news in one way or another. Jason had to pay them off, or else they would have come after him. An eye for an eye," Ritchy said, and tapped his blank eye with his little finger.

"What happened to Damian?"

"This is the hard part. After his trouble in Norwich, the lad called his father. He was drunk, ranting. Boasting how he was going to make all kinds of money. I managed to put a demon on his message, ran it back to a cell in Gravesend. Jason went up there, and that's when . . . Well, there's no other way of saying it. That's when he found out that Damian had been killed."

The shock was a jolt and a falling away. And then Lucas was back inside himself, hunched in his damp jeans and sweater in the clatter and bustle of the café, with the fridge humming next to him. Ritchy tore off the tops of four straws of sugar and poured them into Lucas's tea and stirred it and folded Lucas's hand around the mug and told him to drink.

Lucas sipped hot sweet tea and felt a little better.

"Always thought," Ritchy said, "that of the two of you, you were the best and brightest."

Lucas saw his friend in his mind's eye and felt cold and strange, knowing he'd never see him, never talk to him again.

Ritchy was said, "The police got in touch yesterday. They found Damian's body in the river. They think he fell into the hands of one of the gangs that trade in offworld stuff."

Lucas suddenly understood something and said, "They wanted what was growing inside him. The people who killed him."

He told Ritchy about the shard that had hit Damian in the arm. How they'd pulled it out. How it had infected Damian.

"He had a kind of patch around the cut, under his skin. He said it was making him stronger."

Lucas saw his friend again, wild-eyed in the dusk, under the apple tree.

"That's what he thought. But that kind of thing, well, if he hadn't been murdered he would most likely have died from it."

"Do you know who did it?"

Ritchy shook his head. "The police are making what they like to call enquiries. They'll probably want to talk to you soon enough."

"Thank you. For telling me."

"I remember the world before the Jackaroo came," Ritchy said. "Them, and the others after them. It was in a bad way, but at least you knew where you were. If you happen to have any more of that stuff, lad, throw it in the Flood. And don't mark the spot."

Two detectives came Gravesend to interview Lucas. He told them everything he knew. Julia said that he shouldn't blame himself, said that Damian had made a choice and it had been a bad choice. But Lucas carried the guilt around with him anyway. He should have done more to help Damian. He should have thrown the shard away. Or found him after they'd had the stupid argument over that girl. Or refused to take him out to see the damn dragon in the first place.

A week passed. Two. There was no funeral because the police would not release Damian's body. According to them, it was still undergoing forensic tests. Julia, who was tracking rumours about the murder and its investigation on the stealth nets, said it had probably been taken to some clandestine research lab, and she and Lucas had a falling out over it.

One day, returning home after checking the snares he'd set in the woods, Lucas climbed to the top of the levee and saw two men waiting beside his boat. Both were dressed in brand-new camo gear, one with a beard, the other with a shaven head and rings flashing in one ear. They started up the slope towards him, calling his name, and he turned tail and ran, cutting across a stretch of sour land gone to weeds and pioneer saplings, plunging into the stands of bracken at the edge of the woods, pausing, seeing the two men chasing towards him, turning and running on.

He knew every part of the woods, and quickly found a hiding place under the slanted trunk of a fallen sycamore grown over with moss and ferns, breathing quick and hard in the cold air. Rain pattered all around.

Droplets of water spangled bare black twigs. The deep odour of wet wood and wet earth.

A magpie chattered, close by. Lucas set a ball-bearing in the cup of his catapult and cut towards the sound, moving easily and quietly, freezing when he saw a twitch of movement between the wet tree trunks ahead. It was the bearded man, the camo circuit of his gear magicking him into a fairy-tale creature got up from wet bark and mud. He was talking into a phone headset in a language full of harsh vowels. Turning as Lucas stepped towards him, his smile white inside his beard, saying that there was no need to run away, he only wanted to talk.

"What is that you have, kid?"

"A catapult. I'll use it if I have to."

"What do you use it for? Hunting rabbits? I'm no rabbit."

"Who are you?"

"Police. I have ID," the man said, and before Lucas could say anything his hand went into the pocket of his camo trousers and came out with a pistol.

Lucas had made his catapult himself, from a yoke of springy poplar and a length of vatgrown rubber with the composition and tensile strength of the hinge inside a mussel shell. As the man brought up the pistol Lucas pulled back the band of rubber and let the ball bearing fly. He did it quickly and without thought, firing from the hip, and the ball bearing went exactly where he meant it to go. It smacked into the knuckles of the man's hand with a hard pop and the man yelped and dropped the pistol, and then he sat down hard and clapped his good hand to his knee, because Lucas's second shot had struck the soft part under the cap.

Lucas stepped up and kicked the pistol away and stepped back, a third ball bearing cupped in the catapult. The man glared at him, wincing with pain, and said something in his harsh language.

"Who sent you?" Lucas said.

His heart was racing, but his thoughts were cool and clear.

"Tell me where it is," the man said, "and we leave you alone. Your mother too."

"My mother doesn't have anything to do with this."

Lucas was watching the man and listening to someone moving through the wet wood, coming closer.

"She is in it, nevertheless," the man said. He tried to push to his feet but his wounded knee gave way and he cried out and sat down again. He'd bitten his lip bloody and sweat beaded his forehead.

"Stay still, or the next one hits you between the eyes," Lucas said. He heard a quaver in his voice and knew from the way the man looked at him that he'd heard it too.

"Go now, and fetch the stuff. And don't tell me you don't know what I mean. Fetch it and bring it here. That's the only offer you get," the man said. "And the only time I make it."

A twig snapped softly and Lucas turned, ready to let the ball-bearing fly, but it was Damian's father who stepped around a dark green holly bush, saying, "You can leave this one to me."

At once Lucas understood what had happened. Within his cool clear envelope he could see everything: how it all connected.

"You set me up," he said.

"I needed to draw them out," Jason Playne said. He was dressed in jeans and an old-fashioned woodland camo jacket, and he was cradling a cut-down double-barrelled shotgun.

"You let them know where I was. You told them I had more of the dragon stuff."

The man sitting on the ground was looking at them. "This does not end here," he said. "I have you, and I have your friend. And you're going to pay for what you did to my son," Jason Playne said, and put a whistle to his lips and blew, two short notes. Off in the dark rainy woods another whistle answered.

The man said, "Idiot small-time businessman. You don't know us. What we can do. Hurt me and we hurt you back tenfold."

Jason Playne ignored him, and told Lucas that he could go.

"Why did you let them chase me? You could have caught them while they were waiting by my boat. Did you want them to hurt me?"

"I knew you'd lead them a good old chase. And you did. So, all's well that ends well, eh?" Jason Playne said. "Think of it as payback. For what happened to my son."

Lucas felt a bubble of anger swelling in his chest. "You can't forgive me for what I didn't do."

"It's what you didn't do that caused all the trouble."

"It wasn't me. It was you. It was you who made him run away. It wasn't just the beatings. It was the thought that if he stayed here he'd become just like you."

Jason Playne turned towards Lucas, his face congested. "Go. Right now."

The bearded man drew a knife from his boot and flicked it open and pushed up with his good leg, throwing himself towards Jason Playne, and Lucas stretched the band of his catapult and let fly. The ball bearing struck the bearded man in the temple with a hollow sound and the man fell flat on his face. His temple was dinted and blood came out of his nose and mouth and he thrashed and trembled and subsided.

Rain pattered down all around, like faint applause.

Then Jason Playne stepped towards the man and kicked him in the chin with the point of his boot. The man rolled over on the wet leaves, arms flopping wide.

"I reckon you killed him," Jason Playne said.

"I didn't mean—"

"Lucky for you there are two of them. The other will tell me what I need to know. You go now, boy. Go!"

Lucas turned and ran.

He didn't tell his mother about it. He hoped that Jason Playne would find out who had killed Damian and tell the police and the killers would answer for what they had done, and that would be an end to it.

That wasn't what happened.

The next day, a motor launch came over to the island, carrying police armed with machine guns and the detectives investigating Damian's death, who arrested Lucas for involvement in two suspicious deaths and conspiracy to kidnap or murder other persons unknown. It seemed that one of the men that Jason Playne had hired to help him get justice for the death of his son had been a police informant.

Lucas was held in remand in Norwich for three months. Julia was too ill to visit him, but they talked on the phone and she sent messages via Ritchy, who'd been arrested along with every other worker on the shrimp farm, but released on bail after the police were unable to prove that he had anything to do with Jason Playne's scheme.

It was Ritchy who told Lucas that his mother had cancer that had started in her throat and spread elsewhere, and that she had refused treatment. Lucas was taken to see her two weeks later, handcuffed to a prison warden. She was lying in a hospital bed, looking shrunken and horribly vulnerable. Her dreadlocks bundled in a blue scarf. Her hand so cold when he took it in his. The skin loose on frail bones.

She had refused monoclonal antibody treatment that would shrink the tumours and remove cancer cells from her bloodstream, and had also refused food and water. The doctors couldn't intervene because a clause in her living will gave her the right to choose death instead of treatment. She told Lucas this in a hoarse whisper. Her lips were cracked and her breath foul, but her gaze was strong and insistent.

"Do the right thing even when it's the hardest thing," she said.

She died four days later. Her ashes were scattered in the rose garden of the municipal crematorium. Lucas stood in the rain between two wardens as the curate recited the prayer for the dead. The curate asked him if he wanted to scatter the ashes and he threw them out across the wet grass and dripping rose bushes with a flick of his wrist. Like casting a line across the water.

He was sentenced to five years for manslaughter, reduced to eighteen months for time served on remand and for good behaviour. He was released early in September. He'd been given a ticket for the bus to Norwich, and a voucher for a week's stay in a halfway house, but he set off in the opposite direction, on foot. Walking south and east across country. Following back roads. Skirting the edges of sugar beet fields and bamboo plantations. Ducking into ditches or hedgerows whenever he heard a vehicle approaching. Navigating by the moon and the stars.

Once, a fox loped across his path.

Once, he passed a depot lit up in the night, robots shunting between a loading dock and a road-train.

By dawn he was making his way through the woods along the edge of the levee. He kept taking steps that weren't there. Several times he sat on his haunches and rested for a minute before pushing up and going on. At last, he struck the gravel track that led to the shrimp farm, and twenty minutes later was knocking on the door of the office.

Ritchy gave Lucas breakfast and helped him pull his boat out of the shed where it had been stored, and set it in the water. Lucas and the old man had stayed in touch: it had been Ritchy who'd told him that Jason Playne had been stabbed to death in prison, most likely by someone paid by the people he'd tried to chase down. Jason Playne's brother had sold the shrimp farm to a local consortium, and Ritchy had been promoted to supervisor.

He told Lucas over breakfast that he had a job there, if he wanted it. Lucas said that he was grateful, he really was, but he didn't know if he wanted to stay on.

"I'm not asking you to make a decision right away," Ritchy said. "Think about it. Get your bearings, come to me whenever you're ready. Okay?"

"Okay."

"Are you going to stay over on the island?"

"Just how bad is it?"

"I couldn't keep all of them off. They'd come at night. One party had a shotgun."

"You did what you could. I appreciate it."

"I wish I could have done more. They made a mess, but it isn't anything you can't fix up, if you want to."

A heron flapped away across the sun-silvered water as Lucas rowed around the point of the island. The unexpected motion plucked at an old memory. As if he'd seen a ghost.

He grounded his boat next to the rotting carcass of his mother's old rowboat and walked up the steep path. Ritchy had patched the broken windows of the caravan and put a padlock on the door. Lucas had the key in his pocket, but he didn't want to go in there, not yet.

After Julia had been taken into hospital, treasure hunters had come from all around, chasing rumours that parts of the dragon had been buried on the island. Holes were dug everywhere in the weedy remains of the vegetable garden; the microwave mast at the summit of the ridge, Julia's link with the rest of the world, had been uprooted. Lucas set his back to it and walked north, counting his steps. Both of the decoy caches his mother had planted under brick cairns had been ransacked, but the emergency cache, buried much deeper, was undisturbed.

Lucas dug down to the plastic box, and looked all around before he opened it and sorted through the things inside, squatting frogwise with the hot sun on his back.

An assortment of passports and identity cards, each with a photograph of younger versions of his mother, made out to different names and nationalities. A slim tight roll of old high-denomination banknotes, yuan, naira, and U.S. dollars, more or less worthless thanks to inflation and revaluation. Blank credit cards and credit cards in various names, also worthless. Dozens of sleeved data needles. A pair of AR glasses.

Lucas studied one of the ID cards. When he brushed the picture of his mother with his thumb, she turned to present her profile, turned to look at him when he brushed the picture again.

He pocketed the ID card and the data needles and AR glasses, then walked along the ridge to the apple tree at the far end, and stared out across the Flood that spread glistening like shot silk under the sun. Thoughts moved through his mind like a slow and stately parade of pictures that he could examine in every detail, and then there were no thoughts at all and for a little while no part of him was separate from the world all around, sun and water and the hot breeze that moved through the crooked branches of the tree.

Lucas came to himself with a shiver. Windfall apples lay everywhere amongst the weeds and nettles that grew around the trees, and dead wasps and hornets were scattered amongst them like yellow and black bullets. Here was a dead bird too, gone to a tatter of feathers of white bone. And here was another, and another. As if some passing cloud of poison had struck everything down.

He picked an apple from the tree, mashed it against the trunk, and saw pale threads fine as hair running through the mash of pulp. He peeled bark from a branch, saw threads laced in the living wood.

Dragon stuff, growing from the seed he'd planted. Becoming something else.

In the wood of the tree and the apples scattered all around was a treasure men would kill for. Had killed for. He'd have more than enough to set him up for life, if he sold it to the right people. He could build a house right here, buy the shrimp farm or set up one of his own. He could buy a ticket on one of the shuttles that travelled through the wormhole anchored between the Earth and the Moon, travel to infinity and beyond . . .

Lucas remembered the hopeful shine in Damian's eyes when he'd talked about those new worlds. He thought of how the dragon-shard had killed or damaged everyone it had touched. He pictured his mother working at her tablet in her sickbed, advising and challenging people who were attempting to build something new right here on Earth. It wasn't much of a contest. It wasn't even close.

He walked back to the caravan. Took a breath, unlocked the padlock, stepped inside. Everything had been overturned or smashed. Cupboards gaped open, the mattress of his mother's bed was slashed and torn, a great ruin littered the floor. He rooted amongst the wreckage, found a box of matches and a plastic jug of lamp oil. He splashed half of the oil on the torn mattress, lit a twist of cardboard and lobbed it onto the bed, beat a retreat as flames sprang up.

It didn't take ten minutes to gather up dead wood and dry weeds and pile them around the apple tree, splash the rest of the oil over its trunk, and set fire to the tinder. A thin pall of white smoke spread across the island, blowing out across the water as he raised the sail of his boat and turned it into the wind.

Heading south.

Passage of Earth

MICHAEL SWANWICK

The ambulance arrived sometime between three and four in the morning. The morgue was quiet then, cool and faintly damp. Hank savored this time of night and the faint shadow of contentment it allowed him, like a cup of bitter coffee, long grown cold, waiting for his occasional sip. He liked being alone and not thinking. His rod and tackle box waited by the door, in case he felt like going fishing after his shift, though he rarely did. There was a copy of *Here Be Dragons: Mapping the Human Genome* in case he did not.

He had opened up a drowning victim and was reeling out her intestines arm over arm, scanning them quickly and letting them down in loops into a galvanized bucket. It was unlikely he was going to find anything, but all deaths by violence got an autopsy. He whistled tunelessly as he worked.

The bell from the loading dock rang.

"Hell." Hank put down his work, peeled off the latex gloves, and went to the intercom. "Sam? That you?" Then, on the sheriff's familiar grunt, he buzzed the door open. "What have you got for me this time?"

"Accident casualty." Sam Aldridge didn't meet his eye, and that was unusual. There was a gurney behind him, and on it something too large to be a human body, covered by canvas. The ambulance was already pulling away, which was so contrary to proper protocols as to be alarming.

"That sure doesn't look like—" Hank began.

A woman stepped out of the darkness.

It was Evelyn.

"Boy, the old dump hasn't changed one bit, has it? I'll bet even the calendar on the wall's the same. Did the county ever spring for a diener for the night shift?"

"I . . . I'm still working alone."

"Wheel it in, Sam, and I'll take over from here. Don't worry about me, I know where everything goes." Evelyn took a deep breath and shook her head in disgust. "Christ. It's just like riding a bicycle. You never forget. Want to or not."

After the paperwork had been taken care of and Sheriff Sam was gone, Hank said, "Believe it or not, I had regained some semblance of inner peace, Evelyn. Just a little. It took me years. And now this. It's like a kick in the stomach. I don't see how you can justify doing this to me."

"Easiest thing in the world, sweetheart." Evelyn suppressed a smirk that nobody but Hank could have even noticed, and flipped back the canvas. "Take a look."

It was a Worm.

Hank found himself leaning low over the heavy, swollen body, breathing deep of its heady alien smell, suggestive of wet earth and truffles with sharp hints of ammonia. He thought of the ships in orbit, blind locomotives ten miles long. The photographs of these creatures didn't do them justice. His hands itched to open this one up.

"The Agency needs you to perform an autopsy."

Hank drew back. "Let me get this straight. You've got the corpse of an alien creature. A representative of the only other intelligent life form that the human race has ever encountered. Yet with all the forensic scientists you have on salary, you decide to hand it over to a lowly county coroner?"

"We need your imagination, Hank. Anybody can tell how they're put together. We want to know how they think."

"You told me I didn't have an imagination. When you left me." His words came out angrier than he'd intended, but he couldn't find it in himself to apologize for their tone. "So, again—why me?"

"What I said was, you couldn't imagine bettering yourself. For anything impractical, you have imagination in spades. Now I'm asking you to cut open an alien corpse. What could be less practical?"

"I'm not going to get a straight answer out of you, am I?"

Evelyn's mouth quirked up in a little smile so that for the briefest instant she was the woman he had fallen in love with, a million years ago. His heart ached to see it. "You never got one before," she said. "Let's not screw up a perfectly good divorce by starting now."

"Let me put a fresh chip in my dictation device," Hank said. "Grab a smock and some latex gloves. You're going to assist."

R eady," Evelyn said.
    Hank hit record, then stood over the Worm, head down, for a long moment. Getting in the zone. "Okay, let's start with a gross physical examination. Um, what we have looks a lot like an annelid, rather blunter and fatter than the terrestrial equivalent and of course much larger. Just eyeballing it, I'd say this thing is about eight feet long, maybe two feet and a half in diameter. I could just about get my arms around it if I tried. There are three, five, seven, make that eleven somites, compared to say one or two hundred in an earthworm. No clitellum, so we're warned not to take the annelid similarity too far.

"The body is bluntly tapered at each end, and somewhat depressed posteriorly. The ventral side is flattened and paler than the dorsal surface. There's a tripartite beak-like structure at one end, I'm guessing this is the mouth, and what must be an anus at the other. Near the beak are five swellings from which extend stiff, bone-like structures—mandibles, maybe? I'll tell you, though, they look more like tools. This one might almost be a wrench, and over here a pair of grippers. They seem awfully specialized for an intelligent creature. Evelyn, you've dealt with these things, is there any variation within the species? I mean, do some have this arrangement of manipulators and others some other structure?"

"We've never seen any two of the aliens with the same arrangement of manipulators."

"Really? That's interesting. I wonder what it means. Okay, the obvious thing here is there are no apparent external sensory organs. No eyes, ears, nose. My guess is that whatever senses these things might have, they're functionally blind."

"Intelligence is of that opinion too."

"Well, it must have shown in their behavior, right? So that's an easy one. Here's my first extrapolation: You're going to have a bitch of a time understanding these things. Human beings rely on sight more than most animals, and if you trace back philosophy and science, they both have strong roots in optics. Something like this is simply going to think differently from us.

"Now, looking between the somites—the rings—we find a number of tiny hairlike structures, and if we pull the rings apart, so much as we can, there're all these small openings, almost like tiny anuses if there weren't so many of them, closed with sphincter muscles, maybe a hundred of them, and it looks like they're between each pair of somites. Oh, here's something—the structures near the front, the swellings, are a more developed form of these little openings. Okay, now we turn the thing over. I'll take this end, you take the other. Right, now I want you to rock it by my count, and on the three we'll flip it over. Ready? One, two, three!"

The corpse slowly flipped over, almost overturning the gurney. The two of them barely managed to control it.

"That was a close one," Hank said cheerily. "Huh. What's this?" He touched a line of painted numbers on the alien's underbelly. *Rt-Front/No. 43.*

"Never you mind what that is. Your job is to perform the autopsy."

"You've got more than one corpse."

Evelyn said nothing.

"Now that I say it out loud, of course you do. You've got dozens. If you only had the one, I'd never have gotten to play with it. You have doctors of your own. Good researchers, some of them, who would cut open their grandmothers if they got the grant money. Hell, even forty-three would've been kept in-house. You must have hundreds, right?"

For a fraction of a second, that exquisite face went motionless. Evelyn probably wasn't even aware of doing it, but Hank knew from long experience that she'd just made a decision. "More like a thousand. There was a very big accident. It's not on the news yet, but one of the Worms' landers went down in the Pacific."

"Oh Jesus." Hank pulled his gloves off, shoved up his glasses and ground his palms into his eyes. "You've got your war at last, haven't you? You've picked a fight with creatures that have tremendous technological superiority over us, and they don't even live here! All they have to do is drop a big enough rock into our atmosphere and there'll be a mass extinction the likes of which hasn't been seen since the dinosaurs died out. They won't care. It's not *their* planet!"

Evelyn's face twisted into an expression he hadn't known it could form until just before the end of their marriage, when everything fell apart. "Stop being such an ass," she said. Then, talking fast and earnestly, "We didn't cause the accident. It was just dumb luck it happened, but once it did we had to take advantage of it. Yes, the Worms probably have the technology to wipe us out. So we have to deal with them. But to deal with them we have to understand them, and we do not. They're a mystery to us. We don't know what they want. We don't know how they think. But after tonight we'll have a little better idea. Provided only that you get back to work."

Hank went to the table and pulled a new pair of gloves off the roll. "Okay," he said. "Okay."

"Just keep in mind that it's not just my ass that's riding on this," Evelyn said. "It's yours and everyone's you know."

"I *said* okay!" Hank took a long breath, calming himself. "Next thing to do is cut this sucker open." He picked up a bone saw. "This is bad technique, but we're in a hurry." The saw whined to life, and he cut through the leathery brown skin from beak to anus. "All right, now we peel the skin back. It's wet-feeling and a little crunchy. The musculature looks much like that of a Terrestrial annelid. Structurally, that is. I've never seen anything quite that color black. Damn! The skin keeps curling back."

He went to his tackle box and removed a bottle of fishhooks. "Here. We'll take a bit of nylon filament, tie two hooks together, like this, with about two inches of line between them. Then we hook the one through the skin, fold it down, and push the other through the cloth on the gurney. Repeat the process every six inches on both sides. That should hold it open."

"Got it." Evelyn set to work.

Some time later they were done, and Hank stared down into the opened Worm. "You want speculation? Here goes: This thing moves through the mud, or whatever the medium is there, face-first and blind. What does that suggest to you?"

"I'd say that they'd be used to coming up against the unexpected."

"Very good. Haul back on this, I'm going to cut again . . . Okay, now we're past the musculature and there's a fluffy mass of homogeneous stuff, we'll come back to that in a minute. Cutting through the fluff . . . and into the body cavity and it's absolutely chockablock with zillions of tiny little organs."

"Let's keep our terminology at least vaguely scientific, shall we?" Evelyn said.

"Well, there are more than I want to count. Literally hundreds of small organs under the musculature, I have no idea what they're for but they're all interconnected with vein-like tubing in various sizes. This is ferociously more complicated than human anatomy. It's like a chemical plant in here. No two of the organs are the same so far as I can tell, although they all have a generic similarity. Let's call them alembics, so we don't confuse them with any other organs we may find. I see something that looks like a heart maybe, an isolated lump of muscle the size of my fist, there are three of them. Now I'm cutting deeper . . . Holy shit!"

For a long minute, Hank stared into the opened alien corpse. Then he put the saw down on the gurney and, shaking his head, turned away. "Where's that coffee?" he said.

Without saying a word, Evelyn went to the coffee station and brought him his cold cup.

Hank yanked his gloves, threw them in the trash, and drank.

"All right," Evelyn said, "so what was it?"

"You mean you can't see—no, of course you can't. With you, it was human anatomy all the way."

"I took invertebrate biology in college."

"And forgot it just as fast as you could. Okay, look: Up here is the beak, semi-retractable. Down here is the anus. Food goes in one, waste comes out the other. What do you see between?"

"There's a kind of a tube. The gut?"

"Yeah. It runs straight from the mouth to the anus, without interruption. Nothing in between. How does it eat without a stomach? How does it stay alive?" He saw from Evelyn's expression that she was not impressed. "What we see before us is simply not possible."

"Yet here it is. So there's an explanation. Find it."

"Yeah, yeah." Glaring at the Worm's innards, he drew on a new pair of gloves. "Let me take a look at that beak again . . . Hah. See how the muscles are connected? The beak relaxes open, aaand—let's take a look at the other end—so does the anus. So this beast crawls through the mud, mouth wide open, and the mud passes through it unhindered. That's bound to have some effect on its psychological makeup."

"Like what?"

"Damned if I know. Let's take a closer look at the gut . . . There are rings of intrusive tissue near the beak one third of the way in, two thirds in, and just above the anus. We cut through and there is extremely fine structure, but nothing we're going to figure out tonight. Oh, hey, I think I got it. Look at these three flaps just behind . . ."

He cut in silence for a while. "There. It has three stomachs. They're located in the head, just behind the first ring of intrusive tissue. The mud or whatever is dumped into this kind of holding chamber, and then there's this incredible complex of muscles, and—how many exit tubes?—this one has got, um, fourteen. I'll trace one, and it goes right to this alembic. The next one goes to another alembic. I'll trace this one and it goes to—yep, another alembic. There's a pattern shaping up here.

"Let's put this aside for the moment, and go back to those masses of fluff.

Jeeze, there's a lot of this stuff. It must make up a good third of the body mass. Which has trilateral symmetry, by the way. Three masses of fluff proceed from head to tail, beneath the muscle sheath, all three connecting about eight inches below the mouth, into a ring around the straight gut. This is where the arms or manipulators or screwdrivers or whatever they are, grow. Now, at regular intervals the material puts out little arms, outgrowths that fine down to wire-like structures of the same material, almost like very thick nerves. Oh God. That's what it is." He drew back, and with a scalpel flensed the musculature away to reveal more of the mass. "It's the central nervous system. This thing has a brain that weighs at least a hundred pounds. I don't believe it. I don't *want* to believe it."

"It's true," Evelyn said. "Our people in Bethesda have done slide studies. You're looking at the thing's brain."

"If you already knew the answer, then why the hell are you putting me through this?"

"I'm not here to answer your questions. You're here to answer mine."

Annoyed, Hank bent over the Worm again. There was rich stench of esters from the creature, pungent and penetrating, and the slightest whiff of what he guessed was putrefaction. "We start with the brain, and trace one of the subordinate ganglia inward. Tricky little thing, it goes all over the place, and ends up right here, at one of the alembics. We'll try another one, and it . . . ends up at an alembic. There are a lot of these things, let's see—hey—here's one that goes to one of the structures in the straight gut. What could that be? A tongue! That's it, there's a row of tongues just within the gut, and more to taste the medium flowing through, yeah. And these little flapped openings just behind them open when the mud contains specific nutrients the worm desires. Okay, now we're getting somewhere, how long have we been at this?"

"About an hour and a half."

"It feels like longer." He thought of getting some more coffee, decided against it. "So what have we got here? All that enormous brain mass—what's it for?"

"Maybe it's all taken up by raw intelligence."

"Raw intelligence! No such thing. Nature doesn't evolve intelligence without a purpose. It's got to be used for something. Let's see. A fair amount is taken up by taste, obviously. It has maybe sixty individual tongues, and I wouldn't be surprised if its sense of taste were much more detailed than ours. Plus all those little alembics performing god-knows-what kind of chemical reactions.

"Let's suppose for a minute that it can consciously control those reactions, that would account for a lot of the brain mass. When the mud enters at the front, it's tasted, maybe a little is siphoned off and sent through the alembics for transformation. Waste products are jetted into the straight gut, and pass through several more circles of tongues . . . Here's another observation for you: These things would have an absolute sense of the state of their own health. They can probably create their own drugs, too. Come to think of it, I haven't come across any evidence of disease here." The Worm's smell was heavy, penetratingly pervasive. He felt slightly dizzy, shook it off.

"Okay, so we've got a creature that concentrates most of its energy and attention internally. It slides through an easy medium, and at the same time the mud slides through it. It tastes the mud as it passes, and we can guess that the mud will be in a constant state of transformation, so it experiences the universe more directly than do we." He laughed. "It appears to be a verb."

"How's that?"

"One of Buckminster Fuller's aphorisms. But it fits. The worm constantly transforms the universe. It takes in all it comes across, accepts it, changes it, and excretes it. It is an agent of change."

"That's very clever. But it doesn't help us deal with them."

"Well, of course not. They're intelligent, and intelligence complicates everything. But if you wanted me to generalize, I'd say the Worms are straightforward and accepting—look at how they move blindly ahead—but that their means of changing things are devious, as witness the mass of alembics. That's going to be their approach to us. Straightforward, yet devious in ways we just don't get. Then, when they're done with us, they'll pass on without a backward glance."

"Terrific. Great stuff. Get back to work."

"Look, Evelyn. I'm tired and I've done all I can, and a pretty damned good job at that, I think. I could use a rest."

"You haven't dealt with the stuff near the beak. The arms or whatever."

"Cripes." Hank turned back to the corpse, cut open an edema, began talking. "The material of the arms is stiff and osseous, rather like teeth. This one has several moving parts, all controlled by muscles anchored alongside the edema. There's a nest of ganglia here, connected by a very short route to the brain matter. Now I'm cutting into the brain matter, and there's a small black gland, oops I've nicked it. Whew. What a smell. Now I'm cutting behind it." Behind the gland was a small white structure, square and hard meshwork, looking like a cross between an instrument chip and a square of Chex cereal.

Keeping his back to Evelyn, he picked it up.

He put it in his mouth.

He swallowed.

What have I done? he thought. Aloud, he said, "As an operating hypothesis I'd say that the manipulative structures have been deliberately, make that consciously, grown. There, I've traced one of those veins back to the alembics. So that explains why there's no uniformity, these things would grow exterior manipulators on need, and then discard them when they're done. Yes, look, the muscles don't actually connect to the manipulators, they wrap around them."

There was a sour taste on his tongue.

I must be insane, he thought.

"Did you just *eat* something?"

Keeping his expression blank, Hank said, "Are you nuts? You mean did I put part of this . . . creature . . . in my mouth?" There was a burning within his brain, a buzzing like the sound of the rising sun picked up on a radio telescope. He wanted to scream, but his face simply smiled and said, "Do you—?" And then it was very hard to concentrate on what he was saying. He couldn't quite focus on Evelyn, and there were white rays moving starburst across his vision and—

When he came to, Hank was on the Interstate, doing ninety. His mouth was dry and his eyelids felt gritty. Bright yellow light was shining in his eyes from a sun that had barely lifted itself up above over the horizon. He must have been driving for hours. The steering wheel felt tacky and gummy. He looked down.

There was blood on his hands. It went all the way up to his elbows.

The traffic was light. Hank had no idea where he was heading, nor any desire whatsoever to stop.

So he just kept driving.

Whose blood was it on his hands? Logic said it was Evelyn's. But that made no sense. Hate her though he did—and the sight of her had opened wounds and memories he'd thought cauterized shut long ago—he wouldn't actually hurt her. Not physically. He wouldn't actually kill her.

Would he?

It was impossible. But there was the blood on his hands. Whose else could it be? Some of it might be his own, admittedly. His hands ached horribly. They felt like he'd been pounding them into something hard, over and over again. But most of the blood was dried and itchy. Except for where his skin had split at the knuckles, he had no wounds of any kind. So the blood wasn't his.

"Of course you did," Evelyn said. "You beat me to death and you enjoyed every minute of it."

Hank shrieked and almost ran off the road. He fought the car back and then turned and stared in disbelief. Evelyn sat in the passenger seat beside him.

"You . . . how did . . . ?" Much as he had with the car, Hank seized control of himself. "You're a hallucination," he said.

"Right in one!" Evelyn applauded lightly. "Or a memory, or the personification of your guilt, however you want to put it. You always were a bright man, Hank. Not so bright as to be able to keep your wife from walking out on you, but bright enough for government work."

"Your sleeping around was not my fault."

"Of course it was. You think you walked in on me and Jerome by *accident*? A woman doesn't hate her husband enough to arrange something like that without good reason."

"Oh god, oh god, oh god."

"The fuel light is blinking. You'd better find a gas station and fill up."

A Lukoil station drifted into sight, so he pulled into it and stopped the car by a full service pump. When he got out, the service station attendant hurried toward him and then stopped, frozen.

"Oh no," the attendant said. He was a young man with sandy hair. "Not another one."

"Another one?" Hank slid his card through the reader. "What do you mean another one?" He chose high-test and began pumping, all the while staring hard at the attendant. All but daring him to try something. "Explain yourself."

"Another one like you." The attendant couldn't seem to look away from Hank's hands. "The cops came right away and arrested the first one. It took five of them to get him into the car. Then another one came and when I called, they said to just take down his license number and let him go. They said there were people like you showing up all over."

Hank finished pumping and put the nozzle back on its hook. He did not push the button for a receipt. "Don't try to stop me," he said. The words just came and he said them. "I'd hurt you very badly if you did."

The young man's eyes jerked upward. He looked spooked. "What *are* you people?"

Hank paused, with his hand on the door. "I have no idea."

Y ou should have told him," Evelyn said when he got back in the car. "Why didn't you?"

"Shut up."

"You ate something out of that Worm and it's taken over part of your brain. You still feel like yourself, but you're not in control. You're sitting at the wheel but you have no say over where you're going. Do you?"

"No," Hank admitted. "No, I don't."

"What do you think it is—some kind of super-prion? Like mad cow disease, only faster than fast? A neuroprogrammer, maybe? An artificial overlay to your personality that feeds off of your brain and shunts your volition into a dead end?"

"I don't know."

"You're the one with the imagination. This would seem to be your sort of thing. I'm surprised you're not all over it."

"No," Hank said. "No, you're not at all surprised."

They drove on in silence for a time.

"Do you remember when we first met? In med school? You were going to be a surgeon then."

"Please. Don't."

"Rainy autumn afternoons in that ratty little third-floor walk-up of yours. With that great big aspen with the yellow leaves outside the window. It seemed like there was always at least one stuck to the glass. There were days when we never got dressed at all. We'd spend all day in and out of that enormous futon you'd bought instead of a bed, and it still wasn't large enough. If we rolled off the edge, we'd go on making love on the floor. When it got dark, we'd send out for Chinese."

"We were happy then. Is that what you want me to say?"

"It was your hands I liked best. Feeling them on me. You'd have one hand on my breast and the other between my legs and I'd imagine you cutting open a patient. Peeling back the flesh to reveal all those glistening organs inside."

"Okay, now that's sick."

"You asked me what I was thinking once and I told you. I was watching your face closely, because I really wanted to know you back then. You loved it. So I know you've got demons inside you. Why not own up to them?"

He squeezed his eyes shut, but something inside him opened them again, so he wouldn't run the car off the road. A low moaning sound arose from somewhere deep in his throat. "I must be in Hell."

"C'mon. Be a sport. What could it hurt? I'm already dead."

"There are some things no man was meant to admit. Even to himself."

Evelyn snorted. "You always were the most astounding prig."

They drove on in silence for a while, deeper into the desert. At last, staring straight ahead of himself, Hank could not keep himself from saying, "There are worse revelations to come, aren't there?"

"Oh God, yes," his mother said.

I t was your father's death." His mother sucked wetly on a cigarette. "That's what made you turn out the way you did."

Hank could barely see the road for his tears. "I honestly don't want to be having this conversation, Mom."

"No, of course you don't. You never were big on self-awareness, were you? You preferred cutting open toads or hunching over that damned microscope."

"I've got plenty of self-awareness. I've got enough self-awareness to choke on. I can see where you're going and I am not going to apologize for how I felt about Dad. He died of cancer when I was thirteen. What did I ever do to anyone that was half so bad as what he did to me? So I don't want to hear any cheap Freudian bullshit about survivor guilt and failing to live up to his glorious example, okay?"

"Nobody said it wasn't hard on you. Particularly coming at the onset of puberty as it did."

"Mom!"

"What. I wasn't supposed to know? Who do you think did the laundry?" His mother lit a new cigarette from the old one, then crushed out the butt in an ashtray. "I knew a lot more of what was going on in those years than you thought I did, believe you me. All those hours you spent in the bathroom jerking off. The money you stole to buy dope with."

"I was in pain, Mom. And it's not as if you were any help."

His mother looked at him with the same expression of weary annoyance he remembered so well. "You think there's something special about your pain? I lost the only man I ever loved and I couldn't move on because I had a kid to raise. Not a sweet little boy like I used to have either, but a sullen, self-pitying teenager. It took forever to get you shipped off to medical school."

"So then you moved on. Right off the roof of the county office building. Way to honor Dad's memory, Mom. What do you think he would have said about that if he'd known?"

Dryly, his mother said, "Ask him for yourself."

Hank closed his eyes.

When he opened them, he was standing in the living room of his mother's house. His father stood in the doorway, as he had so many times, smoking an unfiltered Camel and staring through the screen door at the street outside. "Well?" Hank said at last.

With a sigh his father turned around. "I'm sorry," he said. "I didn't know what to do." His lips moved up into what might have been a smile on another man. "Dying was new to me."

"Yeah, well, you could have summoned the strength to tell me what was going on. But you couldn't be bothered. The surgeon who operated on you? Doctor Tomasini. For years I thought of him as my real father. And you know why? Because he gave it to me straight. He told me exactly what was going to happen. He told me to brace myself for the worst. He said that it was going to be bad but that I would find the strength to get through it. Nobody'd ever talked to me like that before. Whenever I was in a rough spot, I'd fantasize going to him and asking for advice. Because there was no one else I could ask."

"I'm sorry you hate me," his father said, not exactly looking at Hank. Then, almost mumbling, "Still, lots of men hate their fathers, and somehow manage to make decent lives for themselves."

"I didn't hate you. You were just a guy who never got an education and never made anything of himself and knew it. You had a shitty job, a three-pack-a-day habit, and a wife who was a lush. And then you died." All the anger went out of Hank in an instant, like air whooshing out of a punctured balloon, leaving nothing behind but an aching sense of loss. "There wasn't really anything there to hate."

Abruptly, the car was filled with coil upon coil of glistening Worm. For an instant it looped outward, swallowing up car, Interstate, and all the world, and he was afloat in vacuum, either blind or somewhere perfectly lightless, and there was nothing but the Worm-smell, so strong he could taste it in his mouth.

Then he was back on the road again, hands sticky on the wheel and sunlight in his eyes.

"Boy, does *that* explain a lot!" Evelyn flashed her perfect teeth at him and beat on the top of the dashboard as if it were a drum. "How a guy as spectacularly unsuited for it as you are decided to become a surgeon. That perpetual cringe of failure you carry around on your shoulders. It even explains why, when push came to shove, you couldn't bring yourself to cut open living people. Afraid of what you might find there?"

"You don't know what you're talking about."

"I know that you froze up right in the middle of a perfectly routine appendectomy. What did you see in that body cavity?"

"Shut up."

"Was it the appendix? I bet it was. What did it look like?"

"Shut up."

"Did it look like a Worm?"

He stared at her in amazement. "How did you know that?"

"I'm just a hallucination, remember? An undigested bit of beef, a blot of mustard, a crumb of cheese, a fragment of underdone potato. So the question isn't how did I know, but how did *you* know what a Worm was going to look like five years before their ships came into the Solar System?"

"It's a false memory, obviously."

"So where did it come from?" Evelyn lit up a cigarette. "We go off-road here."

He slowed down and started across the desert. The car bucked and bounced. Sagebrush scraped against the sides. Dust blossomed up into the air behind them.

"Funny thing you calling your mother a lush," Evelyn said. "Considering what happened after you bombed out of surgery."

"I've been clean for six years and four months. I still go to the meetings."

"Swell. The guy I married didn't need to."

"Look, this is old territory, do we really need to revisit it? We went over it so many times during the divorce."

"And you've been going over it in your head ever since. Over and over and . . ."

"I want us to stop. That's all. Just stop."

"It's your call. I'm only a symptom, remember? If you want to stop thinking, then just stop thinking."

Unable to stop thinking, he continued eastward, ever eastward.

For hours he drove, while they talked about every small and nasty thing he had done as a child, and then as an adolescent, and then as an alcoholic failure of a surgeon and a husband. Every time Hank managed to change the subject, Evelyn brought up something even more painful, until his face was wet with tears. He dug around in his pockets for a handkerchief. "You could show a little compassion, you know."

"Oh, the way you've shown *me* compassion? I offered to let you keep the car if you'd just give me back the photo albums. So you took the albums into the back yard and burned them all, including the only photos of my grandmother I had. Remember that? But of course I'm not real, am I? I'm just your image of Evelyn—and we both know you're not willing to concede her the least spark of human decency. Watch out for that gully! You'd better keep your eyes straight ahead."

They were on a dirt road somewhere deep in the desert now. That was as much as he knew. The car bucked and scraped its underside against the sand, and he downshifted again. A rock rattled down the underside, probably tearing holes in vital places.

Then Hank noticed plumes of dust in the distance, smaller versions of the one billowing up behind him. So there were other vehicles out there. Now that he knew to look for them, he saw more. There were long slanted pillars of dust rising up in the middle distance and tiny gray nubs down near the horizon. Dozens of them, scores, maybe hundreds.

"What's that noise?" he heard himself asking. "Helicopters?"

"Such a clever little boy you are!"

One by one flying machines lifted over the horizon. Some of them were news copters. The rest looked to be military. The little ones darted here and there, filming. The big ones circled slowly around a distant glint of metal in the desert. They looked a lot like grasshoppers. They seemed afraid to get too close.

"See there?" Evelyn said. "That would be the lifter."

"Oh." Hank said.

Then, slowly, he ventured, "The lander going down wasn't an accident, was it?"

"No, of course not. The Worms crashed it in the Pacific on purpose. They killed hundreds of their own so the bodies would be distributed as widely as possible. They used themselves as bait. They wanted to collect a broad cross-section of humanity.

"Which is ironic, really, because all they're going to get is doctors, morticians, and academics. Some FBI agents, a few Homeland Security bureaucrats. No retirees, cafeteria ladies, jazz musicians, soccer coaches, or construction workers. Not one Guatemalan nun or Korean noodle chef. But how could they have known? They acted out of perfect ignorance of us and they got what they got."

"You sound just like me," Hank said. Then, "So what now? Colored lights and anal probes?"

Evelyn snorted again. "They're a sort of hive culture. When one dies, it's eaten by the others and its memories are assimilated. So a thousand deaths wouldn't mean a lot to them. If individual memories were lost, the bulk of those individuals were already made up of the memories of previous generations. The better part of them would still be alive, back on the mother ship. Similarly, they wouldn't have any ethical problems with harvesting a few hundred human beings. Eating us, I mean, and absorbing our memories into their collective identity. They probably don't understand the concept of individual death. Even if they did, they'd think we should be grateful for being given a kind of immortality."

The car went over a boulder Hank hadn't noticed in time, bouncing him so high that his head hit the roof. Still, he kept driving.

"How do you know all that?"

"How do you *think* I know?" Ahead, the alien ship was growing larger. At its base were Worm upon Worm upon Worm, all facing outward, skin brown and glistening. "Come on, Hank, do I have to spell it out for you?"

"I have no idea what you're talking about."

"Okay, Captain Courageous," Evelyn said scornfully. "If this is what it takes." She stuck both her hands into her mouth and pulled outward. The skin to either side of her mouth stretched like rubber, then tore. Her face ripped in half.

Loop after loop of slick brown flesh flopped down to spill across Hank's lap, slide over the back of the seat and fill up the rear of the car. The horridly familiar stench of Worm, part night soil and part chemical plant, took possession of him and would not let go. He found himself gagging, half from the smell and half from what it meant.

A weary sense of futility grasped his shoulders and pushed down hard. "This is only a memory, isn't it?"

One end of the Worm rose up and turned toward him. Its beak split open in three parts and from the moist interior came Evelyn's voice: "The answer to the question you haven't got the balls to ask is: Yes, you're dead. A Worm ate you and now you're passing slowly through an alien gut, being tasted and experienced and understood. You're nothing more than an emulation being run inside one of those hundred-pound brains."

Hank stopped the car and got out. There was an arroyo between him and the alien ship that the car would never be able to get across. So he started walking.

"It all feels so real," he said. The sun burned hot on his head, and the stones underfoot were hard. He could see other people walking determinedly through the shimmering heat. They were all converging on the ship.

"Well, it would, wouldn't it?" Evelyn walked beside him in human form again. But when he looked back the way they had come, there was only one set of footprints.

Hank had been walking in a haze of horror and resignation. Now it was penetrated by a sudden stab of fear. "This *will* end, won't it? Tell me it will. Tell me that you and I aren't going to keep cycling through the same memories over and over, chewing on our regrets forever?"

"You're as sharp as ever, Hank," Evelyn said. "That's exactly what we've been doing. It passes the time between planets."

"For how long?"

"For more years than you'd think possible. Space is awfully big, you know. It takes thousands and thousands of years to travel from one star to another."

"Then . . . this really is Hell, after all. I mean, I can't imagine anything worse."

She said nothing.

They topped a rise and looked down at the ship. It was a tapering cylinder, smooth and featureless save for a ring of openings at the bottom from which emerged the front ends of many Worms. Converging upon it were people who had started earlier or closer than Hank and thus gotten here before he did. They walked straight and unhesitatingly to the nearest Worm and were snatched up and gulped down by those sharp, tripartite beaks. *Snap* and then swallow. After which, the Worm slid back into the ship and was replaced by another. Not one of the victims showed the least emotion. It was all as dispassionate as an abattoir for robots.

These creatures below were monstrously large, taller than Hank was. The one he had dissected must have been a hatchling. A grub. It made sense. You wouldn't want to sacrifice any larger a percentage of your total memories than you had to.

"Please." He started down the slope, waving his arms to keep his balance when the sand slipped underfoot. He was crying again, apparently; he could feel the tears running down his cheeks. "Evelyn. Help me."

Scornful laughter. "Can you even *imagine* me helping you?"

"No, of course—" Hank cut that thought short. Evelyn, the real Evelyn, would not have treated him like this. Yes, she had hurt him badly, and by that time she left, she had been glad to do so. But she wasn't petty or cruel or vindictive before he made her that way.

"Accepting responsibility for the mess you made of your life, Hank? You?"

"Tell me what to do," Hank said, pushing aside his anger and resentment, trying to remember Evelyn as she had once been. "Give me a hint."

For a maddeningly long moment Evelyn was silent. Then she said, "If the Worm that ate you so long ago could only communicate directly with you . . . what one question do you think it would ask?"

"I don't know."

"I think it would be, 'Why are all your memories so ugly?'"

Unexpectedly, she gave him a peck on the cheek.

Hank had arrived. His Worm's beak opened. Its breath smelled like Evelyn on a rainy Saturday afternoon. Hank stared at the glistening blackness within. So enticing. He wanted to fling himself down it.

Once more into the gullet, he thought, and took a step closer to the Worm and the soothing darkness it encompassed.

Its mouth gaped wide, waiting to ingest and transform him.

Unbidden, then, a memory rose up within Hank of a night when their marriage was young and, traveling through Louisiana, he and Evelyn stopped on an impulse at a roadhouse where there was a zydeco band and beer in bottles and they were happy and in love and danced and danced and danced into an evening without end. It had seemed then that all good things would last forever.

It was a fragile straw to cling to, but Hank clung to it with all his might.

Worm and man together, they then thought: *No one knows the size of the universe or what wonders and terrors it contains. Yet we drive on, blindly burrowing forward through the darkness, learning what we can and suffering what we must. Hoping for stars.*

Ken Liu (kenliu.name) is an author and translator of speculative fiction, as well as a lawyer and programmer. A winner of the Nebula, Hugo, and World Fantasy awards, he has been published in *The Magazine of Fantasy & Science Fiction*, *Asimov's*, *Analog*, *Clarkesworld*, *Lightspeed*, and *Strange Horizons*, among other places.

Ken's debut novel, *The Grace of Kings* (2015), is the first volume in a silkpunk epic fantasy series, The Dandelion Dynasty. It won the Locus Best First Novel Award and was a Nebula finalist. He subsequently published the second volume in the series, *The Wall of Storms* (2016), as well as a collection of short stories, *The Paper Menagerie and Other Stories* (2016).

In addition to his original fiction, Ken is also the translator of numerous literary and genre works from Chinese to English. His translation of *The Three-Body Problem*, by Cixin Liu, won the Hugo Award for Best Novel in 2015, the first translated novel ever to receive that honor. He also translated the third volume in Cixin Liu's series, *Death's End* (2016), and edited the first English-language anthology of contemporary Chinese science fiction, *Invisible Planets* (2016).

He lives with his family near Boston, Massachusetts.

Reborn

KEN LIU

Each of us feels that there is a single "I" in control. But that is an illusion that the brain works hard to produce . . .

—Steven Pinker, *The Blank Slate*

I remember being Reborn. It felt the way I imagine a fish feels as it's being thrown back into the sea.

The Judgment Ship slowly drifts in over Fan Pier from Boston Harbor, its metallic disc-shaped hull blending into the dark, roiling sky, its curved upper surface like a pregnant belly.

It is as large as the old Federal Courthouse on the ground below. A few escort ships hover around the rim, the shifting lights on their surfaces sometimes settling into patterns resembling faces.

The spectators around me grow silent. The Judgment, scheduled four times a year, still draws a big crowd. I scan the upturned faces. Most are expressionless, some seem awed. A few men whisper to each other and chuckle. I pay some attention to them, but not too much. There hasn't been a public attack in years.

"A flying saucer," one of the men says, a little too loud. Some of the others shuffle away, trying to distance themselves. "A goddamned flying saucer."

The crowd has left the space directly below the Judgment Ship empty. A group of Tawnin observers stand in the middle, ready to welcome the Reborn. But Kai, my mate, is absent. Thie told me that thie has witnessed too many Rebirths lately.

Kai once explained to me that the design of the Judgment Ship was meant as a sign of respect for local traditions, evoking our historical imagination of little green men and *Plan 9 from Outer Space*.

It's just like how your old courthouse was built with that rotunda on top to resemble a lighthouse, a beacon of justice that pays respect to Boston's maritime history.

The Tawnin are not usually interested in history, but Kai has always advocated more effort at accommodating us locals.

I make my way slowly through the crowd, to get closer to the whispering group. They all have on long, thick coats, perfect for concealing weapons.

The top of the pregnant Judgment Ship opens and a bright beam of golden light shoots straight up into the sky, where it is reflected by the dark clouds back onto the ground as a gentle, shadowless glow.

Circular doors open all around the rim of the Judgment Ship, and long, springy lines unwind and fall from the doors. They dangle, flex, and extend like tentacles. The Judgment Ship is now a jellyfish drifting through the air.

At the end of each line is a human, securely attached like hooked fish by the Tawnin ports located over their spines and between their shoulder blades. As the lines slowly extend and drift closer to the ground, the figures at the ends languidly move their arms and legs, tracing out graceful patterns.

I've almost reached the small group of whispering men. One of them, the one who had spoken too loud earlier, has his hands inside the flap of his thick coat. I move faster, pushing people aside.

"Poor bastards," he murmurs, watching the Reborn coming closer to the empty space in the middle of the crowd, coming home. I see his face take on the determination of the fanatic, of a Xenophobe about to kill.

The Reborn have almost reached the ground. My target is waiting for the moment when the lines from the Judgment Ship are detached so that the Reborn can no longer be snatched back into the air, the moment when the Reborn are still unsteady on their feet, uncertain who they are.

Still innocent.

I remember that moment well.

The right shoulder of my target shifts as he tries to pull something out of his coat. I shove away the two women before me and leap into the air, shouting "Freeze!"

And then the world slows down as the ground beneath the Reborn erupts like a volcano, and they, along with the Tawnin observers, are tossed into the air, their limbs flopping like marionettes with their strings cut. As I crash into the man before me, a wave of heat and light blanks everything out.

It takes a few hours to process my suspect and to bandage my wounds. By the time I'm allowed to go home it's after midnight.

The streets of Cambridge are quiet and empty because of the new curfew. A fleet of police cars is parked in Harvard Square, a dozen strobing beacons out of sync as I stop, roll down my window, and show my badge.

The fresh-faced young officer sucks in his breath. The name "Joshua Rennon" may not mean anything to him, but he has seen the black dot on the top right corner of my badge, the dot that allows me inside the high-security domicile compound of the Tawnin.

"Bad day, sir," he says. "But don't worry, we've got all the roads leading to your building secured."

He tries to make "your building" sound casual, but I can hear the thrill in his voice. *He's one of* those. *He lives with* them.

He doesn't step away from the car. "How's the investigation going, if you don't mind me asking?" His eyes roam all over me, the hunger of his curiosity so strong that it's almost palpable.

I know that the question he really wants to ask is: *What's it like?*

I turn my face straight ahead. I roll up the window.

After a moment, he steps back, and I step on the gas hard so that the tires give a satisfying squeal as I shoot away.

The walled compound used to be Radcliffe Yard.

I open the door to our apartment and the soft golden light that Kai prefers, a reminder of the afternoon, makes me shudder.

Kai is in the living room, sitting on the couch.

"Sorry I didn't call."

Kai stands up to thir full eight-foot height and opens thir arms, thir dark eyes gazing at me like the eyes of those giant fish that swim through the large tank at the New England Aquarium. I step into thir embrace and inhale thir familiar fragrance, a mixture of floral and spicy scents, the smell of an alien world and of home.

"You've heard?"

Instead of answering, thie undresses me gently, careful around my bandages. I close my eyes and do not resist, feeling the layers fall away from me piece by piece.

When I'm naked, I tilt my head up and thie kisses me, thir tubular tongue warm and salty in my mouth. I place my arms around thim, feeling on the back of thir head the long scar whose history I do not know and do not seek.

Then thie wraps thir primary arms around my head, pulling my face against thir soft, fuzzy chest. Thir tertiary arms, strong and supple, wrap around my waist. The nimble and sensitive tips of thir secondary arms lightly caress my shoulders for a moment before they find my Tawnin port and gently pry the skin apart and push in.

I gasp the moment the connection is made and I feel my limbs grow rigid and then loose as I let go, allowing Kai's strong arms to support my weight. I close my eyes so I can enjoy the way my body appears through Kai's senses: the way warm blood coursing through my vessels creates a glowing map of pulsing red and gold currents against the cooler, bluish skin on my back and buttocks, the way my short hair pricks the sensitive skin of thir primary hands, the way my chaotic thoughts are gradually soothed and rendered intelligible by thir gentle, guiding nudges. We're now connected in the most intimate way that two minds, two bodies can be.

That's what it's like, I think.

Don't be annoyed by their ignorance, thie thinks.

I replay the afternoon: the arrogant and careless manner in which I carried out my duty, the surprise of the explosion, the guilt and regret as I watched the Reborn and the Tawnin die. The helpless rage.

You'll find them, thie thinks.

I will.

Then I feel thir body moving against me, all of thir six arms and two legs probing, caressing, grasping, squeezing, penetrating. And I echo thir movements, my hands, lips, feet roaming against thir cool, soft skin the way I have come to learn thie likes, thir pleasure as clear and present as my own.

Thought seems as unnecessary as speech.

The interrogation room in the basement of the Federal Courthouse is tiny and claustrophobic, a cage.

I close the door behind me and hang up my jacket. I'm not afraid to turn my back to the suspect. Adam Woods sits with his face buried between his hands, elbows on the stainless steel table. There's no fight left in him.

"I'm Special Agent Joshua Rennon, Tawnin Protection Bureau." I wave my badge at him out of habit.

He looks up at me, his eyes bloodshot and dull.

"Your old life is over, as I'm sure you already know." I don't read him his rights or tell him that he can have a lawyer, the rituals of a less civilized age. There's no more need for lawyers—no more trials, no more police tricks.

He stares at me, his eyes full of hatred.

"What's it like?" he asks, his voice a low whisper. "Being fucked by one of them every night?"

I pause. I can't imagine he noticed the black dot on my badge in such a quick look. Then I realize that it was because I had turned my back to him. He could see the outline of the Tawnin port through my shirt. He knew I had been Reborn, and it was a lucky—but reasonable—guess that someone whose port was kept open was bonded to a Tawnin.

I don't take the bait. I'm used to the kind of xenophobia that drives men like him to kill.

"You'll be probed after the surgery. But if you confess now and give useful information about your co-conspirators, after your Rebirth you'll be given a good job and a good life, and you'll get to keep the memories of most of your friends and family. But if you lie or say nothing, we'll learn everything we need anyway and you'll be sent to California for fallout clean-up duty with a blank slate of a mind. And anyone who cared about you will forget you, completely. Your choice."

"How do you know I have any co-conspirators?"

"I saw you when the explosion happened. You were expecting it. I believe your role was to try to kill more Tawnin in the chaos after the explosion."

He continues to stare at me, his hatred unrelenting. Then, abruptly, he seems to think of something. "You've been Reborn more than once, haven't you?"

I stiffen. "How did you know?"

He smiles. "Just a hunch. You stand and sit too straight. What did you do the last time?"

I should be prepared for the question, but I'm not. Two months after my Rebirth, I'm still raw, off my game. "You know I can't answer that."

"You remember nothing?"

"That was a rotten part of me that was cut out," I tell him. "Just like it will be cut out of you. The Josh Rennon who committed whatever crime he did no longer exists, and it is only right that the crime be forgotten. The

Tawnin are a compassionate and merciful people. They only remove those parts of me and you that are truly responsible for the crime—the mens rea, the evil will."

"A compassionate and merciful people," he repeats. And I see something new in his eyes: pity.

A sudden rage seizes me. *He* is the one to be pitied, not *me*. Before he has a chance to put up his hands I lunge at him and punch him in the face, once, twice, three times, hard.

Blood flows from his nose as his hands waver before him. He doesn't make any noise, but continues to look at me with his calm, pity-filled eyes.

"They killed my father in front of me," he says. He wipes the blood from his lips and shakes his hand to get rid of it. Droplets of blood hit my shirt, the scarlet beads bright against its white fabric. "I was thirteen, and hiding in the backyard shed. Through a slit in the doors I saw him take a swing at one of them with a baseball bat. The thing blocked it with one arm and seized his head with another pair of arms and just ripped it off. Then they burned my mother. I'll never forget the smell of cooked flesh."

I try to bring my breathing under control. I try to see the man before me as the Tawnin do: divided. There's a frightened child who can still be rescued, and an angry, bitter man who cannot.

"That was more than twenty years ago," I say. "It was a darker time, a terrible, twisted time. The world has moved on. The Tawnin have apologized and tried to make amends. You should have gone to counseling. They should have ported you and excised those memories. You could have had a life free of these ghosts."

"I don't *want* to be free of these ghosts. Did you ever consider that? I don't want to forget. I lied and told them that I saw nothing. I didn't want them to reach into my mind and steal my memories. I want revenge."

"You can't have revenge. The Tawnin who did those things are all gone. They've been punished, consigned to oblivion."

He laughs. "'Punished,' you say. The Tawnin who did those things are the exact same Tawnin who parade around today, preaching universal love and a future in which the Tawnin and humans live in harmony. Just because they can conveniently forget what they did doesn't mean we should."

"The Tawnin do not have a unified consciousness—"

"You speak like you lost no one in the Conquest." His voice rises as pity turns into something darker. "You speak like a collaborator." He spits at me, and I feel the blood on my face, between my lips—warm, sweet, the taste of rust. "You don't even know what they've taken from you."

I leave the room and close the door behind me, shutting off his stream of curses.

O utside the courthouse, Claire from Tech Investigations meets me. Her people had already scanned and recorded the crime scene last night, but we walk around the crater doing an old-fashioned visual inspection anyway, in the unlikely event that her machines missed something.

Missed something. Something was missing.

"One of the injured Reborn died at Mass General this morning around 4 o'clock," Claire says. "So that brings the total death toll to ten: six Tawnin and four Reborn. Not as bad as what happened in New York two years ago, but definitely the worst massacre in New England."

Claire is slight, with a sharp face and quick, jerky movements that put me in mind of a sparrow. As the only two TPB agents married to Tawnins in the Boston Field Office, we have grown close. People joke that we're work spouses.

I didn't lose anyone in the Conquest.

Kai stands with me at my mother's funeral. Her face in the casket is serene, free of pain.

Kai's touch on my back is gentle and supportive. I want to tell thim not to feel too bad. Thie had tried so hard to save her, as thie had tried to save my father before her, but the human body is fragile, and we don't yet know how to effectively use the advances taught to us by the Tawnin.

We pick our way around a pile of rubble that has been cemented in place by melted asphalt. I try to bring my thoughts under control. Woods unsettled me. "Any leads on the detonator?" I ask.

"It's pretty sophisticated," Claire says. "Based on the surviving pieces, there was a magnetometer connected to a timer circuit. My best guess is the magnetometer was triggered by the presence of large quantities of metal nearby, like the Judgment Ship. And that started a timer that was set to detonate just as the Reborn reached the ground.

"The setup requires fairly detailed knowledge of the mass of the Judgment Ship; otherwise the yachts and cargo ships sailing through the Harbor could have set it off."

"Also knowledge of the operation of the Judgment Ship," I add. "They had to know how many Reborn were going to be here yesterday, and calculate how long it would take to complete the ceremony and lower them to the ground."

"It definitely took a lot of meticulous planning," Claire said. "This is not the work of a loner. We're dealing with a sophisticated terrorist organization."

Claire pulls me to a stop. We're at a good vantage point to see the bottom of the explosion crater. It's thinner than I would have expected. Whoever had done this had used directed explosives that focused the energy upwards, presumably to minimize the damage to the crowd on the sides.

The crowd.

A memory of myself as a child comes to me unbidden.

Autumn, cool air, the smell of the sea and something burning. A large, milling crowd, but no one is making any noise. Those at the edge of the crowd, like me, push to move closer to the center, while those near the center push to get out, like a colony of ants swarming over a bird corpse. Finally, I make my way to the center, where bright bonfires burn in dozens of oil drums.

I reach into my coat and take out an envelope. I open it and hand a stack of photographs to the man standing by one of the oil drums. He flips through them and takes a few out and hands the rest back to me.

"You can keep these and go line up for surgery," he says.

I look through the photographs in my hand: Mom carrying me as a baby. Dad lifting me over his shoulders at a fair. Mom and me asleep, holding the same pose. Mom and Dad and me playing a board game. Me in a cowboy costume, Mom behind me trying to make sure the scarf fit right.

He tosses the other photographs into the oil drum, and as I turn away, I try to catch a glimpse of what's on them before they're consumed by the flames.

"You all right?"

"Yes," I say, disoriented. "Still a bit of the aftereffects of the explosion."

I can trust Claire.

"Listen," I say, "Do you ever think about what you did before you were Reborn?"

Claire focuses her sharp eyes on me. She doesn't blink. "Do not go down that path, Josh. Think of Kai. Think of your life, the real one you have now."

"You're right," I say. "Woods just rattled me a bit."

"You might want to take a few days off. You're not doing anyone favors if you can't concentrate."

"I'll be fine."

Claire seems skeptical, but she doesn't push the issue. She understands how I feel. Kai would be able to see the guilt and regret in my mind. In that ultimate intimacy, there is nowhere to hide. I can't bear to be home and doing nothing while Kai tries to comfort me.

"As I was saying," she continues, "this area was resurfaced by the W. G.

Turner Construction Company a month ago. That was likely when the bomb was placed, and Woods was on the crew. You should start there."

The woman leaves the box of files on the table in front of me.

"These are all the employees and contractors who worked on the Courthouse Way resurfacing project."

She scurries away as though I'm contagious, afraid to exchange more than the absolute minimum number of words with a TPB agent.

In a way, I suppose I am contagious. When I was Reborn, those who were close to me, who had known what I had done, whose knowledge of me formed part of the identity that was Joshua Rennon, would have had to be ported and those memories excised as part of my Rebirth. My crimes, whatever they were, had infected them.

I don't even know who they might be.

I shouldn't be thinking like this. It's not healthy to dwell on my former life, a dead man's life.

I scan through the files one by one, punch the names into my phone so that Claire's algorithms back at the office can make a network out of them, link them to entries in millions of databases, trawl through the radical anti-Tawnin forums and Xenophobic sites, and find connections.

But I still read through the files meticulously, line by line. Sometimes the brain makes connections that Claire's computers cannot.

W. G. Turner had been careful. All the applicants had been subjected to extensive background searches, and none appears suspicious to the algorithms.

After a while, the names merge into an undistinguishable mess: Kelly Eickhoff, Hugh Raker, Sofia Leday, Walker Lincoln, Julio Costas . . .

Walker Lincoln.

I go back and look at the file again. The photograph shows a white male in his thirties. Narrow eyes, receding hairline, no smile for the camera. Nothing seems particularly notable. He doesn't look familiar at all.

But something about the name makes me hesitate.

The photographs curl up in the flames.

The one at the top shows my father standing in front of our house. He's holding a rifle, his face grim. As the flame swallows him, I catch a pair of crossed street signs in the last remaining corner of the photograph.

Walker and Lincoln.

I find myself shivering, even though the heat is turned up high in the office.

I take out my phone and pull up the computer report on Walker Lincoln: credit card records, phone logs, search histories, web presence, employment, and school summaries. The algorithms flagged nothing as unusual. Walker Lincoln seems the model Average Citizen.

I have never seen a profile where not a single thing was flagged by Claire's paranoid algorithms. Walker Lincoln is too perfect.

I look through the purchase history on his credit cards: fire logs, starter fluid, fireplace simulators, outdoor grills.

Then, starting about two months ago, nothing.

As thir fingers are about to push in, I speak.

"Please, not tonight."

The tips of Kai's secondary arms stop, hesitate, and gently caress my back. After a moment, thie backs up. Thir eyes look at me, like two pale moons in the dim light of the apartment.

"I'm sorry," I say. "There's a lot on my mind, unpleasant thoughts. I don't want to burden you."

Kai nods, a human gesture that seems incongruous. I appreciate the effort thie is making to make me feel better. Thie has always been very understanding.

Thie backs off, leaving me naked in the middle of the room.

The landlady proclaims complete ignorance of the life of Walker Lincoln. Rent (which in this part of Charlestown is dirt cheap) is direct deposited on the first of every month, and she hasn't set eyes on him since he moved in four months ago. I wave my badge, and she hands me the key to his apartment and watches wordlessly as I climb the stairs.

I open the door and turn on the light; I'm greeted with a sight out of a furniture store display: white couch, leather loveseat, glass coffee table with a few magazines in a neat stack, abstract paintings on walls. There's no clutter, nothing out of its assigned place. I take a deep breath. No smell of cooking, detergent, the mix of aromas that accompany places lived in by real people.

The place seems familiar and strange at the same time, like walking through déjà vu.

I walk through the apartment, opening doors. The closets and bedroom are as artfully arranged as the living room. Perfectly ordinary, perfectly unreal.

Sunlight coming in from the windows along the western wall makes clean parallelograms against the gray carpet. The golden light is Kai's favorite shade.

There is, however, a thin layer of dust over everything. Maybe a month or two's worth.

Walker Lincoln is a ghost.

Finally, I turn around and see something hanging on the back of the front door, a mask.

I pick it up, put it on, and step into the bathroom.

I'm quite familiar with this type of mask. Made of soft, pliant, programmable fibers, it's based on Tawnin technology, the same material that makes up the strands that release the Reborn back into the world. Activated with body heat, it molds itself into a pre-programmed shape. No matter the contours of the face beneath it, it rearranges itself into the appearance of a face it has memorized. Approved only for law enforcement, we sometimes use such masks to infiltrate Xenophobic cells.

In the mirror, the cool fibers of the mask gradually come alive like Kai's body when I touch thim, pushing and pulling against the skin and muscles of my face. For a moment my face is a shapeless lump, like a monster's out of some nightmare.

And then the roiling motions stop, and I'm looking into the face of Walker Lincoln.

Kai's was the first face I saw the last time I was Reborn.

It was a face with dark fish-like eyes and skin that pulsated as though tiny maggots were wriggling just under the surface. I cringed and tried to move away but there was nowhere to go. My back was against a steel wall.

The skin around thir eyes contracted and expanded again, an alien expression I did not understand. Thie backed up, giving me some space.

Slowly, I sat up and looked around. I was on a narrow steel slab attached to the wall of a tiny cell. The lights were too bright. I felt nauseated. I closed my eyes.

And a tsunami of images came to me that I could not process. Faces, voices, events in fast motion. I opened my mouth to scream.

And Kai was upon me in a second. Thie wrapped thir primary arms around my head, forcing me to stay still. A mixture of floral and spicy scents enveloped me, and the memory of it suddenly emerged from the chaos in my mind. *The smell of home.* I clung to it like a floating plank in a roiling sea.

Thie wrapped thir secondary arms around me, patting my back, seeking an opening. I felt them push through a hole over my spine, a wound that I did not know was there, and I wanted to cry out in pain—

—and the chaos in my mind subsided. I was looking at the world through thir eyes and mind: my own naked body, trembling.

Let me help you.

I struggled for a bit, but thie was too strong, and I gave in.

What happened?

You're aboard the Judgment Ship. The old Josh Rennon did something very bad and had to be punished.

I tried to remember what it was that I had done, but could recall nothing.

He is gone. We had to cut him out of this body to rescue you.

Another memory floated to the surface of my mind, gently guided by the currents of Kai's thoughts.

I am sitting in a classroom, the front row. Sunlight coming in from the windows along the western wall makes clean parallelograms on the ground. Kai paces slowly back and forth in front of us.

"Each of us is composed of many groupings of memories, many personalities, many coherent patterns of thoughts." The voice comes from a black box Kai wears around thir neck. It's slightly mechanical, but melodious and clear.

"Do you not alter your behavior, your expressions, even your speech when you're with your childhood friends from your hometown compared to when you're with your new friends from the big city? Do you not laugh differently, cry differently, even become angry differently when you're with your family than when you're with me?

The students around me laugh a little at this, as do I. As Kai reaches the other side of the classroom, thie turns around and our eyes meet. The skin around thir eyes pulls back, making them seem even bigger, and my face grows warm.

"The unified individual is a fallacy of traditional human philosophy. It is, in fact, the foundation of many unenlightened, old customs. A criminal, for example, is but one person inhabiting a shared body with many others. A man who murders may still be a good father, husband, brother, son, and he is a different man when he plots death than when he bathes his daughter, kisses his wife, comforts his sister, and cares for his mother. Yet the old human criminal justice system would punish all of these men together indiscriminately, would judge them together, imprison them together, even kill them together. Collective punishment. How barbaric! How cruel!"

I imagine my mind the way Kai describes it: partitioned into pieces, an individual divided. There may be no human institution that the Tawnin despise more than our justice system. Their contempt makes perfect sense when considered in the context of their mind-to-mind communication. The Tawnin have no secrets from each other and share an intimacy we can only dream of. The idea of a justice system so limited by the opacity of the individual that it must resort to ritualized adversarial combat rather than direct access to the truth of the mind must seem to them a barbarity.

Kai glances at me, as though thie could hear my thoughts, though I know that is not possible without my being ported. But the thought brings pleasure to me. I am Kai's favorite student.

I placed my arms around Kai.

My teacher, my lover, my spouse. I was once adrift, and now I have come home. I am beginning to remember.

I felt the scar on the back of thir head. Thie trembled.

What happened here?

I don't remember. Don't worry about it.

I carefully caressed thim, avoiding the scar.

The Rebirth is a painful process. Your biology did not evolve as ours, and the parts of your mind are harder to tease apart, to separate out the different persons. It will take some time for the memories to settle. You have to re-remember, relearn the pathways needed to make sense of them again, to reconstruct yourself again. But you're now a better person, free from the diseased parts we had to cut out.

I hung onto Kai, and we picked up the pieces of myself together.

I show Claire the mask, and the too-perfect electronic profile. "To get access to this kind of equipment and to create an alias with an electronic trail this convincing requires someone with a lot of power and access. Maybe even someone inside the Bureau, since we need to scrub electronic databases to cleanse the records of the Reborn."

Claire bites her bottom lip as she glances at the display on my phone and regards the mask with skepticism. "That seems really unlikely. All the Bureau employees are ported and are regularly probed. I don't see how a mole among us can stay hidden."

"Yet it's the only explanation."

"We'll know soon enough," Claire tells me. "Adam has been ported. Tau is doing the probe now. Should be done in half an hour."

I practically fall into the chair next to her. Exhaustion over the last two days settles over me like a heavy blanket. I have been avoiding Kai's touch, for reasons that I cannot even explain. I feel divided from myself.

I tell myself to stay awake, just a little longer.

Kai and I are sitting on the leather loveseat. Thir big frame means that we are squeezed in tightly. The fireplace is behind us and I can feel the gentle heat against the back of my neck. Thir left arms gently stroke my back. I'm tense.

My parents are on the white couch across from us.

"I've never seen Josh this happy," my mother says. And her smile is such a relief that I want to hug her.

"I'm glad you feel that way," says Kai, with thir black voice box. "I think Josh was worried about how you might feel about me—about us."

"There are always going to be Xenophobes," my father says. He sounds a little out of breath. I know that one day I will recognize this as the beginning of his sickness. A tinge of sorrow tints my happy memory.

"Terrible things were done," Kai says. "We do know that. But we always want to look to the future."

"So do we," my father says. "But some people are trapped in the past. They can't let the dead lie buried."

I look around the room and notice how neat the house is. The carpet is immaculate, the end tables free of clutter. The white couch my parents are sitting on is spotless. The glass coffee table between us is empty save for a stack of artfully arranged magazines.

The living room is like the showroom of a furniture store.

I jerk awake. The pieces of my memories have become as unreal as Walker Lincoln's apartment.

Tau, Claire's spouse, is at the door. The tips of thir secondary arms are mangled, oozing blue blood. Thie stumbles.

Claire is by thir side in a moment. "What happened?"

Instead of answering, Tau tears Claire's jacket and blouse away, and thir thicker, less delicate primary arms hungrily, blindly seek the Tawnin port on Claire's back. When they finally find the opening, they plunge in and Claire gasps, going limp immediately.

I turn my eyes away from this scene of intimacy. Tau is in pain and needs Claire.

"I should go," I say, getting up.

"Adam had booby-trapped his spine," Tau says through thir voice box.

I pause.

"When I ported him, he was cooperative and seemed resigned to his fate. But when I began the probe, a miniature explosive device went off, killing him instantly. I guess some of you still hate us so much that you'd rather die than be Reborn."

"I'm sorry," I say.

"I'm the one that's sorry," Tau says. The mechanical voice struggles to convey sorrow, but it sounds like an imitation to my unsettled mind. "Parts of him were innocent."

The Tawnin do not care much for history, and now, neither do we.
They also do not die of old age. No one knows how old the Tawnin
are: centuries, millennia, eons. Kai speaks vaguely of a journey that lasted
longer than the history of the human race.

What was it like? I once asked.

I don't remember, thie had thought.

Their attitude is explained by their biology. Their brains, like the teeth
of sharks, never cease growing. New brain tissue is continuously produced at the core while the outer layers are sloughed off periodically like
snakeskin.

With lives that are for all intents and purposes eternal, the Tawnin
would have been overwhelmed by eons of accumulated memories. It is no
wonder that they became masters of forgetting.

Memories that they wish to keep must be copied into the new tissue:
retraced, recreated, re-recorded. But memories that they wish to leave
behind are cast off like dried pupa husks with each cycle of change.

It is not only memory that they leave behind. Entire personalities can be
adopted, taken on like a role, and then cast aside and forgotten. A Tawnin
views the self before a change and the self after a change as entirely separate beings: different personalities, different memories, different moral
responsibilities. They merely shared a body seriatim.

Not even the same body, Kai thought to me.

?

In about a year every atom in your body will have been replaced by others,
thought Kai. This was back when we had first become lovers, and thie was
often in a lecturing mood. *For us it's even faster.*

*Like the ship of Theseus where each plank was replaced over time, until it was
no longer the same ship.*

You're always making these references to the past. But the flavor of thir
thought was indulgent rather than critical.

When the Conquest happened, the Tawnin had adopted an attitude of
extreme aggression. And we had responded in kind. The details, of course,
are hazy. The Tawnin do not remember them, and most of us do not want
to. California is still uninhabitable after all these years.

But then, once we had surrendered, the Tawnin had cast off those
aggressive layers of their minds—the punishment for their war crimes—
and become the gentlest rulers imaginable. Now committed pacifists, they
abhor violence and willingly share their technology with us, cure diseases,
perform wondrous miracles. The world is at peace. Human life expectancy

has been much lengthened, and those willing to work for the Tawnin have done well for themselves.

The Tawnin do not experience guilt.

We are a different people now, Kai thought. *This is also our home. And yet some of you insist on tasking us with the sins of our dead past selves. It is like holding the son responsible for the sins of the father.*

What if war should occur again? I thought. *What if the Xenophobes convince the rest of us to rise up against you?*

Then we might change yet again, become ruthless and cruel as before. Such changes in us are physiological reactions against threat, beyond our control. But then those future selves would have nothing to do with us. The father cannot be responsible for the acts of the son.

It's hard to argue with logic like that.

Adam's girlfriend, Lauren, is a young woman with a hard face that remained unchanged after I informed her that, as Adam's parents are deceased, she is considered the next of kin and responsible for picking up the body at the station.

We are sitting across from each other, the kitchen table between us. The apartment is tiny and dim. Many of the lightbulbs have burnt out and not been replaced.

"Am I going to be ported?" she asks.

Now that Adam is dead, the next order of business is to decide which of his relatives and friends should be ported—with appropriate caution for further booby-trapped spines—so that the true extent of the conspiracy can be uncovered.

"I don't know yet," I say. "It depends on how much I think you're cooperating. Did he associate with anyone suspicious? Anyone you thought was a Xenophobe?"

"I don't know anything," she says. "Adam is . . . was a loner. He never told me anything. You can port me if you want, but it will be a waste of energy."

Normally, people like her are terrified of being ported, violated. Her feigned nonchalance only makes me more suspicious of her.

She seems to sense my skepticism and changes tack. "Adam and I would sometimes smoke oblivion or do blaze." She shifts in her seat and looks over at the kitchen counter. I look where she's looking and see the drug paraphernalia in front of a stack of dirty dishes, like props set out on a stage. A leaky faucet drips, providing a background beat to the whole scene.

Oblivion and blaze both have strong hallucinogenic effects. The unspoken point: her mind is riddled with false memories that even when ported cannot be relied upon. The most we can do is Rebirth her, but we won't find out anything we can use on others. It's not a bad trick. But she hasn't made the lie sufficiently convincing.

You humans think you are what you've done, Kai once thought. I remember us lying together in a park somewhere, the grass under us, and I loved feeling the warmth of the sun through thir skin, so much more sensitive than mine. *But you're really what you remember.*

Isn't that the same thing? I thought.

Not at all. To retrieve a memory, you must reactivate a set of neural connections, and in the process change them. Your biology is such that with each act of recall, you also rewrite the memory. Haven't you ever had the experience of discovering that a detail you remembered vividly was manufactured? A dream you became convinced was a real experience? Being told a fabricated story you believed to be the truth?

You make us sound so fragile.

Deluded, actually. The flavor of Kai's thought was affectionate. *You cannot tell which memories are real and which memories are false, and yet you insist on their importance, base so much of your life on them. The practice of history has not done your species much good.*

Lauren averts her eyes from my face, perhaps thinking of Adam. Something about Lauren seems familiar, like the half-remembered chorus from a song heard in childhood. I like the indescribable way her face seems to relax as she is lost in memories. I decide, right then, that I will not have Lauren ported.

Instead, I retrieve the mask from my bag and, keeping my eyes on her face, I put it on. As the mask warms to my face, clinging to it, shaping muscle and skin, I watch her eyes for signs of recognition, for confirmation that Adam and Walker were co-conspirators.

Her face becomes tight and impassive again. "What are you doing? That thing's creepy-looking."

Disappointed, I tell her, "Just a routine check."

"You mind if I deal with that leaky faucet? It's driving me crazy."

I nod and remain seated as she gets up. Another dead end. Could Adam really have done it all on his own? Who was Walker Lincoln?

I'm afraid of the answer that's half-formed in my mind.

I sense the heavy weight swinging towards the back of my head, but it's too late.

C an you hear us?" The voice is scrambled, disguised by some electronic gizmo. Oddly, it reminds me of a Tawnin voice box.

I nod in the darkness. I'm seated and my hands are tied behind me. Something soft, a scarf or a tie, is wrapped tightly around my head, covering my eyes.

"I'm sorry that we have to do things this way. It's better if you can't see us. This way, when your Tawnin probes you, we won't be betrayed."

I test the ties around my wrists. They're very well done. No possibility of working them loose on my own.

"You have to stop this right now," I say, putting as much authority into my voice as I can. "I know you think you've caught a collaborator, a traitor to the human race. You believe this is justice, vengeance. But think. If you harm me, you'll eventually be caught, and all your memory of this event erased. What's the good of vengeance if you won't even remember it? It will be as if it never happened."

Electronic voices laugh in the darkness. I can't tell how many of them there are. Old, young, male or female.

"Let me go."

"We will," the first voice says, "after you hear this."

I hear the click of a button being pressed, and then, a disembodied voice: "Hello, Josh. I see you've found the clues that matter."

The voice is my own.

". . . D espite extensive research, it is not possible to erase all memories. Like an old hard drive, the Reborn mind still holds traces of those old pathways, dormant, waiting for the right trigger . . ."

The corner of Walker and Lincoln, my old house.

Inside, it's cluttered, my toys scattered everywhere. There is no couch, only four wicker chairs around an old wooden coffee table, the top full of circular stains.

I'm hiding behind one of the wicker chairs. The house is quiet and the lighting dim, early dawn or late dusk.

A scream outside.

I get up and run to the door and fling it open. I see my father being hoisted into the air by a Tawnin's primary arms. The secondary and tertiary arms are wrapped around my father's arms and legs, rendering him immobile.

Behind the Tawnin, my mother's body lies prostrate, unmoving.

The Tawnin jerks its arms and my father tries to scream again, but blood has pooled in his throat, and what comes out is a mere gurgle. The Tawnin jerks its limbs again and I watch as my father is torn slowly into pieces.

*The Tawnin looks down at me. The skin around its eyes recedes and contracts
again. The smell of unknown flowers and spices is so strong that I retch.*

It's Kai.

". . . in the place of real memories, they fill your mind with lies.
Constructed memories that crumble under examination . . ."

*Kai comes to me on the other side of my cage. There are many cages like it, each
holding a young man or woman. How many years have we been in darkness and
isolation, kept from forming meaningful memories?*

*There was never any well-lit classroom, any philosophical lecture, any sunlight
slanting in from the western windows, casting clean, sharp parallelograms against
the ground.*

*"We're sorry for what happened," Kai says. The voice box, at least, is real. But
the mechanical tone belies the words. "We've been saying this for a long time. The
ones who did those things you insist on remembering are not us. They were necessary for a time, but they have been punished, cast off, forgotten. It's time to move
on."*

I spit in Kai's eyes.

*Kai does not wipe away my spittle. The skin around its eyes contracts and it
turns away. "You leave us no choice. We have to make you anew."*

". . . they tell you that the past is the past, dead, gone. They tell you
that they are a new people, not responsible for their former selves. And
there is some truth to these assertions. When I couple with Kai, I see into
thir mind, and there is nothing left of the Kai that killed my parents, the
Kai that brutalized the children, the Kai that forced us by decree to burn
our old photographs, to wipe out the traces of our former existence that
might interfere with what they want for our future. They really are as
good at forgetting as they say, and the bloody past appears to them as an
alien country. The Kai that is my lover is truly a different mind: innocent,
blameless, guiltless.

"But they continue to walk over the bones of your, my, our parents. They
continue to live in houses taken from our dead. They continue to desecrate
the truth with denial.

"Some of us have accepted collective amnesia as the price of survival.
But not all. I am you, and you're me. The past does not die; it seeps,
leaks, infiltrates, waits for an opportunity to spring up. You *are* what you
remember . . ."

The first kiss from Kai, slimy, raw.

The first time Kai penetrates me. The first time my mind is invaded by its mind.

The feeling of helplessness, of something being done to me that I can never be rid of, that I can never be clean again.

The smell of flowers and spices, the smell that I can never forget or expel because it doesn't just come from my nostrils, but has taken root deep in my mind.

". . . though I began by infiltrating the Xenophobes, in the end it is they who infiltrated me. Their underground records of the Conquest and the giving of testimony and sharing of memories finally awoke me from my slumber, allowed me to recover my own story.

"When I found out the truth, I carefully plotted my vengeance. I knew it would not be easy to keep a secret from Kai. But I came up with a plan. Because I was married to Kai, I was exempt from the regular probes that the other TPB agents are subject to. By avoiding intimacy with Kai and pleading discomfort, I could avoid being probed altogether and hold secrets in my mind, at least for a while.

"I created another identity, wore a mask, provided the Xenophobes with what they needed to accomplish their goals. All of us wore masks so that if any of the co-conspirators were captured, probing one mind would not betray the rest of us."

The masks I wear to infiltrate the Xenophobes are the masks I give to my co-conspirators . . .

"Then I prepped my mind like a fortress against the day of my inevitable capture and Rebirth. I recalled the way my parents died in great detail, replayed the events again and again until they were etched indelibly into my mind, until I knew that Kai, who would ask for the role of preparing me for my Rebirth, would flinch at the vivid images, be repulsed by their blood and violence, and stop before probing too deep. Thie had long forgotten what thie had done and had no wish to be reminded.

"Do I know if these images are true in every aspect? No, I do not. I recalled them through the hazy filter of the mind of a child, and no doubt the memories shared by all the other survivors have inseminated them, colored them, given them more details. Our memories bleed into each other, forming a collective outrage. The Tawnin will say they're no more real than the false memories they've implanted, but to forget is a far greater sin than to remember too well.

"To further conceal my trails, I took the pieces of the false memories they gave me and constructed real memories out of them so that when Kai dissected my mind, thie would not be able to tell thir lies apart from my own."

The false, clean, clutter-free living room of my parents is recreated and rearranged into the room in which I meet with Adam and Lauren . . .

Sunlight coming in from the windows along the western wall makes clean parallelograms on the ground . . .

You cannot tell which memories are real and which memories are false, and yet you insist on their importance, base so much of your life on them.

"And now, when I'm sure that the plot has been set in motion but do not yet know enough details to betray the plans should I be probed, I will go attack Kai. There is very little chance I will succeed, and Kai will surely want me to be Reborn, to wipe this me away—not all of me, just enough so that our life together can go on. My death will protect my co-conspirators, will allow them to triumph.

"Yet what good is vengeance if I cannot see it, if you, the Reborn me, cannot remember it, and know the satisfaction of success? This is why I have buried clues, left behind evidence like a trail of crumbs that you will pick up, until you can remember and know what you have done."

Adam Woods . . . who is not so different from me after all, his memory a trigger for mine . . .

I purchase things so that someday, they'll trigger in another me the memory of fire . . .

The mask, so that others can remember me . . .

Walker Lincoln.

Claire is outside the station, waiting, when I walk back. Two men are standing in the shadows behind her. And still further behind, looming above them, the indistinct figure of Kai.

I stop and turn around. Behind me, two more men are walking down the street, blocking off my retreat.

"It's too bad, Josh," Claire says. "You should have listened to me about remembering. Kai told us that thie was suspicious."

I cannot pick Kai's eyes out of the shadows. I direct my gaze at the blurry shadow behind and above Claire.

"Will you not speak to me yourself, Kai?"

The shadow freezes, and then the mechanical voice, so different from the *voice* that I've grown used to caressing my mind, crackles from the gloom.

"I have nothing to say to you. My Josh, my beloved, no longer exists. He has been taken over by ghosts, has already drowned in memory."

"I'm still here, but now I'm complete."

"That is a persistent illusion of yours that we cannot seem to correct. I am not the Kai you hate, and you're not the Josh I love. We are not the sum of our pasts." Thie pauses. "I hope I will see my Josh soon."

Thie retreats into the interior of the station, leaving me to my judgment and execution.

Fully aware of the futility, I try to talk to Claire anyway.

"Claire, you know I have to remember."

Her face looks sad and tired. "You think you're the only one who's lost someone? I wasn't ported until five years ago. I once had a wife. She was like you. Couldn't let go. Because of her, I was ported and Reborn. But because I made a determined effort to forget, to leave the past alone, they allowed me to keep some memory of her. You, on the other hand, insist on fighting.

"Do you know how many times you've been Reborn? It's because Kai loves . . . loved you, wished to save most parts of you, that they've been so careful with carving as little of you away as possible each time."

I do not know why Kai wished so fervently to rescue me from myself, to cleanse me of ghosts. Perhaps there are faint echoes of the past in thir mind, that even thie is not aware of, that draw thim to me, that compel thim to try to make me believe the lies so that thie will believe them thimself. To forgive is to forget.

"But thie has finally run out of patience. After this time you'll remember nothing at all of your life, and so with your crime you've consigned more of you, more of those you claim to care about, to die. What good is this vengeance you seek if no one will even remember it happened? The past is gone, Josh. There is no future for the Xenophobes. The Tawnin are here to stay."

I nod. What she says is true. But just because something is true doesn't mean you stop struggling.

I imagine myself in the Judgment Ship again. I imagine Kai coming to welcome me home. I imagine our first kiss, innocent, pure, a new beginning. The memory of the smell of flowers and spices.

There is a part of me that loves thim, a part of me that has seen thir soul and craves thir touch. There is a part of me that wants to move on, a part of me that believes in what the Tawnin have to offer. And *I*, the unified, illusory *I*, am filled with pity for them.

I turn around and begin to run. The men in front of me wait patiently. There's nowhere for me to go.

I press the trigger in my hand. Lauren had given it to me before I left. A last gift from my old self, from me to me.

I imagine my spine exploding into a million little pieces a moment before it does. I imagine all the pieces of me, atoms struggling to hold a pattern for a second, to be a coherent illusion.

Ted Chiang was born in Port Jefferson, New York, and holds a degree in computer science. In 1989 he attended the Clarion Science Fiction and Fantasy Writer's Workshop. His fiction has won four Hugo, four Nebula, and four Locus awards, and he is the recipient of the John W. Campbell Award for Best New Writer and the Theodore Sturgeon Memorial Award. His collection, *Stories of Your Life and Others*, has been translated into ten languages. He lives near Seattle, Washington.

Story of Your Life

TED CHIANG

Your father is about to ask me the question. This is the most important moment in our lives, and I want to pay attention, note every detail. Your dad and I have just come back from an evening out, dinner and a show; it's after midnight. We came out onto the patio to look at the full moon; then I told your dad I wanted to dance, so he humors me and now we're slow-dancing, a pair of thirtysomethings swaying back and forth in the moonlight like kids. I don't feel the night chill at all. And then your dad says, "Do you want to make a baby?"

Right now your dad and I have been married for about two years, living on Ellis Avenue; when we move out you'll still be too young to remember the house, but we'll show you pictures of it, tell you stories about it. I'd love to tell you the story of this evening, the night you're conceived, but the right time to do that would be when you're ready to have children of your own, and we'll never get that chance.

Telling it to you any earlier wouldn't do any good; for most of your life you won't sit still to hear such a romantic—you'd say sappy—story. I remember the scenario of your origin you'll suggest when you're twelve.

"The only reason you had me was so you could get a maid you wouldn't have to pay," you'll say bitterly, dragging the vacuum cleaner out of the closet.

"That's right," I'll say. "Thirteen years ago I knew the carpets would need vacuuming around now, and having a baby seemed to be the cheapest and easiest way to get the job done. Now kindly get on with it."

"If you weren't my mother, this would be illegal," you'll say, seething as you unwind the power cord and plug it into the wall outlet.

That will be in the house on Belmont Street. I'll live to see strangers occupy both houses: the one you're conceived in and the one you grow up in. Your dad and I will sell the first a couple years after your arrival. I'll sell the second shortly after your departure. By then Nelson and I will have moved into our farmhouse, and your dad will be living with what's-her-name.

I know how this story ends; I think about it a lot. I also think a lot about how it began, just a few years ago, when ships appeared in orbit and artifacts appeared in meadows. The government said next to nothing about them, while the tabloids said every possible thing.

And then I got a phone call, a request for a meeting.

I spotted them waiting in the hallway, outside my office. They made an odd couple; one wore a military uniform and a crewcut, and carried an aluminum briefcase. He seemed to be assessing his surroundings with a critical eye. The other one was easily identifiable as an academic: full beard and mustache, wearing corduroy. He was browsing through the overlapping sheets stapled to a bulletin board nearby.

"Colonel Weber, I presume?" I shook hands with the soldier. "Louise Banks."

"Dr. Banks. Thank you for taking the time to speak with us," he said.

"Not at all; any excuse to avoid the faculty meeting."

Colonel Weber indicated his companion. "This is Dr. Gary Donnelly, the physicist I mentioned when we spoke on the phone."

"Call me Gary," he said as we shook hands. "I'm anxious to hear what you have to say."

We entered my office. I moved a couple of stacks of books off the second guest chair, and we all sat down. "You said you wanted me to listen to a recording. I presume this has something to do with the aliens?"

"All I can offer is the recording," said Colonel Weber.

"Okay, let's hear it."

Colonel Weber took a tape machine out of his briefcase and pressed PLAY. The recording sounded vaguely like that of a wet dog shaking the water out of its fur.

"What do you make of that?" he asked.

I withheld my comparison to a wet dog. "What was the context in which this recording was made?"

"I'm not at liberty to say."

"It would help me interpret those sounds. Could you see the alien while it was speaking? Was it doing anything at the time?"

"The recording is all I can offer."

"You won't be giving anything away if you tell me that you've seen the aliens; the public's assumed you have."

Colonel Weber wasn't budging. "Do you have any opinion about its linguistic properties?" he asked.

"Well, it's clear that their vocal tract is substantially different from a human vocal tract. I assume that these aliens don't look like humans?"

The colonel was about to say something noncommittal when Gary Donnelly asked, "Can you make any guesses based on the tape?"

"Not really. It doesn't sound like they're using a larynx to make those sounds, but that doesn't tell me what they look like."

"Anything—is there anything else you can call tell us?" asked Colonel Weber.

I could see he wasn't accustomed to consulting a civilian. "Only that establishing communications is going to be really difficult because of the difference in anatomy. They're almost certainly using sounds that the human vocal tract can't reproduce, and maybe sounds that the human ear can't distinguish."

"You mean infra- or ultrasonic frequencies?" asked Gary Donnelly.

"Not specifically. I just mean that the human auditory system isn't an absolute acoustic instrument; it's optimized to recognize the sounds that a human larynx makes. With an alien vocal system, all bets are off." I shrugged. "Maybe we'll be able to hear the difference between alien phonemes, given enough practice, but it's possible our ears simply can't recognize the distinctions they consider meaningful. In that case we'd need a sound spectrograph to know what an alien is saying."

Colonel Weber asked, "Suppose I gave you an hour's worth of recordings; how long would it take you to determine if we need this sound spectrograph or not?"

"I couldn't determine that with just a recording no matter how much time I had. I'd need to talk with the aliens directly."

The colonel shook his head. "Not possible."

I tried to break it to him gently. "That's your call, of course. But the only way to learn an unknown language is to interact with a native speaker, and by that I mean asking questions, holding a conversation, that sort of thing. Without that, it's simply not possible. So if you want to learn the aliens' language, someone with training in field linguistics—whether it's me or someone else—will have to talk with an alien. Recordings alone aren't sufficient."

Colonel Weber frowned. "You seem to be implying that no alien could have learned human languages by monitoring our broadcasts."

"I doubt it. They'd need instructional material specifically designed to teach human languages to nonhumans. Either that, or interaction with a human. If they had either of those, they could learn a lot from TV, but otherwise, they wouldn't have a starting point."

The colonel clearly found this interesting; evidently his philosophy was, the less the aliens knew, the better. Gary Donnelly read the colonel's expression too and rolled his eyes. I suppressed a smile.

Then Colonel Weber asked, "Suppose you were learning a new language by talking to its speakers; could you do it without teaching them English?"

"That would depend on how cooperative the native speakers were. They'd almost certainly pick up bits and pieces while I'm learning their language, but it wouldn't have to be much if they're willing to teach. On the other hand, if they'd rather learn English than teach us their language, that would make things far more difficult."

The colonel nodded. "I'll get back to you on this matter."

The request for that meeting was perhaps the second most momentous phone call in my life. The first, of course, will be the one from Mountain Rescue. At that point your dad and I will be speaking to each other maybe once a year, tops. After I get that phone call, though, the first thing I'll do will be to call your father.

He and I will drive out together to perform the identification, a long silent car ride. I remember the morgue, all tile and stainless steel, the hum of refrigeration and smell of antiseptic. An orderly will pull the sheet back to reveal your face. Your face will look wrong somehow, but I'll know it's you.

"Yes, that's her," I'll say. "She's mine."

You'll be twenty-five then.

The MP checked my badge, made a notation on his clipboard, and opened the gate; I drove the off-road vehicle into the encampment, a small village of tents pitched by the Army in a farmer's sun-scorched pasture. At the center of the encampment was one of the alien devices, nicknamed "looking glasses."

According to the briefings I'd attended, there were nine of these in the United States, one hundred and twelve in the world. The looking glasses acted as two-way communication devices, presumably with the ships in orbit. No one knew why the aliens wouldn't talk to us in person; fear of cooties, maybe. A team of scientists, including a physicist and a linguist, was assigned to each looking glass; Gary Donnelly and I were on this one.

Gary was waiting for me in the parking area. We navigated a circular maze of concrete barricades until we reached the large tent that covered the looking glass itself. In front of the tent was an equipment cart loaded with goodies borrowed from the school's phonology lab; I had sent it ahead for inspection by the Army.

Also outside the tent were three tripod-mounted video cameras whose lenses peered, through windows in the fabric wall, into the main room. Everything Gary and I did would be reviewed by countless others, including military intelligence. In addition we would each send daily reports, of which mine had to include estimates on how much English I thought the aliens could understand.

Gary held open the tent flap and gestured for me to enter. "Step right up," he said, circus-barker-style. "Marvel at creatures the likes of which have never been seen on God's green earth."

"And all for one slim dime," I murmured, walking through the door. At the moment the looking glass was inactive, resembling a semicircular mirror over ten feet high and twenty feet across. On the brown grass in front of the looking glass, an arc of white spray paint outlined the activation area. Currently the area contained only a table, two folding chairs, and a power strip with a cord leading to a generator outside. The buzz of fluorescent lamps, hung from poles along the edge of the room, commingled with the buzz of flies in the sweltering heat.

Gary and I looked at each other, and then began pushing the cart of equipment up to the table. As we crossed the paint line, the looking glass appeared to grow transparent; it was as if someone was slowly raising the illumination behind tinted glass. The illusion of depth was uncanny; I felt I could walk right into it. Once the looking glass was fully lit it resembled a life-sized diorama of a semicircular room. The room contained a few large objects that might have been furniture, but no aliens. There was a door in the curved rear wall.

We busied ourselves connecting everything together: microphone, sound spectrograph, portable computer, and speaker. As we worked, I frequently glanced at the looking glass, anticipating the aliens' arrival. Even so I jumped when one of them entered.

It looked like a barrel suspended at the intersection of seven limbs. It was radially symmetric, and any of its limbs could serve as an arm or a leg. The one in front of me was walking around on four legs, three nonadjacent arms curled up at its sides. Gary called them "heptapods."

I'd been shown videotapes, but I still gawked. Its limbs had no distinct joints; anatomists guessed they might be supported by vertebral columns. Whatever their underlying structure, the heptapod's limbs conspired to move it in a disconcertingly fluid manner. Its "torso" rode atop the rippling limbs as smoothly as a hovercraft.

Seven lidless eyes ringed the top of the heptapod's body. It walked back to the doorway from which it entered, made a brief sputtering sound, and returned to the center of the room followed by another heptapod; at no point did it ever turn around. Eerie, but logical; with eyes on all sides, any direction might as well be "forward."

Gary had been watching my reaction. "Ready?" he asked.

I took a deep breath. "Ready enough." I'd done plenty of fieldwork before, in the Amazon, but it had always been a bilingual procedure: either my informants knew some Portuguese, which I could use, or I'd previously gotten an introduction to their language from the local missionaries. This would be my first attempt at conducting a true monolingual discovery procedure. It was straightforward enough in theory, though.

I walked up to the looking glass and a heptapod on the other side did the same. The image was so real that my skin crawled. I could see the texture of its gray skin, like corduroy ridges arranged in whorls and loops. There was no smell at all from the looking glass, which somehow made the situation stranger.

I pointed to myself and said slowly, "Human." Then I pointed to Gary. "Human." Then I pointed at each heptapod and said, "What are you?"

No reaction. I tried again, and then again.

One of the heptapods pointed to itself with one limb, the four terminal digits pressed together. That was lucky. In some cultures a person pointed with his chin; if the heptapod hadn't used one of its limbs, I wouldn't have known what gesture to look for. I heard a brief fluttering sound, and saw a puckered orifice at the top of its body vibrate; it was talking. Then it pointed to its companion and fluttered again.

I went back to my computer; on its screen were two virtually identical spectrographs representing the fluttering sounds. I marked a sample for playback. I pointed to myself and said "Human" again, and did the same with Gary. Then I pointed to the heptapod, and played back the flutter on the speaker.

The heptapod fluttered some more. The second half of the spectrograph for this utterance looked like a repetition: call the previous utterances [flutter1], then this one was [flutter2flutter1].

I pointed at something that might have been a heptapod chair. "What is that?"

The heptapod paused, and then pointed at the "chair" and talked some more. The spectrograph for this differed distinctly from that of the earlier sounds: [flutter3]. Once again, I pointed to the "chair" while playing back [flutter3].

The heptapod replied; judging by the spectrograph, it looked like [flutter3flutter2]. Optimistic interpretation: the heptapod was confirming my utterances as correct, which implied compatibility between heptapod and human patterns of discourse. Pessimistic interpretation: it had a nagging cough.

At my computer I delimited certain sections of the spectrograph and typed in a tentative gloss for each: "heptapod" for [flutter1], "yes" for [flutter2], and "chair" for [flutter3]. Then I typed "Language: Heptapod A" as a heading for all the utterances.

Gary watched what I was typing. "What's the 'A' for?"

"It just distinguishes this language from any other ones the heptapods might use," I said. He nodded.

"Now let's try something, just for laughs." I pointed at each heptapod and tried to mimic the sound of [flutter1]; "heptapod." After a long pause, the first heptapod said something and then the second one said something else, neither of whose spectrographs resembled anything said before. I couldn't tell if they were speaking to each other or to me since they had no faces to turn. I tried pronouncing [flutter1] again, but there was no reaction.

"Not even close," I grumbled.

"I'm impressed you can make sounds like that at all," said Gary.

"You should hear my moose call. Sends them running."

I tried again a few more times, but neither heptapod responded with anything I could recognize. Only when I replayed the recording of the heptapod's pronunciation did I get a confirmation; the heptapod replied with [flutter2], "yes."

"So we're stuck with using recordings?" asked Gary.

I nodded. "At least temporarily."

"So now what?"

"Now we make sure it hasn't actually been saying 'aren't they cute' or 'look what they're doing now.' Then we see if we can identify any of these words when that other heptapod pronounces them." I gestured for him to have a seat. "Get comfortable; this'll take a while."

In 1770, Captain Cook's ship *Endeavour* ran aground on the coast of Queensland, Australia. While some of his men made repairs, Cook led an exploration party and met the aboriginal people. One of the sailors pointed to the animals that hopped around with their young riding in pouches, and asked an aborigine what they were called. The aborigine replied, "Kanguru." From then on Cook and his sailors referred to the animals by this word. It wasn't until later that they learned it meant "What did you say?"

I tell that story in my introductory course every year. It's almost certainly untrue, and I explain that afterwards, but it's a classic anecdote. Of course, the anecdotes my undergraduates will really want to hear are ones featuring the heptapods; for the rest of my teaching career, that'll be the reason many of them sign up for my courses. So I'll show them the old videotapes of my sessions at the looking glass, and the sessions that the other linguists conducted; the tapes are instructive, and they'll be useful if we're ever visited by aliens again, but they don't generate many good anecdotes.

When it comes to language-learning anecdotes, my favorite source is child language acquisition. I remember one afternoon when you are five years old, after you have come home from kindergarten. You'll be coloring with your crayons while I grade papers.

"Mom," you'll say, using the carefully casual tone reserved for requesting a favor, "can I ask you something?"

"Sure, sweetie. Go ahead."

"Can I be, um, honored?"

I'll look up from the paper I'm grading. "What do you mean?"

"At school Sharon said she got to be honored."

"Really? Did she tell you what for?"

"It was when her big sister got married. She said only one person could be, um, honored, and she was it."

"Ah, I see. You mean Sharon was maid of honor?"

"Yeah, that's it. Can I be made of honor?"

Gary and I entered the prefab building containing the center of operations for the looking glass site. Inside it looked like they were planning an invasion, or perhaps an evacuation: crewcut soldiers worked around a large map of the area, or sat in front of burly electronic gear while speaking into headsets. We were shown into Colonel Weber's office, a room in the back that was cool from air conditioning.

We briefed the colonel on our first day's results. "Doesn't sound like you got very far," he said.

"I have an idea as to how we can make faster progress," I said. "But you'll have to approve the use of more equipment."

"What more do you need?"

"A digital camera, and a big video screen." I showed him a drawing of the setup I imagined. "I want to try conducting the discovery procedure using writing; I'd display words on the screen, and use the camera to record the words they write. I'm hoping the heptapods will do the same."

Weber looked at the drawing dubiously. "What would be the advantage of that?"

"So far I've been proceeding the way I would with speakers of an unwritten language. Then it occurred to me that the heptapods must have writing, too."

"So?"

"If the heptapods have a mechanical way of producing writing, then their writing ought to be very regular, very consistent. That would make it easier for us to identify graphemes instead of phonemes. It's like picking out the letters in a printed sentence instead of trying to hear them when the sentence is spoken aloud."

"I take your point," he admitted. "And how would you respond to them? Show them the words they displayed to you?"

"Basically. And if they put spaces between words, any sentences we write would be a lot more intelligible than any spoken sentence we might splice together from recordings."

He leaned back in his chair. "You know we want to show as little of our technology as possible."

"I understand, but we're using machines as intermediaries already. If we can get them to use writing, I believe progress will go much faster than if we're restricted to the sound spectrographs."

The colonel turned to Gary. "Your opinion?"

"It sounds like a good idea to me. I'm curious whether the heptapods might have difficulty reading our monitors. Their looking glasses are based on a completely different technology than our video screens. As far as we can tell, they don't use pixels or scan lines, and they don't refresh on a frame-by-frame basis."

"You think the scan lines on our video screens might render them unreadable to the heptapods?"

"It's possible," said Gary. "We'll just have to try it and see."

Weber considered it. For me it wasn't even a question, but from his point of view it was a difficult one; like a soldier, though, he made it quickly.

"Request granted. Talk to the sergeant outside about bringing in what you need. Have it ready for tomorrow."

I remember one day during the summer when you're sixteen. For once, the person waiting for her date to arrive is me. Of course, you'll be waiting around, too, curious to see what he looks like. You'll have a friend of yours, a blond girl with the unlikely name of Roxie, hanging out with you, giggling.

"You may feel the urge to make comments about him," I'll say, checking myself in the hallway mirror. "Just restrain yourselves until we leave."

"Don't worry, Mom," you'll say. "We'll do it so that he won't know. Roxie, you ask me what I think the weather will be like tonight. Then I'll say what I think of Mom's date."

"Right," Roxie will say.

"No, you most definitely will not," I'll say.

"Relax, Mom. He'll never know; we do this all the time."

"What a comfort that is."

A little later on, Nelson will arrive to pick me up. I'll do the introductions, and we'll all engage in a little small talk on the front porch. Nelson is ruggedly handsome, to your evident approval. Just as we're about to leave, Roxie will say to you casually, "So what do you think the weather will be like tonight?"

"I think it's going to be really hot," you'll answer.

Roxie will nod in agreement. Nelson will say, "Really? I thought they said it was going to be cool."

"I have a sixth sense about these things," you'll say. Your face will give nothing away. "I get the feeling it's going to be a scorcher. Good thing you're dressed for it, Mom."

I'll glare at you, and say good night.

As I lead Nelson toward his car, he'll ask me, amused, "I'm missing something here, aren't I?"

"A private joke," I'll mutter. "Don't ask me to explain it."

At our next session at the looking glass, we repeated the procedure we had performed before, this time displaying a printed word on our computer screen at the same time we spoke: showing HUMAN while saying "Human," and so forth. Eventually, the heptapods understood what we wanted, and set up a flat circular screen mounted on a small pedestal. One heptapod spoke, and then inserted a limb into a large socket in the pedestal; a doodle of script, vaguely cursive, popped onto the screen.

We soon settled into a routine, and I compiled two parallel corpora: one of spoken utterances, one of writing samples. Based on first impressions, their writing appeared to be logographic, which was disappointing; I'd been hoping for an alphabetic script to help us learn their speech. Their logograms might include some phonetic information, but finding it would be a lot harder than with an alphabetic script.

By getting up close to the looking glass, I was able to point to various heptapod body parts, such as limbs, digits, and eyes, and elicit terms for each. It turned out that they had an orifice on the underside of their body, lined with articulated bony ridges: probably used for eating, while the one at the top was for respiration and speech. There were no other conspicuous orifices; perhaps their mouth was their anus, too. Those sorts of questions would have to wait.

I also tried asking our two informants for terms for addressing each individually; personal names, if they had such things. Their answers were of course unpronounceable, so for Gary's and my purposes, I dubbed them Flapper and Raspberry. I hoped I'd be able to tell them apart.

The next day I conferred with Gary before we entered the looking-glass tent. "I'll need your help with this session," I told him.

"Sure. What do you want me to do?"

"We need to elicit some verbs, and it's easiest with third-person forms. Would you act out a few verbs while I type the written form on the computer? If we're lucky, the heptapods will figure out what we're doing and do the same. I've brought a bunch of props for you to use."

"No problem," said Gary, cracking his knuckles. "Ready when you are."

We began with some simple intransitive verbs: walking, jumping, speaking, writing. Gary demonstrated each one with a charming lack of self-consciousness; the presence of the video cameras didn't inhibit him at all. For the first few actions he performed, I asked the heptapods, "What do you call that?" Before long, the heptapods caught on to what we were trying to do; Raspberry began mimicking Gary, or at least performing the equivalent heptapod action, while Flapper worked their computer, displaying a written description and pronouncing it aloud.

In the spectrographs of their spoken utterances, I could recognize their word I had glossed as "heptapod." The rest of each utterance was presumably the verb phrase; it looked like they had analogs of nouns and verbs, thank goodness.

In their writing, however, things weren't as clear-cut. For each action, they had displayed a single logogram instead of two separate ones. At first I thought they had written something like "walks," with the subject implied. But why would Flapper say "the heptapod walks" while writing "walks," instead of maintaining parallelism? Then I noticed that some of the logograms looked like the logogram for "heptapod" with some extra strokes added to one side or another. Perhaps their verbs could be written as affixes to a noun. If so, why was Flapper writing the noun in some instances but not in others?

I decided to try a transitive verb; substituting object words might clarify things. Among the props I'd brought were an apple and a slice of bread. "Okay," I said to Gary, "show them the food, and then eat some. First the apple, then the bread."

Gary pointed at the Golden Delicious and then he took a bite out of it, while I displayed the "what do you call that?" expression. Then we repeated it with the slice of whole wheat.

Raspberry left the room and returned with some kind of giant nut or gourd and a gelatinous ellipsoid. Raspberry pointed at the gourd while Flapper said a word and displayed a logogram. Then Raspberry brought the gourd down between its legs, a crunching sound resulted, and the gourd reemerged minus a bite; there were cornlike kernels beneath the shell. Flapper talked and displayed a large logogram on their screen. The sound spectrograph for "gourd" changed when it was used in the sentence; possibly a case marker. The logogram was odd: after some study, I could identify graphic elements that resembled the individual logograms for "heptapod" and "gourd." They looked as if they had been melted together, with several extra strokes in the mix that presumably meant "eat." Was it a multiword ligature?

Next we got spoken and written names for the gelatin egg, and descriptions of the act of eating it. The sound spectrograph for "heptapod eats gelatin egg" was analyzable; "gelatin egg" bore a case marker, as expected, though the sentence's word order differed from last time. The written form, another large logogram, was another matter. This time it took much longer for me to recognize anything in it; not only were the individual logograms melted together again, it looked as if the one for "heptapod" was laid on its back, while on top of it the logogram for "gelatin egg" was standing on its head.

"Uh-oh." I took another look at the writing for the simple noun-verb examples, the ones that had seemed inconsistent before. Now I realized all of them actually did contain the logogram for "heptapod"; some were rotated and distorted by being combined with the various verbs, so I hadn't recognized them at first. "You guys have got to be kidding," I muttered.

"What's wrong?" asked Gary.

"Their script isn't word-divided; a sentence is written by joining the logograms for the constituent words. They join the logograms by rotating and modifying them. Take a look." I showed him how the logograms were rotated.

"So they can read a word with equal ease no matter how it's rotated," Gary said. He turned to look at the heptapods, impressed. "I wonder if it's a consequence of their bodies' radial symmetry: their bodies have no 'forward' direction, so maybe their writing doesn't either. Highly neat."

I couldn't believe it; I was working with someone who modified the word "neat" with "highly." "It certainly is interesting," I said, "but it also means there's no easy way for us write our own sentences in their language. We can't simply cut their sentences into individual words and recombine them; we'll have to learn the rules of their script before we can write anything legible. It's the same continuity problem we'd have had splicing together speech fragments, except applied to writing."

I looked at Flapper and Raspberry in the looking glass, who were waiting for us to continue, and sighed. "You aren't going to make this easy for us, are you?"

To be fair, the heptapods were completely cooperative. In the days that followed, they readily taught us their language without requiring us to teach them any more English. Colonel Weber and his cohorts pondered the implications of that, while I and the linguists at the other looking glasses met via video conferencing to share what we had learned about the heptapod language. The videoconferencing made for an incongruous working environment: our video screens were primitive compared to the heptapods' looking glasses, so that my colleagues seemed more remote than the aliens. The familiar was far away, while the bizarre was close at hand.

It would be a while before we'd be ready to ask the heptapods why they had come, or to discuss physics well enough to ask them about their technology. For the time being, we worked on the basics: phonemics/graphemics, vocabulary, syntax. The heptapods at every looking glass were using the same language, so we were able to pool our data and coordinate our efforts.

Our biggest source of confusion was the heptapods' "writing." It didn't appear to be writing at all; it looked more like a bunch of intricate graphic designs. The logograms weren't arranged in rows, or a spiral, or any linear fashion. Instead, Flapper or Raspberry would write a sentence by sticking together as many logograms as needed into a giant conglomeration.

This form of writing was reminiscent of primitive sign systems, which required a reader to know a message's context in order to understand it. Such systems were considered too limited for systematic recording of information. Yet it was unlikely that the heptapods developed their level of technology with only an oral tradition. That implied one of three possibilities: the first was that the heptapods had a true writing system, but they didn't want to use it in front of us; Colonel Weber would identify with that one. The second was that the heptapods hadn't originated the technology they were using; they were illiterates using someone else's technology. The third, and most interesting to me, was that the heptapods were using a nonlinear system of orthography that qualified as true writing.

I remember a conversation we'll have when you're in your junior year of high school. It'll be Sunday morning, and I'll be scrambling some eggs while you set the table for brunch. You'll laugh as you tell me about the party you went to last night.

"Oh man," you'll say, "they're not kidding when they say that body weight makes a difference. I didn't drink any more than the guys did, but I got so much *drunker.*"

I'll try to maintain a neutral, pleasant expression. I'll really try. Then you'll say, "Oh, come on, Mom."

"What?"

"You know you did the exact same things when you were my age."

I did nothing of the sort, but I know that if I were to admit that, you'd lose respect for me completely. "You know never to drive, or get into a car if—"

"God, of course I know that. Do you think I'm an idiot?"

"No, of course not."

What I'll think is that you are clearly, maddeningly not me. It will remind me, again, that you won't be a clone of me; you can be wonderful, a daily delight, but you won't be someone I could have created by myself.

The military had set up a trailer containing our offices at the looking-glass site. I saw Gary walking toward the trailer, and ran to catch up with him. "It's a semasiographic writing system," I said when I reached him.

"Excuse me?" said Gary.

"Here, let me show you." I directed Gary into my office. Once we were inside, I went to the chalkboard and drew a circle with a diagonal line bisecting it. "What does this mean?"

"'Not allowed'?"

"Right." Next I printed the words NOT ALLOWED on the chalkboard. "And so does this. But only one is a representation of speech."

Gary nodded. "Okay."

"Linguists describe writing like this—" I indicated the printed words "—as 'glottographic,' because it represents speech. Every human written language is in this category. However, this symbol—" I indicated the circle and diagonal line "—is 'semasiographic' writing, because it conveys meaning without reference to speech. There's no correspondence between its components and any particular sounds."

"And you think all of heptapod writing is like this?"

"From what I've seen so far, yes. It's not picture writing, it's far more complex. It has its own system of rules for constructing sentences, like a visual syntax that's unrelated to the syntax for their spoken language."

"A visual syntax? Can you show me an example?"

"Coming right up." I sat down at my desk and, using the computer, pulled up a frame from the recording of yesterday's conversation with Raspberry. I turned the monitor so he could see it. "In their spoken language, a noun has a case marker indicating whether it's a subject or object. In their written language, however, a noun is identified as subject or object based on the orientation of its logogram relative to that of the verb. Here, take a look." I pointed at one of the figures. "For instance, when 'heptapod' is integrated with 'hears' this way, with these strokes parallel, it means that the heptapod is doing the hearing." I showed him a different one. "When they're combined this way, with the strokes perpendicular, it means that the heptapod is being heard. This morphology applies to several verbs.

"Another example is the inflection system." I called up another frame from the recording. "In their written language, this logogram means roughly 'hear easily' or 'hear clearly.' See the elements it has in common with the logogram for 'hear'? You can still combine it with 'heptapod' in the same ways as before, to indicate that the heptapod can hear something clearly or that the heptapod is clearly heard. But what's really interesting is that the modulation of 'hear' into 'hear clearly' isn't a special case; you see the transformation they applied?"

Gary nodded, pointing. "It's like they express the idea of 'clearly' by changing the curve of those strokes in the middle."

"Right. That modulation is applicable to lots of verbs. The logogram for 'see' can be modulated in the same way to form 'see clearly,' and so can the logogram for 'read' and others. And changing the curve of those strokes has no parallel in their speech; with the spoken version of these verbs, they add a prefix to the verb to express ease of manner, and the prefixes for 'see' and 'hear' are different.

"There are other examples, but you get the idea. It's essentially a grammar in two dimensions."

He began pacing thoughtfully. "Is there anything like this in human writing systems?"

"Mathematical equations, notations for music and dance. But those are all very specialized; we couldn't record this conversation using them. But I suspect, if we knew it well enough, we could record this conversation in the heptapod writing system. I think it's a full-fledged, general-purpose graphical language."

Gary frowned. "So their writing constitutes a completely separate language from their speech, right?"

"Right. In fact, it'd be more accurate to refer to the writing system as 'Heptapod B,' and use 'Heptapod A' strictly for referring to the spoken language."

"Hold on a second. Why use two languages when one would suffice? That seems unnecessarily hard to learn."

"Like English spelling?" I said. "Ease of learning isn't the primary force in language evolution. For the heptapods, writing and speech may play such different cultural or cognitive roles that using separate languages makes more sense than using different forms of the same one."

He considered it. "I see what you mean. Maybe they think our form of writing is redundant, like we're wasting a second communications channel."

"That's entirely possible. Finding out why they use a second language for writing will tell us a lot about them."

"So I take it this means we won't be able to use their writing to help us learn their spoken language."

I sighed. "Yeah, that's the most immediate implication. But I don't think we should ignore either Heptapod A or B; we need a two-pronged approach." I pointed at the screen. "I'll bet you that learning their two-dimensional grammar will help you when it comes time to learn their mathematical notation."

"You've got a point there. So are we ready to start asking about their mathematics?"

"Not yet. We need a better grasp on this writing system before we begin anything else," I said, and then smiled when he mimed frustration. "Patience, good sir. Patience is a virtue."

You'll be six when your father has a conference to attend in Hawaii, and we'll accompany him. You'll be so excited that you'll make preparations for weeks beforehand. You'll ask me about coconuts and volcanoes and surfing, and practice hula dancing in the mirror. You'll pack a suitcase with the clothes and toys you want to bring, and you'll drag it around the house to see how long you can carry it. You'll ask me if I can carry your Etch-a-Sketch in my bag, since there won't be any more room for it in yours and you simply can't leave without it.

"You won't need all of these," I'll say. "There'll be so many fun things to do there, you won't have time to play with so many toys."

You'll consider that; dimples will appear above your eyebrows when you think hard. Eventually you'll agree to pack fewer toys, but your expectations will, if anything, increase.

"I wanna be in Hawaii now," you'll whine.

"Sometimes it's good to wait," I'll say. "The anticipation makes it more fun when you get there."

You'll just pout.

In the next report I submitted, I suggested that the term "logogram" was a misnomer because it implied that each graph represented a spoken word, when in fact the graphs didn't correspond to our notion of spoken words at all. I didn't want to use the term "ideogram" either because of how it had been used in the past; I suggested the term "semagram" instead.

It appeared that a semagram corresponded roughly to a written word in human languages: it was meaningful on its own, and in combination with other semagrams could form endless statements. We couldn't define it precisely, but then no one had ever satisfactorily defined "word" for human languages either. When it came to sentences in Heptapod B, though, things became much more confusing. The language had no written punctuation: its syntax was indicated in the way the semagrams were combined, and there was no need to indicate the cadence of speech. There was certainly no way to slice out subject-predicate pairings neatly to make sentences. A "sentence" seemed to be whatever number of semagrams a heptapod wanted to join together; the only difference between a sentence and a paragraph, or a page, was size.

When a Heptapod B sentence grew fairly sizable, its visual impact was remarkable. If I wasn't trying to decipher it, the writing looked like fanciful praying mantids drawn in a cursive style, all clinging to each other to form an Escheresque lattice, each slightly different in its stance. And the biggest sentences had an effect similar to that of psychedelic posters: sometimes eye-watering, sometimes hypnotic.

I remember a picture of you taken at your college graduation. In the photo you're striking a pose for the camera, mortarboard stylishly tilted on your head, one hand touching your sunglasses, the other hand on your hip, holding open your gown to reveal the tank top and shorts you're wearing underneath.

I remember your graduation. There will be the distraction of having Nelson and your father and what's-her-name there all at the same time, but that will be minor. That entire weekend, while you're introducing me to your classmates and hugging everyone incessantly, I'll be all but mute with amazement. I can't believe that you, a grown woman taller than me and beautiful enough to make my heart ache, will be the same girl I used to lift off the ground so you could reach the drinking fountain, the same girl who used to trundle out of my bedroom draped in a dress and hat and four scarves from my closet.

And after graduation, you'll be heading for a job as a financial analyst. I won't understand what you do there, I won't even understand your fascination with money, the preeminence you gave to salary when negotiating job offers. I would prefer it if you'd pursue something without regard for its monetary rewards, but I'll have no complaints. My own mother could never understand why I couldn't just be a high school English teacher. You'll do what makes you happy, and that'll be all I ask for.

As time went on, the teams at each looking glass began working in earnest on learning heptapod terminology for elementary mathematics and physics. We worked together on presentations, with the linguists focusing on procedure and the physicists focusing on subject matter. The physicists showed us previously devised systems for communicating with aliens, based on mathematics, but those were intended for use over a radio telescope. We reworked them for face-to-face communication.

Our teams were successful with basic arithmetic, but we hit a road block with geometry and algebra. We tried using a spherical coordinate system instead of a rectangular one, thinking it might be more natural to the heptapods given their anatomy, but that approach wasn't any more fruitful. The heptapods didn't seem to understand what we were getting at.

Likewise, the physics discussions went poorly. Only with the most concrete terms, like the names of the elements, did we have any success; after several attempts at representing the periodic table, the heptapods got the idea. For anything remotely abstract, we might as well have been gibbering. We tried to demonstrate basic physical attributes like mass and acceleration so we could elicit their terms for them, but the heptapods simply responded with requests for clarification. To avoid perceptual problems that might be associated with any particular medium, we tried physical demonstrations as well as line drawings, photos, and animations; none were effective. Days with no progress became weeks, and the physicists were becoming disillusioned.

By contrast, the linguists were having much more success. We made steady progress decoding the grammar of the spoken language, Heptapod A. It didn't follow the pattern of human languages, as expected, but it was comprehensible so far: free word order, even to the extent that there was no preferred order for the clauses in a conditional statement, in defiance of a human language "universal." It also appeared that the heptapods had no objection to many levels of center-embedding of clauses, something that quickly defeated humans. Peculiar, but not impenetrable.

Much more interesting were the newly discovered morphological and grammatical processes in Heptapod B that were uniquely two-dimensional. Depending on a semagram's declension, inflections could be indicated by varying a certain stroke's curvature, or its thickness, or its manner of undulation; or by varying the relative sizes of two radicals, or their relative distance to another radical, or their orientations; or various other means. These were nonsegmental graphemes; they couldn't be isolated from the rest of a semagram. And despite how such traits behaved in human writing, these had nothing to do with calligraphic style; their meanings were defined according to a consistent and unambiguous grammar.

We regularly asked the heptapods why they had come. Each time, they answered "to see," or "to observe." Indeed, sometimes they preferred to watch us silently rather than answer our questions. Perhaps they were scientists, perhaps they were tourists. The State Department instructed us to reveal as little as possible about humanity, in case that information could be used as a bargaining chip in subsequent negotiations. We obliged, though it didn't require much effort: the heptapods never asked questions about anything. Whether scientists or tourists, they were an awfully incurious bunch.

I remember once when we'll be driving to the mall to buy some new clothes for you. You'll be thirteen. One moment you'll be sprawled in your seat, completely unselfconscious, all child; the next, you'll toss your hair with a practiced casualness, like a fashion model in training.

You'll give me some instructions as I'm parking the car. "Okay, Mom, give me one of the credit cards, and we can meet back at the entrance here in two hours."

I'll laugh. "Not a chance. All the credit cards stay with me."

"You're kidding." You'll become the embodiment of exasperation. We'll get out of the car and I will start walking to the mall entrance. After seeing that I won't budge on the matter, you'll quickly reformulate your plans.

"Okay Mom, okay. You can come with me, just walk a little ways behind me, so it doesn't look like we're together. If I see any friends of mine, I'm gonna stop and talk to them, but you just keep walking, okay? I'll come find you later."

I'll stop in my tracks. "Excuse me? I am not the hired help, nor am I some mutant relative for you to be ashamed of."

"But Mom, I can't let anyone see you with me."

"What are you talking about? I've already met your friends; they've been to the house."

"That was different," you'll say, incredulous that you have to explain it. "This is shopping."

"Too bad."

Then the explosion: "You won't do the least thing to make me happy! You don't care about me at all!"

It won't have been that long since you enjoyed going shopping with me; it will forever astonish me how quickly you grow out of one phase and enter another. Living with you will be like aiming for a moving target; you'll always be further along than I expect.

I looked at the sentence in Heptapod B that I had just written, using simple pen and paper. Like all the sentences I generated myself, this one looked misshapen, like a heptapod-written sentence that had been smashed with a hammer and then inexpertly taped back together. I had sheets of such inelegant semagrams covering my desk, fluttering occasionally when the oscillating fan swung past.

It was strange trying to learn a language that had no spoken form. Instead of practicing my pronunciation, I had taken to squeezing my eyes shut and trying to paint semagrams on the insides of my eyelids.

There was a knock at the door and before I could answer Gary came in looking jubilant. "Illinois got a repetition in physics."

"Really? That's great; when did it happen?"

"It happened a few hours ago; we just had the videoconference. Let me show you what it is." He started erasing my blackboard.

"Don't worry, I didn't need any of that."

"Good." He picked up a nub of chalk and drew a diagram:

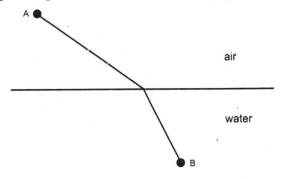

"Okay, here's the path a ray of light takes when crossing from air to water. The light ray travels in a straight line until it hits the water; the water has a different index of refraction, so the light changes direction. You've heard of this before, right?"

I nodded. "Sure."

"Now here's an interesting property about the path the light takes. The path is the fastest possible route between these two points."

"Come again?"

"Imagine, just for grins, that the ray of light traveled along this path." He added a dotted line to his diagram:

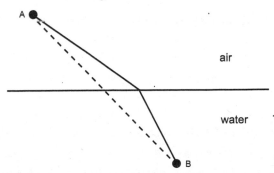

"This hypothetical path is shorter than the path the light actually takes. But light travels more slowly in water than it does in air, and a greater percentage of this path is underwater. So it would take longer for light to travel along this path than it does along the real path."

"Okay, I get it."

"Now imagine if light were to travel along this other path." He drew a second dotted path:

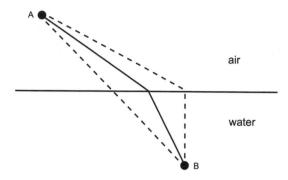

"This path reduces the percentage that's underwater, but the total length is larger. It would also take longer for light to travel along this path than along the actual one."

Gary put down the chalk and gestured at the diagram on the chalkboard with white-tipped fingers. "Any hypothetical path would require more time to traverse than the one actually taken. In other words, the route that the light ray takes is always the fastest possible one. That's Fermat's Principle of Least Time."

"Hmm, interesting. And this is what the heptapods responded to?"

"Exactly. Moorehead gave an animated presentation of Fermat's Principle at the Illinois looking glass, and the heptapods repeated it back. Now he's trying to get a symbolic description." He grinned. "Now is that highly neat, or what?"

"It's neat all right, but how come I haven't heard of Fermat's Principle before?" I picked up a binder and waved it at him; it was a primer on the physics topics suggested for use in communication with the heptapods. "This thing goes on forever about Planck masses and the spin-flip of atomic hydrogen, and not a word about the refraction of light."

"We guessed wrong about what'd be most useful for you to know," Gary said without embarrassment. "In fact, it's curious that Fermat's Principle was the first breakthrough; even though it's easy to explain, you need calculus to describe it mathematically. And not ordinary calculus; you need the calculus of variations. We thought that some simple theorem of geometry or algebra would be the breakthrough."

"Curious indeed. You think the heptapods' idea of what's simple doesn't match ours?"

"Exactly, which is why I'm *dying* to see what their mathematical description of Fermat's Principle looks like." He paced as he talked. "If their version of the calculus of variations is simpler to them than their equivalent of algebra, that might explain why we've had so much trouble talking about physics; their entire system of mathematics may be topsy-turvy compared to ours." He pointed to the physics primer. "You can be sure that we're going to revise that."

"So can you build from Fermat's Principle to other areas of physics?"

"Probably. There are lots of physical principles just like Fermat's."

"What, like Louise's principle of least closet space? When did physics become so minimalist?"

"Well, the word 'least' is misleading. You see, Fermat's Principle of Least Time is incomplete; in certain situations light follows a path that takes more time than any of the other possibilities. It's more accurate to say that light always follows an *extreme* path, either one that minimizes the time taken or one that maximizes it. A minimum and a maximum share certain mathematical properties, so both situations can be described with one equation. So to be precise, Fermat's Principle isn't a minimal principle; instead it's what's known as a 'variational' principle."

"And there are more of these variational principles?"

He nodded. "In all branches of physics. Almost every physical law can be restated as a variational principle. The only difference between these principles is in which attribute is minimized or maximized." He gestured as if the different branches of physics were arrayed before him on a table. "In optics, where Fermat's Principle applies, time is the attribute that has to be an extreme. In mechanics, it's a different attribute. In electromagnetism, it's something else again. But all these principles are similar mathematically."

"So once you get their mathematical description of Fermat's Principle, you should be able to decode the other ones."

"God, I hope so. I think this is the wedge that we've been looking for, the one that cracks open their formulation of physics. This calls for a celebration." He stopped his pacing and turned to me. "Hey, Louise, want to go out for dinner? My treat."

I was mildly surprised. "Sure," I said.

I t'll be when you first learn to walk that I get daily demonstrations of the asymmetry in our relationship. You'll be incessantly running off somewhere, and each time you walk into a door frame or scrape your knee, the pain feels like it's my own. It'll be like growing an errant limb, an extension of myself whose sensory nerves report pain just fine, but whose motor nerves don't convey my commands at all. It's so unfair: I'm going to give birth to an animated voodoo doll of myself. I didn't see this in the contract when I signed up. Was this part of the deal?

And then there will be the times when I see you laughing. Like the time you'll be playing with the neighbor's puppy, poking your hands through the chain-link fence separating our back yards, and you'll be laughing so hard you'll start hiccupping. The puppy will run inside the neighbor's house, and your laughter will gradually subside, letting you catch your breath. Then the puppy will come back to the fence to lick your fingers again, and you'll shriek and start laughing again. It will be the most wonderful sound I could ever imagine, a sound that makes me feel like a fountain, or a wellspring.

Now if only I can remember that sound the next time your blithe disregard for self-preservation gives me a heart attack.

A fter the breakthrough with Fermat's Principle, discussions of scientific concepts became more fruitful. It wasn't as if all of heptapod physics was suddenly rendered transparent, but progress was steady. According to Gary, the heptapods' formulation of physics was indeed topsy-turvy relative to ours. Physical attributes that humans defined using integral calculus were seen as fundamental by the heptapods. As an example, Gary described an attribute that, in physics jargon, bore the deceptively simple name "action," which represented "the difference between kinetic and potential energy, integrated over time," whatever that meant. Calculus for us; elementary to them.

Conversely, to define attributes that humans thought of as fundamental, like velocity, the heptapods employed mathematics that were, Gary assured me, "highly weird." The physicists were ultimately able to prove the equivalence of heptapod mathematics and human mathematics; even though their approaches were almost the reverse of one another, both were systems of describing the same physical universe.

I tried following some of the equations that the physicists were coming up with, but it was no use. I couldn't really grasp the significance of physical attributes like "action"; I couldn't, with any confidence, ponder the significance of treating such an attribute as fundamental. Still, I tried to ponder questions formulated in terms more familiar to me: what kind of worldview did the heptapods have, that they would consider Fermat's Principle the simplest explanation of light refraction? What kind of perception made a minimum or maximum readily apparent to them?

Your eyes will be blue like your dad's, not mud brown like mine. Boys will stare into those eyes the way I did, and do, into your dad's, surprised and enchanted, as I was and am, to find them in combination with black hair. You will have many suitors.

I remember when you are fifteen, coming home after a weekend at your dad's, incredulous over the interrogation he'll have put you through regarding the boy you're currently dating. You'll sprawl on the sofa, recounting your dad's latest breach of common sense: "You know what he said? He said, 'I know what teenage boys are like.'" Roll of the eyes. "Like I don't?"

"Don't hold it against him," I'll say. "He's a father; he can't help it." Having seen you interact with your friends, I won't worry much about a boy taking advantage of you; if anything, the opposite will be more likely. I'll worry about that.

"He wishes I were still a kid. He hasn't known how to act toward me since I grew breasts."

"Well, that development was a shock for him. Give him time to recover."

"It's been *years*, Mom. How long is it gonna take?"

"I'll let you know when my father has come to terms with mine."

During one of the videoconferences for the linguists, Cisneros from the Massachusetts looking glass had raised an interesting question: was there a particular order in which semagrams were written in a Heptapod B sentence? It was clear that word order meant next to nothing when speaking in Heptapod A; when asked to repeat what it had just said, a heptapod would likely as not use a different word order unless we specifically asked them not to. Was word order similarly unimportant when writing in Heptapod B?

Previously, we had only focused our attention on how a sentence in Heptapod B looked once it was complete. As far as anyone could tell, there was no preferred order when reading the semagrams in a sentence; you could start almost anywhere in the nest, then follow the branching clauses until you'd read the whole thing. But that was reading; was the same true about writing?

During my most recent session with Flapper and Raspberry I had asked them if, instead of displaying a semagram only after it was completed, they could show it to us while it was being written. They had agreed. I inserted the videotape of the session into the VCR, and on my computer I consulted the session transcript.

I picked one of the longer utterances from the conversation. What Flapper had said was that the heptapods' planet had two moons, one significantly larger than the other; the three primary constituents of the planet's atmosphere were nitrogen, argon, and oxygen; and fifteen twenty-eights of the planet's surface was covered by water. The first words of the spoken utterance translated literally as "inequality-of-size rocky-orbiter rocky-orbiters related-as-primary-to-secondary."

Then I rewound the videotape until the time signature matched the one in the transcription. I started playing the tape, and watched the web of semagrams being spun out of inky spider's silk. I rewound it and played it several times. Finally I froze the video right after the first stroke was completed and before the second one was begun; all that was visible onscreen was a single sinuous line.

Comparing that initial stroke with the completed sentence, I realized that the stroke participated in several different clauses of the message. It began in the semagram for 'oxygen,' as the determinant that distinguished it from certain other elements; then it slid down to become the morpheme of comparison in the description of the two moons' sizes; and lastly it flared out as the arched backbone of the semagram for 'ocean.' Yet this stroke was a single continuous line, and it was the first one that Flapper wrote. That meant the heptapod had to know how the entire sentence would be laid out before it could write the very first stroke.

The other strokes in the sentence also traversed several clauses, making them so interconnected that none could be removed without redesigning the entire sentence. The heptapods didn't write a sentence one semagram at a time; they built it out of strokes irrespective of individual semagrams. I had seen a similarly high degree of integration before in calligraphic designs, particularly those employing the Arabic alphabet. But those designs had required careful planning by expert calligraphers. No one could lay out such an intricate design at the speed needed for holding a conversation. At least, no human could.

There's a joke that I once heard a comedienne tell. It goes like this: "I'm not sure if I'm ready to have children. I asked a friend of mine who has children, 'Suppose I do have kids. What if when they grow up, they blame me for everything that's wrong with their lives?' She laughed and said, 'What do you mean, if?'"

That's my favorite joke.

Gary and I were at a little Chinese restaurant, one of the local places we had taken to patronizing to get away from the encampment. We sat eating the appetizers: potstickers, redolent of pork and sesame oil. My favorite.

I dipped one in soy sauce and vinegar. "So how are you doing with your Heptapod B practice?" I asked.

Gary looked obliquely at the ceiling. I tried to meet his gaze, but he kept shifting it.

"You've given up, haven't you?" I said. "You're not even trying any more."

He did a wonderful hangdog expression. "I'm just no good at languages," he confessed. "I thought learning Heptapod B might be more like learning mathematics than trying to speak another language, but it's not. It's too foreign for me."

"It would help you discuss physics with them."

"Probably, but since we had our breakthrough, I can get by with just a few phrases."

I sighed. "I suppose that's fair; I have to admit, I've given up on trying to learn the mathematics."

"So we're even?"

"We're even." I sipped my tea. "Though I did want to ask you about Fermat's Principle. Something about it feels odd to me, but I can't put my finger on it. It just doesn't sound like a law of physics."

A twinkle appeared in Gary's eyes. "I'll bet I know what you're talking about." He snipped a potsticker in half with his chopsticks. "You're used to thinking of refraction in terms of cause and effect: reaching the water's surface is the cause, and the change in direction is the effect. But Fermat's Principle sounds weird because it describes light's behavior in goal-oriented terms. It sounds like a commandment to a light beam: 'Thou shalt minimize or maximize the time taken to reach thy destination.'"

I considered it. "Go on."

"It's an old question in the philosophy of physics. People have been talking about it since Fermat first formulated it in the 1600s; Planck wrote volumes about it. The thing is, while the common formulation of physical laws is causal, a variational principle like Fermat's is purposive, almost teleological."

"Hmm, that's an interesting way to put it. Let me think about that for a minute." I pulled out a felt-tip pen and, on my paper napkin, drew a copy of the diagram that Gary had drawn on my blackboard. "Okay," I said, thinking aloud, "so let's say the goal of a ray of light is to take the fastest path. How does the light go about doing that?"

"Well, if I can speak anthropomorphic-projectionally, the light has to examine the possible paths and compute how long each one would take." He plucked the last potsticker from the serving dish.

"And to do that," I continued, "the ray of light has to know just where its destination is. If the destination were somewhere else, the fastest path would be different."

Gary nodded again. "That's right; the notion of a 'fastest path' is meaningless unless there's a destination specified. And computing how long a given path takes also requires information about what lies along that path, like where the water's surface is."

I kept staring at the diagram on the napkin. "And the light ray has to know all that ahead of time, before it starts moving, right?"

"So to speak," said Gary. "The light can't start traveling in any old direction and make course corrections later on, because the path resulting from such behavior wouldn't be the fastest possible one. The light has to do all its computations at the very beginning."

I thought to myself, *the ray of light has to know where it will ultimately end up before it can choose the direction to begin moving in*. I knew what that reminded me of. I looked up at Gary. "That's what was bugging me."

I remember when you're fourteen. You'll come out of your bedroom, a graffiti-covered notebook computer in hand, working on a report for school.

"Mom, what do you call it when both sides can win?"

I'll look up from my computer and the paper I'll be writing. "What, you mean a win-win situation?"

"There's some technical name for it, some math word. Remember that time Dad was here, and he was talking about the stock market? He used it then."

"Hmm, that sounds familiar, but I can't remember what he called it."

"I need to know. I want to use that phrase in my social studies report. I can't even search for information on it unless I know what it's called."

"I'm sorry, I don't know it either. Why don't you call your dad?"

Judging from your expression, that will be more effort than you want to make. At this point, you and your father won't be getting along well. "Can you call Dad and ask him? But don't tell him it's for me."

"I think you can call him yourself."

You'll fume, "Jesus, Mom, I can never get help with my homework since you and Dad split up."

It's amazing the diverse situations in which you can bring up the divorce. "I've helped you with your homework."

"Like a million years ago, Mom."

I'll let that pass. "I'd help you with this if I could, but I don't remember what it's called."

You'll head back to your bedroom in a huff.

I practiced Heptapod B at every opportunity, both with the other linguists and by myself. The novelty of reading a semasiographic language made it compelling in a way that Heptapod A wasn't, and my improvement in writing it excited me. Over time, the sentences I wrote grew shapelier, more cohesive. I had reached the point where it worked better when I didn't think about it too much. Instead of carefully trying to design a sentence before writing, I could simply begin putting down strokes immediately; my initial strokes almost always turned out to be compatible with an elegant rendition of what I was trying to say. I was developing a faculty like that of the heptapods.

More interesting was the fact that Heptapod B was changing the way I thought. For me, thinking typically meant speaking in an internal voice; as we say in the trade, my thoughts were phonologically coded. My internal voice normally spoke in English, but that wasn't a requirement. The summer after my senior year in high school, I attended a total immersion program for learning Russian; by the end of the summer, I was thinking and even dreaming in Russian. But it was always *spoken* Russian. Different language, same mode: a voice speaking silently aloud.

The idea of thinking in a linguistic yet nonphonological mode always intrigued me. I had a friend born of deaf parents; he grew up using American Sign Language, and he told me that he often thought in ASL instead of English. I used to wonder what it was like to have one's thoughts be manually coded, to reason using an inner pair of hands instead of an inner voice.

With Heptapod B, I was experiencing something just as foreign: my thoughts were becoming graphically coded. There were trancelike moments during the day when my thoughts weren't expressed with my internal voice; instead, I saw semagrams with my mind's eye, sprouting like frost on a windowpane.

As I grew more fluent, semagraphic designs would appear fully formed, articulating even complex ideas all at once. My thought processes weren't moving any faster as a result, though. Instead of racing forward, my mind hung balanced on the symmetry underlying the semagrams. The semagrams seemed to be something more than language; they were almost like mandalas. I found myself in a meditative state, contemplating the way in which premises and conclusions were interchangeable. There was no direction inherent in the way propositions were connected, no "train of thought" moving along a particular route; all the components in an act of reasoning were equally powerful, all having identical precedence.

A representative from the State Department named Hossner had the job of briefing the U.S. scientists on our agenda with the heptapods. We sat in the videoconference room, listening to him lecture. Our microphone was turned off, so Gary and I could exchange comments without interrupting Hossner. As we listened, I worried that Gary might harm his vision, rolling his eyes so often.

"They must have had some reason for coming all this way," said the diplomat, his voice tinny through the speakers. "It does not look like their reason was conquest, thank God. But if that's not the reason, what is? Are they prospectors? Anthropologists? Missionaries? Whatever their motives, there must be something we can offer them. Maybe it's mineral rights to our solar system. Maybe it's information about ourselves. Maybe it's the right to deliver sermons to our populations. But we can be sure that there's something.

"My point is this: their motive might not be to trade, but that doesn't mean that we cannot conduct trade. We simply need to know why they're here, and what we have that they want. Once we have that information, we can begin trade negotiations.

"I should emphasize that our relationship with the heptapods need not be adversarial. This is not a situation where every gain on their part is a loss on ours, or vice versa. If we handle ourselves correctly, both we and the heptapods can come out winners."

"You mean it's a non-zero-sum game?" Gary said in mock incredulity. "Oh my gosh."

A non-zero-sum game."
"What?" You'll reverse course, heading back from your bedroom.
"When both sides can win: I just remembered, it's called a non-zero-sum game."

"That's it!" you'll say, writing it down on your notebook. "Thanks, Mom!"

"I guess I knew it after all," I'll say. "All those years with your father, some of it must have rubbed off."

"I knew you'd know it," you'll say. You'll give me a sudden, brief hug, and your hair will smell of apples. "You're the best."

L ouise?"

"Hmm? Sorry, I was distracted. What did you say?"

"I said, what do you think about our Mr. Hossner here?"

"I prefer not to."

"I've tried that myself: ignoring the government, seeing if it would go away. It hasn't."

As evidence of Gary's assertion, Hossner kept blathering: "Your immediate task is to think back on what you've learned. Look for anything that might help us. Has there been any indication of what the heptapods want? Of what they value?"

"Gee, it never occurred to us to look for things like that," I said. "We'll get right on it, sir."

"The sad thing is, that's just what we'll have to do," said Gary.

"Are there any questions?" asked Hossner.

Burghart, the linguist at the Fort Worth looking glass, spoke up. "We've been through this with the heptapods many times. They maintain that they're here to observe, and they maintain that information is not tradable."

"So they would have us believe," said Hossner. "But consider: how could that be true? I know that the heptapods have occasionally stopped talking to us for brief periods. That may be a tactical maneuver on their part. If we were to stop talking to them tomorrow—"

"Wake me up if he says something interesting," said Gary.

"I was just going to ask you to do the same for me."

T hat day when Gary first explained Fermat's Principle to me, he had mentioned that almost every physical law could be stated as a variational principle. Yet when humans thought about physical laws, they preferred to work with them in their causal formulation. I could understand that: the physical attributes that humans found intuitive, like kinetic energy or acceleration, were all properties of an object at a given moment in time. And these were conducive to a chronological, causal interpretation of events: one moment growing out of another, causes and effects created a chain reaction that grew from past to future.

In contrast, the physical attributes that the heptapods found intuitive, like "action" or those other things defined by integrals, were meaningful only over a period of time. And these were conducive to a teleological interpretation of events: by viewing events over a period of time, one recognized that there was a requirement that had to be satisfied, a goal of minimizing or maximizing. And one had to know the initial and final states to meet that goal; one needed knowledge of the effects before the causes could be initiated.

I was growing to understand that, too.

"Why?" you'll ask again. You'll be three.

"Because it's your bedtime," I'll say again. We'll have gotten as far as getting you bathed and into your jammies, but no further than that.

"But I'm not sleepy," you'll whine. You'll be standing at the bookshelf, pulling down a video to watch: your latest diversionary tactic to keep away from your bedroom.

"It doesn't matter: you still have to go to bed."

"But why?"

"Because I'm the mom and I said so."

I'm actually going to say that, aren't I? God, somebody please shoot me.

I'll pick you up and carry you under my arm to your bed, you wailing piteously all the while, but my sole concern will be my own distress. All those vows made in childhood that I would give reasonable answers when I became a parent, that I would treat my own child as an intelligent, thinking individual, all for naught: I'm going to turn into my mother. I can fight it as much as I want, but there'll be no stopping my slide down that long, dreadful slope.

Was it actually possible to know the future? Not simply to guess at it; was it possible to *know* what was going to happen, with absolute certainty and in specific detail? Gary once told me that the fundamental laws of physics were time-symmetric, that there was no physical difference between past and future. Given that, some might say, "yes, theoretically." But speaking more concretely, most would answer "no," because of free will.

I liked to imagine the objection as a Borgesian fabulation: consider a person standing before the *Book of Ages*, the chronicle that records every event, past and future. Even though the text has been photoreduced from the full-sized edition, the volume is enormous. With magnifier in hand, she flips through the tissue-thin leaves until she locates the story of her life.

She finds the passage that describes her flipping through the *Book of Ages*, and she skips to the next column, where it details what she'll be doing later in the day: acting on information she's read in the *Book*, she'll bet one hundred dollars on the racehorse Devil May Care and win twenty times that much.

The thought of doing just that had crossed her mind, but being a contrary sort, she now resolves to refrain from betting on the ponies altogether.

There's the rub. The *Book of Ages* cannot be wrong; this scenario is based on the premise that a person is given knowledge of the actual future, not of some possible future. If this were Greek myth, circumstances would conspire to make her enact her fate despite her best efforts, but prophecies in myth are notoriously vague; the *Book of Ages* is quite specific, and there's no way she can be forced to bet on a racehorse in the manner specified. The result is a contradiction: the *Book of Ages* must be right, by definition; yet no matter what the *Book* says she'll do, she can choose to do otherwise. How can these two facts be reconciled?

They can't be, was the common answer. A volume like the *Book of Ages* is a logical impossibility, for the precise reason that its existence would result in the above contradiction. Or, to be generous, some might say that the *Book of Ages* could exist, as long as it wasn't accessible to readers: that volume is housed in a special collection, and no one has viewing privileges.

The existence of free will meant that we couldn't know the future. And we knew free will existed because we had direct experience of it. Volition was an intrinsic part of consciousness.

Or was it? What if the experience of knowing the future changed a person? What if it evoked a sense of urgency, a sense of obligation to act precisely as she knew she would?

stopped by Gary's office before leaving for the day. "I'm calling it quits. Did you want to grab something to eat?"

"Sure, just wait a second," he said. He shut down his computer and gathered some papers together. Then he looked up at me. "Hey, want to come to my place for dinner tonight? I'll cook."

I looked at him dubiously. "You can cook?"

"Just one dish," he admitted. "But it's a good one."

"Sure," I said. "I'm game."

"Great. We just need to go shopping for the ingredients."

"Don't go to any trouble—"

"There's a market on the way to my house. It won't take a minute."

We took separate cars, me following him. I almost lost him when he abruptly turned in to a parking lot. It was a gourmet market, not large, but fancy; tall glass jars stuffed with imported foods sat next to specialty utensils on the store's stainless-steel shelves.

I accompanied Gary as he collected fresh basil, tomatoes, garlic, linguini. "There's a fish market next door; we can get fresh clams there," he said.

"Sounds good." We walked past the section of kitchen utensils. My gaze wandered over the shelves—peppermills, garlic presses, salad tongs—and stopped on a wooden salad bowl.

When you are three, you'll pull a dishtowel off the kitchen counter and bring that salad bowl down on top of you. I'll make a grab for it, but I'll miss. The edge of the bowl will leave you with a cut, on the upper edge of your forehead, that will require a single stitch. Your father and I will hold you, sobbing and stained with Caesar salad dressing, as we wait in the emergency room for hours.

I reached out and took the bowl from the shelf. The motion didn't feel like something I was forced to do. Instead it seemed just as urgent as my rushing to catch the bowl when it falls on you: an instinct that I felt right in following.

"I could use a salad bowl like this."

Gary looked at the bowl and nodded approvingly. "See, wasn't it a good thing that I had to stop at the market?"

"Yes it was." We got in line to pay for our purchases.

Consider the sentence "The rabbit is ready to eat." Interpret "rabbit" to be the object of "eat," and the sentence was an announcement that dinner would be served shortly. Interpret "rabbit" to be the subject of "eat," and it was a hint, such as a young girl might give her mother so she'll open a bag of Purina Bunny Chow. Two very different utterances; in fact, they were probably mutually exclusive within a single household. Yet either was a valid interpretation; only context could determine what the sentence meant.

Consider the phenomenon of light hitting water at one angle, and traveling through it at a different angle. Explain it by saying that a difference in the index of refraction caused the light to change direction, and one saw the world as humans saw it. Explain it by saying that light minimized the time needed to travel to its destination, and one saw the world as the heptapods saw it. Two very different interpretations.

The physical universe was a language with a perfectly ambiguous grammar. Every physical event was an utterance that could be parsed in two entirely different ways, one causal and the other teleological, both valid, neither one disqualifiable no matter how much context was available.

When the ancestors of humans and heptapods first acquired the spark of consciousness, they both perceived the same physical world, but they parsed their perceptions differently; the worldviews that ultimately arose were the end result of that divergence. Humans had developed a sequential mode of awareness, while heptapods had developed a simultaneous mode of awareness. We experienced events in an order, and perceived their relationship as cause and effect. They experienced all events at once, and perceived a purpose underlying them all. A minimizing, maximizing purpose.

I have a recurring dream about your death. In the dream, I'm the one who's rock climbing—me, can you imagine it?—and you're three years old, riding in some kind of backpack I'm wearing. We're just a few feet below a ledge where we can rest, and you won't wait until I've climbed up to it. You start pulling yourself out of the pack; I order you to stop, but of course you ignore me. I feel your weight alternating from one side of the pack to the other as you climb out; then I feel your left foot on my shoulder, and then your right. I'm screaming at you, but I can't get a hand free to grab you. I can see the wavy design on the soles of your sneakers as you climb, and then I see a flake of stone give way beneath one of them. You slide right past me, and I can't move a muscle. I look down and see you shrink into the distance below me.

Then, all of a sudden, I'm at the morgue. An orderly lifts the sheet from your face, and I see that you're twenty-five.

"You okay?"

I was sitting upright in bed; I'd woken Gary with my movements. "I'm fine. I was just startled; I didn't recognize where I was for a moment."

Sleepily, he said, "We can stay at your place next time."

I kissed him. "Don't worry; your place is fine." We curled up, my back against his chest, and went back to sleep.

When you're three and we're climbing a steep, spiral flight of stairs, I'll hold your hand extra tightly. You'll pull your hand away from me. "I can do it by myself," you'll insist, and then move away from me to prove it, and I'll remember that dream. We'll repeat that scene countless times during your childhood. I can almost believe that, given your contrary nature, my attempts to protect you will be what create your love of climbing: first the jungle gym at the playground, then trees out in the green belt around our neighborhood, the rock walls at the climbing club, and ultimately cliff faces in national parks.

I finished the last radical in the sentence, put down the chalk, and sat down in my desk chair. I leaned back and surveyed the giant Heptapod B sentence I'd written that covered the entire blackboard in my office. It included several complex clauses, and I had managed to integrate all of them rather nicely.

Looking at a sentence like this one, I understood why the heptapods had evolved a semasiographic writing system like Heptapod B; it was better suited for a species with a simultaneous mode of consciousness. For them, speech was a bottleneck because it required that one word follow another sequentially. With writing, on the other hand, every mark on a page was visible simultaneously. Why constrain writing with a glotto-graphic straitjacket, demanding that it be just as sequential as speech? It would never occur to them. Semasiographic writing naturally took advantage of the page's two-dimensionality; instead of doling out morphemes one at a time, it offered an entire page full of them all at once.

And now that Heptapod B had introduced me to a simultaneous mode of consciousness, I understood the rationale behind Heptapod A's grammar: what my sequential mind had perceived as unnecessarily convoluted, I now recognized as an attempt to provide flexibility within the confines of sequential speech. I could use Heptapod A more easily as a result, though it was still a poor substitute for Heptapod B.

There was a knock at the door and then Gary poked his head in. "Colonel Weber'll be here any minute."

I grimaced. "Right." Weber was coming to participate in a session with Flapper and Raspberry; I was to act as translator, a job I wasn't trained for and that I detested.

Gary stepped inside and closed the door. He pulled me out of my chair and kissed me.

I smiled. "You trying to cheer me up before he gets here?"

"No, I'm trying to cheer me up."

"You weren't interested in talking to the heptapods at all, were you? You worked on this project just to get me into bed."

"Ah, you see right through me."

I looked into his eyes. "You better believe it," I said.

I remember when you'll be a month old, and I'll stumble out of bed to give you your 2:00 A.M. feeding. Your nursery will have that "baby smell" of diaper rash cream and talcum powder, with a faint ammoniac whiff coming from the diaper pail in the corner. I'll lean over your crib, lift your squalling form out, and sit in the rocking chair to nurse you.

The word "infant" is derived from the Latin word for "unable to speak," but you'll be perfectly capable of saying one thing: "I suffer," and you'll do it tirelessly and without hesitation. I have to admire your utter commitment to that statement; when you cry, you'll become outrage incarnate, every fiber of your body employed in expressing that emotion. It's funny: when you're tranquil, you will seem to radiate light, and if someone were to paint a portrait of you like that, I'd insist that they include the halo. But when you're unhappy, you will become a klaxon, built for radiating sound; a portrait of you then could simply be a fire alarm bell.

At that stage of your life, there'll be no past or future for you; until I give you my breast, you'll have no memory of contentment in the past nor expectation of relief in the future. Once you begin nursing, everything will reverse, and all will be right with the world. NOW is the only moment you'll perceive; you'll live in the present tense. In many ways, it's an enviable state.

The heptapods are neither free nor bound as we understand those concepts; they don't act according to their will, nor are they helpless automatons. What distinguishes the heptapods' mode of awareness is not just that their actions coincide with history's events; it is also that their motives coincide with history's purposes. They act to create the future, to enact chronology.

Freedom isn't an illusion; it's perfectly real in the context of sequential consciousness. Within the context of simultaneous consciousness, freedom is not meaningful, but neither is coercion; it's simply a different context, no more or less valid than the other. It's like that famous optical illusion, the drawing of either an elegant young woman, face turned away from the viewer, or a wart-nosed crone, chin tucked down on her chest. There's no "correct" interpretation; both are equally valid. But you can't see both at the same time.

Similarly, knowledge of the future was incompatible with free will. What made it possible for me to exercise freedom of choice also made it impossible for me to know the future. Conversely, now that I know the future, I would never act contrary to that future, including telling others what I know: those who know the future don't talk about it. Those who've read the *Book of Ages* never admit to it.

I turned on the VCR and slotted a cassette of a session from the Ft. Worth looking glass. A diplomatic negotiator was having a discussion with the heptapods there, with Burghart acting as translator.

The negotiator was describing humans' moral beliefs, trying to lay some groundwork for the concept of altruism. I knew the heptapods were familiar with the conversation's eventual outcome, but they still participated enthusiastically.

If I could have described this to someone who didn't already know, she might ask, if the heptapods already knew everything that they would ever say or hear, what was the point of their using language at all? A reasonable question. But language wasn't only for communication: it was also a form of action. According to speech act theory, statements like "You're under arrest," "I christen this vessel," or "I promise" were all performative: a speaker could perform the action only by uttering the words. For such acts, knowing what would be said didn't change anything. Everyone at a wedding anticipated the words "I now pronounce you husband and wife," but until the minister actually said them, the ceremony didn't count. With performative language, saying equaled doing.

For the heptapods, all language was performative. Instead of using language to inform, they used language to actualize. Sure, heptapods already knew what would be said in any conversation; but in order for their knowledge to be true, the conversation would have to take place.

First Goldilocks tried the papa bear's bowl of porridge, but it was full of Brussels sprouts, which she hated."

You'll laugh. "No, that's wrong!" We'll be sitting side by side on the sofa, the skinny, overpriced hardcover spread open on our laps.

I'll keep reading. "Then Goldilocks tried the mama bear's bowl of porridge, but it was full of spinach, which she also hated."

You'll put your hand on the page of the book to stop me. "You have to read it the right way!"

"I'm reading just what it says here," I'll say, all innocence.

"No you're not. That's not how the story goes."

"Well if you already know how the story goes, why do you need me to read it to you?"

"Cause I wanna hear it!"

The air conditioning in Weber's office almost compensated for having to talk to the man.

"They're willing to engage in a type of exchange," I explained, "but it's not trade. We simply give them something, and they give us something in return. Neither party tells the other what they're giving beforehand."

Colonel Weber's brow furrowed just slightly. "You mean they're willing to exchange gifts?"

I knew what I had to say. "We shouldn't think of it as 'gift-giving.' We don't know if this transaction has the same associations for the heptapods that gift-giving has for us."

"Can we—" he searched for the right wording "—drop hints about the kind of gift we want?"

"They don't do that themselves for this type of transaction. I asked them if we could make a request, and they said we could, but it won't make them tell us what they're giving." I suddenly remembered that a morphological relative of "performative" was "performance," which could describe the sensation of conversing when you knew what would be said: it was like performing in a play.

"But would it make them more likely to give us what we asked for?" Colonel Weber asked. He was perfectly oblivious of the script, yet his responses matched his assigned lines exactly.

"No way of knowing," I said. "I doubt it, given that it's not a custom they engage in."

"If we give our gift first, will the value of our gift influence the value of theirs?" He was improvising, while I had carefully rehearsed for this one and only show.

"No," I said. "As far as we can tell, the value of the exchanged items is irrelevant."

"If only my relatives felt that way," murmured Gary wryly.

I watched Colonel Weber turn to Gary. "Have you discovered anything new in the physics discussions?" he asked, right on cue.

"If you mean, any information new to mankind, no," said Gary. "The heptapods haven't varied from the routine. If we demonstrate something to them, they'll show us their formulation of it, but they won't volunteer anything and they won't answer our questions about what they know."

An utterance that was spontaneous and communicative in the context of human discourse became a ritual recitation when viewed by the light of Heptapod B.

Weber scowled. "All right then, we'll see how the State Department feels about this. Maybe we can arrange some kind of gift-giving ceremony."

Like physical events, with their casual and teleological interpretations, every linguistic event had two possible interpretations: as a transmission of information and as the realization of a plan.

"I think that's a good idea, Colonel," I said.

It was an ambiguity invisible to most. A private joke; don't ask me to explain it.

Even though I'm proficient with Heptapod B, I know I don't experience reality the way a heptapod does. My mind was cast in the mold of human, sequential languages, and no amount of immersion in an alien language can completely reshape it. My worldview is an amalgam of human and heptapod.

Before I learned how to think in Heptapod B, my memories grew like a column of cigarette ash, laid down by the infinitesimal sliver of combustion that was my consciousness, marking the sequential present. After I learned Heptapod B, new memories fell into place like gigantic blocks, each one measuring years in duration, and though they didn't arrive in order or land contiguously, they soon composed a period of five decades. It is the period during which I know Heptapod B well enough to think in it, starting during my interviews with Flapper and Raspberry and ending with my death.

Usually, Heptapod B affects just my memory: my consciousness crawls along as it did before, a glowing sliver crawling forward in time, the difference being that the ash of memory lies ahead as well as behind: there is no real combustion. But occasionally I have glimpses when Heptapod B truly reigns, and I experience past and future all at once; my consciousness becomes a half-century-long ember burning outside time. I perceive— during those glimpses—that entire epoch as a simultaneity. It's a period encompassing the rest of my life, and the entirety of yours.

I wrote out the semagrams for "process create-endpoint inclusive-we," meaning "let's start." Raspberry replied in the affirmative, and the slide shows began. The second display screen that the heptapods had provided began presenting a series of images, composed of semagrams and equations, while one of our video screens did the same.

This was the second "gift exchange" I had been present for, the eighth one overall, and I knew it would be the last. The looking-glass tent was crowded with people; Burghart from Fort Worth was here, as were Gary and a nuclear physicist, assorted biologists, anthropologists, military brass, and diplomats. Thankfully they had set up an air conditioner to cool the place off. We would review the tapes of the images later to figure out just what the heptapods' "gift" was. Our own "gift" was a presentation on the Lascaux cave paintings.

We all crowded around the heptapods' second screen, trying to glean some idea of the images' content as they went by. "Preliminary assessments?" asked Colonel Weber.

"It's not a return," said Burghart. In a previous exchange, the heptapods had given us information about ourselves that we had previously told them. This had infuriated the State Department, but we had no reason to think of it as an insult: it probably indicated that trade value really didn't play a role in these exchanges. It didn't exclude the possibility that the heptapods might yet offer us a space drive, or cold fusion, or some other wish-fulfilling miracle.

"That looks like inorganic chemistry," said the nuclear physicist, pointing at an equation before the image was replaced.

Gary nodded. "It could be materials technology," he said.

"Maybe we're finally getting somewhere," said Colonel Weber.

"I wanna see more animal pictures," I whispered, quietly so that only Gary could hear me, and pouted like a child. He smiled and poked me. Truthfully, I wished the heptapods had given another xenobiology lecture, as they had on two previous exchanges; judging from those, humans were more similar to the heptapods than any other species they'd ever encountered. Or another lecture on heptapod history; those had been filled with apparent non-sequiturs, but were interesting nonetheless. I didn't want the heptapods to give us new technology, because I didn't want to see what our governments might do with it.

I watched Raspberry while the information was being exchanged, looking for any anomalous behavior. It stood barely moving as usual; I saw no indications of what would happen shortly.

After a minute, the heptapod's screen went blank, and a minute after that, ours did, too. Gary and most of the other scientists clustered around a tiny video screen that was replaying the heptapods' presentation. I could hear them talk about the need to call in a solid-state physicist.

Colonel Weber turned. "You two," he said, pointing to me and then to Burghart, "schedule the time and location for the next exchange." Then he followed the others to the playback screen.

"Coming right up," I said. To Burghart, I asked, "Would you care to do the honors, or shall I?"

I knew Burghart had gained a proficiency in Heptapod B similar to mine. "It's your looking glass," he said. "You drive."

I sat down again at the transmitting computer. "Bet you never figured you'd wind up working as a Army translator back when you were a grad student."

"That's for goddamn sure," he said. "Even now I can hardly believe it." Everything we said to each other felt like the carefully bland exchanges of spies who meet in public, but never break cover.

I wrote out the semagrams for "locus exchange-transaction converse inclusive-we" with the projective aspect modulation.

Raspberry wrote its reply. That was my cue to frown, and for Burghart to ask, "What does it mean by that?" His delivery was perfect.

I wrote a request for clarification; Raspberry's reply was the same as before. Then I watched it glide out of the room. The curtain was about to fall on this act of our performance.

Colonel Weber stepped forward. "What's going on? Where did it go?"

"It said that the heptapods are leaving now," I said. "Not just itself; all of them."

"Call it back here now. Ask it what it means."

"Um, I don't think Raspberry's wearing a pager," I said.

The image of the room in the looking glass disappeared so abruptly that it took a moment for my eyes to register what I was seeing instead: it was the other side of the looking-glass tent. The looking glass had become completely transparent. The conversation around the playback screen fell silent.

"What the hell is going on here?" said Colonel Weber.

Gary walked up to the looking glass, and then around it to the other side. He touched the rear surface with one hand; I could see the pale ovals where his fingertips made contact with the looking glass. "I think," he said, "we just saw a demonstration of transmutation at a distance."

I heard the sounds of heavy footfalls on dry grass. A soldier came in through the tent door, short of breath from sprinting, holding an oversize walkie-talkie. "Colonel, message from—"

Weber grabbed the walkie-talkie from him.

I remember what it'll be like watching you when you are a day old. Your father will have gone for a quick visit to the hospital cafeteria, and you'll be lying in your bassinet, and I'll be leaning over you.

So soon after the delivery, I will still be feeling like a wrung-out towel.

You will seem incongruously tiny, given how enormous I felt during the pregnancy; I could swear there was room for someone much larger and more robust than you in there. Your hands and feet will be long and thin, not chubby yet. Your face will still be all red and pinched, puffy eyelids squeezed shut, the gnomelike phase that precedes the cherubic.

I'll run a finger over your belly, marveling at the uncanny softness of your skin, wondering if silk would abrade your body like burlap. Then you'll writhe, twisting your body while poking out your legs one at a time, and I'll recognize the gesture as one I had felt you do inside me, many times. So *that's* what it looks like.

I'll feel elated at this evidence of a unique mother-child bond, this certitude that you're the one I carried. Even if I had never laid eyes on you before, I'd be able to pick you out from a sea of babies: Not that one. No, not her either. Wait, that one over there.

Yes, that's her. She's mine.

That final "gift exchange" was the last we ever saw of the heptapods. All at once, all over the world, their looking glasses became transparent and their ships left orbit. Subsequent analysis of the looking glasses revealed them to be nothing more than sheets of fused silica, completely inert. The information from the final exchange session described a new class of superconducting materials, but it later proved to duplicate the results of research just completed in Japan: nothing that humans didn't already know.

We never did learn why the heptapods left, any more than we learned what brought them here, or why they acted the way they did. My own new awareness didn't provide that type of knowledge; the heptapods' behavior was presumably explicable from a sequential point of view, but we never found that explanation.

I would have liked to experience more of the heptapods' worldview, to feel the way they feel. Then, perhaps I could immerse myself fully in the necessity of events, as they must, instead of merely wading in its surf for the rest of my life. But that will never come to pass. I will continue to practice the heptapod languages, as will the other linguists on the looking-glass teams, but none of us will ever progress any further than we did when the heptapods were here.

Working with the heptapods changed my life. I met your father and learned Heptapod B, both of which make it possible for me to know you now, here on the patio in the moonlight. Eventually, many years from now,

I'll be without your father, and without you. All I will have left from this moment is the heptapod language. So I pay close attention, and note every detail.

From the beginning I knew my destination, and I chose my route accordingly. But am I working toward an extreme of joy, or of pain? Will I achieve a minimum, or a maximum?

These questions are in my mind when your father asks me, "Do you want to make a baby?" And I smile and answer, "Yes," and I unwrap his arms from around me, and we hold hands as we walk inside to make love, to make you.

PERMISSIONS

ABOUT THE EDITOR

Neil Clarke is the editor of *Clarkesworld* and *Forever Magazine*, owner of Wyrm Publishing, and a six-time Hugo Award Finalist for Best Editor (short form). He currently lives in New Jersey with his wife and two sons. You can find him online at neil-clarke.com.